Michael Scott Rohan was born in Edinburgh in 1951, of a French father and Scottish mother, and educated at the Edinburgh Academy and St Edmund Hall, Oxford. He is the author of twelve fantasy novels and science fiction novels, including the award-winning Winter of the World trilogy, and co-author of three more, as well as several non-fiction books. His books are published in the USA, Japan, Israel, Russia and throughout Europe. Besides writing novels he has been a *Times* columnist, edits reference books, reviews CDs, videos and opera for *Gramophone* and other magazines, plays with longbows and computers, drinks beer, eats Oriental food, keeps up with hobbies including archaeology and palaeontology, sings, argues and travels a lot. After many years in Oxford and Yorkshire, he and his American wife Deborah now live in a small village near Cambridge, next to the pub.

Find out more about Michael Scott Rohan and other Orbit authors by registering for the free monthly newsletter at www.orbitbooks.co.uk

Also by Michael Scott Rohan

The Winter of the World
THE ANVIL OF ICE
THE FORGE IN THE FOREST
THE HAMMER OF THE SUN
THE CASTLE OF THE WINDS
THE SINGER AND THE SEA

CHASE THE MORNING
RUN TO THE STARS
MAXIE'S DEMON

With Allan Scott
A SPELL OF EMPIRE
THE ICE KING

Shadow of the Seer

A Winter of the World Novel

Michael Scott Rohan

www.orbitbooks.co.uk

An *Orbit* Book

First published in Great Britain by Orbit 2001

Copyright © 2001 by Michael Scott Rohan

The moral right of the author has been asserted.

All characters and events in this publication are fictitious and any resemblance to real persons, living or dead, is purely coincidental.

All rights reserved.
No part of this publication may be reproduced,
stored in a retrieval system, or transmitted, in any
form or by any means, without the prior
permission in writing of the publisher, nor be
otherwise circulated in any form of binding or
cover other than that in which it is published and
without a similar condition, including this
condition, being imposed on the subsequent purchaser.

A CIP catalogue record for this book
is available from the British Library.

ISBN 1 84149 041 5

Typeset by Hewer Text Limited, Edinburgh
Printed and bound in Great Britain by
Mackays of Chatham PLC, Chatham, Kent

Orbit
A Division of
Little, Brown and Company (UK)
Brettenham House
Lancaster Place
London WC2E 7EN

This sixth Winter of the World tale is gratefully dedicated to the many thousands of people across the world who have contributed to its success over the last two decades; and, most of all, to you, the reader.

Acknowledgements

Thanks to all those who have helped me create this book, including Tim Holman and Simon Kavanagh at Orbit; Ian Miller; Anne and Bill Macdonald, for unearthing source material I hadn't seen since my childhood; and, as always, for belief and support, my wife Deb.

Contents

Acknowledgements

The Winter Chronicles record many tales of the folk who fled across the great oceans out of the West, to the land of Brasayhal and the realms of Nordeney and Bryhaine, the peaceful settlers and the savage warriors who pursued them. But of the lands they fled from, all too little is recorded, and that unreliable and inconsistent; for the spreading dominion of the Ice, enemy to all that lived and especially all that thought, had destroyed its ancient civilisations, fragmented its cultures and ruined its records. All that remains is dark shards out of long-shattered centuries, more legend than history. Yet among that darkness, some of the shards still gleam, and legends of heroic deeds and stern resistance still strike a momentary brightness, revealing how humanity could still struggle against the advancing gloom.

Wisdom was denied to ordinary folk, knowledge and craft; the wondrous art of the mastersmiths never took root, or was long buried. A more savage mystery took its place in the hearts of men, tapping similar springs, perhaps, but with less understanding, and more superstition; it was used alike by the enemies of the Ice and its servants, from whom its secrets may even have been stolen. At its best it gave suffering humanity insight and power; but it was unpredictable, always open to misuse, often destructive in the demands it made on its wielders. Nonetheless, it is often of these strange folk the legends speak, and in particular one of the best supported. A tale of heroism and strength against vast odds, true; yet also a tale of destruction and defeat, a sharp reminder that against those odds sheer strength, even the greatest, may not in the end prevail.

Yet still a light was lit, that did not easily go out . . .

CHAPTER 1
Dance at the Precipice

IT was the light between the mountain peaks that awoke him, rather than his father's hand. The first long beams fell full on his face, flooding his weary eyes with a wash of blood-tinged flame he could not shut out. It was all too like the vicious dreams that rampaged across his sleep, and he sat up sharply, gasping. Often, he knew, the mind could vastly magnify some slight sound or feeling at the edge of waking; for his father was deep and wise in the lore of dreams. But these apparitions had left him far more seriously shaken than the light could explain, or the touch. His shoulder had been shaken, gently; and his father was not normally a gentle man.

The boy shook his head to clear it, sought to uncross his thighs, and groaned. His father ran a hand down the deep lines flanking his straight mouth. 'You fell asleep, boy.' There was no expression in his voice. The boy nodded mutely, ready for the slap that usually followed. Some time in the small hours he had nodded off where he sat, cross-legged, head sagging over the pattern marked out for him on the earthen floor. Now he was too numb and stiff to move. The slap would almost be welcome; but it did not come.

'You finished the pattern?' demanded his father; but it was not really a question. The boy stared. Somehow, though he could not recollect it, he must have done. All the small stones were set out in their spiralling swirls of ochre-red and yellow-brown sand, interwoven and interlinked with darker swirls of grey ash and black soot, a fierce contrasting energy of movement that led your eye inwards like a steep cliff path, too steep to take slowly; you had either to run with it, or fall away from it into confusion. He must have finished it on the fringe of sleep, his hands moving instinctively with the practice drilled into him since he had spoken his first recognisable word. He decided to say nothing of that. Safer simply to nod and grunt, as his father did.

But the iron-grey voice said, 'You have done well, Alya,' and the boy could not help looking up in surprise at the tone, almost warm, and the sound of his name, which his father seldom spoke. His father squatted easily on his heels beside him, and waved an approving hand over the pattern. 'The sleep is permitted – this time. You have done well to complete the Trail at all. That in itself often brings darkness down over the mind. But if you are to succeed in passing the barrier one day, you must learn to endure, so that you may understand and direct, and explore – not simply suffer what is shown you. Tell me now what you saw.'

The boy shivered; not simply with the cold in the little hut, or need of food and warmth. Those he was used to. 'I saw . . . men, who fought. And more than men. Many, many men, like ants seething in a nest. They fought at the walls of . . . great villages, towns greater than I have seen. You will laugh at me, but . . . their huts were huge and of many floors and of stone, as it seems. Like wonders that I have heard of only in tales. Great walls like whole cliffs of stone, yet . . . yet carven, shaped by some art. Could such things be?'

The older man rasped a thumb against his chin. 'Towns under siege. Towns of stone. Aye, such things were; still are, maybe, in distant corners of the lands. All I have seen are their ruins; and even those are very mighty. Yet they were thrown down, and burned, long ago.'

'Burned! Aye, there was fire! Men outside, who fought to enter, and raised ladders and great engines. And the defenders, men cased in glittering metal, running up and down the heights of those walls like goats on a cliff. They hurled all manner of things down upon the others, weapons, darts, arrows from strange short bows. And then the fire came, fire from above, raining down in great blasting streams . . . I saw it. Like all the evil things in the world, in one unhallowed shape. Scales . . . and claws . . . whirling around in smoke and confusion; and great beating wings. A thing that flew, a great thing but no bird, vast beyond any bird I could imagine . . .'

'Yes?' demanded the older man curtly, as the boy wavered and closed his eyes.

'I do not know . . . More like a bat, as big as a cloud and blacker by far, sending down blasting spurts from its jaws . . . You will strike me, when I say many mouths. Yet only one creature . . .'

But his father only shook his shaggy head. 'Tugarin! The *Buryakud*! Tugarin son of Zamai, eldest and worst of the curses of the Ice!' He breathed out. 'But surely that was long, long ago. You have seen far and well, my son, farther even than I dared hope. It is many an age since that horror was loosed upon the world! You will be a powerful chooser of the paths to your folk one day, a wise Seer. More so than I, maybe.'

The boy glowed with this sudden and unprecedented praise, but his father simply snapped, 'Now, what more? What then?'

Alya closed his eyes again, felt them sting with smoke, although the peat-damped hearth gave off no more than a faint warmth. 'There was fire, fire everywhere, all over the walls. They blackened; and the men fell from them, blazing, or cast themselves into the abyss. Fire . . . They were so majestic, those walls.

The huts behind them, so mighty and tall and fair, like the pillars of the sky. But the fire rolled over all. Still I strove to see, more closely . . .'

His father's face changed, the eyes as intent as a stooping hawk's. 'Yes. And then?'

The boy felt the shudder of fear return. 'Then it was as if the walls changed before my eyes, and become a real cliff! Of rock, black, jagged and fierce, as if weather had never touched it. Yet the blazing spew of the beast still trickled down it in rivulets, so that the very stone smoked. So hot that it burned my cheeks and drove me back, every time I sought to approach it.'

The thin lips turned down grimly. 'Indeed, my son. Learn now, then, that that which you call a cliff is not of any stone that ever was upon this world, even among the Firedream of its first forging. That cliff is a barrier set before you, before whatever you would see of your own will, rather than be shown. It is the Wall, that lies at the end of the Trail. Every shaman, every true Seer must first build it up within himself, and then contrive to pass it, whatever the obstacles it places in his path, whatever the terrors. Only then can his spirit be free to begin its journey on roads it chooses, and wield freely what power it has.'

'Yet I seemed to see across it, beyond it, even as I woke. There was a horizon beyond it, as there is here. Blue, uncertain peaks . . .'

'Most likely these above us, remembered in dreaming.'

Emboldened now, the boy shook his head. 'Father, no! They stood across . . . across an expanse of water, wider than a river, a lake, anything. The hugest trees, larger than I have ever seen; and then the water. Like a great grey beast-fell spread out about the world . . .'

The older man only snorted, and snatched a bundle wrapped in greasy leather from the wall.

'Water to put out the fire, no doubt! Forget it, my son. If you have come thus far, there is work still to be done, and without delay, indeed. Come with me now! Leave all this, and follow. Leave your robe. Take no food. Cold and hunger are the Seer's friends. But bring your bow, in case!'

So they left the little hut, with its floor of trodden earth, where his mother and sister lay still asleep within the wattled inner chamber, plastered with mud and dry grass to hold in the precious heat of their bodies. Had they been awake, they would not have dared to listen to what passed on the other side of the fire, let alone watch. That was men's work, and they knew better than to brave the father's wrath. Women had their own mysteries with which to content themselves.

The tiny knot of huts was barely stirring, the old watchman on the wall nodding in the blessed moment between the perils of dark and day. Yet he sat up straight as the pair passed. He knew the very shadows that stretched before them, as he knew all in the little farm, the older man's tall and lean, but shoulders bowed as if by great burdens. And little Alya, already grown so much like him, almost a man now at his fifteenth summer, with a full chieftain's name to bear, Alyatan-kawayi'wale Atar. The watchman saluted them with hand to brow, and eyes on the ground. Nobody dared watch what paths the Seer took, or cared to wonder what was held within the dark bundle he bore – one reason he was an outliver among his folk, with only a few poor kin in his huts to gather and work the soil for him. When they took the stony path to the valley's ridge, father and son, and beyond that to the mountain-ways, none dared mark their going. Seer and Seer to be, they walked alone on paths lesser men could never follow, and it was known that the hard earth beneath their feet was not always where their spirits trod.

There were cairns beside the path, some mere
heaps of stone, some half concealing a worn stone
stump with some trace of natural shape. From some
cairns the boy watched his father take a stone, and
add one to others, often with a brief clasping of the
hands and a swift, nasal chant. They climbed and
climbed the narrow trails, for long hours, until the
boy felt exhaustion weighing down his limbs, his
belly griping on nothing and his chest sucking painfully at the thinning air. His father gave him dried
leaves to chew, which tasted foul but eased both the
hunger and the pain, leaving only a light, faint giddi-
ness he dared not give way to.

For the last stage they truly climbed, rather than
walked, scrambling across cold, frost-shattered rocks
to a crevice, a chimney and above that, even as the
boy's strength failed, a ledge. He pulled himself on to
the harsh rock, softened by odd patches of mossy soil,
and lay gasping, sickened yet unable to vomit. Gradually the feeling subsided, and he saw his father
outlined against the sky, sitting cross-legged, hands
outstretched as if in supplication to the brilliant
glaring blue sky. 'Come!' was all he said, and the
boy scurried to sit beside him. Yet even as he reached
the edge he stopped, and gaped, and sank to his
knees, still staring.

The elder shaman nodded. 'You see what it is
most fit for a Seer and a chieftain's son to see. Behold
the world, spread out as upon wings beneath you!'

The boy drew breath, deeply, shakily. They had
ascended for hours, but the sun still stood below its
zenith, not far above the peaks at their back, and its
rays reached out like shafts of yearning across the
expanse beneath. The lower slopes it left in shadow,
touching only the very tops of the foothills with
glowing colour, as if the brown scrub burned suddenly from within. But the vale beyond, where grass
still fought to grow above the bed of unmelting ice

and scattered stone in the thin soil, it lit with kindly warmth, whitening the smokes that twisted up from the little scar of tended land that was theirs.

And beyond that, the open expanse that the boy had always seen as featureless infinity extending to the world's edge, it revealed first as a rolling mass of low brown hills and shallow, greener vales, cut by meandering streams with strange little woodlands crouched along their banks, and brown bogs and livid green reedbeds above which flights of birds seemed to float like dreams, among feathery wisps of cloud. Along the water's edge some small herds of great beasts strayed.

'So wide and free,' said the boy, wondering. 'And so passing fair . . . Can we not go out there some day, and see it at close hand?'

'You may live to see more than you wish,' said the Seer, and his son was to remember those words. 'Look now to the northward, whence come those dark rivers that stem not from our mountains. Does that seem so fair?'

It was not so far in that direction, along the black wide streams, that the brown hills seemed to become browner and the green grew less, the trees and bushes lower and scrubbier. The earth showed through them in wide bare patches, and through it in turn the grey bones of rock and stone, rolled boulder and solid, rising ridge. Colour and life drained from the land, till it became a rounded, riven country of stones. And increasingly, as one looked, it grew tinged with white, light and uneven at first but swiftly thicker and solider, till it enveloped height and distance and identity in a hazy featureless mantle that seemed to bleach the very air above. Sky and cloud mingled as one with the earth beneath, a chilly veil behind which lurked some suggestion of massive solidity, massive as the mountains beneath them, and cool, remote menace.

'Yonder lies the realm of the foes of men,' said the Seer, neutrally. His eyes were steady. 'The ancient powers of the Eternal Cold, and their domain, undying citadel and weapon in one, the moving Walls of Winter, the glaciers of the Ice. There, in their stony hinterlands, the warrior tribes they have corrupted, our kin no longer kin to us, dwell – the *Aikiya'wahsa*, the Ekwesh. And thence they ride forth to rape and raid, and take for their own what little men have wrested from the earth to feed themselves and theirs. Well, would you see more?'

'Not of that!' shivered the boy. 'Can we not look elsewhere?'

'It is wise to,' agreed the Seer, and pointed once again. 'Yonder, my son, to the south and the west. There in warmer lands the ancient green of the growing land lingers still among the stones, even to forest and woodland of a kind. There dwell our kin, still, some in settlements such as ours but greater; and perhaps some even in those towns you remember from your infancy – such as have been spared. But for the most part they dwell in isolation and in fear. Their only hope is that the storm will pass them by, and perhaps also their children. Beyond that they do not think, save in idle fancies and foolish visions.'

'Yet you say yourself that even the faintest dream-picture may have deep meaning—'

The slap came, this time, a hard one. The boy bore it as he had learned to, but his eyes burned. His father's voice was unyielding. 'I speak of what is shown us from within, not stupid fictions men confect, to console themselves for what is not. Hear for yourself! These empty heads say that if you only voyage far enough eastward, you will come to some enormous lake, wider than sight or sound, with a greener land, more forested, such as this land once was, along its shores. Well, that is as may be; but they also say it is thick with salt! Think of the hot springs you have seen, mineral-encrusted, stinking. Could anything green grow along such a shore? And there is more. They claim that on its further shore there is a better land yet, where men with white faces dwell!' The elder hawked and spat, copiously, out into the glassy air.

'As if any lake, large as may be, would hold back the cruel hand of the Ice, or place men beyond its grasp! It gathers the world into its cold palms, and who can restrain it? Yet fools have set out to seek that land, following the Eye of the Swan that looks forever eastward – whatever that may be! And indeed by such a fool's portent they may find it! For this could only be the land of the dead, where the pale-faced ghosts dance.' He sighed. 'No, my son. The way of the Seer is wiser. To seek wisdom through the spirit, and guide his folk in ways where the hand of ill does not fall. Learn now, learn swiftly, and be wise.'

Alya was about to ask more, but the sting of his face made him hesitate. By then the Seer had opened his bundle, and with a tender grasp he lifted out a strange sight, that yet was somehow very familiar to the boy. As a toddling infant in dead, distant days, living in a town with others, he had gaped in de-lighted awe at the spirits that came and danced on holidays – at the turning of the year, at the veneration of the ancestors in the sowing and the harvest, and the festivals of children and unmarried girls at sum-mer's height, when the days seemed endless and the Ice far away.

They were like men, these spirits, but with their bodies streaked and circled in glorious gaudiness, bright as jaybirds on rainbows, and their heads stran-ger and brighter still, mingled visions of beast and man with jaws that chomped and beaks that clapped. Their ancestors, the children were told; their fore-bears, at one with the prey they had hunted in richer, more plentiful lands.

Ancestors who would, with enough propitiation
and offerings, bring back the game and the good
seasons. Ancestors who danced out the old tales,
and the prophecies of tales to come, and most magi-
cally of all scattered gifts and sweetmeats to the
children of their children. Ancestors who, after dancing and eating and drinking and coupling with their
descendants till they were dizzy, fell writhing and
shouting into the arms of their fellows. When they
had left the town, Alya saw them no more, though at
times the beat of drums from his father's hut would
bring them back to mind.

But this, here, rising from the box – this was one
of them, itself. It was with deep wonder he saw for
the first time that that awesome head was made of
painted wood and metal, beautifully carven and
shaped.

His father nodded. 'You understand now. The
spirits need us, as we need them. They need our solid
shapes to live within the pleasures of life once more,
and for a while enjoy the offerings we give them. We
can receive them within us only at the height of our
powers, in the grip of the living dream – just as, in
that state alone, can we penetrate the Wall and its
terrors. To scan what lies beyond and share its many
eyes and ears and thoughts, to draw upon its powers
to influence the world – even, for the most supremely
powerful of us, to carry us throughout it, from one
place to another, by unseen paths . . .' He shivered
with evident delight at the idea of the power. 'For
that also we need to take their form, to beguile the
many Guardians. And therefore they taught us how to
don the Shapes that are their aspect, and to dance the
dance of the Mask.'

The old Seer had been building a tiny fire of dry
twigs as he spoke, and kindled it now with a spark of
flint into dry moss tinder, sputtering and smouldering.
He raised the heavy mask reverently above his head,

into the warming rays of the sun. 'This is the dearest of all the shapes given to our folk, most precious of my masks.' After an instant the warming wood creaked and sang, and he laughed aloud.

'Hear the voice of the ancient wood, speaking to its beloved children! It is said that in that foolish cuckoo-country, that ghostland, the pale men make their magics with hammered metal! As if the earth's cold blood could contain any such life force as this once-living wood! As if it could give you eyes to see through, and a mouth to speak and sing!'

Swiftly, deftly, the Seer lowered the heavy wooden shape about his forehead and slowly down, until his face was hidden. The mask seemed to float lightly above his shoulders, long beak with crooked tip, huge eyes painted in red and white, picked out in glittering obsidian, but hollow at their hearts. Then he knelt, pulled the rough barkcloth shirt from his back, and streaked himself with earth from the ledge, and smearings of chalk and coloured sand in fat from the bundle.

'This is Raven, great patron of our folk! Friend of Men, who stole the Sun for them to defy the first coming of the Ice. You are the last Seer of his most ancient line, Alya; so learn now how to invoke his power. You know this dance, this chant; you have been taught it since you could barely walk. See now the use of it, and the meaning.'

He sprang lithely to his feet, and the beak snapped cruelly. Out of the bag he took a small roundel of steam-bent wood, topped with a taut skin of dark deerhide; hanging from it was a short length of antler, polished by many years of wear. On the drumskin were painted symbols hard to make out against the age-blackened hide, stark, sticklike figures in black and red. The Seer tapped the drum once, twice, on different symbols, and then again, in a different, wilder measure. He beat the skin with the antler stick, and the deerhide thrummed and rang. He sang, in a low husky voice, the same syllables again and again, sounds that were not words but were all the more heavy with meaning. The arms, streaked now like rows of dark feathers, flapped once, twice, and thrust out, fingers spread, in a gliding curve. The drum stuttered to silence, the feet stamped and shuffled in the same soft pulsing beat, but the upper body remained still, as it seemed, wheeling and gliding like the dark specks over the woodlands below. Back it swooped against the rockface, then up and away, out to the very edge of the rim as if to join its brethren in the airs below. Small stones skittered and crumbled into emptiness, but the feet did not falter, whirling and kicking with the energy that infused the effortless glide above.

When the arms came down, the drum thuttered again. Alya thrilled at the sight of his Ancestor, felt the pace of the dance in his blood, and drummed exultantly on the moss with his flat palms. He felt no fear for his father, as he trod the thin line of the cliff's edge; to him also it seemed as if the masked figure would take flight and soar any instant, out of the abyss and into the face of the climbing sun. He longed to follow.

The voice grew higher, harsher, and faster, gasping and dry. The syllables merged and blurred into a raw rasping cry. The voice, not of a single bird, but of many, the cawing clamour of a rising flock; and out of the empty air distant voices knew and answered it. The figure stood straight up suddenly, arms outflung. The jaws opened, wider than before, gaping; and within them, set deep at the throat, shimmered the metal mask of a man, smooth-skinned, impossibly serene, the features bland and general save for the white-painted beard, a rare thing among his folk. And yet the boy clenched his fists in wonder; for within it, within the very metal itself, like glimmering trout in a clear stream, flickers of cold light came and went, and the bland metal eyes blazed and glittered into his own. A single rasping cry rang out among the rocks.

Suddenly the cliff face behind them flashed and shone bright as a mirror, as solid obsidian—

Just as suddenly, the light vanished. Warm darkness was around him, the smell of sweat and leather. His father was putting another mask over his head, telling him to try it, to dance with it in place. 'This is an easier ancestor to bear, the Hawk, the young hunter who feeds his brood; he will carry you as far as you should need. Remember the pattern, the earths, the pebbles! Think hard upon its tracks, for it is through the Trail you are dancing. Dancing on your journey, to the Wall; and one day, beyond.' He settled the mask in place, and let Alya swing his head, grow used to its weight.

'How shall a man get there? Seers seldom agree. Some say you may fly over its summit, some say you may burrow under. For that matter, some say it is not a wall at all, but a very range of mountains, in which paths and passes must be opened and explored. Some others seek to ride thither in the minds of birds and beasts, which know no distinction between it and the outer world; or even through the minds of other Seers. But I who am the Seer and son of many Seers, and carry within me now the words of many more, I say it is a Wall; and that for the strong Seer there is but one way, to rise over it himself, by his own power. Unless he is among the great – and they go *through*! Dance now, boy. Dance, Hawk. *Dance!*'

His arms were already outflung; his feet already stamping the moss. The drum rattled, the chant droned on in his father's exalted voice. Dizzy with exhaustion and altitude and the essence of the dry leaves, Alya threw back his head, and felt the short beak clack and clatter. The mask wobbled, ill-fitting, and he staggered. He knew he should stop. His father's singing took on a harsh, angry tone, the contemptuous voice that made him shrivel when he faltered or failed at anything, worse than any slap; and at the very thought of it his shaking legs thrashed harder. He could not stop. He wagged his head to and fro, desperately trying to balance the mask. The chant burst from his lips in an answering torrent, higher than his father's, almost like a wounded bird piping. Beyond the narrow eyeholes there were only the clouds. He thrust back his wings, trembling as he glided, hovered, stooped . . .

The mask half fell sideways, the eyeholes away from his eyes. Hunger shook his legs. Stone cracked and turned beneath his weary feet—

Everything vanished. He was staring into that jagged, glassy surface, silken smooth yet savagely etched and fanged. High above him it loomed, as far below; and flame boiled in the depths. It was as if he were torn in two. He heard a voice scream, knew his own, and the glassy rock wheeled sickeningly as his legs failed him. He fell back, felt the ledge hit him hard in the back, but his head fell back out into empty space.

He stared upside down into the abyss, and the fiery mouths clamoured in his roaring ears. Light and air smote his cheeks once again. Into the distant depths something small turned and wheeled away, and he convulsed with horror. It was the Hawk mask.

He flung out useless arms, but it was far gone. A distant, hollow smash rose from below, and the rattle of a few rocks. He stared in mute horror and humiliation. He had destroyed a thing he knew must be unimaginably precious. What would his father do to him now? He could almost let himself slide after it.

A firm hand hooked in his shirt, hauled him back up, and dropped him hunched and shaking on the moss. He curled up like a baby, shivering, and awaited the rain of blows that would almost be a relief. 'I'm sorry. I let the Hawk fall! I'm sorry.'

'You did nothing,' said the Seer's grim voice, sternly enough but evenly. 'I saw. The mask sat awkwardly upon you from the start. That, it should not have done, not with any man, and never has before. And yet you achieved the pattern of stones . . . Strange. I thought the mask would settle. I should have taken it from you at once. When I did not, it fled you of its own choosing, and for its own reasons. You are not meant to have the Hawk, that is clear.' There was a note almost of sadness as he added, 'And no more, now, am I.'

Deep misery must still have marked the boy's face, for the Raven mask lifted to reveal his father's features, as ever stern and unbending, yet not without a touch of concern. To the boy's surprise he reverently raised the great mask from his own head. 'Here. Don this!'

Passively, dumbly, Alya let the thing be slid over his head, the beak closed once more, the leather lining positively hot to the touch and slick with sweat. It seemed to cling to his cheeks, yet once in place it did not feel too hot. It was heavy, draggingly heavy; but the boy nodded very carefully, and felt it fit across both scalp and jaw, moving with them, but never itself stirring in its seat.

The Seer gave a long, low grunt of satisfaction, and struck the drum hard. So sudden was the thrill that Alya surged to his feet, hardly heeding the wooden weight. '*Now* can you dance?' growled the older man. 'Now, yes? *Yes!*'

Cold fire ran in the boy's legs, where a moment before milky weariness had flowed. He clattered the beak and cawed as his father had, and flung back his head wildly, and as the drum stuttered he once again echoed the chant. Wheeling, diving, the blue sky spun crazily in the eyeholes, but he knew now why his father had not stopped for the cliff's edge, for fear or even for the mildest caution. He could no longer even feel the stone beneath him; but the wind was cool and thrilling beneath his wings.

All at once the light whirled into the spiral of the Trail, the blackness roared in his head and drew him in. The jagged gloss of the Wall arose again, its innumerable facets now mirroring his naked face, bare of any mask. Endless facets, countless faces, eyes wide, jaws slack, gasping for breath – infinite selves. Then hands scrabbled within the dark glass, clawing, burning at their finger-ends even as they reached out. The faces were no longer his. They were faces he knew. They opened to him, in menace or mute appeal, and glows burst from their eyes, their gaping mouths and distended nostrils. Mother, sister, the tillers of the farm, the few friends of his early life – he fought to rise, to break free of their fearful clutches, to soar above them and crest the grim barrier. For an instant he seemed to see through it, to make out a distorted image, such a wide spread of lands as he had seen from the ledge, but from far higher. And among them, standing out sharply, the valley, the farm, the figures around it like dots, and far, far above them the ledge itself, with a figure that squatted grim and motionless, and another that wheeled and turned—

He could not rise further. Instead he struck the black surface, like a windblown bird. Agony speared one arm, and he felt the tangle of limbs, and the screaming, sickening fall.

He was on his knees on the grass, choking and shaking within the mask, desperately afraid. He plucked it off, and it came willingly, for all it had fitted so close. And again, as he stared at it in his shaking hands, the coursing gleams and glows came and went within the metal. They were continuous things, like serpents, like fish that dived in one piece of metal and surfaced in another, as if there was some incredible unity in the metal, threading the painted wooden sections together. The wood had another feeling entirely, something strange under his hands . . .

He cried out as the thing was taken from him, leaving him alone with the fear. His father grunted as he wrapped the beaked form away in its bundle. 'It is well! Well enough for now. Much you have learned, and that is good. For you may need the knowledge swiftly.'

His father's black eyes, dark and remorseless as the Wall, surveyed him, as if weighing up whether to say something. At last he flung the boy a thick collop of smoked meat from his bag, and a large dried oilcake – a rich feast, to a boy raised so harshly, and his first since the evening before. Gratefully Alya fell to, while his father watched him still. The old man did not eat, but simply stroked his chin thoughtfully. When he spoke at last, it was unexpected.

'It is often the strongest of Seers, when young, who find the craft most thorny to grasp . . .'

Greatly emboldened, if only by a greater fear, the boy stared back. It was hard to imagine his father needing to learn anything; or even young; and yet . . . 'My father! Did *you*?'

The Seer nodded, distantly. 'So hard, I thought the mask would wring blood from my eyes and break my neck like a stalk. This very mask. Your grandfather also, as he admitted to me only in his age. He reached his eighteenth summer ere he completed the pattern, his twentieth ere he even saw the Wall; and that after weeks of fasting in the wilderness.' He rounded on the boy. 'But do not take that as a licence to idle! Every seeker of the paths is different! It's rare that the Sight endures through so many generations, as it has in ours – and through your mother's, also. Once our ancestors were more than shamans! Once they were

wonderworkers who dwelt in great halls of stone,
and travelled the world at will, and spoke with the
Powers whose task it is to steer it. And in the bones I
cast at your birth, while your mother still screamed
and strained you out of her, it was written that you
would yourself speak with Them, one day.'

There was both pride and trouble in his harsh
voice. 'But which Power? There are many it is ill to
speak with, unprepared. There are some it is ruin to
encounter at all! For such a destiny as that, Alya my
son, you must be strong. And strong I shall make you.
From your mother you will learn tenderness; I have
none. Others will teach you to be happy; I would not
know how. But from me you will learn a warrior's
pride and honour, and reverence for the Powers –
yes, even for those who hate us, for their might is
awesome, and not to be taken lightly. And you will
learn your duty as a Seer, to those who will one day
depend on you.'

Never before had the old man spoken so openly;
and in years thereafter the boy Alya wondered
whether it was something he himself had seen that
provoked it. If so, his vision was not clear enough; or
the tale of Alya, and of Savi, and of the Mask, might
have turned out very differently.

The Winter Chronicles, archives of the ancestors
of legend, record it only as a legend in their terms,
brought by the incomers who fled across the ocean to
the haven of Nordeney. They mention many versions
and variations, with as many embellishments as there
were tellers; but equally they insist that the tale itself
was true, and that many who acted within it, for
better or worse, lived to bear witness.

A dark legend it is, too, as befits those times. Yet
it is not without its shafts of light, showing that even
in those lands west of the sea which the glaciers and
their lords most thoroughly overran, that even in their
shadow the sparks of defiance could still catch fire in

human minds. And that even deep within the bitter heart of the Ice itself, with its devouring hatred for all that lived, with the myriad deaths it contained and contrived, the ashen fires of life could sometimes still be rekindled.

The sun now plummeted across the sky, behind clouds infused with purple, edged with blazing gold; across them, untouched somehow, a great feathery, wispy sweep of grey stretched like a heron's wing. The Seer studied it, and shook his head. 'Come! I had thought to spend the night here, for we could lap the dew from the rocks. But the best path for us is downward, I see. All has its place and time. We need severities to train and toughen you. Life provides them all too readily. Yet it seems we cannot even choose the time. Such it is to be a Seer.'

The boy looked back as they turned away; and for a moment the unimaginable misty distances of the Ice became a haze of gold. Yet through it, in the low light, he thought he glimpsed great crags, less high than the abyss, and yet more terrible by far. 'Yes!' said his father, though he had said nothing. 'For this mountain is made of stone, and fixed, changing only with the slow rhythm of the world. But those white walls, they are a marching army, slow though they seem. Their patience is deadly. Many fair lands they have already laid waste; and one day even this, too, they shall grind down. For who can fight them?'

His voice took on a cold sneer. 'But we men may at least slip and skip about their feet, like granary mice. Survive thus, perhaps, until a change of days. Till then our Sight must be our greatest friend, closer even than wife or child; for it serves the greater good. On the far side of the Wall lies all we know, all we can achieve; and that you must surmount, to find it.'

'It seems hard,' said Alya guardedly. 'But I will succeed.'

'It is. You will. There are easier paths. One can

reach out to touch other minds, and be carried by
them across the Wall. Chiefly those of beasts; for all
creatures, and birds especially, slip to and fro over its
bounds, all unknowing, as if to them it is a dream – or
our own world is. But you cannot direct the sight of
beasts, as you can your own. You will see only what
they can see – or what they are shown. Such glimpses
out of the dark are hard to trust. You can ride human
thoughts, if only you are stronger than they; but
Seers who try this too often inevitably come to grief.
Sooner or later they will touch a mind stronger than
theirs – even the mind of a Power. The Seer who rides
one does not live to dismount. So follow the firmer
paths, stony though they are; and trust in yourself.'

Their way down was slower, as is often the way,
slipping and sliding over steep ways they had
bounded up. The boy had time enough to ponder
those words, and to find himself in some ways at war
with his father's wisdom. It was a new experience,
and one he found half daunting, half exhilarating.
Slipping and skipping! Like granary mice indeed, for
sooner or later the cat took them, to play with and
slay. Surely they could do more! Surely they could
fight!

And the mention of these far lands intrigued him,
as such tales always did. Alya the boy would keep his
countenance for now; but one day soon Alyatan-
kawayi the Seer would look farther afield, to the very
ends of the earth.

He forgot that, though, as they wound their way
through the foothills at evening, and looked no
farther than home, whose odours the wind brought
them, first woodsmoke and then roasting meat. That
would be from a deer he had brought down with his
father three days since, another time of freedom and
delight. He was shaping into a fine huntsman, the
workers said.

But as they rounded the slope into the last small

vale, minutes from sight of the farm, Alya saw the
smoke plume ahead, against the last luminous blue. It
billowed dark; and far too high.

The sight held them rigid; and then the Seer
slapped hand to side. No sword hung there. 'Accursed am I,' he breathed, 'that I heeded your Seeing
so much, and my own so little! Come, boy!'

Both were weary, neither in prime manhood;
and yet their leather-hard legs bore them in great
loping strides across the twilit slopes, scarcely feeling
the grass that twined around their shins to trip them,
the patches of soft wet bog that sucked at their
deerskin shoes, the bite of briar and thorn. The
boy strung his bow as he ran, as if this were the
hunting trail, and the father grunted approvingly.

Fear ran cold in their bellies as they crested the
vale's rim; and grew colder yet. The farm was ablaze;
had been, for some time, so that already the low roof-
ridges with their bark shingles were consumed and
gone, and the fire roared at the top of the encircling
walls. Even as they watched, a gable-end collapsed in
a flare of yellow flame, spilling blazing beams across
the ground before them; and by its light they saw only
too clearly what awaited them.

The horses, the kine, the goats were rounded up,
tethered in lines to be led away. Their wagon stood
out, its shafts to the heavens, ready for its team; and
by it, still unloaded, lay their stores, and what little of
their goods was worth plundering. Their people . . .

By the fire's edge Alya saw the bodies stacked,
naked save for slathered blood, sprawled and broken,
his mother's dark hair, so much younger than his
wolf-grey father, spilling grotesquely from under the
watchman's shrivelled flank. All, save one he sought.
But he saw that also, by the light of a lesser fire; the
child's arm that dangled above it, skinned, stretched
out and split, broiling on a makeshift spit.

The same harsh flame had also shown them to

the men around that fire – not many, some ten or
twelve men much like themselves in kind, with
ruddy-brown skin, swarthier than their own, hard
bony faces, and straight dark hair. Theirs was cut
short about the neck and caught up in black rags; and
they wore black breastplates of stiffened leather,
studded with nailheads and streaked with white
patterns that echoed the markings smeared on their
scarred faces, making them look like cruel masks
themselves.

'*Aikiya'wahsa!*' groaned the Seer, as they
snatched up swords and spears. 'The Ekwesh! Wolves
of the Ice!'

He clutched Alya by the arm, and snarled like a
wolf himself. 'One single tear, and I disown you!
Linger, and I curse you!'

He thrust the boy away with a force that sent him
staggering, but himself dashed forward into the glare.
A blazing beam he stooped and caught up, and even
as it kindled his sleeves he bore it forward, against the
oncoming raiders. The first of them yelled as it swung
at their faces, and fell back, but the force of his rush
carried them with it, against the three behind. Swords
flashed, but he seemed not to feel their bite. Their
hair flamed as they stumbled and fell, blinded and
burning; one man was slammed against the glowing
house-wall, and ran howling in a banner of flame. The
rest gave back before the blazing madman and his
mace of fire, into the dark. The Seer laughed a great
screeching laugh. 'So, so! Pretty, pretty! Let others'
women do the weeping! Run, Alya! To the south and
east, to the warmer lands! To our kin! *Run!*'

He hurled the beam across the fire, and the
attackers scattered from its rolling onslaught. Then,
catching the mangled body there by its hair, the old
chieftain lowered his head and ran into the flame-
filled doorway of the farmhouse. It roared like an
open mouth.

Alya, stepping instinctively forward, tripped over something cold and sank to one knee. The bundle his father had thrown down—

A spear hissed. Broad-headed, not meant for throwing, it would still have skewered him, otherwise. It gashed his side and stuck quivering in the ground.

One of the raiders, stalking forward, paused blinking at the edge of the firelight to see if he'd hit his mark. In a frenzy of fear, ignoring the pain, the boy drew his arrow to his chin and loosed. It hissed past the bow's fur wrapping and sailed almost lazily to its mark. The boy had hit rabbits running at greater range. With a snapping thud the arrow sank deep beneath the lower lip of the breastplate, and the man screamed and doubled over around it, tugging at the shaft.

Alya ground his teeth, imagining the barbs biting home in the liver. He had slain beasts in the hunt, but never before a man. Even now he hardly felt he had killed one, for this horror kicking away its life was worse than a clean animal.

The others shouted, seeing the peril of arrows out of the dark, and backed hastily into shadow. His heart pounded, but his stomach was steady. They would circle around, now, and come after him. But he would not be here, and they could not know the ground as he did in the dark.

He ran, light and fleet, wishing they would come after him on their horses, so he could shoot a rider and steal one. But he knew the rest of the raiders, hardier men on horseback, would soon catch him up. Better to be small, and slip by unseen. Over rough ground, marsh and trackless scree lay his safety, such as it was; and his long wandering he knew must be, with naught but the few arrows at his belt and the bundle that bumped at his shoulder, already a burden.

The night flooded Alya's spirit, chilly and black. He felt nothing, not even the long gash in his side. Even when he glanced back at the dying flame it was to see if it showed him another enemy. His mouth was set and thin; his eyes dry. He would never come back, that was certain. He ran.

CHAPTER 2
The Citadel

ALYA ran; and it was as if the lands flew past beneath his feet, as night gave way to day. When light came the dark plume was a streak against the low hills; and pursuit, if there was any, he had left far behind. Nor did he fear he would be tracked. Beyond their sheltered valley the land was as hard as he had seen it, at best rolling hills crowned with brown grass, more often bare and stony, with great outcrops of weathered rock that held no trace for long. He had cut across these many times to hide his trail. He was alone, now, in every sense.

But the barrens held a worse peril for him. At this season, with the spring snows barely melted and the icy underfloor still unthawed, they offered little that lived, still less he could eat.

A day passed, in growing hunger; and another, worse, a pain to add to the fire in his side. There were some signs that men had lived here, but too long ago to be of any help. Only once did he see any other living men, and those a baleful sight. A column of black-clad horsemen, all too like those at the farm, came riding in a number he could not reckon across the plains, following the ghost of a great track, barely visible in the lank grass. They made no attempt to conceal themselves, and he had plenty of warning. They passed in cascading thunder no more than a few hundred paces away, kicking up the brown earth in a great scar, and sped northward in a close column whose regimented lines looked to him both ridiculous and sinister, with wagons rattling along at their tail. They spared scarcely a look for the land around, let alone for the thicket that hid him.

Alya watched them go with hatred, wondering how these men, if men they truly were, could come to serve the Ice and its Powers, that were supposed to hate all things living, and most of all men. Hunger gave his mind an edge of false clarity. He wondered cynically if there really were such things as Powers. His father had thought so, had revered them deeply, had believed his son would speak with them; and what good had that faith done him?

He missed his father more than he could say, for all his grimness; and his mother's voice, his sister's laugh. The farmhands and their simple banter, friends since he could first remember. All stilled, horribly; nothing but the low wailing of the wind on the open plain. More likely Powers were lies or deceptions, mere reflections of human hopes and fears. More likely these black-clad beast-men had shaped deities in their own image, to justify their own cruel desires.

He saw no man else. He was alone.

Otherwise he found only relics of huts very like those at his home, low rings of stone, many cracked and whitened by ancient flames. His father's huts must look like that, now, and the farm with them. Its remains would soon be overgrown; but not these. How folk had lived in such a barren land was hard to understand, unless it had not always been barren. More immediate was how he could manage to survive; for he was not ready to give up the only thing that had been left to him, not yet. He journeyed on, in bitterness.

Alya was well schooled in living in the wilds. Shelter of a kind he could contrive from the scrubby bushes that grew in patches, and even, when he could find dry kindling, fire. But what he roasted over it was scanty – frogs from the many rivulets, tiny fish he had scooped up, snails that rasped the red lichen from the rocks, such roots as grew in the bleak cold soil. At need he ate even fat worms and slimy dark things from under rocks. They would hardly sustain him for long.

Before many days, though, he passed the spring snowline, where the ground grew softer. It was too early for berries, but there were more small animals. He was able to set snares, knock down an occasional bird with a throwing stick, and twice he felled a young deer, though others escaped him. He did not dare risk his few arrows too often. But he had been hungry to start with; and though the gash in his side seemed to heal, bound up in its own blood, the effort of throwing and drawing his bow soon opened it. He tried to staunch it with chewed herbs, but he had little lore of healing, and his weakness told; it would not close, bled often, and burned him more and more fiercely as the days passed. As they grew into weeks he felt his strength ebbing, his head grow light, his stomach sicken; and grief and solitude clawed at his heart.

The night within it sustained him, like cold iron stiffening his spine; but the night also brought terror. For as he lay curled and sweating under his fan of branches, though he was never warm, the Wall seemed to rise up unbidden behind his eyes, and in its dark glass show him visions no man should see. There came to him then his mother, as he had seen her on that fell heap, and his sister, their eyes hollow, their faces beseeching, their ravaged bodies all too clear in the red light. His sister raised up one blood-streaked hand, and the roar of the devouring fire would fill his ears. Then he would start awake in blank terror, scattering the branches, to see only more blackness, moonless and comfortless. It would be long before fear and cold brought their own numbness, and allowed him to sleep once more.

But a day came, after a night of storm and driving rain, when a sudden warmth shone through his meagre shelter, on to his wounded side, and seemed to ease its stabbing a little. Alya sat up, wincing, and found the rays of a red dawn creeping over the world's rim, warming the chill rocks under whose lee he had taken shelter, among the heavy undergrowth that cloaked them. He saw with wonder that they were not rocks at all; they were a wall, of loose flat stones, built rough but very thick and heavy. Tall as a man, in most places, it was the highest he had ever seen; and the outline of the ruin he made out through the foliage suggested it had been taller still. Grooves and scratches on some of the stones might have been carvings once, though now they were no more than rain-channels. He remembered the towering houses of his vision; but they were taller yet, and more strongly built. He wondered who had made this and lived in it, and whether any folk still remained in the land.

Alya stood, carefully, and looked around. Perhaps he was coming into those warmer lands, at last; but they did not look very encouraging. There might be more trees, now he thought of it; but there was less grass about, save by the small streams. The ground looked drier and stonier, the soil more dusty, as if warmth drank up the water. But perhaps there was better country about. The southern horizon looked a little greener. It could even be trees, many trees – a woodland, such as he only dimly remembered. This might be the region where his kin could still live. Somewhere like the noisy townlet of his first and faintest memories, a place full of giants. His father had fled it with his family and household, foreseeing its destruction – but had he simply foreseen his own doom, and run to meet it?

At any rate he must seek somewhere. He could not live long like this, not now. How long had it been since the raid? It had happened under the last new moon. Where was the moon now? Well, tonight he would see, if the sky stayed clear. Meanwhile there were small holes here, made by burrowing creatures; and no shortage of stones.

The little brown beasts were fast, scurrying and chittering between their burrows, with sentinels posted like warriors; their white-striped flanks confused their outline, and Alya's hand was no longer as steady as it had been. In two frustrating hours he felled only a brace, barely a dog's meal for a long day afoot; but it would have to do. He cooked them both, poorly, and saved one for the end of his march. That might be all too soon. He trudged on, until the sun fell downwards into thin cloud, and thence into the dark. If there was a moon, it was too faint to penetrate the cloud. It must be new again, probably; but he hardly remembered that many days passing.

He tried to gnaw the miserable little carcass, sought sleep in the shelter of some thorn-bushes, but his burning side kept him awake and shivering. It bled no longer, but formed a yellowish crust that cracked painfully with every sudden movement. Eventually, at the first hint of light, he rose and stumbled on, sucking the last flesh and marrow from the bones; but then he was violently sick. His head swam as it had with the height, and his side was raw and swollen, and wept slow tears, not blood. His ears sang, and swift things seemed to flicker around at the margins of his vision, long-limbed insectile shapes which danced and mocked like sawflies. They grew bolder as the day advanced and the sunlight dazzled him, as the edged reddish granite which everywhere poked up through the soil tripped and cut him, as the faint paths he found among the unyielding stones seemed to swim and diverge before him. He was stifling with the heat, yet he knew the chill of night would be worse; and he had no idea which way to turn.

If cold and hunger were a Seer's friends, he had
never had better company. And it came to him then
that he might indeed make use of them.

He fumbled for the mask, but at first he could not
even untie the bundle. Then he had it free, set it on
his head, which seemed slick with sweat, and held up
the drum. The figures on it seemed to caper and
cavort, mocking him, and he struck at them, pulsing,
and tried to match their antics. But all he could do
was sway and stagger painfully, unable to dance but
too bewildered to remove the heavy mask. He
struggled not to fall on the sharp raw stones.

His mind roared, his eyes dimmed. The landscape faded into pinkish cloud, that flickered and
pulsed alarmingly. Then all of a sudden it billowed
like a storm-rent veil, blackness blazed with fire, and
the Trail crackled swiftly before him. He dropped the
drum, felt it smash underfoot. A spurt of flame
coursed along the curves and windings of the Trail,
and the coloured earths flared and turned ashen. He
was toppling helplessly forward into it.

There was a fearful rushing and roaring in his
ears, and he felt as if a flood was carrying him off,
turning and tumbling him through a myriad chill
eddies and currents, scraping him past sharp stones.
The Wall towered in his mind. The firelit corpses
whirled and gyrated, thrust out wild arms to stop
him—

His head jarred within the mask. He clawed at
the ground, trying to get up, to crawl forward at
least; but fell back gasping. He saw nothing now, he
could feel only the dry crumbly soil beneath his
fingers. He bore up the mask with his hands, managed to lift his head, and stared. Had he been
stumbling about for hours? The view had changed.
He was looking at raw earth, turned and loose, in
neat rows. Tilled and planted; shoots were poking
through, already gnarled, but alive and growing. His

arms gave, and he slumped down, gasping at the burning blade in his side.

'See!' shrilled a voice. 'See! What'd I tell you?'

'Is it a man? Is it a bad man?'

Children's voices – his sister's, maybe. Something dabbed at his side, hurt him terribly. He moaned, stirred but could not move. The voice fled, shrieking.

'*Baad maaaannn—*'

The voice seemed to spiral away into echoing emptiness.

Then, shockingly, he was swaying, sickeningly. Stones rattled, voices cursed; the sky hurt his eyes—

The mask! He flailed around, choking on his dry throat. It had gone.

'Easy, boy!' said a calm voice, a man's, in his own tongue and accent. 'Lie still now, we mean you no harm. You are heavy enough to bear already.'

There was a hissing rattle, like a small rockfall. His eyes were so gummed he could hardly keep them open. His cheek lolled against something dry and taut, smelling faintly unpleasant. A hide, with four heavy brown hands clenched in its edges, bearing him along like a new-born babe. Gingerly, he realised, as if over unsteady ground. Another sharp swaying, curses, more rocks falling. He tried to croak a question.

'The mask? Safe and in good hands, boy. The drum – well, that's got burned, by the look of it, but we have it also. You're a Seer, then? Young for it. I also, though I don't see far or clear. We have a better man, for that. But your mask's kept for you, fear not. Lie still. You will soon be safe in the Citadel.'

Alya could do little but believe him. His head rocked so with fever that he hardly noticed when at last they set him down; the solid earth still swayed beneath him. The drum had burned? How? And how had he got here? He slid away into dreams of churning darkness.

Agony shot him awake again, a fresh sting in his side. Hands seized his limbs, quelling his struggle. He broke into a convulsive sweat and retched.

'Easy!' said a quiet voice in his ear, that he thought was his mother's. 'Your side's been cleaned, but it needs stitching up. Only one more to endure. Here, hold my hand . . .' The fingers felt slender and blissfully cool. He was afraid he might crush them, when the pain came again. When it did, it was blinding; yet somehow more bearable than the sickly ache it pierced. His hand was squeezed gently. 'There! That is all. Here . . .'

Water trickled on to his face, cracked the encrusted dirt about his mouth, freeing his tongue, loosening his throat. He gulped it greedily.

'So, so!' said the soft voice, with a severity that still had a touch of the child about it. 'Too much at once will make you more ill. So my father says, and he is our chieftain!'

An old woman's voice cackled. 'Savi! If you must wag your jaw, help chew these bitter leaves!'

The boy relaxed, remembering his mother chewing herbs to poultice his cuts and grazes. The sting of warm water on his side was breathtaking, then blissful; and he sighed as the cool dressing drew the sting. 'Bear up now, lad,' said the old woman, 'so we can bind it!'

Hands lifted him, while soft ragged cloth was wound gently about his body. His head still sang, but he found he could look around for the first time. He was in a room of some sort, but no hut; more like a cave, with sunlit greenery at its mouth. The roof was rock, but the walls on either side were a mess of piled stone and crude mud-bricks, plastered with pale earth. Around them, around him, sat a ring of women, all ages and kinds, looking at him with pity and concern. The one who tended him was a walnut-faced crone, though her eyes twinkled very black and

bright among the wrinkles. But at his other side dark
eyes shone with a softer lustre in a face that was only
just finding its true shape. They held his; and from
that moment forth, so says the tale, to them both all
other eyes seemed dim.

But the sunlight was barred suddenly, and all
eyes turned away at the sound of a harsh voice. 'How
does he fare? Does he wake yet?'

The old woman half rose from her knees and
pushed back the figure that stooped in. 'Away now,
Ushaya! This is women's business!'

He thrust her aside with a wiry arm, a rangy,
goatish man with greying braids and a sour, bony
face. 'It is everyone's business, old fool! It was wrong
to bring him here without first consulting me! Am I
not the chiefest healer? And who knows how he
came here, or what he brings with him? There is a
cloud about him, in my sight. The ways he trod are
hidden. We must be sure he is not of the *Aikiya'
wahsa*, their slave or spy!'

'I am no man's slave,' croaked the boy indignantly. 'My name is Alya, as was my father's, an
outliver in a sheltered vale in the shade of the northern mountains. The men of the Ice you name came
down upon us, and slew all my family. He died in
helping my escape, bidding me seek out our kin far to
the south.'

The women groaned with sympathy. 'Hear! Our
kin! Does he not speak our tongue as we do?'

The grey man angled his head, like a nod. 'Near
enough. Though I have never heard of an outliver
called Alya. Whence came your line?'

'I . . . remember only a town. Many huts. He
took us all from there when I was small. I believe he
foresaw its downfall.'

'He was a Seer? Ah. The mask, yes. Seers often
knew one another by name and repute, in the old
days. The Seer Alya . . . Yes. Alyatan-kawayi'wale

Atar. Of Teoquhan. So that is what became of him! I
heard much of him, in my youth. And Teoquhan the
town was indeed laid waste, in war. So, then.' He
glared at the women. 'Turn away. Here is men's talk!'

They snorted with disdain or annoyance; but
they obeyed. The old man squatted beside him,
and dropped his voice to a whisper. 'Are you a Seer
also, that you dare bear that mask? Have you passed
the Wall?'

'I have come close. Seen over it once, I think. My
father said I was on the path, and should keep trying.'

The old man sat back, as if disappointed. 'Perhaps it would not be much use, not now, without
him. Such a mask should only be used by a Seer of
great experience, such as he was. I will take it for you,
and if you show promise I will train you as I train my
own son . . .'

'You will take nothing!' blazed the girl suddenly,
thrusting a bundle behind her back. 'My father orders
it kept for him! He knew your greasy fingers would be
itching for it!'

The old man looked at her contemptuously. 'I do
not answer to a child. If he seeks refuge among us,
this boy, he must win his place. Power misused may
doom us all! And if he seeks to become a Seer, he will
achieve that only with my guidance. I will tell your
father of that, and your insolence.'

'Go shake your ears!' shrilled the old woman
after him, as he stooped out under the rock arch. The
women laughed, but there was a nervous edge to it,
and the girl shivered.

'He is a terrible man,' she whispered to the boy,
as she helped him lie back on the hide once again. She
smiled, and it seemed to him like a new dawn in his
life. 'He can see both life and death, they say, and
move between their worlds freely; and to look at him
I can believe that. But do not fear, my father holds
him on a tether, and he has many times served our

need. And his son is a fine boy, you will like him. So rest now, and heal – Alya! You are safe among us of the Citadel. Safe, and welcome!'

Such was Alya's coming to the place that became his new home, and the nurturing of his extraordinary life that was to be. But how it was he came there out of the wilderness, he only began to guess.

He was given a drink of sour herbs, that refreshed him deeply, and a little mess of beans and brown wheat. He slept long, and awoke stiff and sore still, but shed of his fever. The old woman who kept watch on him gave him more food, and when he mentioned another need she helped him to the mouth of what he had thought was a cave. There he looked for the first time on the strange place the Chronicles name the Citadel.

It was a peaceable village, as it stood then, of only some three hundred folk; yet so great, and so defensible, that it could have held a whole garrison and their people, large as a town. That place was not a work of man, in its beginning; but men had made it what it now was. It had no high towers, no outthrust buttresses, battlements or any other defence traditional to citadels; yet it stood no less secure. It was a mirror of a citadel, behind walls which did not rise, but sank deep into the earth.

Too narrow to be a true valley, it was a great cleft sliced deep into a slope of stone, by a fast-flowing stream that now meandered along its floor. On its way down the water had cut through layers of softer rock to create great ledges and overhangs. And into these, struggling along sheer cliff-faces and treacherous scree-falls, its builders of a bygone age had cut first narrow pathways, and after that piled up walls of stone and mud-brick to turn the space beneath the rocky overhangs into chambers that might hide and hold an army and its stores. The paths were left narrow and treacherous, for those who did not know them well, cutting across the perilous scree slopes. Seen from within, those steep flanks did look like the sternest of citadel walls; yet from without they were almost invisible, till you stood on the very rim. From any distance it seemed nothing but another gully. It was a place of power, and a strong force was quartered within it, dominating the lands about.

Now, though, only the villagers dwelt there. Some said they were the descendants of the original garrison, soldiers turned to peaceable farmers when their kingdom fell apart about them; others that they had arrived later, in flight from other lands and towns the Ice and its agents had laid waste. Probably both tales were true.

They had taken over the ancient strength, dividing and extending its halls to make storerooms and dwellings. Its high gatehouse at some time collapsed, or was thrown down, and never repaired; but the rubble was used to narrow the valley entrance and keep it defensible. Windows and doors were left as few and as small as possible, against both foes and weather, and on the bare lower flanks they planted trees and thorny bushes to screen them, and hide the paths. Most of these they left as narrow and uneven as before, adding only a few wider platforms before the granaries and storerooms. The old muster-ground, before the tall rock hall that had been the commandant's and was now their chieftain's, they made a gathering place with a firepit, shielded by more trees, where of an evening they sat and talked. Their fields they kept at some distance, beyond a barrier of wiry woodland.

In this way the strength of the Citadel was largely hidden. It was difficult to find, harder still to attack, and by then it had already endured long after many greater towns had been swept away.

'For we want nothing of little kingdoms and brief alliances,' said Saquavan the chieftain that night, having called a much-restored Alya to eat in his house. 'They rise from villages, within a generation or two. They build their walls and their palaces, they play a little while with peace and war, bask in the reflected glories of the past. And then one day the Ice stretches forth its fell hand, and all is brought low to the dust.'

The chieftain looked up, into the shadows of the uneven ceiling above. Alya saw that there, upon the vast wooden beam that supported its man-made portion, hung a blackened, cobwebbed shape. It was of a length that might reach from a tall man's waist to his ankle, flat and broad; and it drew Alya's eye strangely. 'There is a relic of one such. A blade from another age, a sword that was of our ancestors, traced with wild old characters none can read. Some say, the mighty Zvyataquar, greatest of our line, in whom strength ran like fire in the blood; and who, when old age stilled it, did not die, but turned instead to indomitable stone. What good did his heroism do him? His land lies now beneath the Ice. None now draws that blade, for it is too weighty for even the mightiest among us. I would beat its metal into hoes and ploughs, if I had the means. Better it hangs useless there, as a symbol of a way that has failed.'

He scooped beans from his bowl with a coarse crust. 'Even now, within ten days' journey of us, beyond the forest to the south, another little kingdom puffs itself up, rising within the ruined walls of a greatness long departed. We could ally with it, if we wished, have trade and traffic and a richer life – if we cared to leave our hoes and hunting-bows, and draw that sword. And with it we could fall. Better to live simply, as we do. Make no wars, hoard no wealth, but dwell in peace by the smoke of our cooking fires, and leave no mark upon the world of our coming and going. We can do no better.'

Alya was silent a moment, enjoying his corn porridge. He was inclined to like Saquavan, a tall

man in early middle age, whose calm face and quiet
manner carried great authority. And for the girl
Saviyal, whose dark eyes and high cheekbones
gleamed in the shadows on the women's side of
the fire, he felt more than liking. He did not want
to contradict her father; but a resentful flame kindled
in him.

'You are wise, chieftain,' he said, carefully, with
the courtesy his father had taught him. 'And concerned for your folk. I am lucky to have fallen among
you, grateful that you have accepted me so readily.
Yet forgive me, but could we not at least seek some
other way of defying the Ice? Less openly than of old,
if we must – but defy it still! For otherwise do we not
simply shape our own prison, and save the Ice the
trouble?'

He heard the quick gasp in the shadow; but the
chieftain only nodded. 'Your tongue is quick, with
something of the serpent's. That is as it should be, for
you are young. Some thirteen summers, yes? Much
the age I was, when I said the same thing. I yearned
for some way to strike back – or simply to escape, to
that land over-sea that men tell of. But I never found
such a way, and I no longer believe those idle tales.
The Seers can tell us nothing certain. All we can do is
endure.'

Alya almost choked on a mouthful, but the chieftain leaned forward and spoke more quietly. 'For my
days, at least. But in yours – who knows? You, boy,
you are a Seer in the making. Perhaps already, in the
world of your dreams, you make out the first steps of
some path others have missed! And that is one reason
I welcome you among us. Ushaya . . . he is our best
Seer, many times proven right. But he is a man to
value his own interests highly. And those of his
son . . .' He glanced into the shadow, and chuckled.
'Ushaya sees it as rightful that his son should succeed
him as both Seer and chieftain. That I do not like.

Vansha is a fine lad, strong as a horse and fond of a laugh or a scrap, but he is unproven as a Seer. And though he might make a sturdy chieftain one day, he is, well, headstrong. I think it safest to place our folk's safety in more than one hand. And destiny sends us another Seer! One who owes nothing to Ushaya. One who may prove stronger. One who will at least give the people a choice.'

Alya sat silent. Young he might be, but already he saw clearly enough into the minds and motives of men, as a Seer should. The chieftain's kindly welcome he had not questioned; but that Saquavan should so firmly deny his own Seer the mask he coveted . . .

Now he understood why. Kindness, yes; but more than kindness. 'You place great trust in me, chieftain. I too am unproven.'

'So far, perhaps. And yet you found us easily enough, did you not? Promise me that you will keep trying to learn, even while you share our daily labours. For all our sakes. For the sake, let us say, of your dream.'

Saquavan was not chieftain for nothing, Alya realised. Deftly and without fuss he had been told his role among them – thankless enough, yet one he must accept. He wondered what this Seer's son would make of it; for he too would surely see beneath the surface. And he wondered also what thoughts might lie behind those firelit eyes.

He had not long to wait. They gave him a little hut no other wanted, a single room that was a relic of the ancient gatehouse. There he woke before dawn, and the first thing he knew was that his side, though still stitched, was no longer badly inflamed. Thunder crackled, somewhere far off; from the north whence he had fled, perhaps. Then he saw the figure that filled the low entrance, dark against dark.

'Awake then, little Seer?' said a light voice, a boy's. 'And feeling better, surely?'

'No worse than tender, thank you.'

'Well, then. Among we plain farmers even a Seer must sometimes earn his keep. I'm sent to ask if you feel fit enough to join our labours!'

Alya stood up, slowly. The words were amiable enough, the tone even; yet there was that in it he disliked. He could guess who this must be. 'I'll do all I can. What's wanted?'

'Oh, a hunt's afoot – a band or two setting out. Or, if that's not to your taste, there's planting and weeding enough for any.'

Alya could not see the boy's face, but he could hear the smirk it must wear. Putting on a performance for cronies lurking outside, perhaps. Alya picked his answer carefully. 'I would hunt, gladly; but the spear wound's still stiff, I would hinder you. I do not scorn to work the fields with the women and children, until I am well.'

That left little room for mockery. He'd wager these boys had never faced a spear in anger.

There was a moment's silence. 'As you wish.' The tone was dull, disappointed. The new brat hadn't been provoked. 'You're to eat the daymeal at the chieftain's fire. Come now!'

The three or four boys in the dimness outside – Alya had been right – shuffled along behind as Alya limped down to the chieftain's hut. The path was especially difficult in this light, and from the sniggers at his back he guessed that they were pretending to push him – along, or over the edge. He ignored that; but he knew there would be more. Their feelings wreathed around him like acrid smoke, but until they reached the chieftain's house he did not look around.

There, in the growing light, Alya and Vansha, Seers' sons, beheld one another for the first time. Neither liked what they saw.

Vansha, perhaps a year the elder, was already the image of a man in his hunter's garb, little more than

'No worse than tender, thank you.'

'Well, then. Among we plain farmers even a Seer [] sometimes earn his keep. I'm sent to ask if you [] fit enough to join our labours!'

Alya stood up, slowly. The words were amiable [] ough, the tone even; yet there was that in it he [] iked. He could guess who this must be. 'I'll do all I [] . What's wanted?'

'Oh, a hunt's afoot – a band or two setting out. [], if that's not to your taste, there's planting and [] eeding enough for any.'

Alya could not see the boy's face, but he could [] ar the smirk it must wear. Putting on a performance [] r cronies lurking outside, perhaps. Alya picked his [] nswer carefully. 'I would hunt, gladly; but the spear [] ound's still stiff, I would hinder you. I do not scorn [] work the fields with the women and children, until [] am well.'

That left little room for mockery. He'd wager [] hese boys had never faced a spear in anger.

There was a moment's silence. 'As you wish.' The tone was dull, disappointed. The new brat hadn't [] been provoked. 'You're to eat the daymeal at the [] hieftain's fire. Come now!'

The three or four boys in the dimness outside – [] Alya had been right – shuffled along behind as Alya [] imped down to the chieftain's hut. The path was [] specially difficult in this light, and from the sniggers [] t his back he guessed that they were pretending to [] ush him – along, or over the edge. He ignored that; [] ut he knew there would be more. Their feelings [] reathed around him like acrid smoke, but until they [] ached the chieftain's house he did not look around.

There, in the growing light, Alya and Vansha, [] ers' sons, beheld one another for the first time. [] either liked what they saw.

Vansha, perhaps a year the elder, was already the [] age of a man in his hunter's garb, little more than

having called a much-restored Alya to eat in his house. 'They rise from villages, within a generation or two. They build their walls and their palaces, they play a little while with peace and war, bask in the reflected glories of the past. And then one day the Ice stretches forth its fell hand, and all is brought low to the dust.'

The chieftain looked up, into the shadows of the uneven ceiling above. Alya saw that there, upon the vast wooden beam that supported its man-made portion, hung a blackened, cobwebbed shape. It was of a length that might reach from a tall man's waist to his ankle, flat and broad; and it drew Alya's eye strangely. 'There is a relic of one such. A blade from another age, a sword that was of our ancestors, traced with wild old characters none can read. Some say, the mighty Zvyataquar, greatest of our line, in whom strength ran like fire in the blood; and who, when old age stilled it, did not die, but turned instead to indomitable stone. What good did his heroism do him? His land lies now beneath the Ice. None now draws that blade, for it is too weighty for even the mightiest among us. I would beat its metal into hoes and ploughs, if I had the means. Better it hangs useless there, as a symbol of a way that has failed.'

He scooped beans from his bowl with a coarse crust. 'Even now, within ten days' journey of us, beyond the forest to the south, another little kingdom puffs itself up, rising within the ruined walls of a greatness long departed. We could ally with it, if we wished, have trade and traffic and a richer life – if we cared to leave our hoes and hunting-bows, and draw that sword. And with it we could fall. Better to live simply, as we do. Make no wars, hoard no wealth, but dwell in peace by the smoke of our cooking fires, and leave no mark upon the world of our coming and going. We can do no better.'

Alya was silent a moment, enjoying his corn porridge. He was inclined to like Saquavan, a tall man in early middle age, whose calm face and quiet manner carried great authority. And for the girl Saviyal, whose dark eyes and high cheekbones gleamed in the shadows on the women's side of the fire, he felt more than liking. He did not want to contradict her father; but a resentful flame kindled in him.

'You are wise, chieftain,' he said, carefully, with the courtesy his father had taught him. 'And concerned for your folk. I am lucky to have fallen among you, grateful that you have accepted me so readily. Yet forgive me, but could we not at least seek some other way of defying the Ice? Less openly than of old, if we must – but defy it still! For otherwise do we not simply shape our own prison, and save the Ice the trouble?'

He heard the quick gasp in the shadow; but the chieftain only nodded. 'Your tongue is quick, with something of the serpent's. That is as it should be, for you are young. Some thirteen summers, yes? Much the age I was, when I said the same thing. I yearned for some way to strike back – or simply to escape, to that land over-sea that men tell of. But I never found such a way, and I no longer believe those idle tales. The Seers can tell us nothing certain. All we can do is endure.'

Alya almost choked on a mouthful, but the chieftain leaned forward and spoke more quietly. 'For my days, at least. But in yours – who knows? You, boy, you are a Seer in the making. Perhaps already, in the world of your dreams, you make out the first steps of some path others have missed! And that is one reason I welcome you among us. Ushaya . . . he is our best Seer, many times proven right. But he is a man to value his own interests highly. And those of his son . . .' He glanced into the shadow, and chuckled. 'Ushaya sees it as rightful that his son should succeed him as both Seer and chieftain. That I do not like.

Vansha is a fine lad, strong as a hors[e] laugh or a scrap, but he is unproven though he might make a sturdy chiefta[in] is, well, headstrong. I think it safest to p[ut] safety in more than one hand. And des[ire] another Seer! One who owes nothing to [ ] who may prove stronger. One who will [ ] the people a choice.'

Alya sat silent. Young he might be, bu[t he] saw clearly enough into the minds and [ ] men, as a Seer should. The chieftain's kindl[y] he had not questioned; but that Saquavan [ ] firmly deny his own Seer the mask he cov[ ]

Now he understood why. Kindness, [ ] more than kindness. 'You place great trus[t] chieftain. I too am unproven.'

'So far, perhaps. And yet you found u[s] enough, did you not? Promise me that you w[ill] trying to learn, even while you share our daily l[ ] For all our sakes. For the sake, let us say, o[f] dream.'

Saquavan was not chieftain for nothing[,] realised. Deftly and without fuss he had bee[n] his role among them – thankless enough, yet [ ] must accept. He wondered what this Seer [ ] would make of it; for he too would surely see b[ ] the surface. And he wondered also what th[ ] might lie behind those firelit eyes.

He had not long to wait. They gave him [ ] hut no other wanted, a single room that was a[ ] the ancient gatehouse. There he woke befor[e] and the first thing he knew was that his side[,] still stitched, was no longer badly inflamed. [ ] crackled, somewhere far off; from the north [ ] he had fled, perhaps. Then he saw the fig[ure] filled the low entrance, dark against dark. [ ]

'Awake then, little Seer?' said a light [ ] boy's. 'And feeling better, surely?'

loincloth and light sandals, his skin oiled for warmth, with bow at his back and quiver and bag at his side. In him his father's gauntness looked sleek as a snowcat; his muscles moved with careless feline ease, and his narrowed eyes had the same glitter. Beneath his oil-spiked hair his face was hard but very handsome, and his open smile suggested he knew it all too well.

It also told Alya that he looked like a gawky starveling by comparison, his bony limbs ungainly and ill-proportioned, his protruding ribs marred by the blood-blackened gash. His face was flecked with scratches, scars and spots, and to him it seemed ordinary, oafish and blank, accustomed since childhood to hide any outward feeling. It did not occur to him that he wore marks of experience the other did not, of enviable strength and achievement beyond his years; or that some might also think him handsome.

'Don't want to hunt!' anounced Vansha, making it sound contemptible. Alya was aware of the girl Saviyal, though she would never meet his gaze.

'But when I heal—'

'Then we'll see how well you handle a bow,' said Vansha crisply.

'You may see that now,' said Alya, and held out his hand.

Vansha unwillingly passed his over. Alya strung it, a little clumsily because it hurt his wound, flexed the string a couple of times, then drew it to his chin, swung around and loosed. The effort burned along his side; but the arrow hissed into the pines some hundred paces away, and struck a narrow sapling with a humming thud. A flock of pigeons erupted in protest. A second shaft struck a span below it. Vansha made a great show of being impressed, then lazily handed him another shaft. Angrily Alya seized it and drew, but his side stabbed at him suddenly and shook the strength in his left hand. The shaft went into the ground some ten yards short.

Vansha shook his head as he hurried to retrieve
it. 'Bad for a hunting point. Now I'll needs sharpen it.
Never mind, boy, we'll make a hunter of you yet.'

And so the seal was set upon their meeting. As it
was then, so it was to be.

Always Vansha was the leader among the other
boys. They took their tone from him; and, less obviously, the rest of the village echoed them. That first
day, though his side still ached, Alya worked with the
women and children and old men. He dug the stony
ground with hoe and stick, till by evening his hands
blistered and his wound cracked a little, mingling
blood with sweat. But when the hunters returned
Vansha greeted him with a ringing cry. 'Hoi there,
Alya, you lazy bag of bones! Did you foresee the fine
deer we've caught you? It'll fatten you up for a man's
work!' He spoke merrily and without open malice;
but the others laughed, and Alya saw his labours set at
nothing.

From then on, whatever he did, Vansha put his
laughing words upon. The good was made negligible
and slight, the ill a matter of laughter and tale retold;
and soon Alya could do no right.

In the eyes of many. But the chieftain seemed to
be sympathetic, and was careful to praise Alya when
he could. And of Saviyal's regard, Alya was never sure;
for though he could never meet her eyes, he often
found them upon him. But they would always turn
instantly away. That first day in the fields he had seen
her, working like all the rest stripped to the breech-
cloth, and he had admired her litheness, thinking
how slender and willowy she seemed among so many
plump village girls. He had tried to work his way over
near her, not so hard in this shapeless patchwork of
fields; but he got no more from her than a quick smile
and a turned head. Yet that smile's warmth heated
him more than sun or labour, and eased more than
one pain.

When he was well enough to hunt, Alya hoped to win better opinions; for he had always been a keen tracker and a good shot. But at first he did not shine, for hunting and tracking in this barren land was different from the well-watered vale he had grown up in, at the mountains' roots. He learned, soon enough. He had more patience than most of his age, and a tenacity even Vansha could not mock. He would track his quarry beyond all hope, and often bring it back. But it did him no good. Whatever he took, Vansha would exert himself to take more of. Often he shadowed Alya, as if teaching or guarding a helpless child, and would loose his own arrow too early, either to claim the quarry himself or scare it away. When their arrows both struck, he would claim the kill, for none would believe otherwise, and belittle Alya in the guise of praise.

With Vansha it was always words. He might have dominated Alya with force, but never did. Some of his oafish cronies joked that since Alya was fit only to work with the girls, they might use him as one. But they found him agile enough to evade their grasp and strong enough to leave bloody denials on their faces. The stone that smashed a ringleader's nose settled the matter. They never bothered him again, but they often sought to trip him, soak his bowstring or steal his catch, and suchlike mean tricks.

All this Alya bore, because he knew he had no choice. But often, in the long cold nights, when only the watchfires still burned and all others huddled together on their mats and skins for warmth, he would sit naked in his hut door, feel the icy night-breath on his skin, and think, slow and deep. He had many memories to relive, good and bad; and many questions to ask of himself. At first, he wondered how he had come here, whether he had simply wandered in blindness and fever, whether the mask or something behind it had guided his steps, or whether some

other force had somehow come into play. As the
weeks wore on, though, and his battle for regard
grew ever harder, he no longer wondered how, so
much as why, and whether he could leave, and start
anew. But that was no doubt what Vansha wanted;
and there was the girl.

Often, from behind the carefully loosened stone
in the wall, he would take out the hide bundle, and
reverently unwrap the mask, and the drum he had
remade as best he could, repainting the figures from
memory on a scrap of gut. He strove to pursue his
discipline, as the chieftain wanted; but that too
seemed increasingly hard and hopeless. These days
he would don the mask, dance a little, trace the
smoking path of the Trail on the soil and in his
thoughts; but with no serious intent, save to savour
the sense of power, and the memories of his inheritance. But these, like tears, he held back; for they
might yet serve his purposes.

At last, though, there came a night when his
blood was hot, and bitterness in his mouth. He had an
urgent question to ask, a path to seek; and for the first
time it was neither vengeance nor guilt that filled his
heart. The mask slid on as always, and, very softly, he
began to tap the drum, to shuffle his feet on the
trodden earth floor. This way and that he swayed,
relishing the extra swing the mask gave his head, the
pulse in his excited blood. The pattern flickered and
grew, the Trail smoked like a maze of incense, leading
him inward and upward, as to the foothills of a range
of mighty cliffs. The darkness of the hut came rushing
in upon him suddenly, glittering, solid, shining black
as ice on wet stone or deep water; and he was staring
at the million facets of the Wall.

The flames were gone. Instead there was a
churning, seething mass of pale forms in motion,
threshing fish in a tightening net. But they were
not fish. Now, though, instead of accepting what

was shown him there, he drove against it in rebellion, in desperation, striving to see something in its place. He summoned up the face before his eyes, the look he had at last met and held for an endless second; and his blood seemed to boil with the sudden urgency of his need.

For an instant, as the air trembled between, and he shook with it, he thought he glimpsed something, some glimmer beyond the fleshy turmoil. Instinctively he reached out – and found the Wall solid under his hand. Solid, and cold, numbing cold – and razor sharp, on its faceted rim, like the obsidian it resembled, stinging his hand as if he clutched a handful of reeds. He let go with a yelp, and fell, plummeting away down into infinite dark below. He landed with a thump, on his knees, on the hut's earth floor, panting. A figure squatted at the low door; and he felt giddy with achievement.

'Alya! Is anything amiss? I'd risen – I heard you call—' She had a skin clutched around her, and moonlight shone on one bare shoulder, translating copper to silver.

He rose, still in the mask, and stood looking at her. His call? Of voice, or of mind? She gasped a little, shrank back as if to run; and he realised what a frightening sight he must make, imbued with the awe that surrounds a Seer. Quickly he plucked the mask off, ducked down to clutch her hand.

'It's nothing, Savi. Please don't go! I sought a path, that was all. And found it – blocked, guarded. As always.'

She shivered, visibly, and still did not cross the threshold. 'It must be a great mystery. And a great power. Vansha always tries to make it sound so, but I think he doesn't really know much, yet.'

'I think so too. But thank you for your concern, Savi. For coming to me.' It occurred to him, crazily, that he could even ask his question directly, now. 'But

. . . why will you not come to me in the day? Even for a quiet word? There is so much I would like to tell you!'

She hesitated a little. 'What might that be?'

'How kind you were to me. How much that meant. How beautiful you are, the most beautiful creature in all the world, sleek as a doe and as tender, as bright-eyed as a bird. Why can I never tell you that under the sun, Savi?'

'Because I shall be of marrying age in only a few months. Because of Vansha.'

'Vansha!' Alya made his name a curse. Always Vansha! 'What of him? You are a chieftain's daughter, you may speak to whom you like.'

She ducked her head from side to side, a sign of denial; but this was almost like a writhe of pain. Alya felt his blood burn, his heart grow heavy. 'You are not bound to him, are you? Not before you are of age?'

The writhe again. 'No! Though he would have me so. Long since. We have . . .' She looked away. 'We have touched one another since we were children, and it pleased me well enough, though he was rough. He was always fair and strong and full of cheer, bright as the sun, and made much of me. But I have watched him grow more like his father, and liked him less and less for it. Then you came. And I saw how he looked at you from the first. He hates you. He has done so since you first appeared, the very look of you, the face of the Raven, the tale you told. He hates you so much his heart grows cold, his merriment hollow. Because you are everything he is not. He fears you, also. For what my father plans.'

'That I guessed. But it always seemed like scorn and jest!'

'That is how Vansha would have you, how he is happy enough for now. But if he finds any cause to fear you, to think you a real rival – then he would do worse, Alya! He might hurt you!'

She seized his hand in her entreaty; and he caught it, and drew her over the threshold. 'Don't be seen out there if he worries you so! Vansha doesn't frighten me. Remember how I ran rings around Chaquala and Miale, and flattened Balka's nose across his warty face?'

'But not Vansha. They are only what he made them, their own strength broken against his. He is stronger and cleverer.'

'Let him be vicious as a bear-dog, if he wants!' said Alya. 'But if you do not want him, Savi, he shall not have you!'

'Once . . . Oh, I do not know! I thought him so brave and strong once, and he is. But he is not . . . good, not as you are good, that I can tell. When I saw you, so full of sorrows and yet more than that . . . The flame in your eye is darker, yet it dimmed his to an ember. Yes, I want you! With him I might be happier, who can say? But it is you I want!'

Their people seldom kissed on the lips; but they held one another, tightly, and he let his face rest against hers, upturned, their foreheads and noses touching. Their eyelashes fluttered against one another, their breath mingled. He had hardly remembered he was naked; it meant little among their folk. But he became fiercely aware of it now, and of her warmth against him, the skin held from him by no more than the stiff hide. He drew his lips down her face, her neck, to where the moonlight had made her shoulder shimmer like the enchanted metal of the mask. And from there, down, against the stiff stale hide, pressing against the warmth of her small breast beneath. She caught her breath, and leaned back in his arms, and ran her hands up his thigh, clutching at him. Panting, he buried his head in her shoulder again, slid his own hand beneath the hide, between her legs, held her as she him. They leaned together in the darkness, clutching and breathing as one, aware of little else and deeply content.

She left him, after a time, with scarcely a word, threading her way back among the trees to provide an excuse, if she were seen. He watched her in the faint light, long bare legs steady on the rough slope, until she was out of sight. Only then did he begin to wonder how the world had changed. For the better, beyond doubt; yet it might bring so much evil with it.

How much, he soon discovered. Neither said anything, and next day she shunned him as before. Yet before long something new infected Vansha's jibes, an edge of spite that came worryingly close to a challenge. Perhaps a warning vision had come to him, though he was showing no other talent as a Seer.

Old Ushaya, now, powerful and malignant, able to direct his sight by arcane means – he might well have perceived something. Whatever the cause, Alya knew a challenge would be disastrous, though his fiery heart ached. By fighting the village's favourite son he would gain little, win or lose. When Savi became ready, then something must happen. Perhaps by then he could better his standing in other ways.

By that crucial day he had lived in the Citadel perhaps a year and a half, and there had been few other intrusions from the outside world. From time to time strangers would pass by, of many kinds. They would spy the folk among the fields, and there they would be met and welcomed, eagerly greeted as bringers of news and diversions from the round of life. Never, though, would they be suffered to see where the Citadel lay, or its true size and strength, even the most harmless of them.

There were travellers to and from one or other of the little kingdoms dotted about the land, wandering pedlars selling salt, spices, knives and trinkets and suchlike simple trade goods. Now and again there might even be a minstrel or jester, telling stories, singing to an instrument or juggling and tumbling, taking up a collection for his evening meal. But none had come for a long time already, and it was six months longer before another new voice was heard.

Six months in which Alya and Saviyal stayed apart by day, and by night met rarely and briefly. Six months in which Vansha grew ever harsher and more contemptuous, so much so that a few in the village remarked it with displeasure, and showed some sympathy with Alya. That only made Vansha more disturbed. Alya came to hate that crooked smile, that smooth, commanding figure lounging its way through life, like a rock against which others might break, the greater their efforts. But he practised patience by day, and by night he sought guidance in his visions once again. He never conquered the Wall, but he began to master the fleeting images in its depths, just a little. He glimpsed much, and felt more in his heart. And it was through those warnings, perhaps, in his inner feelings, that he and Saviyal were never caught in their trysts; which, brief and restrained as they were, would have given his foes the excuse they wanted.

But there came a night when another vision came to him, clearer than any yet, a glimpse beyond the Wall. With a soaring effort, his feet stamping the floor of his hut, he seemed to whirl above it for a brief instant, wheeling high against a bright blue sky, and glimpse a fragment of what lay beyond, before he was hurled bodily, as he felt it, back to earth. He brooded on his vision afterwards, struggled to piece together his shattered memories. A broad land he might have seen, and across it paths, a double way to far horizons. At their joining stood a crossroads with no marker-stone; and as he hesitated there for that single brief moment, he saw from horizon to horizon. But above them rose two very different skies.

It was the task of a Seer to be a scout for his folk,

to be the pathfinder of their destiny amid such brief
and enigmatic glimpses. None save legendary figures
had ever achieved clear and consistent prophecy; and
the clarity of his vision startled him. All day long he
debated with himself whether he should bother the
chieftain; and plucked up courage to do so only the
next morning. Nobody else would listen, that was
certain; save of course Saviyal. But as he was about to
go to the Great House, he heard a rush of hooves
through the narrow gate not far beyond his hut, and a
stir and hubbub within the village beyond. Ducking
beneath the low lintel, he ran out to see.

It was a rider, on a tall chestnut horse that picked
its way surefootedly down the path. Alya had never
seen such a fine mount, nor such clothes as the
rider's, dusty and travel-stained as they were –
breeches and shirt of some full brown cloth, thickly
woven, a jerkin of heavy leather richly worked, a long
rider's cloak of black waxed material that could be
stretched out over saddlebags and horse's crupper,
and to conceal the crossbow and sword at his saddle.
His face was weatherbeaten and hard, but he did not
bear the look of the raiders, nor their markings. His
dark hair was gathered in a horse-tail at the crown of
his head, bound with fillets of gold and silver, swinging from side to side. Rings gleamed on the bare arms
he raised in greeting.

'Your chieftain, good folk!' he called, as he
reached the narrow open space before the Great
House. 'Your Seer! I bear great tidings for them!'

Saquavan himself, tall and calm, came out to
meet him with raised and empty palms, but also a
forbidding frown; and many others had weapons to
hand and ready, Vansha included. 'You do well to ride
so calmly into this vale of ours, stranger; for we take
great pains to keep it apart and hidden, and the paths
are difficult. How came you upon us so, and past our
sentinels? Upon what cause?'

The weatherbeaten face cracked in a smile. 'I did not mean to upset you, chieftain, nor to intrude. I came here because I knew of this place already, and had been told the ways and the paths. The first, from the old accounts of its finding and making; the second, in all secrecy, from one who dwelt here long ago, by name Atuqua.'

'Him!' snorted Ushaya, and several other grey heads nodded. 'A wild lad, cracked in the head. Thought himself a Seer, and hared off into the blue after his visions.'

'A Seer he was, nonetheless,' said the stranger calmly. 'One of the greatest in the realm, until his death years past. It was he sent me off into this part of the land, in search of those folk who might still scratch out a perilous living here.'

'Ah,' said the chieftain, with a wry smile. 'You would be from the court of Volmur, then? What's his interest in us now? Another message of brotherhood, or is it taxes and tribute this time?'

The stranger chuckled. 'I think he has ceased to expect either, and has other concerns. From his court I come, for it lay on my road, but I am none of his. I am from the Eastlands, now, out of the rising sun and the Sea; and from thence are the tidings I bring.'

'Then you've wasted your journey,' said Ushaya curtly. 'The sun sends us his light from there, and nothing else need concern us!'

Saquavan held up his hand sharply. 'We need not be discourteous. Come within and tell us your tidings, stranger.'

The man bowed slightly, but still made no move to dismount. 'I thank you; but what I have is for the ears of all. I am Tuma, Rider of the Lynx clan, born a paramount chieftain's son in the forest realms of the coastlands, where men may still live as men, yet see the advancing threat more clearly than many closer to it. There we remember what once we had, and treasure what remains of it, and do not cling to brief mushroom kingdoms like Volmur's. And there before us we have the Sea. It is daunting, but it also brings hope. Many have fled across it before; and now, before it is too late, many of us also plan to flee. We are calling men to us, all that we may; we are felling the great trees for planks and masts, and building huge ships. Already thousands flock to us; but thousands more do not yet know. So messengers like myself are being sent forth into the inner lands to gather all the friendly folk they may.'

The tall man stood in his stirrups, letting his voice carry down the vale. 'To unite before doom comes upon us one by one. As assuredly it will, if we delay! I beg you, leave this place, this prison, safe as it may now seem. Turn to the east, follow the sun that rises over new lands out there, safer and richer. Help build the ships that will carry us there—'

'*Enough!*' said Ushaya imperiously. 'Is it not known among all Seers that the Sea is the world's end, and that the lands beyond its mists can only be the Lands of the Dead, the ghostlands? Why should we hasten there?'

'That is not so!' protested Tuma.

'How can you say?' demanded Saquavan, almost as angry as Ushaya. 'You may believe honestly enough, my friend – but why force your belief upon us? Have you trodden those lands? Has any living man? All we have of them are tales and legends long past, misty shores fishermen sighted, strange strands they beached upon once and dwelt in for a few seasons. How will you find them, if the waters are so wide as legend says?'

'They are. You have only to look upon them to know that, to see the broad waves roll up towards you over the distant curve of the world. But it is said that there are currents and prevailing winds, that will guide us much of the way as on a road—'

'*It is said!*' Ushaya sneered. 'And by what marks

shall you know, over trackless waters? By what way-side stone or tree?'

'Yet a mark there is,' responded Tuma calmly. 'The ancient lore says so. The tales of those who sailed there, as you say, who spoke with the pale folk and learned of them ancient arts we have forgotten, or been denied. Our loremasters seek out that mark, and in fair hope – the Eye of the Swan, some call it. But if it cannot be found, we will send out scout ships until the path is clear.'

Saquavan tossed his head in exasperation. 'A word, here and there. A mark not yet found. Pale folk with strange arts – who can credit all that? Who would dare?' He threw his arms wide. 'I, I must weigh the fate of my folk, Sir Rider! Shall I cast them into the scale against mere hope?'

'The Seers—'

'All the Seers I know say nothing of your lands! A Seer am I myself, in some small wise. And in pursuing any thought of leaving this place, I have seen only a long bleak road, and the smoke of destruction!'

Vansha, who had been lounging in the background as usual, suddenly stepped forward beside his father. 'If we went to the coasts,' he said quietly, 'we would have to stay there. We could not return, not safely. Landless, without shield, we would be at the mercy of those who dwell there now. Much might be demanded of us, in the name of such a dream, many sacrifices for some future good. Shipbuilding we might indeed be set to; but would that not make us, in the end, their slaves?'

It was so wise a caution, and so sinister a prospect, that even Alya faltered. But he too stepped forward. 'Chieftain, forgive me, but I must speak. You know my heritage. Two nights past it showed me something also, a vision close to yours.'

'Then I wish you had spoken at once,' said the chieftain. 'But do so now, freely.'

Alya's mouth was dry, with the awareness of the eyes fixed upon him. 'I say nothing of what it means; I can only describe it. There was a way, yes, a double way. There was smoke indeed, shadow and smoke, among which the way grew dim and threadlike and cold; but it lay only across the way westward. The eastern way was uncertain, misty, yes; it led strangely, into a region of haze. And yet this seemed filled with light, as if . . . As if it heralded the sunrise.'

Ushaya flung a glare at him like a spearshaft. 'Another outcomer!' he grated. 'Sent to prepare the way for this popinjay!'

The chieftain shook his head wearily. 'He walked too close to death for that. No, boy, I believe you are sincere. It does sound like what I saw. But which way the path led, I could not be sure; and perhaps you only read into it the image of your own desires. Tuma, you have spoken enough. Now, go your way in peace and seek others who may serve your turn. We cannot. None shall leave here, save alone and without aid. And if they try, they will never be allowed to return, or be received back among us. In the wilderness they shall meet the unseen enemy, to which all succumb, and leave their bones to wolf and bird. That is my decree. Go, and never return.'

'I am sorry for it,' said Tuma, and looked down at Alya. 'Boy, you at least see clearly. There is a place for you among us, if you can make your way thither. I must pursue my mission and spread my word.'

'Though few be fool enough to listen!' sneered Ushaya. 'Off with you, and give your masters this blessing from us!'

Before the chieftain could move Ushaya had thrown a rock, one he must already have had in hand. It struck Tuma on the breast, and rebounded; there was the clink of mail beneath his shirt. Ushaya roared with laughter. 'Hear! He came prepared! He must have found others are not such fools, either!'

Vansha laughed, and hurled a stone of his own, and his friends joined in. Tuma had no choice; armour or no, he must escape or fall. They were stoning the horse's legs already. It reared, and he hauled on the reins, twisting it around so it all but fell on the uneven ground, and spurred it towards the path. Away they galloped in a shower of stones and filth, whatever came to hand, hooves skidding on the uneven slope of the path, and away, to the malicious laughter of the crowd. But as the rider vanished among the trees at the summit the laughter hesitated and died before Saquavan's anger.

'*That is enough!* Am I yet chieftain? Did I not reject the man in courtesy, and was not that enough? Ushaya, your mean spirit will work us all harm one day; and you, Vansha, you grow too like him. Come with me, both, and hear some schooling you will not soon forget! The rest of you, to your labours! If you wish a peaceful home, keep peace among your-selves!'

Alya, face burning with shame and anger, saw many faces turned towards him as the crowd drifted away, some in contempt but also some in doubt. He had not seen Saviyal, and started when her voice spoke close beside him. There was something strange in its tone. 'Do not look around at me. I also thought him sincere. And you.'

'I believe him still,' said Alya, staring out into the trees. 'I would go, and seek his people and their ships, and the great sea.'

'Why should you not?' she said, her voice slightly tremulous. 'Why should this little place hold you, when the wide world is yours?'

'Surely you know!' he said. 'While you are here, Savi, I will never leave! Never! Unless you wish me to.'

'You know I do not! Do not make it me that holds you! I would not be your fetter!'

'Come, then! Come with me!'

Her voice shook. 'I do not want to – no, I do, I
do! But I was born here, here my mother died and her
ashes are scattered, I have never seen anywhere else!
Alya, I am frightened. You, you are strong and brave,
you have fared far already. I cannot go, not yet. And
there is . . .'

'Yes. Always. Will you come to me tonight?'

'I will . . . try.' Then she was gone, like smoke,
gliding light and graceful over the rough paths.

She came that night, for a moment; and then not
for many nights. Alya strove to settle his restless mind
with the disciplines of the Seer; but even the chill of
the nights did not cool the fever in his mind. He
starved himself of sleep, of food, but still his yearning
blood distracted him as he danced, and all his vision
turned upon her. The Seer's vision felt more and
more like something false, a gloss men laid upon
mere dreams and fancies, something he was outgrow-
ing. Why should absurd self-torment lay bare any
truth? Why should prophecy be born of frenzy and
pain?

Like as not he had been deluding himself as his
father had taught him, turning himself into some
swollen-headed charlatan like Ushaya, snarling like
a stray dog at every foot lest it spurn him. He told
himself again and again how free he would feel if he
abandoned this fruitless quest, how liberated from
lying shackles. But one night when Savi had promised
to slip out, but did not, there came a change.

It was harvest time, and she might well be weary
and asleep. Even hunters helped in the fields now,
and this year the crops had been especially plentiful
for such stony ground. The sun was blistering, the air
heavy. Even now it was hot and hard to breathe.
Everyone was exhausted, himself included, and tomorrow would bring more toil. Yet he danced still, to
subdue his angry disappointment. He danced in the
dark before his door, for there was neither moon nor

star, and the air hung heavy in the vale, where no breeze could shift it. Unfair to expect her; yet still his resentment and jealousy simmered in the stamp of his feet. Soon it must be decided. Soon he must speak to the chieftain. Soon she must decide. Soon he must face Vansha . . .

It was as if the drumming of his feet found some echo in nature. Thunder rumbled, far distant, and the sky flared and pulsed along the rim of the world, from end to end of its canopy. It was a great storm, certainly; but seemed still greater, as if something magnified the lightnings that leaped like dragons between the hummocked clouds. He thought of the mountains of his homeland, and how sharply they had stood out under moon or storm, as their light was mirrored back by the vast white spaces beyond, the realm of the Ice.

With that thought, he was suddenly back on the ledge. He was looking, through the eye-slots of the Raven's countenance, straight into his father's long-dead face. Yet behind that stern, stony gaze, the dark sky still erupted with flickering fire; and the lightning traced the path of the Trail.

All at once it was no sky, but a glassy black barrier, jagged and terrible, its depths alive with flashing flame. Sinking down into them was the face. Stifling a cry, he reached out his arms, pressed his own face against the sharp stinging facets of the Wall. But white fires rushed by, and swept it away. Or were they fires? They rolled and roiled along a narrow channel, pent and fierce, glittering white . . .

His foot skidded sideways. His ankle turned. Stones shot out into emptiness, rattling against the valley face below. He danced at the path's very edge. Stormlit trees swayed across the mask's eyeholes, and he fought for balance. The gulf below was not so terrible as the ledge, but steep and deep enough to end him easily enough. He kept his foothold, but his legs trembled violently as he staggered back, and he sat down hard at the path's edge. He snatched off the mask, and shook.

There had been human limbs in that turmoil, pathetic pale limbs dashed this way and that. Was that no more than some imaginary fancy, for the credulous to twist into meaning? He ought to believe that; but he was finding it unexpectedly hard. His whole being shouted against him, bidding him believe.

At last he clambered to his feet, plucking small sharp gravel from his scraped thighs. He could make nothing of the sight, no revelation, save the terror of that bleak face, still shaking his mind. He struggled to think instead of Savi, mingling her clean sharp scent with the resinous pines; and he succeeded, long enough to stow away the mask and fall exhausted upon his bedmat. Yet even as he sank into sleep the vision rolled over him once more, chill and unresolved.

When he awoke, at first light, it still hung haunting in the stifling air. But he could get no hold upon it, to see it more clearly or rip it apart, if need be. It clouded his mind as he arose to join the others who tramped past his door, on their way to the fields. Vansha, he noted grimly, was nowhere to be seen; he hated field-work, and avoided it when he could. No sign of Savi either, which awoke sinister little fancies in his mind. He looked so miserable that some of the married women swept him up, laughing, and took him off berrying with them along the sheltered banks of a nearby stream. It was labour much less backbreaking than the open fields, and one could dip in the stream when the heat got too much; but he hardly noticed it, drifting off to gather by himself.

The voice at his back made him jump. There was Savi, standing nervously in the water, limbs glistening red-gold with droplets. 'I'm sorry I could not come,' she whispered. 'I was so tired, I slept . . .'

A burden lifted from Alya's heart. 'I also!' he lied, springing down the bank and taking her in his arms. 'We could have snored together!'

She laughed softly, looking constantly around, but making no move to free herself. 'Maybe tonight, then.'

A harsh laugh sprang them apart. There stood Vansha, angry and sullen, with a bruise on his cheek, no doubt from his father. He skidded down the bank and splashed into the water. 'So that's where you've wandered off to! Well, I shouldn't leave you alone with this outcomer brat – never know what he might get up to!' He seized her arm. 'Come! Back to where real men work!'

She shook her arm free, but stalked off down the stream, with the two splashing after her. Alya guessed she would not side with either openly, but he could not hold back; he had had more than enough of Vansha. The other women stared and whispered, while the two boys glared and sneered. Alya's blood was up, roaring in his ears—

Alya stopped where he stood, staring; then he turned and shouted to the watching women. '*Get up!* Get out of here, all of you! For your lives!'

The stared, as well they might, so wild was his demeanour. Some of them turned, some hesitated. Then all of a sudden Vansha screamed at them, and at Saviyal. '*Get away!* Something's coming!'

The gatherers believed him now, and turned to run; but Alya shouted, '*No! Not that way!* Up! Get up the bank! *Up!*'

Seizing Savi, he thrust her to the edge. Vansha, beside him, grabbed her other arm and they heaved her out of the water. The other women were moving up the bank now, but some went only a little way, looking back and whispering to each other. Then the air was suddenly roaring like a beast, and they screamed and scattered as the vast brown wall raced frothing around the bend in the little stream.

Saviyal shouted, and sprang like an antelope for the top of the bank, turning as she reached it to grab first Alya and then Vansha by the hand. Both of them were plucked from their feet as the torrent rumbled past, but they had already hold of the edge, and with Saviyal's hand to pull on, they fell over the top of it, crashing together in a heap with gouts of spray breaking over them. Beneath their feet raced a turmoil of mud and rock and bushes, tumbling together. And, held in horror, they saw among them like pale sticks the limbs of some who had not heeded the warning fast enough, already stripped bare in the mêlée. Outstretched, pleading for help; but among that turmoil they had no answer.

The young folk picked themselves up, bruised and sorry. Along the bank lamentations went up, frantic cries as one searched for another, mothers for children, sister for sister. In that close-knit tribe everyone heard the names that were called, and the silence that came after. Saviyal knelt and wept. Vansha cursed, monotonously, staring at the angry stream. Alya put his face in his hands to shut out the sight; but it was there behind them already.

The waters soon subsided, leaving a mass of tangled debris where there had been fruitful bushes; and, here and there, a worse loss. Saquavan, grim-faced, ordered the bodies borne back by their nearest kin, but put the rest to work all the harder. The harvest must still be gathered; more swiftly, if the rains were so close. But it was silent work, without the usual laughter and singing. Ten lives had been taken, among less than three hundred. Everyone knew them and their kin.

The villagers trailed back to the vale as the light began to fail, weary and despondent. And as they clambered along the rough paths to the granaries and foodstores of the Citadel, some were beginning to wonder aloud why so great a disaster was not foreseen, by those who claimed the art.

'But it was!' said Saviyal excitedly, as she emptied her baskets at the storerooms. 'If they'd only heeded Alya . . .'

Vansha came leaping down the loose rocks beside the path, and caught her sharply by the arm. 'What d'you mean – *Alya*? I gave warning, I!'

'You're hurting me! You called, yes – but only after he did!'

Vansha caught her again, by the shoulders this time. 'What's this?'

'It was Alya I heard first!' put in one of the women who had worked with him.

'Only after I'd called!' insisted Vansha. 'I, I was first! You, girl, would you make me lose face before the whole village?'

He shook Savi in his anger. Alya sprang forward, but she raked her nails into Vansha's arms, hard, and he let her go, cursing. 'What does your fool's face matter?' she shouted. 'People have died! And you, you did not see it! Alya did and you didn't! Alya, tell them!'

'I wish I'd seen more, or more clearly!' said Alya grimly. 'Last night, in – in a dream. Nothing clear – just a confusion, a turmoil in a narrow place. Bodies. I saw no when, no where for it. Would that I had!'

'But I saw it clearly!' snapped Vansha, in desperate triumph. 'A great sudden flood, racing down the stream's cut!'

'So clearly?' demanded Alya, furious. 'Then by heaven and earth, Vansha, why did you say nothing sooner?'

Vansha stood very still, his eyes flickering from side to side, as the watchers gathered around them and murmured. Alya looked at him suddenly, more keenly. With Seer's eyes, perhaps; or simply the eyes of a rival.

'Unless . . . Vansha, you never did see it, did you? Not by yourself; nothing clear, anyhow. It was your father who saw; and he told you of it secretly, to warn us! To make you look like a good Seer, worthy to succeed him!'

Then sudden horrified understanding came upon Alya, and he blurted out, 'But you – you wanted to make a show of it! So you delayed to the last moment. Then you came upon Savi and me. And you forgot . . .'

Vansha's face went suddenly dark with fury. '*You! You little bastard brat!* Who are you, to say what I did and didn't do? Come crawling up out of your wilderness ditch, sneaking among us, stirring things up, sniffing after the women's backsides!'

He rounded upon the villagers with fists clenched, knuckles white. 'All of you! Do you believe this little pissing puppy, any of you? Him, rather than me? Me, you've known all your lives, me – *me*?' He was almost screaming in his rage, as if he could blast the doubts out of their minds, and perhaps his own. 'Any of you?'

Savi drew herself up. 'I heard and I saw. I believe him.'

Vansha's voice was a wild dog's snarl. '*So*. It's like that. Steal a man's girl, poison her mind against him! Well played, puppy! But I'll send your skinny scut back where you came from—'

He rushed on Alya, arms flailing, as if to sweep him out of sight by sheer speed. Alya had barely a moment to brace himself, to fling up his own arms against a rain of blows. He staggered under the impact; but not as far back as he might have, or as badly. It was Vansha who reeled back, only momentarily. Then he flung himself forward again, to bear Alya down. Alya met him, grappling with him as his father had taught him, and they stumbled and rocked back and forth across the stony platform.

Saviyal was screaming at them to stop, but neither listened. Vansha was screaming and spitting, his face contorted and suffused with blood. But though Alya's arms and shoulders filled with pain, he found himself hanging on, clutching tighter with wiry strength. Vansha yelled and threshed, in pain rather than anger now, and slammed up a knee. Alya's father had taught him the counter to that; he twisted, took the blow on his taut thigh, and while Vansha was still off balance, threw his weight against him. The taller boy's leg twisted in its socket, and he screamed aloud. In pain and panic then it came to Alya that he might even be the stronger man, as he was the Seer. Alya tore free an arm, and punched his enemy twice in the face.

Vansha howled, and threw his arms around him again, in a grip that was truly crushing. Alya grappled with him, and Vansha gave way; they whirled back across the open shelf. Suddenly Vansha's face sagged and he reeled back. Alya was dizzy with burgeoning strength. Vansha was afraid of him! He had won—

Saviyal cried out again, other voices with her. The chieftain, shouting. A foot skidding, a stone rolling beneath him, another. He was on a scree slide, he had been manoeuvred there; and Vansha's streaming face hard against his, Vansha heaving at his arms, hissing words in his ear, straining violently to break their bond. He could not. Alya *was* the stronger!

But his feet scrabbled beneath him, and there was a sudden, sickening falling away, a rustle and rattle of stone. Vansha's words – '*I'll break you before her, you bitch's whelp*—'

A thunderclap slashed the sky from end to end. The breath blasted from his breast in a great snapping spike of pain. A crack, like dry wood. Lightning lanced through his body, keener even than the pain, in every part of him wildly beyond bearing.

Then the pain was different, duller, and he was still alive, awake even, staring up at the sky. Faces over him – the chieftain's, bloodless and grim; women, pressing round. Vansha, blood-smeared and blustering, as if he was about to weep. Saviyal, weeping incoherently; that old swine's snout Ushaya, greyer-faced than ever, asking if he could feel anything.

Old goat! Of course he couldn't; it was too painful. Everything hurt, his head, his arms, his back; at least his legs didn't. It hurt as they swayed him back to his hut on a hide; he wanted to ask if it was the same hide, but he couldn't speak properly somehow. Ushaya was fussing over him; but he was the healer, of course. Serve him right if it had been his own son. Why was he looking so sick, like that? Why was the air so hot, the sky singing?

When he woke next, it was days later, and he was feeble and thirsty. He had drifted off into something deeper than sleep. Ushaya, squatting by his mat, told him frankly enough that he had not expected him to live. And when Alya, startled, struggled to sit up, he felt first that branching lightning stab, then, save its tingling echo, nothing. He could not stir his legs; he could not even feel them, not properly. He knew they were there, but they were dead weight.

He had fallen on a rocky outcrop, said Ushaya, looking away. He had broken his back. He might live many years, and there was much to hope for; men with such injuries had often walked again, often. Eventually.

So Ushaya said, not without some compassion in his withered heart, made keener by the burden of his son's deep guilt. But he remembered then that he was speaking to a fellow Seer; and under Alya's gaze he knew better than to lie.

CHAPTER 3
The Strength of the Earth

So began the long night of Alya's life, in which every minute seemed a weary age, leading to only one hopeless end. Yet its dawn was to come, but in no way that even he could foresee, fearful and terrible; and destined to leave him in a predicament almost as great, and incomparably more strange.

From that first terrible moment, as he lay helpless on his mat, he wished often that Ushaya had been less skilful in his care, and simply let him die. But the old man did not, if only to ease his son's ill deed. He tended Alya with uncommon skill, even bracing the single cracked bone in his back with fine gold wire and rigid splints to help it heal firmly once again. But as Ushaya had admitted, even when the bruising faded, leaving only a slight scar, it was too late. That small wound had somehow frayed the delicate cord linking body and mind.

Once or twice Alya's arrows had done that to the rabbits and other beasts he hunted. He remembered them dragging their legs helplessly, screaming. Sickened, he had ended their misery swiftly. And now he saw himself the same – severed from himself, no more than half a man, a living ruin.

His legs recovered a little feeling, a faint perpetual tickle or tingle that often grew to stabbing pain. They might twitch when he sought to move them, or kick in meaningless spasm like a baby's. Then all too often bladder or bowels would fail him, though those at least he could normally control. So he

no longer even tried. When he had to move, he
crawled on his hands, just like the rabbits; and like
them, though silently, he screamed.

But most of the time he simply sat. He could
labour in the fields a little, for his arms grew much
stronger than before; but he had to be carried there,
hard work for the scant help he could give. The
villagers soon ceased to bother, leaving him increasingly to himself, to do nothing much; and in that life,
to do nothing was to be nothing.

In fine weather he sat on the doorstone of his
hut, in worse weather on a wooden seat within, a
smooth-barked section of log. He sat always bolt
upright, head erect, though not without pain and
effort, for the shred of dignity it gave him. Sometimes
he might whittle and carve spoons and pegs and the
like, when they brought him wood; but he had no
great gift for it. More often he simply watched the
flow of life go by; and it went, increasingly, without
heeding him. For he grew bitter and hard to speak
with, so that fewer and fewer of the villagers sought
him out. At best they would wave a greeting they did
not expect him to return.

Even the chieftain no longer came near. He was
not an unkind man, his sorrow for Alya was real. He
had taken the boy in, for better or for worse; and it
was another of his village who had done this. The
village would see him fed and cared for, as best it
could afford. But Alya was no longer any use to him.
His hopes were disappointed, his worries renewed.
He could spare no time for failure, but must look to
his folk and their future.

It might well include Vansha. For many months,
as Alya, pale and grim, sat like a living reproof, the
young man laboured under the heavy wrath of the
village, and of his father. There was even talk among
some, remembering the matter of the flood, of exiling
him, to find another home or grapple with the unseen

enemy in the wilderness. But the truth was lost in the confusion of the fight, and there were many to find excuses for him – that Alya had provoked him over Saviyal, that the fight had been fair between rivals, that Vansha had never intended what came to pass. Ushaya, furious as he was with his son, could hardly be blamed for clinging to these.

Alya knew better. He might have accepted it, if he had not felt himself manoeuvred to the slope, if he had not felt the older boy cunningly seek to tear free as he slipped. And if he had not heard that taut whisper. Vansha, looking over Alya's shoulder, must have been able to see the rock sticking out of the scree-fall, and schemed to hurl him down upon it. To kill, without appearing to.

But that had been in the heat of the fight. Afterwards, the Seer's son was deeply shocked and chastened by what befell – more so, maybe, than if he had managed to kill. Vansha summoned the courage to face Alya in his first painful days, to beat his forehead on the earth and swear his sorrow and regret, and that he would be a better man henceforth. And Alya did not wholly disbelieve; but forgiveness was far from him.

'The hurt I might forgive one day, perhaps!' he answered, though the words came hard. 'But I am the last of my line, the survivor of my murdered kin. Their spirits will walk unavenged now. Of them I cannot quit you! Nor of my own unrest, if I die thus. Unless – yes. You are strong and brave, in your fashion. Unless you will take my burden of vengeance upon yourself.'

'Your revenge?' Vansha sat up and stared, startled out of his self-abasement. 'Upon whom? Upon the Servants of the Ice? Upon the Eaters of Men? Man, what could you ever have done to *them*? What could I? I would only end my line along with yours, and in madness!'

Alya looked back at him, calm as the cold black

lake about his heart. 'Then you have no more to say to me. Go.'

Vansha went; but more than once he seemed to look back, to be bursting to speak more. But he stayed silent, and bowed his head.

Gradually, though, it began to lift, and his features lost their troubled furrows. Vansha busied himself hard in the village, forever making himself useful in ways large and small. His vigour and dash could not long be suppressed, and his skill in the hunt seemed redoubled, now he no longer had a rival. And although he acknowledged his fault readily enough, the old smile reappeared and was not quenched, and with it his belief in himself, though he was quieter about it. The village said he was a changed man, and came to rely upon him. And so, increasingly, did Saquavan.

Savi did not. That same night Alya fell, while Ushaya laboured to save his life, before all the village she bitterly rejected Vansha, utterly and forever. Saquavan thought that well enough, then; but now he was not so sure. For she showed no interest in any other, save the shell that had been Alya. While he lay abed she tended his every need. When he recovered, as far as he might, it was she who came most often to bring him his bowl of food and talk with him, to wash his few clothes, to trim and braid his long hair. It was she who struggled to help him to better places to sit, or even, with great effort, to join the villagers at their evening talk before the Great House. But he soon gave that up, and sought no other company; and before long he scarcely seemed even to welcome her. She would have curled up beside him, through the nights; but he would not let her.

'Why?' she demanded, both tearful and indignant, of the boy who sat rocklike before her. 'In what am I to blame? Did I do this terrible thing? Do I not also suffer from it?'

Alya sighed, and looked down. His legs already seemed thinner, compared to the heavy arms that leaned upon them. 'I am like a withering stalk . . . Yes, you too have suffered. Can't you see that's just what I don't want? Bad enough I sit broken in body and spirit – but to see *your* life ruined . . .'

'Fool!' she breathed. 'Say the word, and I'm your wife tomorrow! Just let my father try to gainsay it, and I'll warm his ears for him!'

She startled even herself with the force of her words; and Alya almost laughed. 'You're no longer a child, sure enough,' he said. 'Ripe to lead some good man a hard time! But what can I do for you? I cannot put food in your bowl, nor children in your belly.'

'Are you so sure?' she demanded, archly.

'Yes,' said Alya flatly. 'Not wholly dead, perhaps, but too lifeless to give life. And what I might father, I cannot feed. Shall our children beg of some other man? You are as young as the spring sun, and as warm; you should not have a cold bed. I can think of two or three good lads—'

'Then do you marry them yourself, and leave me to choose my own covering!' It was sharply spoken, but it ended in tears.

He cradled her beside him. She smelt like a summer harvest, but even her small breasts against his side did no more than feed his inner fires. And before long holding her thus awoke the pain in his back once more, sending spasms coursing up and down his limbs as though firebrands played across them. So painful were they that his eyes blurred, and, though he fought not to wince, Savi realised what was wrong, and pulled free. She would have had him lie down and be massaged, but he refused. 'Pain is better than nothing!' he said savagely. 'Pain is feeling, feeling is freedom. Maybe along that road some healing lies.'

'Maybe. But don't forget I also feel the pain.'

'I will not. Nor shall I be stupid enough to chase you from my side again. But we should not marry. If in time it became a burden, or your choice fell else-where—'

'It will not! I would face the Ice for you!'

'As I for you – if I could. Let us wait, Savi, and see what time brings.'

'Should I be content with that? It's not you who have rivals, it's I! Every day you hug them to yourself more dearly than me – suffering, and pain!'

'Perhaps!' Alya said, and his voice was not that of a half-grown boy. 'Perhaps I must embrace them, to stand them at all. Perhaps they give me strength. But without you they would overwhelm me, be sure of that! Savi, I beg you, come to me again, as long as it pleases you!'

Nonetheless he was uneasy, almost glad when she left him. His head still spun with the pain, but when he sought to move his legs in the slightest they failed him as before, and his innards also. He barely crawled to the door in time, and into the trees, to avoid humiliation. As he crawled back on knees bloodied yet numb, something stirred in him, in the back of his mind, a rising wave of darkness. Giddy, sick, he felt he was going to faint, and slumped forward over the threshold. For a moment he thought it was the old nightmare returning – the night of destruction, the walls of fire, the bodies and the flame. But it was more.

In the time he might draw a breath, he saw that the vision was reflected, distorted, in a crazed and faceted dark mirror. Without dance or mask, along a trail of suffering, he had reached the Wall.

Nine months, perhaps, passed since the harvest and his fall, and with them the long hard winter. Like many he had caught chills and agues then; but he was not yet wasted enough to die. Of what another winter might bring, he was less sure. For now, he could sit in the returning sun by day, even find some small tasks that made it worth carrying him up to the fields again, throwing stones to scare birds and suchlike. He was sorely tempted to hurl something larger at Vansha, bounding back from the hunt with all his former grace, but held himself back. That way lay folly, maybe madness.

Alya himself was almost seventeen now, also a man by his people's reckoning, for in that harsh and ill-fed place the eldest rarely saw more than fifty summers. Saquavan, at forty, was ageing; Ushaya, at forty-eight, already growing old and stooped, rheumy and mumbling, no longer the forceful figure he had been, no longer the clear-eyed Seer. Vansha, almost nineteen, was a figure of young manhood. Savi, in her fifteenth summer, had been marriageable for six months now; and, to the village's astonishment and her father's growing displeasure, she had picked nobody.

Alya knew that something must happen soon. And, much as he liked Saquavan, he suspected that it might be the discovery of his own body on the valley floor, having no doubt fallen in accident or despair. So Savi would be freed to live her life once again, the chieftain would reason; and a sad burden removed from the village. But Alya knew now there was a way that he could prevent that evil destiny, if he could only achieve it in time. And throughout the dark hours he fought battles within himself to recapture that moment of vision.

So it was that one night, exhilarated, he plucked out the stone that had stayed shut for so long, scraped from within the dry cavity the soft skin bundle, and slid the weight of wood over his head once again. It felt more snug than before, still more a part of him; and when he crawled across the patch of moonlight flooding in through the hut door, he and it together cast a strangely uniform shadow, man becoming bird smoothly, without joint or hesitation. He hauled himself to the log, and pulled himself to his seat. And then, tapping the drum softly, he sat bolt upright.

By now that was enough. He knew how to sit, what to do, how to provoke the pain and the reaction. He clutched the drum as he had clutched Savi, half to one side, and the lightning burst inside him with a roar he could almost hear. Pain seemed to shake the very floor beneath him. His mind numbed, his eyes dimmed, and suddenly he was lost on a long road, in the blackest night. Then the Trail lit the darkness, a thread of racing wildfire, and he was blown like a driven leaf towards the rising, glittering Wall.

To his astonishment he struck it, painfully, helplessly, as if it was a solid thing; and the gust of pain hurled him upwards, helpless as a leaf, dashed against the black blades of glass and off again, whirling ever higher. Confusedly he saw things stir within its shadows, images, visions, chaotic scenes of face and form – riders, battlements, great misty rivers with boats upon them, strange forests that seemed distorted to his sight after the stunted trees he knew. A bleak expanse of snow beneath a jet-black sky, but with a handful of brightly coloured jewels glowing in a hollow. A woman's body, naked, floated in emptiness, among a whirling wash of light. Not Savi's; a young shape, it seemed, and yet her skin was weirdly pale and her hair could not be human, shining ashen white and gold. A wind whirled among high columns of coloured stone, and whipped at the bright robes tall men wore. And lastly smoke curled upwards, from sprawling shapes along a strange wide strand, and the smoke also was turned to red and gold by the sunrise, spiralling higher, ever higher . . .

Until there were black summits below him, the peaks of a glassy mountain range, and he whirled and wheeled in the light and the smoke he could actually smell, tinged with wild scents and strange spices. Tossed helpless upon the gusts he soared, and looked down, down . . .

. . . to glimpse the farther side of the Wall.

Something stirred far below, sounds came boiling up, as if he now heard what he had only seen in the glass. Horses galloped over stony roads, voices shrilled and bellowed and swords clashed on shields, women screamed, bodies fell crashing down into darkness.

'*Show me!*' he commanded, and strove to gain control. He was blowing back and forth about the summit, catching only the faintest glimpses. He must ride the wind, master it so that he could swoop low among the landscape of visions laid out before him there. He was a dry leaf; he must become a bird. But even as he thought of that his mind would no longer obey him, wheeling away swiftly with a harsh gull's scream over a terrain turned suddenly eerie, white and blank. It split apart, opening a cleft of sulphurous fire from which dark things scuttled, ant-like. Screams and roars erupted, and above him some black edifice toppled in a cloud of flame. Frantically he flung himself aside, and saw passing beneath him the burning rooftrees, the heap of corpses, the hideous feast on the threshold of his home. He clamped his eyes tight shut, and felt the sudden weight of the mask about his head like a dull hammer-blow.

When he opened his eyes again, there was only his shadowed room, and the wind whispering in the pines outside, and the constant undertow of pain. Alya's eyes ran with tears, he was sweating and more exhausted than he had ever been since his wounding; yet also he was happy. For a moment he had broken free. What he had seen, he was hardly sure; but in time he would learn to control that, to winnow the truth from the tangle.

What mattered was the seeing! He had

channelled his suffering as surely as any ritual ordeal. This was deeper than any starvation or self-laceration! He had seized his troubles and hammered wings of them, to carry his spirit on its quest. He had shown that maimed as he was, he could still serve the Citadel's great need. Broken he might be, but not beyond use.

Tomorrow he could tell Saquavan that, and with him Ushaya. He savoured the thought. That with help – and yes, with training, that might appease the old man – he could still serve the chieftain's plans after all. Let Vansha be chieftain, if he had truly changed for the better. But now Alya could fairly earn support and sustenance, and with them Saviyal.

He plucked off the mask and set it in hiding once again, and crawled to his mat with a heart full of light.

He woke to turmoil. The dull blare of a bark horn, abruptly cut off. Other horn-calls, like none he knew, clearer, harder. And with them shouting, screaming, a flurry of movement past his door. The village curs barking hysterically. The legs of a horse, galloping.

Startled out of dreams, he tried to spring up. He fell, twisting his body sharply, and agony contorted him. He screamed, but it was lost in the cries outside. Sweating, breathless, he pulled himself over to his seat, hoisted himself up on it, arms hanging over, and saw a black horse come wheeling past the opening, so fast that it skidded and scrabbled on the rough powdery surface, almost sat, slid and crashed out against the bushes and through. Down the steep slope beyond toppled beast and rider, screaming, cascading into the depths of the valley. Yet behind them, hardly glancing at where the horse had fallen, came another rush of men, with the glint of steel among them, and harsh shouts. Bows sang against the flat crack of heavy whips; voices yelled. There was a rush of rattling scree that brought a chill to his heart, a frenzied shriek that fell away into emptiness. Women howling, children screeching. He struggled to raise himself.

The doorway darkened. A tall figure ducked under it, a man, and in his hand flashed a short, broad-bladed spear. He was all too familiar. His breastplate of thick pressed leather was black and metal-studded, like the straps covering his kilt. The white markings that curled across it matched the painted patterns on his flat harsh face. The spear darted at Alya, and thudded into the log as he fell back helpless. The man looked closer, kicked Alya's thigh with his steel-toed sandal, and laughed contemptuously. He grabbed Alya's hair and tried to haul him to his feet, but Alya fell clumsily, agonisingly once again, and the raider laughed louder, baring jagged teeth. There was no pleasure in the sound, not even cruel relish. He laughed as he would rape without great lust, because it was another victory, another humiliation. And there was a nervous edge in it, like the fears of a drunken man.

'You! You broken spear, hah? You no fight. You cut man!' He spoke Alya's tongue carelessly, harshly, as if it were much like his own, yet still beneath contempt. Alya flailed at him, but his wrists were caught and pinioned in iron-hard arms. The raider, still laughing, swung him about and slammed his head against the hut's crumbling clay wall. It was old and loose. The clay surface split and fell away, the loosened stones beyond slid outward. 'Hah!' panted the raider, as Alya slumped down, dazed and bleeding. 'We show you fun, uh?'

With a great heave he swung Alya's head against the bared stones, sending a mass of them spilling down out of the wall. Alya's head was thrust right out through the gap, and the raider pulled him up by his hair. 'There! No squat in dark! Now you see!'

Dazed and sick as he was, Alya saw only too clearly. The Citadel was in chaos. The raiders had found it at last.

They must have surprised an unwary night watch, and come rushing down in force. Along the narrow paths little groups of black-armoured men pursued fleeing villagers, or strove fiercely with a few who turned to fight, some at bay, others to let others escape. He saw some go tumbling down into the valley, friend and foe together in fierce embrace. Along the scree slope where he himself had fallen ran a deep gouge now, and the rock that had both saved and destroyed him bore a great slathered smear of blood.

Another horse, perhaps. The raiders were not having it all their own way, and they had been foolish to trust to horses along such paths. Now they were hastily dismounting, some seized and beaten down by villagers' staves as they did so. But others pressed recklessly on towards the square before the Great House, against the little knot of villagers there. Some of the folk had weapons, rusty swords, hunting bows and spears, others poles and hoes, and a few had even won themselves the enemy's own broad thrusting spears. Men and women alike, they barred the narrow way while others were hurried away into the sheltered chambers and granaries towards the rear of the vale.

There was no sign of the chieftain, but Alya made out Vansha among them, loosing his great bow and plucking a rider right out of his rope stirrups, to fall kicking under the feet of his fellows and send two more sliding out to their deaths. Vansha, his open face distorted to a raging mask, felled another man with the bowstave, wrenched away his spear as he staggered and slashed him face to throat, then gutted the man behind as he fell. Others were no less valiant, and for a moment, though his eyes were blurred, Alya thought he saw Savi, wielding an enemy's short sword. But the press of raiders came against them then, and the defenders were forced slowly back.

Some raiders, though, had turned away from the fight, and when Alya saw why, he cried out and fought still harder to free himself. 'Yes!' laughed his captor, forcing him back down. 'Slaves! We keep, work, fuck, hah? But best, the beauty – we give to *Them*!'

The man put a great shiver of deep feeling into the word, that might have been awe or worship or terror. '*Them! Them!* Always the best we offer up to *Them*!' He shook Alya with the same cold laughter, and hissed in his ear. 'No honour like that for you, boy, huh? You young, we eat young – mmh mmh!' He made a play of smacking his lips. 'Maybe you!'

A tall warrior cantered his black horse very carefully round the turn of the path, shouting urgent orders at a group of foot-men. They were chivvying a wailing train of village women up the path, hurrying them on with kicks and blows and light jabs with their spears. Suddenly the mounted man saw Alya and his tormentor, called out and spurred his horse over to them. Long robes, brightly patterned, trailed over his crude saddle; he wore leather breeches and boots beneath. A wide-brimmed hat, painted with strange beast-shapes, shadowed his eyes as he leaned down to inspect Alya. The raider laughed. 'This? Cut man. Half man! No walk. No come! I show him real man's fun! We roast, huh? Kidneys first!'

The chieftain did not laugh. He reached down and plucked Alya's head back by his bloodsoaked hair. 'This? Young meat, yes.' He too spoke so Alya could understand, but with no trace of accent at all. His eyes weighed up the bleeding boy, terrible eyes like none Alya had ever seen. They were eyes that could gaze upon horrors, and find them no more than tedious. 'But crippled, is unlucky. We will not eat his bad fortune.'

'Kill, uh?' Alya's throat poised against the stone. The chief's expression did not change. 'No.

Leave this bad fortune to those that remain, as a sign
and a punishment for defying us. Let them keep him
alive if they will. They still have a few women, back
there, that they were so keen to defend. Well, let
them breed from this!'

The raider grinned and shook Alya. 'So! Make
babes! She-boy make she-babes, so worth we come
back some day!' He heaved Alya back into the room
and flung him into the corner, like dead meat.

Alya sprawled there, helpless and stunned, while
the voices passed on the outward path, shouting,
weeping, pleading, quelled by occasional angry
shouts and the hissing crack of whips. The clamour
passed swiftly, as it seemed. The silence that followed
it was almost more terrible.

Alya lay, and did not move. What he had seen at
the last, he could not be sure, not with those blows to
his head, the blood in his eyes. He might have been
mistaken. Any man might, after such treatment. But a
great dread welled up in his heart, and slowly, painfully, he forced himself to crawl forward again, nails
clawing at the shattered clay, the unsteady stones,
hauling himself up to the gap in the wall. He could not
stand; he fell half through it, paining his head terribly.
The vale seemed empty; but at its far end, beyond the
Great House, he could see shapes just beginning to
stir. His head reeled with the effort, then. He vomited
violently, and hung there half conscious on the shattered wall.

It was long before anyone came to him. But at
last he heard footsteps, an exclamation, and found
himself being lifted back through the wall and sat
down on his log. Someone poured him water from
the cracked bowl and pitcher in the corner, and he
drank it down in desperate need, and another bowl-
ful, before he saw who was helping him.

It was Vansha; but it was not the Seer's son he
knew. The handsome face was dusty, haggard, dis-

figured by a great bruise across one cheek, his hair dishevelled and spattered with what looked like caked blood. He had cuts and weals across his broad chest and shoulders, and more blood on the breech-cloth he wore. But the true wound was in his eyes, dark-rimmed and more haunted than Alya could imagine them. 'They left you for dead, no doubt,' Vansha said dully. 'As I did, almost. There are so many.'

'Saquavan?'

'Into the valley, at the stirrup of a raider, horse and all. The cliff-edge gave. My father was clubbed witless, though he may recover. Shachuwa, Seequan, so many strong men – speared at their hut doors. So many . . .'

'And they took Savi.'

Vansha seized his shoulders. '*They?* You saw? Oh, Powers, I've been searching for her! There are still . . . still some on the cliff or in the river, some I could not recognise.'

'No,' said Alya grimly. 'My mind was blurred by blows, but I am sure now. I saw her taken, even as you led the fight, over there. I saw her taken. And I couldn't so much as stir these putrefying limbs!'

'I did not even *see*,' said Vansha, through lips bloodless and quivering. 'When they came crowding in on us, it must have been then. And we were forced back up the vale – but I could not have helped her then, hale as I am. No more could you.'

His voice became almost a wail. 'If we could only *follow*!' He struck fist to palm, hard.

Alya closed his eyes. 'How many live?' he asked, at last.

'In all, maybe a hundred and seventy. Sixty men fit to fight – though perhaps we should count the women also, after the struggle they put up!' He grinned savagely. 'We held them off well enough, at the end, you know that? We would have turned the fight against them, if they'd only dared to linger, with the Fortress to help us. We even took three or four of their horses.'

'They seemed in haste to go, right enough. And there were not so many of them, Vansha! How many warriors could you—'

'None.' The Seer's son laughed bitterly. 'You think I didn't try? We found their tracks, headed westward and northward a little – towards those Great Roads I've heard tell of, maybe. Some forty horse in all, with a few wagons. We have more, though on foot. But nobody would go on. They cower like whipped curs. Their spirit is broken. They won't stir.'

Alya groaned. 'But even a few of us, if we could only fall on those devils unlooked-for – they would never expect *that*! I would do it, even if there were no hope.'

'I know! I also. Because what more is life worth? Powers! If we only had you hale, with your spirit . . .' The two young men looked at one another, a long while. Then Vansha sagged back against the wall, and closed his eyes. 'You're wounded. Do you need anything?'

'More water,' said Alya thickly. His tongue seemed to be swelling. 'My pitcher . . .'

Vansha quickly filled it at the well outside, poured him cup after cup, trickled some over his face. 'I must go tend to my poor old father. He foresaw nothing of this, nothing. I'll send someone over later with food, when we have fires lit and the worse wounded in care. Maybe we can still think of something, you and I.'

It was twilight before one of the women came to bring Alya a bowl of beans and parched corn. She took time to tend his head, washing the worst blood away and binding his forehead with rags; but she said little, her face pale and vacant. All along the valley voices echoed, weeping and bewailing so much loss. She slipped away, and misery closed its fist about him once again.

All day long, his body aching and his head reeling, he had sat there in his grief, while from every shadow his mother and father and sister and the folk of the farm called out to him. Terrible as the thought was, he had sought Savi among them, but she was never there. She was nowhere he could see her, it seemed; and she would never come back again, now, to comfort and console him. He would never see her graceful shadow slip in the door, never hear her voice, soft yet strong, never catch the delicate scent of her beside him, feel the touch of her in the blackness that bore the name of life.

More powerfully even than those pallid faces with their voiceless cries, still clearer now in the growing dark, the valley called out to him. A crawl, a fall, and what had been begun would be completed. He could sleep, then, and forget his own brief, meaningless existence.

Of all the struggles of Alya's life, perhaps the greatest was the one he won that night in the half-ruined hut, with the moon shining skull-white on the narrow path outside, and the gulf beyond whispering words of painless rest and quiet. Two thoughts alone stopped the valley claiming him. One was the restless power within him, the Sight that he had promised to use wisely. Had it sought to give him some kind of warning? Maybe. Maybe it could do more yet. And the other was the thought that somewhere in the infinite, unkind, unbearable world, Savi yet lived.

So long as her shade did not join the rest at his shoulder, pleading and cajoling with soundless gaping mouths, he would go on believing. But that only brought home his misery and helplessness more keenly. And a horrible idea came building up to haunt him. What had provoked that attack? It had followed so closely upon his happiness, his rediscovery of the Trail – even as the attack on his home had come so close upon his first steps along it.

A shaman in the spirit's flight could latch on to other minds, to help him, even over the Wall; so his father had said, back then. What if, in the undirected, leaf-blown whirling to and fro of his thoughts – what if some other mind had latched on to his? What if they had seen the Citadel, seen where it lay, seen its secrets, seen its women . . .

What had been dammed up for so long broke in him, all the harder. He blamed himself, shook off the guilt, blamed himself again; he could not decide. The thought alone was enough. He slumped down and wept, endlessly it seemed. But when the convulsions no longer shook him, and his swollen eyes felt dry in their sockets, he sat up, and he dragged out the mask, and sought to don it as before. But it jarred agonisingly on his wounds, and though he got it on at last, its weight was blinding, and the long curved beak pulled his head down on his chest. There he let it hang, in bleak despair; there was no more he could do, not even this. And without realising it, he sank down into sleep.

Yet in the extremity of grief and exhaustion, it was no ordinary sleep that enshrouded him; for he felt that he was falling once more, from some infinite height, but slowly. Perhaps he crossed the Wall again, all in that moment, without perceiving it; or perhaps his dreams bore him back to the memories of his great vision. Whatever the way of it, he was suddenly wheeling again in emptiness, borne up on winds of pain against implacable clouds. But now it was dark. Below him the cleft of fire, the toiling, scurrying shapes – and at its heart, something he could hardly make out, a wild and shimmering shape that dazzled the eye, unstable, shimmering in every hue as if shaped of purest light itself. Then, out of the barren whiteness beyond, a different wind blew up, a dark wind gusting like great wings that caught him and whirled him, struggling helplessly, back down upon the peaks of the Wall, into the shadow.

'*Help me!*' he screamed, and it came out as a wordless bird-screech, a lonely, tragic call that echoed off the bleak rock-faces in a confused clamour. '*Help me! Help her! Whatever the price! Help her!*'

Desperately he fought, and only at the last moment turned his fall and swept past the sharp-edged peaks, their edges slicing the very air between. Momentarily he saw a flat bare land beneath the moon, a great crossroads, a tiny group of waggons ringed by horsemen. Then that too was gone, past, and away into blackness, into doubt and dark once more.

His head sagged, and the great beak of the mask passed between his knees and touched the trodden floor. He whimpered with the pain. Thunder rolled in the distant mountains. The bird-mask fell open slowly, to reveal the shining human face within. Moonlight touched his eyes. He was awake. He fought with his last strength to raise himself, his masked head, his arms flung wide to the sinking moon that shone through the shattered wall. And he shouted, as a boy might shout for his father, yet more loudly; and all in the village were awakened by it. Some did not sleep again that night.

'*Father! Show me a path! Show me a way! Help me!*'

The moon touched the broken bricks, silvering the dust a moment, and was gone. Alya tore the tormenting mask from his head, leaned over to lay it down carefully, and fell, exhausted, upon the hard floor. He had not even the strength to reach his crumpled mat.

He awoke, sharply, as the blackness was leached from the sky, to the everyday sound of steps outside.

He would have crawled to the door, but thought
better of it, and though it was slower and more
painful, he pulled himself up to his hard-made window instead, where the stains on the stones were
turning brown. There, hanging by his elbows, he saw
the remaining villagers passing by. They were silent,
grey-faced, neither chattering nor singing, but otherwise they were on their way to work in the fields, as
they did every day.

'Is that all?' he shouted. 'Is that *all*?'

A woman darted out of the throng to leave him a
bowl of corn mash, and quickly refill his pitcher from
the well. 'What would you?' she whispered softly.
'Life must go on, the seasons go around. And you of all
of us can do least about it. Be still now, and we'll take
you out another day.'

He sank back, defeated. He had no appetite for
the food, nor for sitting on the step. There was
nothing to see. The village was empty now, of even
the voices of children; those still left had been taken
out to the fields. The Citadel was a vale of silence and
death, save for the harsh cry of carrion birds; for
many bodies still lay in perilous places around the
slopes, where none could reach them, and must wait
till the bones fell. All that long day he sat in the near-
dark, and felt as if he were one of them.

Towards the end of the afternoon, as shadows
grew long and the sun traced a circle of warmth upon
the wall, he found himself bored and sleepy, nonetheless. His aching head weighed down with sleep,
and he no longer bothered to brush away the flies that
buzzed around his clotted bandage. His chin sank on
his chest for a moment, as it seemed.

Then he snapped upright again. Something had
awoken him, he knew; strange sounds. It took him a
moment to know it as music, for it was not like any he
had ever heard, an airy ripple of plucked strings that
sounded light and sweet at first. Then suddenly it

took on an heroic skirl that sent a shiver down his
spine. Its rhythms spoke of riding far and free, of
running on his own two feet with the wind fresh in
his face, and no burden of body or mind to hold him
back. Again he hauled himself upright to the window,
though it cost him skin in his haste. He saw, upon the
inward path, two figures striding slowly down into
the village, two ridiculously gaudy apparitions in this
place of recent death.

They wore the brightly patterned robes and tall
hats that were the dress of wandering entertainers in
this part of the world, perhaps more sombre than
some. These were old men, one leaning upon a heavy
staff wrapped with rough cloth, the other plucking at
whatever the strange instrument was, so they would
not be jugglers or tumblers, although they bore the
usual bags for their gear. They seemed not at all
surprised to find a settlement here, and looked about
them with a casual air, so they had probably come
this way before and learned its location. That mattered little enough now. They paused in the open
space by the well, seemed about to raise their voices
to summon an audience; so Alya hailed them.

'Fathers! You are welcome enough, but you may
save your songs!'

'Who speaks?' demanded the older; then, seeing
Alya at the broken wall, he bowed deeply and elabo-
rately. The player followed suit, though Alya caught a
flash of a sardonic smile that made him uncomfortable.

'Greeting, young lord!' boomed the older man.
'Are you now the gatekeeper of this hospitable village? You see before you two men of wisdom and
learning, come straight from the court of King Volmur, their heads and hearts full of splendid ballads
and ancient lore!'

The other man struck his strings a great clamour.
'Songs and tales of heroes and Powers and fair ladies,
as performed before the King himself! Tales of magic

and love and the slaying of fell beasts. Songs to stir the
hearts and loins of all who hear! Songs of other lands
and other times, before the grim advancing of the Ice.
Songs of heroic deeds and dragonslaying, of forbidden loves, desperate quests and daring elopements,
all for your delectation at the most reasonable of
rates—'

Alya held up a warning hand, and they must have
read his face, for they fell silent. 'Old fellows, I'd
gladly hear your ballads. My heart longs to be reminded of such things. But save your voices. The
village has lately suffered great loss, and at this moment stands empty. Save for the unburied dead; and
me, a useless cripple.'

'With the arms of a great warrior!' observed the
old man. He must once have been formidable enough
himself, Alya realised. Beneath the shabby gown the
bowed shoulders were broad, and the mottled hands
that gripped the tall smooth staff were still long and
muscular. To Alya's eye his windblown white mane
and beard looked venerable enough, but almost lu-
dicrously long and thick, for in his race beards were
rare; but what they did not hide of the old man's face,
the great hook nose and deepset dark eyes, was
strong and commanding, though strangely pale of
skin.

'That's so,' agreed the other old man, though
there was something less friendly in his level gaze –
mockery, almost. Or a challenge. This one's face was
also oddly pale, and deeply chiselled with lines of age
and what might be ill temper, or suffering; but it had
once been handsome in its fashion. His hair and beard
were shorter but just as thick, grey-black and white-
streaked like an old wolf's mane; and in his flashing
glance there was also something of the wolf. 'A
broken man is not weak, if all his strength flows into
his remaining limbs – or into his heart and mind! He
could still be a leader. Others have!'

Alya glared. That was easy for him to say. Old as he was, he could stand staff-straight, his shoulders more massive than his fellow's, his chest deep, his limbs robust.

'A cripple may be many things,' Alya agreed sarcastically, 'if others will only let him! Not make him a burden, and an embarrassment. If they only listen to him, once in a while! But the troubles weighing on me now, kind fathers, they need a whole man to answer them. I might still lead, perhaps, if only I could find any men fit to follow!'

He throttled down his rage. It was not, after all, their fault. 'Two days ago this place was raided by the man-eaters of the Ice. Many were slain, many carried off. The rest cower in the fields and seek to pretend that nothing has happened. They will have little stomach for hero-tales, I warrant you – so, fathers, you must earn your dinners elsewhere.'

'That is hard news,' said the string player, more sympathetically than Alya would have expected. 'I grieve for you and your friends. And I guess in these concerns, your deeds would be worthy of song, no doubt, themselves. But I admit it is a blow to us also. For beyond Volmur's kingdom there are few large settlements left within easy reach, and jesters and singers were always kindly treated here. We counted on earning at least a bowl of food to see us on our way.'

Alya smiled wearily. 'Well, that at least I can provide, and without demanding a song. Take the bowl of corn that lies just inside the door there.'

'Surely that is your meal,' said the older man. 'Your only one, I guess.'

'It is,' said Alya. 'But I have no stomach for it. For drink, I can only offer you the gatehouse well, there. The raiders had no time to pollute it.'

'Drink we carry,' said the player cheerfully, fetching out the bowl, 'of the finest! And for your courtesy, my lord, that we will share with you.'

'Some lord!' laughed Alya. 'Lord of the half-dead!' But he found his heart grow lighter, simply at having someone new to talk to, and especially these cheerful old fellows. He could imagine having such a grand-father; though his, it seemed, had been grim to the point of cruelty. 'I am not even of this place, low and landless. In debt to them for the roof above my head—' He stopped.

'And also for the legs which will not bear you?' demanded the old man, sitting on the well's rim and slurping cheerfully at the corn. 'I wonder which side now owes the most! But not all lords are born. Some earn their honour.'

'I have no wish to be one,' said Alya, firmly. 'All that I desire is to be my own man, whole again, and together with she who is the half of my being, torn from me! That I want with all my soul, with every breath I breathe! Whole, together, free of all en-tanglements and mysteries. Free to live as folk should live!'

'Nobody is ever altogether free of mysteries,' growled the player, licking his massive fingers robustly as he finished the rest of the corn. 'How else should life keep its savour? Ah, that's better than all these town kickshaws, eh, brother? Plain, but sustaining!'

'All the more so when given with a good heart!' agreed the elder. 'And we have something to share with you, now!' He rummaged in the great purse at his side, and came out with a substantial wineskin. The player rinsed out the bowl at the well-bucket, and the elder man poured in a generous helping. He tasted it and smacked his lips at his fingers. 'Mead,' he said happily, 'such as only kings can afford to brew!'

The grizzled player chuckled, and brought the bowl over to Alya. 'Indeed! This'll set your soul to dancing again!'

Alya had little taste for drink; but he did not want to refuse the old men the courtesy. If he did, they might start singing again.

He received the bowl. It felt unusually heavy, as if the mead were thick, and in this grey light the honey liquor bubbled bright as molten gold, gold you could drink. Once, at home, Alya had tasted a little mead; but this was surely a stronger brew. Its fumes were a distillation of drowsy summer twilights, heavy with hot flower scents, poppy and honeysuckle, and the drugged buzzing of bees. He sipped at it gingerly, and a sunbeam seemed to shine warmth into the chilly pit of his belly.

'Drink deep!' urged the player, with a lopsided smile. 'We have all that we require, and more. Song-makers seldom go short of the true mead!'

And he struck another tune from his strange box of strings, solemn, noble, a rising phrase repeated in a higher pitch, as if climbing in stages to the skies.

Alya needed no urging now. He tilted the bowl and his head together, and drank, swallow upon swallow. Half the bowl went down in that blissful instant, and he held it up, rejoicing.

A thunderbolt seared through him.

His flesh flamed and smoked. He smelled his very hair burning in wisps. Pain ate him from the inside out, as the small worm the larger. The drink burst through his gullet and burned his bones to falling ashes. It gushed out of him, every way it might, and flayed his skin off him as it ran. His scalp wrenched and tightened, so he could not even close his eyes, but must see his nails blench and blacken, burst into smoking smoulder and crumble away from his fingers as fire spurted from beneath them. His back erupted in agony that bowed him backward, halfway to a hoop, then flung him forward as his muscles convulsed. His very eyelashes smoked and blazed up like wicks. He retched, and light burst out of his open mouth and burned the cracking mud upon the walls. He coughed out horrible steam, his limbs twisted, his convulsing thighs locked in a vicious rictus.

He sought to catch himself against the wall, managed it, staggered, sweating violently, and convulsed as another shock ran through him, top to toe, and another. He would have spilled his bowels, vomited himself dry, but he seemed to have nothing within him but light. Infinite needles snapped at his nerves, and he stamped with the breathtaking pain.

The thunder underfoot shocked him. Cracks burst open, racing serpent-like across the stone floor and out beneath the wall. The cliff shivered, stones flew from the wall, the trees outside wavered in frenzy as amid the roar and rattle of scree the fragile lip of the cliff crashed down into emptiness. The broken wall sagged, slid and subsided outward on to the path, with almost a rattling sigh, as if his prison was glad to crumble.

Alya was standing, free, on his own two legs.

He found himself staring straight into the eyes of the player. There also fires danced, darker, warmer, deeper than the blaze that still crackled away within his spine and legs.

The earth still shivered like a frightened horse, and new cracks raced across the path. Alya cried out in ecstatic delight, and raised the bowl still seething to his lips once more. With a sharp cry of warning the older man's staff lashed out. It struck the bowl from Alya's fingers. Slowly, as it seemed, it fell to the trodden earth and splashed the mead in a great viscous golden flood. The cracks drank it up in an instant, and vanished.

'Earth's strength returns to earth!' said the old man, with grim satisfaction. 'Another drop, and the ground could not have borne you, down to the very roots of stone. But now the fire will subside.'

Alya felt it ebb, and with it a sudden waft of sheer shock. He sagged down upon his seat; but he felt firm muscle beneath him, not waste and numbness. The hand he thrust out to steady himself felt about to dig deep into the very wood. He saw almost to his surprise that he still had fingernails; but they were glass-smooth, with a golden sheen in them that was echoed in his skin. He flexed his fingers, felt the sheer force in them, and crinkled his toes in childish delight. And then, with a wild shout, he sprang to his feet, and the filthy bandage fell free from his head, without pain. His hair was loose, an untamed mane that flailed about his shoulders like a mantle, and beneath it he felt no wound.

Then, remembering himself, he dropped to one knee before the strangers. Laughing hysterically, he bowed his head, would have prostrated himself and kissed their feet, and beaten his brow on the earth. He was still a boy, and he wept. The player's hand caught his shoulder and raised him.

That touch sobered him swiftly. His own new strength he felt like a live thing apart from him, a mighty beast he rode. But for every ounce of it, in the clasp of those aged fingers he would have been less than a withered leaf.

He looked at both the strangers in an awe that was all the keener for being suddenly calm. At first the older man had seemed the kinder. But now, if kindness was anywhere, it lay in the player's quizzical glance. A faint smile curled the corners of the older man's beard, and there was something strange behind it – not malice, exactly, but little short of it. It was the smile of the successful imp, the prankster whose prank has taken root, yet has a long way still to run.

But Alya could not feel anything small or mean in what had been played upon him. It was more as if he had been sucked, somehow, into a much larger,

much more lasting jest – though one at which he
might not laugh.

'I thank you!' he gasped, although he was no
longer short of breath. 'I bless you, fathers! Whoever
you are, from wherever you stem! But *how*?'

'Hospitality should be repaid,' said the player,
mildly. 'And from one who has little, your gift was
great. It was fitting that we also give as greatly as we
can, in return. Yet every gift bears some burden with
it, some manner of destiny. We may have given you
more than enough for your taste.'

'I will use it well!' declared Alya, feeling the air
sweet against his sweating skin.

'Will you?' asked the old man innocently. More
than ever his venerable age looked assumed; and with
deep unease Alya saw that the fabric about the staff-
head had come a little unwound. A massive spearpoint peeped through. 'You will have every chance!
And if you do not, then woe to you! Yet even so, this
strength may not always serve you as you wish. For
whatever a man may be given, he remains no more
and no less what he is.'

The player chuckled, more reassuringly. 'Even
so; all the old tales bear it out. A strong arm and a
sharp sword are the least of things that make a hero;
and a hero is not always the wisest thing to be. Stick
to your word and your purpose, boy, for that is your
best chance of coming through it all! And of giving us
a new song to sing!'

He struck the strings decisively, rippled his fingers across them, and with no other word they turned
both of them on their heels and strode away, up the
path, into the lengthening shadows. Their voices
echoed across the valley, surprisingly strong and sure.
But the simple song, mere repeated pairs of notes
high and low, still had about it a rhythm of chanting
mockery, and an undertow of icy warning that Alya
felt he barely understood.

Songs of gods and songs of mortals!
Tales of terrors long ago,
Ballads brave and ballads bawdy,
Always make a moral show.

Any story we can tell you!
Stories in the telling grow.
Many a story has no ending,
Others spark but never glow.

Lovers joined may yet be sundered,
Others sundered reunite –
Which is tragic, which is happy?
Where the shadow, where the light?

Learn that no man sees all endings,
Learn that ill can conquer good,
Learn that no man wins forever,
Learn that love cannot stay blood.

Hear a tale, be slow to live it,
Steel your heart before you bend,
Matchless might and constant virtue
May not triumph in the end . . .

The chanting died away in the rustle of the screen-
ing trees. There was an instant of silence. Then the
wind rose and reasserted itself once again, and the
falling sun flashed a flickering streak of light across
the vale.

Alya stood; and simply revelled in the sheer fact
of existence. He raised his arms to the skies as if he
might lift them off the foundation of the mountains,
and lay bare the secrets of the universe.

He could hardly believe what it was to feel whole
once again, and without the gnawing teeth of constant pain. His arms had grown strong, indeed; but
now he had legs to match them. No more than his

birthright, maybe, the body an austere and active life would have shaped. But there was more than that to it. He could feel the energy that flowed within him, the force of sheer life, swifter and stronger than the blood that carried it, a surge of pulsing, tingling fire.

He snatched up a great stone from the wall that had confined him, and hurled it hard, saw it whistle through the trees and out across the vale, to shatter against the opposite cliff in a shower of splinters. He tore up a stick and swished it through the air, so hard it hummed and snapped. He laughed; and a thought came to him, and then a rush of thoughts, one upon another, tumbling over and over in their implications. Still rejoicing in the ease and poise of movement, he stepped over the ruined wall and out along the path that led deep into the vale, to the Great House.

Then, with a wild rush of exultation, he began to run.

It was almost sundown, and the workers in the fields laid down their numbing activity, and turned wearily homeward. It was a fine evening, and already the consoling routine was reasserting itself. Many began to sing, the old work songs, and that in itself was so comforting that the others joined in. But as they came out of the trees and on to the deeply cut path that led down into the vale, they shuffled to a stop, and the words faltered upon their lips at the sight of the figure that stood there.

Some did not recognise him, and screamed, fearing the raiders had returned. Those at the front did, and cried out all the louder. Some fell to their knees, many because they feared it was a spirit awaiting them; but others less credulous were struck with fear, nonetheless. He did not look changed, save that he stood, his body full-fleshed and firm. His new strength did not show itself unnaturally. But his very stance spoke of power, his limbs were firm as young branches, and his eyes, no longer dimmed by pain, flashed and glittered. Health glowed in his very skin like sunlight, and he wore fine boots and garments that had once been the chieftain's. Across his back was his fur-trimmed bow, that had long lain unstrung, and a hide bundle at his belt; and cradled in his arms was a shape of menacing darkness.

They knew it then, the ancient sword of Zyya-taquar that had hung smoke-blackened among the rafters of the Great House; but none in their memory had ever drawn it. He paid them no apparent heed, but when he laid hand to hilt, it parted to reveal a glint of steel. Caked in soot and dust though it was, the old blade left the scabbard with an easy hiss, and its blade glittered greenish and strange in the failing light, its traceried characters rippling through the metal like dragons sporting among cloud. Some virtue was upon it, that sword, such as the mastersmiths of Brasayhal or Kerys could confer; and time had not touched it.

Then many villagers remembered cruel taunts and heedless slights, scornful regard, cold charity and grudging kindnesses, their failure to stop Vansha in his bullying, and most of all in that final fight. And they sank down, and wailed, and beat their foreheads on the stony path; for clearly here was one upon whom destiny had set its hand.

Only one man kept his feet: Vansha, forcing his way forward among them, looking as haunted as any, but chilling his pride to steady limb and voice.

'Well, son of a Seer! You're strangely healed. You may well take any vengeance you wish. But spare the rest, who have suffered enough. My father lies in his last sleep. So make good your wrongs upon my head, alone!'

Alya felt flame stir in him, but he held his hand. Only his voice lashed them, as they cringed. 'Learn that after all the ancient Powers have not deserted you. Little as you deserve it! They have returned me to

you as your champion, to lead you! To deliver those
who were taken! That's the only revenge I care about.
This sword, that was left you for your defence, that
you chose to forget – I claim it now, by right!'

There was silence in the little vale, save for those
still whimpering. 'Speak then!' snapped Alya. 'You
see what has come upon me. Is that not a sign? You
yourselves are broken now, far worse than ever I was.
Yet you too may find healing, if you seek it. Speak
then! Which among you will follow me?'

Silence hung upon his words, heavy with shame.

'Say!' barked Alya, unable to believe what he
saw. 'Who will come? Is not one among you man
enough? And yet you dared, *dared* to call me half a
man?'

Vansha's face went pale beneath his red-brown
skin. His voice held more than a hint of the old
contempt. 'If the Powers'd spared us all such a gift,
now, that might've been different! We fought bravely
enough without it, didn't we? But what can we do
now, for all this strength of yours? The raiders are a
day away already, and we have few horses. The cause
is lost, beyond hope, Alya. Even for her!'

Alya stared him hard in the face. 'Does any true
man or woman abandon . . . a good cause, merely
because it's lost? What remains, otherwise? To squat
and scratch a living from a ruined land, in a Citadel
you can no longer defend? Isn't that a lost cause?
Better to die resisting! Better to run up the spear that
strikes you, and slay the wielder! Better by far!'

And it was as if his fires poured into Vansha's
cold cheeks, and he plunged through the clawing
villagers. 'A true word! For that, I am with you, and
come all the rest!'

'They'll not trample you in the rush,' observed
Alya drily.

'Then to the Ice with them all!' shouted Vansha
furiously. 'To rescue Saviyal, or to death and dam-

nation, without regret! I'll not falter, though my strength's my own and no more. But remember this, son of a Seer – I will not, not ever, *follow* you!'

Alya shrugged. 'The weakest form of pride, as my father often said; but it will serve. Let us swear, and shame these fools who witness. To go forth to rescue Savi, and any others we can, and never turn aside. In full trust of one another, together. As brothers.'

'As brothers!' echoed Vansha, his voice fierce. 'All quarrels forgotten, while our bond endures! Never to turn aside, never till we taste certain success or final failure!'

'Till then, never!' agreed Alya. 'Sworn!'

They clasped hand to arm then, in the fashion of their folk. 'Now let us go!' said Alya, but Vansha shook his head.

'Not so! Not on foot, without preparation! We will take those fine mounts we captured, and food. But what will two accomplish, even with the strength of the Powers? We must fetch help!'

'We'll find little enough here!' said Alya sourly. 'Where else?'

'Volmur!' said Vansha. 'They say our local king seeks men of valour. Why should we not seek aid from him, in the name of proving ourselves? At the least we might gather a few more men!'

Alya tossed his head impatiently. 'But that capital of his is far off – a good week's ride, I've heard! And to the southward!'

'That would be too long!' agreed Vansha, the two ignoring the villagers who gaped around them, many still on their knees. 'But there is a shorter way – though perilous. I know it. Two days, three at most.'

Alya writhed. The very idea of delay clouded his mind.

'If you demand it, brother,' persisted Vansha, 'I will ride with you right into the raiders' camp! Or steal in by night, if you can bear even that much delay! What then? Can even two strong arms stand against the forty or fifty we saw? And they may well be part of some larger band. At most we'll give Savi the joy of seeing us cut to pieces! Whereas with twenty or thirty – ten, even – there might be a very good chance! If we ride now, no matter how perilous the way!'

Alya looked keenly at him. For all Vansha's oath, he was being tried here, tested once again. But then he would also be testing Vansha, and that did not displease him.

'Some chance,' he said, grimly. 'They ride west and north . . . We could cut across the plains from – what's the name? Volaghkh? Volaghkhan? Pick up their trail in maybe two days . . .'

The thought of what might have happened to Savi, what might be happening even now, was a sickening pain in itself. Alya had dreamed of rushing headlong to her rescue, but this made sense. Three days at least . . . but better that, than waste his gift. Perhaps that had been the warning in the song, or part of it.

'Very well, then – *brother*! Choose us the best of the horses. The women will bring us food.' Alya said it as a calm certainty; and when he clapped his hands, with a frightening crack, the women rose and scurried to fetch all they might want. The men slunk after them. Alya watched them go, and snapped the great sword back into its scabbard. 'And when that is done, nothing need hold us here any longer. Nothing at all, now.'

CHAPTER 4
Into the Night

EVEN as Alya, in fear and dread, turned his thoughts to her, Savi's, for all the terror and discomfort around her, were no less upon him. The bullock cart, clumsy and ill-made, was jolting her this way and that, against the girls on either side, and they back against her. Bound in a line as they were, they could not avoid it.

'*Peasant!*' panted the girl on her right, a stranger, for the hundredth time that day – the only thing she had said. The plump girl on her other side sat hunched into her own misery, saying nothing even when Savi tried to talk to her. She knew her well enough – Kaqual, from the Citadel, as were many others in the cart.

There had been more. Only the young women were here, no older ones, no children; what had become of them all Savi hardly dared to think. What had happened to these girls here was bad enough, and what might yet happen.

They had been torn away during the fighting, stunned or otherwise subdued. Savi, brandishing a rusty old weaving-staff, had fought with the fury that often surprises peaceable people when they are threatened. Her father, with no surviving son, had taught her a little of handling weapons. She had held her own, even snatched a proper sword from a dead raider and dealt a wound or two, until the crush grew too great and the villagers' line gave back. She remembered little enough then, but she could still feel the bruise at her midriff where a heavy fist had struck the wind from her. They'd dragged her away, sword still in hand, as if she were no threat worth considering. They seemed bored, almost, as if their brutalities were normal behaviour, without excitement.

All the women taken were swiftly gathered at the feet of a snake-eyed chieftain, who had painted some marks on their foreheads with an ink-brush. Different marks, it seemed; though she did not know what her own was. Then they were roped together at throat and waist; and it was only then they finally took away her sword, as an afterthought. That rankled with her, foolish though it felt, almost as much as the liberal dose of kicks and flicks of the lash with which they'd driven the string of wailing women out through the trampled fields, out of their old life. Forever, Savi knew; for she had seen her father fall, her home ravaged, herself torn out of it. Come well or ill, nothing would ever be the same.

And Alya – what would have happened to Alya? That was her endless torment. If these fiends came upon him, they would surely have slain him where he sat. The thought stabbed at her, bitterly. He might have been fortunate. Apart from the rest, unable to come out and fight, they might have missed him. But would he think that any kind of good fortune?

He who had had so little would now have less. Even if he did live, who would care for him now? She felt a dreadful helpless emptiness. More likely he was dead. She should accept that, and end that one of her worries, at least. She was uprooted, and must find new sources of strength.

Yet, somehow, she could not shake off the concern, although she herself had enough to fear.

The raiders were disciplined. No man did worse than paw or strike the women, according to his humour. But their whole manner was gloating, mena-

cing; and their drive relentless. In the hours that
followed, the women were herded along swiftly by
anxious-looking raiders, as if they feared some rescue
bid. But none came. The women were goaded and
lashed to a stumbling half-run, a dreadful pace. One
older woman, her face puffy and bruised, fell, dragging on the rope. Whether through rough handling or
exhaustion, she was barely alive. The guards simply
cut her loose and flung her by the wayside, and drove
the others on into the gathering twilight. Wolves
were howling on the road, and Savi realised they
were following, drawn by the smell of blood.

No more than a few miles further off, there were
horse-carts waiting, rough, miserable things tilted
upon two wheels and draped with patchwork cover-
ings of cloth and hide. The women were split up, and
chivvied into these, on to their bare board beds,
and lashed crudely to the sides by their ropes at
hand and waist. And the moment the last knot was
secure, commands were howled, whips cracked the
air, and away the carts lurched.

Westward and northward they went still, over
marsh and mire by many trails, but always keeping up
a pace that punished beast and man alike, and jolted
the women unbearably. That night they made hardly
a stop, though the horses were staggering. At last,
upon the next day's dawn, the ground grew more
level and the rumble of the carts changed. The air
seemed warm, still, but unusually moist, dark and
heavy and suffocating to someone used to drier air.
They were following an old road, she guessed, across
barren brownish-green heaths, the stones booming
hollowly beneath the iron-shod wheels, and it soon
brought them out into what looked like a great flat
land, crossed by dark, sluggish rivers.

The raiders and their catch made only brief halts
to drink at streams, until late that evening, when the
carts thundered across a great stone bridge, though

its causeway was as rough and grassy as the road on
either side, and as briar-riven. On its far side they
came upon a larger camp of the same folk, set up in a
hollow, with strong pickets posted against any pursuit. What then became of the women in the other
carts she never saw; but those from hers, the youngest, were taken to a row of slightly larger carts laden
with baggage and some booty, and, roped to a couple
of these, another line of women captives. The newcomers were simply strung on to it. Their necks were
freed, and they were given food; but that night, as
they found what sleep they could, huddled beneath
the carts, some were attacked. Some, not others; and
Savi soon realised that no woman with a particular
forehead mark was being harmed. She had had to
watch Kaqual brutally raped, twice, next to her. But
when she had done her best to kick and buffet the
young men doing it, they pinned her down and
threatened her horribly; but nothing more.

Shortly before dawn, deep straw had been piled
into the cart, and all the women herded into it, still
roped together. Even as the last knots were tied, the
whole caravan, with fresh horses now, went clattering off. The straw was a lot more comfortable, but
few of the captives seemed to notice or care. Kaqual,
once plump and laughing, sat speechless and locked
into herself. Her nose bled often, but she simply let
the blood trickle down her chin. Savi had tried to put
an arm around her, but she shrank away. Some of the
other women sobbed helplessly and incessantly; most
seemed sunk in dead-eyed resignation. Only the tall
girl beside her, the pretty but haughty one from
somewhere else entirely, seemed at all alive. She
bore the protecting mark, some days old and smeared
now; and by the look of her she too had not been
touched. She seemed a few years older than Savi, and
the fine clothes that hung in rags about her, and her
cold disdain, suggested wealthy origins. Whenever

Savi tried to speak, she only flashed her eyes contemptuously, and sniffed.

Savi fumed. 'You may think yourself a cut above the rest of us,' she said sharply, at yet another rebuff. 'But, my fine madam, you are in the same cart and on the same rope, and facing much the same fate as any of us, perhaps. It might become you to be less standoffish with those you may be needing, soon enough.'

The woman looked down her long nose. 'That I doubt. I am a princess of the Chaquan line, from the kingdoms far to the west of this barren place – as these uncouth creatures have doubtless recognised, by according me better treatment. Not that it will help them, when my uncle's troops catch them up! I could hardly address you on equal terms.' She unbent slightly. 'But if it is my help and protection you supplicate, when we reach our destination, you or any of you are welcome to it.'

Savi snorted. 'I am a chieftain's daughter myself, with no need to kiss anybody's pretty bum! And but for that last answer, high and mighty, I might have taken you by your long hair and shaken you!'

The girl turned away. 'Your petty rank can hardly be compared with the serene blood of Chaquan. But you may address me as Lady Ulie, if you wish, respectfully.'

Savi lowered her voice. 'I might be more respectful, my lady, if it wasn't so obvious you wet yourself thoroughly a while back! Keep up a bold face, if you wish; but I don't think it was for any fine treatment they spared you and I what they gave poor Kaqual. They don't seem too worried about any troops following, either. More likely we're to find ourselves under some hairy old high priest, or smoking on an altar. Best we accept that, and make common cause.'

The compressed lips, still reddened by bright salve at the corners, showed a sudden tremor. 'But what can we *do*?'

Savi tried to collect her own panic-ridden thoughts. 'Keep our heads. Find out more. Get around some of them, if we can. Captains, men who count.'

Ulie's face crumpled. 'Get around . . . You mean . . . but I am a virgin!'

'So am I,' sighed Savi; and again the image of Alya welled up in her mind. 'Unfortunately. But better bed with a brute than be a baked offering. That's what these folk go in for, at times. The lesser evil you might at least shake off, eventually.'

Ulie burst into silent shaking sobs. Savi sighed. So much for finding other strengths; she had only shattered what little this woman had. She did her best to comfort her. The princess's skinny body, short on muscle, felt like a dry stick in Savi's arms, slender though she herself was. More like a princess in a tale than a real ruler. No spirit. But then, neither had the rest, the village women.

Savi herself had never been so scared in her life; but something, somewhere seemed to be sustaining her. In part, the memory of her father; in part, sheer anger at the fate that had dogged her and others so cruelly. And the worry she could not dismiss was also, against all sense, an insistent source of hope. She found she could not abandon Alya to memory just yet. He was too alive for her; and perhaps, somehow, she might return to him still. Whatever it took, that she would do. When she thought of it like that, it almost made life simpler.

The ascending sun soon showed them that the Ekwesh had taken a new and more northerly direction. Savi, as usual thinking hard to keep down her fears, found herself puzzled. The raiders were riding as if they had something urgent to deliver, urgent and precious. Yet there were not that many of them, forty in all perhaps, a fraction of the whole band; and not that much booty – apart from the women. It was as if they themselves were the main point of these raids.

One thing soon became clear. They were following the wide river, very black and chill to look at, that
flowed more or less southward, though from where
and to where Savi could only guess. Towards midday
they halted briefly, by a sheltered hollow on the bank.
Reaching the bank seemed to please the raiders, who
drank great toasts in captured wine and beer, as well
as some thinnish grey mess of their own, that left
them reeling merrily in their saddles when they
started out again. Snatches of song ran along the line,
and Savi was not too surprised to see the stinking hide
cover flung open at the tail, and a leering guard climb
into the cart, belching a gust of wine. She knew him,
one of the men who had raped Kaqual and others. He
floundered forward, and a lurch sent him on top of
the princess, who pushed him off in a hysterical panic
that would not have deterred a fly. But by chance she
caught the man a sharp blow in one eye, knocking
him sprawling back over Savi's legs, howling with
rage. He nursed the eye frantically for a few minutes,
while the women shrank back. Savi struggled to push
him off, back out over the tailboard, but the others
were no help.

He recovered, still clutching his eye, glaring
malevolently from the other. It lit on Kaqual. He
lurched up and over her, hauling at her skirts as
she tried to roll away from him, flinging her arms
about and shrieking. Savi grabbed at the guard, but he
lost patience suddenly and seized Kaqual by the hair,
dragging her back to the tail with him. Savi and the
princess were hauled along with her. He dropped
back to the ground, trotting to keep up, and yanked
Kaqual out after him. She landed on the rough road
with her bare feet, stumbling to keep up, still screaming. Savi tried to haul her back in, the princess too;
but the guard, springing up again to sit on the tailboard, knocked their hands away and drew his sword
threateningly. Kaqual was forced to run at the pace of

the cart. She managed it, but before long, inevitably, she began to trip and falter. With a sudden impatient laugh the guard lashed out a foot, and kicked the legs from beneath her. She fell flat, and Savi and Ulie were almost hauled out after her. Clinging to the tailgate, they saw her bounced and dashed over rut and rock, her head banging on the stones.

Suddenly a robed man drew his horse up beside the cart, and shouted something angrily at the guard. He leered and shrugged. Ulie screamed words, and the chieftain barked an order. Sullenly the guard reached down and hauled Kaqual up bodily, by the rope. He was not strong enough. In only those few minutes she had become a limp weight. Savi hauled as well, the princess tried to, and the other women joined in. Sagging and bloody, Kaqual appeared over the tailboard; but the guard lifted her head, and it flopped back loosely. The chieftain spat something at him, and he simply severed the waistrope. The girl dropped back from sight. Savi and the princess sprawled flat. The other women wailed, and the guard rounded on them furiously, as if it were their doing. Then he dropped back off the tailboard, and let the cover fall once again.

Savi found she was crying with both horror and sorrow, and also, to her shame, relief. She struggled to choke it off. But Ulie, strangely enough, sat silent. 'You understand their tongue!' said Savi. 'What did that dog's-head say?'

The princess shook her head, dazedly. 'You would understand also, if you listen hard enough. It is much like yours or mine, but with an uncouth accent, and they do not use so many words. He said . . . he said she was more trouble than she was worth. And the chieftain told him that was not for him to decide, that women were urgently needed, young women, as many as possible – and virgins especially. Needed – needed by – there was a name, or a title . . . Needed. That was the word.'

'Needed,' repeated Savi. She hated to think what for. It seemed too close to her worst imaginings. But as her shock and grief subsided, her anger grew. If they were going to do something that terrible to her, then she could hardly make it worse, could she?

When they made camp that night, the women hardly moved, but stayed huddled together in the carts. Savi, though, insisted on going out to wash herself in the sandy shallows, and after a little hesitation managed to persuade the princess. Together they hauled the others, lamenting, out and down to the bank. The princess washed decorously, without removing any clothes; but despite the chill water Savi took her time, under the gloating looks of the guards.

When they went back to the cart a number of the younger men came idling around it; but Savi, sitting swinging her long legs from the tailboard, refused to give them so much as a glance, until she caught the glance of one in particular. He came sidling over at once, twirling his drooping moustaches and eyeing her sidelong, leering as widely as he had when he climbed aboard the cart. She hitched up her legs, slowly, and sent him an even slower smile. He looked this way and that, obviously petrified lest a chieftain see him. Savi shot him one more inviting look, and ducked back beneath the cover. Only seconds later there was a scrabble on the tailboard, and the guard was in among them once again. The women whimpered, but he snarled them to silence, tossed his sword against the tailgate, and made a clumsy grab at Savi.

'If you untied me, we could be more alone!' she cajoled him.

'And I lose head!' he hissed. 'Don't mind watcher! Show what they miss, hah?'

Savi curled her legs tight around him, and ran her hands across his broad back. Then, as he fumbled at his thick belt and between her legs, unable to manage both at once, she locked her crossed ankles tight, made as if to pull at the loosening belt, and plucked his eating knife out of its scabbard. With a quick gasping breath she clutched it in both hands, and, shuddering, rammed it deep into the spot she had chosen.

The guard screamed like a baby in tantrum, and jerked upright, out of her grasp. His face scarlet and convulsing, he grabbed frantically at his back, over the kidneys, and fell backwards through the hide flap. Ignoring the horrible heat of the blood on her hands, Savi caught up the discarded sword and lunged out after him, dragging the others on their faces through the straw. The guard rolled off the tailgate on to his feet, staggering. Savi's thrust took him below the breastbone, and he wheeled about, wrenching the sword from her fingers. He jerked the blade loose and slumped down against the wagon, doubling over and vomiting.

Her gorge rose, but she struggled to reach the blade. She managed it, and began to hack at the rope, but the row had drawn other guards. One ran up and smacked the hilt from her hand with the flat of his broad spearblade. Others seized her, hurled her down with spearblades at her throat. But at a sharp command they fell back, and the cold-eyed chieftain came striding over.

'What has happened here?' he demanded, in clear speech. He kicked the writhing man, who howled louder, then stared at her bloodied hands. 'You, bitch! Did you do this?'

Savi sat up, none too eager to look. 'He murdered one of my people, cruelly! I am a chieftain's daughter!'

The guards threw back their heads and roared with laughter. The chieftain chuckled, more coolly. 'Better you should have been his son! No man would have challenged you till you were old and grey. I was not wrong, it seems.'

'You?' she demanded. 'Not wrong? How so?'

He contemplated her, with no intention of answering. His bored eyes sparkled with amusement. He dipped a finger in the spattered blood, and drew a second sign on her forehead. 'Do not wash it off! Now,' he said to the remaining guards, 'fetter her with iron, but easily, padded.' He kicked the dying man again. 'To remind the new guard of his obedience, let him drag this carrion over to the marsh and sink it. I will have these women left in quiet by all, even chieftains.'

Savi picked herself up. 'Give me back my sword, then!'

Again they roared.

'No!' The eyes narrowed, but not, as she thought, with wrath. 'Take mine!' The chieftain drew his short sword and tossed it to her.

Savi was so startled she nearly dropped it. But the guards laughed again as she seized it neatly by the hilt. It was a crude, weighty blade in dark pitted iron, of the kind called *sax*, single-edged save at the recurved point, and bright only along that edge. She hefted the sword under that cynical look, and found in it a kind of admiration, however distorted. She had no doubt this dead-eyed, depraved creature would have raped her, if he were free to, or worse. He had given her a sword mostly to discourage any further assaults. But his own? She had touched his humour, such as it was, and perhaps even some remnant of admiration.

Had she done right, if it pleased such a one?

She swished the heavy blade back and forth once or twice, surprised at the fierce joy she felt. She had never taken any delight in weapons, but in her present plight this felt as though it gave her back some fragment of herself. Even as they clamped an iron belt about her waist, binding it first in soft hide, she held herself proudly, and slapped away hands that probed too close. And when she was returned to the cart, the other women hugged her and wept, even Ulie. From that day forth she was their champion and chieftain; though the new guards, whatever their eyes held, kept their hands and all else strictly to themselves.

The sword was a support she needed; for as they journeyed on, at a cruel pace, across these wide lands, the country became so different from her own that it felt like another world. She saw less than she would have liked, for the guards kept the cart's cover fastened now. Whether fearing escape or temptation, they were quick to thrust back anyone who looked out, and she could only spy about her by stealth, through the tiny gaps beneath the cover's edge, or by their brief daylight halts. The world seemed to pass by in hurried glimpses.

The great cold river was always with them; when the road seemed to move away from it, it was only to return. Along its banks the scrubby trees gave way gradually to huge clumps of cane, tall and rattling, and then to greater canebrakes, and at last, as far as they could possibly see, cane everywhere. Cane ahead, at their sides, between them and the river, bowing and rushing like the sea under the passing gusts of wind, rustling and chattering as if it had a mind and spirit. They heard things stirring in it, small scuttling things by day and once or twice larger, blundering masses by twilight; the warriors rode close by the carts, and at night they built fires and fences of sharpened canes.

Something happened in that time, though what, Savi was never sure; but the guards grew still more distrustful, riding with readied spears, and looking around them continually. The princess noticed that at least one guard had been replaced, as she remarked, by another even dirtier; but where the first one had gone, they never found out.

The canes lasted for some days, long enough to lose track; but they seemed to end quite suddenly, and give way to a greener land beyond. Few would have called it lush, but to Savi, used to hard stony ground with little water and grudging growth, the sombre greens of this riverine landscape seemed overwhelmingly full and fertile, well watered by driving fronts of rainclouds and heavy with tall grasses, and bursting with a richness of life she found startling.

In her homeland large beasts were rare; but here great herds grazed wide across the rolling hills, especially strange long-haired oxen whose shaggy backs and curiously bowed horns, like saddles, she knew only from old carvings. And there were beasts that fed on these herds. In her own land the largest were the great wolves, though they were rare, and a smallish hill cat, usually starveling and mangy, a peril chiefly to children for lack of easier food. So were the great carrion birds, black-winged, evil heads naked and grey; but they were rarely seen now. Other than that, snakes were the chief peril, and not hard to avoid.

But here, for the first time, she glimpsed bounding bear-dog packs, and once or twice even pairs and prides of fearsome daggertooths loping across the rainy fells, thick-bodied, heavy-legged, their shaggy coats making them even bulkier. One stopped and roared as it saw the caravan, and in the dull stormlight the stabbing fangs gleamed briefly huge and menacing, in a massive head held man-high from the ground. Her heart leaped with the fear and the majesty of the beast, and she gripped the sword more tightly. But whatever the raiders had feared, it was not this. They jeered and rattled spear against shield, spun their helms on their swordpoints and raised a great clamour. The beast turned and loped off into the drizzle, behind its mate. Savi imagined such a brute carrying off whole oxen, until she saw, still further off, the herd these beasts were really shadowing.

The caravan was passing along the rim of a wide shallow valley, above the course of a meandering stream; and she peeped out from below the cover to look down on a carpet of rich grass, still with a few faded flowers. But she was puzzled by the massive boulders strewn along it, like some ancient toppled tower. Almost at once, though, one stirred at the sound of hooves and wheels, tossing back its great hummocked head and brandishing serpentine tusks, almost all that was visible in that hill of earth-hued hair. The trunk she had seen depicted, and hardly believed, curled upward, and its trumpeting cry of warning sent the whole band of them plunging away, their stiff-legged gait rolling like boats in a rapid, while she watched in utter wonder. For a time she even forgot her pain.

Before long, though, that same wonder brought it back to her renewed. Why was this land as it was? By the stars she could guess they had come some way west, now, as well as north. It was colder; the wind that bore the life-giving rains bit more keenly. Yet it was richer land than her own, and all this plenty, that could have fed a host of towns far greater than the Citadel, stood deserted, while her kind grubbed a scanty living among dust and stones. Her suspicions were confirmed at last, when she saw lines of hummocks in the grassland, too regular to be natural, and among them, where the earth had slipped away, vast stone blocks one upon another. These really had been walls and towers, walls many times taller than the Citadel was deep, perhaps the very ones Alya had dreamed of. Long ago, in the days of legend, men had lived here; but their work had been overthrown, and they were driven out, never to return. War, or plague? Or some worse force, the same one even that had brought her here now?

She had time to ponder this, more than she desired. The answer came to her sooner than she wished, and bearing an even deeper chill. The rivers they had crossed flowed mostly southward. The wind blew harshest from the north. She knew much, from her father and from Alya. She knew that across the north of this land there was only one ultimate source for anything. This blossoming of life, denied to the wider, warmer lands, was fed by the outflow of meltwater from the Ice.

It seemed a horrible jest, that so much life should subsist beneath the shadow of its greatest enemy, living on its casual leavings, like gold dust dribbling unregarded from a stolen purse. But through the long and jolting hours, silent and brooding among the stinking straw of the cart, she came to understand. For all its hatred of living things, the Ice had to maintain its living thralls, these *Aikiya'wahsa* as they were called, or shortened in her own speech, the Ekwesh. They could hardly grow food on its icy plains, and it was well known they despised the tilling of the land, as they did all high arts of civilisation. This enclave must be their preserve, a tolerance to let them hunt and gather.

And more than that; for as the caravan forded the stream somewhere and followed the black waters northward, she saw what could only be cultivated fields go by. They passed through several of the miserable little communities that farmed them, a scatter of blind hovels huddled along the flat and marshy banks. The riders paid them no heed whatsoever. Savi herself would not have known them for houses, save for the smoke threading up from their rooftrees; and, here and there amid the misty glooms, an occasional burst of dim yellow light from low door or blocked window, hastily put out.

It spoke so much of life and home to her, that simple light, that she wanted desperately to weep, to howl and tear her hair. Yet she dared not, among the other women, lest she terrify them also. They were grudgingly let out, to bathe themselves as best they could by the cold river, drying themselves at a fire afterwards. The others slept in an untidy tangle, Ulie the princess with her thumb in her mouth; and there at last Savi let her head sink on her knees, and wept silently. Much as she longed to be even a little cleaner, she hated the touch of that dark meltwater, and feared the influences it was said to carry into better, cleaner lands.

It was no mere qualm, that fear. More and more, as the women curled up to sleep in the carts, strange cries and noises encircled them in the dark. At times the marshes sucked and moaned like living souls, and the quaggy earth shook and quivered in places, as if to drink down the cart. At twilight pale glows danced in the distant mists, and the silhouettes of half-decayed trees swayed eerily over the carts, trailing stinking brown strings of fungus against unwary faces; but even dead trees soon became rare. The raiders themselves still ringed their camps with large watch-fires, and tended to stay well within the overlapping circles of light. Yet late one sullen night there were terrible shrieks, and the next day the guards were moody and savage, beyond the usual. But nobody was foolish enough to ask. Only slaves would dwell in this country, indeed; and she could not escape it.

Soon thereafter, though, there came a day when, among the dawn mists, the carts turned away from the road; but not inland. To everyone's surprise they went bouncing down a much rougher road, sloping quite steeply downward towards the river itself. The guards drove the caravan slowly along the bank, evidently careful lest they slip a wheel on the path's edge and topple into the black waters, now so close. Savi wondered if there would be a ford, but was surprised when the carts were drawn up, and then laboriously manhandled on to what were evidently wide flat boats. Most of the women had never been on board any such thing before, and moaned with terror at the swaying sensation, uneasy at every step or shift of weight. When the barges were poled off the bank and out into the stream, Savi didn't much take to it either, but tried to stay composed. Her fear would break the rest, panic them even; and this was no time for that. The motion was gentle enough, though; and compared to the bruising jolts and jarrings of the road, it was peaceful. By the first day's end she was almost enjoying it.

Almost; for this was still no quiet land that went by them, as the barges were drawn north against the current, sometimes by the horses along the bank, sometimes by the guards with their long poles. By day, when the mists lifted, the winds moaned, and the river ran slow and heavy past sighing banks of reeds and sedge; all else was barren and bleak. Green soon faded from the land, to be replaced by dull browns, like a perpetual late autumn. They saw no more herds, but heard the harsh cries of beasts they did not know and could not see. Even the birdsong seemed muted and sad. And by night, as the barges were brought in and moored, and the guards built their fires, the land grew fearful.

Evening wisps of mist drifted across the river, taking strange shapes, like phantoms, that even the reivers balked at and avoided. Wings fluttered in the dusk, small insects sang strange songs, and the hard-faced men with their pitiless eyes moved the horses nearer the fires, and muttered over amulets and charms.

Savi's was her sword.

That, and the need of those around her. She would not be seen to fear by the other girls, and clutched the carven hilt close. But in the darkest night, sometimes, when cries like distant laughter awoke her, or some great beast wallowed by too close to the cart, she would give way to her loneliness and fear, hugging her breasts as if other hands comforted her.

And then one such night the terror struck deepest of all into her soul, pinning her down, as it seemed, like some helpless creature speared to the earth. That chill midnight, as the murmur of the camp, already muted, faded into silence, she risked looking out of the cart with its stinking straw and rank jumble of bodies, to snatch great lungfuls of the clear, crisp air.

She threw her head back to the chill, baring her neck and breast, wondering as ever if Alya also looked upon this full cold moon and star-silvered sky, and whether he still thought of her. She had little enough hope; but to think otherwise was too painful. But then she saw another gleam across the horizon, that seemed to reach back up from earth to heavens, silhouetting even at this great distance a range of shadowy clifftops studded with jagged mountain-teeth, as blue and bitter as edged steel.

Thither they were heading, she could have no doubt about it now. That way lay their journey, straight to the heart of all she had most cause to loathe and fear. There lay her destiny, and fettered both by iron and the role she'd assumed, there was nothing she could do to prevent it. The barrier was already past and down behind her; for what would she do in these terrible lands? She had seen her way only in brief glimpses. Even if she should escape, somehow, she would never, ever be able to find her way back out of them, not with their legendary evils. She knew, without being told, that she looked upon the light of the Great Ice.

'Can we not ride faster?' demanded Alya, for the hundredth time. 'This is taking us away from her, every step!'

'Only to bring us closer in the end!' said Vansha patiently, for an equal number. 'Much faster and we'll kill these poor beasts! But we'll be at the Forest of Birds soon enough. All too soon, maybe!'

They were heading south and west, and it felt ridiculous. Such tracks as they had found led west and north – not that that would be hard to guess, for that was where the land of the raiders lay, in the arms, it was rumoured, of the Ice itself. Alya shuddered at the thought of Savi, alone and helpless, without him, borne towards that terrifying embrace. He had the strong fancy of the Seer, the power to shape living images in the mind from scanty hints and clues; and the pictures that constantly came upon him made him goad the black mare still more sharply. He found himself digging his heels into its flanks as if the poor brute was somehow responsible for every delay. But he was not cruel, and realising that made him stop. 'Right enough, Vansha. The next river we come to, they can rest and water.'

'That's wise. So can we. You seem to be living on the fire in your belly, but it won't hurt to stoke it once in a while. Once we get more mounts, more weapons, some followers – then we can ride harder. I wish I could be more sure . . .'

'Of what?'

Vansha looked dark. 'Nothing. Hope isn't what we chase, is it?'

Alya shook his head. 'But hope there is, of a kind. If she were dead – I would know.'

Vansha shrugged uncomfortably, and said little more. He was looking across the open plain ahead. For the first time in two days' hard riding there was something new there, some definition to the endless horizon – a low smudge of dark green, shadowed and strange beneath the hazy grey sky. A steely thread wound its way among the low hillocks that lay between.

'That's it?' demanded Alya.

'It is. And there's the forest river, flowing down from the north-west. The horses can smell it already.'

It was midday when they halted by a dark pool between the hills, but the sun remained hidden under gathering clouds, and the air was heavy. Vansha dismounted stiffly, with many oaths. 'Too unused to riding,' he groaned, easing his leather breeches about his thighs. 'And never this far.'

'But you've been to the Forest before!'

'Its outskirts. Once. And not in such long rides.'

Alya surprised himself at how easily he swung down, and how relaxed he felt. The fire in his back was no more than a welcome tingle, for now.

'Aren't your hams even aching?' demanded Vansha enviously. He turned his horse loose by the stream, and sank gratefully down among the sparse grass. 'They should be, damn it. Longer still since *you* rode! And yet you don't even seem tired.' He shivered. 'What is it about you, man? What happened to you?'

'You did, maybe.'

Vansha's face twisted. 'I know. I know! But have some mercy on me, at least, now such a miracle's healed you. I was just a boy, then, still. I was terrified of you, you know that?'

'Of *me*?' Alya snorted.

'Yes! Of you! The Citadel was my home, all I'd ever known. Oh, I longed for better, but I was going to stay and look after the folk, like my father said. Little use as a Seer, but better than nothing, he said. You know, this – here, to the Forest's edge – this is as far as I've ever been from the Citadel? As much of the world as I've ever seen? I hadn't even done that, back then. And suddenly, into my narrow world bursts this wild lad who's lived twice the life I ever had, been places, seen twice the things, and they're written all over his face – and he's a Seer to boot. As good a shot and hunter, easily. And fairer, at that.'

'Better-looking than *you*?' Alya laughed.

'Savi thought so,' said Vansha sullenly, not laughing in the least. 'There I was – and she hardly seemed to notice me any more. Nobody did, not the way they used to. You, always in the forefront, always striving—' He choked, for a moment. 'I was fighting, for my life – my old life! I had to keep a brake on your wheel, to pull you back down all the time. Or you'd have had everything. *Everything!* Whisked the mat right out from beneath my feet. Oh aye, there was plenty to be scared of. Most of all Savi . . . Savi . . .'

Alya drew breath. 'I knew you always sought to diminish me. But I never wished . . . I hardly knew what I was doing to you! Could you not have told me? Spoken to me?'

'Would it have made any difference? Then, that fight, that was the last straw . . . Powers, how I hated you! How I feared you! Because on top of all else, you were winning! Winning! In my village, before my people, my girl, in my home that you'd usurped! Would it have made any difference, to speak, to plead with you?'

Vansha rose abruptly, strode over to the stream where it flowed fast over fine gravel, and splashed his face.

'No,' said Alya, quietly. 'I don't think it would have.' He flopped down on the grassy bank and began to scoop up water in his cupped hands. 'We won't take time to light a fire, not now.'

'No,' agreed Vansha, looking anxiously around. 'It might . . . attract attention. Among the trees. Just a bite or two of bread and trail-meat, cold, for now. Then onward.'

Alya gazed at the trees. 'The Forest of Birds, that doesn't sound so bad. Are you truly afraid?'

'Yes. I am. When I came here with the hunters . . . it was bright sun then, and there was still a shadow among the leaves, and a cold breath of breeze

that sucked the heat out of the day . . . *There!* Did you
feel it?'

'There's no shortage of breezes, within or without. Was there more?'

'Oh yes. Lights, at night, deep among the trees.
We were camped back up there, on the hill, about a
thousand paces away, and we still saw them. Not
natural, like firelight or torches. More like will o'the
wisps, or rotting fish – you know? And there were
voices on the wind, horrible voices, whining, whistling. That was autumn, when night came earlier. We
can try to get through by dark, at least to the other
margin; and that means moving fast. Where's that
bread?'

'The cloud'll make it darker, though,' said Alya,
around his mouthful. 'Especially if that breeze brings
up any more. Whew! You're right. Feel that chill!'

'What did I tell you? But listen, man, you're a
Seer, are you not?'

'While I did no more than sit in pain, I saw,
almost without willing it. But it was never enough.'

'Well, now you can dance again! Why not try and
spy out something of our path?'

Alya stared. 'I should have thought of that. But I
didn't – why not? I'll surely give it a try.'

Vansha stared at the mask, as Alya slipped it on;
but he said nothing of his thought. There on the bank
Alya stamped and spun in the old remembered
rhythm, this way and that; and the Trail traced its
smouldering path behind his eyes, leading him on and
in. In his mind the image growing in his mind of
wings, wheeling black wings against the deeper
blackness of the Wall. High, soaring above a country
of arid stone, able to glimpse the cloudy depths of
distance that lay beyond the distant barrier, higher,
ever higher. It was the sun on black wings, maybe,
that growing heat . . .

He was on his knees, panting, while the flare of

red cleared from his eyes. He felt as if he had looked straight into the noonday sun. Vansha gave him cold river-water to drink, and sprinkled the rest on his sweating face. 'Well? Was what you saw so terrible?'

Alya shook his head. 'I saw nothing!'

'Not even the Wall?'

'Within sight of it, from far off. But then something stopped me, cast me down! Something that stung me like, like a shower of cinders at the smith's. As if it was forbidding me, somehow. Holding me back.'

'I've eaten enough!' snapped Vansha, snagging the trailing reins and, for all his stiffness, springing back into the saddle. 'And done lingering!'

Alya shivered, and ruffled his mount's mane. 'I think you're right!' He also did not want to think about what had just happened, not even for a moment. Much longer, and they would lose their nerve. He swung himself up, and the two young men turned their mounts towards the wall of trees.

It ended quite sharply against the grassland, with only patches of bushes and other low growth as a barrier. The trail among it was clear but narrow, an animal trail more than human, printed with the notched hooves of deer. Vansha swore as stinging plants brushed his bare ankles, and sharp thorns needled through Alya's breeches. But as they came beneath the shade of the trees the growth seemed to diminish, and the path opened out. Vansha looked back, and pulled his horse up sharply. Alya wheeled, hand on blade.

'What's the matter?'

'*Look!*' whispered Vansha. There was no trace of a trail behind them; the greenery bulked close and undisturbed.

'Because we brushed through it!' said Alya, unconvincingly. 'Well, we weren't planning to go back that way, especially.'

'Just as well!' whispered Vansha. 'Ride on, then! Even with the branches overhanging, a trot is less of a risk!'

The forest floor was soft beneath their hooves. Where the trees were densest, it was soft damp leaf mould and made little sound, but where the trail branched into open space, the choking greenery returned. All the time, though, the trees were becoming thicker and of kinds Alya hardly knew, broadleaved and broad-limbed, like canopies rather than evergreen pillars. Their limbs stooped low, and before long the young men had to dismount to avoid rapping their heads continually.

'I think I'm growing bark!' complained Alya, tugging it out of his thick hair. 'And this miraculous healing doesn't stop lumps on the head, obviously. If this isn't a cone.'

'My eyes seem to be full of twig! This is useless, we'll have to lead the mounts. For a while, anyhow. From what the other hunters told me, the main trail starts to rise here, towards the wood's heart, and then falls away somewhat on the other side, a more thinly wooded slope. So most probably the worse part will be before then.'

'So be it! But we must be ready to mount and flee at need. I am not going to leave my bones and quest here together.'

'Nor I.' Quickly Vansha strung his bow and laid it ready across his pommel. Alya clutched his great sword, and led his horse forward. It came willingly enough, glad to be without his weight, no doubt; but every so often, at some noise within the wood, some quick sharp scurry among the leaves or flurry within a bush, its ears would go back and its eyes roll. Vansha was reacting much the same way, suddenly twisting this way and that; and eventually he stopped and snarled.

'*I* know what's been bothering me! Bird Forest

be damned – have you ever heard so few among trees, and at this time of year?'

'I have not!' agreed Alya, in sudden wonder. 'There were some calls, at first – at the edge. But not now, none at all. As if something—'

A sudden flurry of wind whipped around him. A leaf danced high in the air above him, then struck, viciously as it seemed, down into his eyes, so hard he ducked. Rain came after it, dashed in his face almost in handfuls, and the branches sprung and whipped about him. The air howled, and drove them all staggering backwards, men and horses both, into the tangling embrace of the trees.

Then other howls arose about them, as figures sprang up from the thickets around.

So wild, so shapeless they seemed that it was hard to be sure what they were; long-limbed apes, maybe, baring yellowed fangs, slashing with filthy claws. The pungent stink that surrounded them was animal, if not worse. But the claws were metal, and what hung around them was not pelt but rags; and the wild eyes were still, after a fashion, human. As the wind failed the young men broke away, the horses rearing and plunging wildly; Vansha grabbed his bow as it fell from the saddle. The brigands, seeing their surprise had failed, hung back, tittering slightly, holding their weapons ready in long limbs, lank but strong-looking. Alya counted nine, but suspected a couple more among the greenery.

'What d'you want of us?' shouted Vansha. 'We're not rich! We've nothing!'

'Horsies!' jeered one of the creatures, smacking his lips robustly. 'Your stickers, your slicers! Throw'm down an' we won't hurt yous!'

'Have you home t'eat!' sniggered another, and slurped back his drool as the others giggled. 'Friends, huh?'

'You want our weapons?' demanded Vansha. 'Have one!' Unseen by them, he had already nocked an arrow to the string, and now he raised the bow, drew and loosed with a hunter's smooth speed. Instantly, as it seemed, the leading brigand kicked up his legs and fell back into the green. Another sprang over him, screeching with rage, but Alya's sword swept from its ancient scabbard. He felt his back and shoulders blaze, and he swung it. He was no swordsman, but it weighed like a light stick in his fingers. It smashed the brigand's dagger from his hand and slashed down across his chest. Alya hardly felt the impact, but it sent the man flying backwards among the ferns, spraying them with red.

The others skipped back with shrill yells, and that gave both boys the moment they needed to mount. They spurred the horses forward, stooped low against their necks, and rode down any who sought to block their way. Shrill cries sang after them like a rookery disturbed, stones and sharp flints whizzed into the trees around them, but nothing new or dangerous. The wind whistled about them, and the trees bent and slapped at them as they passed, but there was no pursuit. 'All right?' called Vansha cheerfully enough, when they were far enough ahead. He reined in, looking as rattled as Alya felt, but also as relieved. 'Pretty pathetic, those outlaws. Can't get many travellers through, these days. Must live on rats or something most of the time, no diet for any man.'

'I don't think they were men,' said Alya, reining in alongside and looking back. 'Not any more.'

Vansha shivered. 'The smell . . .'

'Yes. Gets your hackles up, doesn't it? And those long limbs. They say the Powers can change some people, over generations, make servants of them.'

'Yes. You think these ones were serving some-one? Something?' Vansha seized his bow again, and looked angrily about. 'Damn them, they might be driving us ahead! Making us feel we'd scored some kind of victory! And all the time herding us just where they wanted us to go—'

The whistle of wind that cut off his words was deafeningly shrill. The boughs above them stooped and struck, dead twigs and mast flew up off the forest shore and stung their eyes.

'No – ordinary – storm!' yelled Alya, struggling to steady his horse. 'Only one safe way!'

'Right!' yelled Vansha. 'Run, now! Right into the teeth of it—'

The two young men struggled to subdue their frightened horses, to head them into the wind. It gusted a great roaring laugh about their ears, whipping Alya's long hair into his eyes – a monstrous, threatening sound. They shouted to counter it, cracked the reins across their horses' cruppers, and the frightened beasts sprang madly away. Alya's hair streamed out in the rain, Vansha's gleamed slick with water as they crashed through bush and briar, the horses breasting the seething undergrowth and snapping branches in their eagerness to be gone. Alya, holding reins and saddle with one hand, slashed at bush and branch with the great sword, while Vansha, clinging with his knees, fitted another arrow and cast about.

Faster and faster they raced, sending great sprays of leaves up and dancing in the stormy air. A wild laugh erupted to one side, and Vansha, bow still in hand, loosed the long shaft at the source. Through the leaves it sliced, and stuck quivering in the trunk of an ancient elm. More laughter rumbled. A huge branch flailed into their path; Alya slashed at it, but only scored the bark. It whipped back, there came a great shriek of wrath, and a blast of wind that strove to lift them both from their saddles. Alya ducked as the branch flailed back, and together, cresting the wall of trees, they burst out into a wide clearing right at the brink of the hill.

Nothing grew here within that wide oval, though one dead tree stood at its heart on a hillock of half-exposed roots, blackened and twisted as if by lightning. Even the earth seemed barren and dead, slipping away from the hilltop to lay bare its stony heart – and with it, half buried, a heaping scatter at the tree's foot. Some of it was stone, carven and shaped, though worn now almost beyond all recognition; here and there a stony face gaped like a skull. But around and between that lay mostly human bones, scattered, skulls and ribcages with all manner of other bones between them, but cracked and split, glistening in the mire.

The horses reared and plunged, the rain lashed like flails, and the booming voice spewed mockery in their ears. A loud whistle blasted the air, and the wind charged against them like a beast, sending them staggering. Again the whistle, and they were almost hurled across the clearing, hooves dragging among the bones but finding no purchase. The whistle changed, and they were spilled back again, stunned and winded. Again that horrible laugh sounded, and it seemed to shake the ground beneath them. But it had a source now. It came from above; and looking up with dazed eyes they saw it, squatting high on the branch of the dead tree like some form of horrible growth or parasite, a shapeless bundle of fur with skinny limbs dangling in the air below.

Vansha yelled in answer, 'What are you? We want nothing of you but to pass!'

The bundle stirred. 'But there's much I want of you. You're in my realm now!' The voice was human, casual, though it seemed impossible it should come from that spidery shape.

'What d'you want?' demanded Alya angrily. 'The flesh on our bones?'

'I? Perish the thought!' A young man's voice, drawling, amused, using words Alya barely understood. 'My devotees insist on that. The ones you've already met. Poor fellows! A relic of their long servitude to the Ice, when they were taught to think of mansflesh as the reward of chieftains. They are no chieftains now, but I must let them have their way. I once tried a little myself, but frankly . . .'

'You want something else. Like what?'

'Oh, that's terribly hard to define. Essence? Being? You'd never understand, so why waste time?'

Vansha understood even less than Alya, and that made his anger boil over all the more. His bow hung ready, and he swung it up, drawing and aiming as one movement, and loosed as the string reached his chin. It was a fine shot, and the arrow soared into the tree. But just as swiftly a thin white arm darted from the bundle, and with an almost easy accuracy long fingers plucked the shaft from the air.

The creature giggled, and pushed back its fur hood to reveal a face that Alya was startled to find so human. It grinned, a wide, thin-lipped gape, raised the arrow to its mouth and made great show of picking its teeth. Then it stuck the arrow in its lips, point outward, and spat. Vansha just managed to duck as it sang past his head on a whistling blast.

The bundle uncoiled suddenly, swift as a snake's strike; the thin limbs tensed. The first shiver of a whistle almost too high to hear hurt their ears and blurred their eyes. Hardly less swiftly Alya raised his sword, but the rising wind clutched the blade, shook it in his hand, shoved it rudely back; and the whine grew to a stabbing ache. The horses tossed their heads and threshed, too terrified to move.

The new fire burned along Alya's arm. He let the blade be driven back, gathering his strength. Then, standing suddenly in his stirrups, he flung it from his hand, as once the boy hunter had hurled sticks into rising flocks of birds, straight into the face of the wind.

The blade-edge cut the air like gossamer silk. The sword flew straighter than the arrow, and struck, both the branch and the leg that dangled from it. The thud shook the tree from top to bole. The tree-limb, half cut through, creaked, tore and snapped, and the bundle was swept shrieking out into the air. Down on to the hillock it toppled, hit the upturned roots and bounced, curled up like a spider, to roll down among the bodies at the foot. It half opened; and then the sword came hissing down from the air, and stuck quivering in the earth a finger's breadth away.

The little monster curled up sharply, and the white limbs trembled. Blood trickled from the deep gash in one thigh, blood too dark to be a normal human's. Alya sprang down and grabbed the thing, though the fur felt unpleasant in his hands, and Vansha after him.

'Now *that* was a throw, brother!' he laughed. 'And what a pretty little birdie it's brought down!'

He grabbed the head by what might have been fur or hair, and forced it back. The face leered up at them, and both men recoiled. Not that it was inhuman, or monstrous; it was human, in its fashion, indeed almost ordinary if the skin had not been so pallid, the mouth so heavy. Even so, the features were wholly unlike their own, rounded, smooth, puffy in the cheeks. It was a boy's face, still half a child's, wholly unlined. But the eyes were as dark as the slitted lids were white, and they peered out between them like pits of black malice, so strong it struck both men like a blow. This was a man, in its shape; yet they felt that some kind of creature grinned at them, the fat pale lips stretching unpleasantly wide over the large yellow teeth. The lips pursed suddenly. Vansha thrust his dagger to its side; Alya clamped his hand on its throat. It bucked at the touch, and the lips subsided.

'You'll whistle through every hole and a few new ones if you try that again!' warned Vansha.

'So you've caught me!' mocked the voice. 'Stars, that's a handy talent, that sword-throwing. I must practise. But now, what're you going to do with me? Can't squat here holding on to me forever!'

'What's wrong with killing you, whatever you are?' Vansha suggested.

The bland face smirked. 'Everything. People like me, we never wholly die, you know. We always come back. We change, but we come back, eventually. And then you'd be very, *very* sorry!'

'I've heard that said about the Powers!' grunted Alya.

'That's right!' tittered the face. 'That's me. Oh, a very minor one, I grant you, but still nobody to trifle with—' It shrilled. Alya's grip had closed. He hauled the now silent creature upright.

'Power or not, you can be brought down. You can be choked, I think. Feel the strength in my hand. It runs through my body. That is the strength of Powers, as much as any whistling tricks of yours. Tell me now why it should not destroy you. You might be slow to return from *that*.'

The fur quivered, and a deep shuddering breath whistled in the constricted throat. 'Because – because I can serve you?'

Vansha chuckled incredulously. 'A Power serve a mere mortal? There's a comedown!'

'I *am* a Power!' it squalled petulantly. 'Oh, my mother was a mortal, maybe! She died. But I didn't. Not ever, not in many lifetimes of men. Some Power had got across her, who'd made himself human, no doubt. They can do that, you know! Oh, easily enough, all but the greatest ones. And equipped his nice new body with human seed he probably never thought of; and that seed made me!' The creature gave a high wheezing cackle, and tossed his tousled mane. 'For that I'm deeply indebted to him – me, half shaped, pale of cheek, strong in magic but weak in limb, never dying but never young, hating the strong and the happy, despising fools who ride free through the world! Their lives are my true food, their essences make me live as their carcasses feed those beast-witted worshippers of mine! Well, now you know. So go ahead, slay me now and watch my cursed blood stain your swords forever. Or take me for what I am!'

Alya considered those black eyes for a moment. He could imagine himself weakened, helpless, staring into them and feeling his life draining away, all his memories, his experiences – his essence, pouring out into that hungry mind.

'Why should you prefer that, creature? What lure is in it for you, better than a death you claim not to fear? And why should we trust you?'

The voice grew almost serious. 'Because you are a hero of the Powers. You are the first such ever to cross my path, in year upon year; but I know you, oh yes, I know. I cannot see your strength, but I feel it, feel the thunder of it, fire that flows beneath your skin like waters racing beneath the earth. Strengths like that are given to cut fiery courses across this cold world. I want to follow it awhile, and see where it leads.' Again the giggle. 'And because somehow, despite all this, despite a gift that mortals rarely taste, you are not – either of you – happy.'

Vansha's dagger moved across its throat. 'Never less happy than looking at you! I say, speed him on his journey and rid the world of one more foulness. Let him find his own way back, if he will!'

'Look at his thigh!' said Alya. Vansha snarled. There was no more blood; there was not even a scab, only a brown mark.

'We could hew him in pieces—' began Vansha. The creature shrilled horribly.

'Maybe,' said Alya thoughtfully. 'He is uncanny

enough; but then so was my healing. You, creature or man, you have not answered us fully. Why should we trust you? Why should we sleep easy with you at our heel, you and your Powers?'

'What, strive against you, now that I know you? Look where it got me last time. No, you're one to run with, not against, as all but fools can see. So, bind me if you will, gag me even – oh, cruel torment! – and I'll be your outrunner, before your horse or beside you. Not behind, I don't like the view. And a sword I can be to you, greater than that you bear. I will fell your foes, defend your friends, drink only the lives you give me. I will be another strength to you, such as you now possess! And maybe even make up for the brains they never gave you!'

Vansha spat; but Alya, after a long moment, lifted his hand and Vansha's from the narrow throat. Beside him the sword stood half its length in the earth, but he did not lay hand to it. 'Do you have a name, creature?'

The head waggled. 'None I can remember. My followers called me the Nightingale, by times. For the grace and beauty of my song, upon moonlit nights in the wild wood.'

'I can see why. Well, Nightingale, you'll have your wish. I will spare you, unless and until you menace us ever again! You'll be something to show to the King.' Alya silenced Vansha's protest with a gesture. 'But something more will bind you. Your word – no, spare me! You need not swear to either of us. You would break that the first time we turned our backs on you, or slept. But to the Powers that poured this strength into me – to *Their* purpose, whatever that was.' The creature sat up with a squeal, its white face suddenly livid. 'To *that*, to Them you will swear. And bring down *Their* wrath upon you, should you fail.'

Nightingale scrabbled backward on the ground,

uttering little shrill cries; then stopped, as suddenly, as he ran into Vansha's dagger. Alya tugged his sword from the ground, and wiped it clean of soil against the oily furs. 'I do not force you. My friend is only too eager—'

Nightingale's eyes narrowed. 'You don't know what you ask! You don't even know the fire that burns in you! That alone would consume me in torments!'

'Every moment of which you deserve. Consider this a chance to make amends. And do not delay, in the hope your hungry devotees will free you – what's left of them, and when they catch up. Now, or never. Vansha?'

'*Now!*' shrieked Nightingale, and a gust thrashed the branches at his very word. 'Now! I swear, I swear, to the Powers whose strength you carry. I'll help you, I won't betray you, I won't, I won't . . .' He fell forward, foaming and drooling, almost in a fit as it seemed.

Vansha picked him up bodily by the scruff of his skinny neck. 'Heard and witnessed, demon! And the first wrong move you make . . .'

Nightingale, dangling from his fist, smiled suddenly, and there was malicious strength in that smile. 'That *I* make? If you must worry, handsome fellow, worry over yours! Oath made, oath kept, for me!'

Vansha snorted. 'See that you do!' He set him on his feet, where he stayed, shakily, like an ugly child in ragged furs, stooped, thin and starveling. 'Think he'll be strong enough to run a step, let alone pace a horse?' jeered Vansha. 'We'll end up carrying him!'

'If we must,' answered Alya, feeling a strange mixture of excitement and relief within him, as one might who has passed a barrier, or a test. 'But Master Nightingale has more surprises for us yet, I think. Vansha, you have the way of knots; bind him tightly enough, but leave him ungagged. I think we might do well to endure his rattling and railing, for the specks of truth within.'

Nightingale stole a look from under his fleshy brows, and giggled. 'What's this, brains between a hero's ears? Coming up in the world, clearly. We live in an age of miracles. But be swift now, or my votaries will get their nerves and their appetites back, and perhaps include me. False god would be top of their table.'

'Don't give yourself airs,' grinned Alya, as Vansha knotted two narrow cuffs at the end of a length of thin hempen cord. 'You'd supply the toothpicks. Now lead us out of here, by the quickest and safest way, towards the city.'

But when they hauled themselves into their saddles once more, it was the false god who set off at a startling pace out of the clearing and down the further slope, his skinny limbs skipping over roots and underbrush more lightly than their mounts could follow. Vansha cracked the rope. 'Slow down, ghoul! I'll not have you steering us into any pits or peat-bogs!'

'They're all on the other paths!' Nightingale cackled, his furs bouncing and shifting as he loped down a winding path that none could see save he. 'Along with worse things, holes and voles and bears in lairs with more bones outside than mine, and hanging vines that are no vines, yet hang very neatly by the neck! But we can take the pretty route, if you insist!'

'Another day!' said Vansha, looking uneasily around. The sun struck slanting beams down between the trees now, and the air was heavy, and sang. Dust motes sparkled, and insects glittered lazily this way and that. The slope was steep, and they came downhill faster than they would have liked, the horses whinnying as their hooves slipped in the loose soil. The trees changed around them, with fewer evergreens and more leafy crowns, and mercifully thinner underbrush. But it was still impossible to move quietly at such a pace. Over the crashing of their horses' hooves, Alya was sure he heard other sounds, distant but distinct, keeping pace with them.

'Nightingale!' he snapped, after a moment. 'Something's pacing us! Many things. I thought it was your men, but they sound smaller, faster. Like a pack . . .'

'No wolves here!' snapped Nightingale, and bounded, if anything, faster. 'Don't ask! Just come, and be clear of the trees ere nightfall. They won't strike till then.'

'That suits me very well!' snapped Vansha, though he had to duck under a whipping stand of grey ash saplings. Alya felt the same, though it cost him also a lashing, and once a fall, with his horse plunging around in fright before he caught and calmed it, while Nightingale capered and gibbered in his haste. The rushing sounds were louder now, and closer, and sometimes they were also in the tops of the trees as well as along the ground. And there they leaped and skipped among the leaves, like squirrels; only they were many times too large for that.

Birds shrilled from the trees at their clumsy passage, jays like screaming sapphire darts, woodpeckers cackling mockery overhead, catbirds trilling eerie calls that belonged to no other bird they knew. Tiny chickadees spun and swooped before their eyes, making them flinch and almost lose their seats; pheasants burst from the scanty undergrowth, startling the horses. Crows thrashed and jeered overhead, sending down showers of twigs, and Nightingale jibbered back at them. Alya, fighting to keep his seat, envied him the breath.

Vansha's horse reared suddenly, kicking at the

air, and he fought to control it. Alya wheeled around to help him, but his own horse was suddenly almost as startled, its ears flattened back, head tossing. He saw why, in the earth at his feet; a single chance print, perhaps, but very new, the water still oozing back into it. A bird's it was, surely; but of such a size that his own two feet together could scarcely match it.

Even Nightingale stared. Then he hauled bodily at the rope. '*Come!* Race for the light, or I am not answerable!'

Their mounts wanted nothing better, and crouching low in their saddles the riders dug in their heels and clung. All above them was thrashing turmoil, a storm of greenery speeding by, spraying down leaves and twigs upon their heads. Out of it something stooped, and Alya yelled as talons raked his ear. But then they were among tall slender beeches, on a clear and open floor, and beyond them, in the distance, hints of open sky, and the steep slope flattening out. A single screeching cry sounded behind them, and Nightingale, wheeling about, urged them on. But nothing followed, and gradually they slowed the horses to a walk.

'Forest of Birds!' said Vansha feelingly. 'When we took this creature, I thought it was all we had to fear in here!'

Nightingale leered around at them. 'All woods and forests are the Lord Tapiau's – did you forget that? And throughout his domains he has many servants, jealous as any distrustful peasant of his petty square of earth and dung. This one I could withstand, while I laired in my clearing, for my whistling could topple many trunks; and it let me be. But now it has seen me bested and bound by pissy little men. It is still not safe to linger. *Come!*'

Vansha growled. 'He'd better be the help you expect.'

Alya, fingering his stinging ear, smiled. So much power there, if he could only unleash it; if he could only win its trust. 'I think he will be. For a time, anyhow. Who knows? I cannot feel it, not yet; but perhaps he is our first glimmering of hope.'

CHAPTER 5
Darkness Answers

'WILL you look at the size of the place!' exclaimed Vansha.

He was sitting back in his saddle, openly gaping at the jagged line of walls that sprawled across the river-plain ahead, in the sinking sun's long shadows. Walls with rooftrees behind them, great and small, and here and there like vicious teeth a tall tower. The greatest tower of all rose at its heart, its pinnacle a dull green gleam.

'How many folk d'you think live in there? Must be hundreds upon hundreds!'

'Thousands, I'd guess,' said Alya. 'Maybe tens of thousands. Smells like it, doesn't it?' He had seen greater in his visions, much greater; but this was real, and here.

Vansha shook his head. 'But how do they all *live*? Not by honest farming or hunting, that's for sure!'

Nightingale, squatting at their feet, cackled. 'One upon another, the way of the world. Wolf upon sheep, cat upon mouse, flea upon smaller flea; so all kingdoms are. At least my folk ate up men honestly, and did not tell them it was good government, and their loyal duty to lend their bones for gnawing!'

Alya glanced at him. 'For one who never stirred from his forest, you seem to feel you know a lot about ordinary men.'

'I was not born in the forest! I fled the ways of common men. And I have drunk up the minds of many, lived a thousand lives. Some is with me yet.'

Nightingale fingered his full lips. 'Let me see . . . Ah, yes. There was a lord not long since, fleeing through the forest, when others were being clapped in dungeons or simply chopped up in public. Though he could have saved himself the trouble, heh! *He* knew this Volmur. Proud, selfish, weighing everything from wine to women by what makes him stronger and grander, increasing his wealth or his name. You'll need to impress him. Mighty thews find favour, but only if it's him they serve.'

Alya nodded. 'For that I thank you. And I think we should do something about you, in return.' He unhitched a sack that had held their food, and tipped what little was left into a saddlebag. 'You should be able to fit into this.'

Nightingale screeched like a daw. 'Into that? I'll choke!'

'Then would you rather be led openly through a place where you're a known bugbear? Where many might recognise you, from legends if nothing more? I thought not!' The pale creature had skipped instantly into the bag and squatted down, pulling it up around his head. Once again he weighed surprisingly light in Alya's hand, but the horse shied nervously as he was hung at the saddlebow.

'Don't blame the poor brute, either!' said Vansha. 'Well, here we are, my brother – two bare-assed country lads, come for to see the King. How're we going to get within spitting distance?'

'Two country lads who've bagged a local demon,' said Alya lightly. Vansha looked at him, sharply.

'Not half so miserable as you were, are you?'

'Are you? We're getting somewhere, at last. If we can find the power to save Savi anywhere, it's here. Fast horses, armed men . . . You couldn't call it happiness, brother; but it'll serve till happiness comes along!'

They turned their tired mounts to the slope, and

trotted down to the broad road that ran through the wide fields below. When they reached it, it looked less impressive. It had been cleared and levelled, once, long ago, and a sturdy roadbed laid, of great stones and gravel well drained; but the surfacing had been allowed to wear away for so long that deep ruts were worn in the top of the very stones, and much of the gravel was gone. Here and there it had been mended, clumsily, with jumbles of stone and even great logs, now half rotten and slippery. Carts came clattering and thumping by, drawn by lowing oxen, their iron-shod wheels striking sparks from the flints in the road; and their drivers cast curious eyes at the young men on the proud horses, ill-clad but well armed.

Neither man paid them much heed, for they could not take their eyes off the walls that loomed larger ahead, marking off a wide section of the plain between two broad streams, no doubt for both water and defence. It was their sheer size that fascinated Vansha; but for Alya it was something more.

They rose in two distinct parts. Uppermost, and most visible, was a strong wooden palisade of massive treetrunks, visible beneath a clumsy facing of clay that would make them harder to fire or hew. The top of the palisade was not neatly level, but rose and fell like jagged teeth. Around it ran a rough battlement, also of wood, with here and there a roofed shed for archers to shoot from. It all looked quite new and recent. But at the front of the wall, most massive and dominating, the trunks were rooted in something else entirely, a huge cliff-like course of stone that ran from channel to channel like one of the very bones of the earth itself, lying exposed.

And as he stared, Alya felt a great thrill of wonder; for this enormous thing was not natural. Worn and battered, and in places strangely calcined, but still immensely strong, it was the remnant of a

wall made by men, and in the same manner as the
buildings he had seen fall.

Vansha refused to believe it. 'Shaped, maybe, out
of some ridge already there. But d'you see any chinks,
or joints? No. Even in times past they weren't that
mighty!'

Yet as they came at last under their looming
shadow, he was forced to swallow his words. The
wall of Volaghkhan was irregular, creating the jagged
profile above; and it had once been carven with many
shapes, blurred now and broken. Seams and joints
there were, but even in ruin impossibly clean and
close, visible only where the rock had flaked a little or
been hewn, or where streaking water had hardly
made an impression. The seams made the outline
of the vast stone blocks all too clear; and indeed, here
and there before the wall, more blocks as vast and as
carven lay strewn, too huge to remove. It must once
have been at least as high as the palisade.

'Were they giants, the folk of old, to raise such a
thing?' marvelled Alya. 'And did they shape stone
with their hands, or their teeth, or what? Some art
we have lost, surely!'

'One that's been taken from us!' grated Vansha.
'I'd never have believed it, till now – but once we
must have been so much greater. We wouldn't have
been mere yokel dungboots, you and I, but heroes,
loremasters, men of power . . . Maybe this Volmur
has the right idea, after all. At least he strives to shape
some kind of new beginning!'

The road led them to a clear gap in the wall,
though the palisade continued above it, unbroken, on
a bed of logs and timbers, sagging somewhat in the
middle. There the stone wall ended and began again,
with inner faces so sheer they might have been
sword-cut. In both of them were embedded the rusty
remains of hinges so vast that they suggested gates of
a ridiculous height. Fit for giants, indeed; but nothing

remained of these. Some way behind, on massive worn flagstones, a much lower gate of ironbound logs stood open, but with a barrier in front, and spearmen lounging by it, the picture of bored arrogance. They did not bother to raise their spears as the young men approached, but nor did they raise the barrier.

'Market's all but over, country boy!' said one, as they approached. The others grinned.

Alya, who might once have been abashed, grinned in his turn. 'We're not here to buy or sell. We've something to show the court.'

'That should be worth seein',' said the guard, with complete lack of interest. 'Toll's three-farthing each for mounted men, but since it's late we'll pass the pair of you for a penny.'

Alya bridled, but Vansha's answer was immediate and contemptuous. 'What d'you think we are? If the King levied tolls, he'd have 'em posted, to stop you lining your pockets!' He swung from his saddle, right before the barrier.

'Didn't say it was the King's toll, did I?' said the guard sullenly. Alya saw spears swinging up to the ready. 'One of our perks. You're not townsmen. If you shitkickers never get in here, the King's not going to hear much about it, is he?'

The spears were at Vansha's chest. Alya almost reached for his sword; but then thought better, and caught one spear by the shaft and snapped it with a twist of the wrist. Vansha snatched a spear in either hand, and slammed them down on the barrier with his full weight. A hunter's sinews stood out in his shoulders. The shafts bent and broke, sending their wielders staggering. He seized the barrier and threw it back.

The first guard cursed and poised his spear. Alya caught him by the scruff of his mailshirt and lifted him flailing from the ground. 'Kicking all that shit builds up a lot of muscle!' he said quietly. 'You should try it some time.' He rode through the barrier and dropped him on the other side. Vansha had already re-mounted.

'Oh yes,' Alya added, turning in his saddle. 'That reminds me – which way to the court, an't please you?' The bag at his side gave a sudden screeching cackle.

One of the soldiers pointed, mute. 'Thank you kindly!' said Alya, and they rode off. They had the sense to get around the next corner before they burst out laughing.

'Country boy!' gurgled Alya.

'Shitkicker!' chuckled Vansha, and then, more seriously, 'But they had a point. That's what we are – how we look to *them*!' He waved a hand at the scurrying crowds of folk on foot, jostling past the horses in the narrow street. 'That's how we'll look to the King. Think he'll give us a hearing?'

'Maybe you've a feeling for all this,' admitted Alya. 'But we've no money for finery – hardly even food,' he added, aware the air seemed to be alive with mouthwatering smells of roasting and baking. 'We daren't sell the horses, and we can't stop to earn some! So how are we going to even get in to see him?'

Vansha stooped, and seized the sleeve of a hurrying passer-by. 'Good sir! We need to come to the King, and swiftly! How best can we reach him?'

The man looked hunted and careworn, but he took in the weapons and the horses swiftly enough. 'Depends, young masters! Most days I'd say bribe a servant at the King-House and wait a week. But today's been Spring Market, and he's out and about the town, showing off his fine self. He'll come back soon and hold feast in the Great Hall tonight. That's why everyone's so busy. Got to clear the street!' Even as he spoke, there was a great blare of horns and drums, and he looked round swiftly, with a face full of alarm. 'There! What'd I say? The Great Beast is coming! Time for mere humans to hide!'

Everyone seemed to be scattering for the side-roads, even the better-dressed folk. Two runners came by, beating bronzen tubes like bells, and then a line of pikemen, weapons lowered, forcing the way clear with the shafts. They balked a little at two hefty young men, mounted; but Vansha and Alya backed their horses into the mouth of an alley, forcing back those already there, and the pikemen prudently decided that was enough. None of the other folk protested, even when the horses trod on them. 'I think even just having a mount and a weapon makes a man of you, here,' whispered Vansha. 'That's encouraging.'

Alya agreed. 'Says something about how they think! Let's see what we make of this Volmur!'

Even as they spoke drums stuttered, discordant trumpets wailed, and the pikemen began to shout in time to them. The head of a procession wove its way out of one of the side-streets and into the main street. Wove, because it was swaying from side to side across the full width of the street.

'Are they drunk, or dancing?' muttered Alya.

'Looks like both!' grinned Vansha. 'Cheerful, anyway!'

It was colourful, certainly. The procession was led not by warriors, as they'd expected, but by dancers and tumblers in gaudy rags, juggling with balls and beakers and rusty swords. Another, on his own, was tossing up what they recognised as the black helms the raiders wore. One spun flaming torches in the air, and Alya almost yelped with surprise as he suddenly sprayed fire from his mouth.

But immediately behind him, with a great clamour of bells and drums, came something more startling. A great snaking thing the length of many men wound down the street, a long green and yellow body

rearing and plunging from side to side, rolling to
reveal massive golden scales on its belly, flapping
ridiculous little wings on its back. Before it, rearing
still higher, rose a monstrous green head with rolling
eyes and red lolling tongue. It stooped, snapping its
jaws at the squealing crowd; but another head, blue-
scaled this time, swung up beside it, and yet another,
in bright red, bit playfully at the crowd opposite.

It was only as the young men saw the capering
dancers who lifted the heads on poles, and the line of
legs beneath the winding body, that they fully realised
this huge serpentine horror wasn't real, saw that its
scales were painted on to cloth, the heads of crudely
carven wood. 'But why three heads?' demanded Alya
of the walnut-faced man behind him. 'No beast like
that could exist!'

The man shrugged. 'Why? Why not, young lord?
'Tis the Great Dragon that stands for the Ice, and
that's how they allus shown him, time out of mind,
since I were a nipper! Three heads, one each for the
three mighty lords that they say rule the Ice, Taoune
and his lady Taounehtar and the Frost-King Surdar!
Allus with the fire-eater going before!'

'And the King coming along behind!' said Vansha
drily. 'I see!'

They could hear now what the pikemen were
chanting, and some of the crowd. '*Hail to Volmur!
Hail to the Bright Daystar, the Winter Sun! Hail, all
hail!*'

Behind the monster, as if driving it, trotted a
double line of mounted warriors, wealthy ones by the
look of their gear, with their lances at the hunting
port, though they swayed in their saddles and sang.
Spearmen and bowmen ran about their feet like
hounds, brandishing their weapons. And behind
them, on a high seat borne on poles by twelve mailed
men, there came a hardly less awesome figure. He
stood rather than sat, hanging on with one hand so all

could see him; and indeed he was a splendid enough sight.

The renowned King Volmur was a man of huge frame, taller than most men and looking taller still as he rode, massive about the shoulders and breast, though they sloped off to a great spreading bow of a belly. Robes of red, red as a winter sun indeed, poured across him in folds and falls, trimmed with great swathes of the finest furs, marten and ermine, with beaver across the shoulders to bar rain. About the wide sleeves ran cuffs of rare spotted daggertooth fur.

'A sign his splendour's worth at least one life!' whispered Vansha. 'For every skin that's brought back, a hunter's life is lost, and the price is set high accordingly!'

The King's face, what could be seen of it, was scarlet as his robes, rolling-eyed and roaring thunderously, though not a word could be heard above the hubbub. Angrily he tossed the black hair that fell about his shoulders. It was streaked with grey, but his spreading beard, unusually thick among all these folk, was curled and glossy black still. A circlet of gold crossed his brow, wreathed now with spring leaves; but beneath the robes the glitter was gilded mail, and in his free hand he brandished a long sword as if it were a huntsman's whip, to lash on his minions in the monster's tracks.

The procession's message was clear: King Volmur is driving the Ice before him.

But though the crowd was whooping lustily enough at the colour and the spectacle, the cheers did not seem that much warmer for the King's own person, and not all took up the chant. The tumblers had had as much acclaim, or more. And the files of warriors who trotted behind him, mounted men and foot, were not intent on the dragon but upon the crowd, eyes swinging this way and that, and they were grimly sober – a bodyguard, and an alert one, against a living threat.

They made a human barrier, too, between the King and the mounted lords who followed, many flanked by smaller bands in mail and livery matching the colour of their banners. Some were drunk, others merry and shouting; but Alya was struck by one face in particular, a tall, lean man who rode soberly and alone. His grey hair was foppishly curled, and he was gorgeously robed as any in green and gold over a coat of dark green mail; but he sat straight and firm in the saddle, and the long sword at his side had a well-worn look. His deeply lined face was flint-hard and set, his eyes narrowed with ill-contained anger and impatience, and they seldom left Volmur. The lords who followed him, themselves with only a few followers, were openly laughing and pointing; but the tall lord appeared not to notice.

Behind them the procession tailed off into random ranks of armsmen, sometimes with mounted captains, sometimes with only a sergeant and a few drummers striding at their head, drill and discipline sadly disarranged by drink. The pikemen had relaxed, and Alya exchanged a swift glance with Vansha. 'Well?' demanded a muffled voice. 'What're you waiting for, a formal invitation on red paper? A fair wind?'

'Shut up, demon!' growled Vansha, and together they urged their mounts forward, as the procession wove towards their side of the street. The startled pikemen were thrust aside by the horses, and sent staggering before they could say anything. The horses, evidently used to riding in formation, were eager to join this parade. The two young men fell in quite naturally at the head of a particularly drunken band of soldiery, and their mounts swung with it across the street and away, in the wake of the dissolving procession.

The crowd was already spilling into the street

behind them, and cries, if any, were lost in the hubbub. The head of the procession, tumblers, dragon, king and all, had already vanished in the tangle of streets ahead; but Alya saw, not far beyond, the top of a high tower over the rooftops, the tallest one they had made out from the hill. The gables were dragons and demons and other fabulous monsters, all wildly carved and painted, and the roof itself was metal sheet of some kind, probably copper.

Vansha cocked his head. 'That'd cost a bit, wouldn't it? Even for city folk!'

'Most like!' Alya agreed. 'A king this rich—'

'Yes. Surely he'd barely notice the cost of a war party! And look at those gates!'

The gates were even more extravagant than the gables. They were nowhere near as gargantuan as those in the ancient wall must have been, but the arch loomed impressively high over the weaving line of weary revellers, and the gates themselves seemed to be made of glinting greenish metal. The guards did not seem to be stopping anyone, or even looking at them very seriously. The delicious aroma of roasting meats from the courtyard beyond drew all attention, and Alya found his mouth dripping as the gate drew leadenly, slowly nearer.

'Are they going to let this rabble in at all?' whispered Vansha thickly. 'Shouldn't we move up the line?'

'Not now! They'd tear us to shreds and dip us in dripping! We'll need take our chances!'

They held their breath as the archway loomed still closer. Not only from excitement; there was a nastier taint to the air as they passed beneath, over-riding even the roasting, and not far to look for its source. Over that massive arch dangled an array of heads, not carven but real and human and decaying, tarred and impaled upon rusting pikestaffs, crowned with squabbling crows and buzzards. The bag stirred, and chuckled softly. 'As at my door, so at his! Yet who calls him a brigand?'

'Peace, little chickadee!' said Alya quietly. 'Save your huff and puff till it's wanted!'

They saw now that the imposing gates were only rough logs, like all the other walls; but some effort had been made to cover them in copper sheathing, not mere metal sheets but great plates finely embossed with mythical scenes, and curlicues of foliage, and strange lurking beasts. They looked age-worn and out of place, as if they too were fragments salvaged from some vanished past.

The procession entered the courtyard at last, as the sun dropped behind its walls. In shadow it was a wide place defined by fires and greasy smokes, carcasses crackling on spits over roughly piled embers, turned and basted by scurrying figures like demons in a pit. Behind the smoke the newcomers could see not one single palace, but a mad jumble of smaller buildings clustered around the tower, some with the high-crowned shingle roofs and smooth walls covered in painted figures, others mere flat-roofed log-piles stopped with mud. The ground between them, too, was trodden earth, strewn with dung and litter. Only here and there was there any paving, and that old and cracked and badly laid, by the look of it yet another crude salvage from the past.

At the heart of this ramshackle complex rose a massive, uneven hall, darker than shadow, with a wide spreading staircase of huge logs and painted pillars leading up to its high-peaked doors; and from one corner of this that tall tower arose. Before the stair the largest patch of paving was spread out, and all across this were strewn rough benches and planks on trestles. On the wide stairs higher tables were set, and on the highest, before a shadowy door, a high seat of black wood gilded and painted. There sat Volmur, surrounded by guards and attend-

ants, and before him men were making obeis-
ances.

'As well now, as ever!' muttered Vansha. Instead
of dismounting as others did, they trotted their horses
forward between the fires, coughing as the sputtering
smokes wrapped around them, and through the ranks
of benches. Men already filling cups and wooden
trenchers glanced at the young men curiously, but
they rode on as if they had every right, until they
came almost to the foot of the wide stair. Suddenly
hard hands seized their bridles, but before spears
could be raised they kicked free of their stirrups and
slid to the ground, nodding amiably to the guards left
holding their horses.

'Hail, King!' shouted Alya, and his clear voice cut
through the festive hubbub of the court, so loud that
most heads turned, and the men on the steps rose and
stared. 'We wish you joy of your feast, Bright Sun! But
we come to report a great wrong, and to seek your aid
and justice!'

They could not see Volmur's face as he heaved
himself up from his throne, and gestured to one
beside him. It was that man who answered them,
striding down the stairs flicking his long robes about
him, as arrogant as his tone. 'There is a time and place
the King hears grievances, and this is not one! Begone!'

'I am sorry to offend!' said Alya stoutly. 'We
know nothing of the court's ways. But we have come
a long way and a hard one to have our hearing, and
the matter will not brook delay!'

'That is for me to judge!' snapped the courtier,
motioning to the guards. But a word from above
stopped him in his tracks; and Volmur himself lumbered to the head of the stair.

'Well, then, peasant?' he demanded thickly; and
his voice held little encouragement. 'You will have
your say! And then, consider that I will have mine!

What is this wrong so great that it must spoil a royal feast?'

Vansha swallowed. 'The raiding of the village known as the Citadel, three nights since; the murder of its chieftain, my father the Seer and many other folk; and the carrying off of young women.'

Neither was prepared for the gust of laughter that went up around them, or the scorn that hissed in Volmur's voice, like fat upon the embers below. 'And by whom? By my command? No! But it might have been, indeed. For I had a mind to turn my gaze upon the Citadel one day, when I had the time to spare, and come to claim the dues and fealty it has long denied me, the garrisoning of my troops!' He snorted, and wiped his beard. 'Then you curs might well have lost more than lives, and the women you were too cowardly to protect! And you may yet lose more, in your insolence!'

Alya shook his head. 'King, that is as may be. None denies your power. But the town did stand against the raiders, and slew many – these their horses as our witness! The raiders were our common enemies, the *Aikiya'wahsa* that men call the Ekwesh, the bloody right hands of the Ice. Shall it be said that you permit them to rampage unchecked across domains you claim, a threat to all alike? Shall we not stand together against them, lest we be taken piece by piece? There is still time to punish their impudence!'

There was an uneasy silence. Volmur broke it with a defiant roar. 'I stand against the jackals of the Ice wherever they show their painted faces! Eh, lads?' The court cheered and howled in answer; but when the row died down it was evident that he had been using the diversion to think.

'But riding out against them, now – that is a costly exercise, and I must be sure it's worth the lives I venture! Three nights since, you say?' His voice grew darker suddenly, and more menacing than before; and he came rolling down the stairs to confront them, barging his guards out of the way. 'But how can that be? Three nights, as you claim, from the Citadel, on the northern borders of my realm?' He loomed above them, arms akimbo, close enough so Alya could see his narrowed eyes glinting blackly. 'Say then, and quickly – even on swift mounts, how could you be standing here before me now, so soon?'

'By riding through the Forest of Birds, my lord,' said Alya calmly, and his face did not change in the storm of laughter that followed. Even Volmur laughed; but there was no merriment in his face, only scorn and wrath, more of thunder than of sun.

'You look remarkably well for that! Well, mere overbold bumpkins I thought you. I might even have found you a place in my guards, after your floggings! But now you have over-reached yourselves. Through the dark Forest, indeed! You seek to draw my men out into some snare or trickery, or to distract from some other assault, I doubt not. Perhaps you are even fingers of that icy hand yourselves! But whatever, we shall find out – eventually!'

He snapped fat fingers to his guards.

'King Volmur!' shouted Alya. 'I do not blame your doubt! Yet pass we did. And brought you a token there is no disputing!'

He threw open the bag from his saddle, and reaching within seized the squalling Nightingale by the scruff of his neck and drew him out. He dangled the childlike figure high, one-handed, effortless. Ignoring the sudden clamour around him, he grinned at Nightingale. 'Now, demon, show them who you are! Whistle up a good blow!'

Nightingale kicked his legs delightedly, stuck his grubby fingers in his gape of a mouth and took a deep breath. Even Alya, braced against the sound that came, shuddered at its impact; and yet he could scarcely hear it.

He felt it, as one feels the scrape of a knife over rough earthenware or the screech of chalk upon slate, up and down his spine, with shrivelling force. Vansha clapped his hands over his ears and winced; the guards dropped their spears and did likewise. Volmur's courtier, standing straight in its path, rolled up his eyes till only the whites showed, and fell in a fit upon the stair. Volmur himself staggered back, hands on ears, face screwed up in anguish. Nightingale screeched with malevolent pleasure. And then the air seemed to gather itself in stifling folds about them, and unleash.

The torches were extinguished with snapping force. The cooking fires lifted in great swathes of flame, and went out. An icy roar swirled through the courtyard, spinning weathercocks, rattling doors and rooftiles, plucking at robes, lifting tabletops from their trestles and heaving benches over and over. The roasting carcasses toppled with a crash and hissed in the embers. Around Vansha and Alya the air was still, while all about them men stumbled, leaning into the gust to keep their footing, waving their arms as if swimming.

Still it grew, plucking fur hats from wealthy heads, rags from serfs, helms from the guards, sending them bowling madly together across the yard. At the stairhead above, the high seat tilted and toppled back with a crash. The doors and shutters that had rattled burst open now, and the screaming from within mingled with the howling air. Jugs, chairs, anything loose was plucked up and hurled. Men fell flat and scrabbled to the earth for a handhold, or caught at pillars as their legs were plucked from under them by the rushing air. They hung there by their hands among wreathing smoke, as if the world had turned upon its side.

On the stairs Volmur was not borne away, but on his hands and knees he struggled forward, grabbing at his sword. And off to the side Alya saw one man who still stood upright, bow in hand, struggling to aim an arrow. He loosed, and the blast blew it straight back at him, over his shoulder. It was the unhappy lord of the parade, looking like a tall grey feather the blast should pluck away. But, far from that, he hurled his bow from him, drew his sword; and he too began to inch forward against the wind, step by leaden step.

'Enough, little bird!' cried Alya then, and as suddenly the air was deadly still, like the hush before a storm. The grey lord staggered with the sudden release, and the men who had been holding on slumped down exhausted.

In the silence Nightingale's snigger was all too audible. Hastily Alya bowed his head to Volmur, picking himself up, and forced the Nightingale to bow also, though the creature was still giggling to himself.

'Your pardon for the damage, great lord!' said Alya deferentially. 'But it is not too hard to set aright – and there was no other way to convince you what we have conquered, and what power we hold. A power against which only your mighty self could still stand – and in some measure this other gentleman here. Say, is my good faith now proven?'

Volmur was breathing heavily, and his glowering eye burned with wrath, but he contained it sensibly enough. 'It is, though I could wish it less forcible. Very well, boy, you have shown you are no man to gainsay! And you have rid that bloody woodland of its worst menace among many, which is no small service to me. For that alone I must forgive you the damage and more. But now, you will cause me the keenest of delight by striking the head from that stinking abomination there . . .'

Vansha looked deeply relieved, but Alya again bowed, and returned Nightingale struggling feebly to the bag. 'Your pardon, King, but I took a pledge that I would spare him, for his surrender and service. And such power as his we may yet have need of, when we set out after the savages of the Ice.'

Volmur scowled. 'Well, I suppose that is true enough; and if the Powers have given you might enough to subdue that thing, then there is little to be gained from pursuing the matter. You shall join us, and welcome!'

Nightingale put his head out of the bag and waggled a long pale tongue at him, but the King ignored it. '*Serfs!* Shift! Get off your lazy scuts and renew the feast at once! Set all this mess aright, and lay two more trenchers on my table, for—' He paused.

Alya bowed yet again. It always seemed to be the right thing to do. 'I thank you, my lord. My friend is Vansha, son of Ushaya-awale, late Seer of the Citadel; and I am Alya, son of Alyatan-kawayi'wale Atar, late Seer of the town of Teoquhan.'

'*Teoquhan!*' The grim man, leaning languidly against a pillar, stood suddenly erect. 'You are old Alya's son? It must be thirty years since he left us. Whatever became of him?'

Alya, dismounting, stared. 'I am his son. He chose to become an outliver, with his young wife and household; and with them he was slain, three years since, by the raiders. He died in saving me. How came you to know him?'

The grey man drew himself up. 'Because I am the Lord Asquan, son of Atiya, inheritor of Teoquhan domain, last of the ancient lands, and it was my father he served.' Volmur snorted loudly, but the grey man ignored him. Suddenly he looked by far the more regal of the two. 'My father it was whom Alya sought to warn after his fashion. My father, whom he left, and went into the wilderness. And thus, some five years after, he escaped the sack and destruction of Teoquhan, town and lands, by the Ice. Few enough of us did.'

Asquan rubbed his cheek with beringed fingers,

and Alya saw there a white line scored across it from brow to throat, a terrible jagged scar. 'I have often thought we should have listened to him, harsh and impatient as he was. Yet it seems that in the end the all-seeing Alya could not save himself from just the same fate!' His smile was more crooked and mirthless than a sneer, and it stung Alya fiercely.

'A Seer cannot predict everything!' he snapped. 'Often what concerns himself, least of all. The realm beyond the Wall is not mapped or tracked.'

Volmur had been listening with keen interest. 'You speak of what you know. So you yourself are a Seer?'

'I was, though my schooling was not completed. But, as you say, the Powers have chosen to give me a greater strength.'

Volmur shook his head dubiously. 'I often wonder if there can be any greater might than a Seer's. A king may command the strength of giants in his armies, but if he lacks the foresight and the knowledge to wield it, then it is as nothing. But come, eat and take your ease, and we will ponder what way your service can best be rewarded.'

Alya caught Vansha's eye, and they were wise enough to content themselves with that, for then. They were eager for the meat that still caressed their nostrils, as the fires were relit. The courtier who had sought to dismiss them now came to invite them to the King's tables upon the stairs, and his bleak face revealed no more than his courteous bow. Alya found himself and Vansha in a place of honour among the lords, and they deferred to him in all things. There was boiled grain in plenty to timber the belly, and deep bowls of fine herbs and sauces to flavour it, and a huge pinch of white salt for every man; and if ash or earth still clung upon the carcasses restored to their spits, on the joints that reached the King's table none remained.

The young men ate like wolves, while Nightingale in his bag crouched beneath the table and crunched and cracked bones that Alya passed down to him, sucking out their marrow. But as time passed and their bellies filled, Alya became aware that the Lord Asquan had moved unobtrusively down the table to sit near him, though he only inclined his head gravely, and did not speak. Only when Volmur's attention was wholly elsewhere did he speak, looking straight ahead, not moving his lips, and too softly for any other to hear.

'Alya's son, I should not look to Volmur for too much help, if I were you.'

'Why so?' demanded Alya fiercely. 'Do you say he means to betray us?'

'Not that, no,' said the grim-faced man. 'Not unless it served his turn in some very important way. Volmur cares how others see him, and he will honour you, as you no doubt deserve. But I came to Volaghkhan and his father, more than twenty years past, for aid in regaining the lands of Teoquhan. Much was promised me, when the time was right; and much I have earned, by faithful service. He has been good to me, in his fashion; but I have little left that is mine, and must depend on him to live. Yet here I am still, and Teoquhan is a wasteland where only the Ice holds sway. And there may be a very good reason for that.'

He broke off and hailed another, and Alya realised there were eyes upon them, including those of the courtier and Volmur himself. But it seemed that the King only wished to speak their praises; and at his command, as they relaxed between courses, men brought them each a fine suit of the royal livery, coat and hose of deep blood-red such as his captains wore, with shirts of mail and bright helms, and a hefty sword for Vansha, and to the cheers of the crowd they were arrayed in them where they stood. Toasts were drunk to them, and, ironically, to the Nightingale when he was hauled out from his lair. 'For you are clearly warriors of no common kind,' said Volmur jovially. 'Too good for mere farmers! You shall be soldiers in my service, and learn the ways of arms. Put down your roots here, and become lords ere long!'

They rose, feeling strange and itchy in their new garments, and bowed in all directions, and drank the king's health, as they had seen the lords do; but after Asquan's warning, Alya felt he had to speak to Volmur, now and quietly, before he became too drunk again.

'King, you honour us, and we bask in your favour. When our quest is done and our oaths are fulfilled, then your service is what I know Vansha would want; and,' he added carefully, 'I can see no nobler prospect myself. But for now we must serve you in our own fashion, by pursuing those raiders. Our oaths leave us no other path.'

Volmur's face darkened; but he was too well aware of the power that had been unleashed within his walls. 'You are bound by oaths? That is bad, for I will have no oaths in my kingdom greater than those to me. My laws forbid them. But yours were sworn first, I suppose; and I can hardly compel loyalty in the face of them. I will aid you, then. But it will take some time to assemble sufficient men, for I have hardly enough for the garrisons and patrols I must maintain now, to discourage this same endless raiding that whittles away at the borders of my realm. A constant drain upon my revenues! I mean to strike into the outer lands, indeed; but not hastily. When the time is right. And strong lads like you can surely help me prepare!'

There was something in his voice that Alya could not comprehend, and he fought to marshal arguments that could not be taken as insults. 'King, that is noble of you; but for the women's sake we must follow, now, before the trail grows too cold! It has been three days already, and it will be more before we can gain it again. We must take up the hunt with no more delay!'

Volmur said nothing; but his gaze went beyond them, and lit upon Asquan, in a way that chilled Alya's blood. Vansha leaned across the table, his voice urgent but quiet. 'King, in your wisdom you must see that is so! We have already cleared a danger from your land, gone some way to opening a new path your troops may use northward, even. Will you not help us to serve you now, to your own greater glory? Imagine the blow against the Ice in your name, imagine how it will look to your folk. How it will discourage those raiders! For they need to be discouraged, do they not?'

It seemed to Alya that Vansha must perceive the mind of the King more keenly than he himself, for the wrath faded somewhat from Volmur's brow, into lines of thought. 'I have told you,' he said at last, 'that I can spare no troops right now, not on such a wild premise – not my costly regular troops. Had you been patient, I could certainly have managed much more, soon.' He shrugged, and smiled benignly. 'But I sympathise with your desire for speed. And indeed, I feel strongly that your best chance will lie not in mere numbers, but with deftness and cunning. So, I will spare you aid worth many mere soldiers. I give you the Lord Asquan, to be your guide and leader!'

Volmur smiled into the ensuing silence, and this time it was not at all benign. 'The Powers know he has been pestering me for action for long enough! And it is evident,' he said blithely, 'from this chance meeting, that your destinies and his must run together. So that is decided! Of course, you will need men. Well, I give you my warrant to recruit any who will follow you. You may scour my gaols freely, for example. That, and the war-gear I have bestowed upon you, is the best I can do, for now; but your valour is such that I have every confidence.' Before anyone could answer, he raised his goblet. 'Hail, avengers of Teoquhan!'

Asquan, who had been contemplating the King with ironical detachment, rose and bowed. 'Hail to King Volmur!' he said drily. 'I rejoice that you are so keen to keep your word, to one grown grey in your service. Perhaps riding out with these young hot-heads will renew the youth I have given you. May our example inspire a new and unceasing campaign against the Ekwesh!'

The air was heavy with things unspoken, like the advent of a storm. Volmur's eyes narrowed again, but he simply raised a hand in mild benison. 'Then it is decided!' he said. 'Draw up the warrants at once. Meanwhile, let us continue the feast, and honour our gallant friends, while we may. For they will not wish to linger even a single day longer!'

When Volmur had drunk himself almost into insensibility, the feast was declared closed. The young men and their captive were led into the great hall behind, heart of the rambling King-House, on whose boards many men lay already asleep and snoring by the dim smoky light of the fire-trough in the middle of the floor. There they were given furs and blankets, and wished a good night. Nightingale, pledged to behave himself, curled up in the blanket he was given and slept at once; but though they had drunk far more than they were used to, neither of the young men felt at all ready to copy him.

'We must talk!' Alya whispered, and Vansha cast a cold eye around at the sleeping throng.

'Aye, but not here! If we could only seek out some quiet corner in this great jumble of a place—'

'I may be able to help you there!' said another voice, equally soft. It was Asquan, with a mantle of dark fur shrouding his form and face. 'Say nothing, and follow!'

Into the dark at the end of the hall he glided, and under the shadow of a great wall-hanging there, a cloth painted with a gory hunting scene. Behind it, almost hidden, was a small door, and through that he led them, quietly, and out on to worn flagstones. In this chamber, miraculously, the walls were of stone, and the ceiling also, an arching vault carven with many strange shapes, stars and comets and round shapes Alya did not recognise, and between them many figures of women and men.

'This is the way to the tower,' whispered Asquan, 'the only part of the King-House left from the old times, wrought in stone rather than wood. The only part that will not burn, and therefore the last redoubt against a besieger. Few come here otherwise, for it is thought to be haunted.'

'Haunted?' Vansha looked nervously around.

Asquan's lined face twisted into a smile. 'A legend I encourage. Things have been seen here, but they were mostly me, for I value my privacy in this seething nest of spies and informers. Yet it is probably true, all the same. Here, if anywhere, there should be spirits. Shadows of a bygone better age, brought low at last by the treasons and terrors of the Ice. Men massacred and men deceived, brought even to worship that which wished them ill. Blood soaks these derelict stones, and their cries for just vengeance go unheeded. Like all such, in this land now.'

'I guessed as much,' said Vansha, still nervous. 'From what you said, and from the King's look. He does not seem to want to take action against the raiders, and there must be some strong reason for that.'

Asquan's smile was colder than ever. 'You might make a courtier one day, young man. But this is still no place to talk of it. Admire the ceiling, depicting the

Powers. You will see it better from the stairs, at hand here; but watch your step.'

They were as worn as the rest, spiralling upward, and the walls deeply worn by many steadying hands; but they led out at last on to a wide floor of wood, surrounded by a strong wooden wall, breast-high, dimly lit by moon and star. From here rose the rest of the tower, but in timber only. 'Do not go near the edge, or you will be seen!' said Asquan. 'There is a sentry at the top, a thankless task reserved as punishment. He will not chance to come down the stairs before daybreak, lest a passing breath blow out his lantern – as so often happens. So we may talk unheard, if we are quiet. And acknowledge the truth of your suspicions, Master Vansha. Our Bright Sun dare not take action. Can you guess why?'

'The reasons he gave?' hazarded Alya. 'It would cost too much, his troops are too few—'

'Yet he has many times hurled them against neighbour kingdoms and smaller domains, with ruthless freedom. And swelled his revenues thereby. His troops live better than most men in his kingdom, and he could raise more any time he wished. No, it is not that; and yet Volmur did not altogether lie. Too much of his revenues does indeed go to fending off the raiders.'

Vansha gasped. 'He pays them tribute?'

Teeth gleamed briefly, in Asquan's warped smile. 'That, and more. You have not plumbed his depths, yet. He pays them, not only to spare his realm, but also to harry those who oppose it, or simply stand free of it – such as the Citadel, perhaps. I long suspected it, but only lately have I become sure. He bribes them with great stores of provisions and other necessaries, luxuries even. They are taken from his warehouses and left in mysterious outlying hiding-places, supposedly for later operations; but it is not his own troops who empty those hiding-places! I guess the Ice must always need sustenance for its human servants, so it is ready enough to tolerate such a pact. Perhaps the situation amuses them, for now.'

Alya winced. 'So we have wasted all our journey!' A black veil of anger and bitterness descended.

'Speak more softly, boy! I would not say that. You have that formidable creature, your servant. You have fine mail, and much honour, upon which you may trade in many ways. And you have me.'

'Yes.'

Asquan chuckled waspishly. 'Please don't faint with joy. I am more of an asset than you might think. True, Volmur is only too glad to get rid of me. I have not been a popular figure at court, arguing for some real effort against the forces of the Ice, and not against our fellow men. Since his father's day I have spoken for alliance instead of conquest, union instead of exploitation; and railed against those who preferred to grow fat on the proceeds. Or who served still darker ends, agents and devotees of the Ice itself; for such a dark and hidden cult exists, they say. There have been intrigues enough against me, plots and assassination bids; but Volmur and his father always protected me. Why? Because they found me very useful. Now you may, too, perhaps.'

'Why did you bear it?' demanded Vansha. 'Why not simply go somewhere else?'

'Such as where?' Asquan shrugged. 'The unknown West? The Eastlands, by the Sea, where the world ends? There is nowhere else, not near enough to give me the help I wanted, that I dreamed of. I dreamed that because these kinglets praised me and upraised me and gave me what seemed like wealth, they would one day keep their word and help me. Dreaming, I endured, and because there was little else meaningful I could think to do. I fought hard, and drowned my doubts in pleasures of every kind. Now I grow old, and the pleasures wither on the vine. The

end of my usefulness is in sight, and my inconveni-
ence grows. Volmur has become different to me;
perhaps he suspects what I know. The wealth dries
up, and with it the hope. I know I will never find my
lands again, and reunite my scattered folk, and I taste
bleak despair. But in aiding you I may at least sweeten
it with some revenge. And if I must seek death, do so
to some purpose!'

The dry voice spoke of despair and death without a trace of feeling, unless in its utter calm. But
there was a trace of something more in it, as he
turned to Alya. 'And I also believe in destiny, now and
again, Seer's son.'

Vansha also looked to Alya; but Alya remained
silent. Asquan seemed to him a mere courtier, effete
and dandyish, fit only for intrigues and stratagems,
not to be trusted. How Volmur had found him useful
was hard to imagine. And Volmur was wishing him
off on them. Yet his words rang true; but then, what
else would one expect from an intriguer? He felt as if
this weird old palace were truly a labyrinth, and
himself one of its lost spirits; and over the distances
his heart yearned for Savi.

'We have cause to be cautious, my lord,' said Alya,
at last. 'But I also have more reason than most to
believe in destiny. Help and counsel is what we
desperately need, Asquan. We would be glad of yours.'

A hand was stretched out to him in the dimness,
like a claw emerging from the cloak. Alya took it, arm
to arm; and it clamped closed with quite startling
strength. He answered it with his own, very carefully.
Asquan drew breath sharply, and then nodded. 'You
are much stronger even than you look, Master Seer.
But then so, I think, am I.' He clasped hands also with
Vansha, who glared, but bore it. 'Well, then! We make
a masterful three.'

'Perhaps,' said Alya, still guarded. 'But still only
three. What can so few hope to achieve?'

The lord shrugged. 'Much, if I judge you two aright. But perhaps not enough. If you wish my counsel, we should seek out other men. We cannot expect many; ten, perhaps, and not the army you would wish.'

'*Ten?*' Vansha sounded horrified. 'There were at least fifty raiders! We need no fewer, surely!'

'We could not arm and provision such a party in less than a week, not without Volmur. And it might be too cumbersome. I believe a small band may be better, if they are seasoned men. We should seek them at once.'

'Yes!' said Vansha excitedly. 'We could ask for volunteers among the guards!'

'Who would be forbidden to accept, upon pain of immediate death,' sighed Asquan. 'No doubt the orders are being cut even now. Not that many save the bad lots and the madmen would be interested in changing their comfortable billets for such an uncertain prospect. Still less so the common folk. They have a measure of peace and even some prosperity to live for. Why should they quit the comfort of their wallows and sties for folk they don't even know? No, it's into worse mire we must descend to find the kind of men we need, worse and deeper, an abyss beyond light and hope. It's a place I know well. Come, make its acquaintance!'

Vansha stood at once, but Alya held back. 'Where to, then?'

'The depths. Where even our darkness may seem like a little light.'

Along long passages he led them then, still among stone, and down stairs where every whisper seemed to be magnified, every echo a rustling, chattering answer. He kindled a torch, but its uncertain flicker seemed only to add more darkness to the shadows forever flickering at the edge of sight, like a threat of blindness. The walls here were still stone, but thick with ancient nitre, the roofs heavy with dripping spikes of it, save where it had been shattered, as by something heavy hurled against it; and here and there the light showed darker stains and smears. These were ancient ways, but the feeling in them was much newer, and the faint acrid stink that grew upon the air.

Vansha's arm was shivering, when Alya brushed against it, but he said nothing. Before long a glimmer of light grew in the darkness, but so also did the stench; and they came to a small open chamber, and a chair in which a great brute of a man sat dozing beneath three large lanterns. But the moment Asquan stepped out of the passage he sprang up with a startled cry and fell back against the wall.

'Easy, man!' said Asquan irritably. The oaf stared, then wiped a greasy arm across his sweating forehead, and bobbed a semblance of a bow.

'Ah, my lord! And you, young gennlemen! Took you for – dunno what, poppin' out of there like that. You know how it is with these passages; and them forever chatterin', back there in the blackness like that! Nobody ever comes that way, 'ardly. I'd have it stopped up if they'd let me.'

Asquan smiled unpleasantly. 'The King has many uses for the ways beneath his halls. Seeing how alert are his gaolers, for one. But that is not our charge tonight. The King sends us on a perilous mission, and has given us warrant to seek help wherever we choose, even in his gaols. We need men who would sooner face death than rot in the dungeons.'

' 'Ere?' The gaoler spat. 'Dunno what you hope to find 'ere, my lord. Scum in here'll mostly say yea, and cut your throat the moment your back's turned. *They* don't care.'

'Precisely. It must be the right men. Take us in – right in – and we will decide. Your trouble will be amply appreciated. Now, and afterwards.'

The gaoler looked unhappy, but his fat palm closed swiftly around the coin Asquan put in it. He lit another large lantern, and looped the strap of an iron-headed cudgel about his wrist. 'Well, as you wish, my lord. But you, young gennlemen, you've not been here before. Watch your footing – and your backs!'

Asquan smiled his crooked smile. 'They can handle themselves at least as well as I can, man. Lead on!'

Keys jangled, one after another; and at last the great ironbound door creaked menacingly inward. Both Alya and Vansha exclaimed in disgust at the stench that washed out over them. Two more gaolers, seated by their lanterns at either side of the door, grinned at the softmarks who complained. Asquan sniffed the air like fine wine. 'The stink of human stupidity, my friends! Enjoy it. The King's main prison is a stockade, where lesser offenders and those who can pay may dwell in elementary comfort. This, though, is known all too accurately as the Hole. It would take little effort to maintain a modicum of hygiene here, but few of its delightful inmates are very interested. So they die of innumerable distempers, and make room for their replacements, and that suits the guards well enough. An ever-changing tapestry, and a ceaseless flow. I see new faces each time I come here.'

'The gaoler seemed to know you well enough!' said Alya, wonderingly. 'You come often?'

'It suits my view of humanity,' said Asquan. 'A microcosm – but you would not know what this is? Yes? Of course, your fathers were Seers. A world in a little space. A realm of chains and torment, where the stronger fastens on the weaker amid the slime. I almost said "feeds upon" – and that is not unknown, down here. Oh yes, I have come here often enough.'

The gaoler motioned to one of the guards, who held the lantern high. They saw they were in a vaulted chamber, lower and wider than the rest, held up by rows of squat pillars supporting the broad flattened arches. The work looked strong, ancient, but void of decoration or finish. The pillars seemed to grow out of the miry floor, as if it had risen to envelop them; and they were hung about with chains. Here and there a gaunt figure was chained right up against the stone, immobile; but others had enough slack to move away, to sit or lie upon the filth about them. They hid their eyes as the light fell upon them, ragged, half naked and half skeletal, like dark spirits flinching from the dawn. But some moved swiftly towards it, only to shrink back from the gaoler's cudgel, snarling like beasts.

When they saw Asquan, though, their manner changed. Some catcalled insults and jeers; some launched shrill invitations. Asquan acknowledged them with a regal wave, and once even stopped before a crouching, staring woman to run a light caress over her matted hair. But he said nothing of their errand, until he had led the way deep into the chamber, and still not found its further wall.

'A sorry crew, gaoler,' he remarked carelessly.

'What'd I tell you, my lord? Scum, and starveling scum at that.'

'Indeed. I want those whom chains will not hold. I want the manner of men who break away from the herd. I want the ones who when they were banished to this place banished it from themselves. I want those who have had the strength to found their own place apart in the heart of this infernal realm. *Come out, all of you!*' His voice echoed beneath the roof. '*I know you are here! Come and show yourselves. Or have you forgotten the sun?*'

And, astonishingly, they came.

It was as if the darkness itself swelled, a mere curtain billowing. As the lanternlight swung this way and that they appeared, never in its centre, always as

it passed, half-seen shapes that slid cautiously from
behind pillars, or darted forward an instant and
skittered back, thin, spidery, insubstantial. Alya's
hand went to his sword as a pair of eyes glinted
suddenly on a level with his own, and another; but
they came no closer, hovering, ready to escape.

Asquan looked around. 'You know who I am. I
have given you food before now, some of you, to
increase the little you wrest from the vermin still
enchained.'

'Given?' said a thin voice, whether man's or
woman's Alya could not tell. 'Traded, rather. You
give us nothing. You feed our bodies, and feed upon
them in return.'

Asquan shook his grey hair with calm disdain.
'How else could I help? What I took from some
among you only repaid my risk. I had nothing better
to offer. But now I do. You are all beyond the
common herd, here. You are all proud enough to
prefer your own small shred of freedom to mingling
with the beast-men nearer the door, even with their
faint chance of release. You are the uncounted, the
disappeared, the living dead. You survive no more
than months, but you are not afraid to die free. I need
a few who would sooner face death under the sun.'

'And what filthy favour buys that?' demanded a
woman's voice. 'What new sport have you dreamed
up, Asquan? There are only men and women, more or
less. And a body only has so many portals, you know!'

There was a little soft laughter among the pillars.
Asquan seemed not at all concerned. 'I offer you
freedom, in a good cause. You will offer your lives.
We are going up against the Ice, and very likely few
will return. I do not greatly expect to.'

Silence grew, till it seemed to press on their
chests like a dead weight. 'Against the Ice?' said a
voice that seemed to belong to the dark, cavernous
and deep. 'In what manner? On what cause?'

'Hold that lantern up!' snapped Asquan. 'That is never you, Kalkan? Not after so long?'

'Some endure a little longer here, my lord!' growled the voice. 'If they are willing to do what they must to survive. Has Volmur sent you to gloat?'

'Volmur sends me to my death, my lord. And I was never your enemy.'

'You were never my friend.'

Asquan sighed. 'Your folly was your own, in attacking Volmur so openly. Why should I share it? But does your son live also?'

The blackness was silent a second, before it answered. 'He is free.'

Asquan sighed again. 'Truly, I am sorry. Even Volmur's wrath seldom extends so far; but you frightened him, and that was very unsafe. But I offer you light now, and a slim chance at life. We need men who will not cut and run at once, who will not prefer the life of a hunted brigand to death with honour! Take what you can, man, and come!'

'Leave me here!' snorted Kalkan. 'I want no light, to show me the injustices of men!'

Alya stepped forward. 'Hear me! Three days since, our home was raided, by the men of the Ice, that are called the Ekwesh. Women were stolen – dear to me and others. Volmur gives us scant aid to pursue them, save Asquan and whomever we can recruit. Do you dare complain of injustice, yet skulk in darkness while others suffer?'

Kalkan laughed, loudly. 'Your women are dead, boy, or whores to the Ekwesh, beyond reclaiming! Your cause is lost. Abandon the burden of hope and live for yourself. Dig no others from their graves.'

'I was given hope!' snapped Alya furiously. 'I was raised from a living grave worse than yours! And since when was a lost cause less worthy? One way or another, you shall see the light!'

Alya seized the chains that hung from the nearby

pillar, some four or five in his hands, and pulled, hard.
Two of the chains snapped at once, and flew up
jingling. The gaoler and the guard gave back, and
gasped. Alya set his foot against the stone and hauled.
From the roof above, nitre cascaded into the lamplight, and small fragments of stone rattled down in
falls of dust. With a horrible grinding squeal the
mighty blocks in which the chainrings were set rose
slowly from their sockets, and the pillar trembled.

The gaoler yelped. 'Make the mad bastard stop!
He'll have the tower down on us!' The guard dropped
the lantern, and ran.

In the sudden blackness Alya felt a hand laid on
his arm – lean and greasy, no doubt with the filth he
smelt, but strong and steady. 'Hold, boy! From a
worse grave than mine, you say?'

'The tomb of my living spirit! The prison of my
own ruined body, barely able to crawl. The Powers
gave me healing, and the might of ancient heroes!
What they give, they give for a purpose! Will you dare
gainsay them?'

Asquan had retrieved the lantern, and at the click
of his tinderbox it sprouted a feeble flame. The eyes
that suddenly stared into Alya's, half hidden by
tangled hair, were bloodshot, and very intent; but
they did not look demented.

'You are a mere boy!' boomed the voice. 'But
you feel as if you are filled with fire! You make me
think. While such a flame is loose in the world, shall
any hatred of mine stand idle? In hating Volmur I had
half forgot the Ice, maybe.'

'The Ice is the reason Volmur is,' put in Vansha.
'In happier times men will find better lords!'

Asquan simply laughed. But Kalkan stood silent a
moment. 'It is good that you believe so, perhaps. I do
not, not any longer.' Alya could hear the effort in his
voice. 'I fear to emerge, as I have feared little in this
world. But you remind me what it was to have a belief

and a goal, and the free air on my face. If you can truly get me out, I will come.'

'Thank you!' said Alya. 'And can you find others with that much spirit?'

Kalkan snorted. 'Few. Fazdshan, stand forth! And you, Darzhan! Chiansha, Almur, what say you? The enemy rolls across our land like black smoke. Shall we not raise a spear where Volmur dare not?'

Darkness took on another voice, younger, bleaker. 'We come to your call, as we are sworn to. As we would from the grave, if we could!'

Other shadows deepened in the darkness. They moved hesitantly, yet it was as if they grew taller, as if the blackness and the mass of the stone above no longer weighed upon them so heavily. Kalkan appeared to see them perfectly. 'The old days are not wholly gone, then. But Tseshya? You also? You mere inky-arsed bookworm, you have never borne mail!'

'A scholar can ride. And shoot a bow from the saddle. I have hunted so. And I cannot read or write in darkness. As the poet Paiolan says: *I would have horse in hand again, were there no roof but the sky*.'

'You shall,' said Asquan. '*The just cause affords its own shelter* – as the poet Dzhanmur wrote, shortly before he froze to death.' He glared around, as if he could summon more faces out of the darkness. 'Is this all that remains of your knights and followers? What of Quyan the Landholder?'

'Dead these last two months, as I reckon them. And Marshal Jianshu took his own life after only two weeks. Shashan, Uien; even my old sergeant of horse Pazhen. My kin from the northern frontier, Landholder Laomer, Ulimer the Commander of Footmen, Hazhya of the Seventh Fort, Djakan of the Fifth Battalion. All dead, of festering wounds and deep despair. Volmur spared us only for a dirtier and more miserable end. Some others have turned away from me,' Kalkan added grudgingly, 'and from the line of duty. Taken to thieving and suchlike, joined the filthy herd that are content to squat by the door there for their muck-rations, aye, and your kind of bounty, my lord. I don't recognise them now.'

'A useful skill, maybe, thieving,' said Vansha drily. 'But timidity and turning coats will not serve us. I hoped for fifty, not five! Can't we persuade any others?'

'None that you'd want to have by you while you slept!' answered Kalkan, ushering them towards the speck of light that was the distant door. 'How swiftly do we leave? I doubt Volmur's bounty will last too long, if he learns whom you are setting free!'

'Agreed!' said Asquan sardonically. 'Gaoler, here is my warrant. Set down any names you will for those we are engaging. But if you will take my advice, let them be . . . everyday names. Free of associations!'

The gaoler chuckled, as something chinked musically inside the warrant. 'The Lord Kalkan perished of a plague four years past, my lord, the very day his gyves fell empty. Saved me a mort of explanations, that. No idea whom this fellow is!'

'Very good,' said Asquan, glancing around. 'Did we not have a guard with us?'

'Maybe, maybe,' said the gaoler uneasily. His face was glossy with sweat. 'Then again, maybe not. Could be wandering round anywhere, he could. He'll turn up. Or not. Not a good idea to leave the lamp, down here, if you take my meaning! Now, my lords, if you'll follow me . . .'

He stopped dead. The glow that was the door vanished as if a curtain were drawn across it. Their own lantern guttered and dimmed to a feeble red glow. Instinctively they drew together. Kalkan growled; and a voice spoke out of the darkness.

'Forgetting a woman may have talents, too, my lords? I should not waste time seeking that poor guard of yours, by the way. I saw him go by with some friends!'

'Rysha!' barked Kalkan. 'I smell you, vixen! What does such as you want with us?'

'No more than any woman with any man, old crow! Bartering and bargaining, as usual. What we've got, for what we're grudged. That's how it always works.'

Kalkan spat. 'I don't want any of what you've got! We're—'

'I know. I'd sooner deal with this nice young lad.' Alya shivered suddenly. Long fingers, icy cold and strong, slid beneath his waistband and down across his stomach. 'Or the sleek one!'

Vansha yelped; but he was standing feet away. The smooth soft voice was suddenly back behind Alya, so close he could feel the breath on his ear. 'Ah! Now, *they've* got something to offer a lady, maybe. If they didn't have their own little biddies so firmly in mind – no? Not two biddies, is it? One? Well, would you credit that, gentles? Whatever are they going to do with her – share her? Alternate days? Alternate ends?'

Alya cursed and twisted away from the snaky grasp.

'What's amiss?' sneered the voice, as silkily as before. 'Don't like playing games in the dark?' The words seemed to come from all around them. 'Never mind, you'll learn! It's better that way. You don't see the end of it all.'

The darkness seemed to recede a little. The yellow lanternlight picked out the merest suggestion of a form, a woman's body, naked, defined only by vague curves and hollows, and by the faint fluttering rise and fall of quickened breath. A man's mind might draw a vision like that upon unyielding dark. There were sharp breaths and exclamations all around, and someone – Vansha – stepped forward.

There was no warning. The change was immediate. The face that glimmered in its own light, a finger's breadth from Alya's own, was livid, horrible, a mass of oozing decay. The nose was eaten away, maggots crawled about the pus-rimmed eye sockets, the lips hung yellowed over teeth that rotted in the pallid gums. But it was alive, and all too recognisable. Vansha's cry was despairing as much as appalled. A shriek of laughter echoed across the roof.

'Don't like it, do you? Whoever it was you saw? *I* don't know, not Rysha. Nobody tells her, no! But *you* know. Because what you saw there – it's in you! *That's* the end of all your piddling desires. *That's* what you all chase!'

'Don't worry, friends!' said Kalkan loudly. 'She can't keep this up! She can only work her little tricks in the dark, and for a few breaths. If she could do anything meaningful, she'd have been out that door long since.'

Alya himself recoiled, less at what he had seen than at the malice behind it, more visible to his inner eye than his common sight. The dark shape seemed almost to glitter with it. She must be a Seer, of a rare kind he had heard his father mention, with dire warnings; one whose power turned outward, almost always through malevolence and resentment, not to cultivate farsight and wisdom, but to obscure the minds of men with illusion and ill-will. But one with power such as this, however brief, he had never heard of.

'A spae-wife . . .' he said, aloud, and the woman called Rysha laughed again, more softly.

'A witch!' Vansha was horrified. He had been brought up to fear such creatures, man or woman, almost more than the Ice. And it was true that they could work dreadful havoc in a tight-knit village, setting brother against brother or child against parent. Most often they were mobbed, if discovered, and stoned or hanged; few survived for judgement. And many innocents died in their stead.

'She drove her husband to his death,' said Kalkan, with savage relish. 'His son slew him at her goading – if she didn't do it herself! And then she did kill the son. Cut his throat while they coupled, and sought to blame it on the father, as if they'd killed one another. A merchant's second wife, with kinfolk prosperous enough to spare her the disgrace of fire or gibbet. But they didn't want her out of here. Nobody does!'

'Who would?' hissed Vansha. 'We've got one demon too many, already. We don't need her!'

'That's right, lad!' said Kalkan roughly. 'Setting folk at each other's throats, that's her little fancy! Been more trouble than the guards, down here!'

'How many breaths has it been dark now, old crow?' Rysha jibed. 'And you, pretty one – you'll need me, all right! I can ride like a man! I can fight like one, too! Which means I don't have to kowtow to pretty boys! Though before your friend, now – I might just tag along!'

'That is not your decision,' said Alya evenly. 'Yet she might be of great use. You have the power to cloud the sight, Rysha. But how clear is your own?'

Suddenly, sharply, he reached out, following only his instinct. Whether through luck, or some element of inner sight, he caught a bare arm, clamped his fingers about it, and heard the startled hiss. The lantern flame swelled suddenly. He hauled hard, and a woman stumbled into the spreading patch of light.

He had expected the desirable vision to be nothing like her, save in mockery; and that was right enough. She was younger than he expected, though, a few years older than himself, tallish and rangy, though her soiled and shredded rags made it evident that she was better fleshed than most here. Her filthy hair, still shaded at the ends with henna, framed a face that surprised him, neither fair nor otherwise, not ill-shaped but lean and deeply lined, with furrows between the brows and around the nose and mouth. That face must normally hide its demons, behind eyes of weathered glass like river pebbles; it could be a mask of blandness even a husband might not penetrate. Yet it was not hunger that had pinched the nose or hollowed the cheeks before their time, or set the harsh twist to the mouth as she hawked and spat in his face, struggling to tear her hand free and failing utterly.

Then she sagged. Only in the dark had the devils been unleashed, and they faded even as he saw them. She stood suddenly meek and demure, eyes downcast.

'Look at me!' said Alya, and when she would not, he tilted her chin up, sharply. 'What I offer is not mere escape, understand that! You may live through it, or you may not. But you must forswear this vicious pleasure of yours.'

She nodded, hesitant, eager to please. He thought of the long, cold salamanders that concealed themselves among the stones of the river bed, unseen, immovable, until the small fishes passed too close. 'Hear me!' he persisted, seizing her shoulders, shaking her, striving to drive understanding home through that frosty glass barrier, as opaque as the Wall, and as dangerous. 'Save it for our foes, if you must. We are so few, and in so much peril, we can only live by depending on one another, utterly. And the moment you endanger our search, I promise you – I will strike you down.'

There was something in the face at last, a flicker of expression. 'You?'

'I'll spare him the trouble!' said Kalkan. 'I should have done so, long since.'

'And yet you didn't!' remarked Vansha idly.

Alya nodded. 'I thought the same. You are not

wholly immune to her, my lord. But it only shows what an asset she may be.'

'I will not . . . worry you,' Rysha said earnestly, in a breathy young girl's tone, as if the voice from the dark belonged to someone else entirely. 'I want to live. I want to breathe. I will come.'

'I did not ask,' said Alya sternly. Asquan looked at him, surprised, but nodded approvingly. 'You have heard too much, to be left behind in all your malice. You have no choice. Come, gaoler! Our tally's complete.'

When the great door boomed shut behind them, it was like a cloud lifting. The passage no longer seemed so dark and haunted, as if its spirits had fled back to the deep at the sight of still more inhumanity. The men around him, anonymous hulks of hair and filth and rags, stood suddenly straighter, and though they carried the gaol-stench with them, they sniffed at the air like keen hounds. Kalkan almost seemed to be sobbing, and the scholar was running long fingers along the rough wall as if he moved in some world of dreams. Rysha, back in the shadows, stood silent, which might be a good sign.

'Do not linger!' said Lord Asquan urgently. 'The night is well gone, and they must be made ready, bathed, fed, equipped – especially bathed! Volmur will sleep late today, after his last night's sousing, and we can take our leave quietly. But he will awaken late, and with a sore head on him. And by then I wish to be well beyond his reach!'

CHAPTER 6
Beyond the Wall

ALYA reined in his horse atop the rise, and watched as the rest came circling around to join him. The sight gave him a thrill, despite his black mood. For the first time they looked like quite a formidable little warband; and they were at his command.

And Vansha's, of course. He would do better not to forget that, too often.

In name they were the joint leaders; but he was only too aware of how soon that might change. The soldiers were evidently used to obeying Kalkan, and he to obeying nobody much. So far he had taken their orders with genial enthusiasm, as if he were joining in a boy's game. What he would do when they met any real problem was hard to tell. Asquan seemed to daunt him, though, loudly as he despised him. And Asquan, so far, was astonishingly helpful, always deferring to the young men and prompting them, if at all, from the background, spending his money freely to equip the little force, seizing every quiet opportunity to school them in using their new arms.

Alya had asked Kalkan and his men to instruct the less soldierly in their use, himself and Vansha included; but to his surprise they had all deferred to Asquan. And, slight and effete as he might be, he must once have been a skilful fighter, and proved a good instructor even now. With his support they could command, for now; but how fully could they rely on that? The man was a complete enigma. And strong as he showed himself, he was old. They would be less able to rely on him when any real fighting started.

And suppose Alya and Vansha came to clash? As they might, especially if Alya did not pay the older boy proper regard. Alya decided he simply could not let that happen.

If he died, Vansha was Savi's only real chance. None of the others even knew what she looked like; none of them had the same drive to help her. Assuming they even kept their oaths. Vansha had strengths of his own; and they were his own, owing nothing to whatever the forces were that seethed constantly in Alya's limbs. In his new armour he looked much more the handsome hero than Alya, as he and Asquan trotted easily up the slope and waved a casual salute. 'You've found some signs, then?'

'It wasn't too hard,' answered Alya, but his pleasure faded. He had ridden back towards the Citadel to scout out the raiders' tracks, and found all too much, too clear. 'They had wagons waiting, it seems. So the tracks say. And a use for them. I found bodies.'

Vansha stared. 'The women?'

'Only one or two. Something had been at them, but I knew them well enough. Kemashal, the digger's wife, she was one. And Lamatyal, Usha's mother. She spared me a fowl's wing, once.'

'Older women,' said Vansha, after a moment. 'So . . . you think they took the younger ones in the wagons?'

'There are more small footprints, but they don't lead away anywhere. Just the horsemen and wheels, heading west and north. Swiftly enough, by the look of it, but no desperate hurry. You never know, they might have decided to camp somewhere for a day or two.'

'No more than a night!' said Asquan. 'Volmur does have the odd warband out on patrol, at times.

For appearances' sake; and they wouldn't know
about any truce. They'd attack.'

'Well, there's an even odder band on the loose
now!' said Vansha scornfully. 'Look at them! I imagined us riding out with lines of horse, not a handful
of starveling townie gaolbirds. And worse!'

Alya nodded. 'I also. A few more hardened
warriors, at least. But I like them well enough, for
all that! And there is this good – king's horsemen we
could not have commanded, or restrained.'

Vansha's face darkened. 'True! We'd have been
mere hangers-on, to them.'

'There are good men here, I'm sure. They may be
more use to us, in the end.'

'We'd better hope so. Since you're sure of the
trail—'

'For now. But it may not last forever. We must
always be looking for more guidance, however we
may come by it.'

Vansha clicked his tongue impatiently. 'Time
enough. Well, do we ride, my captain?'

'We do!' said Alya, and with a gentle tug of the
reins he cantered down the slope towards the rest,
who waited there with spare horses in tow. Whatever
Vansha thought, they already looked far from the
shaggy, half-naked wrecks who had stumbled out
of the gaol's gate, blinking even in grey dawn light,
and drinking in the dank, dungy town air as if it were
the free wind of the peaks. All this time Alya had been
fighting against the feeling that he had been landed
with a crew of grotesque scarecrows, an absurd crew
to even think of challenging the iron-handed men of
the Ice. But drawn up here in order, armed and on
horseback, they presented a different picture.

Half-starved frames were already filling out again,
and not one of them but sat his or her mount well,
better than he, probably. The soldiers wore their mail
with stiff-necked pride, and trailed their cloaks like

banners, hefting weapons that meant independence and trust; and Vansha aped them well. Asquan and the scholar Tseshya, though they sat easier in their saddles, looked all the stronger. That also was satisfying. Even Rysha seemed more cheerful, once the dungeon lay behind her; she rode, as she said, like a man, and seemed at ease under her mail. And she was the only one, so far, who had tried to escape.

That had been at Asquan's lodging in a side building of the royal compound, to Alya's eyes a huge and lordly apartment, but which Asquan himself seemed to find mean and comfortless. 'There's no satisfying some people!' whispered Vansha, fingering a wall hanging of some impossibly smooth fabric. 'Why, he's even got his own bathhouse out back!'

'And there you can scrub the prison off you!' said its owner sardonically. Evidently his ears were sharper than most. 'It's being readied now. I've sent for fresh clothes, and we'll buy our other gear in the town. Dead men's armour's always to be had, and cheaply.'

Rysha, though, indignantly refused to enter the bathhouse with the men. Vansha and Alya found that funny, but nobody else, apparently. 'Been married, hasn't she?' demanded Vansha, smelling suspiciously at peculiar oils and pumice stones. 'Knows what it all looks like, close up.'

'Yes, well, we town-dwellers have our strange little ways,' sniffed Asquan. He did not join the bathers himself, but leaned against the wood-planked wall, apparently enjoying the spectacle. 'Though the lady is of modest origins, I gather, and used enough to life in the wild. Still, after a year in that stinking hole I would expect cleanliness to overcome shyness—'

Asquan broke off abruptly, turned on his heel and stalked out. There was an outburst of shrieking

and cursing somewhere outside, and he returned
dragging a snarling Rysha by one arm and her ear.

'Halfway across the roof,' he said laconically, and
with little effort tipped her bodily into the earthen-
tiled pool among the rest. She surfaced, spat at him as
she clambered out, and with no inhibition at all
stripped off her rags, keeping only a scrap of silken
neckscarf, and began to scrub herself down at the hot
tub with a bag of oilseed chaff.

Asquan watched her, as well.

Alya thought how pallid and bony she seemed
compared to Savi. Vansha spared her a look, no more.
Her fellow gaolbirds glared, though Almur, the youngest, let his gaze linger. Kalkan saw that, and bridled.
'Think yourself lucky we don't just drown you here
and now, you stupid bitch!' he growled, as she came
back to the pool. 'Traditional, for such as you!'

'Who's the more stupid?' she demanded. 'The
curs who run right into the bear's mouth, or the bitch
that slips away? After all, what have I to lose?'

'Doesn't how you die matter?' demanded Alya.
'And why you risk it?'

She glanced at him under her thin lashes, as if
surprised. 'There's only one way to die,' she said,
swirling her hair around on the surface with surprising care. 'And that's the wrong one. Life's all you've
got. They tried to ruin mine, and I paid them. I just
didn't move fast enough.'

'Does she mean then, or just now?' muttered
Vansha.

However that might be, she had chosen armour
and weapons as readily as the rest, demure, downcast, silent. Only when she encountered Nightingale,
perched uneasily like a beggar-child atop one of the
baggage horses, did she show any feeling, and that
seemed to be genuine fear. Understandable enough,
for the creature's black eyes fixed on her with an
unhealthy intensity, and his tongue lolled and slav-

ered like a dog's. But when Alya rebuked him, he only cackled, a little wistfully. 'I never got many women, stuck out there in the wood.'

'Shouldn't think you'd want this one!' said Vansha curtly. 'I wouldn't want a murderess witch in *my* bed!'

'Oh, I don't want *her*,' cackled Nightingale. 'Not like *that*. But there'd be a heady life to drink, eh? All those tasty memories and feelings, writhing up together like a ball of fat wet worms! All those hates and spites and loathings, and herself most of all. Give her to me! If she offends you, give her to me!'

'I might just do that!' said Vansha, loudly enough for Rysha to hear. 'One demon deserves another!'

She sneered, and mounted up, when the order was given, in a sullen fury. But she took her place in line readily enough, set where Asquan could watch her; and as they rode down through the morning bustle of the town, she had made no new attempt to break free.

When they filed out through those enormous gates the guards, seeing Asquan's standard, sprang to throw aside the barriers, and Vansha was amused to see how they all but grovelled before this well-armed and aristocratic-looking party.

'If they only knew, eh?' he tossed back, rather too soon for Alya's liking. But it raised a laugh along the line, and caught their lightening mood. Just emerging from the looming shadow of that wall, raising the first dust from the yellow road, shed a deadly burden from their shoulders, the weight of Volmur's anger.

He might pursue them now, when he found what had happened, but that would hurt his prestige. Most likely he would brush the matter off – unless, of course, they fell into his hands again. Wherever Alya and Savi might go now, it could never be back to the Citadel. Alya could not feel that mattered too much.

There would always be somewhere, if only it could be with her.

Now he waved to the horsemen at the hill's foot, without stopping, showing them the way; and at Asquan's command they moved off in a swift canter, no longer in line but in such files as the rough track permitted. Alya stood off a little, watching, and was interested to see Rysha riding quite close behind the Nightingale, her eyes as fixed upon him as his had been on her.

'Those two will want watching!' grunted the Lord Kalkan, riding up beside Alya. 'Too strong, too wicked. Too alike.'

'True. But they may yet be our greatest hope.'

Kalkan shook his head, and the look in his eye was strange. 'Don't forget yourself! I've never seen anyone like you, not even a Seer. Half a country lad, and half – I don't know. Something out of old tales. The Powers don't hand out that sort of strength for nothing. And you've a strength of mind, too. There's some destiny in you, working itself out.'

'I feel so, maybe. But for your good, or mine? The Powers have larger purposes, as I've heard; and woe to the little men who get caught in them. And we're going up against some others at least as mighty.'

'That's all true,' said Kalkan, sounding little concerned. 'But ill or well, it's got me out of that living tomb, and that alone's enough, my lad. Would only you'd come a little sooner, and saved my boy! But that wasn't to be.'

He wheeled his mount then, roaring at the scholar Tseshya to have a care of those baggage nags, and did he want all their food in the roadside mire?

Alya watched him join the column now, and take over the reins, whipping them to his own saddle and guiding the horse expertly on to the smoother part of the way. They were a fascinating study, these new followers of his; and one he had better take up at once, to make the best of what hope they represented.

Washed and barbered, Lord Kalkan revealed a formidable presence, a square, heavy-boned face with hard lines and creases still etched in the loose skin of his starvation. He had kept his moustache, and it drooped grimly over a hard, set mouth. It was a stern, proud, habitually scowling countenance, but not, somehow, an angry or brutal one, far more open and readable than Asquan's. He could imagine Kalkan conspiring against a corrupt king; he could also imagine him getting caught.

The followers he had chosen were men in his own mould, warriors by birth and soldiers by life. They all seemed much alike, hard, sturdy men despite their long confinement, more than a touch dour but open of face and heart, with little learning or breadth of mind, and obviously loyal to Lord Kalkan first and foremost. They would want watching, too, in their way.

Tseshya was a harder study, a burly, square-faced young man who had been studying to gain a post as a tax official, one of the few stable positions in Volmur's ramshackle government. Bigger and stronger than Alya's idea of a scholar, he was evidently learned enough, but also as good an archer as he had claimed. He was genial and talkative, compared to the soldiers, but often nervy and irritable also; and as Kalkan was currently pointing out in no uncertain terms, preoccupied and careless in everyday ways. He was fatter than the others, having suffered no more than a few weeks in the dungeons, consigned there for a drunken satire on Volmur. 'If I'd only been a whit more sober,' he mourned, 'the bastard would never even have understood it!'

'I think he still might have guessed,' objected Asquan. 'From the way you painted it on the palace latrine.'

'No! My style was the most refined in my year! Anyone learned enough to get all the references would hardly have given me away!'

Asquan tugged at a stray lock of hair. 'Perhaps not. But the picture you drew alongside it might have. Effective, I thought, but somewhat exaggerated.'

'Well, it was just a joke. I didn't *really* believe Volmur went in for . . .'

'No? I thought the likeness was excellent. It was the horse that seemed a little strained.'

Definitely careless, thought Alya. That could be a problem. But compared to Rysha, he was as open as one of his own scrolls. She was an enigma, and a nasty one; and yet she might be the key to their success.

Ten against forty – and that assumed Rysha was any use as a fighter, as she claimed. It was one thing to slice open a man's throat, as Vansha acidly pointed out, when you had him at a disadvantage – quite another to meet him in open fight. But then, in open fight the odds would doom them, anyway.

'Our best hope must be stealth,' Alya told Vansha and the others, that first evening of their chase. 'To ride up close to their camp or stopping place, when we find it, sneak in and free her by stealth – and any others we can, of course. Only rely on force to cover our escape.'

Asquan nodded. 'And that more as a diversion. To exhaust them, make them feel it's not worth the following. It will cost a few lives, I believe.'

'Then shouldn't we just ride in?' objected Vansha, prodding angrily at the fire they sat around. 'Stir up the camp. Fire their tents and wagons, drive off their horses, that kind of thing. We'd at least be sure of getting Savi away properly, then!' Kalkan nodded vigorously.

'Would you?' mused Asquan. 'Not if the *Aikiya 'wahsa* think as you do, my friends. That is what they will be prepared and organised to cope with; as you are, my dear Lord Kalkan, posting your watchers each night. With a larger force we could risk it. But as things are, our chances lie in mist and moonshadow!'

'More in my lord's right hand!' grumbled Darzhan, and the others rumbled their agreement.

'Touching, aren't they?' Asquan leaned across to Alya. 'I swear, if Kalkan threw a stick, they'd fetch it! But they seem to take to your friend, at least.'

That was true, and interesting, for Alya. They all called both the young men lords, even Kalkan; Alya found that embarrassing, but Vansha turned to it like a sunflower. He seemed to be on easy terms with them already, far easier than with Alya. Alya knew little enough of men; but he felt he was learning, not least with Asquan's constant acid whispers in his ear. The ageing lord seemed to believe in nothing, not even himself; and that was an education, if you didn't take him too seriously. Nothing was obvious about the man, everything concealed; and yet even Kalkan seemed in awe of him. Alya wondered what Asquan whispered to others about him, behind his back. Let Vansha make friends; Alya felt he would do well to win some of Asquan's trust, before they were much further along the trail.

This led them straight enough in the days that followed, down well-worn paths and tracks across the open grasslands. At first they found odd ruins, or heaps of stone that might once have been more, now cemented into the earth as if it was pulling them back down. The sun rose on brown grasses, whispering in the perpetual wind; but they seemed to hold no secrets, for when it sank little was different. They might almost have been riding the same stretch of land over and over again, for only the details changed.

At first; but before many days passed the first changes became apparent, beneath their very feet. Here and there the stony brown mud of the ways exposed a patch of rough stone roadbed or, to

Vansha's astonishment, even the paving that had covered it, like protruding bare bones. Alya's father had told him of the mighty ways of stone that had once crisscrossed the whole land, but it was a very different thing to be riding over them now, thousands of years gone. 'What could they have used such things for?' demanded Vansha.

'Trade, war, women!' Asquan told him. 'Filling your belly or your girl's, emptying someone else's. What does any human use anything for, otherwise?'

'Huh!' put in Fazdshan, Kalkan's man. 'Heard you've filled a few other things, in your time! Honour, my Lord Vansha; honour, power, that's what they meant to us. That's what the Ice stripped from us!'

Vansha stared angrily down at the remaining paving, cracking beneath his mount's hooves. 'We could have had so much!' he whispered, almost to himself.

'I'll settle for Savi, right now!' snapped Alya, urging his horse forward. 'We can't be far behind, but their wagons will go faster on this stuff! Ride on!'

Soon they were finding more than bare paving. Someone had tried to restore these roads, someone recently; but the effort had been clumsy, tamping broken rocks into potholes, banking earth to support the collapsing roadbed. 'Primitive!' snorted Tseshya, whose horse had just stumbled over an ill-filled crack. 'Like the way they did it under the last king. Volmur at least set people to study the old skills, to see it done properly!'

'I was thinking that myself!' remarked Asquan. 'But the old king's writ never ran this far north and west. Someone else has been doing this.'

'The raiders?' suggested Fazdshan, scanning the horizon hopefully. But anything that broke the bleak skyline soon resolved into a cluster of rocks or scrubby trees, growing out of some sheltered dip or hollow.

'Hardly. No, there may be some other folk stirring here, beginning to unite once again. And that would be something to watch for, wouldn't it?'

'As friends or foes, either way,' agreed Alya.

'We hear rumours of folk far westward,' said Asquan thoughtfully. 'Nascent kingdoms even, like ours, warring with one another. Some even talked of settling in these inner lands. But this is right on Volmur's bounds! And I see no other sign for thousands of paces in any direction – not so much as a wisp of smoke.'

'Well, it's one more thing to watch for. Any signs – anything. We had better pass the word on.'

At last, when the trail became hard to see in the dusk, Alya was persuaded to halt once more, though his heart misgave him.

'The wagon ruts are still wet! They could be only an hour ahead!' he raged.

'Or days,' said Vansha grimly. 'We are used to a drier country. Even your family's place was highlying, but this is low, with rivers, they say. Anyhow, even if the bastards are that close, we'd likely blunder past them in the dark.'

'Unless they light fires!'

'Then we would see them from here, if at all!' said Asquan firmly. 'It will do us little good to come upon them weary and half starved, too. Be wise, sit and eat!'

They found themselves not far from one of the smaller, scrubbier patches of woodland. Shelter and firewood were rare enough, so that they made eagerly towards it. 'But under the eaves only!' commanded Alya. 'And nobody must stray deeper! Woodlands here can hold all manner of strange perils!'

'Like me!' fluted the Nightingale, and tittered. His large eyes glimmered unhealthily bright in the gloom. Alya noticed Rysha staring sidelong at the creature once again, and her thin lips writhed. She was not smiling.

Nobody gave an order; but everyone drew their weapons. The trees were quite young, birches mostly and much of an age, and at this time of year their foliage was yellowing fast. They grew densely, on a small rise, surrounded by thorn thickets as tangled as those in Nightingale's wood.

He was looking around suspiciously, and sniffing. 'Funny place, this! Smells strange!'

'How so?' demanded Alya quietly. 'Tell us more. You must try to be helpful.'

Nightingale ducked his face down petulantly. 'How'm I supposed to be sure? All these stinking men around. Stinks, all of them; and that she-devil there, she stinks! There's another here. That's all I know.'

'Another stink?' Asquan swung his horse this way and that, towards the fringes of the wood. 'They tell of beasts in these lands – but I see nothing.' Then he exclaimed, and his horse shied as Nightingale shot up, like a bolt from a bow, off the back of the baggage pony and on to its crupper. From there he bounced again, apelike, and seized an overhanging twig of birch that did not look able to bear a bird's weight. Up it he sprang, to the branch and along, on all fours. He looked so like a small child playing that Alya almost called him back; but Asquan held up an abrupt hand. And indeed, Nightingale was moving through the trees now with a speed and agility that were less and less childlike, downright sinister in fact. Alya and Vansha exchanged glances. Perhaps they had been lucky he had been lazy and complacent, and not scurrying around above their heads.

He had vanished completely into the twilight now. 'And will it break my heart if the little demon doesn't come back?' muttered Vansha, into the silence. 'Not much!'

For long moments there was only the soft swishing of the branches, and Alya began to wonder. Then there was a sudden heart-stopping flurry, and down came the Nightingale in a shower of leaves, on to Alya's saddle.

'Helpful!' he panted, ducking his snout of a face, and his waxy fingers thrust something into Alya's hand.

'A – what is this?' demanded Kalkan, peering over. 'Some piece of mason's trash.'

'A trowel. Caked with mortar, but very rusty.' Alya hefted it. 'Somebody's been building something. Show me, Nightingale; and thank you! Stay back, the rest of you!'

But when he reached the trees, he found Vansha and Asquan still at his back. 'Well, brother, someone should at least know what happened to you!'

Alya sighed, and crept forward after Nightingale. Now wasn't the time to start arguing about authority, least of all with Vansha. Apart from anything else, the little creature seemed immune to thorns, and Alya, whatever his gift could do for him, was not. Swearing under his breath, he struggled through to the crest of an earthen rise, trying not to dislodge any stones, and raised his head very gingerly, in the direction Nightingale pointed.

'A bloody house!' exclaimed Vansha, when Alya waved them on. 'Houses! Right down in the dip! Could be a whole village, smack in the middle of the wood! Solid stone walls, better than ours by the look of it! Who'd be building there?'

'Someone who didn't want to be seen!' said Asquan quietly. 'A clever ruse in a hard land. See there, by the bottom of the bank? There are foundations there, for a surrounding wall, I guess. A solid one.'

Vansha snapped his fingers. 'The road repairers! We wondered where they were! Why, every patch of woodland we've passed could hold a hidden settlement, a town even.' He reached for his sword. 'They might be back any moment!'

'I think not!' said Asquan. 'The trowel has been lying for a while, a year or two. And there is weed overgrowing the walls, in places. And see! At that wall there, that could be fire damage. And that one is toppled. I do not think they will be back, somehow, these builders. They grew overconfident. If they had stayed far from the roads they might have remained concealed. No, they will not be back.'

They cast about them swiftly, as if the trees might hide watching eyes; and went swiftly back to their horses and their followers. 'A timely warning!' said Tseshya drily, as they dismounted to make camp. '*The hunters who blunder upon the bear's lair—*'

'*Fall prey, little wonder, to beast who lurks there!*' capped Asquan. 'Very quaint, I'm sure. What our proverb-peddler is trying to say is that we want to come up with the raiders, but carefully. Tonight we set a double watch!'

They hid the fire as best they could, in the lee of thorn bushes. These billowed the smoke back around them, in the flaws of wind, but at least kept the light hidden at any distance. Alya, obstinately taking first watch while the others curled up in their blankets, scanned the night urgently for some other flicker of flame; but saw none. The night invaded his spirit, as he watched; and only exhaustion drove him off to sleep.

His awakening was hardly more welcome. Over a cheerless mess of biscuit, water and smoked meat, Asquan spelled out his deliberations. 'If this land has been raided so recently, there is a good chance there are more raiders about than the Citadel force. It always seemed so small to me, a mere detachment, perhaps. So we must be on the alert, constantly. I suggest we get going at first light, but stop and look about carefully, every hour or so.'

Alya ground his teeth. 'That will slow us still further!'

'He's right, though,' said Vansha unhappily. 'We could run into a large band of them! Or just some mingled tracks, even, but end up following the wrong one! I'm as impatient as you are, brother – but we've got to be sure!'

'Then the sooner we're away again, the better!' snapped Alya, and shouted angrily to the rest. There was some cold satisfaction in the way they scrambled to mount up again, but little joy. He scanned the horizon, under lowering cloud, thinking of Savi's face, framed in her long hair, wondering if she looked upon that same wintry sky, if indeed she was still beneath it. Every hour seemed to be taking her further from him, every setback. The flames flickered beneath his skin, the eternal maddening tingle in his back and thighs. He should have ridden on her trail straight away, on his own if need be, however little sense it made. He dug in his heels, and they cantered away.

Before the day was out, however, he realised how right Asquan had been to be cautious, and said so. This land, that looked so empty, was a living scar, marked with wars old and new. There had indeed been a recent attempt to settle it, by a folk whose clothes and weapons, what scraps remained, nobody recognised. They had built their stone walls in the heart of woodlands and the shelter of steep vales cut by the small streams that increasingly crossed the land, invisible behind thorny undergrowth, some of which seemed to have been deliberately planted to conceal fields and plantations. It had done them little good.

There had been whole villages, some larger than the Citadel, small towns almost. Even these had been burned out wholesale, leaving only skeletal remains of birches still standing, leafless and charred, about their margins.

'But some of the fields have been planted more recently,' puzzled Vansha that evening. 'This year, I mean. *After* the towns were destroyed. There would have been a harvest; but it's been left to rot. Not even weeded.'

'If you say so,' sniffed Asquan. 'I have always kept a healthy distance from horny-handed dung-slingers and their toil – preferably upwind.'

Alya said nothing. He was scanning the way ahead, as usual; and Nightingale with him.

The next day brought them closer to the truth, for about midday they came upon something new. Another wide river crossed the land, slow and marshy; and across it, as derelict as the road but still standing, ran the remains of a stone bridge. Ruined as it was, it was still passable; and the enduring might of it made them stop and stare. Even Asquan could not belittle it. 'I have seen the rubble of others like it, far away to the west and south; but this . . . What this must have been, when it was new-built!'

'Like Volmur's walls,' said Alya. 'That gate. I can believe in it, now!'

Kalkan tugged at his beard. 'There were mighty folk here, before the Ice and its jackals came.'

'There still are!' said Vansha, his face as hard as the smooth-chiselled stone; and they rode across in bitter pride.

But what awaited them at the other side soon whipped it out of them. All along the bank the ground was muddy and churned up, and there were the remains of many fires.

'More of the swine!' said Alya, between his teeth, as they searched the trodden ground.

'A great many more!' said Tseshya, who seemed to be a good tracker. 'As if this was another rendez-vous. It's certainly another crossroads, with ways in every direction.'

'Could be, couldn't it?' agreed Alya thoughtfully. 'Strange that they're both by rivers.'

'But not very navigable, and with no easy landings. That's a nasty-looking rapid up there to the north. So I don't think anyone's gone off by boat, if that's what you're thinking.'

'I suppose so. But I remember my father saying that the meltwaters flowing down from the Ice can carry something of its evils with them.'

Tseshya nodded thoughtfully, as he scanned the ground. 'It's written. They say fell creatures follow the watercourse, sometimes, as if it still carries influences to direct them. But that's only up north, while the water's undiluted and icy still. I shouldn't imagine it would matter much here. Well, I give up on this. They've ridden over the wagon tracks. It's been raining, too. They're all blurred now.' There was a hint of relief in his voice, like a child eager to go home.

'We can't give up!' Alya spurred his horse down off the bridge, glaring at the ground as if it had offended him. The fires glowed within him, but his heart was cold. Anything could have happened, and what trace would remain? Here and there ran what might be ruts, but he could not tell how many, or whether they were still the same. Alya sprang down. 'There must be some indication . . . See, here – horses, wagons . . .'

'Too many!' groaned Vansha, joining him. 'This is an army! And our quarry's muddled up in it all, and I can't find which way they go! You?'

'No! There was one wagon with a traceable wheel-track, a jagged seam in the metal tyre; but it's lost in the mire and mess. Some one way, some another . . . !'

'Some, days back,' added Tseshya.

'This is serious!' said Asquan quietly. 'We city folk are not your match as trackers, even the hunters

among us; we will not find what you cannot. We will
have to search the countryside around, and that will
take still more time!'

And indeed that was all they could do, spreading
out, looking for some trace of the wagons with the
women. But what they found first was not a track at all.

'Smoke!' called Tseshya. The others, still searching afoot, came running up the low hill to join him,
dropping down so as not to be seen on the skyline.
There, away to the westward, there was indeed a
faint thread rising, greyer than the afternoon sky,
from among a patch of low rolling hills little more
than a thousand paces ahead.

'I found what looked like wagon tracks, leading
west!' said the scholar urgently. 'Followed them a
little, to see if they became clearer. Then I saw that!'

'And then you made trouble for yourself!'
grinned Alya. 'No excuse to slope off now, is there?'

Tseshya groaned.

'Never mind, scribbler!' chuckled Kalkan. 'One
more thing to be philosophical about. Besides, where
would you have gone?'

Tseshya shrugged. 'Somewhere! Far to the east,
maybe, to the remains of the kingdoms by the Sea.
Maybe even off on one of those ships they're building.'

Most of the others laughed and jeered. 'What, to
the land of ghosts?' Fazdshan scoffed. 'I could show
you a quicker way!'

'The polished man travels easily and without
haste,' said Tseshya austerely. 'And at least I might
find some educated company!'

'It doesn't sound so stupid to me!' said Alya,
wistfully. 'I should like to try that, myself. I saw their
messenger. He believed!'

'I saw him too, brother!' said Vansha grimly.
'Maybe he did; but fools believe in many things.
For now, we must move after that smoke!'

'With care,' said Asquan. 'But I do not see them making camp in the middle of the day. We must be prepared to find something different.' He glanced at them, sidelong. 'Perhaps worse.'

What they found, though, was not what any expected, good or bad. The smoke rose from the side of a suddenly steep down, and huddled against its lower flank, surrounded by burned-out trees, they found yet another farmstead, broken and burned, but still half standing. The smoke did not look like left-over embers, and so Alya and Lord Kalkan dis-mounted and made their way down, with great care, while the others covered them from above with bows. When they reached the yard, it seemed to be empty and devastated, and there were no signs that anyone had been there lately, raiders or other-wise. The smoke was escaping from under the burned-out rooftree. Kalkan found a door, and with Alya flanking him, kicked it hard and sprang aside.

It was merely propped up, not on its hinges, and it fell in with a deafening crash. There was a cracked shriek from inside, but when they peered in, the room looked empty, save for a little fire of leaves and debris. Suddenly they both jumped, as what passed for a heap of rubbish in one corner stirred.

When Kalkan stalked forward and prodded it with his spear, it squealed in a human voice, old and cracked. The heap dissolved in a flurry of scrabbling terror, to reveal an old man, filthy and skinny, barely alive, his eyes the colour of stale milk. He could talk, though, and in words they more or less understood, though the dialect was strange. When they gave him a little food, he accepted at last that they were not going to slay him, and he told them something of what had passed over his land.

'War, my lords, battle and war! All my life, and am I not of seven score summers and more? Aye, and me the one my Lord Balhur once called the greatest

manslayer in his service! Towns I laid waste, fields I
burned, enemies I slew before the faces of their wives
and children, I!' His voice became a screech. 'And
now my lord is long in his grave! And what am I, but a
bundle to be left behind by the cold hearth, an
inconvenient burden my cowardly piss-pant grand-
children choose to forget when they flee the Ice-
wolves!'

'I also have been left as a burden,' said Alya
wearily. 'And I also have suffered from these same Ice-
wolves.'

'Ah, them!' hissed the old man, and his voice
trembled still further. 'Them, we should have been
ready to face! Had the others not been so obstinate,
had they but acknowledged my Lord Balhur as their
rightful overlord, and not followed base pretenders!
And now they suffer for it, aye, their homes razed, their
fields smouldering, their women dragged off screaming in wagons, who knows where!' He sniggered. 'But
why, he-he, that all men know! Only the other day I
watched them – bathing in the river, he-he-he . . .'

'You watched what, old man?' demanded Alya
fiercely. 'You spied on the *Aikiya*? Saw the women
they'd taken?'

'Couldn't light a fire while they were here!'
mumbled the old man. 'Didn't dare! Had to watch
'em, well hid. See when they went. Westward, most
of 'em.'

'The women? Westward too?'

The old man shook his head tetchily. 'No, fool!
Why westward? That's not their home, the savages,
the maneaters, no! North, that's where they live,
north, under the eye of their cold masters. North,
that's where they take the women, whole wagonfuls,
he-he . . .'

Alya seized him by his ragged shirt. 'And this
time? Did they take these wagonfuls north, this time?
Due north?'

The old man, startled and frightened, shrank down into himself. 'N-no, my lord! There was only one wagon this time, of women. Watched 'em bathing, he-he-he . . . Might have saved themselves the trouble, for those dirty bastards—' He squeaked, as Alya's grip tightened. 'Not north, my lord! There's no good way north, not any more. North and west, the river-road, the rough road. Road to nowhere, we called it; though there'd been towns there once, they said, greater towns even than my Lord Balhur's! And now they're paid for it, homes laid waste, fields smouldering, children devoured, he-he-he . . .'

'It is clear what has come about,' said Lord Asquan, when Alya told him the tale. 'Pretty much as in the days of Volmur's grandfather. A lord seeks to set himself up above the rest, to build a kingdom; or perhaps many do, not just this Balhur. There is civil war; but out here, nobody wins conclusively. Perhaps the agents of the Ice foment it; maybe their forces lend one side or another a hand, at first. It drags on, till recent times, even. Then when all sides are exhausted, when there's a first faint shiver of peace, folk beginning to build again and till the fields – then the Ekwesh descend upon the remains! These folk have dug their own graves.'

'And by the sound of it,' put in Kalkan, riding close behind, 'that old bastard dug deeper than most. I grudge him the food!'

Alya looked back. They had left him with what little they could spare. 'I do not. He has done us a great service. And his is a living death now, with only a still more miserable one to follow. At least it may sustain him till his family return, if ever.'

'A touching reunion, that will be!' said Asquan delicately. 'Audible from here to the horizon, I doubt not. But, as you say, he has served us. This road seems to parallel the river, all right; and if I am not mistaken—'

Vansha swung a long leg over the saddlebow and sprang down to look; then as quickly remounted. 'Wagon ruts! One with that jagged seam! That's our spoor!'

'Provided that wagon still bears the women!' said Asquan absently, peering into the grey distance.

'The old goat seemed sure enough!' grinned Kalkan. 'A shame you could not wring the time out of him! But we may find more signs ahead.'

'As I said,' remarked Asquan, still oddly abstracted, shading his eyes. 'What we find is not always what we want . . .' Suddenly he urged his horse to a light gallop, ahead of the rest, away off the west of the road towards a stand of scrubby trees. Alya and Vansha, puzzled, led the others after him.

'It can't be the raiders! Or he wouldn't—'

Vansha had the keener eyes. 'He's getting down! It's something there.' A scatter of black birds rose, cawing and screeching. Some were bare-necked buzzards. Vansha reined in his horse suddenly. But then Alya had seen it too.

The body lay almost under the branches; Alya was surprised that Asquan's ageing eyes had picked it out, sooner than their own. The more so because it was already blending with the setting, the bright-hued shreds of clothing dulled and dirtied, the livid brightness of raw flesh brown and shrivelled now, blued and greyed with decay.

'Beasts have dragged it. Wolves, perhaps,' said Asquan, still detached. 'And taken their fill, I fear.'

'Yes,' said Alya. Vansha said nothing.

'Might you nonetheless . . .' Asquan paused, looking from one to another with bird-bright eyes. 'Recognise . . . her?'

The body had been eviscerated, the flesh gnawed off the limbs. The ribs gaped bare and empty. Other things, the birds included, had taken the eyes and much else, and more had been removed by dragging. The limbs were no longer complete, the lower jaw was gone. The hair remained, a nightmare frame of normality to the scarified, desecrated portrait of someone they had known.

'Yes,' said Vansha, rubbing the back of his hand across his lips. 'Yes.' He looked to Alya as if for confirmation, or perhaps simple support.

'Kaqual,' said Alya. He could not say how he might be sure, but he was. 'I think it's Kaqual.'

Asquan nodded. 'Not—'

'No! Not Savi, no.'

Not Savi! yelled his inner self, exultant with relief and horrified at itself in the same instant. He remembered Kaqual as a nice girl, jolly and plump, fond of dancing and singing. How did he dare feel relieved, let alone rejoicing? But he could not help it; and to judge by Vansha's glassy expression, he was suffering the same inner battle.

Asquan squatted down, calmly prodded the pitiful remnant this way and that with a dead stick. 'Her head was wounded, seriously. And her ribs, I think, though it is hard to tell. She would have died quickly enough – and to judge by the condition of the body, three or four days since.'

'The time would be right,' agreed Alya neutrally, trying to control his stomach.

'We should bury her!' burst out Vansha suddenly, then looked from one to another, to Kalkan in particular, as if to be sure he'd said the right thing. 'I mean – even though we're in haste?'

As if he feared to be too sentimental before all these warriors, thought Alya, grimly amused despite himself.

'Damn right we should, lad,' said Kalkan warmly. 'Not poke around the poor thing more'n we need to, either!' he added, with a glare at Asquan. 'Stones'd be more use than earth, or something'll just be digging her up. Jump to it, you all, and gather some!'

There was no shortage of big stones in this rich dark soil, and it took them less than an hour. Anger fuelled them, and visions of brutalities they could not prevent. Rysha, silent as ever, joined them without prompting, and Alya saw her lift some substantial rocks easily enough. Only Nightingale, dozing among the baggage, took no part. Asquan stood by, arms folded; but at last condescended to add a few rocks to the top.

'Why not, my lord?' rumbled Kalkan. 'Somebody might do as much for you, one of these days!'

'Might even remember to kill him first!' put in Chiansha, and the others laughed. Asquan simply smiled his faint smile.

'Well,' he remarked, as they mounted up once more, dusting the soil from their hands as if ready to grab Ekwesh throats, 'the trail is all too clearly marked. But so is the distance. Do you still wish to continue?'

'All the more!' snarled Alya impatiently; and the other men bayed with anger. 'What in Hella's name are we waiting for now?'

'Only to remind you that every way has a destination, and two directions. This may not be the only group of raiders travelling it. However hard we ride, we must still keep close watch!'

Vansha spat and swore; but on seeing Kalkan's sober nod, he said nothing. There was something to be said for Asquan's coolness, Alya decided; a lesson for himself, however brightly his inner fires burned.

They rode in column then, and every so often one would gallop ahead, to spy out the road and the land around, for the least sign of life. But for the first two days there was little enough of that, save birds: small birds in the bush, and greater ones gliding through the grey airs. Once, spying from a low hill, Alya saw a great mass of them wheeling against the clouds, far to the west and south – almost like vultures over a prey, and yet their silhouettes seemed different, somehow. Vansha, straining his eyes, thought they had long necks, and that there were smokes in the air there, dark smoke. But that was far from their route, and perhaps better so. The river bent westward and northward now, and the road more sharply so.

At first it merely cut off the river's meandering curves, and they were glad enough of that. It was good to be away from it for a while, and not only for the cold dank airs it carried, the haze and fogs and clouds of small stinging insects it spawned. Its dark water was uncomfortable company, racing and boiling through shallow stony rapids one moment, then lingering in deep uneasy pools and lakelets, outwardly calm and yet crossed with sharp swirling undertows that could make bathing or fishing dangerous. Some of the deeper ones, shadowed under great rocks, were not places any sensible man would want to bathe, so uncanny they seemed; long smooth shadows glided beneath the surface, strange bubbles welled up. Even Nightingale, uncanny enough himself, preferred not to linger there; though he never bathed anyway.

Now, though, the road moved further away altogether, across brown fells thinly cloaked with grass and heathery scrub. As if it followed some faster, more direct route; but to where?

It was some days later, in the early evening, when Fazdshan, their scout, did not wait as usual for them to catch him up, but came galloping back at full tilt.

'Smack atop the road!' he panted. 'In a notch above a river-bend, two thousand paces on, nice and cosy and damn near out o' sight!'

'Who, man?' demanded Lord Kalkan. 'Raiders?'

'Who bloody else?' demanded Fazdshan, wheezing with his haste. 'As well we didn't come sauntering round that bloody bend straight, or we'd have ridden straight under their camp!'

'What exceptional luck we're being so careful!' murmured Lord Asquan. 'How many?'

'Fifteen, I counted. There's a couple might be captives, but I couldn't see clear!'

'We could handle that many!' grinned Kalkan. 'Eh, lads? In our sleep! Ride down, and—' He made pigsticking gestures with his lance.

'Unfortunately I remain awake!' snapped Asquan. 'If we have no alternative, we must attack by stealth only! On foot!'

Kalkan and the others looked dubiously to Alya, which both pleased and burdened him. 'I also would like to ride over them!' he said heavily. 'But we cannot take chances, not yet. We'll see! Rysha, we've asked little enough of you, thus far. But it'll be dusk soon. Will you help? Your . . . shadows?'

She fiddled with her hair, and said nothing; but at last she nodded. Her bony face smirked a little. 'Since you ask the shadows nicely, my lord. Not when we're right on top of them, mind. Even then it won't be as dark as the dungeon.'

'We'll ride closer, strike faster. The wind's in our faces, at least; it won't carry the sound of hooves. But stay quiet, all the same!'

The track was stony, but clear and largely dry, and it was less than half an hour before Fazdshan gave the signal. Alya halted the riders, and sprang down even as the others drew up, staring at the bluff the soldier indicated, topped with a line of windbent birches against the darkening sky.

'Below that! Smell the fires?'

'Only just!'

Fazdshan shuddered. 'They know how to keep down the smoke. I'd have damn near tripped over the bastards, if they hadn't been having some shouting match over something!'

'But you didn't,' said Alya, and clapped him on the shoulder. 'Rysha, to me! Can you get us past that, unseen?'

She eyed him sidelong, and scratched her head. 'Miracles, my lord? No. Too many of us, with the horses and all. Easiest if there's only a few, three or four. Maybe more when it's darker – maybe. But then a horse'd whinny, and—' Her gesture was brutal.

Alya nodded. 'Then we've no choice; we go in. One lot to attack, the rest follow. Vansha can lead them, and keep Nightingale with him in case of real trouble. In the vanguard, you, me; you, Fazdshan – and a fourth, a really strong fighter. Kalkan, I guess.'

Rysha snorted. 'That big oaf? Asquan, you mean!'

Alya stared. 'The old fellow's a good counsellor, but – Fazdshan?'

He had expected an explosive disagreement, but none came. The big soldier simply looked embarrassed, and shrugged. 'They are both strong, my lord.'

From someone so fanatically loyal, that was a serious admission.

'Asquan,' said Rysha bluntly, and only added, 'My lord!' as an afterthought. Asquan solved the problem by catching them up, along with Vansha, and Alya gave out his commands. He was relieved when Asquan only nodded approval, and drew his sword. For the first time Alya thought how heavy it looked in those spidery hands, already lined and spotted with age.

They moved forward, the four, to below the crest, now rimmed with a faint glow of firelight. At first they walked swiftly, from clump to clump; then they ducked and stooped under the trees, and at last they crawled through the scanty undergrowth. Alya was relieved at how well the older man kept up. He wormed through the bushes with serpentine speed and energy, far more easily than the clumsy Fazdshan. Rysha was muttering to herself as she followed, an

unpleasant, insistent sound at the edge of hearing,
like some litany of spite or injury; her long bony
hands looked almost animalistic as she crawled.

At the crest, before the firelight could touch him,
Asquan halted, cupped hand to ear. Alya could hear
them then, the same harsh voices that had marked the
most terrible moments of his life, the brief braying
laughter; and a great loathing swelled in him, swollen
by the grief and guilt of those who survive when
many die. He did not live for vengeance, not yet; he
could forget, if not forgive, if only Savi were somehow his again. But stilling some of those deadly voices
would quieten his own heart.

He turned sharply at the soft touch on his arm.
Rysha's face was already shadowed and unreadable;
her whisper was unusually low, but that was only
sensible. 'We must touch, my lord, to share my
sending. Now?'

Alya tapped Asquan, and nodded; but he was still
not ready for the blackness that rolled over him. It
was cold, sunless and stifling, it had the shock of an
icy welling wave, making him gasp for breath; then it
ebbed a little, and he could see – not well, but
enough. He remained crouching, but Rysha slowly
rose, and held out her hand to him. Asquan's claw
closed on his arm, the other on Fazdshan's, who
flinched at the touch. It seemed weird, unnatural
to stand like that, so clearly, overlooking death;
stranger still, when they simply stepped out of the
bushes and down the rough grassy slope towards
their enemy's firelight, as casual as travellers approaching an inn.

Rysha was breathing heavily, her free hand
clamped on the hilt of the short hunting falchion
she had chosen. Asquan stalked along supple and
catlike, treading lightly, his broadsword drawn and
held close to his leg. Fazdshan, hefting his heavy
lance-spear, trod intent and wary, of Rysha as much

as anything else. Alya himself was racked by a weird tumult of feelings, beyond understanding. His heart pounded, his thoughts were in turmoil, the fires rolled and boiled within him, as if his limbs were each a flame. He was not afraid; he was too furious to be afraid. This felt right, it felt more than right. He could make the scrubby grass catch fire under his shoes, or so he felt, or shatter the pebble that merely skipped away; and no obstacle seemed more substantial than that.

One of the figures squatting by the fire below looked up, out, straight at them. He squinted around uncertainly; but when somebody called, he gave only a slight shrug and went on peering into the dusk. The others ignored him. Then, as they drew nearer, he sprang up, hefting his stabbing spear; but he was looking in the wrong direction. They were so close now, yet not close enough. Another moment, and the man would place them.

Alya felt Asquan's grasp free his arm. Before he could say anything, there was a rush, and the old lord was no longer at his side, no longer in the shadow. It made little difference. He was still a shadow as he glided forward, too fast to move, too silent to hear. The raider, aware of something in the dusk, tried to cry out, to spring back. Too late by far; a wind sighed, and the man flew backwards, his head turning in the air on a scarlet streamer.

From beside the fire the others sprang up, brandishing spears; but they ran only towards Asquan.

One crossed the path of the shadow. He spun around, with fear and fury on his blunt face; too late. The painted features, the firelight, the whiff of roasting meat on the breeze, they triggered Alya's memory, and with it all the frustrations, the times when he could not strike out. Not now!

His blow was almost a reflex, the impact a shock.

The raider was flung aside in a tangle of limbs, almost unnoticed. The jarring bite of the blade, the dark blood; that was real. Then he was in a howling mêlée of men and weapons.

He had thought the fire hot in him before, but now it roared like an open furnace, its tingle grown to a needling, goading force that scorched along nerve and sinew. He swung and struck, a sweeping, swinging stroke of the whole body that Asquan had shown him, a wide battle-clearing slash, a living shield that scarcely needed to connect. The hero's sword, weightless in his hand, seemed almost a solid line of steel, that nothing crossed intact. At what he struck, he was only half aware.

One face, contorted. Painted; a stabbing tongue of a spearhead flashed firelight in his eyes. He hewed the air, saw face and blade flung back into the dark, and did not know whether the roaring was in his ears or his throat. Another face, a spearhead thudding harmlessly across his mailed chest, and that too he struck down into the dark. Snarling, scarred faces, spears, slash, strike, shrieking mouths and swinging shields, till the pain in his ribs startled him, caught at his breath, a stab that skipped across his mailrings and lodged, hard, spinning him about. He rode with that, lashing out, two-handed, his feet skidding in blood-greased grass. He thought he had missed; but the spear did not come. A noise like axe on tree, a cry, a rustling fall in the dark. He pressed forward, driving the faces back.

He hardly glimpsed the others, Fazdshan wielding his lance like a quarterstaff against three enemy spears, driving under their shafts to stab, swinging down the loaded butt to dash out brains. Asquan, sliding lithe as a dancer through a tangle of blades, his broadsword sliding swiftly here and there, one instant stabbing and biting with the delicacy of a striking snake, the next hewing and slashing with a strength that looked too brutal for such lean limbs, and vanishing behind another wall of assault. Rysha, apparently at bay as two warriors rushed down upon her. Then a ripple, as in summer air, and something stood in her place. To Alya it was unformed, shapeless, and she was clearly visible; but the warriors screamed and threw up their hands. The first warrior clutched at his throat, choked and doubled up. Alya had not seen her move; nor did the man behind, till he stared down at the falchion hilt-deep in his belly. He staggered; and with a deliberate twist she yanked it back, and he fell. The mêlée closed around them again.

Heads turned, eyes widened; more shouting. Alya barely stopped himself striking at the new figures on the slope. One more glimpse of Rysha, plunging her blade with both hands into another man's back, straddling him as he fell kicking, stabbing down and screeching with laughter. Then the mêlée broke, revealing Asquan, leaping after fleeing men, striking from side to side. They fell, and over the last, flung writhing on the grass by a great cut over the spine, he stood with blade poised. The man twisted and convulsed, unable to rise; but Asquan did not strike.

'He's waiting!' said Rysha, coming up beside Alya; and it was only then he realised the shouting had stopped, that the hero's sword he held was a foul steaming mass, that the fight was over. Everything was silent, save for the wind and the crackling of the fires.

'He's waiting?' began Alya, minded to tell Asquan to kill the dying brute cleanly, to do it himself, even. But then, in his agony the raider rolled over, staring straight up at Asquan with terror-filled eyes. Asquan smiled down at him, put his swordpoint to the man's hardened leather breastplate, and slowly, very slowly, leaned upon it. The sword bent slightly; the scream was tearing. Alya, angered and sickened, looked away.

'Very neat!' said Asquan's dry voice. 'Twenty-one, I think? And none of ours? *Very* neat!'

'Kalkan!' wheezed Alya, desperate for some distraction. 'Vansha! Well done – but did you delay?'

Vansha laughed. 'Delay? We were right on your heels, the moment they spotted you. A few heartbeats! We were hoping you'd leave us some!'

'Heartbeats? It seemed so long . . .' Alya struggled to clear his head. 'Look, you and Kalkan – you'd better take two men, make sure none of them are still lurking. And look for prisoners!'

'I'll take Nightingale!' said Vansha. 'Seems the little stinker can see in the dark, trust him! We'll get their horses, too.'

'Well thought of!' said Asquan approvingly. He sounded quite at his ease; but he was wiping his sword on the kilt of the man who still twitched at his feet. 'Do I make that six? Oh, and of course, our over-observant friend back there. He may have had a touch of the Seer's discerning talent in his head, but not enough to keep it on his shoulders. Seven, then; but I must bow before your distinguished tally.'

'Mine?' Alya blinked around, astonished. His gorge rose. Behind him, like a trail trampled through cornstalks, lay a swathe of figures sprawled and still – how many, he could hardly count, but more than six. Here and there a black-and-white breastplate gaped wide with great slashing wounds, a lopped hand or head; one figure, almost at his feet, was cut quite in two. Darkness welled around his boots, and he stepped away hastily. He felt he wanted to vomit, and then realised he was not going to. There was nothing in him, nothing save the ebbing fire, its prickle cold and satisfied. He could hardly loathe Asquan as he had begun to, not when he himself was capable of this. He stabbed the sword down into the clean grass and earth, once, again, scraping the clotted mass from it, and from his hands, stabbing, scraping, wiping, furious and intent.

'This one's alive!' called Tseshya. He turned over one of the outflung bodies by its shoulder. The raider moaned, writhed a little. His face in the firelight was heavy, flat, impassive; but the eyelids flickered, the mouth twitched in agony. Alya stooped over him, but looked up as Vansha reappeared with a train of horses in tow, shaggy sturdy creatures like their own captured mounts. In the yellow glow the young man's face looked waxen and cold.

'Lucky you weren't there. No prisoners; but there were . . . joints roasting. Young men, boys even. We tipped what was left into the fires, piled on more wood! *Why?*' The word became a thin-lipped noise of contempt. Vansha booted the half-conscious raider savagely in the side, making him convulse and groan. 'Why do they do it? *Why?* Plenty of ordinary meat in their packs – smoked fish, fowl, meal, clean provender we can surely use. *Why?*'

'To drive home their victory!' suggested Kalkan. 'To humble those they've overcome still further.'

Asquan's eyes were hooded. 'More! To savour the pain they inflict, the cruelty even after death. It nurtures their manhood, in the very awfulness of the act. The taste of the flesh, even . . .'

Tseshya grinned nastily. 'Sounds like you understand them pretty well, my lord!'

Asquan sniffed. 'They are a crude people, but an interesting study. Their outlook is original, there are insights to be gained. Pain, understood properly, is a defence, a weapon, a servant and a friend. A close friend. Have your researches never shown you that?'

Tseshya shifted uncomfortably. 'Maybe mine were a bit less arcane, my lord. I do remember one chronicler, a man they held as thrall awhile, who managed to escape. He said the sacrifice and the eating, the darkness of the deed, bind them into a brotherhood, not ruled by the restraints of ordinary men. And that makes the deed ultimately an offering to their living gods, the Powers of the Ice.'

Asquan smiled coolly. 'Indeed, but there is more to it than that. They believe, it seems, that their lives are only at the gift of the Powers. By destroying other lives they earn their own place in the world, and their right to have children; and they believe their own lives are worth many others. If ever a man dies in the service of the Ice, whatever the cause, they believe it's because he hasn't cleared away enough other lives to make room. A dozen children sacrificed to earn a year's life, maybe; a hundred, to get a wife and brat of one's own. That is how they see it. Or rather, how they are shown it. The Ice has many ways of clouding the minds of men.'

'*Very* clever,' breathed Vansha.

'Very evil!' said Alya sharply, and the others echoed him. 'Can we waken this one? I want a word with him.'

'There's a stream down there,' said Kalkan. 'Hoi, Chiansha! Bring a couple of good helmfuls! Bastard's cut up more than somewhat, but it's worth a try. You're a mighty fighter, my lord!'

Alya said nothing. He would have to be many things he was not, no doubt. Including another, maybe, any moment. Would the inner fires carry him through this?

Water slapped the twitching face, spilled between the thin lips, over the jagged teeth. The face twisted away, choking, and the stricken raider half raised himself, but sank back with only a grunt.

'You!' said Alya. 'D'you understand me?'

The raider sneered, closed his eyes again. But they had looked more alert than Alya expected. Tseshya tried a harsher dialect Alya could barely understand. 'Answer the lord!' He prodded the

man with his swordtip. 'You're cold mutton in our
hands! But we might just let you slither away free, if
you answer us fairly. *Look at me!*' He jabbed the
sword in, harder. The man glared at him and twisted
away.

'He understands, all right!' said Vansha contemptuously, and planted his foot hard on the man's
injured side. 'Listen, you – *aie!*'

The raider had sunk his teeth in Vansha's leg,
above his boot. The young man lashed out with his
sword, but Asquan parried the blow.

'No! That's what he wants, just to spite us!'

'He's going the right way to get it!'

'There's another way.' Asquan looked at Alya. 'I
somehow don't think you'd like it, mind you . . .'

What Alya really did not like was Asquan's little
lopsided smile. 'Is that necessary?'

'Nothing less will make them speak, except
sheer defiance; sometimes not even that.' Asquan
smirked. 'Believe me, I have plenty of experience.'

Vansha looked around at the others. 'I would not
stand in your way.'

The man understood, no doubt of that. 'Do your
worst, old louse!' he croaked.

Defiance, thought Alya. 'Why? You don't even
know what we want to ask!'

'You want. Is enough! My folk do worse to you,
soon. Don't waste time talking. You dead, now.'

'Are we?' demanded Alya quietly. 'Maybe not.
Maybe your masters aren't as all-powerful as you
think. Look at me. For years I lay a helpless cripple.
Then the Powers healed me in a moment, and poured
into me the hero's strength I longed for. The strength
you felt! What have your cold lords ever given you,
save fear and hatred?'

The raider laughed. 'Powers? Young little
Powers, maybe. Rebels, latecomers, scabby tramps!
Old Powers we serve, they freeze them in walls of

Ice!' He hawked and spat blood on Alya's boot. 'Fault is ours. We hungered for life-meat. We left great band, we leave Their shadow, under the Choosers' wing. Else you never take us! Choosers of Slain, in their shadow, never. Never! Soon they find you, the Choosers. Then no Powers save you. Can't trust Powers!' He lay back, wincing, and laughed again. 'I know! Bred to serve them – I know! Never for man. For Selves only. Never give. Take only. Your strength, digs your own grave deeper. Better like me.'

Alya looked down at the man. 'Very soon you may not think so. Some of your breed murdered my family – you, perhaps. The Powers know how many more!' The fires leaped in him, feeding the embers of his hatred, spilling over in a way he knew was wholly unlike him, yet no more possible to resist. 'What you know could save lives. More delay could cost them. You leave me no choice, but to let the Lord Asquan do with you as he likes.' He looked at Asquan. 'Call me when—'

Asquan picked up a fallen spear and stood the blade in the nearby campfire. 'You will hear.'

Alya turned away. From what he was ready to allow, he told himself, his stomach cold and lead-heavy. The little ripples of fire along every limb seemed to be mocking him. *Coward! Your foe, your vengeance – your decision! Why should you not enjoy it?*

Then he jumped, violently; for he found himself facing the Nightingale, and that long animalistic countenance was no good thing to come upon so suddenly, in a fireshot dusk.

The creature hopped and giggled, like Alya's voices given flesh. 'Nervous, aren't you? A great big manslayer like you! That was fun, that; like being back home. What now? Oh.' His tongue lapped delicately at his lips. 'I see. Just for fun, or is there something you wish of him?'

Alya shivered. 'We need to know almost anything he can tell us. The women – did they see them? Where might they be taken? Where the way leads, through what lands, to what end? Anything could help.'

Nightingale twittered, and his big black eyes gleamed. 'Silly, silly, silly! Never truly listen to me, do you? I told you, and you never listen! Give him to me! Whatever he knows, I will know, I will tease out for you, I will tell you! Give his life to me! Quick now, before that nasty old man lets him go to waste!'

Without waiting for a word the Nightingale spun around and let out a fearsome, penetrating whistle. A gust of wind whipped and whirled around the clearing; the leaves billowed from the bending birches, the campfires blazed up, streamed out sparks and tongues of roaring flame. It was a hungry, horrible sound. Asquan, advancing on the fallen raider, hurled down the blade and clapped his hands over his ears, and all the others fell back. The Nightingale pushed and slithered between them like an insistent child, scuttled up, pushed Asquan aside and hopped upon the wounded man. He seized the raider's head in those long skinny fingers, almost tenderly, gazing deep into the narrow eyes as if to suck out a soul through them.

Till then the raider had made no more sound, even at the sight of the spear. But now he screamed aloud and struggled; but he could not overturn the creature, and his head shifted not the breadth of a hair in that pale spidery clasp.

Then Nightingale opened his mouth.

That long jaw gaped wider than any human mouth, like a biting snake's. The bloodless lips slipped back over great stubby ape's fangs, with the thin tongue lolling across them, dripping. The raider yelled in mindless terror, but Nightingale's head darted forward. The jaws closed.

The watchers all sprang back with cries of revulsion. Vansha stood like stone. Rysha sank to her knees in fascinated horror, her hard mouth twitching. Kalkan and the soldiers, hard men all, seemed completely helpless, and Asquan stared in appalled fascination. Not one tried to stop the creature; not the bravest would have touched him, not then. Alya shut his eyes, but that only made the noise worse, the popping, crushing sound and the awful liquid noises, lapping, sucking.

'*Stop it!*' Somehow Alya managed to choke out the command. Then he wished he had not; for Nightingale looked up from his feeding, and smiled, and that was a sight not to be easily borne.

'Why, lord? I'm not yet finished. When I have, you may ask me anything you will. Ahh, I have hungered, hungered. And this is a tasty, tasty life!' He bent to his meal again.

Vansha spun on his heel in disgust. 'Is this a fit thing for a man to allow, brother? I thought he meant some kind of, I don't know, reading another's soul! All those broken skulls at the foot of his tree, remember? Ach! I wouldn't have spared that little monster for a moment, if I'd known. Lords they call us! Should lords allow this?'

Alya drew breath. His sickness was all in the mind, his body whole and fell. Even as he had feared, there was a part of him could almost relish this, with bitter-cold enjoyment. 'Lords have done worse, brother. You were ready enough to watch one, just now. Consider this the more merciful way!'

'Merciful!'

'Compared to Asquan's way? Yes! And if that little ghoul serves our need, I may well unleash him again. Have to! The power in me tells me I must! Think, man – this is for Savi! This may be what'll bring us to her!'

'The fires tell you that?'

'As surely as they make me walk. As strongly as
the force they lend my arm!'

Vansha whistled softly. 'They've changed you,
brother. Maybe more than you know.'

'Many things have changed me. But yes, the fires
among them. Not least by depriving me of Sight, of
the Trail, of the Wall – of my father's legacy.'

'Are you so sure? Could you not at least try once
again, rather than – that?'

'Has he finished?'

'Sounds like it.'

'My lord! My lord! I am done, done, done!'
Nightingale was crouched over the prostrate body,
leaping up and down on all four sticklike limbs at
once, gibbering with delight. 'Ask me, ask me anything! This man has *lived*!'

'You learn everything about him by eating . . .'

'No! No! Not *learn* – *live*! All he has done, seen
. . . As it lived in his memory, in his soul . . . I have
both! I have everything, to keep, to chew over, to live
again. Till I forget it all, bit by bit. And find more.'

Alya tried to turn from the creature's breath, and
not to look at what lay beyond. 'Well! Say, then! Look
back, how long . . . Ah. A week or so since.'

Powers, no longer than that?

'A village set in a deep vale. A raid. Many women
taken.'

'Hmm . . .' Nightingale looped a long arm over
his head to scratch his other ear. 'No, not there, are
we? We hear, though. When Wasp clan meets us with
the rest, at stone bridge. Wagonload of villager
bitches. A couple worth the eye. Chieftains mark
them all off, worse luck. For themselves, as usual.
Or for the Great Ones!' Something had changed in the
cretinous piping voice, as if a darker colour stained it.

'For the Great Ones?' demanded Alya, forgetting
his revulsion, feeling as if he stood on the brink of
some vast understanding.

'Surely. As ever. Word down from the top –
They, Themselves. Glad it's not *my* detail! Women;
gather women. Stuff booty, forget weapons – just
women. Young women, any kind, many as you can.
Bring back safe and whole. A choice!'

Alya seized the narrow shoulder. 'But *what for*?'

'And who,' put in Asquan, sounding distinctly
shaken, 'are *They*?'

'*They*? What for?' Nightingale laughed, an unpleasantly familiar bark. 'For life-meat, altar-food, surely! Or
something special. Straight to the Taounehtar her sweet
self, maybe. So not a finger laid on them, not even when
the skinny one skewers that simpleton Wasp! We laugh:
serve the bastard right, all balls, no order. Stands to
reason. What the Ice takes for its own, only a moron
touches. Only a moron!' He chuckled, quietly, a sound
wholly unlike his normal laughter. 'Fiery little bitch,
though. Skinny, but sharp. The Taounehtar's in for
some fun, maybe. Set her sizzling, for a change! No
wonder idiot Wasps lose so many, down there!'

'Down there?' demanded Alya, breathless.

'That dungpit valley. Chieftain's daughter, she
said. Might look in that way myself one day, see if she
has little sisters!'

Alya clenched his fist, shaking with relief and
excitement. 'Thank you, Nightingale! That's she
whom we seek!' Savi would show them, right enough; leaving him a trail even in the minds of their
foes. 'But where they've taken her – does he . . . do
you know?'

Nightingale giggled. 'That one? Nice. Big eyes,
like me. He was right, though – skinny. No meat.'

Alya held Vansha back. 'Where, Nightingale?
Don't ruin it all now!'

The creature shrugged petulantly. 'Northward.
Westward, turning northward. Where else is there,
for the Ekwesh? The only place they are at rest. North,
along this road. In wagons. We see them go.'

'When?' put in Vansha. 'How far ahead?'

Another shrug. 'Not sure. A day and a night? Two days? Three? He was drunk. All drunk.'

Vansha groaned. 'You useless little vermin! If we only knew—'

'We don't need to!' snapped Alya. 'We know she's on this road ahead, and that's enough! We'll ride out at once!'

'Agreed!' said Asquan, who had stood fascinated. 'To horse now and as fast as we can! Did you not hear? The Ekwesh have some kind of guardians. Choosers of the Slain! The Powers alone may guess what that means, but I know I'm not lingering till they find what we've done here!'

'I think I can guess!' said Tseshya grimly. 'And if I'm right, my lord, so are you!'

Alya nodded. 'That's it then! You can explain later, scholar. Ride with the Nightingale meanwhile, learn as much from him as you can about the road; how long? What might we meet along it? Such things. Do you have the skill to make one of these pictures, these map things? Then begin as soon as you can!' He reached for his saddle, and winced as his bruised side complained. 'Wounds and smarts will have to wait, too. Darzhan, Chiansha, Almur, rope up the new horses, any food as well – we'll sort out what we can stomach later. We'll be riding in the dark, but don't complain. It may save us worse troubles!'

Within minutes they were mounted and away, the captured horses trailing behind. The way was so deeply shadowed that they could risk nothing faster than a trot, and Alya watched the horizon uneasily. The overcast was ragged, there; and before long it would be moonrise. Normally he would welcome that; not tonight.

Suddenly Vansha's tall silhouette rode up, breaking into both his line of sight and his black thoughts.

'Alya, brother! I must speak! This damned demon –
now he's demon and Ice-warrior in one!'

Alya held up a hand. 'I know. Do you think I
haven't been turning that over and over? Can we
possibly trust anything that lives – that feeds – like
that?'

'*Yes!* How can we? Powers, how *can* we? He
seems so harmless! Just a little gawk! You start
thinking he's halfway human, a brat almost – and
then . . . Ach, Powers! My guts won't stand the
thought!' His horse whinnied softly as he sagged in
his saddle.

'Then don't think it. He may be the best guide
we can find. And I believe he may be true enough, in
his way. He simply isn't human, and you cannot
blame him for that alone.'

'Maybe not! But that makes me feel no better.
Could you not at least try your Sight once again? To
check on what he says?'

Alya sighed. 'I could not! You saw, when last I
tried. It was – difficult. Painful, even. As if there were
a barrier across my path – across the Trail. The same
feeling this new strength gives me – but turning
against me, like a shower of hot sparks in my head.
And there was more. Another vision entirely, not
within me; from outside. Wings . . . great wings,
against the clouds. Maybe not a vision. Maybe something that saw *me*. Like a hawk that hovers an instant,
before it falls . . . And it might be on the lookout,
once more.'

Vansha sat silent awhile. 'My father could never
believe I had little of the Seer in me, you know that?
When I understood nothing of what he prattled
about, when I could see nothing, he thought I was
pretending, wilfully. He said I was his son, I could not
disgrace him so. He called me lazy, weak, coward; he
thrashed me, till I grew too big to take that! In the end
he made me pretend, so as not to shame him, so as I

could still be chieftain and shaman both. He was wrong; and I have seldom been so glad he was wrong. I wouldn't want the troubles that Seeing brings you. Yet I still wish I had at least a fraction of his power, to try, at least. To try!'

Alya hugged himself in the darkness, jerking the reins, making his horse toss its head and whinny. 'All right. When we stop, I will try.'

They halted at last, in the early hours, when weariness swayed them in their saddles. The moon was weltering in slow, heavy clouds, and showers of cold drizzle came and went; but they found only the grudging shelter of a clump of birch-scrub and black-thorn against the flank of a hill. There was nothing to be done then, and they curled up for what rest they could find. By dawn they were aching and clammy with the trickles that had somehow condensed under their oiled cloaks; and they greeted even the invisible sunrise and its thin glow with relief. Kalkan and Asquan began to bicker about building a fire, and whether it would cause too much smoke, if there were enemies nearby; which, of course, nobody knew.

'Same old problem,' observed Vansha. 'Alya?'

Alya nodded. Now he had made his mind up, it no longer seemed so terrible. 'Yes. Now would be a good time, I think. Hunger and cold are the Seer's friends. Meanwhile, you can also wake up the Nightingale and set him to work with the scholar.'

'A pleasure.' Vansha hobbled stiffly over to the ponies.

Alya sat for a moment, cross-legged, head in hands. He would have to think about this, move carefully at every step. Better not to dance, at first; better to remain in control, ready to fall back at any moment. He had no sand, but under the bushes he grubbed up drier handfuls of the rich crumbly soil. After a moment he sat back, and crossed his legs. The others saw his eyes flutter closed, and his hands move, trickling the earth out on to the damp ground. After a moment it was exhausted, but still his hands moved as if pouring something fine and precious, with deadly care. It was a strange sight; but when Vansha returned he watched, fascinated, and they saw the sweat break out on his brow.

'That is the true Path!' he whispered to the others. 'I know it! It draws me as I watch . . .'

Then Alya jolted as if struck, and slumped forward. They rushed to raise him, and found him pale and sweating, but awake. 'Only . . . a glimpse . . .' he panted, before they could ask. 'Blood, death – confused – but I saw it . . .'

'You crested the Wall?' asked Vansha softly.

'I tried . . . I drew near, I was hurled back . . . then I touched thought . . . more as if I was caught up and borne over it . . . from a vast height, terrifying . . .' He struggled to separate the impressions in his mind, a confused whirl of images and colours through sight that seemed far sharper than his own. 'Vansha, I saw; but not by crossing the Wall, not directly. I saw through other eyes!'

Vansha nodded. 'My father said something about that. How you could see across the Wall – using the minds of beasts and birds . . .'

'Mine told me that, too. Said it wasn't the best way. But the fires bar me, whatever way I seek directly.'

Vansha scratched his head. 'If the front door's blocked, hop around the back!'

Alya nodded. 'I'll try again. I have the Trail still, I think.' He looked at the others. 'It might be better if you leave me alone. Go down the slope.'

Maybe being alone would give him more strength, and in a high place, as high as there was in the lands around, anyhow. But after a few interminable minutes he shrugged, went to his saddlebags and drew out the crooked beak of Raven, and placed it reverently on his head. Then he stiffened; the fires had flamed up suddenly, driving a dart of pain down his back, from the crown of his head to the sinews of his ankles, breathtaking, icy. But he tapped one hand into the other in slow rhythm, like a drum; and gradually made it faster, clapping now, loudly, to the beat of the song he intoned beneath his breath. He stamped his feet to the beat, twisting this way and that; until at last, forgetting where he stood, forgetting all else, he began to dance across the hillcrest, shuffling and sliding his feet in a wide twisting pattern, the way of the Path.

He found the pattern of earth written on the darkness, pulsing with the pulse in his eyelids, and he traced it further, as he had before, found it ran ahead of him like a burning thread, faster and faster, turning with the force of the fire . . .

The flames roared, the dark glass towered over him; but he ignored them, searching upward, searching for wings. Something found them, not sight, not sound; simple awareness. Abruptly they were his, and his eyes opened on dripping greenery flashing by on either side. It could be the bushes at his back, probably was; a small bird, a low flier.

'I need hawks!' he gasped, to whom he could not imagine. 'Something greater! Give me height! Give me sky!'

The stinging shower filled his mind, but it seemed less tormenting, more distant. Then suddenly he was through it, and into a dazzling realm of light, flashes of whiteness, slashes of blue, pure blazing light that exploded into rainbow hues on the margins of his wide vision, inhumanly wide. The whiteness was the eternal clouds; but he was above them now, where the sun shone in a constant cold blue sky. He wheeled and dived among the troughs of grey moisture, screaming for the sheer delight of it. And then he

turned to the northward, by the sun; and saw the Wall
once more, its dark facets flashing the rays of the sun
into lancing spears. He was level with it; he was
looking across it – and suddenly there was no Wall
there at all, only a vast, an infinite landscape over
which he drifted, desperate to orient himself, fighting
to pick out the details that flashed by with the stark
clarity of a dream.

So much seemed to be happening, wherever he
turned. He could see right across the lands he knew,
as it seemed, and beyond, from sky to sky. It could not
be a real landscape, to be seen in so much detail; and
yet all that it showed him was real enough, a glimpse
of the moment throughout the real world. That he
knew, both from his father's teaching and from the
feeling in his bones; yet what he saw came as a
revelation.

He had thought these lands so empty; but they
were not. To east and west, all across these great
expanses of brown and green and stony grey, veined
silver by a net of southward-flowing rivers, were
scattered little pockets of humanity, towns and cities
like Volmur's. Some seemed to have risen up on the
bones of others more ancient, looking weak and
scrappy among those massive grey relicts. They were
everywhere he looked; but they were just too far
apart, the nearest four weeks' ride or more, usually
much more – too far to be neighbours, near enough
to be remote rivals, a distant, uncertain threat. And
across the lands, as he saw, long lines of dark-
armoured horsemen rode, not merely a few reiving
bands but huge campaigns. And here and there black
smoke curled above a city's towers, or from the
scorched lands close around another, held in a tight
ring of siege.

Seeking the way, he scanned the rivers nearest,
and swiftly saw what looked like the great bridge
they had crossed, the trampled camping ground, the

greater road westward. He was about to follow their track, when smoke caught his eyes. Out along the other road it lay, and looking that way he saw a burst of red light, too early to be the sunset, too intense.

His eyes – could he call them his? – followed it to its source, and he went dropping down the wind in search. It could not be that far beyond the bridge, surely; a few weeks' march. Already, at this distance he could take in buildings in flames, whole streets outlined in curling blossoms of fire, already dying down as their hearts turned ashen. A city, of sorts, as great as Volmur's; yet not nearly so great as those he had seen in flames, in his distant dreams. Without will, his flight somehow carried him low towards it, almost into the flames, as if sporting with their licking heat. Nothing stirred; and still shapes lay among the burning streets. This must have been the task of the main band of raiders; and indeed there were files of horsemen and laden wagons leading away from the ruined walls, and lines of chained captives, men and women both. Leading away across the brown lands to the northward; and there was nothing he or his could hope to do for them. Dark wings circled the column of smoke, wings that beat in slow unison, massive shapes that rode the heated air and climbed away skyward. He thought of the great vultures of the mountains. Even the carrion birds had finished their task here.

It had been easy to forget his purpose, for a moment, in the sheer joy of this airy existence, both real and unreal, in the hunger to take in all that it showed him. But the sad sight brought it all back to him, sharp as a spearthrust, and guiltily he sought to gain height again, to turn the eyes back the way he sought. It was not so easy; they seemed to be growing recalcitrant, and the clouds and the land plunged and whirled around him for long moments. Struggling to fix them, he saw the river go by, and the bridge once again, even the dell where he knew he must truly be. Beyond it, stooping once again, he made out a great strip of the landscape that looked rougher, taller than the grassland, like a forest; and yet he could imagine no trees of that strange grey-green hue, flecked with dark yellow.

He struggled to see more closely, saw instead green hills beyond it, a hue richer even than the mountain valley he remembered, and not without woods and other greenery. A fair enough country, yet ominous somehow, draped in trailing mists that rolled leadenly along the dark metallic rivers. For to the north of it, here and there where the haze grew thinner, he saw the green vanish quite suddenly and give way to brown, a brown that spoke of bleaker lands of a kind his father had told him about, thinner soil, scrubbier grass, and beneath it, even under the hottest sun, an undying layer of frost.

And it was not far, not far at all from the margins of this brown land, that he at last made out the thing he sought, the same road that he and the others now followed; and upon it a train of wagons. Like many others he might have seen that day, he guessed; save that this was shorter, and its escort light, and it moved more swiftly than he had expected. There was real urgency upon it, a constant speed that kicked up a trail of dust even in these dampening lands, and jolted and bounced the wagons along the track. At first he hoped devoutly it was not the one; but as he struggled to hold his vision firmly in mind he knew with a failing heart that it must be. The road unrolled beneath him, before and behind, back into that strange greenery and out again, across the brown fells ahead, straighter than the river it paced, with little compromise to the lie of the land; and there was no other such train upon it, not anywhere.

Further ahead than he had tried to promise himself, far further. And at that pace . . .

His sight was wrenched away again. He could not be sure how far; he had not seen enough to guess. Bitter, desperate, he fought the mind he touched, struggled to stifle its will with his own; but whatever creature it was, the steadiness he wanted was not in its nature, and he could not maintain it. He imagined a swift or a swallow or a small speedy hawk, a living, shrilling arrow made for dashing and diving through the air, suddenly constrained to sail steady as an eagle or buzzard, unable to evade its enemies or hunt its prey. He was asking too much of it. Eagle or buzzard indeed, that was what he needed; or one of those great vultures he had seen. He set his thoughts upon them, and sensed the easy gliding, the wind whistling beneath broad unflapping wings. He cast loose his hold upon the other, which shot away with explosive grace, and opened a new pair of eyes.

Blankness greeted him, blind pallor that terrified him for a moment, till blue sky gleamed through a breach, and the cloud around them thinned. The first he saw was other wings, to either side; vast black wings; and others beyond. Vultures did not fly in formation, though; and these wings looked broader, the necks longer. But then they burst out of the cloud, and he forgot all else in the breathless awe of his vision.

They were higher indeed, far higher. Lesser clouds hung between him and the landscape, gleaming in the cold sun. The rivers mirrored them. There was his; they were diving towards it now! A steep, plunging descent that took his breath away, as if he were falling from sun to earth like some ancient demigod. There was the great road, a line scored through the lands, there was their own way, a thread alongside the seam of the river. There that weird forest, there the hills, sweeping past his sight as they turned; their covering dwindling, their trees shrinking, huddling to the earth, vanishing, the very green fading all too swiftly to that drained, half-barren brown, and beyond it only a deathly grey. And there the river again, blued steel fading to black, and over it, gleaming here and there with rainbow hues in the sun, a white haze that hid the horizon.

Or did it? The horizon shimmered in the sun; but it was not all mist. Beyond cloud and hill, at the margins of what could be seen, a flash of dazzling light lit the edge of the world, and showed it jagged and broken, as if the very stuff of the rocks had been shattered by a titanic blow, and the world split away. There the land lost its colours. It looked to be a country of stones far colder and deader than the worst deserts east of the Citadel. They were dying lands, maybe; but this was long dead. The low rolling hills shone pale and colourless, the flat scraped land beyond them a stony, speckled grey-white, the mists that wreathed and rolled about it whiter still. Yet all looked pallid and tainted compared to the dazzling blue-white rim. There were cliffs there, cliffs that followed the very curve of the world to the ends of sight; white mountain-walls rising out of those mists, and opening only upon more of the same.

He had reached the limits of his vision. He knew that from this great distance he looked upon his ultimate enemy and all men's, all things that truly lived and were glad; he saw at road's end the Walls of Winter, the fortress, domain and weapon of the Great Ice.

Their sheer extent and scale struck terror into him, as well they might into the boldest of men: the grasp that encompassed half the world, and yearned with icy desire for the remainder. Before that his concerns, his self even, seemed diminished and daunted; he did not want to look upon it any longer, he did not dare. And he must concentrate upon the road!

This was as bad as the other mind, this slow

wheeling dive. He could hardly see straight. It was there! The road, the dust, the wagons once again, far below, far ahead but drawing nearer. If he could only dive a little lower, see the wagons, some trace of what they held! He bore down upon the eyes he looked through, strove to have them level out and fly straight, straight along the path he sought . . .

The thoughts he touched looked back at him. And they looked with appalling force.

Who? WHO?

It was like a voice, like a bird's cry, screaming in his ear, so loud the very bones of his face seemed to reverberate.

Show yourself!

He had never felt less like obeying an order. Yet something told him that it would be deeply dangerous to stay silent and submissive.

'*You show your own damned self!*' he panted, and undying fire leaped to his thought. The landscape heeled, violently. His sight vanished. Darkness enveloped him. There was nothing except a horrible, sickening fall, into more dark; and in that blackness a face – a mask, not unlike his own, a bird's countenance but shorter and flatter in the bill. Black, with white markings and eyes outlined in red; staring, terrible eyes. Something struck at him, a frightening collision that brought exploding lights of pain; and another mind assailed his own. A rush of disjointed thoughts poured over him, as if to drown his by their very force. Like his own, but more smoothly, the mask dropped open. Within it, eyes closed, mouth open as if gasping, was the face of a girl.

It was not Savi. It was nobody he had ever seen, like nobody he had ever seen. The cast of it was strange, the eyes, the cheekbones, the hard planes of the jaw, everything; and the long hair, strange to tell, was not black, like all normal human hair, but curling threads of what could have been pure gold. He thought it very fair, yet frightening. It was spattered, as was all the face, with small smears of glistening red. And even as he admired its serene calm, like living ivory, the eyes narrowed and the expression shifted to incandescent fury.

WHO?

Like claws fixing in his flesh, raking, digging deep for the veins—

He hurled himself back, he remembered familiar sights good and bad, he clung to them, he ran to them, to himself. He sought Savi, but she blurred and became that beautiful face, swooping down on him with terrifying force and a vast thunder of wings. Once again the river wheeled beneath him, a broad bend lined with reedbeds and little inlets and side streams, and far away from it now, the road, the distance . . . He tore free, and flung himself away back. The last he saw, those wide dark wings, many of them, all around him, beating with appalling strength; yet all of them spotted and slathered with clots of bright scarlet . . .

Light burst in on him, long golden rays of the rising sun stabbing through the clouds. Somebody was panting, so hard they were almost sobbing. Himself. He found himself, back on the hillcrest, on his knees, panting, with the mask at his feet. He staggered to his feet, limp and bewildered, to find the others on the slope below, staring up at him.

'Are you—' ventured Vansha, and got no further.

'What've you seen, lad?' demanded Kalkan. 'You were doing some strange things—'

Alya blinked about him, about the lands around, struggling to regain himself, to understand. Then he saw the river, gleaming barely a couple of thousand paces away, and in sudden fright he scanned the northward sky.

Dark against the cloud they wheeled, as if in anger or distress, wide-winged shadows against the shining air. He snatched up the mask, and bundled it into its bag. 'Get out!' he yelled. 'Get to cover, fast! Hide the horses! That body, too! Anywhere!'

Vansha opened his mouth, but Alya hissed, 'No time!' Nightingale, watching him wide-eyed, gave one sharp sniff of the air, yelped, and bounded for the baggage ponies. Asquan was already seizing the horses, and Kalkan and the soldiers after him, experienced enough to know an alarm when they heard it. Chiansha scooped up the protesting Tseshya, and together they swung the body into the bushes, then grabbed their horses and drew them in after. Rysha rolled headlong under a thorn-bush, yelped, and stifled it at Alya's glare. The little glade was suddenly empty of all save meaningless debris.

Alya peered up through the veil of twigs at the sky. It remained obstinately clear, and he was just beginning to relax when a half-dozen huge shadows, at least, swept across the space from a wholly unexpected direction, so low the downdraught pressed down the twigs overhead, and blew dead leaves in gusts from the mould. With strange, lonely cries they wheeled about the clearing, and were gone.

It was long minutes of silence before anybody stirred, lest they come around again. 'What in the world was *that*?' demanded Vansha, in Alya's ear.

'I'm not sure,' admitted Alya. 'But they were dangerous. Searchers in the sky. Their thoughts were all of battle and war.'

'I might guess a name for them,' said Asquan quietly. "Or Tseshya."

Alya shrugged. 'So might I. I don't know. But they will search a while longer. For now you'd better lie low, hide yourselves! Hole up here awhile. I . . . I need one of the fresher horses. There's something I have to seek, to understand.'

'Alone, brother?' demanded Vansha. 'You'll need me along, at least!'

'No, brother! You least of all!' Vansha, being who he was, could wreck everything, but there was no way to tell him that. 'You must stay with the band; someone must survive who knows Savi. Keep northward on this road and you should find the wagon tracks again. I believe she is with them still; but they are days ahead, even further than I feared. If I do not return – greet her for me. And you, Asquan, stay also.'

'You must take someone!' protested Asquan.

'Part of the way, then. My Lord Kalkan?'

'At your service, lad. Whither away?'

'Towards that river there. Towards a great reedbed. I think I can tell the one. But you must stay well back. What may be there is a mystery no man can match.'

'Except you, eh?'

'Except, perhaps, me.'

They galloped down from the hill into the rising sun, across grassland that was smooth and easy going, and down on to the flatter floodplain beyond, where growth was richer and more tangled, the ground boggier and harder to pass. After a short time they dismounted in the shelter of low trees some hundred paces from the great river bend, while he scanned the banks. There were reedbeds aplenty, but one, in the crook of the stream, extended out a good wide way into the water, with a more solid shadow at its heart that stood out beneath the growing disc of gold. 'That one!' said Alya decisively, and Kalkan picked up his spear.

Alya barred him. 'Come with me no further! One may succeed where two would be seen!' He hurriedly stripped off mail and jacket, belt and boots, keeping only shirt and breeches, with his dagger in the waistband.

'You know something,' said Kalkan, tugging at his moustache. 'Whose thought did you touch, Seer?'

'Cold ones, warrior. You would not be glad to

know more. I need you to wait, and watch, my lord!'
Which brother Vansha would not have been content
to do. 'If I call, come help! Otherwise, wait till all is
quiet, then ride back as if demons were after you. Or
they may be! Get the others to the road again. It will
be no use looking for me.'

Kalkan nodded calmly. 'Makes sense. Good luck,
then – weather-luck, weapon-luck, woman-luck, a
man can never have too much of those!'

'Truer than you know, my lord!' The reeds
hissed in the wind, mockingly. 'There. That's where
I'll be.'

The river bank was an illusion. Only a little way
beyond the trees it grew soggy and moss-ridden, and
here and there patches of bog sucked noisily at his
bare feet. He winced at every sound, thanking the
Powers that the wind was in his face; and at last he
cast himself down and slithered like a serpent across
the quaggy ground, as silent and as subtle – or so he
hoped. He came to the edge of the reeds, and there
was water under his breast; but he hardly heeded its
cold caress, when he saw the arrowhead of wings
come gliding down the sky. Keeping ever low, he
pulled himself forward, half crawling, half swimming
through the matted vegetation to the low island in its
midst, scarcely more than a sandbar. The cold bit at
him; but fire drove his limbs where plain strength
might have failed. The water was so thick with rotting
debris that he had to struggle to sink down, but he
managed it, smearing mud over his exposed face.
Only just in time; for the swans circled low over the
water with wings widespread and feet outstretched.
They left hardly a ripple as they settled on the calm
dark water

Swans; but black. A kind he had never seen –
huge birds, as great as the vast vultures of the high
steppes and mountain airs, glossy black in plumage
and bill, with red-rimmed eyes. With regal grace they

came sailing in towards the reeds, like the ships he
had dreamed of, and he watched in growing awe. He
guessed what was to come, but he was no more
prepared when it happened – the swans, as they
reached the reeds, rearing upwards in the water with
a great thrash of wings, outspread as if to buffet an
enemy. For a moment primal terror, colder than the
water, struck him breathless, the numbing fear that
lies in all things beyond nature.

Yet then a wonder no less chilling took its place,
as he saw the black plumage drop away from pale
bare shoulders, whirled off like so many cloaks, and
be cast down upon the sandy shore. One fell within
feet of him at the water's edge. Where the swans had
been, nine naked girls splashed in the shallows,
frolicking as carefree and shrill as any young peasant
girls, and with as little dignity.

Yet peasants these could never be, nor anything
within the common run. No two were akin; for their
skins were of many hues, and their hair of shades
he had never guessed at. Only two had the black hair
and level eyes that were the only human kind he knew,
and of those just one a ruddy-brown skin like his own;
lithe and lean-bodied, small breasts bouncing, she
reminded him heartstoppingly of Savi. The other
was paler and yellower, like fine parchment, and
her features smaller and less distinct: like a doll's, he
thought. But compared to the rest she looked normal.

Some were dark, one so dark he wondered if she
were still part-swan; but her skin shone glossy brown
in the water as another girl washed her back. Her face
was strange but fine, cheekbones high, lips full; and at
least her hair, however strangely curled, was a decent
black. Others were deathly pale in his eyes, their skin
white enough to be shaded by the blood beneath, like
the white-bone demons he had heard of in his youth.
One of these had short dark hair that seemed normal
enough, a slender frame and neat features; but the

others were startling. One, taller and more stalwart by his standards, had long straight hair like a fall of gold indeed, and as she turned, running her hands through it, he recognised his vision, the face in the mask. A troubled face, if he could read those unfamiliar features, less blithe than the rest. He could guess why.

But eeriest of all was another, also tall and strongly built, but with a skin that was pale to transparency, save where it was oddly mottled, like a beast's, all over cheek and shoulder and thigh – mottled the same terrifying hue as her shaggy crop of hair. The very sight of her appalled him. These had to be shape-shifting demons, surely; for what remotely human creature could have red hair?

Yet he was seeing them here unguarded, as themselves, and they behaved as girls. He remembered the tales of the men beyond the wide waters. Could these creatures reflect different races, shaped by different climes?

The idea fascinated him; and so, for all his thoughts of Savi, did their bodies. He had never imagined beauty could come in so many different guises, so strange and yet so much alike. Nobody in the village had concerned themselves much about nakedness, among folk they had known all their lives; yet lads still spied upon girls bathing, older ones especially – and sometimes, Savi had told him, the other way about. As an outcomer they had usually barred him, but this had the same tinge of mischief about it, spiced with a more adult shiver of danger.

They stirred his blood and his body, those girls, so that even with Savi in his mind he ached to be there among them, to seize one or many of those bodies, search out their secrets and the heat of their pleasures, the taste, the scent, the sheer essence of woman that he missed so much. But his blood needed no chilling; who could say what would happen to him if they so much as sensed his presence?

Demons they might not be, the human form came naturally enough to them – might once have been their own, even. And yet now they were scarcely more human than if they had been swans, indeed, wearing hands only to wash themselves clean. That was the purpose of their game, though it pleased them also, perhaps, a pleasure whose wildness hinted at their nature.

That, he had no wish to arouse; yet the ache drove him to be foolhardy. Them he could not touch; but he eased forward, still hidden under reeds and murky water, till he could stretch out and stroke the nearest cloak.

He almost gasped aloud at the touch. Feathers indeed; but they felt not like a discarded garment, but a living fell, with quickening flesh beneath. Something about it was sticky and congealed. The girl with light-brown skin exclaimed, turned quickly to her sisters, then to the swan-cloak where it lay. But Alya's hand was beneath the surface again, and he lay deadly still. She would have seen him, had she waded over; but she shrugged, and turned again to steeping her long black tresses. He slid slowly away, breathing as shallowly as he dared, propelling himself with his trembling fingers, no more. He knew now of what they cleansed themselves, what had spattered the fair face. He had touched blood.

He drew back barely in time; for they took up the swanhames, and drew them through the water, combing them with their fingers, preening almost. He watched the bend and sway of their haunches and breasts, drawing a wry pleasure from the mingled menace and allure. So strange, yet so ordinary, young girls in nature, as if that nature ran far beyond the confines of the mere body. He knew now what he had come to make sure of, that the things he had glimpsed through the eyes of the golden one were true, and not some delusion or extension of his fancy.

Had there been another reason? Had he hoped to see this kind of a sight? He realised he probably had. Foolish; but human, for all the might of the Powers that had been thrust into him. Perhaps Powers could also be foolish; and in that there might lie some obscure hope. At least now he might make some sense of the jumble of thoughts he had picked up from that other overbearing mind.

He watched the girls still, as they shook their cloaks free of water with careless strength, like great wingbeats, and shrieking laughter as they soaked one another once again. Then one, the girl with parchment-shaded skin, flung hers about her shoulders once more and ran splashing through the shallows; but she flung wide her arms, and it was a swan that rose into the noon sun. With a vast fluttering rush, like a great breath, the others lifted in a cloud behind her, not paddling along the surface like ordinary swans, but soaring up into the light, heading straight and swift to the northward. His desire soared with them; and the fires surged in his blood. What he had seen was true. That was the way he must go.

'What did you see?' demanded Vansha, as they plodded back into camp.

'Down there?' growled Kalkan. 'He's been for a paddle, but he won't say. Few ducks off the river, that was all I saw.'

'I saw . . .' began Alya, shivering over the miserable little fire that was the most they dared kindle. His desire had succumbed to bone-chill. 'I had a vision; more than one. Tseshya, have you and Nightingale got anywhere with your map?'

'Somewhere!' grunted the scholar, glaring at Nightingale. 'A lot further, if I could hold his attention for two breaths in three! And talking of his breath . . .'

He caught Alya's glare, and hastily thrust a leaf of reed-paper at him. Alya nodded absently, turning it this way and that, trying to read Tseshya's impossibly

ornate letters. 'Yes,' he murmured, more to himself.
'This here – and here – this is what I saw! Through the
bird's eye – and hers. In the rush of the wind—'

Flame flared in him, and he was no longer cold.
Memory brought the crude page suddenly to life. He
had striven to find what he should be able to see, the
line of the great road, and saw it pass crazily by. The
wagons, the dust – he had yearned for some sight of
her, some confirmation. And yet he did not really
need it. He traced the line of the road, saw how true
its path lay – for indeed, it came from the mind of one
who knew it – and saw also in that a devastation of his
hopes.

'Well?' demanded Vansha.

'A good map. I can add to it. I saw them, brother
– just here.'

'There? But on that measure . . .'

'Yes. Well on their way. They move faster, those
wagons, than ever we gave them credit for. They
drew fresh guards from the main army, no doubt,
fresh horses. So now they are five days ahead, even;
and getting further.'

'But when can we hope to catch them up?'
demanded Vansha anxiously.

'We cannot,' said Alya, and was amazed at how
calm he felt. 'Not as such. They will have reached
their journey's end long before, if I am right.'

Vansha crumpled and grew angry, all at once.
'How so? Where will it end, then?'

Alya's fingers strayed across the blank area at the
upper edge of the leaf. He had reached the bounds of
his memory, and suddenly he was back among the
others again, squinting at mere paper in the feeble
firelight. But he realised, with deepening astonishment, that it was not wholly blank. There were no
roads, no rivers marked; but within its very bounds,
there were a few lonely circles.

He looked up at Tseshya, in speechless astonishment; and the scholar nodded, grimly. 'Within it, yes. So the man's memory says. Within the walls of winter, its very heart and substance.'

Circles, the signs the scholar had used to indicate towns.

Vansha closed his eyes. 'You tell me – they're taking her into the Great Ice itself?'

Alya flung his hands wide. 'Where else? Should that stop us trying? At least we know now where we're headed, my friends. Do we not?'

Once again, very lightly, he tapped the map.

CHAPTER 7
Children of Powers

SAVI woke, as always, with a start. Her dreams had been bad; and that too was usual. The straw in the wagon was flattened and stale, no longer even slightly comfortable, crawling with vermin, stinking of bodies too little washed, and of worse than that: of despair. Since the barge had landed them again they had moved away from the river into low hills, with only small streams, and both these and the weather generally had become too cold to allow all but the most perfunctory wash. Some of the girls had let themselves go, sinking into despondency and inaction, caring no longer about themselves or each other.

One, whom Savi had known all her life, had begun to cough and grown feverish and delirious, and the guards had cut her loose lest she infect anyone else. Probably she had been left dying on the brown hills. Another had seemed well enough, though silent; but around the time the sliver of brown beyond the flapping canvas turned gradually to snowy grey, she had begun, very quietly, to injure herself, on the wagon side, the ropes, once on Savi's sword and finally on anything else she could reach. They had had to bind her wrists and ankles. In the end she seemed to grow reconciled, promised to stop; and that night bit through her tongue and bled to death. They had thrown out as much of the bloody straw as possible, but it still seemed to be adding its sickly smell to all the rest. Her body was dumped in the snow-sprinkled barrens that had depressed her so much.

In such a time Savi was grateful for the princess Ulie, whose head now seemed almost impossible to upset. Even her prissy habits, her pathetic attempts at neatness and polite behaviour, became virtues, because they were surprisingly good defences against the ugliness around them. Savi took to following her poise and her speech, when she could, and coaxed her to tell tales of her life at court. She was only too eager, and her stories let Savi imagine herself among lords and ladies and their intrigues – although, reading between the lines, the court was evidently a shadow of past glories, and its nobles not so different from ordinary villagers with their little jealousies and scandals. The Princess, in turn, began to ask about the Citadel, and seemed to take equal delight in the idea of living a simple rustic existence, as she put it. She and Savi set the tone for the rest, and were their leaders in all things. When they laughed, fear lifted a little from the others, and they hardly dared be seen to falter or weep. That was a burden indeed, and the Princess bore it better than she.

So it had been for long weeks now, of slow jolting along stony roads and rutted trails, an increasingly snowy landscape. The wagon had become viciously cold, though the guards gave them warmer rags and even tattered, greasy old grey cloaks which added another smell to the cart. They huddled together at night. Then, one bitter blowy afternoon, they felt the road start to slope beneath them, and the ironbound wheels had begun to crunch and furrow something other than stony earth. A wholly different sound they made, a popping, squeaking noise that somehow caught at one's guts; and the wagon ploughed this way and that. There were always black-clad guards following along close to heave at the wheels, now wound in rope for traction, or lever the wagon along when it began to skid. A desperate cold crept around the cart, that bit through rags and straw, so the women's only defence was to huddle close, almost in a heap; and only those at the centre were warm.

They could see little, still, save through the tiny gaps in the cover, the open flap behind. But they knew then, the women, that they had come at last to the fortress and fastness of the forces that had over-shadowed all their lives, the fear that had hung over them all, high and low, all their lives. They were crossing the surface of a glacier; and who had not heard that the glaciers were the Walls of Winter, the realm and palace and home of the ancient Powers of the Ice?

That had been just as the last moon shrank to nothing; and last night the new moon had glittered fiercely between the flaps of the cart, blotting out the dying campfires outside. Their guards had allowed them only a few minutes to exercise and answer nature, then bundled them unceremoniously back in. The air was so still it seemed to drink sound, until they heard the vast sobbing cry of some unimaginable beast echoing across the wastes. Savi had slept clasping that sword so tightly she had nicked herself a little between arm and breast, and woke with a sticky trickle of blood across it. The princess's sharp eyes caught it at once, and widened in alarm.

'An accident!' Savi whispered. 'Fear not, I'm not going the way of the other. I'd sooner make a few raiders bleed, and most of all the brute that's had us dragged here!'

The princess smiled wearily. 'May I live to see it! May we all!'

The other girls were stretching, complaining, accusing one another of stealing a crust of dinner or breaking wind overmuch in the night, a mild familiar squabble that was almost comforting. They waited for their brief release, for their dish of scraps in hot broth; and when neither appeared, and the wagon simply jolted into motion, the protest turned into screaming confusion. Guards ran up, flung open the rear and started screaming too, which helped not at all. The dawn air that flooded in was cold beyond belief, and so utterly dry it bit at eyes and nose and throat, sucking out the moisture. Beyond them the background was blotted out completely, white, featureless, so that the cart seemed to dangle in terrifying emptiness. The women gave back, their throats drying out; and finally the princess quelled the uproar. Savi, careful to remind the guards of her sword, angrily demanded food and release.

'No food!' snapped the guard. 'None left!'

'Your moustache is still greasy!' she snapped back.

'We need! We work! We hurry! You just ride. Soon, 'fore sundown, we there. Then you eat! You wait, you shut up, we let you out when we rest!'

They vanished, and the wagon lurched and heaved horribly.

'If I have to piss over the side,' fumed Savi, 'I hope it's when his shoulder's to the wheel.'

The girls shrieked. 'Let's all do it! One of us is bound to score!'

'It'll freeze and kill him!'

Perhaps the guards overheard, for they were let out within the hour, briefly. Savi, with her feet wrapped in wisps of straw, stepped down gingerly, on to snow that squeaked and crunched like dry sand, and did not melt even for a moment. The guards lay about exhausted, and it took little effort to guess how murderous the ice track behind them must have been. As the women looked back they could still see nothing. A mist of sparkling ice hung in the air, so solid that moving bodies appeared to leave gaps and trails through it. Every movement seemed to suck the heat out, and stiffen the limbs, and the ground bit at their feet.

'We hurry!' remarked the princess quietly, wiping her face with a little powdery snow. Savi tried to wash herself with more, and yelped.

'We'd better not be reduced to this for long! Pray to the Powers they do get us off this awful stuff before tonight!'

The princess was not looking at her. 'Before tonight? I would not waste your breath, my dear. Look! The mist is lifting!'

Savi gulped, and the icy air in her lungs felt deadly. The fog rolled and billowed in a wispy breath of breeze, and it was as if the ice crystals condensed into a whole new world. Behind them, a slope of greenish-white, glittering ice, strangely rutted and scored, overlain with clean white snow in low drifts; save where, here and there, bare black rock broke through like a clean obsidian blade, shining with rime. To either side, the same; and ahead, more level, a plain of ice, almost free of snow, that shimmered dazzlingly all the way to the distant slopes where it met blue sky and white clouds.

Every bit as bright and clear, these, as on a fine spring day at home; but here they were sharper, clearer, cruel, because all things were. This land was a threat to life itself, made solid. And Savi could clearly see that, early in the day as it was, there could be no way out of it before the light vanished.

'Mustn't tell the rest!' was all she muttered; and the princess nodded. Their destination must surely be death on the ice, as sacrifices, perhaps, to who knew what; and she clutched at the sword that was her only hold on destiny. Should she sell her life dearly? Or kill the others, to save them from worse? The idea nearly broke her spirit. Even stripped of hope, she simply could not do that. But she would send a few raiders on ahead, to make a sacrifice of her own.

If, that was, she still had the strength. She felt now how the journey had drained her, the imprison-

ment, the scanty exercise, the poor food, the continual jolting upon her body and her mind. And as
always she thought of Alya. She had always believed
she understood what his imprisonment had been like,
in a ruined body and a place where he had no real
home or family. She knew now, a hundred times
better; and she could not hold back her tears. She
would never be able to tell him, now.

But the chill wind both explained the tears and
dried them, and she mounted the cart again stony-
faced, glaring as hard as she could at the guards who
had lied to her. Those two – any two she could reach
– and then rest, and forgetting. There were worse
prospects than that. She sank into black thoughts, and
not even the princess dared disturb her, so much so
that she hardly noticed the change that the afternoon
brought.

'We're going downhill!' she said suddenly, as she
felt herself sliding to the end of the cart.

'My dear, we have been for an hour at least,'
observed the princess mildly, examining a cracked
nail. 'It's just growing steeper. May I use the tip of
your sword?' She pared away the ragged edge gently.
'That's better. I believe the cold must make them
brittle. Yes, this does seem more than just another ice-
slope. Deeper.'

Savi absorbed what she was saying. There might
have been something they couldn't see back there,
some vale hidden among the white. She reached up
to the endflap, dragging the others with her, and
risked peering out. There was nothing but an ice-wall
behind them, but it looked worked in places, as if cut
away; and it shifted past them as they watched,
exposing cliffs of cracked black rock. The cart was
turning.

'As it has once or twice already,' remarked the
princess. Savi nodded, imagining a road zigzagging
down a steep hillside. It still did not sound good; but

there might be something here. The wheels were biting into something harder than snow, and no longer skidding and slipping over ice.

Then the cart shook and shuddered, and the girls clung together as they heard the rattle and swish of falling stones. Some drummed across the cart's taut cover. The horses neighed, men cursed, and underlying it all was a deep rumble they felt as much as heard, the voice of a mountain grumbling. Even in the fetid cart a strange, rotting odour seemed to tinge the air.

'Like some great beast!' said one of the girls fearfully.

'A dragon,' whimpered another. The princess snorted her derision.

But that was not the greatest strangeness. The rumbling stopped, and the voices outside did not seem more fearful or angry than before. But another noise grew over the trundling of the carts, low but different, a droning hum that changed constantly; the harder you listened the less clear it became. The slope beneath them was growing shallower all the time, and the wheels crunched in what might have been stony soil or gravel. The hum was growing in intensity swiftly, other sounds surging suddenly up out of it like fish leaping and falling back.

The princess wrinkled her nose. 'That sounds almost like . . .'

'A village!' exclaimed one of the girls. 'A market day!'

'A town, more like,' said Savi. 'But it'd be too big for that, even – and you're forgetting where we are! Maybe a big waterfall or something . . .'

They could see nothing through the back of the cart, save the grey-white hillside losing its gleam in the failing light. Yet here and there a different kind of light flickered faintly across it, like firelight on a wall; and the air felt almost warm. The noise was increas-

ing, a roaring, a growing tumult. Savi sat feeling more
and more uneasy, desperate to see what was out
there, but afraid of what it would show her, making
her fate too clear. She guessed the others felt the
same; and that made her impatient.

'I'm tired of seeing nothing but where I've been!'
she snapped, and stabbed her swordpoint through
the taut cover. 'Let's have a really good look at
whatever their devilry is!'

Red confusion swirled across her eyes. She recoiled, startled; and then, so as not to make the others
anxious, she pressed her eyes to the wide slit again.

She was looking out into deep shadow. She
could just see a strip of sky, pallid and dim now
the sun had set behind the glacier slopes above. All
below was a pool of gloom. But the shadow had light
of its own, shades of many colours, flickering and
leaping, a whirl of movement about her. She was
surrounded by fire.

By a host of fires. By innumerable spots and lines
of light in the dark, whose very brightness concealed
their source. Some might be bare hearths and firepits,
maybe, peaks of leaping flames and beds of glowing
coals. Others, like flashing gems coming and going in
the dark, might be ovens and furnaces, with here and
there a splash and trickle of flame, a shower of sparks.
Lesser gleams might be lamps or braziers, sending up
every kind and colour of flame, orange, blue, green,
blazing red like the blood of the very earth itself,
vibrant sunflower yellows, all mirrored and magnified
by the wintry walls of the snowy ice-slopes looming
above, over crags of black stone.

No wonder the air felt warm; no wonder it stank
of sulphurous smoke. No wonder it carried that low
roar and mutter. Shapes were solidifying in that firelight as her eyes grew accustomed, shapes solid and
huge, shapes moving, flickering, skeletal shadows
passing to and fro, demonic in the red-gold light.

Fire, within a killing chill. Life, within a deadly embrace, nestled many days deep within the steel-hard, snowbound heart of the Ice.

'Well?' shrilled the other girls, as she sat back.

'It . . . it *is* a town,' she said, shaking her head in wonder. 'Like a town of fire and smoke, but real – huge, even . . . Rooftops above the murk, streets, people. A town. Here. But that's impossible.'

'No, it isn't!' remarked the princess quietly. 'Listen to them! Listen to the voices. Like a waterfall, indeed – a torrent of them. And all the other sounds . . .'

The torrent seemed to envelop them even as they listened. Loud voices, shrill voices, screaming voices, rising above the general roar. Sudden sharp explosions of shouting outside, as if their guards were exchanging insults with people passing. The harsh blare of a trumpet, a rattle of feet on hard ground, running past. Whips cracking, children wailing, dogs barking, beasts bellowing – oxen, probably, though no kind she knew. What sounded like loud drumming in the distance, ferocious and frenzied. Flashes of wailing chants, squabbles, a little harsh laughter. Bellows wheezing, hammering and clanging, the spitting hiss of quenched metal, wheels that rumbled and squeaked worse than the carts – all familiar sounds, and yet a whole dimension larger, louder, more insistent.

Savi thought her head was going to split. The waft of odours didn't help; she had thought the cart stank, but the air carried in a greasy stink of humanity hardly washed and poorly drained, overladen with unimaginable fumes and smokes. Her lungs laboured, and she thrust the others away from the slit again, desperate for freer air. It was only a little better. She could taste the stench, even, and it made her feel sick. They were passing some kind of log palisade, heavy but crude, and stacked against it, little surprise, was a stinking midden—

Savi fell back in shock, shivering. The others clustered around her, clamouring, but she would only sit there, shaking her head, sweating. There had been rats running over it, and she hated rats, but what they were running over . . .

By the time she could look again, it was long past. They were going by walls, few of them high yet rough and ugly, little more than heaps of some kind of ashy-looking porous stone, clumsily slathered in crumbling mortar. Others were just log-walls, similarly sealed with mortar or something rougher, mud or dung maybe. Windows were small and high and always shuttered tight; small wonder, as strange wisps of mist continually flowed around them, emanations perhaps from the ways below, glistening with filth and puddles into which the cart was constantly lurching. Here and there at the base of a wall a grille flashed and flickered with the continual firelight, and darker smokes boiled up. Around these a few weeds had sprung up. Nothing else grew, that she could see, anywhere; and nothing lived, save the odd diseased dog or rat slinking through the narrow alleys, and hurrying humanity. Always hurrying, whether it was riders on horseback or hobbling crones, wild-looking children or chained files of slaves with their drivers lashing at their legs. The perpetual firelight had more lasting life in it.

But behind the crest of one wall she caught a brief gleam of something startlingly different, something that did not fit at all, rising above this sink of flame and turmoil like a stark reproach. The cart turned again, and it was hidden; but she clung to the opening in the cover, hungering to catch just one more glimpse among all this undreamed-of ugliness. For there at its heart and summit, rose a vision equally unexpected. It was more than beautiful; it seemed to purify the very light that welled up around it, and reflect it like a towering jewel. That much she had seen, no more. She flung herself across the cart, overturning the others, eagerly stabbing at the cover on the other side; but it showed her only more bleak walls.

'What was it you saw?' asked the princess urgently, but Savi could only gesture helplessly. Her life had never needed words for any such vision.

'There was something else, too . . .' insisted the princess.

'That was horrible, yes. On a midden . . . bones. Almost; burned, roasted even. Small limbs, a head still with the hair . . .'

The princess seemed to shrink into herself, folding her tall frame, hugging her knees desperately. 'We are near the end,' she whispered. 'For better or worse . . .'

'There are folk out there,' said Savi. 'If they live, so may we.'

The princess sighed. 'But will we want to?'

Savi said nothing. She had to catch her balance. The angle of the cart had changed again. It was climbing a slope.

The two of them sat watching the slits in the cover. The other girls sat watching them. Neither wished to move. For all their hunger their stomachs were leaden, and Savi tasted a tang of sickness. And then the ground levelled off suddenly. The cart plodded forward, but just as Savi reached desperately for her spyhole, she was thrown flat among the stinking straw. The cart stopped dead.

The tailboard fell with a crash, the cover was thrown back. A guard sprang up, and jerked a thumb. 'Out!' he said harshly. 'All you!' He kicked the nearest girl and dragged her out by her hair, the others hastily sliding after her. Savi, looking down for her footing, saw neat cobbles slick with black water, pooling between them, mirroring . . .

The cobbles hurt her feet, but she hardly noticed.

She looked up, up, devouring the vision she had only glimpsed from below, and that from a distance greater than she guessed. She stood now at the apex of a low hill, an outcrop at the high end of the little vale; but higher still towered the shape that crowned it. To the height of the surrounding snows it rose, with a glittering, bitter beauty that mirrored their own, less remote perhaps, but scarcely less chill, an eerie, inhuman loveliness. So in the tales of her lost childhood the palaces might appear; so to mere mortals a legend might take shape, out of words and fine-spun glass.

Liquid, almost, it looked; liquid and live, as if it had frozen suddenly in the process of becoming something else, and might any moment flow and change again. It had a tall roof, high-gabled, and beneath that rows of pillars and colonnades any lordly hall might have envied, but it was not regular or foursquare as human buildings are made. Rather, it seemed a single flowing shape in which no part could be detached from a whole that scarcely seemed solid, more like an instant of existence. All of its massive substance was translucent, and about it, within it, light coursed, all shades, all hues in constant change.

The smoky scarlet of the town below it took and split apart, shattering it with all the cleaner fire of a brilliant gem, scattering it from facet to facet of its endless surfaces. But there were other lights too, shimmering glows that coursed across its tall roof and danced about the rooftree, burned at the gable like lanterns or sank slowly down the walls in a wash of blue like a summer twilight. Behind the columns an inner wall welled deep green as an ice-island in winter seas, then faded swiftly to the grey skies above it, with racing snowclouds. Savi had seen neither, yet somehow she knew what she was being shown, captured there like the tints in smoky quartz. There were no windows, and she guessed it would need none, this luminescent form; but there were high doors gaping blackly, above wide steps of gleaming white stone that gave on to a court of what looked like the same stuff, extending almost to their feet here. And out of the doors, down the steps and across the court beneath, figures were hurrying. Towards them.

A hand sought Savi's, and on the other side the princess's bony fingers entwined with hers. This was new; this was strange.

Some of the newcomers wore robes, of a fashion she had not seen. Those around them bore arms, the short spears and swords of the raider men; and the same black kilts and jerkins. But though they were all of the *Aikiya-wah'sa* kind and caste of face, with the swarthy red-brown skin and heavy, muscular build, not a single one of them was a man.

Doubling swiftly across the cobbles, the armed guards gathered around the little knot of captives, their spears held at port. But then the robed women caught them up, and at a word the spears relaxed. A thickset older woman in a fine blue robe moved unhurriedly forward, others fluttering in her wake; and Savi guessed this must be their chieftain, maybe even the one who had ordered them taken. She tripped slowly along the ragged line, looking the captives up and down, and then she snapped a couple of words to the wagon guards. They ducked their heads and turned away hastily, as if glad to, and the stinking cart that had been their cell these past weeks rattled off into the dark.

Savi had no time to feel any relief. The woman turned back to the palace, and the female guards closed in behind the captives and prodded the girls along with their shields, their faces as harsh and unreadable as any of the men's. The court and the steps were so shiny even their bare feet slipped, weary as they were. One girl fell to her knees, and a spearshaft slapped her to her feet.

Then the air seemed to fill with a thunderous yawning roar, and the stairs shook beneath them. The girls screamed; some staggered, others sought to flee in panic and fell sprawling, almost pulling Savi and the rest off their feet.

'Silence, fools!' snapped the woman in tones as harsh as the raiders, and the guards laughed raucously. 'Keep feet, or lose them! Happens all times here! Grow used to it!'

Savi and the princess exchanged swift glances. To grow used to anything they would have to be alive.

The doors loomed vast above them, like caverns in the Ice, and yet the air was warm, clement almost. Their footsteps echoed startlingly as they were hurried through, and across a dark forecourt beyond, to where a still vaster arch opened up. And at its entrance the coarse-voiced woman Savi had assumed must be the chieftain ducked her head, bowed low as any servant, and stepped aside.

The woman who stood waiting within was yet another contrast, as tall as the princess and as thin, with a curious cast of face, and a look like chalky water in her eyes, as if she were going blind. Her robe was finer than the other's, pale grey but glossy and shot with iridescent lights, as if river pearls could be spun for thread; and her hair showed only a few black strands among much the same shade of grey. Silver clasped the robe, fastened her hair, twisted through the fine jewelled fillet about her brow, and she leaned on a short staff of what looked like clear glass.

To Savi her step spoke of power, her manner radiated command. This was a much worthier mistress for such a hall, a queen of this strange realm. She could almost imagine her some creature beyond the mortal, some legendary enchantress or demi-power.

Her image shone clear in the dark floor as she stalked slowly towards them; and she too looked the new arrivals up and down, one by one. Those calcareous eyes seemed to see with little difficulty, and in her clawed hands there was strength. One girl's rags she tore at, letting her breasts fall free. Another's chin she tilted back, pulled back her lips to examine her teeth. She lingered when she reached the princess, fingering what was left of her fine fabrics, examining her hands, caressing her tangled hair, and when the princess haughtily shook her off, the old woman nodded as if in deep approval.

Then when she came to Savi she stopped dead. Her staff tapped the sword that still hung at Savi's waist, and her thin eyebrows raised in a silent, severe question.

'The chieftain gave it to me,' stammered Savi. Her throat seemed very dry. 'After the guards raped some of the others, murdered one. Gave me it, so I could protect the others.'

The voice was like withered leaves, on a breath of dried flowers. 'Why you, child?'

'Because . . . because I killed the guard who did it.'

'Mmmmmh.' It was almost a sigh. The claw touched her chin, tilted her head this way and that, slid her filthy cape off one shoulder and bared one breast. Her claw touched the nipple. 'You have not given suck. What age have you, child?'

'Fifteen . . . my lady.' She found the right title in the princess's tales. She wondered if she should bow; and decided she was damned if she would. She felt a flush of anger, and realised it must show. But to her astonishment she was simply patted on the head, and the old woman moved along to the next girl. Her, too, she half stripped, and one or two more; and at the end of the line she clicked her fingers. There was a rattle as of spearblades, some of the girls squealed in terror; but only the foul chains and waistbands fell at their feet, in pieces, and they staggered to catch their balance. Savi, rubbing gratefully at her chafed waist, half expected to see the vile things squirm.

Instead there was another deep tremor in the earth, somewhere between a sound and a sensation, rising through their feet to shiver almost ecstatically through their bodies. It was a terrifying feeling, as if one were shaken in a vast hand, and Savi herself could not hold back from squealing and ducking, as if the roof might collapse.

The old woman smiled thinly. 'You will learn to tolerate that. Nothing but natural forces, I assure you; and held well in check.' She sniffed her contempt. 'Down there in the town they will tell you it is the ancient dragon Tugarin, son of Zamai, that stirs and bellows in his chains; but in all my life I have never seen him. If ever he lived, he is long dead. Here in the palace you must learn clearer thinking. The Great Ice, in whose grasp and upon whose sufferance we all live, lies heavy, infinitely heavy, upon the stone that is the bones of the earth. It forces up the fires beneath, by which we fragile fleshly creatures are kept warm and lit. A tremor or two is small pain to pay for that! Give thanks to the Ice that tolerates us, unworthy as we are, and banish your fears. Our lives are all in the gift of its august masters, whom we live to serve, for as long as they alone please. Go now, and see for yourselves!' Nodding slowly, she turned away, to the depths of the hall, and bowed as deeply as the other.

The shields pushed them forward again, out into the hall and across the pale floor, covered with designs Savi hardly noticed. Her eyes were fixed on the back of the great chamber, where the light was sinking now to a deepening twilit blue, so that she almost expected to see stars come out between the line of massive pillars. Instead, as if out of infinite distances, a single arching streak of white light shot

across the blue; and with it the shields vanished from
their backs. Savi and the others turned in astonishment, to see the young women guards face down
upon the mirror floor, their heads in their hands, eyes
covered.

And then the air burst into light above their
heads.

Some of the captives had seen the Northlights
before; for they came far south in those days, the
heralds and banners of the conquering Ice. But here,
beneath the vaulted roof, rippling out over their
cowering heads, they were terrifying, like shimmering curtains of flameless fire flung across the hall,
their greenish glow turning faces livid and dead. Still
more terrifying, because the very air crackled and
spat with the forces at play, and the girls could feel
their hair ripple and rise in otherworldly breezes,
their skins prickle. The women guards wailed in awe
and terror as their spearpoints danced and shimmered with answering glows.

For a moment only the Lights blossomed there,
first green, then blue, one colour and another coursing through them. Then their flicker slowed, and they
sank down like steam condensing, drew in towards
the line of pillars and the steps that led up to them.
Suddenly they were gone; and between the middle
pillars hovered a deeper glow, a single spinning core
of rainbow colours fading to white, a vortex high
above the steps. The crackle rose to a singing, agonis-
ing note, and within the vortex something took
shape, spinning swiftly at first and then slowing,
stilling, floating in the void. A form, a human form,
framed in a great plume of pale gold streaming out
into the void, billowed by that same unseen wind.

The singing note vanished beyond the edge of
hearing. A wind, a real wind filled the hall, rushing
and singing, blowing their hair this way and that,
plucking at their clothes. Its note seemed to change,

to rise and fall; and suddenly it took a tone and timbre, and voiced words.

I am Taounehtar.

I am the mistress of this place, and of all the realm about you, and of all whom it holds in thrall.

And you have been brought here to serve me.

Down to the steps sank the last bright corona, still shimmering, dazzling, swelling. The glassy pillars caught the light unbearably. Everyone averted their eyes, barely in time. A brilliant flash shone through hands, eyelids, everything, picking out the bones beneath the skin. But then the wind died, the air was instantly hushed. The sense of presence was so strong that Savi simply had to lower her hands and look.

There upon the stair stood a young woman, and about her, writhing and rippling still, the pale aureole of white gold that was her hair. Such a colour Savi had never seen, and she clapped her hands to her mouth and almost laughed with the sheer beauty of the sight. Quite naked the woman stood, her flesh pale against the deep glow of wall and pillar, and astonishingly fair; yet she seemed wholly unconscious of her nakedness, her stance curiously graceless, clumsy, almost, casting about her with eyes tightly shut. She gulped in air, her breasts heaving as if she were struggling to speak; but her speech, when it came, was still the voice of the wind.

You are to teach me how to be as one of you.

You will teach me how to be a living woman –

The last word was almost a gasp. She staggered suddenly, this vision, her limbs sprawling this way and that, and fell heavily on the black steps. Savi heard her head strike them, quite hard; but she did not cry out or even seem to understand. She curled up like a newborn, shivering visibly; and Savi was astonished to see flakes of frost fall from her bare skin.

Suddenly stirred, greatly daring, Savi stepped

forward hesitantly and, slipping the filthy cloak from around her own shoulders, draped it around the shaking figure on the steps. It slipped off, and instinctively Savi stooped to lift her a little and tuck it in. She felt light, this woman; almost fragile. Her face was blank, unlined; but as Savi touched her it crumpled suddenly into a mask of pain and trouble. The eyelids flew open. The eyes within were utterly void and dark; yet they fixed Savi in a gaze of almost physical force. Her mouth fell open, and she screamed, loudly, like a baby; again, and again.

Savi turned to shout at the servants, still grovelling at the far end of the hall; but they came running, their slippers slapping on the glassy floor, and gathered around the writhing girl. One tore away the cloak, and slipping off her own smooth robe wrapped it around her, but the girl cast that away, struggling, and they had to seize her limbs as if she were in a fit, leaving Savi holding her tossing head. She retched and tried to vomit, but her stomach was empty; she seemed to lose control of her body with little more result, and her beautiful lips champed with bloody foam as she bit her tongue. Savi wiped it with a fold of the robe, trying to place it between her teeth to prevent worse, and yelped as her own finger was bitten hard; but she found herself stroking that beautiful hair and murmuring words of calm, as she might to a child, as she had to Alya.

Suddenly, alarmingly, she saw that the eyes were no longer empty. That gaze was fastened on her with frightening, angry intensity. The lips spat out the robe, and hissed in voiceless fury. A hand pulled free, came up and slapped her open-fingered with such force she was sent sprawling back on the floor, her face bruised and burning, the lining of her cheek cut against her teeth. '*You!*' demanded the voice, and it was no longer that of the wind, but low and clear and forceful. 'How *dare* you?'

'I was only trying to—' wailed Savi; but her face hurt so much that her anger overflowed the words.

She struck back. The pale cheek cracked like a whip, and the rattle of spears was instant. She was thrown on her face, and cold points jabbed into her back.

The golden-haired woman sat up on the stair, clutching her bleeding mouth, and whimpered, 'Made . . . bite . . .'

'I *didn't!*' Savi protested. 'I was trying to stop you doing it! You were flailing about and - and—'

The woman looked at her askance a moment, and then at the others who were still holding her legs and one arm. 'So,' she said, and waved the spears back. 'Not . . . easy. Cannot . . .' She waved a hand, vaguely.

Savi guessed that was as much apology as she could expect - more than usual, to judge by the astonished faces of the serving women. 'Come!' said the woman slowly, beckoning to Savi. 'Help. Head . . . it hurts.'

Savi was startled to see slow tears roll down that lovely face. She wiped them away, and took the woman's hand, but she still could not get up. At last Savi had to pull her arm about her own shoulders and more or less hoist her to her feet. Her skin felt soft and warm, more like a child's than an adult's, and with the same bready smell. She leaned her head on Savi's shoulder a moment.

'This shape - not often. Worse . . . than before. Less . . . self. More truly . . . human. Not enough. I forget. Forget what . . . all does. Cannot will them.' It was a strange speech, fighting for words, yet still a voice of command, the tones of one accustomed to obedience. 'Anger . . . in head. Becomes . . . fire in blood.' She paused, breathing deeply, still leaning on Savi. 'And fear. I struck . . . fear.'

Savi nodded. 'I do that, sometimes. I understand.'

Startlingly, the young woman rolled her head round and smiled, a cold, crooked quirk of her full lips. 'Indeed? Maybe . . . more human . . . than I thought. But, to be human . . . must lose much . . . of self. That . . . you . . . not know.'

'No?' said Savi softly. 'Half of myself I lost. When you had me brought here.'

'So?' The woman looked at her again. 'You . . . hate?'

Not like someone who knows too little of a tongue, thought Savi. She used words that sounded old and learned. Someone who knows too much, and must fight to say deep things simply. 'Perhaps,' she answered quietly.

'Perhaps . . .' the other echoed. Then she gasped, and stumbled, clutching still at Savi's shoulder, sinking to one knee. She shook her head, desperately, and tears rushed down her expression-less face, great racking sobs shook her slender frame. The other girls sidled closer, astonished, apprehensive. Whatever any one of them had feared or dreaded, it was not this. Yet the princess reached out to take the young woman's other hand, almost comfortingly, and the others gathered round, tentatively touching that beautiful, eerie hair.

The young woman's voice was a bleak husk, hollow with fear.

'I do this . . . I must. No other . . . can trust. All alone. Time since . . . I was as I am. Now . . . what? Self, memories . . . dream. Far away . . . fleeing. All I could do, all I am. Torn from me. Only . . . shred . . .' She was weeping now, open-mouthed, inelegantly, clawing at the robe her horrified servants were still trying to wrap around her. 'Hurts! Beast in trap! Alone. Alone . . . again. Never so. Help. Cannot. You . . . hate. You . . . help . . . me?'

It was pathetic, and to Savi at that moment the gulf between the eerie vision and this lovely, stumbling child-woman seemed truly infinite.

Impulsively she hugged her. 'Never mind,' she said. 'We'll help you, somehow. I'll help you.'

The land before them had no horizon. The road had led Alya's little band down out of the low hills and dells, to a wide, low-lying expanse of country, a massive floodplain as it seemed, cut through by great cold rivers such as the one that led them, carving their way down across it from the North. Only their meandering, blackish-brown flows broke the constant flatness of the surface; but it looked no more firm than they. Alya wondered if the sea would be like this, a green waving expanse stretching out into misty infinity. To the eye there was no solid land at all. Even the road was hidden, visible only where it emerged briefly along the banks of the great stream ahead. Near or far, the landscape waved and surged like a grey-green swell in the constant, biting wind, and though Vansha claimed he could make out small plumes of smoke rising from what must be wide clearings, far in the distance, the only life to be seen above it was wheeling, plaintive birds.

It was not water, though there was marsh enough beneath. It sighed and rattled down the wind like the dead mocking their own bare bones. It was a vast field of tall cane, the stems of all sizes green shading to yellow, the leaves long and spearlike, sharp at the edge. It grew taller than a mounted man, and it clustered ever closer about the road, on both sides, until it became hard to see more than a few paces through it. And at last, rustling and heavy, it blotted out even the remaining patches of weak grey sky, and closed in a roof over the narrow road. A shifting, hissing roof, yet solid and stifling; it drew the force from the wind, and the air hung heavy and

clammy about them. Kalkan, leading the way down
the narrow road, rose in his stirrups to spy out the
way, and cursed as it leant and bowed over him,
almost mockingly.

'My lord Kalkan?'

'Nothing, my lord Asquan! I see only more
bloody canes. And Vansha and I are the tallest, and
with the sharpest eyes. We'll see nothing of what's
ahead, until we reach one of those open patches.
Unless . . .'

'No!' said Alya firmly, as everyone looked to him.
'It's too dangerous. I very nearly drew down disaster
on us all. I won't risk that again, until there's real
need.' *Even if I still can*.

'Then we plod on!' shrugged Kalkan irritably.
'But I can't even tell what hour it is, beneath this
infernal cane!'

Tseshya grinned, and poked his spear upward,
parting the topmost leaves. 'Not so long till evening, I
think. At least we'll have a dry camp, and plenty of
firemakings. Hot soup.'

Vansha stretched in his saddle, rubbing his backside. 'Sounds good! I might even go fishing, if the
river's near enough. We could smoke ourselves up a
few days' worth, too.'

'Maybe,' said Alya. 'But fish from cover. I'm
growing wary of what might frequent these rivers.'

'I'll take Rysha!' laughed Vansha. 'Maybe she can
blind the fish, as well as men.'

Rysha sneered. 'It's harder. Fish have more sense!'

Vansha chortled. 'You think? Try giving them a
sniff of your pants, they'll be leaping out!'

Rysha spat a word at him and rode on into the
rustling green. Alya caught Vansha's eye. 'You
shouldn't antagonise her so! Look at how much
she did for us, back then!'

Vansha looked sulky. 'Maybe! But you can't trust
her! You ask Kalkan, he knows!'

'Will you always take your cue from Kalkan, brother?'

'Sooner that than Asquan! Hate to think where he got his wisdom, as you call it.'

'Through experience! He's done so much, seen so much more of the world. And you've seen how he fights!'

Vansha lowered his voice. 'Oh, aye! Asquan can fight, I'll give you that. Little as I'd have credited it! Like a shrivelled old snake on a rock, you think it's dead till it ups and strikes. And he's been places, all right! Just the thought of them makes my eyes water! I wouldn't trust that scrawny old debauchee with my bloody sheep, let alone anything more precious.'

'I might, brother. Maybe sooner than Kalkan. Oh, Kalkan's sensible enough, a straightforward upright man. Too upright for his own good! And from all I've read, sometimes your upright men find it all too remarkably easy to accommodate their desires. Do you think he only plotted against Volmur out of public duty? Who was supposed to take the King's place, d'you suppose? Or benefit from the grateful successor?'

Vansha was silent. Alya chuckled. 'Whereas, yes, Asquan's a puzzle. He's probably tried anything you can think of, and a few you can't! And yes, it makes me shudder, sometimes. But do you not see? He's found them wanting. He's disappointed. And I guess that's stripped away a lot of self-deception. He knows what he is, better than you or I; his dreams have died. He has nothing, and wants nothing he can still have. I suppose that makes ambition or treachery pretty meaningless. I don't understand him, not fully; but I do believe he's really glad to find an honourable task once more. Oh, I know Kalkan's your friend, I'm grateful to have him along. We'll need him and his men. But we need the others, too. For just the very reasons you don't trust them!'

Vansha sat a moment, then shrugged. 'If you say so, brother!' He laughed, and rode on. That closed it, as near a quarrel as they had had of late; and Alya gave it little more thought. Natural enough, he reflected, that Vansha, being who he was, should prefer the open-air, right-and-wrong, sword-in-hand values of Kalkan and his men; so might Alya, normally. He still shivered at the memory of Asquan's faded eyes, brightening briefly at unspeakable prospects; at Rysha, laughing as her enemy died beneath her; at the Nightingale's feeding. But like it or not, the twilit world that Asquan and Rysha and that uncanny creature inhabited had its uses and values also; and they could be of more service on their road ahead. Its perils might leave little room for squeamish hesitation.

And at least, for all the bickering, nobody showed the least sign of turning back; that was something.

Not even Rysha. She did go with Vansha on his fishing, that evening; and he came back with a fair number of fish, familiar river types but darker and less brilliant, as if coloured by the muddy water. Some they cleaned and set to bake in a clay earth-oven under cane fronds, while Rysha gutted and scaled the rest for smoking later. Alya came to help her, though she did not seem to care.

'Thank you for all this,' he said to her. 'Your darkness, and your fighting hand.'

She shrugged. 'I'm no warrior woman. I'm a witch and a murderess, aren't I? I was just doing what seemed natural.' She slit a fish's belly and held it up to check for worms.

'It was valiant, all the same.'

'Pig dung. I didn't fight anyone much, just sneaked up or scared 'em and stuck them, mostly from behind. Get a thrill out of that, at times.' She dug in her fingers and drew out a mass of guts, along with a tail of straggling white things.

'You haven't tried to hurt any of us. And you're cheerfully going along to what might be your death.'

'Me? Don't get your hopes up. Can't kill what they can't see. And that's not my only trick. Watch out for the scales.' She flicked the knife expertly down its flank.

'But there's more than that,' said Alya softly.

'Is there?' She picked up another fish. 'If you say so. Nowhere much else for me to go, is there, now we're out here? Back home I'd have been forever living on a knife-edge, and a dull one at that. Those towns on the steppe are deathtraps, that's clear enough. And the dungkicker villages like you came from don't sound like much fun. Specially if the word got round about who I am, what I did. Men don't seem to take to that, somehow. They fear you; or they use you, to show they're not afraid. No, this'll do for now. I don't ask much more from life, and I quite like the killing.'

She flicked guts away, too close to him, and eyed him. 'I do, you know. Not screwing. That makes me sick, with anyone, man, woman. Plain sick. Dunno who invented it. Dirty. You just lace into your killing, I saw that. *You* don't think. But take it from me, when you down the other man—' She gave a little shiver. 'You never felt more alive! 'Cause life's what you're taking away, right?'

'No. And when you spoke of it, you suddenly said "you", instead of "I". So is it really that great a pleasure for you?'

She snorted with derisive laughter. 'Clever little man! Really got to watch the mouth with you around, haven't I? But – yes, there's a thrill in it. Maybe not as much as I like to say, but – yes. Bit like that old goat Asquan and his torture lark, I guess. Maybe he'd teach me!' She chuckled nastily. '*On* me, like as not. Just to put some wag back in his tail, the dirty old bugger. What men always do, isn't it?'

She sighed. 'Don't like me much, do you? No, don't answer. I'm who I am, that's all. Rysha who murders men, no getting away from it. If I live through this, maybe I'll find a way not to be. Maybe I'll have had enough. Get myself a home, settle down, see if waving my legs in the air makes any more sense. But I wouldn't wager on it. Are those fish done yet? My belly's flapping.'

Vansha was taking them out of the oven, breaking away the clay and the skin with it, and the others gathered swiftly, gobbling down the fish with grain they had boiled beside the oven. But as they finished, Alya's chewing slowed, and so did the others'. Only the Nightingale munched on, giggling to himself, but looking around nervously as if somebody might snatch the fish away.

'This tastes a little strange,' said Asquan. 'Just a faint aftertaste, but . . .'

'Dull,' agreed Kalkan, spitting out a bone. 'Muddy. You can eat it, but, well . . .'

'It's a muddy river,' said Vansha, inclined to defend his catch. 'Healthy enough. That must be why the cane grows so high hereabouts. Lays down good fertile silt. It'd do wonders for grain – rice, even, with all this water.'

Fazdshan grunted. 'Think so? Nobody seems to want to use it. They've all been living in the stony hills and steppes back there. Must be something wrong, here.'

'There were those smokes!' objected Vansha. 'They could have whole farms deep in this lot, almost hidden. Like they tried to among the trees, but better!'

'Hope we find 'em!' said Chiansha, rubbing his broad stomach. 'Pick up some proper food, maybe!'

Alya swallowed a last unrewarding mouthful. 'They might not want to sell, remember; they might not produce enough. They can't have much use for silver, out here. And what else have we, that they want?'

'Almost everything, I'd have thought,' said Tseshya cheerfully. 'Why would they be here, otherwise? Not from choice, surely!'

He looked around, as if expecting applause.

'Go on,' prompted Alya.

'But isn't it obvious? This is rich soil, like Vansha says, plenty of water – mild enough clime, even. Not as sunny as further south, but not as dry either. You could clear this lot easily enough, make yourself a big farm, a plantation even. You could get your grain down south to trade easy enough, by the river maybe; keep boats either side of the rapids.'

'Thinking of settling down and doing some honest work, inkslinger?' grunted Chiansha.

'No! And neither has anyone else. If there are farms here, they're smaller than they should be. So, why not?'

Kalkan shrugged. 'Too lonely?'

Asquan snapped his fingers. 'The raiders! They must keep this road open. The *Aikiya 'wahsa* would scare anyone off!'

'That's part of it, my lord,' said Alya quietly. 'But I think I see what our scholar is leading up to. If he's right . . . well, we'll have to tread very carefully indeed.'

'Very carefully,' agreed Tseshya. 'But leave it at that for now, Lord Alya. We may see, soon enough.'

'Maybe even a farm-girl or two!' grinned Almur.

The soldiers hooted and whistled, but quietly, experienced enough to be cautious in this first camp in new country. Fazdshan glanced around. 'Might be glad of some new blood, in a dank hole like this is!'

'Probably all got six fingers!' suggested Darzhan. 'And webbed!'

'Growing moss, more like!' put in Vansha. 'Great fat thighs, all covered in moss!'

'It'll rub off!' said Almur confidently.

Kalkan and the others chuckled, even Rysha.

'But there may be no farms, nobody at all!' Alya reminded them sharply. 'And even if there are, do you think we can afford to linger? We're in the chase, remember?'

He knew as he said it that he had been too curt. The atmosphere changed, and not for the better. But Asquan was contemplating him with narrowed eyes. 'Somehow I don't think lingering's on anyone's mind!' he said suavely. 'Quite the opposite, in fact! I suspect their speed will amaze them!' They chuckled again, Alya with them, and the feeling improved. 'But we'll see soon enough,' the old lord added. 'We must, ah, contain ourselves in patience till then!'

Asquan could put a leer into the simplest word when he wished, and it caught the general mood. They settled down in their blankets among a hail of banter on the general theme of containment, and Asquan offered to take first watch – to put down, as he phrased it, any outbreak of blanket-tossing. When the others were snoring soundly, though, Alya joined him as he sat and watched the patchy moonlight through the shifting ceiling of the cane.

'Thank you for that, my lord. For repairing my mistake. I should have left them their daydreams of food and women, they were harmless enough.'

'My pleasure. Yes, let them dream. We all need dreams, the Powers help us.'

'I can't share theirs!' said Alya, with quiet savagery, feeling the tensions that racked him whenever he allowed himself too much thought. The fires leaped up in stinging answer. 'They gall me, them and their dung-headed lip-smacking over nonexistent farm-girls! Even Vansha! There are real girls in danger out there, deadly danger! He at least should know better! I don't know how they can talk like that, how they can rest when—'

'I do,' said Asquan quietly. 'To most of them, of course, your girl's no more real than their own fantasies, and less interesting because she *is* yours. To your friend – well, he feels less deeply than you, I think. Perhaps for that same reason. But he may be wiser.'

'How so? In caring less?'

'In not dwelling too much upon what he cannot alter. Say, cannot yet alter, if that disturbs your faith. In dreaming sweeter dreams, and sleeping while he can.'

Alya rubbed his eyes. 'My dreams always hover on the brink of nightmare.'

'Naturally. But at least you have them. It is one of the things that makes folk follow you. Only one.' Asquan looked at him keenly. His spidery hand hovered close to Alya's thigh.

Then, to Alya's deep relief, he appeared to change his mind. 'What's to come, farm-girls or fiends, that we shall see in good time!' His hand fell on his own knee, as perhaps it was always intended to. 'Go now, find happier times to sleep in – ones to come, maybe. I shall take your watch, and keep company with the moon, what I can see of her. We are old lovers, she and I.'

Unnerved, and yet strangely comforted, Alya slid gratefully away. When he awoke at dawn, he felt that he had slept better than of late, for all the seeping dampness of the ground; and he was surprised to see Asquan still sitting up, as grey as the light around him, listening to the breeze that rattled like a skeletal horse through the cane.

'I smell smoke,' he said, as the others stirred and stretched wearily. 'Just faintly, but smoke it is. The wind is from the north. So perhaps our friends will get their fat thighs and six fingers soon enough, after all.'

But that day brought them nothing save more

damp winds driving dank mists, and the lonely calls of waterbirds, and the cane, always the cane. The next was no better, and the next and the next after that, wary but infinitely dull. For long hours nothing changed, least of all the canopy of canes. Alya was growing to hate its rustling, rattling voice, and its shrouding blindness, which blotted out any sense of progress, and the dripping caress of its spear-shaped leaves, decanting the mists and dews in droplets down their necks.

'We should have you huff and puff and blow all this away, demon!' said Kalkan.

The Nightingale was hunched in among the baggage for warmth. 'Mist? Little use! Fast as I blow one way, in it rolls another.' He leered up at them. 'Much prey it's cost me. Many tasty lives!'

'That's enough of that!' said Alya sharply. He hated this dank obscurity more than the rest. At times he felt it was a trap set for him, to wander around forever in circles, while the world passed him by outside and Savi was drawn further and further from him. The others seemed to feel much the same, and the wind bowed their heads and whipped away words. Nobody spoke; they all seemed lost in thought, in memory perhaps, while the horses plodded patiently on.

When the winds blew strongly, it was like a rainstorm under the green canopy, and when they were lower and gusty the mists trickled between the stiff stalks in disturbing shifts of shadow and movement. Things would plunge through the canes, large things by the sound of it; but always at a distance, never visible; and whether that was curse or relief was hard to be sure. Every so often one of the fighting men would curse and lunge out with his lance at something he saw from the corner of his eye; but there was never anything there, not, at any rate, by the time the spear arrived. Once Tseshya loosed a

precious arrow at a fleeting shadow, and they were
rewarded by a wild pig's squeal, a welcome promise
of meat; but the beast broke the shaft and fled.

'At least we know it was a real pig,' said Darzhan
with evident relief. 'And not . . .'

'Not what?' demanded Alya. There was a sullen
silence.

'They've been seeing things!' said Vansha scornfully.

'Not us!' Fazdshan sounded defensive. 'Your
little pal on the baggage-moke. The Nightingale. He's
saying there's been something around us here, something that doesn't smell right. Like nothing still walking around has a right to smell!'

'What's it to him?' demanded Vansha. 'Couldn't
be anything much spookier than him! Could there?'

But when he and Alya let themselves fall back
down the file to the baggage ponies, he found the
Nightingale's white face and wide black eyes peering
apprehensively out from among the panniers. 'It's not
there now!' was the first thing he said; and the only
thing, for a while, except to gibber. Eventually they got
some sense out of him. He had been seeing things, all
right, and since they first entered the cane, it seemed.
Only at night; but his eyes were better than anyone's,
then. What he saw, though, was uncertain. Once or
twice, far distant, there had been something hairy and
bestial, perhaps no more than a bear. More often there
was some kind of laughing demon, which could take
on the semblance of a woman. And sometimes it was
dark and shapeless, a tall shadow slithering through
the canes or gliding through the river mists.

'We need to know so much, in these perilous
places,' mused Alya. 'I wonder if these mist-creatures
devour lives as you do, Nightingale? And what would
their own memories be like, then? Very useful to us,
perhaps. I may set you to catch us one. If you do, he's
yours.'

He was only half joking; but Nightingale whimpered and shrank down at the very prospect.

'Well, that's something new!' observed Vansha drily. 'A monster afraid of monsters!'

They all chuckled; but equally they all caught themselves glancing around at the cane, and the soldiers put hand to weapon.

Asquan nodded. 'Just so. Were there not evils enough abroad in your wood, Nightingale?'

He looked up, sullen and sidelong. 'Knew those! Simple things, near mindless. Could smell their purposes, make them serve me if I wished. This is more! No commanding, no touching it even. Smells cold, cruel. More like human evil!'

'And that's worse, is it?' said Tseshya. 'Fascinating. I don't know about you, my lords and masters, but I'd be glad not to spend another night in the open!'

'We can set fires, mount sentinels as usual!' said Alya. 'It hasn't harmed us yet, has it?'

'And build a cane fence!' rumbled Kalkan. 'Cane sharpens like spears! But I don't mind admitting I'd still feel better behind a door! If there are any farms around here—'

'We'd be mad to stray off the road to seek them!'

Kalkan thumbed his beard. 'Aye, maybe. But if we come upon somewhere . . .'

They did. At first it was the smoke that trailed them, tantalisingly near, this way and then that, flirting with them on the wind. But it was only when dusk made the canes into a tangle of grey web that they saw anything, a faint flickering point of red that seemed like the only colour left in the world.

'That can't be far off the road!' said Darzhan hopefully.

'Might even be on it!' said somebody, and there was a general rumble of encouragement.

'And it might be full of Ekwesh!' snapped Alya.

He was feeling the oppression of the canes as badly as anyone.

'You do well to remind us,' said Asquan. 'Ekwesh or worse. We'll scout it out, first, a couple of us.'

'Better we stick together!' said Darzhan rebelliously. 'Won't get me rattling off through that stuff on my own – eh, lads? Even if Almur's girl's at the end of it!'

'Especially if she is!' chuckled Chiansha. 'Fair shares alike, eh, Almur?'

Almur said nothing. He was usually quiet; but when Chiansha looked around to repeat his question, the words died in his mouth. Almur was nowhere to be seen.

Even Asquan was startled. 'What? What d'you mean, gone?'

'I mean, not frigging there!'

Alya was shocked to see how straggling their train had become. 'Close up!' he hissed. 'My lord Kalkan, please gather them up!'

'Of course!' snapped the old warrior. 'Can't have this! Worse than women out berrypicking!' He sent his mount cantering back down the path, gesturing to the others as he went, and they hurried forward to join him. There was still no sign of Almur, or his horse.

'He was bringing up the rear!' said Tseshya, sweating. 'Like Lord Kalkan always wants a soldier there. He was behind me, last I saw, but with the canes, and this hazy light, that was . . .'

'You didn't hear anything?'

'He never says much!' protested Tseshya. 'Not to me, anyhow!'

'Can't imagine why!' snarled Kalkan savagely. 'You're so bright you couldn't even spare an eye for him now and then?'

'None of us were looking,' said Alya pacifically. 'That's a mistake we'll not make again in a hurry! But the important thing's to find him.'

Kalkan snorted. 'He's a warrior! Maybe he's just stopped for a leak. Or dozed off and wandered into the cane.'

'His horse wouldn't,' said Alya. 'They follow one another.' He bit his lip, imagining a silent something reaching out from within the cane. It wasn't as hard as he would have liked. 'We'll have to go back and look. Damn the hour! I don't want to make camp this early.'

'I don't think anyone wants to make camp,' said Vansha, glaring around. 'I think we want anything with walls and a roof, if we can find it, and maybe a door to bar!'

'He's right!' snapped Fazdshan, and the other warriors agreed. 'We want to seek out that house!'

'How d'you know it's even a house?' protested Alya, but he could almost feel the cold aura of fear that surrounded them. These men might fear little enough that was human and could fight, but their terror of the unnatural was almost more acute. Even Asquan the unbeliever looked cold and grim in this grey light. Whereas he himself—

Alya had his fires within him, and his driving purpose; and he had touched minds whose menace he could still taste. Mere shadows among the canes he found less immediately frightening. But he knew he must give in.

'All right then! Darzhan, Fazdshan, Tseshya – go back after him, as far as you think worthwhile, while there's any light at all. Look for any sidepaths or tracks he might have taken. Shout, if you think good; but save horn-calls for real trouble. The rest of us will spy ahead. That way, if there is any trouble at least one group can try to get the others out!'

Darzhan nodded glumly as he urged his unwilling horse around, chivvying Nightingale's out of the narrow way. 'Best we all keep our eyes open!'

'On all sides!' added Kalkan. 'All, scholar!'

'If I were Djalmur of the Thousand Eyes, I might manage that! I'll do what I can!'

'If you were Tseshya of the Half a Brain, I wouldn't need to tell you!'

But for all their caution the main group came upon their object quite unexpectedly. They had expected to see clearings among the cane-brakes, as they had for the other farms; but not here. Alya, in the lead, pulled up his horse hastily, and looked around in case someone collided with him, they were huddling so close now. He waved at them urgently, to dismount, and swung from his own saddle to stalk closer

'Well, will you look at that?' breathed Vansha in his ear, and he jumped. 'Our little home from home, isn't it?'

Alya had hardly been able to tell it from the vegetation around. The building, if there was no better word, was made entirely of the cane, darkened with mud, moss and age. The rooftree stood about the height of his head, and sloped almost down to the ground; the few gaps in it, covered with crude smoke-blackened shutters whose every chink shone dully red, were almost at ground height. He thought it could not be a house, till he saw the steps leading down to the low dark door, large enough for a man of medium height. The other buildings behind it were no taller, and they lacked either door or shutter – granaries or stores, maybe. But for what? They were as dilapidated and moss-grown as the larger. And there was no trace of fields or cultivation, save what might be a small patch between them.

Vansha grunted. 'So much for food or girls! Skinny little starvelings who slam the shutters tight at the sight of us, more like.'

'Miserable enough,' agreed Asquan, and Alya jumped again; he had materialised silently at their side. 'Well, if our scholar is right, you can't blame them.'

'What's all this mean?' demanded Rysha. Everyone was clustering together again, unwilling to hang back too long. 'What's the bookworm been chewing now?'

'A possibility, that's all,' said Alya. 'A point we didn't need to raise unless we came across somewhere – somewhere close to the road, like this. Asquan thought the reivers must know of the farms, tolerate them.'

'Yes. Well?'

'But the farms are much smaller and poorer than they should be. Why?'

Kalkan's heavy brows knitted. 'Ignorance?'

'No! You know a lot, my lord, but not about the growing. Even with the simplest farming this ground should yield great harvests, far more than a few peasants can eat up. And if they're trading the food, why aren't they richer?'

Kalkan's breath hissed. 'So somebody's taking it all!'

'More, my lord,' said Alya patiently. 'This is not the work of free hands. Why farm here, however rich it might be, if you did not have to? Slaves do only the least work they can get away with, and can you blame them? Why should they strive to increase what will never be theirs? Most likely the reivers do more than suffer them; they most likely put them here in the first place, and for a reason I can guess. The mortal servants of the Ice, those towns the Nightingale placed on our map, this must be what feeds them. Farms all across this flat land. We thought we were still far from the dominions of the Ice. I believe we are already within them!'

That thought silenced them all. The shadow of the canes above them became suddenly less sheltering and more oppressive, and they looked around nervously.

'The rivers flow from the Ice!' said Vansha suddenly. 'The taste of the fish . . .'

'Harmless enough for now, I guess,' said Alya. 'But further north, who knows?'

'That gives us more immediate worries!' said Asquan. 'Nightingale, do you smell anything?'

The creature's head poked nervously out of the baggage. His snout snuffed the air. 'Smoke. Stale food. Stale bodies, some yours. Others, but not many. That's all. No more!' He ducked back.

'Stale,' said Asquan thoughtfully. 'No worse. Yet he seems afraid of something, all the same. Well, behind that door we will almost certainly find Ekwesh slaves – and maybe their masters. Still, I am tired of this wind and bone-rattling. Mine are doing quite enough of that as it is. And we must look for that wretched boy! So we can do little but knock – my lord Alya?'

Alya nodded, and he and Asquan rose to their feet. Alya rarely touched the spear and shield Asquan had insisted he have, but he pulled them from their rests on the baggage-pony now. The shield would help if there were archers lurking, at least. Asquan slithered – there was no better word for it – swiftly around through the canes and flattened himself against the low wall. Alya was in plain sight of the house now, but there were no alarmed cries, no shutters slamming, no rattle of weapons. He strode quickly forward, stooping to peer through a warped shutter, but saw nothing but smoke and red light. Asquan, watching the other windows, shrugged slightly. Alya levelled his spear and rapped lightly on the door, a simple slab of bound canes set at an angle, like a cellar hatch. Still nothing moved or made a sound. He reached down and flipped it back with a crash. Red light shone out at him, like an oven, but cooler. Faces stared back up at him.

Women's faces; blank, unreadable. He cleared

his throat, feeling ridiculous. 'We mean you no harm.
We'd be glad of shelter and a hearth, while we seek
others of our party. There are . . . several of us. May
we come in?'

The eldest face – not old – surveyed him, guardedly. A jerk of the head. 'Come, then.'

Three of the faces vanished swiftly. Alya gathered his fur cloak and swung himself down the steps
of tamped earth and cane, his shield still before him.
As his eyes adjusted he was pleasantly surprised. He
had expected a stinking, squalid den. This was bare
enough, certainly, a single round room with cane
inner walls and a trodden earth floor, little furnishing
save reed mats; but it smelt clean enough, and it was
well warmed by the big stone stove at the centre.
Asquan followed, glancing round like a malign bird.
There seemed to be nowhere anyone hostile could
hide, though, and nobody in sight save the four
women, three of them quite young, even pretty in
a round-faced peasant way. The fourth was in early
middle age, her face hardened by toil and care, but
indeed, not old. They watched, unspeaking, as the
others clambered down into their room, exclaiming,
for all their talk, more at the sight of the stove than the
women, and flocking to warm clammy hands and
damp backsides. Nightingale slunk away into the
shadows beneath the sloping wall, unnoticed.

'You are . . . warriors?' asked one of the young
women.

Alya smiled at her. 'Just for now. To help somebody.'

'War helps nobody,' said the older woman
sharply.

Asquan looked at her. Hard-faced indeed, with a
strange, intense look about the eyes. 'Where are your
menfolk? Are they hereabouts?'

'They are two years gone,' said the woman
harshly. 'My husband, my sons, taken to fight. These

are their wives, poor creatures. They have not returned, unless their ghosts waded the streams northward. We live and work what little we can of the land,
but cannot manage it all without them; and when we
have enough, the *Aikiya* take it, and insult us for it.'

One of the girls spat juicily into the stove. 'Men
in armour, like you. They stole our men, now they
steal our food.'

They looked plump enough, though. Alya
guessed the overgrown appearance of the farm
was a front to let them keep more food for themselves. More credit to their wit, then. 'Not like us. We
will take nothing. We have food we will share with
you, if you like, as the price of a night's lodging.'
Nobody demurred. He itched to get on, but even if
they found Almur it would be too late. And even he
felt it would be good to seize a night under cover
while they could.

'There are others to come,' he added. 'They've
gone back to seek one of our band who seems to have
strayed—'

The older woman sniffed contemptuously. 'One
lost? Then like as not you'll never see him again.
There's perils in among the canes, as none know
better than us as dwell here. Shapes to deceive fools,
visions to lead them astray. They come from the river,
mostly. With the mists. And before that, from the
Walls, perhaps.'

'You mean the glaciers? The Ice?'

'Quiet!' she snapped. 'Those we don't name. But
. . . perhaps. For sure they're worse the further north
you go, like all things. Men don't live on farms there,
but must huddle together, far from their fields.'

'Demons that eat flesh!' chipped in one of the
girls. 'Worse even than the Ekwesh.'

'I've encountered one of those,' said Alya evenly.
'He didn't give me so very much trouble.' The Nightingale looked hurt.

The woman smiled coldly. 'You may be a hero, then, out of old tales. But one is not a hundred. I'd think about turning back, if I were you.'

Alya shrugged. 'We can't. We're sworn. Another life depends on it, maybe more.'

The woman shrugged. 'It's nothing to me. Stay if you like, so you don't foul the place up. Sleep on the mats, piss in the field out back, keep your paws off the girls. Show me your food and I'll start the sunset meal.'

She was already boiling up grain when the door crashed open, and Darzhan's massive frame came stamping through, followed by the others. They made for the stove with rumbles of relief, but little joy; and there was no fourth man.

'You didn't find him, then?' demanded Alya.

'We found him,' said Tseshya grimly. 'He's across my horse out there. His, we didn't find.'

Silence fell. Asquan hissed softly between his teeth. 'So how did the poor boy meet his end? Could you tell?'

'Tell?' Darzhan shivered. 'Just a guess, mind you, but having his head smashed like a pumpkin might have something to do with it! Stripped and smashed, not a stitch to know him by. Hardly have recognised him, if we'd not been looking!'

Alya felt suddenly cold, despite the stove. Asquan's mouth twisted. 'I believe I should examine him.'

'You're welcome!' said Tseshya.

'Just don't paw him around!' shouted Darzhan, as Asquan headed up the steps. The other soldiers echoed him.

'Never know where you are, with that skinny old bugger!' rumbled Kalkan. 'Go after him, Chiansha, if he takes too long! Where did you find the body, lads?'

Darzhan scratched his head. 'Off the road, about

two thousand strides back, where the land dipped by that stream. The scholar tracked his horse, found him lying some five hundred strides deep in the cane, nothing round him but blood and, and, well, him. And tracks, but nothing we could make sense of. His horse went deeper into the cane, but we didn't want to follow. Not with night coming on.'

The picture that painted struck everyone silent for a moment. Alya felt a dreadful cold possibility forming. Then, almost at once, Asquan reappeared. 'The old bugger can at least use his eyes, where young oafs cannot,' he said crisply. 'The blow was a terrible one, but the poor boy never felt it. He was dead already. You should have seen from the blood on the saddle; though perhaps the ride back opened the wound again. He was stabbed in the back first, a small wound but deep. An arrow or a spear, I would say, with a narrow round point unlike any of ours; and his heart was still beating when it was made.'

'I won't ask how you know!' said Kalkan gruffly. 'But it explains the silence, at least, if somebody took him from the rear.'

'But not the straying from the path!' said Alya. 'Hey, Nightingale! These things you've seen! Were there any of them around that last stream we crossed?'

'Maybe,' said the muffled voice in the shadows. 'Maybe . . .'

'As strong as a mule,' sighed Asquan. 'And about as intelligent, or fanciful. He wouldn't have turned aside lightly, not without raising the alarm. Something made him. Some kind of illusion, if this woman's right.'

'Well, don't look at me!' said Rysha. 'I need the dark, remember? It was no more than grey afternoon. If there's things here can swing that in broad daylight, they're more powerful than I. A hundred times!'

'They are,' said the older woman, and turned to

the stove. The younger women huddled back and watched them, fearfully as it seemed.

'Then tell me, woman,' enquired Asquan, 'how do you live here?'

'We watch our backs,' said the woman calmly. 'And go about in pairs. They seldom come near houses, anyhow, or anywhere there's more than one person. Your horses should be safe out the back. It'll be on the road you're in trouble.'

'Still don't think he'd go haring after one, alone!' suggested Chiansha.

'Without warning the rest of us?' grunted Darzhan. 'No! Almur was green enough, but not that stupid! Tseshya was nearest, he'd have told him!'

'Except for the baggage ponies!' Chiansha reminded him; and his voice changed. 'Maybe he did tell someone! Maybe he told that little vermin! Who happened to forget to tell us!'

Nightingale shrilled. 'No! He would have told me nothing! He hated me! He thought I killed his father!'

'Who disappeared in your wood, certainly!' said Kalkan slowly. 'But how did you know that, creature? He told me, once, when I pressed him; but no other, as I advised him. He was a quiet fellow. He would have hardly told *you*!'

The picture that had momentarily vanished burst fully formed into Alya's mind. 'I thought it could not be you, Nightingale!' he said quietly; and no other spoke. 'When I heard of the smashed skull, I wondered. For a moment.' He did not need to elaborate. Perhaps they had all felt the same. 'But the stab? You have neither the strength nor the weapon, that I can see; and why strip him? So I dismissed the thought. But it seems you have knowledge you cannot account for. And you were very nervous, and trying to make us see all manner of monsters in the cane. To distract us from the one closer at hand? Well?'

The creature whimpered in the gloom. 'No!

Noble lord, master of masters, no! I keep my word! Bound by my bond! Did not slay, never slay, never, never, save as you command me!'

Kalkan seized his spear from the wall where it rested, and the Nightingale's shrills rose in hysterical crescendo. 'Never! *Never! I did not, I did not, didn't!*'

A child, wailing over some unfairness. 'Wait, my lord!' said Alya softly. 'Nightingale, you are no infant, and you choose your words too carefully! You did not slay Almur, you say – but what else did you do?'

Vansha gasped aloud; but there was no response, only the suggestion of a whimper. 'Well, Nightingale?' demanded Alya sharply. 'You were tempted, weren't you?'

Another whimper; but then Alya put hand to sword, and it became a shrilling scream. '*No! Noble lord, master, no!*'

'Why not? You have served me faithfully in your own way. I know it must have been hard for such an one as you. But now it seems – no? Then you must tell me all!'

'Saw him . . .' said the voice, more childish than ever. 'Kept watching, looking back . . . Something in cane, something I smelt, saw only a little, a shape . . . scared! Then saw him ride off suddenly, looking about, as if he didn't want to be seen . . . Nobody else in sight, nobody to tell! I wait, he doesn't come. So I leave horse, go after!'

'Liar!' spat Fazdshan. 'The scholar or I, we'd have seen your tracks, for sure! And you were afraid, you said!'

The voice sneered at him out of the dark. 'You too, if you had any brain worth the eating!'

Fazdshan yelled in rage, but to Alya's surprise Kalkan thrust him back, before Alya had to.

Nightingale tittered. 'You, ape, you stomp in the mud. Me, I go through the cane! High up, where nothing sees me, nothing gets me! And I go fast! I hear

man cry, I hear horse run, I come on him almost at
once lying out all white in his blood – sweet blood, so
savoury!'

'But did you see anything?' demanded Asquan
furiously. 'Anything, any*one* else?'

'Or did he?' demanded Alya. 'Do *you* remember?'

'Something!' shivered Nightingale, like a man
forced to face an accuser. Once again his speech
changed, grew clearer. 'It moved, it glided – maybe it
called. But a mist was about it, and the call was not for
me! Yet I understood it, through things I have tasted
through many others, eyes and lips, long hair over
white skin and supple limbs, hot huddlings and
beastly ruttings – funny, they seem to me! Yet him
they beguiled. And still . . .'

'Yes?'

'I am not sure of men in myself. But from all I
have tasted, I do not think such visions alone would
have called him, enough. Not away; not alone, and in
silence. And . . . yes! In his thoughts they did not.
There was more, something more solid . . . But I do
not see, not clearly. All is blurred by the sudden
struggle, the confusion, the pain – so great! And there
he fell, as I found him. I went, to see if I might help –
no, lord! True, lord! To help, as you would wish!
Though my heart burns, and my mouth flows; and I
have not dined these many weeks, and little enough
of common food. But he is twitching and shivering,
and the shivers fade already, I see the light die in his
eyes – and I must take and eat, what would otherwise
run wasted and be lost. So now, yes, he lives in me, a
little; and I remember. But I am not guilty of his blood.
Not I!'

Fazdshan snarled in furious disgust, and others
echoed him. But Vansha, with an incoherent noise of
rage, simply lunged forward with drawn sword and
slashed before Alya could stop him. Nightingale

screeched loudly, and sprang away, racing on all fours for the stairs, dribbling dark blood from his side.

'No, Vansha!' shouted Alya; but Vansha was on the creature's heels, his sword thudding into the wooden doorpost as Nightingale wriggled out. Vansha bounded up the steps, and Alya, appalled, ran after him.

Outside on the twilit road he saw what he feared; the horses, milling about at their tethers, and Vansha flat on his back in the dust, his sword lying beyond his reach, and the wounded Nightingale astride his chest, pinning him down with one skinny hand to his throat.

'No, Nightingale!' shouted Alya despairingly; but the creature only turned those pit-deep eyes upon him and snarled a few half-formed words. Then the terrible jaws parted, the lapping tongue emerged, and the great blunt teeth lunged for Vansha's forehead.

Alya sprang; and the flat of his sword knocked the creature backwards, but left no cut. Nightingale sprang up, arms swinging, and Alya opened his mouth, to speak to the milder half, the gentler aspect of what stood before him; he knew better than to call it the human side. But a spear hissed past him, far too close, and struck between the creature's feet as it flinched, and another followed it, as the others came running up. Nightingale swelled with rage; and that extraordinary mouth pursed itself into a whistle.

The note was piercing, though soft at first, almost hard to hear among the rattling canes. But it swelled with frightening intensity, and the red tongue turned it to a stabbing, vibrating trill that shook the air and them with it. They stood, wavering on their feet, held by the shuddering power of that whistle. Kalkan and many others spurted blood at the nose. And then the gust came.

The canes bowed sharply; the shutters rattled

and slammed. Vansha, scrambling up, was hurled
from his unsteady feet and sent tumbling. Those still
standing planted their feet hard, and held, though
dust whipped up and into their eyes, and pebbles
leaped and stung. Tseshya staggered and lost footing,
but he fell on to the wind, and it picked him effortlessly up and slammed him back against the house
wall. Vansha was dashed sprawling into a roadside
ditch, and the others were whipped around or sent
staggering away. Another moment and they would be
hurled into the canes, perhaps impaled on them. Only
Alya held his footing; and he inched forward, step by
step, and caught hold of a whipping cane, as thick
around as his arm but still creaking with the strain.

Nightingale, seeing this, turned the full force of
the whistle against him, and the air juddered about his
head, hammered on his breast. He could not breathe;
and he allowed the force of it to fling him back. But he
did not let go of the cane; and it flung him around,
right around the cane-stem and out of the focus of the
blast. The fires in his limbs roared still louder as he
sprang. The hero's sword slashed the very blast
asunder, and sliced as effortlessly through the bristling fur. The Nightingale spun around with a shrill
bubbling hiss that came not from his throat but his
lungs, and was caught up in his own whirlwind even
as it sank and died, laying him almost gently upon the
earth.

His dark eyes were wide, his uncanny face distorted in agony. The thin lips writhed, and he pawed
up at Alya who knelt beside him, horrified.

'Kept . . .' was all he could make out, and he
nodded. He hoped the creature saw him, because the
eyes were already still, and even as he watched the
red tongue lolled, and they grew fixed. The wound
bubbled, the entrails gurgled and emptied, the limbs
kicked and spasmed, but without any effort. The dark
pulse died.

'Black blood!' said Vansha sombrely. 'Stinks worse dead than alive! Thank you, brother!'

'Thank me?' demanded Alya bitterly. 'For what, brother? For destroying our best hope?'

And he rose in wrath against Vansha. 'For destroying our most powerful ally? And why? For nothing, brother! Could you not have held your damned hand? He didn't kill Almur! What he did do, I also loathed! But it was his nature! And not against his pledge to serve us! That he kept, in his fashion!'

'Kept? He was trying to kill us all!'

Alya seized him by the shoulders and shook him as a hound, a rabbit. 'Aye, kept! It was you who broke it, you and your temper! He kept faith till then, and he reproached me with that as he died! And he was right!'

'You owe nothing to a thing like that!' said Vansha tautly, unable to move in that grip. 'Think of all he's killed, and fed on! But you owe it to me – *brother!* – not to humiliate me thus! Who made you the only voice in command?'

'I try never to think what I owe to you,' said Alya, and the words were like sharp-edged stone. He dropped Vansha on his feet. 'You have your life, brother. I preferred yours to his. Be content with that. But it has cost us dear. Our best hope, perhaps.'

'Come now!' rumbled Kalkan. 'Come! The lad was a shade hasty, I'll agree – but don't blame a man too much for acting on decent feelings! And our best hope, surely that's the strength in your arms! Why, a mad bull would hardly have stood against that blast!'

'I am not a bull,' said Alya numbly. 'Mad or otherwise. And I do not think either madness or strength will avail us much against the forces that stir the glaciers.'

'Would the little monster?' enquired Asquan. 'Useful, I grant you; but no more decisive than your strength, or your other powers. What will serve us best, we still have; in you, most of all. I have served few men gladly; but I count it an honour to follow you.'

And hand on heart, he bowed. But whether it was to Vansha as well, it was hard to say. Kalkan, surprised, bowed likewise, but to them both.

'Feel the same way m'self!' he said stiffly. 'Bold fellows, smart as well. Salt of the earth. Good huntin' with you!' And all the others bowed as he did, which left Alya no alternative but to bob up and down to each in turn. Last of all he saw Rysha, still standing on the steps with the women, as if guarding them; and she had not bowed. But to his surprise she gave him a slight toss of the head, like a nod; and again, to him alone.

'Well, we've two to bury or burn,' said Kalkan heavily, and order was restored. 'Which, my lords?'

'Bury,' said Vansha. 'An unusual smoke might attract attention. But we can toss that thing in—' And then he exclaimed in disgust; for where the Nightingale had fallen there lay only bones and a black puddle; and the bones looked barely human, a crude likeness, flattened and translucent as fishbones.

'A poor caricature,' said Asquan gravely. 'They say many Powers have great trouble passing as human, that our bodies and our minds are hard for them to counterfeit without long labour. This one's father made a rotten job of his seed. Small wonder he brought forth a monster.'

Even as they watched, the ribcage bent inwards, and the sutures of the skull, still free as in human infants, fell apart and subsided. The thighbones withered to bare fibres, pitiful remnants. Vansha looked around at their faces, and swallowed uneasily. 'Well, then, bury him where he fell, I suppose. Not all his fault, maybe. I want my dinner!' He stalked away into the house.

'I wonder how many others there are in the

world like that,' mused Asquan. 'Better counterfeits,
perhaps. The leavings of a Power who hungered to
taste a little human love, such as it is.'

'They say that's how we all came about,' grinned
Alya, though he had little good humour left in him
then.

'Shaped by the Powers? Aye, out of the earth, or
the waters, or the back end of some hairy southern
ape – I can believe that of us only too easily! But if so,
at least we were shaped deliberately, with care. Think
of other casual by-blows, looking human, living human, yet never wholly humans, doing things because
others do but never really understanding why.'

'I could credit that of some,' mused Alya, fascinated by the idea despite the fears and preoccupa-
tions that welled up around him. 'Some of the great
tyrants and villains in the old tales, maybe.'

'And some great heroes, perhaps. Provided they
were on the right side. Selfish, ruthless, fearless,
victorious. A handsome exterior would help. Whatever their origins, such men exist, believe me. But
you at least are not of that breed, young lord. Therefore be wary of them, look for them in those you
meet. For now, though, the river mists are rising. Let
us go in and eat. Eat, and forget.'

Alya let himself be ushered inside once again. At
another time he might have pondered long over the
old lord's words, but now he was preoccupied, both
with what had happened and its aftermath, and the
new worries that arose to entangle him. He still felt
bad about the little monster's death, richly deserved
though it might be; and whatever others might say, it
had indeed robbed him of his most potent weapon.
Now he had no vision at all, no source of information
on what lay ahead. Ghastly as its method was, the
creature might have provided that, have given him
some substitute for what the fires had blinded. For
the first time he truly could have cursed his gift, felt

that the old men, whoever or whatever they had been, had played him the cruellest of jokes. Immensely strong, but stripped of insight – they had made a real hero out of him, indeed.

He could not hope to cross the Wall directly, not now; and riding the thoughts of others was now grown too dangerous, given the cold minds that searched for him and his. He had to find some other way to see ahead, to spy out his path; and what that might be, he could not imagine. He sat and thought, hardly tasting the bowl of meat and meal that Rysha thrust into his hand. The others let him be, at Asquan's command, though they hardly needed orders, so much they were in awe of him now.

He grew tired, at last, and his thinking faltered. Little by little he became aware of the others once again – Rysha, talking desultorily with the peasant women; Tseshya, preoccupied and gloomy, already wrapped in his blankets. Nobody had the heart for much talking, let alone singing. The wind rattled the door at times, and blew the flames of the crude rush lamps low. They jumped, half expecting someone to walk in – Almur, perhaps, or Nightingale. Finally Kalkan could stand it no longer, and with drawn sword he threw the door wide, to find himself facing impenetrable whiteness. The mists had been blown off the river, and hung thick about the house. The woman plucked the door from his hand and shut it, quietly, jamming heavy bars across it.

Kalkan and the soldiers grew more cheerful, then, glad to be within four warm walls. Almur's fate no longer weighed on them; they were warriors, after all, and to them it seemed his killer had been paid, and they were well rid of something unpleasant and, to them, unnecessary. They lounged around on the mats, exchanging their usual jokes and darting sly eyes at the peasant girls; and though they received little encouragement in return it did not seem to depress them. They sought to cheer up Vansha, still nervous and brooding; for he had done just what they wanted to do, and been given no credit for it. Curled up on his mat, he did not respond at first, but when darkness thickened the mists and the stove was damped down, and the women retreated to their side of it to undress, Alya saw him roll over and stare into the shadows with the others. 'Maybe they'll be freer in the dark!' muttered Chiansha. 'It's often the way!'

Fazdshan chuckled quiet agreement. 'Leastways if we get any little hands stealing up our breeches now, they won't be bloody Nightingale's!'

'One worry we're shot of!' remarked Darzhan. 'Mind you, there's still my Lord Asquan!'

They snorted with half-stifled laughter, though Asquan seldom appeared to hear such jibes. 'That's enough of that, lads!' said Kalkan, without heat. 'Get your dreams in while you can – unless you've something better in hand!' And on that, his usual line, he rolled himself in his blankets and slept.

So, eventually, did Alya. He had hardly noticed the presence of the women; but when at last, surrounded by snores, he managed to shake off his mass of worries, he found that other thoughts took their place, almost as disturbing. At first it was Savi only, and that he almost embraced, for she seemed so real to him tonight, so close. It was as if the hint of her presence, the warmth of her skin, her faint fresh scent, hovered in the darkness about him, almost close enough to reach out and touch. As if he might see her small breasts swing as she stooped over him, in the faint light of the stove, as if he might reach up to stroke his hand across her thighs.

Knowing he could not made him furious. He writhed uncomfortably in his blankets, turned this way and that and found it only made matters worse. Women, any women, danced before him; he had known few enough, hadn't he? And they were here, not far away, in convenient shadows. He slipped down into a fitful sleep, troubled by vague frustrated dreams which seemed constantly about to take clearer shape. Then his eyes fluttered open, though he was still half asleep, and he saw her, half crouching there before him, the curve of shoulder and flank outlined in the red glow. One of the girls – which, he hardly knew. Beckoning him; standing slowly up, turning away to show herself to him, cocking her head slyly to the steps and the door, beckoning again.

His wits were clouded, but that made the lure all the stronger. Hardly thinking, he heaved himself slowly to his feet. The air smelt hot, heavy and sweet, as if there was incense in it, or a drug; little he cared. He stretched out a hand to her, touched her only with his fingertips and stumbled forward as she skipped lightly away, towards the door. Her small chubby fingers closed about his and led him on, and that light touch alone made his heart leap and pound. Sweat broke out on his brow, and he grabbed out at her. His mind flooded with visions, a thrilling turmoil of what might be. What he wanted now was fierce, crude, nothing to do with Savi – or was it? Wasn't that what he really wanted from her, too? Wasn't that all there was to want?

Visions . . . but he had lived all his life in visions, steered them to his will. And Savi was all he truly desired. With leaden efforts he gathered his thought, and bent it upon the alluring shimmer before him.

It changed. Behind the naked figure of the girl, a jolting, looming sense of presence. As if someone else stalked suddenly through the misty light, a tall sweeping shape whose head was wreathed in many-coloured shadows, hues that shone in every hanging droplet and set it softly ablaze. The girl shrank away; he staggered back, stumbled and fell. He was dimly aware of the tall shape bending over him, and then it was like sliding back helpless into a cool dark pool of sleep. For a moment he lay quiet, as it enveloped him swiftly and smoothly, stifling even the turmoil of his dreams; but then he tried to stir, and his limbs felt enmeshed, as if in heavy, cold dark arms. He struggled, hard, but for every limb he tore free another seemed to become more heavily enmeshed. If he could only shout . . . but his voice was paralysed, caught in his throat by the writhing darkness. He threshed, strained; and then suddenly the dark was shot with racing fires.

He sat bolt upright in his blankets, sweating, heart pounding. He lay in his bed, still, as if he had never stirred from it, never risen to the vision of the girl. A dream, then; a nightmare, even. They often ended like that, a threshing struggle between sleep and wakening. He breathed listlessly in the damp air, and longed for more light; no wonder his dreams had stifled him!

At least there was the stove, no more by now than a faint sullen glow. And he was uneasily aware of another need, one that might explain the dreaming. Out the back, the woman had said; he did not like the idea of either door, at this hour, but he need not go far. He shuffled over to the back door, stumbling over someone as he passed. He half expected them to wake up with sword in hand, but they only mumbled and turned over. As well it hadn't been Vansha, with his savage reactions!

Alya reached the door, and was trying to find the bar when he tripped over something, a discarded blanket, touched the door and felt it swing loose and open. The bar had been lifted; to let someone else out, or in?

He was wide awake suddenly, as if ice-water were tipped down his back; and he skipped hastily back to find his place and his sword. It might be nothing, another on his quest; or it might be . . .

Another blanket, discarded.

A thought struck him, and he looked beyond the fire.

'What is it?' Asquan was on his feet, though his speech was thick with sleep. 'You gasped.'

'A dream. Two empty blankets. An open door. And the women are gone . . .'

'There's more than perfume on the air!' Asquan's chuckle was cynical, but it choked as Alya's hand clamped on his arm.

'They wanted walls and bars! Would they quit them? Even for that?'

Asquan's voice was suddenly alert; and reaching into the stove he seized a heavy smouldering cane-stem. 'Then come on! Wake the others!'

CHAPTER 8
Jewels in the Snow

ASQUAN flung back the door, and stopped dead. The mist filled the misshapen frame from floor to roof like a wall of pearl, and cascaded in about him, spreading its pale chill tendrils across the floor. He swung the brand high, fanning it to flame; but it showed them nothing save pale shadows that might be cane-stems a few feet away.

'Wake the others!' he said savagely. Alya nodded; they must not go rushing out into that, only two of them. He prodded the first heap of blankets, but it only stirred and mumbled. Kalkan, by the sound of it. He prodded harder, then kicked; but Kalkan snored loudly and rolled over, not waking even when Alya shook his shoulder. The same for the next, Darzhan, and Fazdshan beside him. 'As if they're drugged!' hissed Alya.

And the next space was empty. Vansha's. Beyond that Chiansha mumbled insults, even when Alya kicked him with bruising force, and curled up like a child. Alya cursed and ran back round to the door, but stumbled over one more heap of blankets, and stooped to shake its shoulder furiously.

Instead he found his hand on a flat breast, and his wrist clamped in a clawlike grip; but not thrust away, met instead with a sleep-sodden chuckle. 'You? Of all people! Never'd have thought it! No wonder, all these dreams!'

'It's not that, woman! Wake up! Something's happening!'

'What?' The dreamy slur vanished from Rysha's voice.

'Two of us are gone! And the women! Outside!'

She started to snigger. 'What, to water the cane together? Or a round of—' Then she saw the mist that billowed across the floor, rising in eerie curlicues around the warm air of the open stove. 'Out in that?' She scrambled to her feet, still in her shirt, hopping to jam feet into boots. 'Not bloody likely, is it?'

'No! And the others won't wake up. Only me and Asquan.'

'Half done myself. Feels like something dragging me down, still. You're right, my lad, there's something stirring here. Besides your hand. Be a bit less rough next time, eh? Or a bit lower down?'

Alya swore in exasperation and dragged her after him.

'Just her?' hissed Asquan. 'Better than nothing. Can you do anything, woman?'

'Can I do anything!' she sneered. 'Sight more than you can, I'll wager! Piss out that light, for a start! It'll only serve to mark us!'

Asquan shook his head. 'Anything out there can surely see without light. Or doesn't need to! Hurry, woman! You make your tricks shine in darkness. Can you kindle a better light for us?'

'Not light! Just the look of it. To be seen, not see by.' She bit her lip between long teeth. 'Not so common down our way, mist; but maybe I can use it. Can't lead you to whatever's out there; but maybe I can do it the other way around! Supposing you've the nerve, this is!'

'Stop wasting time, woman!' snarled Asquan.

'I kneel before you, oh master!' she sneered. 'Or would you rather I bent over?' She laid hand on the door of heavy canes, then turned in surprise, waggled it, then thrust her fingers into the leather hinges. 'Well greased. Silent. Might've guessed. So—'

She flung her arms high above her head; and Alya gasped. She and Asquan were gone in the instant, in only a faint shimmer of the mist. Out of nowhere the brand was thrust into his hand.

'Here! You're so fond of feeling around in the dark – you lead the way!'

Alya shivered, but they'd wasted enough precious seconds already. He stepped out into the fog, shivering at its clammy embrace, and the lank cold touch of the cane-leaves as they brushed his bare shoulders. A mocking whisper came from behind him, so close the breath tickled his ear. 'Hold that brand up nice and high, now; and look stupid! Stupid and horny – shouldn't be too hard! We'll be right behind you – you hope!'

Alya ignored her. That was what he was supposed to do, after all. He was the logical choice, the youngest and the strongest, the inevitable choice – for bait. He plodded on into the mist, zigzagging around, pushing the canes aside as stealthily as he could; that still made a degree of noise. He hoped it would be enough.

After twenty minutes or so nothing had happened, save that he had come across what might have been a winding path, or maybe just an animal trail; and that he was helplessly lost, all the same. He stopped, gazing around, and saw nothing at all, nor heard any voice. Were the others still with him? He couldn't tell. Nothing but milky shadow, and rustling canes. Then, ahead of him, he did see something move. He hefted his sword, and stared hard. It seemed human enough, and small. A human shape indeed, in white, with long hair; and making its way towards him. Demons might have red hair, they said, though the girls he had seen were all shades; but this was black like his own, and straight. Just as he finally saw it clearly, only some ten paces ahead, it stopped.

It was one of the peasant girls, legs bare beneath

a short shift, patched and stained-looking. She saw him too, clearly, and stood hesitantly, legs rubbing together, biting her finger nervously. Like an animal poised to run—

He stepped forward, raising the brand again. 'Don't worry! I won't hurt you! I just—'

She lowered her hands, and smiled at him, a little nervously still, her fingers playing with the hem of her shift. Then, very smoothly, she drew it up, over her shoulders and off, and stood there naked, swinging it in her hand, the misty torchlight gleaming on breast and belly.

The sight aroused him with startling force. He almost forgot where he was, or that there were others there, and he started towards her at a run, dashing aside the canes with the flaring torch. She squeaked, turned and scuttled back a few paces, swinging her shift playfully, then ran in earnest, giggling loudly. He plunged and bounded after her, but she was faster than he at first, slipping nimbly between the canes. He stretched his legs and felt the fire take hold, and the canes part before him as if no more substantial than the mist. She saw him gaining, squeaked again in fright and swung around a canebrake, so close he could almost reach out—

She sprang, not forward but aside; and out of the mist there loomed a monstrous shape, tall and in-choate, crowned with a huge head. For an instant the torchlight caught a wide white eye, a dark streaked muzzle and snarling jaws full of glittering teeth be-neath a lapping tongue. Then the brand flew from his hands as he lost his balance and skidded forward into the gaping mouth of a pit.

Only his speed saved him, that much faster than an ordinary man's. As it was, he did not clear the pit, but falling, struck its far side, hard. Instinct, more than thought, led him to reach out, to clutch a clump of young cane there. It crackled and snapped in his fingers, but held him long enough to let him slash out with his sword, drive it into the earth there and hang, dazed and winded. The rich ground was soft, the blade pulled free almost at once, but he dug in his other hand among the cane-roots and struggled to haul himself up. But the mist rolled above his head, and in the faint glimmer of the dying brand he saw the monstrous shadow stoop over him. From one side something stabbed at him, struck the earth a finger's breadth from his arm; something else whistled down across his sword-arm with stinging force. He yelped, the sword became a burning, deadly weight, the hilt slid through his fingers. And looking up, he saw descending the tip of a stiff cane, cut at a steep slant to create a deadly point; and he knew then what had stabbed Almur.

Then there was a whistle in the mist, a high thin song; and a piercing scream. The point flew past him, and in desperation, snatching up his sword in his bruised arm, hanging on as best he could, he slashed out at that monstrous stooping head. It was not a strong cut, by his lights; but it connected with jarring force, and a shattering sound which was not that of flesh and blood. With a hoarse shriek the whole shape toppled forward and flew past him into the depths below.

Not so deep; he heard the thud of its landing almost at once, an agonised cry, and beneath it, a lower, darker groan. As if something had been disturbed, a terrible stench welled up, and he flailed desperately for fear of he knew not what terror stirring beneath his dangling feet.

Hands seized his arms, and he tried to shake them loose. 'Stop that, you silly bastard!' snapped Rysha. 'Or we'll let you fall into the shit where you belong!' She moaned with the effort as she and Asquan hauled him up over the lip of the pit. 'Powers aid the stupid bitch you do catch up with, you great stirk! You'll grind her to pieces!'

Alya sprawled gasping on the earth. 'Right behind me, was it? Right bloody behind me? Where in Hella's name did you get to?'

A boot caught him in the ribs, and not lightly. 'Right where we said, child! Till you went haring off after that little slut's tail! We're supposed to keep up, are we? I wonder you fell down anything, I'd have thought your prick'd get in the way! Wish this girl of yours could've seen you! If you'd only gone after her that fast, we'd never have had this—'

Alya caught the boot as it was about to land again, and thrust it back. 'Shut up, you murdering bitch!' he hissed, springing up. '*Shut up!*'

Rysha jumped back, hand to mouth in a gesture oddly like the peasant girl's, her eyes wide and gleaming in the faint light.

'Or what, my lord?' demanded Asquan drily. 'We've just saved your life, she and I, and that despite your best efforts! Though I think there was some force at work here, something you couldn't control. Something that lured out the others . . .'

'The others . . .' Alya staggered around.

'Yes. Best we go back and get some light, the moment you can walk. I think they're down there. And someone else is, too.'

'Some – *one*? Who, then?'

Asquan gestured with his sword, and held up the brand. Cowering on the ground were the three girls, one naked, the other two in shifts. One was clutching a wounded arm, the other covering her eye where she had evidently been hit. 'They had cane spears. The peasant's weapon. We took 'em away. The other had one, too.'

The older woman was nowhere to be seen.

Alya drew a shaking breath, and then reached out to Rysha. She flinched, but he only laid a hand on her shoulder. 'I am very sorry, Rysha; and very grateful. Something did come over me, I don't know what.

But maybe I behaved like your idea of any man. Thank you for saving me, both of you.'

She shrugged. 'Any man; not the worst. I had dreams too. More interesting than usual, maybe, but nothing I've not tried out. Guess it was aimed more at men.' She sniggered suddenly, and kicked the naked girl to her feet. 'Explains why it didn't hit his lordship here too hard, either!'

'Evidently being of refined tastes was some defence – as well as merely well-worn!' said Asquan acidly, and slapped the wounded girls with the flat of his sword. 'You! Back to the house, all of you! We'll deal with you later! Which does not explain,' he resumed smoothly, 'why our healthily amorous young friend was only affected at a late stage!'

'It hit me earlier,' said Alya miserably. 'But I kept thinking of Savi. I always think of Savi. Almost always.'

Rysha jerked one of the girls ahead of her by her hair. 'Almost is as much as anyone manages. Think she's still saving it for you?'

'I *know* she's still true to herself,' said Alya. 'So I would be, also.'

Rysha was silent a moment. 'Going to have a lot of catching up to do. Rub it raw, both of you. Virgins?'

'Not quite.'

'That's something. Do all the funny things. Don't get one up her too quickly, or it might go sour. That's what happened to me.'

'You had a child?'

'Till he kicked it out of me. Because I wasn't performing. Saved the kid a mort of trouble, I guess.'

'You took the words right out of my mouth!' said Asquan.

'Brave of me, seeing what's been in there!' She jerked the girl's hair till she squealed. 'Hey, notice something, or are you blind with flogging it? The mist's thinning!'

Back at the house the others were stirring, especially Kalkan, furious at his bruised ribs, and rousing the rest. He was already at the door with a spear when they came in sight, hair and eyes wild, and he broke out cursing when he saw the girls.

'What's this? Are you all right, my lords? And where's young Vansha – and that damned scholar?'

'Down a hole, I fear – where I would have been, but for Asquan and Rysha. Get lights, fast, and rope from the baggage!'

'And keep these little bitches close guarded!' added Asquan, in a tone that chilled Alya's blood. 'I will want words with them, later!'

Alya had other concerns, though, as they slashed their way back out through the cane, under the light of flaring torches and brands. The mist was all but gone now, but the moon was low, and cast long, deceptive shadows among the cane.

'Monsters!' muttered Chiansha. 'So much for that little tale! Did they get Almur, this crew?'

'A cane spear did!' said Alya. 'And within a close ride of here. *And* he was lured off the road . . .'

'We know how, don't we!' muttered Fazdshan. 'And how many more, I wonder?'

'A good many, I wager,' said Rysha flatly. 'That's of *Aikiya*, of course.'

'Ekwesh?' Fazdshan stared.

'Well, who else comes along here?' she demanded as she stalked past them, still clad only in her shirt and boots. 'Damn few. Maybe none. Maybe the *Aikiya*'s all they've ever known.'

The soldiers stared after her. 'What's she mean by that, then?'

'Leave it for now,' said Alya, though he thought he guessed. 'And keep your eyes open, there may still be real perils lurking! For now it's finding the others that matters.'

Even if it's only to bury them deeper.

But the first thing they heard as they neared the pit was a groan, and then a croaking call for help. A man's voice, though they hardly knew it; and when they ran to the edge, some nearly sliding in, their torches showed them Vansha, mud-smeared and bloody, scrabbling wearily up the crumbling side.

'Aha!' said Kalkan jovially. 'Trying to dig your way out, eh? Take you about a day, I'd say. Want a hoist?'

Vansha's gesture in return was weary but un-mistakable, though he did not speak. When they hauled him out, they soon saw why; though they recoiled from the stink. 'Tried to strangle me, the bitches!' he croaked, when they poured watered wine down his throat. Even in the uncertain light the raw seam around it was obvious. 'To hold me still, while they speared me! But then they gave up sud-denly, and just kicked me down that bloody hole! And then someone else on top!'

'Tseshya?'

'No. Don't think so. He . . . I saw him go out. With one of the girls. I . . . went to stop him!' He scowled defiantly when some of the others chuckled.

'Forget that for now,' ordered Asquan, who had stayed leaning over the hole, apparently untroubled by the stench. 'Something else stirs down here!'

In the end they lowered him over with Darzhan, dangling torches from other lines, igniting the meph-itic air in little splashes and spurts of blue light.

'Only about ten feet!' called Asquan, coughing. 'But the foot – faugh!'

They heard Darzhan vomiting; and when Chian-sha looked over, so did he.

'Someone alive!' shouted Asquan. 'And . . . an-other! It's the scholar! Send me down a line!'

'Two lines!' said Rysha flatly.

'But the other one . . .'

'Two,' said Alya. 'But Tseshya first.'

The scholar was unconscious when they found him wallowing among the unholy mix of filth and carrion, half naked, bleeding from cuts and grazes about his head and one bad wound in his side, again from a cane spear. Luckily his shirt seemed to have held it back somewhat, and staunched the worst of the blood. 'Miracle he didn't drown in that mire!' growled Kalkan.

'Would have, most like, if he'd been properly out when they threw him down!' said Fazdshan. 'Tougher than he looks, this lad!'

'He'll need to be! Chances are it'll fester. What of this other, then?'

'She's half dead, too!' grunted Alya, as he hauled up the second line, and Rysha dragged the inert and filthy shape over the edge.

'Our gracious hostess!' said Asquan, following her up. 'But something more than that, it seems!' And he held up several pieces of something, into the torchlight - a strange shape, monstrous, gaudily painted.

'It's a bloody mask!' exclaimed Chiansha. 'Or it was till lately! Like those louse-ridden Seers use for their tricks - saving your presence, o' course!' he added hastily to Alya. 'Savin' your presence!'

'Feel free!' said Alya wearily, looking at the fragments his sword had made of the gaudy, potent thing. 'I'm no longer much of a shaman. But I'd remember this design if I'd seen it before. It's none I know of - an Ekwesh totem, probably. Scales and feathers - some sort of serpent-spirit, I guess. Beautiful and powerful; you can feel it. Not a drug, then. She was working on our minds directly. I should have been on the alert for that. And she could gather the mists somehow, too. Well, we've got to get them all back to the house, and tended - yes, her as well! I've questions to ask her.'

He lingered, fingering the broken edges left by

his blow, and the fall that followed. 'But this thing – I could have used this! Maybe found another path to the Wall, one I could still take!'

'Can it not be repaired?' asked Asquan.

'As wood and metal, yes. As the guise of a Seer, no.' Alya sighed. 'It'd need to be refashioned in many ways. As soon make another from scratch, almost; and even then it would lack the strength these things gather with time and use. This one was very old and potent.' He held it out over the reeking pit and let the pieces fall, splashing back into the liquid mix of sewage and the carrion corpses of those the mask had lured. 'Now that's the best we can do with it. Let's get back with the others.'

Nobody wanted to sleep. It felt uncommonly good to bar the door behind them and stoke up the stove to a blaze, and when Asquan demanded hot water to tend the wounded, they formed a party of five to go down to the river. They came hurrying back in earnest, looking anxiously into every shadow.

'Did you see something?' demanded Alya, as they scuttled down the steps.

'Nothing much!' admitted Chiansha. 'But you start at every shadow. Even a few swans flying low . . .'

'Swans?' Alya swung out of the door and up the steps in haste.

'To the north!' called Chiansha. 'Flying north!'

Alya scanned what he could make out of the sky, but it was little enough, and he came back down thoughtfully. 'Big swans?'

'Very big. Didn't see much more, the moon being so low. They were just shadows. Funny, now you mention it; you'd have thought they'd shine more, being white an' all!'

'Maybe they weren't!' said Alya. 'Come on, let's get this water to the stove!'

They boiled it in the women's crude earthen

cauldrons and pots, and Vansha washed himself, while they sponged the stinking mire off the wounded. 'Duck your head and I'll wash your hair!' Rysha told him, then, as he surfaced, dripping, she gleefully added, 'Probably won't be the first head there's been in here!'

'What d'you mean?' croaked Vansha.

Rysha grinned evilly in the smoky red light. 'You should know, where you've been playing around! All those remains – don't think they let all that good meat go to waste, do you?'

'I thought they looked plump enough!' said Alya, chilled. Vansha turned very uneasy, but Rysha sniggered.

'How does Tseshya fare?' asked Alya hastily, as Asquan came to the stove

'Oh, he'll live to study more follies!' said Asquan cheerfully, rinsing away clotted blood. 'A dunt on the head and a shallow stab, nothing vital pierced. They made a careless job of butchering you both, my lord Vansha. Just what you'd expect from a woman!'

'It worked well enough, for all that!' said Alya.

'I call it a nice neat trick!' said Rysha calmly. 'Lead a man by the cock, out to where you can cack him undisturbed. And he'll even keep quiet in case the others all want a bit, too. That's how it was, eh, me Lord Vansha?'

Vansha snarled and mumbled something about witches.

Asquan glared at the women cowering around the older woman, washing her clean, and the blood from head and arm. 'And I can guess what wondrous visions they showed young Almur!' sniffed Asquan. 'Not just one, but two or three of you, innocent little things surprised in the bushes . . . Oh yes, pretty please, but don't let the others see! Gah! You and your demons and monsters!'

'They're real,' said one of the young women sullenly. 'You wait. You'll see!'

'They'll be cleaner company!' snarled Kalkan. 'Murdering bitches! Stabbing decent men, eating them, even! And selling their armour, I don't doubt!'

'We should certainly make them pay for it!' said Asquan evenly. His eyes looked dull and fixed as a dead man's, and they shrank away.

'Make *us* pay?' It was the older woman's voice. Awake now, livid of face, she half rose on her sound arm, laughing hysterically. 'Funny, funny! Pay more than we have already? How can you do that?'

'I can show you, soon enough,' said Asquan icily; but Alya waved him back.

'What have we ever done to you? Did we not share our food, and trust you?'

'Didn't you hear me? You've taken our men, taken *their* sons and daughters to be! Never to come back, save on the ghost-rides! Thralls to their death and thralls thereafter, fodder of war, my boys, my boys . . . You – *men*! You – *warriors*!' She made them the foulest insults she could spit.

'I told you,' said Alya quietly. 'We are not the *Aikiya*, the Ice-wolves, we are their enemies. We're rescuers. We are not even warriors, first and foremost.'

'You? You might be something more, or think you are. Her, maybe. But the rest of you? Him, the cold grey one? Him, with the iron face? Him, like a sharp new knife?' She meant Vansha. 'Slayers all! Wasters all!'

Kalkan strode forward and caught a girl by the hair. 'Permit me to show you a reason!' He threw her at Alya's feet. 'Let Asquan have his way, my lord!'

She snarled up at Alya. 'Oh aye! Like your little tame demon! Whom like sots you slew for the deed we did!' She spat at his feet, and made an obscene gesture in his face. 'Some rescuers! Excuses for more

blood! You're as bad, you're all alike! You ruin our
lives with our fighting, then foul our bodies. Why
shouldn't we gnaw on your bones, if we can?'

Kalkan took a stiff step forward, but suddenly
Rysha was in his way. 'That's right!' she said softly,
her voice almost caressing. 'Why shouldn't they?'

Kalkan menaced her with his open hand. 'One
murdering witch dares speak up for another? You
forget your place, woman!'

'So do you, my lord!' she answered. 'So do you!'

In the stove-lit dimness of the hut she seemed to
fade suddenly, to grow. In her place, almost as tall as
Kalkan, stood a lean young man, pale, cheeks pinched
with famine and fever, the old lord's unmistakable
image. His eyes bright with delirium, his lips cracked
and raw, he mouthed soundless pleas and waved his
fleshless arms in desperate entreaty. But suddenly his
cheeks sank in, his eye-sockets hollowed, his lips
drew lividly back over fixed and grinning teeth.
The lower jaw sagged and fell away.

Kalkan screamed aloud, a racking, high-pitched
sound to come from such a huge man, and sank to his
knees. His soldiers, riveted with horror, turned their
weapons on the image, but it was no longer there.
Nor was Rysha.

'We all do things we'd never think possible,
don't we, my lord?' she said, from the surrounding
shadows. 'When he died, you had food, didn't you?
Not much, but some. I knew, b'lieve me! I was just
itching to get my paws on it. But you knew he was
dying, and it'd be wasted if you gave it him; whereas
you could still live. So you didn't. And so you did.'

She giggled. 'Nicely put, that! Still, can't have
been easy, can it? Your own son! But it was right.
Why? Because it was striking back. Like I was doing,
when they used me worse'n their bloody dog, my
dear husband and his dad! And that's what we're all
doing, aren't we, in our different ways? Else why

exactly are we spending what life we have left chasing some little skirt most of us've never even seen? Striking back!'

Alya felt a deep chill about him, like a wind from another world. 'But their way was cold-blooded murder! As if we were Ekwesh. I told them we weren't!'

'So?' she snapped. 'What d'you think they know about anything? Like I said, the Ekwesh are all they've ever seen of the world outside, and I mean *all*! Expect them to make nice distinctions? To them you *are* all the same!'

The round house was silent a while, save for Kalkan's dry sobbing. Alya gestured to Darzhan and the soldiers, and they came up to lead the old lord away. Alya ran his hand over his brow. 'Asquan, let her go. Rysha is right. Or rather, she makes a good defence.'

Asquan's clawed fingers caressed the shaking girl's neck, like a casual talon. 'They sought to murder us, without cause. It might have been worse, far worse. Your girl left without any hope of rescue.'

'I know. I will not easily forgive. But they have suffered badly for the attempt, and that in itself grew out of suffering. That's enough. We won't make it worse.'

Vansha began a disbelieving shout, but it died in his throat. There were no other protests, not even grumbles of disagreement, but the silence was almost worse. Nobody made a move. Then Asquan shrugged, without any heat, slapped the girl back and forth across the face, hard, and left her sobbing on the trodden floor. 'As you will, my lord. Shall I see how the older woman fares? Her wounds also will likely fester. I should examine them, if we're to spare her life.'

And hurt her a hundred times over, no doubt! But Alya found he could summon up no great guilt over that. 'Do so, my lord. She may be able to tell us a great deal of interest, not least about the road ahead.'

Asquan nodded thoughtfully. 'So be it! I may have a little talk with her now, in case fever or festering set in.'

The mood relaxed, at last; and weariness drove them back to their blankets. Alya went over to where Kalkan sat, head in hands. 'Come, my lord, try yourself no further. He would have understood, your son.'

Kalkan looked at him, absently, his eyes watery and vague. 'Would he? Do you truly think so? I wonder. It was not only that, you see. It was after he died, when there was no more food . . . Flesh of my flesh, you see. Was that an act of reason, of love? And then next day they sent whole baskets in, after so many days forgotten. Heavy with rich scraps from some banquet . . . It was that, that made me sick. Not what should have done. Not him. So you see, I am no better than them, my Lord Alya. Not truly.'

Alya found it hard to speak. 'I would not say so, not by far. Nor would your son. The vision you saw was a cruel lie. Sleep now, and banish the memory!'

He rose, and went to find Rysha, now laying out her mat protectively before the young women. She smirked up at him. 'Come to take up where we left off?'

'I doubt it,' he said shortly. 'That was a terrible thing you did to Kalkan. Never do it again.'

'He would have slain them, otherwise. He, steeped in his own guilt!'

'After a fashion. As you, in yours.'

She mocked him, making as if to whip up her shirt, as the girl had. 'And what would you have been deeper in, my lord, but for me?'

'I know. Myself, and Vansha, and Tseshya. And I'm grateful. If I could give you much more than gratitude, I would.'

She posed a moment, considering, hands still on the hem of her shirt. 'Who knows? But not now, not tonight. Go dream of your little bit.'

Alya bowed, and made his escape. Vansha, rubbing himself dry over the warm updraught of the
stove, grabbed his arm as he made for his mat.

'You think it all serves me right, don't you? This,
after—'

'I didn't say that, brother. That was a strong
sending the woman set upon us, with that mask.
Using our own minds to increase its strength, maybe.
My father said that could be done, though he never
told me how. But you didn't just follow Tseshya, did
you?'

'Unh. How did you know?'

'A girl came to me, as well. But I – well, I was half
asleep, half dreaming. I must have just dropped off
again. And perhaps my Seer's training helped block
the spell; or these forces I've been given. But mostly I
was thinking of . . . well, other things.'

'Don't say it! Savi.' Vansha groaned. 'You must
think I don't know what of me. That I'm an oath-
breaker or something . . .'

Alya felt bone-weary. 'You didn't swear off other
women. Just not to abandon the chase. I'm not
standing in judgement, anyhow. It caught up with
me, eventually.'

Vansha sighed in anguish. 'You know what she
did to me, brother? It was the little one, the round-
faced one. I woke up with this hand feeling around
me, and . . .'

'Don't. Rysha's bad enough.'

'It's been a long time. I just . . . I felt . . . A statue
would have been stirred! Wouldn't anyone? And the
bitch said we'd be all right out back. And, Powers, it
was all right, it was damn good and she was enjoying
it too, pumping away like . . . with those little legs
waving, and then . . . They waited until, you know,
and they whipped something around my throat,
pulled it tight. And you know, under that damned
'fluence it felt . . . crazy. I struggled . . . broke a spear,

they couldn't get a proper stab at me, kept jabbing. But then they got into a rush and just dragged me off kicking and threw me into that . . . that vat of Hella. Couldn't even cry out! Isn't that something could happen to anyone?'

'I'm for my blankets again,' yawned Alya. 'I won't tell Savi, brother, if that's what's bothering you. Provided you let me sleep out the night!'

That was not to be. He slept almost at once; but the groans and whimpers of the wounded invaded his sleep, and the uneasy stirrings of the others. Towards dawn Darzhan erupted out of a yelling nightmare which set the women off in hysterics. Vansha showed no sign of nightmare, but hardly seemed to sleep; he sat up muttering to himself, not in terror so much as anger, darting sharp malevolent glances towards the women. The smell of blood and sickness, and the lingering taint of that ghastly pit, seemed to invade the room and foul the air. It oppressed Alya as he lay there, unable to sleep again or to think properly. When he shook off the horrors, other images haunted him, filling him with great uncertain fears; and though at last he drifted off, it seemed only a moment before Asquan was shaking his shoulder.

'Mmmnh?'

'The sun is well up, my Lord Alya. Or would be, if cloud and mist and cane did not obscure the light. And I was right about our wounded. That filth has set festering and fever in all, even Vansha. Not too seriously, however.'

Alya struggled to sit up. 'Thanks to your care and skill, my lord, I'm sure. But you're saying we can't ride on today?'

'Nor for three days at least. Perhaps more for Tseshya, for all that he insists he will be ready tomorrow – when he isn't delirious, that is.'

Alya twisted his blankets in his fist. 'More delay,

more! These bloody-handed whores! Maybe I should've let you have your way, after all!'

'Maybe. But your notions of chivalry and justice are oddly becoming, in their way. I do not wish to rid you of them, not wholly. And the woman is certainly well paid! That was a savage cut you gave her, my lord!'

'In a savage snare!' shuddered Alya. 'Will she die?'

Asquan shrugged. 'Her shoulder is slashed deep, into the bone, her jaw less deeply. If her own filth poisons her blood, perhaps; I have not the skill to amputate. But I think not. And I did persuade her to speak a little last night, of our road, and other matters that might be worth hearing, since we must wait in any case.'

Alya sat up stiffly. Someone was frying smoked fish, a smell he normally quite liked. Today, with the sickbed reek still stronger, it made his gorge rise. He could tolerate none of it. Wrapped in his great cloak, he strode up and down the wide hut like a caged bear, while the women cowered, and the others kept well out of his way. Once he kicked a stone out of the floor, smashing a cane in the wall. Finally Vansha called him over to where he lay by the stove.

'Sit, brother! You've walked halfway there already, you deserve a rest!' And, more softly, his voice still croaking, 'Can you not see how you unnerve them? Just when you need to hearten them? We've lost our first man, and near enough more!'

Alya slumped back against the bricks. 'And that's why we must press on! We mustn't lose the scent, not now – they're so far ahead already. And now – three bloody days, says Asquan! Or more! But Tseshya thinks he'll be all right tomorrow—'

'Only because he's scared of you,' said Vansha. 'Scared you'll leave him behind here, with the witches. Small wonder, the way you're behaving.'

'*I'm* be—' Alya shrugged. 'You know why, none better. Anything could be happening to her.'

'It could,' said Vansha, grimly. 'Think I don't remember that, brother?'

'Did you – last night?'

'That was nothing! I'm not made of stone, it's been a long time. But her I loved before you ever came between us! That I do not forget!'

'Whatever else! Better you remember it's me she loves!'

Vansha shifted painfully. 'If we were not oath-brothers—'

'You could strike me down for that? Brother, you already did!'

The air simmered between them a moment, and then Alya folded his arms. 'I'm sorry! That's done now. Rescuing her is more important, and our brotherhood. I must be tired.'

Vansha shook his head. 'It's far more than that. You've changed, brother. For the best, I thought; but now I wonder. The change is not stopping. You no longer look like a boy.'

Alya stared at him, half in laughter; but Asquan, coming to tend Vansha, overheard, and nodded. 'We've all remarked on it. You've filled out; you look far stronger, and your face . . . Not much older, a year or two, but grimmer. I wonder . . .' He lifted off the dressing he had bound over Vansha's deeper cuts, and clicked his tongue. 'The swelling eases, and more splinters come into sight. Filthy weapons, cane spears . . .' Vansha yelped as he plucked out a couple, but sat back relieved. 'There, it will drain better now.' He pressed freshly pounded herbs under the cloth pad. 'My lord Alya . . . forgive me that I suggest this, but even the friendlier Powers have been known to play strange tricks on men, for reasons no doubt good to them. I wonder if your mysterious wanderers in fact gave you anything extra in that vast strength of yours.

Or have they simply caused you to use what you already had, that much faster? Could that inner fire really be burning up your life?'

Alya sat back, thunderstruck. But he was startled to find how little he cared. 'I don't believe that! You don't look so young yourself, Vansha. What we've been through would age anyone! But if that really is their price, so be it! If I can only live a shorter life, so long as it's with Savi I don't care!'

'Then you are still young,' remarked Asquan calmly.

None of them spoke for a few minutes. The wounded woman whimpered upon her bed. Condensing mist dripped slowly from the roof.

Vansha said, almost casually, 'If you're so nervous . . .'

'I'm not nervous!'

'Chafing at the bit, then. Could you not at least try to spy out our way again?'

Alya growled. 'I've said already, man: I dare not! Not now I know what's about out there. His taunts were true, that Ice-wolf we slew. The Choosers of the Slain. We'd be fools to draw their attention. Chosen fools!'

'They were with the war-band, he said, protecting it. They may be far away now.'

'Maybe. But this is all the realm of the Ice.' Alya shivered. 'Those creatures, those minds . . . If I could only find some other way, believe me!' He clapped his hands over his eyes. 'I'm afire with impatience! What use is a Seer who can no longer see? I'm sorry now I wounded the woman so! She at least has power . . .'

He stopped suddenly, thinking hard. Then without another word to Vansha he sprang up, and padded over to where the woman lay. She groaned and shivered as Rysha bathed her injured shoulder and jaw, but she was conscious and staring up at him as he knelt beside her.

'Now you know we are not Ekwesh,' he said. 'Or their kind. And I know also what you are. Where did you get that mask?'

'From – father,' she mumbled, her voice shivering even more than her jaw wound and her fever could account for. She was terrified, as she had not been a moment since. Of him; not of what he might do, simply of what he was. Had suffering heightened her own sight, as it did for him? And what then could she read? 'He . . . from his. And forefathers, deep into years. It would have been . . . my son's, my son's son.'

'But you learned to use it. All too well. Woman, you must know much that passes, in this land.'

She said nothing.

'Much,' he repeated. 'Tell the others all you can. For now, you need only tell me one thing. Is there some place around here, some pool or island, where the black swans bathe?'

The woman almost started up in her fright, but the pain she caused herself, too fierce for a scream, made her sag back with a hissing gasp, pawing feebly at her bandage. Rysha protested, but Alya held her back. 'I need to know, woman,' he said, implacably.

She rolled away from him on to her good shoulder, huddling into herself. He reached out to turn her back, but her voice stopped him. 'There may be such a place. Where the rivers flow apart, north and west, two days' walk, a few hours' ride. A thousand strides short of the ford there. Where the other flow curves around tall rocks, a high bluff. A river island, a heap of sand, little more. I know nothing sure; and I did not tell you. Leave me be!'

Rysha glared at him. He shrugged, and rose to his feet, thinking hard. Was he really no longer a boy? He still felt like one. He did not want to grow older and more cynical, weakening his love for Savi, maybe even making him too ready to accept the possibility he might lose her. Even in thinking that he was

already losing hope! He needed heartening, as badly
as any of them. The risk would be well worth it. Had
he truly changed? Then let him make full use of it!

'My Lord Asquan!' he said, at last. 'If they really
need time to recover, I must leave them in your
charge. I cannot waste it. I must go off for a day
or two!'

'What?'

'On my own! For something only I can do. No,
don't ask! I couldn't explain. A gamble, but it's worth
taking. A throw that might win us much – or everything!'

The others, hearing this, were gathering round,
questioning, protesting, and Alya was surprised at
how nervous they sounded; but he shook his head.
'I leave them all to your command, until Vansha
recovers. Wait four – no, five days, longer only if
you must. If I haven't returned by then, follow the
road north. Either I'll meet you along the way, or—'
He shrugged. 'I'll be careful, of course. And leave the
women safe, whatever!'

'Will you have enough food?' demanded Kalkan.
'At least take your cloak!'

Alya shrugged ruefully. 'Hunger and cold . . .'

'Don't be a fool!' croaked Vansha, sitting up in
his blankets, his hair plastered about his forehead
with the sweat of a breaking fever. 'Wait till I can
come, at least—'

'Only I can do this. Anyone else would be in far
greater danger, and endanger me, maybe. No, go on
and find Savi. Keep your head, listen to Asquan. And
never, *never* give up!'

Alya gathered up his gear and sword, with cold
ripples of excitement surging through his spine,
blazing highest in his old wound, as if goading him
to action. The others were wishing him all kinds of
luck, but though he nodded softly and smiled at them
all, he hardly heard.

It must be near noon, surely. He strode to the door and opened it, as casually as he could. He found himself looking out over the green canestalks once more, woven with only faint wisps of mist; and through them, a pale sun glittering faintly upon the river. He picked up his saddle and, deep in thought, he went out without looking back.

He did not know it, but Kalkan, at Vansha's suggestion, shadowed him some part of the way. The old lord returned to the farm hut that evening, puzzled. 'Lost him among those damned canes, eventually. Can't stay close without giving yourself away! But it was a funny thing. Took stuff from his saddlebags, and went down to the riverbank first, gathering something. Couldn't see what!'

'Sand,' said Vansha unhappily. 'For the Trail. As dangerous as any he can walk in this world.'

Even as they spoke, Alya sat in a small stony clearing some way to the north and east, not far from the river, just south of the great fork of which the woman had spoken. The ride had been long, but he had enjoyed it, and the walk thereafter, for he had left the horse a good hour back, tethered among sparse grass. It felt good to be on his own, surprisingly so. Strength seemed to burgeon in his limbs, till he felt he no longer needed the horse, but should be able to race to the hidden horizon in a few long strides. It felt so right that he found himself wondering if this was truly why he had been given his strength, to do great deeds all on his own, without others to help or hinder – and without endangering them, either.

But I was only a boy! I didn't imagine what I could do. I thought I needed the villagers; and when Vansha volunteered, I was glad not to be on my own. Then I thought I needed the help of a king, proper warriors, troops of horse . . . I was only a boy. If they wanted me to do this on my own, why didn't they give me confidence, understanding,

*knowledge? And they should have left me the power
that was rightfully mine . . .*

So he had landed himself, instead, with this
strange band of misfits, the hopeless and homeless
and reckless. As he should have expected, for who
else would follow such a chase? Strong fighters, he
had no doubt of that now; yet they had hardly had to
do any fighting, so far. He and Asquan had done most.
If anything, he felt they had held him back, so that
Savi was far from him now, and facing whatever her
fate must be. Now, with a single bold move, he might
discover something of what lay ahead. He might find
whether he still needed them or not. He might even
discover some sign of Savi. And maybe, though it was
a remote hope, achieve a thing still greater. But to do
it he must turn the hunt back against the hunter, the
minds that sought him into his prey.

The cane was growing thinner here, and no
more than a hundred paces ahead the bluffs the
woman had mentioned reared high above it, against
the sunset sky. He could not see the river, but he
heard the water lapping among the rushes, a lulling,
peaceful note that was good for his mind to fasten on,
as he let the sand whisper through his fingers in the
serpentine patterns he could not forget, and the
words trickle as softly from his lips. After a while,
without taking his eyes from the pattern, he reached
for the mask; and then, rising and setting it upon his
head, he began to dance.

Slowly; for though he trod the Path, he was
aiming not at any soaring frenzy, but at control. Till
now he had been desperate to fulfil his father's wish,
to win past the Wall and into the realm beyond it; but
he guessed now that that would only have been one
step among many. If his way was still barred, he could
explore others he had only touched upon by chance.
To direct his thought, for one; to fasten on a goal, a
mind . . .

His feet scuffed the stones, but did not turn
aside. Already the black glass rose behind his eyes,
and he glided across its mirroring surface, seeking,
searching. Blood led him, and the smell of smoke, the
stench of burning roofs and bodies beneath; for that
also was deeply graven in his memory. And the blood,
on black feathers.

He was looking, suddenly, through other eyes.
He was circling above what had been a place of
conflict, once, and now held only bones and broken
weapons, already sinking into the land and being
absorbed. The spurting blood that had drenched
the field had already fed three summers' worth of
the brown tundra grass, and soon those who passed,
if any, would see no trace at all. But she felt it, as she
had then, fouling her armour, her clothes, even her
hair and mouth. The blood on her was always fresh.

To wash it off – a picture came into her mind, of
whispering rush beds, rattling cane-brakes, the swift
currents beneath the bluffs, and the deep lonely pool
its constant eddies had carved in the shelter of the
small sandbar. She did not stop to wonder how she
remembered it; there had been so many places, so
many times. She turned in the heights, and came
diving down the curve of the sky, towards the river.

The water was chill, and that very chill strength-
ened Alya's still exalted state. Beneath the surface he
lay now, among the reeds below the shadow of the
bluff, and he waited. Himself he suppressed, his
thoughts, his desires, losing himself in the urge to
be cooled and cleansed. The brush of the water on his
skin seemed only to intensify her longing, through the
faint unconscious thread that still joined them, bearing little more than instinct and sensation. What came
back to him was uproar, violent, heady, confusing.
Greatly daring, he sent that also back to her, magnify-
ing and redoubling itself, dulling her awareness and
heightening her longing for rest and quiet. But that

intensity cut both ways; the shock of cool water upon breastdown was breathtaking, and when it changed suddenly to bare skin he almost fainted. Floating half hidden as before, he pulled himself around the sandspit, and saw.

He was closer to her than he expected, far closer. She floated like any human girl, barely at arm's length, and in the mellow evening light she blazed upon the waters, ivory skin set in a golden aureole of hair. He had not known it would be this one, the least like his own love, yet to him the most potent of all in her beauty. The shock of the sight also passed back and forth between them, and for a minute they were stunned, seer and seen, by its intensity.

That Alya had not expected. It almost unmanned him, but perhaps it also saved him. For one long moment the girl lay rapt, transfixed by the sheer redoubled radiance of her own loveliness in his eyes, like an image thrown between paired mirrors. That gave him the moment he needed to pounce. Not on her, but upon the cloak that she had laid down to drain away the slathered blood into the clean sand.

He landed full in its centre, and his knees dug deep into the black silken lining, with all his weight. She doubled up violently in the water, drowning her terrible cry. He had the cloak then, bundled up with his belt. She thrashed in desperation, rose and hurled herself at him.

She was as tall as he, perhaps taller. Her hands went for his eyes, his throat, her knees for his belly and his groin, with the heedless ferocity of some Ice-spawned predator. He met the blows, though they bruised him; her strength in this shape was only mortal, or at least no greater than his. He caught her wrists, and threw her down upon the sand; and pinning her down, he bound her at wrist and ankle with the heavy straps from his saddlebags, and her mouth with a length of clean cloth. Then, because she was what she was, he murmured words of keeping and binding over them. They should work; it was in her thoughts he read them. Then he rose, wincing, and looked at his prize.

The link was shattered, but glory still coursed in his blood. It fuelled deep and disturbing desires, and he struggled against the urges it awoke, knowing such beauty was an art natural to her, deeper than anything in her human aspect. Whatever shape she chose, she would have scorned to seem anything less than lovely; and the same cold pride flowed out of her now, bound and helpless as she was. She did not struggle, but fixed him with eyes that might have flayed any man less well protected.

Gingerly he stroked the wet tangles of hair back out of them; but she still did and said nothing, though he could see her arms strain against the straps. His hand brushed down her cheek and throat, hovered a moment at her breast. But she was not Savi, and he was not Vansha; and knowing her for what she was killed all true desire.

He dragged her up the narrow strip of sand, beneath the edge of the reeds. 'I regret I must do this to you. I have no choice. I cannot simply bend your mind to my will, and I must seek knowledge, at whatever cost.'

The eyes spoke: *I will tell you nothing, save of death.*

'I know,' he said. 'I will not harm you for that. But force me, and I will subdue you, if I must. You might never escape this trap, save at the cost of this flesh you wear. Will you suffer what you have done to so many others? Then lie still.'

He splashed ashore to find his tunic and jerkin, which he had left dry, and covered her with them. Still she made no move.

'You see, I know something of you,' he said. 'I have touched your sisters' minds, and yours also, a

little. You are a Chooser of the Slain, a lesser Power,
under the dominion of the Lords of the Ice. Your
thought is less cold and cruel than theirs, perhaps.
Yet you are their slave and soldier, nonetheless,
speeding over land and sea at their command. You
are the living banner and command of their armies,
flying above them, seen or unseen. Like this.'

He had the cloak unbound in an instant, flinching slightly at its living touch; and before it could
move, he had wrapped it around his own shoulders.
The girl went rigid before him, her back bowing,
belly and thigh muscles standing taut as cables. The
cloak fought him like an enraged bird, beating and
thrashing as he strove to hold it across his shoulders.
Without the undying flame he might never even have
held it. It beat him to his knees; but then, thrashing
forward, it touched the mask he still wore.

The girl cried out. The transition was abrupt.
Suddenly the cloak was clinging, not thrashing, melting against his arms with almost seductive warmth.
The mask was no longer a weight upon his head, but
as close as skin, its beaked forepart no longer black
before his eyes but bright red. His body rippled
around him like water, and he knew instinctively
all that he must do.

Without a look back at the bound girl he sprinted
down the sandbar into the water, and hurled himself
forward as he had seen the others do, as he saw in her
mind. Suddenly the air was enfolded in his cloaked
embrace. There was no pain, no transition, yet the
feeling was intensely physical, his whole body hurled
into one vast effort. He felt his feet trail briefly across
the water. Then he beat vast wings, and he was
soaring high into the evening air.

The fires raged now in his arms, and he laughed
aloud at the seething tingle, the intoxicating surge.
This was power, this was escape; this was pursuit no
longer dogged and grim, but swift and sure as the

winds that bore him. For this, surely, he was given that great measure of strength. Would they bar him from riding the minds of others? Then he would ride upon their own black wings.

Far below him, on the narrow sandbank, he looked for a human figure, and saw none. She was hidden from road and river and sky alike; and for a moment he felt a qualm. Then he left her and all thoughts of her, and turned northward. There was little enough time.

Down the river he flew, to the place of its branching into many streams, and northward from that along its wider, colder parent, a sheet of black water. He saw with relief the canes fade away, and the wider, greener lands that opened up, with the narrow roads winding between the rolling hills. He gazed in wonder at the vast herds of beasts that roamed the land, and longed to swoop down and explore; but he knew he must not. He might have little enough time; and this, peaceful though it seemed, was the domain of the Ice, and might contain many strange perils.

He looked down with unaccustomed contempt upon the little farms that huddled at wide intervals throughout the land, starved and shrunken things among the rich fields around them. He remembered how the Citadel's folk had struggled and toiled for their food in a parched and barren land; even Volmur's kingdom was poor compared to this. And with those memories stirring he gazed with cold hatred upon the bands of horsemen that made their way north along the roads, like ants toiling back to their nests to serve their bloated queen. Something seemed strange about them, but he was too angry to think, and too impatient. It came almost as a relief when darkness rolled down upon them as the sun sank beneath the rim of the world.

The hours passed, and he flew easily, without effort, and saw the first long rays creep across a land that was growing flatter, scrubbier, starker. Even the farms were gone, save here and there by the river a village of hovels that evidently struggled to exploit the last lowly scraps of fertile green.

Beyond the last of these all things grew smaller and meaner. Trees turned to wiry thickets, creeping across low brown grasses. Those in turn gave way to bare patches in the earth, and soon stones, with no more growing things than shrubs and lichen, and mere winding tracks where the roads had been. And beyond them more stones, less soil, grey land and black water, sterile and cold and bleakly ugly. So ugly, that the sudden sprinkling of whiteness seemed like a benison, a glittering, patterned beauty to compensate for the end of life; and along the river margins, instead of reeds, the grey-white crusting of ice.

Over the snowfields he sped, following the black vein that was the river through the icy whiteness. White as the girl's skin, he thought once, and as cold. But most often he thought only of his own tiny shadow pacing him, skipping and sailing over the country's flattened curves. So it was that at first he did not see what lay ahead, but looked up to find it rear in front of him, as it seemed, impossibly vast in his eyes, a glassy blue-white counterpart to the obsidian of the Wall itself.

From one horizon to the other a mighty range of cliffs stretched across the land; and their name in the tongues of men was glacier. Winter's coming made bitterly solid they seemed, a winter that would admit no spring. The gold of sunset fell upon their ramparts, and was cast back chilled and drained. But the rising moon, faint against their own grey horizon, took fire from them, as it seemed; for over the unbroken fields of the Ice there were no clouds to hide it. Back they stretched from those outer walls, far back beyond the

curve of the world into blackness, as if the glaciers
grew out of the cold Void itself.

So at last Alya the Seer's son, in a guise he had
never dreamed of, set eyes upon the walls of winter,
upon the mighty vanguard and fortress of the realm of
the Great Ice. And the sight pierced his heart with a
splinter of pure chill, for the majesty and grandeur of
the force he dared to challenge.

But its advance was not uniform or even. This
was a realm with a coastline, and the snow for
beaches beneath. Almost all the land lay obliterated
by white, save where here and there black bones of
stone, rime-enshrouded, still protruded slightly
through the snow-capped glacial bays. Once tall
mountains, perhaps, now they were ground down
to mere memory, like skeletons scoured by a desert
wind.

Here and there the contours of the land still
baulked the glaciers, but past such obstacles they
reached out long icy fingers, as if preparing to close
and crush them. Elsewhere, for causes no longer
visible, they formed bays and peninsulas, and these
riven with valleys, crevices, cracks and caves, from
whose shadowy depths the black rivers spewed out
across the land.

All of these he noted as he flew towards the Ice,
as well as he could hope to. It seemed to him that he
flew slowly now, against a headwind. When at last he
crossed the awesome battlements, and the white
lands spread out beneath him, it came as a shock
to see the sun so low. He fought to rise higher and
higher, till by virtue of his great wings he soared
beyond the height of most birds, and the thin dry air
burned his lungs. Yet he soon realised that he sped as
before; it was only the vastness he confronted that
made him seem so much slower.

Then the sun sank at last, and the sky around him
turned black as the rivers beneath; and the Ice

assumed its terrible crown. Far above the whiteness that crown rippled and floated, as if to carry the blazing moon in its corona; and Alya found himself soaring amongst it, the Lights of the Northlands themselves. Towering curtains of light rippled and rained down around him, and the air seemed to shiver with a crackling force. So high was he now that he saw little colour in them; yet below him they turned to greens and pinks and glowing purples, shaking suddenly like a windblown sail and shifting hues. But it was to either flank that their true stature became apparent, shimmering sheets of whiteness filled with a gleaming rain, as if great hands scattered dust of stars and white diamonds down out of the void, like time itself raining down from the eternal stars. Across his very wings cold fires raced, and green flame crackled among his feathers.

He grew giddy with the sight, and the thin air. It seemed to him that some of the showering gems were piling up in the crevices and the hollows of the bare brown rock beneath, forming gleaming pools of gems, rubies and emeralds, sapphires and pure blazing diamonds.

As above, so below. The white light was mirrored in the ice. The moon swam in the glaciers, and drew the stars after her in a trail of fire. Somewhere in the depths of his mind he knew he must descend, or plummet from the sky like some dark fragment of the night. With mighty wings outstretched he glided, tasting the chill air with his pinion feathers, feeling the rush and flow of it. Gradually the pain in his gullet eased, the fatal lightness in his head. Yet the giddy bewilderment remained, the sense of dream or nightmare, of sailing through a mad vision; for this was no place meant for life to be, and he saw through an alien shape, and eyes not his own.

He no longer knew which way he flew. In sudden panic he saw himself speeding on to perish

among the lifeless wastes. Frantically he sought a
fixed point amid this fleeting icy light, and found
it. The stars, shining steady now in the black void
above, no longer twinkling, formed the familiar con-
stellations, marking the corners of the world. He
found the North Star, for which he was indeed heading. He went wheeling wildly about, careering down
the sky with the starsigns cavorting above him. The
Sickle, and the Hunter, the Bow – he could guess his
heading from them now, he could find the way back
without track or signpost. And the wind was changing, a faint cold breeze growing stronger at his back,
buoying up his weary wings.

For a time, resting, he rode it, marking how the
angle of the stars changed at the margins of the world.
That the world was a sphere in the Void, he had been
taught; but that seemed only a philosophical truth, a
device of understanding. It was something else, a
demented dream still, to see land that seemed so solid
actually bent to a curve, and the oppressive Ice that
lay upon it. It made even that cold vastness seem
smaller, somehow, and more limited. There were
realms even the Ice could not conquer, to which it
must seem as small as he to it. The Void was vaster
yet, and colder; and that thought, bleak as it was,
helped pierce the glittering madness in his mind.

And then he saw the jewels once again, from
lower down. It had been no illusion; they were
indeed pooled here and there across the glittering
expanse, as if the Smith of the Powers had set vast
treasures into crystal and white gold. There were not
many; one gleaming on the westward horizon, glinting against the night; another eastward, almost behind him now, shining in the lee of bare rock. But
ahead, almost in his path lay the largest pool, seething
and shimmering in the bitter air. In astonished curiosity, forgetting fear, he swooped down towards it.

It was further than he expected, quite near the

margins of the Ice, cupped within those outstretched fingers. Further and larger, as he skated down the sky; a vale of gems, a deep ring of shining facets, winking blood-red, deep and warm, but shot with gleams of blue and green like frozen memories of hues no longer alive here, skies and trees embalmed from the warm morning of the world. But all their colours were no more than accents to the brilliance at their apex, that gleamed one moment pale and cool, then flashed the sharp-edged blue of lightning, colder and harder even than the moonlit Ice, as it might be a diamond set among pearl. It drew him, and he thrashed the wind with his waning strength, plunging down upon that bright pool in the waste.

Into his sight swam the vale and its margins, flanked by overhanging ice-falls like embodied menace, the thin line of bare black cliffs beneath, and the steaming vents of the earthfires that kept them thawed. Only then did the size of what he saw there begin to fix itself in his tormented understanding. Out of another life swam the memory of Tseshya's crudely sketched sheet of paper, the immensity around him insolently marked off by a single line. And within it the circles that stood for the incredible: life within death, the sprawling, seething veins and arteries of a verminous nest, the fires and smokes and squalors of a town of men.

He could hardly take it in, the size of it, where no such place should be; but he knew he had to fix this place in his mind, everything he could of it. He glided lower, wondering only vaguely what would happen if he were seen, marking out the rambling streets, swimming with meltwater and steam, the myriad and many-hued fires and furnaces, flares and braziers, the endless hordes of ramshackle compounds and tumbledown buildings scattered and tangled across the vale's wide floor like an uncovered maze of rat burrows.

Spirals of warm air rising warred with the bitter Ice-wind, rolling and boiling beneath his wings; but they stank, of steam and sulphur and rotten eggs, and above that the crowding of men and beasts and their mingled filth. At the vale's far end, as the ground lifted towards the cliffs, the ways grew wider, the air cleaner; but the towers, though taller and stronger, were no more than windowless shadows beneath the feet of what arose above. The apex of the jewel, as he had seen it; and this alone still seemed jewel-like as he flew towards it, this alone more terrible and fair. Its pale light blazed across the vale, flashed and flickered against the very Ice above, mirrored and repeated among the cold cliffs.

That was what drew him! Called him, almost; as if some force worked upon the wearer of the wings. That he must resist; but it was harder than it seemed. Even the warm airs warred against him now, cooling and falling as he bore down upon them. He was falling fast; and he saw the jewel beneath him, the milky jewel with the bright heart. Even wheeling as he plunged, he marvelled at it, like no building he could ever have conceived. Its soft-edged walls might have been formed whole in some mighty shell, so smooth was their opalescent sheen, tinged with rainbows, so seamless their lustre. But they were the setting only for the brighter, hard light of adamant, and he wondered at the pulse and shimmer of it among that mighty colonnade in its front face, in all the shifting shades of sky and forest.

There were people in the square before the palace, tiny stick-like figures that resolved themselves as he struggled to rise, hurling his wings against the air. He could see them more clearly by the moment, black-clad men standing guard, unloading wagons, hurrying about other business. Women, too; some clad as warriors, some in longer robes. And they could see him, as he sank down the failing wind.

Some pointed, gestured, called out; others came running from within. He saw bows, and feared a drift of arrows; but none arose. Instead they were falling, down there, black-clad and robed women all alike, dropping to their knees as he passed above them, like cornstalks scythed by his racing shadow. Kneeling, bending their brows to the ground.

They were saluting him, revering him almost. He was descending still more steeply now, right towards the steps of the great building, and he no longer struggled to slow himself. Lower still, so low he could see the wide space between the pillars now, and the people who ran to look up, only to fall on their faces. Wavering crazily now, above the blazing roof of the palace, faces – older women, younger – staring up at him from the high gallery that encircled it, as a golden clasp a pearl. Faces . . .

He almost plummeted from the sky. Young women, in a group, young and fair, clad richly but too lightly, as it seemed, to stand upon that palatial thing of ice. Some chattered and pointed; but at the rear a tall young woman with a haughty look of command stood aloof, though she too gazed upward in wonder. And beside her . . .

He thrashed the air with desperate strokes of those vast wings, till they cracked like thunder in his own ears. He stretched out his neck and shouted aloud; but of course it came out as a wild wordless cry, as lonely as any he had heard across the moors of his earlier life.

Beside her, wide-eyed, ruddy-skinned, raven hair falling strangely coiffed across strong bare shoulders, yet seen beyond mistaking even with eyes other than his own—

A face that filled his sight. Eyes that blazed brighter to him than all the palace, brighter than the distant sun itself, scored more deeply in his mind and heart.

'*Savi!*' screamed the wild swan, in unbearable joy and anguish. '*Savi!*'

Almost the name took shape within the cry, and he saw a momentary look of puzzlement cross her face. Seizing the very air, he swooped upon the roof, cursing that he did not wear the guise of so great a bird of prey. Then he might have scooped her up in flight, borne her off dangling to some remote eyrie. But he had no talons. He would land, though, and somehow make her understand, change back if he had to. Could he bear her away, on his back even, beyond the walls of the Ice, to a new life? Could even the fires hurl such force into his wings? They would. That was the utmost deed he had dreamed of, to fulfil his quest and oath himself with the gift given him. He wheeled about and back, sending the women shrieking and scattering below his thrashing pinions, gliding down in strength over the tessellated pavement of the gallery.

Upon the steps he saw her standing, her face alight with anxious wonder and what seemed a joy half formed, not wholly understood, as if his frantic thoughts already touched her. Closer yet – then he might make her understand! He would! He reached out.

And saw, behind her, behind the taller girl, another taller still. Her face of milk and ivory might have made her the swan-girl's sister, save that the fall of hair which framed it was a whiter, ashen hue. And proud though the swan-girl seemed, this one stood higher and prouder yet, wide of shoulder, imperious and keen, with a hard set to the full lips and the wide blue eyes alight with freezing fire. One hand she rested upon Saviyal's bare shoulder, as if to steady herself; but the other she raised a little in a gesture of command. For all her manner there was uncertainty, as if she doubted at whom she aimed her order. That, and that he had not already alighted, were what saved him then.

It snatched him, the command; it drew him hard – to come, to land, to fall at her feet and acknowledge her. He fought it, and it tore at him; in that guise he could hardly have withstood it an instant. But he was still in the air, unable now to shape his wings to brake himself. His momentum carried him soaring across the gallery, no higher than their heads, and his shadow swept across them. Savi and the other girl ducked; even the ivory woman flinched and threw up her hands.

And he was past, away, free of the awful summons that had locked his muscles and his mind in helpless spasm, riding another spiral of warmer air up the barren flank of the vale and higher, into the rushing Ice-wind and the bitter Northlights once again.

At his back, as he wheeled and flapped for height, he still felt the summons in another fashion now, insistent, angry; but the palace was already a distant pearl, and he could ignore it. What truly called him back was stronger still; but in his heart he knew that it would be useless and worse. And as he wheeled around once more he saw other wings glide across the moon, three or four vaster even than his own. Again his whole being thrilled to a call; and he knew who they were, and why they had been summoned. Yet they were not in swan guise now. The wings were curving, broader, with pinions spread like great fingers. These were raptors, sea-eagles perhaps, shapes of beak and talon, speeding to an urgent alarm. But he laughed, for they were far behind, still circling the fiery vale; they had not seen him, not yet. He hurled himself away down the wind, speeding to the southward, seeking among all the threads of the outflowing rivers the one he had followed.

He found it, black as it was, pouring out of a high shattered glacial wall, among great banks of mist. Its wide waters glittered beneath the sinking moon, with long keen shadows gliding across them. He did not dare stoop in his rush to look; from the mind he touched, he guessed what they must be. So there were sentinels down here also, and already alerted! And across the snowfields beneath the glittering cliffs thin harsh trumpets echoed, and horsemen were starting out. No doubt other less visible sentinels were also stirring, around and within the Ice, seeking out the unknown intruder. So swiftly! As swift as thought, the alert had passed. And as thorough. It augured ill for any road in he could imagine, to that awful fortress and its jewelled heart.

All the same, that hardly seemed to matter against the greater joy that came thrilling up from beneath, like the first warmth of sunrise. The only jewel that place held for him was alive and well, even safe, by the look of it, for now. He had seen her, all but touched her. He would dearly have done more, but that was only a matter of time and perseverance. He would come back for her; surely she would understand. He was happy. He had only to find out how.

After a while Alya looked back again. The wings were circling no longer, above those remote white walls; but he guessed that they would not have given up. He was heart-weary now, but the fire crackled along his limbs, undiminished, and that was as well. They must be far behind him now, but sooner or later they would overtake him.

That was not his only constraint. How long those straps would hold the girl, words or no words, he could not tell; and it had been a whole night and day since he left her. Any mortal woman he would never have abandoned in such a plight for so long, whatever the need; so he hoped, anyhow. But this one would come to no harm. He was less sure about himself.

So he rode a fast tailwind above the bare lands, skimming the high cloud-peaks, and his pursuers were still lost even to his keen sight. The swanhame's owner, whose pulse still beat within it, could not have flown faster; yet still he envied the wind itself its speed.

At last the sunset turned the river to a polished steel ribbon, and showed him the distant green of the canebrakes, and the bluffs at the bend. For all his urgency, he felt a deep pang for what he must now give up. He sank down swiftly, riding the lesser breeze until he hovered almost, then glided slowly in to the channel beside the sandspit. There beneath the rushes she lay still, the strange golden-haired one, shaped in the image of a race far from his own. Could this be what the folk beyond the waters looked like? Very strange, if so; but they must be just as human, and no doubt facing perils of their own. Would he ever see them? And what would they make of him and his kind?

The water was bitter out of the sun, and he landed awkwardly, sinking, struggling to throw the fell from his shoulders. At first it would not come. He could hardly remember what it was like to have human limbs. Then it gave, almost painfully now, and he sank again, cramped and struggling. But the water was shallow enough; he found footing and stood, coughing. When he drew the mask off his face, the leather lining seemed to flay his cheeks, and he was thankful he had little beard as yet. He waded to the shallows, shaking out the cloak, and pulled his dry clothes off her as she lay. She seemed less sleek than he had left her, bedraggled, exhausted, her eyes red-rimmed now and deeply shadowed, as if she, not he, had flown for all those hours.

Merely looking at her, he felt the pain and the indignity behind that terrible gaze. A flood of remorse overcame him. 'I'm sorry,' he said, idiotically. 'I had to. But I've come back. I had to,' he repeated, and sat down beside her, drained.

'You are very fair,' he said, suddenly. 'You're my enemy, I suppose, but I bear you no ill-will in yourself. I had to do what I've done, for a cause that's life itself to me. Do you understand that, I wonder? I've seen you and your sisters at play. I've touched your pride and your wrath. But do you love at all, who are so well made for it? Do any of you have hearts?'

He sighed, and began to dress. 'I'm talking nonsense. Your sisters will be here soon. They'll find you and release you.'

He stopped. He read something else in that gaze. 'You don't want them to find you, do you? Not like this.' He chuckled, a little crazily. 'Powers, I can understand that – Powers? What am I saying? Release you myself? Sorry, what kind of idiot do you take me for?'

Her gaze said nothing, nothing at all. She was as opaque as the river. She was not going to plead, or beg. Impatiently he snatched out the gag, and hurled it away, half expecting a deafening scream, or long white teeth to meet in his finger. Instead she coughed a little, spat inelegantly, and looked at him once again. The look was cold, considering; but it had no added power of its own. The voice was startling, low, quiet, but so forceful it made his neck hairs bristle.

'You know more than most of your kind. But we are beings beyond your understanding. We have some regard for bravery. You are braver than most, or more foolish. Was your cause really worth throwing your life away for, so casually? Release me, or leave me, it matters little. I will be free soon, and then I will kill you, and you will serve me till I weary of your shadow. Whereas you cannot kill me, at all.'

'I can cut you to pieces,' said Alya brutally, 'very slowly. I can burn this fine cloak of yours. None of that will kill you, but it will cause you great pain, and weaken you for a long time.' She said nothing, and he sighed. 'Or I could hide the swanhame far away, in the dark. That would be wisdom, maybe. But I will leave it on the bank, not far off.'

He rolled her over, a little roughly, and tugged the straps free. The heavy leather looked stretched. She doubled up in cramps. He snatched up the cloak and his gear, and splashed out frantically through the reeds to the shore. He dropped the cloak hastily in a nook of the bank, and then he ran for dear life through the canes, as silently as he could. Even as he threw himself beneath the trunk of a toppled willow, he saw her rise and stretch painfully, silhouetted against the still-glowing sky, the thongs dangling from her wrists. They fell free, unheeded, as she came limping through the reeds, in exactly the direction he had taken. His hair bristled as she drew nearer; and then she walked straight to the cloak, though she could not see it, and snatched it up. She glanced around, this way and that. He stilled his very breathing. She would kill him; and then he would serve her? *Then?*

She stood for what seemed like an age, while the dusk deepened. Then suddenly she was no longer there, and a black swan's silhouette soared high into the last of the light.

Alya stayed where he was. It wheeled once, not especially near him, not in the direction of the farm, and sped away, straight and unvarying, towards the distant north. He waited a long time after it disappeared from view; but the time was not wasted, as he searched what glimpses he had had of her mind.

It was dawn when he rode back to the farmhouse, shivering with hunger and unspeakably weary, his limbs cramping with agonies even the fires could not burn away. As he flung the door wide the others sprang up, and ran to catch him as he all but fell down the steps. But he looked up at them with eyes wide and urgent.

'*I've seen her!* Get that door shut, stay out of sight! I tried to break up my tracks, but they have such senses . . . She didn't do anything! But the others . . . Vansha, she's alive, I've seen her!'

Vansha's face stiffened. 'Where? Not . . . beyond the Wall?'

'No! In the flesh! In . . . In the Ice! Right in the middle of . . .' He yawned violently, and shivered. 'Give me some of whatever's cooked, in the name of all the Powers, cold or not! The Nightingale and Tseshya, they were right! And I know where. Vansha, you should have seen her, she's . . .' Gobbling with his fingers, he gestured wildly, flicking dabs of thick gruel about the place.

Vansha, much recovered, hunkered down by his side. 'Saw her? Well, I'm . . . Is, is she all right? How did she look?'

'Beautiful! Well. Well clad. A slave or servant or something. There seemed to be a lot of them about. But that was her! And I know the way now, all the way! Get ready, everyone! We're riding out! No, not now, fools! Soon as it's safe!'

'It's not that long till nightfall!'

Alya seized his arm. 'D'you want to rescue her or not?' He wavered, shook his head, leaned on one arm, and then subsided on to the mat. 'Soon's safe . . . soon.' He rolled over, and fell instantly asleep.

Asquan prodded his buttock with a toe, not too gently, but he only stirred and snuffled. 'Ah,' said Asquan. 'True love.'

'You should try it some time,' grunted Kalkan. 'Or is that too novel?'

Asquan put on a sad face. 'Oh, I have, I have. Believe me. Each time truer than the last. And found it like any scarce commodity – a little sweeter, a lot more expensive.'

'So that's your way of weighing it, my lord?' sneered Vansha. 'By what it costs?'

'Oh yes,' said Asquan, with a withered smile, still contemplating Alya as he slept. 'But I wasn't talking about money. Not entirely.'

Alya sat bolt upright. The shadows that clustered around his dreams slithered back, just to the edge of awareness, no further. A sharp biting breath caressed his cheek; and a long lance of sun stabbed straight at his eyes, through the gap in a shutter. 'How long have I slept?' he demanded of the air. 'We should be on our way . . .'

'No, we should not,' said Vansha with sleepy irritability. 'You've slept since yesterday afternoon, and it's only early morning now!'

'You don't understand!' fumed Alya. 'There's little enough time, now! They must be riding already!'

'Who must?' demanded Kalkan, sitting up just as sharply, with his spear beside him. 'More bloody raiders?'

Alya shivered. 'No. Not exactly. Servants of the Ice. They were there on the river, like great insects skating about on the surface . . . The woman! Is she still alive? Has she told you anything?'

'Many things!' yawned Asquan irritably. 'Some true, perhaps. Much that is rubbish, or sheer superstition. Is it essential that we go through them all now?'

'Maybe! Far in the north . . .'

Asquan scratched himself irritably. 'Far means more than three days' walk, to her. About where human habitation ends is what she meant by that – but you don't credit *that* tale, do you?'

'I've cause to! At the least it's worth looking into. The Ice—' He shivered in the cold air. 'You've never seen anything like it! But it's well guarded; and I believe I know something about some of the guards. Terrible things; but they may give us our door in. And perhaps out, also. If we can only seize the hour, then we may have a chance. But it will be perilous. That's why I want to leave, now!'

'Will an hour make that much difference?' demanded Vansha, wincing as his wounds pulled. 'I thought not. Eat, then. What good will we do her if we reach her too weak to help?'

The sense in that held Alya back just long enough. While the others were still licking out their bowls and rinsing their mouths, he was already saddling his rebellious horse, and impatiently scanning what he could see of the sky. But it was clear and bright, and although there were many arrowheads of birds, they none of them came near, or wheeled as if searching. So at last, when the others were making ready, he returned to the house.

The women were still there in the shadows, gathered around the elder one on her mat, but silent as ever. She looked up at him with fever-sunken eyes, but said nothing. 'You mentioned the ghost-ride!' he said; and the woman whimpered slightly, and tried to turn her head away.

'Tell me!' he said sharply. 'It will make up for some of what you deserve.'

'I know little!' she said sullenly, at last. 'What is to tell? Those who survive the service of the Ice may sometimes be released, to ride home to their own lands. But so, sometimes, do those who do not. Them, they cannot stop and find rest. He who once ruled the Ice now only guards its approaches. Him they must serve. Ask no more!'

Alya nodded. 'I do not need to. We are leaving now. We have taken some of your food, but left enough for many months yet. It was bought with dead men's armour, I don't doubt.' Rysha, standing in the door, made as if to say something, but stopped dead at the look he gave her. 'When we pass this way again, we will see how you fare; and we will do you no more harm, if you offer us none.'

He turned on his heel, and went out. 'When you pass?' shouted one of the girls, at his back. 'Some chance, the way you're heading!'

'You'll know all about the ghost-ride, soon enough!' jeered another, emboldened now.

Alya paid them no heed; but Rysha looked down on them, from the steps. 'I'd be leery of mocking ghosts!' she said shortly. 'You've enough of your own to worry about. And believe me, that's no joke.' She followed Alya out.

'The bitches were right, though!' sniffed Tseshya painfully, as they helped him on to his horse. 'When we pass this way again? We'll be treading another road soon enough!'

Kalkan laughed. 'Which you'd have done soon enough in King Volmur's shit-pit, my good scribbler! You can always stay here with the ladies, you know!'

'Aye!' grinned Darzhan. 'They might even acquire a taste for you!'

Tseshya glared. 'I'll take my chances, thank you!'

'Right!' chuckled Kalkan. 'After all, who's freer than the dead?'

Alya turned sharply. 'Don't be so sure, my lord!'

Kalkan shrugged. 'At least we'd be free of these accursed canes! You say they end soon?'

'We'll be free of them by tomorrow.'

'Then I'll breathe freely again. And open hills after that? Fine; at least we'll be able to see any enemies coming. I've been afraid we'd run into some band of raiders around any corner, without warning!'

'There shouldn't be any danger of that!' said Alya. 'There are none within reach. I saw many, but they were all bound northward.'

'All?' demanded Asquan. 'None headed south, at all?'

'No,' said Alya slowly. 'Not now you mention it, no . . .'

'Won't ask how you know,' muttered Kalkan gruffly. 'But you're sure?'

'Yes. It's something to think about. It's not raiders we'll have to watch out for, in the open. It'll be birds – yes, birds! Swans. Black swans. Or something else large.'

'Swans,' repeated Chiansha. 'Like the ones I saw, uh?'

'The ones we all saw,' said Asquan. 'I think we should know—'

'Not now!' said Alya fiercely; and with that they had to leave it. But Alya remained nervous all that day, most of all when they came near to the river fork in late afternoon, and had to cross by the ford to which the road led them, deep and uncertain.

'Mind how you cross!' growled Kalkan. 'These deep slow streams, they drown twice as many as faster ones!'

'Wise words!' agreed Asquan crisply. 'And be wary of what lies on the far side also. One man should go first, with a rope – and a spear!'

'Fazdshan!' ordered Kalkan. 'You're the biggest—'

'But I'm the strongest,' said Alya; and there was no gainsaying that. But as he felt his way across with the spearbutt, skidding on slimy stones and tangling his legs in weed, he spent so much time scanning the river and the sky that Asquan hissed after him impatiently, 'The far side, my lord! What better place for brigands to lurk, or worse!'

He was right, of course. Alya clambered out carefully, and looked around as he made the rope fast to a beech tree that rose among the thinning cane. 'It's all right!' he called back, wringing out his breeches. 'But hurry!'

They came splashing across on horseback now, with Asquan bringing up the rear, winding in the line. He dismounted as he reached the bank, to untie it from the tree; and as he did so, he froze. 'All right, you said, my lord?'

They gathered round, staring down at the single clear footprint in the waterlogged soil. 'Only a little oozing,' said Kalkan. 'Not long made. But what in Hella's tits is it?'

'A bear?' suggested Rysha.

'No kind I'd know!' said Vansha. The other hunters muttered agreement.

'It's got claws, of a sort,' said Alya. 'But short, and blunt . . . and the size!'

'More like those great apes in the southern forests!' said Asquan. 'You would not have seen them, of course. But, yes, bigger . . . And it stood upright.'

'It stood here!' said Vansha sharply. 'For some time. As if . . .'

'As if it was watching?' They all looked around, as one, peering out among the thinning canes, into the undergrowth and trees that briefly reasserted themselves here.

'In the early hours, I think!' said Asquan. 'Fortunate that we did not decide to press on, as you wished, my Lord Alya!'

Alya gulped, and nodded. 'There might have been others around!' He snapped his fingers. 'Maybe they picked up my scent, last night . . . I think we should press on now. Be clear before dark.'

'Nobody's arguing!' grunted Chiansha, and clambered back into his saddle.

Vansha rode up alongside Alya as they moved off, spears at rest as before. 'It sounds as if you were right.'

'About what?'

'About spying out our way. Being too risky. I shouldn't have pressed you.'

'But it was worth it!' Alya seized his arm. 'Vansha, you should have seen her! So fair – even in that place, among—'

Vansha loosened his grip, wincing. 'Indeed I should!' Alya caught the edge to his tone, and remembered Vansha's forlorn hopes of being a Seer. 'But at what price? If we've called the Powers know what down upon us . . .'

'I doubt it. The print may be something else. They would have come themselves. And sooner, I think. The Choosers!' he added softly, answering Vansha's unspoken question. 'But don't tell the others. Not till we must!'

'The Choosers,' said Vansha between his teeth. 'So that's who you've been a-roving with! The name that Ekwesh bastard threatened us with. A name I've heard before. Things my father hinted at.'

'Mine, too, I think. I'd say they're true.'

Vansha whistled softly. 'So! Are they as fair as folk say?'

'Every bit. Like breeds of women you can't imagine, yet always young and beautiful. And deadly. Either way, to stop your heart.'

Vansha crooked an eyebrow. 'Strange. You'd think they'd want to seem fearsome.'

Alya nodded. 'I remember my father saying that that's how the Ice sees itself – how the Powers who rule it imagine themselves. As victims, not oppressors. As defenders of a great beauty, that living things disfigure. They despise ugliness; so that whatever form they borrow, they make as fair as they can. I read something of that, in among her thoughts.'

'In her thoughts!' Vansha looked bleak. 'And what else? No, don't tell me. Not unless I need to know.'

'Not yet, anyhow,' said Alya, and glanced around the canes once more, just as all the others were doing. They had had enough shocks for now.

The river fork marked the great change in the land, and what grew upon it. There the floodplains ended, and with them the canes. Long before the

day's end it was trees and bushes they scanned, with
only rare canebrakes; and between them they could
see open hills. The upper river itself was wider and
less meandering, flowing faster and deeper through
the channel it had carved out between their slopes. In
mid-afternoon the little party passed out from between the arms of the trees at last; and Kalkan let
out a great bellow of relieved laughter.

Alya was about to rebuke him, when from
among the greenery a horrible noise arose, a howling,
hungry screech that was louder far and larger, though
it seemed to come from only one throat. It lasted only
a moment, but it sent small birds flying up in frantic
clouds, and made the horses shy. Nothing could be
seen, and nothing made any move to come after
them; but in the silence that followed, nobody spoke.
But Alya raised his eyes to the skies; and so did the
rest.

They saw nothing that day, and they made camp
that night undisturbed. Indeed, in many respects the
days that followed were the most peaceful part of
their journey; for Alya knew the way now, and the lie
of the land, and they passed without any great in-
cident. They were anxious, at first most of all, constantly watching the clouds above and the great slow
river on their right flank – slow, save where it drove
through narrows, steep and rapid. Then the enormous weight behind it became clear, transformed
into raging white waters no boat could pass, even by
portage. 'Such a mass of water,' mused Asquan,
watching the flying foam. 'And yet the Ice constantly
throws out many hundred times as much, and never
misses it!'

'More than that!' said Tseshya, now much restored to his old self. 'It recoups it constantly, through
winter snows. And the waters carry its chill southward, and carve its path, for glaciers are but frozen
rivers, in a sense.'

'The rivers carry many things, indeed,' said Alya slowly. 'And in more than one direction.'

Most of them thought he meant the birds, as usual; but Asquan looked thoughtful. Later he rode up alongside Alya, apart from the rest. 'I also have been scouting out the land, in a sense. Following your orders. I talked to the women, while you were . . . away; and very wearisome and confusing it was. I have spent time since, piecing together much that was no more than legend, weeding out the fancies and the spiteful lies, weaving a slender thread of truth with what you have told us. And I believe I can guess something of what you are planning.' Alya said nothing, and the old lord's smile grew more like a lizard's. 'Bold, as I would expect. But dangerous. Appallingly so.'

'Can you see it so clearly?' Alya smiled ruefully. 'That's more than I can. I've no master-plan already mapped out in my mind. No more than . . . an idea. An opening I saw, a chance we might be able to use, if only we can seize the moment. And it need not be so dangerous. We might be able to do it all without fighting. I would like that, if I can.'

Asquan frowned. 'Beware it does not lose you more lives! Fighting is why you brought these men, remember; and me. Fighting is not the worst of evils. And it may well come to that in the end, if the girl is as close to the heart of the place as you suggest.'

'Then I would delay it as long as possible! I cannot shake off the feeling that I was meant to tread this path alone, and risk no other life!'

'Who decides what is meant? Those who gave you your strength also left you the freedom to use it as you will. No, be as cunning as you like, but accept that some may well still die.' Asquan chuckled. 'After all, if we do not, we'll just have to find some better way!'

'And if this is a bad way? Worse than any I can imagine?'

Asquan looked more serious than usual. 'If it is the right one in all other ways, then we must still risk it. But for now, let us say no more of it, and enjoy the peace while we can!'

It was not so hard to do. Indeed, they marvelled at the richness of that land as Alya had, and at the wealth of life and growth within it, even compared to the best of Volmur's kingdom. And like him they grew ever more furious with the Ice, that had locked away so much water, and starved the southern lands to the verge of desert. 'Look at these vast herds,' cried Kalkan. 'These huge things with the long snouts and teeth – mammuts, you say, scholar?'

'They'd never survive down south,' agreed Alya. 'So, my lord?'

'So, if we could tame them, herd them! Think of them for labour, for dragging carts – such strength!'

'And just possibly for beasts of war, my lord?' enquired Alya. It was a barbed question worthy of Asquan, which worried Alya a little.

Kalkan shrugged with boisterous innocence. 'Well, perhaps, perhaps! Since you mention it! Be bloody terrifying, wouldn't they? And you could armour them against spears and arrows, around the legs too. Once they got in among the infantry – the cavalry, too, even, you saw how the horses don't like 'em . . . Rulers must take such things into account, yes. But maybe the meat tastes good, too. A royal banquet on four legs, eh? What a show on parade!'

'With a couple of daggerteeth on chains to lead them!' grinned Vansha. 'Or pull your chariot!'

The soldiers laughed. 'What price Volmur and his cardboard dragon, then! All hail to King Kalkan! Down with his foes!'

Asquan, who had said nothing throughout, simply raised an eyebrow to Alya. He understood, well enough. These were men who thought of fighting, even in times of peace; it was natural to them. And

Vansha seemed to think much the same way; even Tseshya, to some extent. Perhaps he should worry less about setting their lives in jeopardy; and yet he could not. To him that would be too like the Ice, and the way it treated men; and that was often before them.

If the peasant farms had seemed mean from high above, they looked worse below. Alya saw now how prosperous the women had been, by comparison. Sometimes there were no real houses at all here, merely lean-to sheds covering the mouth of some sordid cave or cleft, often dank and stinking. Often they were little more than wide shallow pits dug into the soil, roofed with canes or bundled branches. Inside, the houses were usually smoky, filthy tangles alive with dogs, infants and vermin, all uncontrolled. After their experiences with the women, Alya and the company were wary of sleeping beneath another's roof. They usually sought the barn or granary; and they soon found they had the best of it. The barns were relatively sound and well kept, because the peasants had at all costs to store grain and produce for their masters, and the effort that might have gone into better houses went largely to the stores.

Their inhabitants were little better, a peasant people beaten and degraded, noticeably smaller and squatter of frame than the southerners, as if crushed by the burdens of their existence. Literally so; they had few draught animals, except a few huge wagon and plough oxen, and bore most weights on their own backs. Most were surly and suspicious towards the strangers, though some became a little friendlier when they realised these were not raiders. Even those who had the look of the *Aikiya'wahsa* themselves, small wonder on such a road, showed little love for them. There was evidently little chance Alya and his party would be betrayed – even had there been anyone to betray them to, for the road was as empty as it had seemed from above. The peasants knew no reason; they were only relieved. They cared little about anything beyond their near neighbours, and the overlords who came to snatch away almost all their toil produced. That was their world, and its triumphs and tragedies lay in concealing some food, and some children – but not too much of either.

From one such homestead to another the company passed in some two weeks' long riding, or a little more, and with each day their anger and hatred grew for the Powers they faced. With each, it became clear, the ground was growing ever poorer, the soil thinner, the grass less lush, browner and tougher, the fields more sparse. As the woman had said, the farm buildings no longer stood alone now, but lumped together in gaggles of tiny huts that hardly merited the name of village. Only the road remained clear and straight, with no more than small rough paths and drovers' tracks leading off from it; so that it was a surprise for most of them, one bleak and misty afternoon, to find it forking ahead, and still more so sloping away towards the right, leading only down to the river.

Alya was not surprised; and neither, he guessed, was Asquan. 'That is our way,' he told them. 'And a reminder to take care. We've ridden far and hard, but free from hindrance. Now that may change. I wanted to get here in time for something, and I think we have, just barely. But that means we have to be ready for enemies!'

'Fine by me!' said Chiansha. 'These peasants are getting me down! I need a neck or two to wring – preferably Ekwesh!'

'Be wary of wishing!' warned Asquan sardonically. 'You may find it all too generously granted!'

Alya grinned, and urged his horse down the road. He was startled to hear the sudden ring under his mount's hooves. This was a way of great flagstones, like the roads away south, some leftover from a forgotten past. It was mostly overgrown now, and in places sunken to spongy bog; but it led them through without a break, into the mists that rose from the river every evening, that at last closed about them.

For a while all was raw, cold and quiet, save for the odd bird-cry eerily flattened by the dank air, and the gurgle and ripple of water near and far. Twilight dimmed the mist still further. Vansha came riding up to the fore. 'Are those lights out there ahead?'

'Should be,' said Alya, squinting. 'You always did have good sight. Keep it in use now. Single file, and be careful!'

Lights there were indeed, faint and red in the haze. Alya trotted on towards what looked like the nearest, a dim red glow apparently hanging high in emptiness; and the others saw him loosen his sword in its sheath. Then they saw the light clearly all of a sudden, a battered lantern hanging on a heavy wooden post; and just then Alya's horse's hooves drummed suddenly hollow. He reined in sharply, and they rode up about him as usual; but he held them back.

'Listen! D'you not hear? You might go riding straight into the river!'

Carefully he swung from his saddle, and his feet also boomed on wood. 'Take care, it's narrow. And slippery!'

The others, behind him, saw a mass of shadows, low and long. He stood on a grey outline of planks, and all around it was dim and empty, filled with the cold chuckle of flowing water. Another light gleamed in the distance, over what might be another jetty; but there were others still further off in the deep dusk, the glow of fires, perhaps. There was a hint of smoke in the still cold air. It smelt like winter, although in their own lands winter was still far away.

Vansha also dismounted. 'Slippery? Powers, it's half rotten!'

'You do surprise me!' said Asquan, peering into the murk. 'Made with wood, bodged with cane – has anyone seen a tree lately? I thought not. I shudder to think what the ferry will be like. Over the other side; it always is, isn't it? I suppose one simply shouts.'

'Seems so,' agreed Alya, and he cupped his hands and cried out. His voice echoed out over the dusky river, but nothing stirred. He called again and again, with no result, and his voice cracked.

'*Hoi!*' bellowed Kalkan, deafening. 'Stir your stumps, ferryman! And stumps he'll have,' he added more quietly, 'if we don't get some answer soon!'

'First time I've missed that Nightingale and his whistles!' said Darzhan. '*Hoi!*' Sticking his fingers in his loose mouth, he whistled deafeningly. Ahead in the greyness something creaked, and they saw the shape of an opening door picked out by a dim lantern. The lean figure carrying it limped down to what must be the far jetty.

'Who's there?' The voice was tremulous, but not especially old. '*Who's there?* I got a bow!'

'Then stick your head in it and let loose!' snarled Vansha. 'But first come ferry us over!'

The man held up the miserable lantern, that barely lit his own arm, and peered into the gathering dusk. 'Who's that? What manner of men are you?'

'Just men,' said Alya, not unkindly. 'We won't hurt you, or take you away. But come now, before it grows dark!'

'No ferry after dark!' said the man sullenly.

'That's why we need you to come *now*!' exploded Alya. 'There's a reward for you, if you do!'

'And if I have to swim over there,' roared Kalkan, 'you'll be ferrying a different River soon enough! One with no returning!'

To their astonishment the man almost dropped the lantern, and fell to his knees.

'Didn't think I was *that* horrible!' growled the old warrior.

'Oh you are, my lord, you are!' said Asquan blithely. 'Utterly unspeakable, I assure you. At least our lazy boatman seems to be hurrying now.'

They could see him hurrying indeed, practically sliding over the jetty on all fours. From out of its shadow slid a long craft, wide and flat and riding low in the water, lifting only a little at its square-edged prow and stern. The boatman was poling it across vigorously enough, with little drift downstream; but a few yards off their shore he dug in the pole to hold the ferry in place, and held up his lantern.

'Come nearer!' he said, in a quavering voice. 'Need to see who y'are!'

'Why, when you don't know us from the dead?' demanded Asquan.

There was silence for a moment. 'Come closer, I say! You look strange! Or – or swim, and do your damnedest!'

Alya shrugged, and picked his way gingerly along the decaying jetty, nearer the light. 'Well, then? We are from far in the south, but we don't bite!'

The boatman was a scarecrow figure in a ragged loincloth and coarse jacket, a rag around his greasy hair. 'You look well enough – master! And these others?'

'My followers, yes! Do we have your august approval now?'

The ferry drove in alongside the jetty. It was bigger than it looked. 'Three at a time, masters! Three men, three horse, no more, step careful. Don't worry, I come back as often as need be.'

'Well, that's a change!' spat Vansha, as Kalkan manoeuvred his huge horse on board. 'Practically grovelling, now, the little snotrag!'

'Got to be careful, lord, careful who one takes! This night of all nights most of all! I thought—'

'I understand,' said Alya quietly.

The boatman sighed. 'I'll make all haste now, master. You wager your head on that!'

He made no attempt, in all his journeys, to ask them why they were there or whither they were going. He ferried them fast and well, with all his strength, so that it was still a misty dusk when the last of them came to the far side. From the jetty they could see the source of the lights looming up, the ramshackle hovels of yet another village grey and hunched in the gloom.

When Alya offered the ferryman some small coins that the farmers had accepted, he simply stared and said, 'What should I do with these?' But he seized a chunk of salted meat greedily, tucking it under his jacket and looking about. 'Never seen any of this in a year! Welcome, masters, welcome! No, no lodging in the village. Go to the headman's out beyond on the East road, he's a man of your quality, he has a big hall and food for wayfarers. Only mind; he'll have the door tight barred, this night!'

The village was all too familiar, save for its size, three times that of most others they had passed, and the quality of the road, also of laid stones, but clearer and in better repair than on the other bank. And the headman's house, when they reached it, was also a surprise. It bulked large in the dusk, larger than anything they had seen since before the canes; and as they came up to it, they saw walls of great stone blocks, evidently laid long ago like the road, and by men who knew their work. Now, though, they looked cracked and ramshackle, and the great beams above them were of wood only. Yet even these looked ancient enough, and richly carven; and so was all the wide front of the house, a hall indeed that squatted among the much older stone for shelter and strength. Faces glared out of foliage, deer fled and dogs sprang, bears lumbered and leaped; and above

the arch of the double door itself the heavy central
beam bore lines of intricate, elegant characters none
of them, not even Tseshya, could read. Alya thought
they looked familiar, but he had more urgent concerns. The doors themselves were shut.

Alya rapped on them with his glove, but nothing
happened, though he thought he could hear stirring
within. He struck louder, and getting no answer
hammered loudly, and called, though courteously;
and this time a voice answered him.

'Who are you? Can you not see the signs that bar
my door? Be on your way!'

'I see signs, but they are nothing I can read! Nor
can most in this land, I guess!'

'You cannot . . .' The voice seemed startled, but
it grew harsh again. 'I bear you no ill-will, but you
have no business here tonight! Go!'

'I'm going to kick those bloody doors down
around his—' began Vansha, but Alya shook his head.

'Will you refuse harmless strangers shelter and
fire, or at least a barn to sleep in? When they can pay
for it?'

'Strangers? From another land?'

'Indeed. Cold and weary ones!'

There was a moment of confusion within, as if
people were arguing. Then, very suddenly, bars
slammed back within, and the doors boomed open
in a flood of golden firelight. 'Come on then! Come in
quickly! Bring your horses! But quickly now!'

The man who hurried them in was something
different from the usual miserable peasants, though
he was dressed as raggedly as the others who lurked
down at the back of the hall, men and women and
children. He was no taller than most, but spare and
wiry instead of squat, with a deeply lined, sunken face
and watchful eyes; and as the doors were slammed
and barred behind them, he met the newcomers with
what seemed like a shadow of ancient formality.

He bade them take their places at his board, and had the horses led through the back of the hall, past the central firepit, to a stable at the rear. 'It's stood empty these many years,' he told them. 'But it will serve your beasts for the night. For you we have only these wooden platforms near the old fireplace, but we can at least see your bellies filled first, and build up the fire for you. You will not want to go out again tonight, I think.'

It was a flat statement. Alya saw no need to challenge it. 'For all that, I thank you. If it would cause hardship, we have food of our own. Or we can pay coin.'

The headman stopped him. 'We grow plenty, though we do not grow fat upon it. I would sooner you have it than the *Aikiya* who spare even me and mine only the same poor portions, however much we grow. I am Oshur of the Hall, headman of this village and a descendant of this region's ancient lords – though much that matters! You will pay me for your stay only with news of the far world from which you come, and lighten my cares.'

'I doubt we can do that. All grows darker, as we have seen it, and even hope seems corrupted.'

The headman smiled. 'Yet you are here, by your speech from lands whence none have come since my childhood. In itself that eases my heart of a great burden, and I shall not feel quite so alone this night. Sit and eat your fill.'

While they waited, and his household brought wooden bowls and cups, they told him as much as they dared of the outer world. 'So there is Volmur's kingdom,' Asquan concluded, 'ramshackle as it is. Others to West and East, in the warmer lands. Yet the raiders reach ever further, and treachery and corruption further still. We know many are under attack. And we hear of none strong enough to stand against the Ice, as of old.'

'Yet you are here,' repeated the headman, 'and for some purpose – no! I do not ask, and I am sure you would be wise not to tell. Yet it can only be to serve the Ice some ill, even if only to bring back word of its evil grip. Whatever it is, I wish you well. I would not betray you even if I could. My course is almost run, and I have few fears left in the world.'

'You are no older than I am!' said Asquan. 'And you have your home and your folk, as I do not.'

The headman's chuckle was cold. 'What do I have, that is mine? I cannot protect my people, not even my own family. They not only drive us as slaves in their fields, they levy our young men as foot and horse troops. In the first breath of spring they take them, as their campaigning season begins; and only at the end of harvest, when it ends, do they let some return, to help with the gathering in. All but a few are now back; and the last are expected tonight. The last.'

'Yet the ferryman was less than eager to come out.'

'We all dread the moment.' It was said so curtly as to discourage any deeper enquiry; but Vansha would not let it be.

'Why? Because so many will not return?'

'All return!' said the headman sullenly. 'It is the manner of their return. Some stop, some ride by. Some . . . wish to stop, and may not. That we dread.'

The meal was plain enough, little more than grain and vegetables, but it was no less welcome. After it they relaxed, and told the headman more tales, for his curiosity was insatiable and he seemed to treasure every word.

'You are like a ray of sun into a shuttered room!' he said, shaking his head. 'A wind from the outer world, telling me of sights and deeds such as are only distant memories. To our shame!'

'Not so!' said Alya. 'This sword of mine was some hero's, once, shaped with spells we no longer understand; but it hung in the roof of a chieftain's house for declining generations, gathering dirt and smoke. That is the Ice's doing – but now it is borne against them once again!' He slid it out a short way, and was about to snap it back, when the chief's hand stopped him.

'May I see the writing upon it? I am one of only a few in the land who preserves the skill, save among the *Aikiya* – and what they read, I have no wish to!' He pored over the characters, but sighed. 'No. I can no more read them than the characters on my own lintel. They resemble them, as if they came from the same era, but they are not the same . . . So much is forgotten!'

'Yet you asked us if we could see them.'

'That was different. I know what they mean, and what they are for, but I cannot draw that meaning from them. They prevent—' He stopped.

'Evil from entering?' suggested Tseshya.

'Evil? No. Not exactly. I cannot say—'

The door boomed, and the blood drained from the headman's face. Kalkan gestured to Fazdshan, sitting nearest the door, but the headman gestured urgently. 'No! Leave it be! Leave it be!'

They heard hooves on the earth outside, the weary snorts and scuffles of tired beasts, but never a voice of men. Another sharp blow rattled both the doors. They all jumped. The others laid hand to sword; Alya half drew his again. The headman shook his head.

'Oshur!' came a voice from without. 'Master Oshur!'

The headman rose, like a man in a dream, and went slowly towards the door. 'Who calls my name?'

Again the blow, high up the door, as if from a mounted man; and a harsh voice. 'Oshur! It's I, alive and well!'

The headman started violently. 'Tavao?' he demanded.

'The same. And ten of our lads with me, going to our homes.' The door rattled again. 'Hear that? I can see it well enough!'

The headman ran to the door, and scrabbled at the bars. At Alya's sign the others rose and came behind him with hands on swords. When the doors swung back they saw shadowy shapes of horses out in the mist, and one man, hard-faced and swarthy, leaned down from his saddle into the lamplight. Alya stiffened; he wore a battered Ekwesh leather breastplate.

'Tavao! Welcome, welcome! Come in, warm yourselves, these are strangers but friends, with tales to tell, and no friends of – but are there only this ten with you? No more? Only ten?' The headman's face was creased more deeply, a sweating mask.

Tavao's face was stiff and expressionless. 'No more, old man. I am sorry.'

'Only ten. Come and talk to me, then, Tavao.'

'I hear, headman. I will come. But best not tonight. Best we get to our homes.'

The horses moved off with dragging pace, and the headman slammed the doors and slumped back into his carven seat, his lean shoulders drooping.

'Perhaps we also should leave you,' said Alya quietly.

He looked up, with a crooked smile. 'No, you should not. It does me good to have others here, who do not share our troubles. And I would not send you out into the night, not now. There may be others coming west along the road, even if the ferry will not carry them. I would not send you in their company . . .'

'What others, headman?' demanded Vansha keenly. '*Aikiya'wahsa* vermin, do you mean?'

'*Aikiya*?' snapped the headman. 'We are the *Aikiya*! And you may well be, yourself, for the blood of many lines has fed that dark soil! All whom the Ice overruns and binds in thrall, all whom it raises and corrupts to be its ruthless slaves, oppressed that they may oppress – that name is now given them. But once that name was honourably ours! And before that, long before that, it stemmed from the great realm and empire the glaciers first destroyed, the first flowering of men.'

'And you know something of this?' demanded Tseshya keenly. 'Here, in this remote corner beneath the very shadow of the Ice, when everywhere else it is hardly more than a legend?'

'As it is here,' said Oshur sombrely. 'A legend to my ancestors, even. They had nothing of it but distorted tales, and a vision, that men had once been greater, better, wiser and more civilised. That, and a few remote records; the stones from which those characters were traced, I believe, and others. Perhaps the characters on your sword came from such a source, copied and recopied, as was our inscription. But what little my ancestors had, they fought to keep! Even as we were cut down, reduced from kingdom and town to a folk of clan and village, chieftains and Seers struggled to keep some shred of our past pride alive.'

Alya and Vansha looked at one another. 'It sounds like our home!' exclaimed Vansha. 'Just as we knew it – Savi's father, mine . . .'

'And my father!' said Alya. 'Fleeing a doomed town, to try to keep alive some little of its wisdom and its skills . . .'

Oshur bowed his head. 'As many of our folk did, some hundreds of years since. And as we are now, so your folk may be one day, unless the Ice is somehow halted.' He smiled thinly. 'The common folk still recall that time as a golden era of peace and plenty. They mix it up with legends older still. But in truth it must have been savage and divided, for it was then that the lineages were established that became the clans of

the *Aikiya*, the raiders accursed of all other men. Do
you know, I am of the Herons myself? Though now
the feathers are deeply caked with blood!'

'We apologise,' said Asquan gently. 'We did not
realise these things. We see the Ekwesh only as the
bloody hands of the Ice.'

'I cannot blame you for that. Raiders! Yes, they
are us – as the Ice has made us, and makes us still!' He
brooded a moment. 'So, yes, in a sense it is raiders
who come, now. In a sense . . . Though the ferryman
will not take them unless by terror or force, still they
come. They come, sometimes they knock, they
speak; they want to stay. But we cannot allow them,
although once they were dear to us. To harbour them
brings great ills. The summons is too strong.'

He was sweating, still, and clamping his leathery
hands on the rough table as if to tear it board from
board. Alya felt as if he were poised over the brink of
a great tragic secret. 'Can you tell us more? For our
own good? Who are they, who summons them?'

'They who pause and pass by – they are the Lost.
The Answerers of the Summons. They are riding to
the realm of Taoune, along the fringes of the Ice. For
them its serfdom has no end!' He tore his fingers from
the wood, and bowed his head.

'Taoune!' breathed Asquan softly, and something
in his voice was more awful than all the headman's
racked anguish. 'There is a name out of the dark! They
say he was lord of all the Ice, once.'

'They say truly,' said the headman, with deep
feeling. 'Lord, of all its might and all its ruling Powers,
when it was stronger even than it is now. When he
and his pale consort Taounehtar last drove it forth
across the world. And Taoune was opposed by the
men of those days, and the Elder Brethren who dwelt
among the hollow hills, and the younger Powers, the
cunning of the Raven and the fury of Ilmarinen. And
they drove Taoune and the glaciers back into the

North and South, it is written, and so into the scorn of his own kind. They say it was his own consort who toppled him at the last and took his place, greater and more terrible than ever he was. Now, his might dwindled, he is Lord of the Grey Lands only, gate-keeper and doorward to the Ice, guarding all its frontiers and marches. And to do so, he gathers those who have already lost all in the service of the Ice.'

Vansha looked puzzled. 'How, lost all?'

'Their lives!' barked the headman. 'Those who have been slain in its service! And not even that earns them rest!'

Kalkan snorted derisively. 'How can that be? Once you're dead, you're dead! Or you're somewhere else!'

The headman looked at him. 'Not if you are marked before your death. The Ice makes some impression on your mind, sets some barb within your spirit. It makes you cruel and evil, if you are not sufficiently so already; it makes you a fanatic for the cause of our cold masters. But it does more. When the campaigns are done, and the warriors ride home, then by that barb the spirits of those who have perished are also called back. And they must come. Within Taoune's realm they are given some semblance of solid shape once more, to become his warriors and his sentinels.' He stared into some endless void. 'And his toys! It is said that for his black diversion they fight eternal futile battles, each day dying to be revived the next. Until time itself shall end, perhaps.'

'A fable to frighten you, old fellow!' scoffed Vansha, and Kalkan and some of the others rumbled agreement.

'A legend the *Aikiya* sell you, no doubt!'

'It is *true!*' grated the headman.

'Ach, how'd you know?'

'*Because we see them!* If we are foolish enough

to look! Riding by, never returning . . . our own
folk . . .' The voice was perilously close to a scream.

'My friend is only trying to comfort you, in his
fashion,' said Alya quietly, with a black look at Vansha. 'We would not cast doubt on what you say. But
he thinks, perhaps, that this may be some cruel
deception of the Ice.'

The headman closed his eyes once again. 'Would
that it were. I understand your doubt. Forgive my
certainty.'

'I had already heard something of it,' said Alya
quietly. 'That these shadows return at this time, this
night; and that they ride upriver to the Ice. I believe it.
We seek to follow them.'

Vansha and the others stared, but Asquan
slapped his thigh. 'I *thought* that was your plan!
Follow them, sneak past the guards on the river,
and find a way in through the walls of the Ice! Into
this town or whatever it is!'

'That is it,' Alya agreed. 'If it works as I hope, it
might smuggle us into that place, that town. Once
inside, we may be able to lose ourselves. It looks large
and turbulent. And . . .'

'Follow . . .' Vansha's speech failed him. Even
Rysha was gaping. Over the crackle of the fire they all
heard it now, faint but clear; more horses, approaching from afar. Slowly, stumbling, as if they were not
merely weary but utterly spent; but they were definitely drawing nearer. Only Fazdshan spoke, hollowly.

'Where the dead go, can the living follow?'

'We can only try.'

'Will they not seek to stop us?' demanded Asquan.

'They may not even notice us, if we are careful.
But there would always be sentinels; this way may
help avoid them.' Alya's mouth was dry. 'I had
hoped, almost, that we would not find it open to
us, that we would simply have to go scout out others

into the Ice, and trust to luck to find the right one. But this will lead us far more surely and swiftly. Perhaps, for all its terrors, it will even save us perils and hard fighting. Well? Is the terror too great? Will any refuse?'

Kalkan squared his massive shoulders. 'No way's free of peril. We'll do as we pledged. It's been better than rotting in gaol, anyway!'

There was no murmur of agreement; but nobody demurred.

Oshur shook his head. 'You are bold men indeed! Heroes of old such as I would never have dreamed I would see! But you will surely perish in the attempt!'

'Will we?' demanded Alya fiercely, amid a disquieted rumble from his followers. 'They take boats, and row north, against the flow, under cover of the dark. So will we! We will find another boat, and take it along behind them. The guards will see only one more boat.'

'There are such boats,' said Oshur slowly. 'I can tell you where they lie, openly; for none would wish to touch them. But you will not succeed; for who do you think the guards are? They are Taoune's creatures also; and who knows what they may sense, even in dark and mist?'

Alya sagged back on his seat, and the others fell silent, even Asquan. 'I am sorry—' Oshur began; but he was interrupted by a soft sound, the rustle of horses' hooves upon the gravel, the soft snorts and whinnies of weary beasts seeking a stable. But Oshur sat without moving, and again the sweat shone on his brow. Now there were men's voices, and he rose, and then slowly sat down once again.

Then a voice cried out, softer than Tavao's, a young man's tone. 'Father! Open the door, Father!'

The headman trembled like a leaf. 'Akkur? Akkur, is that you?'

'Open the door! We've ridden far, Father! We're cold and hungry!'

Like a puppet on strings Oshur rose, and stumbled towards the door, brushing off restraining hands as he passed. The few of his people still in the room drew back and melted away.

'Open, Father!' cried the voice again. 'I want to come home!'

Oshur halted, breathing like a man running a course. 'You are home, my son! But I cannot open the door to you! Not yet! Not till sunrise!'

'It is dark, Father! The mist is heavy! There will be no sunrise, for many days, perhaps! Let me in!'

'I will, my son, I will!' gasped Oshur. 'I will unbar the door at once! You have only to knock, and I will open!'

Silence reigned for an instant, save for the headman's breathing. A log fell in the fire, showering sparks. Then the voice wailed again, despairing. 'Father! Open! Please!'

'Then knock!' screamed Oshur. 'Why do you not knock?'

'Father! I cannot even *see* the door . . .' The voice tailed off, to an incoherent wail, and Oshur plunged his face into his hands. Only for a moment; and when he straightened once again, his expression was stern.

'Then begone, my son! For now I know what has become of you, and what must be your fate. It is written above the lintel; and you would do no more than drain the life from us all, if I let you in. And soon enough you would leave, as now you must. Do not deceive us any further, my son, nor ask more blessings that I cannot give. Now go your way, and trouble us no more.'

There was no answer; but the sound of horses lingered. The headman turned sharply away, and returned to his seat by the fire. The others stared at him, with sorrow and pity. There were tears even in Rysha's eyes; and they streamed down Kalkan's furrowed cheeks.

'The third,' said the headman softly.

'Your third?' asked Rysha softly. 'Your third son? Have you others?'

'Four. I had four. The first two were taken together. The others, only this spring . . . when the fourth was only twelve. I had hoped he at least would come back tonight. But not . . . so late. Perhaps he would have been with his brother; but I did not ask.'

'I understand. Not to know will leave your hope alive for another year.'

The old man, for now he seemed so, nodded. 'It is better, in any case. Those who pass thus never stay long. And while they do, there are more deaths; and those they love the most die first. Even the sight of them leaves only misery and bitter memory. And helpless wrath, at the cruelty of the Ice. Better to make an end.'

'I have read much of such things,' said Asquan into the long silence that followed. 'That was how I divined my Lord Alya's intention. All I have read bears out what you say. It is as if such returners from the dead draw the life from the living. The superstitious believe they drink their blood. So you are wise, Master Headman, to do as you do. But there is more that I can offer you for your comfort. I have read that such creatures are not in truth the people they seem to be; but only the shadows of such people in the memories of the Powers that master them – in this case Taoune.'

'This I have read also!' put in Tseshya. 'That is why they exist only within his realm, and by night, when illusions are at their strongest – as our friend Rysha will confirm. Some say it is because the Ice cannot tell the difference, because it thinks all men are mere shadows, with no spirit of their own.'

'Indeed,' said Asquan quietly. 'Your son is surely dead, and I am sorry. But he does not walk in torment or slavery, nor have you turned him from your door this night. This I most firmly believe!'

'If that is so . . .' Oshur sat up, and his face also ran with tears; yet there was a dawning gladness on it, as clear as any sunrise. 'And I begin to believe it must be, indeed . . . Then you have done me a comfort and a solace beyond my power to thank! May such grace follow you also! I cannot think how more to thank you!'

Alya leaned forward. 'But perhaps I can, head-man. That thing in the image of your son, it said it could not even *see* that great door of yours! Why? Because of the mist?'

The headman smiled grimly. 'No indeed! Because of those ancient characters. That is their purpose, that their effect. For that they were graven into stone, many thousands of years since, and for that copied and recopied, ever since! Let me show you.'

He rose; and going to his high seat, he pulled out a clumsy key, unlocked the carven lid, and returned bearing something wrapped in cloth, which he laid carefully on the table. The scroll he drew out was slender, silver-mounted, in a style nobody recognised; and the coarse parchment crackled and flaked as he drew it open upon the table. 'There they are!'

'This is very old,' said Tseshya, studying it intently. 'A text, surely, though none of us can read it!'

'Indeed,' said Asquan, puzzling over the text. 'It defeats me. But of course you would expect to find such a defence preserved in a place where it is most needed.'

'And yet only the first couple of lines seem to serve. Where they stand, all things of ill-omen are blind. That is how we endure, against the awful things that haunt this land; that, and giving up what is rightfully ours to the Ice . . .' Oshur cocked a wise eye. 'You are thinking of painting this upon your boat, perhaps?'

'That might do,' agreed Alya. 'But better yet would be closer. Can you let us have brush and ink, headman?'

'Easily enough; but there is little good paper—'

'On our armour, our clothes, our skins themselves!' said Alya. 'Then we will be able to follow them close, indeed!'

Even Oshur in his grief had to laugh at the scene that followed, as they stripped down stark naked and traced the text across one another, over and over again. Rysha gave him as host the honour, as she put it, of painting her. 'At least he has a flatter paper to work on than I do!' said Vansha sourly, as he scrawled the characters across Alya's broad back. 'Hold still, damn you!'

'Watch where you put those bristles, brother!' said Alya warily. 'Or I'll have my revenge in full, next!'

But it did not take so very long, and soon they were dressed again. Alya sat with Oshur, talking quietly but urgently about their route; but the others he sent out to paint the horses. 'In large letters!' said the scholar sourly. 'I'll get kicked!'

'Isn't that always a scholar's fate?' chuckled Kalkan. 'Now you can truly call yourself a lettered man!'

'You could be a rather skinny scroll yourself, my lord!' said Asquan cheerfully. 'The official sort, with the tasselled knob on the end—'

'At least I'll contain something fit to read! Yours will read like an indictment of universal vice!'

'Ah!' sighed Asquan. 'If only . . .'

Oshur watched in amazement. 'All this, and no fear of where you are going, what you are doing? You are warriors out of the ballads, indeed!'

'I'm afraid,' said Alya quietly. 'Perhaps we all are, even the strong men, the soldiers. But more afraid of failure, perhaps, of being no better off than we are now, with few satisfactions for all this effort, coming all this way. Unless we succeed, we will have nothing, no life to go back to, no homes . . . nothing.'

'We do not have much more,' sighed Oshur. 'Enough to make a difference, maybe. I would offer you homes with us, for I pine for such company, and honour you. But folk such as you could not endure what we must, at every turn. I do so only because I must protect those beneath me, as my ancestors did.'

'If you weary of that,' said Alya slowly, 'or your folk do, let them leave. Let them strike out eastward, for the coast, for the sea, for the new lands I believe lie across it, in strength and freedom. That way I will turn, when my task is done. Then perhaps we will meet again.'

'I fear not, boy. But you have only to knock upon my door again, and it will be open to you.' He stopped, listening. 'More horses on the road! But no more live ones, now, of that I am sure! Go, with the blessing I had to deny my son!'

Swiftly they led their mounts through the hall once more, and Oshur nervously opened the doors a little. 'You need not look out,' said Alya. 'Shut it behind us, think of us also as shadows that have passed. Yet not without remembering your kindness.'

'Can I forget yours?' said the headman, and his voice sounded weary but strong, as a man who has shed a burden. 'I bless you and your coming, for your wisdom has lifted a weight from my heart. Fool that I've been! I should have understood sooner what these shadows must be, no more than the discarded skin of a snake, or a lark's empty eggshell in the fields. The bird itself has flown. That, at least, I need suffer no more, nor my people. And by that much the malice of the Ice is driven back!'

'Whatever blow we strike,' said Alya, 'your arm will be behind it. But now we must set out ourselves.'

He opened the door wider, and the rustle of hooves came softly through the mist. It was strange that so gentle and plain a sound could strike such a mordant chill into his heart.

Even Kalkan stood hesitant. 'You truly mean to follow that . . . shadow? Into shadow?'

Alya met his eyes. 'I do, my lord. It is our only road, though it may end for all or many of us. I am sworn, and so are you. Break your oath, if you will, and stay!'

'I made no oath to follow a madman!' hissed Fazdshan.

Rysha gave a slight shrill giggle. 'Yes you did. We all did! I thought I could shroud myself in night and fear, and be safe! But that out there's a deeper night than any I can bring, and more fearful!'

'It is,' said Alya calmly. 'And I hold you to your word.'

Even Vansha was shuddering. 'I don't believe this! You saw! Death is out there!'

'So is Savi. So is life.'

Asquan alone smiled. 'The world draws in, and our road grows narrow. I see only death and pain for us all before its end. Yet I am curious! I would see this path you've chosen for us, Seer!'

Alya nodded. 'Then do not mount, but lead your horse and follow. It will not be far. You others, follow, or be forsworn in life and death alike. Headman, farewell!'

The old man nodded. 'Even so. Yet even the darkest paths may find unexpected light. Strike hard!'

Alya and Asquan led their horses out into the dark; and Vansha was at their heels. One by one, with a curse or a groan, the others followed, trudging on unwilling feet, till before his ancestral door, with its unknown signs, the headman stood alone in the mists.

CHAPTER 9
The Eye of the Swan

THEY walked on in silence, and the mists clung about them, lit only by the moon. They could hear and see nothing, save Alya and his horse leading them; and of what he saw and heard, he told them nothing. But one thing was all too clear to them, as the hours of the night passed. Following any band of horsemen, there would be signs: tracks, dung, cropped plants, human debris. These left nothing. Alya felt there would not even be marks on the compacted clay of the road. Yet when the others closed up to him, on a difficult patch, they seemed to hear now and then an indistinct rumble of voices, a few harsh words.

'What d'you suppose they're talking about?' muttered Chiansha.

'If they're only spirits, why should it be anything?' whispered Vansha.

'They do what their masters imagine humans do, I think,' said Alya quietly. 'I don't believe the Ice really understands these things aren't real.'

'You mean, they think we're all just . . . chattering shadows?'

'Yes. Just the sum of our memories. Because it suits them to believe that.'

'Like it suits a cruel man to believe his horse can't feel pain,' said Kalkan, unexpectedly. 'Or his slave. But if these things act like the men they were, couldn't they turn on us? Might be bastards up ahead there we've slain already!'

'You think that hasn't been worrying me?' demanded Alya wryly. 'Stay as quiet as you can! But it's worth sticking so close. They may shield us, this band!'

'They may soon get the chance!' rasped Asquan. 'I think . . . *they*'re stopping. *What's that noise?*'

'Water!' said Alya curtly, halting them all with a gesture. 'On wood – a boat's timbers, I guess. Keep quiet! We're back near the river, now, but much higher up. Near where Oshur said the boats lie. From where the . . . the horsemen will make their way back up to the Ice.'

'By boat?' Darzhan shook his head. 'I can't figure this. Spooks need boats? Why?'

'These . . .' Alya shivered. 'As I understand it, these aren't spirits. The opposite; and worse. They're the dead, walking. But more like . . . puppets. Shadow-puppets, maybe. Only the strings aren't of horsehair, here. And the shadows . . . of the mind, I guess! Minds remade, from their memories, with all the skills, the experience they had in life, within a greater mind. A mind that can pull many strings.'

Darzhan's whisper was shaky, in the darkness. 'Puppets? They bring the bodies back to life?'

'I don't know. Oshur didn't think so. Nor did the . . . other minds I touched. But they seem all too real, that's for sure! They need boats just as we do. Great longboats. I saw them out on the river, when I scouted ahead. There should be many moored all along this bank.'

'But won't there be sentinels?' demanded Tseshya.

'There are always sentinels. But they're posted more to keep escapers in, than people out. They don't guard the boats, for who would want to go near them?'

'Now I see!' said Vansha, with a great gust of relief. 'You think one boat full of live men won't be noticed?'

'I hope not. Not with the writings to help shield us; and in these mists especially. Oshur says they often hold for days, at this time of year. Maybe the riding is chosen for that, or maybe the mists are raised to shield it. But we must get past the guards somehow, or they will call out the Choosers. Don't ask me of them!'

'Did you also find all that out, *scouting*?' demanded Asquan sardonically.

Alya looked at him. 'Much that I couldn't understand and don't wish to. I saw this, from paths you could never tread.'

Asquan nodded curtly, though his eyes were hungry. 'So be it, Seer. Listen!'

They all heard it, the soft boom of boat timbers underfoot, the slop and wash of river water as the boat rocked, the quiet whinny and snort of uncertain horses led aboard.

'Are you sure they're not . . .'

'Very.'

'But they sound so alive!' protested Rysha fearfully. 'D'you think . . . d'you think all men can come back, thus?'

She had her reasons for asking that, of course. 'I guess not,' said Alya at last. 'Only those the Ice sets its mark on; those in its service, or within its bounds. Listen! More oars!'

They sounded very soft and slow, as if, like the shadow at the door, they were reluctant to depart. Two boats plashed quietly out into the mists, and a third cast off, in eerie silence; they could even hear the splash of the mooring rope, left trailing by uncaring hands.

Only too easily Alya could imagine himself sitting there, head hanging, the iron of endless servitude already fixed in mind and heart. He would not be real – but would he know it? Or would a new mind take shape, out of the old self? He battled furiously with

the thought, the shapeless terror of death and extinc-
tion that borrowed its force from the deep wells of his
mind. A great impatience surged up within, all the
worse because he knew he was only giving a new
guise to his fear. Yet it helped him, because it let him
spare neither himself nor the others.

'That's long enough!' he grated. 'No more noises.
Asquan, with me! On our bellies, and *quiet*!'

Asquan said nothing, but downed his weapons
and slithered off like a snake – no easy task in a
mailshirt, as Alya discovered among the coarse grass.
The mist grew denser down towards the water, but
they found the path easily enough. Asquan stared, and
waved his hands in some deep emotion; but it took
Alya a moment to realise what he meant. When he
did, he shivered; the faint moon-gleam in the mists
showed him prints on the wet clay, of man and horse,
so fresh the haze was still condensing out in them.

But he shrugged, and slid forward. A moment
later he caught the shadow of black water, and the
glistening timbers of a ramshackle mooring. Beside it
stretched three or four long, wide boats, shallow of
draught or wholly flat-bottomed, and big enough for
some ten places a side. They too looked old, their
crude timbers slimed with moss and mould; but they
rode the river easily enough, and they stood empty,
the wavelets splashing against their low gunwales.
There was no other sound all around them.

'Paddles!' exclaimed Asquan in disgust, as they
sought the safest. 'And a sculling oar! Almost big
enough for two men! Evidently the Ice doesn't trust
its folk with arcane devices like oars!'

'This one's been repaired recently!' said Vansha,
testing the bottom gingerly. 'You're not telling me the
spooks keep a boatyard?'

'The Ice has plenty of living servants!' said Alya,
coaxing his nervous horse aboard. 'These it no doubt
values for their greater terror and indestructibility;

but they cannot take shape far from the Ice. Under
the sun they are powerless, so Oshur says. They exist
fully only within the Grey Lands, Taoune's domain.
Within his thought, you could say.'

'Which is where we're going,' said Fazdshan
sullenly.

'Which is where we already are!' snapped Alya.
'Make the best of it! Get in, and I'll do the work!'

It took time to get all of them into the chosen
boat, and make it stable and secure. Their nervous
mounts had to be tethered to the slimy thwarts in the
centre, and stood there shaking their heads and
pawing the timbers uneasily. But at last all were
aboard, and Alya seized the great scull and pushed
them away from the crumbling mooring, out into the
swirling mists.

Asquan tried to cast off the forward rope, but
under Alya's impatient strength it simply snapped.
The stern rope flew off, taking a rusty cleat with it,
and the boat veered out into the current. On the stern
platform Alya clumsily fitted the scull into its socket,
but he had little idea how to work it, until Asquan
tactfully showed him. Then Alya's arms shot the boat
forward against the current as if it weighed nothing at
all. The others took up the paddles, but only to steer,
and that seldom. Alya kept the boat in the heart of the
current as if he could pierce the mist with his gaze.

The others could not; but when they caught up
with the other boats, they were all too keenly aware.
Not only from the soft plash of the paddles in the
waters ahead, the low rippling wakes on the green
glassy surface. The deeper chill in the mist told them,
and their faltering hearts. Around those unseen presences life itself seemed to gutter like a dying candle.
They would have lost the will and the strength to
drive the boat onward, if Alya had not held the scull.
He felt that chill as they did, but the fires that raged
within him only leaped the higher in answer, as he

called upon them to the full. And since encountering
Oshur there was a colder rage building up alongside
them, that was wholly his own. And, before all else,
there was the vision of Savi drawing him on. The
others looked back at him, and drew strength from
his tall figure at the tiller, and his implacable features,
set flintlike against fear.

For hours he drove the boat on, deep into the
night, and towards the dawn, such as it was. What
light spilled through the mists was grey and grudging,
and showed the little band only each other's haggard
faces. They were bleary and dirty, but they did not
dare wash; the ink that tautened their skins was
already blurring in the moist air. Alya would take
no rest, but drove the boat on as if he were some
fearful mechanism of steel and stone, untouched by
fatigue or fear.

The water flowing around the hull seemed heavier now, black and glossy as onyx. And now and then
in the murk strange shapes seemed to swirl to the
surface and vanish again, with a glimpse of a slimy
black back, or an arch of armoured scales, and a brief
musky stink. The horses whickered and panicked at
that; and once one, Tseshya's, broke its rein and
sprang overboard in mindless panic, swimming away
beyond reach, into the mist. A minute later they heard
a swirl, and a brief high scream; nothing more. They
held the other horses more tightly, after that.

The light dimmed once more, as evening came
to the mist-bound river. Alya heard the paddles ahead
grow louder, as if they were slowing, or making more
effort. Which way they lay he could not tell in the
mist, and fell back a little. Night swirled about him,
grey and hopeless; but the fire gripped him as firmly
as his hands gripped the scull, and drove him as
fiercely. Time rolled on, and he saw heads droop
to knees, his followers sink down even on those slimy
thwarts, worn out; but he felt no such urge. He knew

how far they must go to pass the river guards; and he was too deeply afraid to stop.

So it was that the next dim dawn found him, still strong in his limbs but worn out in his mind, barely able to keep his reddened eyes open. Asquan and Fazdshan between them took over the huge scull, while he lay sprawled across a thwart in his saddle blanket. He awoke towards evening, stiff and clammy, with the boat still shrouded by the mists; but they were chillier and thinner now, and as they swirled and boiled, the watchers caught glimpses of a shore that was green or brown no longer, but barren and white with snow, often deep in drifts. Chiansha and Vansha had the scull now, but when Alya saw the thinning mists he came staggering aft in a fury. 'We must keep up!' he raged.

'We're doing our best!' hissed Vansha. 'So did Asquan and Fazdshan, and they're worn out now! We don't all have the Inmost Flame to stoke our sinews!'

Alya seized the oar. 'Don't you understand, you fools? We must keep within the mists! When they're this thin, we're too far behind! And there are other watchers. If we can see, we can also be seen – can't we?' He gave the oar a massive heave. 'Never mind! As you say, you did your best! But now I have to catch up!'

So he did, all that long day labouring at the scull, with the mists blowing ever thicker around them, until the splash of paddles ahead sounded alarmingly loud. They waved at him to slow down; but Vansha and Asquan had to shake the oar in his hands before he would pay heed. Nor would he rest, even then. He was pale and grim, but he denied he was tired, and he took the food they gave him as he rowed on into the night, his bleary eyes forever fixed on the mists ahead.

Nevertheless, at last his head also drooped a little, though his arms did not slow at the scull. His

eyes closed, for a second as it seemed; and then he
started awake. An icy breath passed across his cheek,
as from ghostly lips, and he had barely a moment to
hiss a warning to the others before the faint gleam
grew stronger, and the growing breeze rolled back
the grey veils overhead.

They revealed first a sky still dark, and heavy
with menacing clouds; but touched with a faint hint
of dawn. But even that dismal light kindled a glitter
among the thinning heights of the mist, a bitter gleam
that drew every eye and struck fear into it. That light
seemed to fill the way ahead, as if the mist was
solidifying around them. And indeed, the mists
tumbled and cascaded down its surface, like sea-
waves that broke impotently off granite rocks, rolling
back to fill the river basin. But this was not granite, it
seemed, but glass, clouded yet shimmering faintly
blue and green even in this gloom with captive light.

Across the tortured earth they stretched, between the horizons, the ends of sight and sky; and
he knew well how much further. But his long flight
had not shown him everything. Among the upper airs
he had missed their truest and most terrible aspect, a
glistening blade that slashed earth and air asunder,
and held the scar apart. Straight ahead they rose with
infinite, forbidding grandeur, blue-white and translucent as jewels, the walls of a vast battlement older
than any other, fortress and fastness, mighty, uncon-
querable, the mountainous ramparts of the Ice.

In Alya's weary eyes they loomed taller and more
terrible than their black counterpart. Yet, white or
black, these walls also he must overcome, to have any
hope of making his life his own once again. The
stronghold of his ultimate enemy had become the
cradle of his last slender hope.

There was nothing smooth or solid about them.
On the contrary; they were deeply riven, fragmented,
cracked, worn and eaten away with the rigours of

unimaginable time. At their feet whole cliff-faces lay
shattered; shards greater than whole palaces stood
half detached and poised to crash down in ruins upon
those that had fallen before, like those fragments of
the Great Ice it was said could fall from the heights
beyond the air, from the abyss of the stars.

Ravines an army could enter opened in many
places, stairs a giant could climb, caves like the
burrowings of monstrous worms from which half-
frozen streams tricked down in icicles the height of
foothills. Craggy crenellations tore at the rainclouds
that hung above them. Yet behind all those flaws and
breaches there was no vulnerability, no defended
heart. There was nothing but the immense realm
of the glaciers themselves, stretching deep beyond
sight to the further half of the world, forever replen-
ished from its heart by the waters it drew down and
captured, as snow.

That sight held them in silent awe, every one.
But at its centre was something that brought home
the deadly reality of their situation. Just such a
crevice clove the wall before them, a vast triangular
gap in the cliff's base. Though it reached barely
a third of the way to the summit, it could have
swallowed the highest towers of human make.
The boiling cauldron of the mist hid its base, but
left little doubt this was the river's source and outflow. And still less doubt that it was into that slash of
blackness the shadow-boats were headed.

The mists, driven down from the clifftops, still
filled the river basin; and Alya strained at the oar to
stay among the thickest banks, to wring all the concealment he could from them. There was something
horribly watchful about those heights, as if keen-eyed
sentries patrolled them. And the shadow-boats were
near enough to hear. A minute more in hiding might
make all the difference.

But he was weary; and the mists were unpredictable, banking and thinning at random. Suddenly, very close, a shadow took form among the whiteness, a figure at its stern. It stood just as Alya stood, leaning on the great scull; and it gave him a horrible fantasy that the thinning mist might show him familiar faces in the other boat, blank and dead, and upon its face, his own. He hissed a warning, but there was no need. His followers already sat like their counterparts, hooded heads bowed with oppression and despair.

Easily, careful not to seem too eager, he sculled past the other, keeping as clear as he could from the sound of their paddles. But the mists betrayed him. The same dank breeze blew once more, bearing scents of bare stone and hard earth, edged with dark frost. It flicked a chilly rain-speck against his forehead, and another. Drizzle thinned the haze around them, and outlined the silhouettes of the other boats.

'There are more!' exclaimed Kalkan hoarsely. 'More than the three we followed! Sentinels!'

'*Paddle!*' snapped Alya, and bent hard to the scull, steering for where the mist still rolled thickest, seeking to plunge into the murk once more. The hull creaked as the paddles hurled it forward, its blunt bow planing over the rain-pocked river. Whiteness parted before them, then rolled and boiled around them once again; and it seemed as if they were safely hidden. Then they saw within it the shadow-shape of yet another boat, driving in on where they had been, and about to pass them very close. Somehow they had been seen.

Rysha waved her hand suddenly, pointing at it. Puzzled, Alya glanced down at his; and a splash of spreading blue landed on his knuckles, blurring the characters there. The rain was washing the ink from his forehead and face, and now his hands also.

A thin stabbing chill swept over them all. The horses tossed their heads and whinnied in dismay. They heard no word spoken, but water boomed and

gurgled against another hull, and the shadow swung
sharply about. Kalkan sprang up, making the flat boat
sway and ship water over its low gunwale. Asquan
hissed in fury and rose to balance him. 'Keep paddling!' growled Kalkan, but Asquan ignored him.
Kalkan hefted his heavy spear, Asquan drew his
sword. Alya drove the boat on, wondering what
would fly out of the mist, a challenge or simply an
arrow in the back.

There was a voice suddenly, with guttural words
he couldn't understand. A harsh plain voice, yet
something in it made his heart leap and labour.

'Don't answer!' hissed Asquan softly. Alya realised he must be right. The creatures in that boat
could not see them clearly, not yet. They might still
give it the slip. The drizzle grew stronger. Something
chill stung his cheek, and again; then his ear. Something hard, among the rain, and now there was more.
A sudden gust thrashed his shoulders; hailstones,
small but fast, and growing larger. The mists sank
before them, a slanting, steely curtain. They hammered on the boat's timbers, stinging, blinding. The
others could do nothing to protect the horses, who
shrilled and tossed their heads. That was enough. Like
a blade through mail, steering straight down upon
them, came the shadow-boat.

Now there was no challenge, and the characters,
what remained upon their skin, could help them
little. They could see and be seen clearly enough
now, by the other crew. Among its paddlers
crouched other shapes, picked out in the grey light
by the sullen sheen of helm and spearpoint. Alya gave
one last immense thrust, feeling the scull bend dangerously under his hands, turning his boat unexpectedly towards the other. Then he heaved the scull
from its socket.

Kalkan had had the same idea. His spear was
already levelled, braced in both hands, and as the

shadow-boat slid alongside he swung it. A broad spearblade stabbed past him and thudded into the timbers, but his longer lance scythed across the gap and struck. The shadows in the other boat were struck sprawling across their gunwales, with a re-assuringly solid crash and splash. The boat rocked with the reaction, and the other shadows ducked.

'You can be hit hard enough!' hissed Alya. He saw the armoured men spring up, and swung the scull in both hands. He glimpsed faces hard and scarred like any Ekwesh, and felt a ridiculous reassurance; surely these were living men, at least. Then he met their eyes.

The scull swept right across their deck. Living, dead, or neither, they were hurled down on one another, over the thwarts, upon the paddlers, into the black water, leaving the boat a tangle of thrashing limbs. But it was a completely silent tangle, without a scream or a curse; and out of it figures sprang up at once, stabbed out and leaped. One landed on the gunwale above Vansha, and Asquan hewed the legs from him. Another fell right in the bottom of the boat, and Rysha yelled in fright and clubbed him down with the butt of her paddle. The dark helmsman loomed up. He too had raised his oar like a quarter-staff; but Alya was ready. His lunge drove the other's scull back in against him, and hurled him overside.

Then they were past, with the horses still rearing and plunging in fright, the planking booming alarmingly. Fazdshan ran to calm the beasts – and Rysha squealed again as the warrior she had felled sprang up, spear still in hand, and struck. The creature flew up, kicking on the end of Kalkan's spear; but Fazd-shan sagged, clawing at his shoulder, blood spurting through his fingers. The creature was hurled over-side; and the dark boat, unsteered, slid away into the mist.

With unsteady hands Alya locked the scull again

and pulled furiously. He looked back to where the
dark boat had disappeared, but it might never have
been. He felt a moment of mad relief. Its mere
presence was somehow deeply shocking.

Rysha was supporting Fazdshan, while Tseshya
struggled to staunch his wound with his neckcloth;
but then the mist swirled. The scholar screamed,
jerked violently and fell back, snatching at the arrow
in his hip. Another thudded into his mailshirt and
broke, but he doubled up in pain. Vansha dragged
him down out of sight. Kalkan dropped as other
arrows hissed over the boat. Asquan cursed as one
hit him a glancing blow on the side. Then two of the
horses screamed, and one dropped dead where it
stood; the other fell kicking and writhing, while its
fellows threshed and whinnied.

Alya winced, but he had to leave them to the
others. Another gust of hail stung his eyes, and
shielding them stopped him seeing what lay ahead,
till the last moment – the other boat, riding still in the
water, full in their way. He swung the scull sharply,
but he was not practised enough to backwater fast.
The boat glided obstinately down against the bow of
the sentinel craft, and arrows hissed down among the
hail.

Alya skipped sharply as they split the stained
timbers around him. Vansha, in the bows, wrenched
one loose, drew his own bow and sent it winging
back. It struck into the breast of one of the shadows
gathering along the gunwales ahead, and the thing fell
back; but others pressed into place, massing as if to
leap. Fear wreathed about them like smoke.

Kalkan growled with rage, and swung up his
spear butt-first. Alya wanted to shout; they would
shoot the old man down at once. But Kalkan took two
short steps forward. His spear slammed down on the
deck timbers, and with a wild roar the old lord
vaulted on it, right over the gunwale, right on to

the approaching bow; and even as he landed the spear was swinging over and down. The nearest of the massing shadows was clubbed down, the stabbing spearblades were scythed apart, and Kalkan stabbed and swung among them.

'Follow me, lads!' he bellowed. 'Let's scour this dung-barge good and proper!'

Darzhan was already poised to follow, Chiansha came leaping down from the bow, and Vansha threw down his bow and drew his sword, ready to follow. Fazdshan also sprang up, sword in hand, as if unaware of the clotted rag dangling from the torn neck of his mailshirt. Darzhan vaulted, Chiansha after him, but Fazdshan, with his long legs, simply pushed Vansha aside and leaped. A gust of hail caught him as he landed, and he skidded to his knees on the platform; but even as he fell he was thrusting out, catching one of the shadows on his sword, slashing another across the thigh and into the river.

Vansha sprang up to follow, but the gap between the boats was too wide now, and he could only watch in astonishment as Kalkan and his men cut a swathe through their foes. Shadows they might be, but they fought like living men. And could be cut down like them also; or tipped into the river, to be whirled away by the strong slow current. In moments Kalkan was at the stern, crossing spears with the shadow-steersman, with Darzhan guarding his back, and Fazdshan stabbing frantically at anything that still moved. Alya was struggling to pull their boat around, and managed at last to bring it alongside.

'Come back!' Vansha roared at Kalkan. 'We've got to get clear!'

Even in his battle-fury Kalkan heard, and with one last sweep of his spear he whirled and came staggering back down the listing boat, pushing the others before him. They reached the bow, and Kalkan was squaring off to leap when one of the mangled things they had left in their passage reared up and hewed with a broken pike. Kalkan bellowed and staggered. Darzhan caught him, Chiansha pinned the flailing thing to the timbers and Fazdshan hacked it in half.

Darzhan more or less threw Kalkan into Vansha's arms, then jumped back himself, sprawling across the gunwale. Chiansha followed, landed on top of him and narrowly missed transfixing Vansha with his spear. Seeing this, Fazdshan turned to the stern. Alya reached out to catch him. But a hand clamped on the hem of the warrior's mailshirt, and he fell sprawling on his injured shoulder. Bodies, unable to stand, slithered up like serpents and swarmed across him as he screamed. Broken blades and haftless spears rose and fell like threshing flails. Blood poured across the platform and dripped off the edge.

Then they were past, with Kalkan groaning and cursing in the bow.

Even as they cleared it, though, Alya saw movement at the edge of sight. He swung the scull, barely in time. Timbers crashed and splintered, and the impact almost threw him from the stern. Their boat swung wildly in the water, rammed by the first boat, which had come up behind them again. But more by luck than skill, Alya had suddenly offered them the craft's solid stern instead of its low flank. Half-rotten timbers splintered under his feet, but the other's entire bow had given way. The shadow-boat sagged down and subsided slowly, as if dissolving back into the black waters. Its stern rose, sliding its shadowy crew in a heap, and it rolled over and vanished.

There were shouts ahead, then, and it was not Alya but Vansha, with a hefty paddle-stroke, who turned the boat aside from another impact, barely in time. Kalkan, the side of his mail stained red, hefted his spear to strike at the other boat; but he made no move. There on the other bow stood Fazdshan, mangled and bloody, but straight and intent. And as Kalkan hesitated, staring, the warrior lunged out, without a sound, and struck his spear right through Kalkan's body, mail and all.

Vansha's sword smashed the spearshaft, and the old lord slumped over with a crash. The impact toppled Fazdshan, or his likeness, into the water between the two hulls. They met and ground in a shower of splinters. An arm was flung up, momentarily, to clutch their gunwale; but it flew up as the hulls parted, and sank back into the river. Then there was a rush of hard boots on timbers, and a dark wave of shadows broke over them.

Alya upended the scull and brought it smashing down among them, breaking the rush; then swung it around and fended off the other boat, as Kalkan had sought to. It tipped violently, shipped water, and many still aboard it were spilled into the river. But their own boat was rocking with the struggling mass of bodies, falling to this side and that.

The remaining horses neighed and plunged in frantic terror of what ran by them, breaking their tackle or the timbers that tethered them, and sprang for the black water. There was no time to stop them. Asquan was almost dancing across the thwarts, his sword slashing left and right with a terrible craftsman's precision. Vansha, standing astride Kalkan, the dead encircled like dogs, and he hewed at them violently. Chiansha and Darzhan stood back to back, the one grunting stolidly with each spear-stroke, the other wide-eyed and raving, laying about him with his broken spear in one hand and a paddle in the other. But though bodies slumped around them, it was not enough to drive them back, and Rysha and the wounded Tseshya were flailing away desperately at the ones that slipped by.

Alya glanced around. No other boats were in sight now; and the horses were gone, to what end he could guess. He shipped the scull, drew his own sword and sprang down into the boat, awash with bodies.

They did not cry out; they did not bleed; and their eyes were no emptier as they lay than those who still fought. Mindful of Fazdshan's fate, he hewed them as he passed, and kicked some overside. He reached Tseshya, and the shades around him sprang away; but that only showed him the spreading pool of blood in which the scholar struggled. To Alya they seemed like swarming vermin, and he lashed out in furious loathing, his skin crawling even as he struck. The flocking shadows fought back with grim intensity, but they awoke no fire in him now, only cold disgust and even a kind of pity, remembering the lonely shade at the door. Yet his arm rose and fell with its full force, and his ancient sword brooked no contest. From elder and better days that edge and temper came, and wherever its great weight struck, it severed, and sent broken shapes flying this way and that, into the river.

They did not break, as living men might well have, but they gave back, freeing Vansha, and then the other two. Then together, though Darzhan was wounded and gasping, Alya and the other closed in with Asquan, driving the shadows between them to the edge. The boat rocked, almost tipped. Vansha tried to drag Kalkan back from the side, but the old lord retched and vomited a great gout of clotted blood down his breast. He struggled to his knees and waved them on, with an incoherent roar; and then sagged against the thwart. But there was little left to do; the last boarders were driven over the bow in a welter of splashes, and Alya kicked their listing craft away into the rain. Darzhan, still screaming, began hacking at the fallen; Asquan heaved them overboard, while the others ran back to Kalkan. He lay there, held half on his side by the spearshaft sticking out from his back; but he still lived.

The old warrior shot Alya a wide grin. 'Thanks for hoicking me out of the dark, boy!' he wheezed, quite cheerfully. 'Doubt I'd have lasted many more weeks. Kept going longer out here. And better. Still say no woman's worth all this, mind you.'

They raised him up, but there was all too clearly nothing to be done. He struggled up on one elbow, looking at the spearshaft. 'Least it's one of ours, not a rusty ripper like theirs! Ach, a louse-ridden place to pop off, here. Me! Here! Me that could've been a bloody king! But better than fat-arse Volmur's shitpit. And they won't stick their bloody strings on me – not me! That's f'sure! Hey, you old bugger!' he gurgled at Asquan, who was hastily tipping the last body over-side. 'You won't need to do that f'me!'

Kalkan supported himself on Vansha's arm, and reached out to jog Tseshya's shoulder, making him yell with pain. 'Hey, scrivener! Looks like you've had your last disputation, an' all!'

Tseshya grimaced weakly. 'Not . . . dead . . . yet!' Alya was appalled to see the scholar's leg was a welling mass of blood, where some great artery had been cut, beyond all staunching.

Kalkan glared at him with grim satisfaction. 'That's not ink you're spilling, boy! Five minutes, and you might as well have wiped your arse on all those old scrolls, for all the good they'll do you. Care to join me?'

The old man lifted his moustache in a lopsided grinning wink to Vansha, as if about to show him a special trick. Then he seized the broken spear that still transfixed him, and with a massive, twisting wrench he hauled it out. Blood and bile and innards spilled down his mail, and he fell face down on to the planks.

Tseshya, his face the colour of pale parchment, gave back in horror, and clutched in agony at his leg, and then at his temples, as if his head pained him still

more. 'Plain as Qualian's precepts!' he muttered, and
bent down, as if to duck his face in the river; but with
a sudden convulsive heave on the gunwale he thrust
himself right over. Rysha, shaking violently, made a
half-hearted move to stop him. Nobody else did. He
slipped easily into the water, without a splash, and
vanished, leaving only a few bubbles and a barely
visible thread of blood.

Asquan, clutching his side and wheezing with
effort, came limping up, thrusting Darzhan and Chiansha aside, thumping Alya in the chest. 'What're you
gaping at? Get back and scull, you stupid bastard!'

Alya, dazed and horrified, ran astern, staggering
and slipping in the blood. The rain was slackening
now, and the mist much lower and more straggling.
He could see now that they must have entered some
wide pool, a lakelet almost, where the sentinel boat
had been moored and the current was slack; but they
were drifting back out of it now, and into the mouth
of the river again. And that way two dark shapes were
converging out of the mist, fighting their way up the
current. He snatched up the scull once again.

'One more effort, and we'll make it!' shouted
Asquan. 'Come on, boy!'

Alya felt weary as he had not felt for an age, as it
seemed, another life. He seized the oar and bore
down on it, and again, and again, while Vansha
and Chiansha dug in their paddles, frantically swinging the unwieldy craft about. Darzhan crouched over
his spear, muttering insistently and looking around
for another attack; but Rysha and Asquan took up
paddles at the bow, and the old boat groaned and
creaked back across the pool. Slowly, as it seemed,
they gathered momentum; and in Alya's arms the fire
took hold once again, and the boat leaped onward.

The mists were sinking all across the river now.
He could see a hazy line that must be the nearer bank;
but ahead of him, nothing. He looked up, and the

great crevice loomed impossibly close, almost over them already. A brief glimpse of the sky was left him, and the weeping rainclouds; then its blackness closed around them like the jaw of a hunting beast, and the roar and tumult of the enclosed river shook the air.

Darzhan sprang to his feet, staring in fascinated horror at the mass overhead, and began backing down the boat, as if he could somehow avoid being taken underneath. Even when he tripped over Kalkan's body he did not tear his eyes away; and when he reached the stern he looked around wildly, threw down his spear and tried to seize the oar from Alya.

'Don't you hear?' the tall man screamed, slavering and wrestling with him for the heavy shaft. 'Hear what it's shouting? Get us out of this place! We'll die here, and join their stinking sentinels - forever! *Get us out! It's shouting—*' Vansha tried to pull him back, and was knocked sprawling. The big soldier began to rave words that made no sense, and his spittle flew in Alya's eyes. They thrashed back and forth, the broken platform creaking under their struggling feet.

From out of the mists behind came a flight of arrows, aimed no doubt at the echoing voice. None struck, but Darzhan swatted at them as if they were insects. Then he snatched up the broken spear.

'*Turn the boat about! Don't you hear it? Get us out—*' There was a noise like an axe splitting wood, and he lurched forward suddenly, choking. The madman stared at Alya, wide-eyed and reproachful as a baby; then the dull sound came again, and he staggered, tipping the gunwale dangerously deep. Vansha seized Darzhan's shoulder and thrust hard once more before Alya could shout. The front of the tall man's mailshirt burst, and he gaped down at the dripping point. He gasped, a reproachful question, '*Don't - hear—*'

'*Vansha!*' snarled Alya.

Vansha's boot thrust the flailing man off the

blade, and over the stern, arms outflung, screaming
into the water.

'He was going to kill you! He'd have had us
overturned! Or caught!'

And indeed, in that moment the dying mist
seemed to darken as the twin shadows slid alongside,
too close on either flank to turn; and along their sides,
defined by gleams of spray-dulled metal, the files of
spearmen tensed to spring.

Rysha leaped first, to her feet, arms above her
head; and Alya remembered they were no longer
under the sun. It was as if blackness dropped a veil
about them, and where Rysha had stood, a vicious
rock outcrop took shape, jagged and deadly, so life-
like that he almost flung up the scull to fend it off.
Dimly, through the pulsing blackness, he saw the
spearpoints veer sharply away. He could have
cheered.

But then he heard the first crash, the hollow
splintering, and felt the oar judder violently in his
hand. No screams, no shouts; but more smashes on
either side. Something struck the bow and whirled
past; and it was only then Alya understood what
Darzhan had been trying to tell them. '*Rysha!*' he
yelled, though the river's tumult drowned out his
hope. 'Lift the dark! *Lift*—'

The dim cavern light sprang up around him
again. Rysha was on her knees, coughing. Asquan
was already in the bow, striking out with a paddle. It
stuck an instant, as if uncertain; then the barge was
hurled contemptuously past its pursuers, bucking and
bouncing on the foaming water of the rapids. A fantail
of spray threw Asquan back and drenched Rysha,
who was crawling astern, moaning. Another rock
loomed up, Alya steered wide and the water picked
them up again, hurling the groaning boat into a more
open channel.

The thunder of the rapids was appalling, and he

saw rather than heard what Vansha yelled in his face. '*We must turn to shore!*'

Of the boats that had pursued them there was no sign among the boiling water; but that was no longer their main fear. Alya had expected to find some kind of landing stage or jetty, but among the great weirs and channels of worn boulders they had passed, there could be none. Now they all saw it together, the spit of black sand outthrust by some quirk of the channel, and beyond it a mirror-calm pool. That was hope, and he heaved at the scull with all his strength.

The boat boomed and jarred. The floor timbers were stove in amidships, splintered on some tooth of the roaring beast they rode. The boat whirled broadside to the water and rocked sharply; the scull snagged, then bent and snapped violently under Alya's hands. He was hurled down into the bottom of the boat as it rocked free – right on to the heaving current. It slapped the hull hard once, almost overturned it and threw it forward. Alya had a momentary vision of the faintly glimmering roof high above; then the disintegrating boat struck hard in a deafening smash of timbers, and the roof seemed to shatter and fall in on him. It struck agony into his head and breast, and he fell into the dark.

'What is it, Savi?'

The Princess Ulie was staring at her with her odd wide eyes.

'Do you feel cold?' demanded the other young woman, still stranger of face, still nameless. 'You shivered.'

Savi almost laughed. Here, among walls of perpetual ice, cold was what she surely ought to feel, yet never did. 'No . . . no. It was as if I heard something, something . . . unhappy. I don't know what!'

'One hears so much here,' said the other, rising and walking to the balustrade. 'Noises, voices – I

cannot make sense of it, it makes my head ache when
I try. Do you still hear it?'

Savi sat listening an instant, then slumped back
among the cushions. 'No. Voices, maybe. Screaming.
I felt afraid.'

The princess smiled faintly. 'Still? You, of all of
us . . .'

'Are you distressed?' demanded the other girl,
quickly. 'In pain?'

'No!' said Savi, quickly. 'No, not at all, just . . . It
seemed far off. In the town, I guess. Perhaps it
reminded me of something. It was strange. Like that
great black swan.'

And all my memories seem so far off . . .

'We will go in,' said the nameless girl, with a
decisive toss of her golden hair. 'Where such crude
things cannot disturb us. The swan . . . I demanded
some answers over that, but I have had none. Strange
. . . Princess, that will be all for now, you may retire.
This afternoon we shall discuss deportment once
again. Do you find me an apt pupil?'

The princess made her an elaborate courtesy,
flicking her gown to one side with a smooth sweep of
the arm. 'You know I do, lady. You gain every day in
grace.'

The courtesy was returned, much less fluidly.
'And lose in other things I should remember. But be
that as it must. Fetch me some of the village girls for
later, to tell me more of their life. Savi shall rest
meanwhile, or divert her mind, perhaps, to keep it
clear for me. I need clarity, who find so much
obscure. Walk with me, girl.'

It was strange being called girl, by someone no
older than herself; and try as she would, Savi could no
longer think of this creature with hair like the sun and
skin like the moon as anything else. She even walked
like a young girl, gawky and uncertain; the princess's
instruction had not yet rid her of that. Savi herself had

picked up the manner more easily, and now reined in
her brisk stride, so that she could wear the gorgeous
gowns she was given with a becoming grace. And
she followed all the other instruction as quickly, or
quicker; for the golden girl would increasingly keep
Savi at her side, at first to help and care for her when
her body betrayed her.

It often had, in the first few weeks. The girl had
some memories of human shape; but she could hardly
remember how to walk, and tumbled continually on
the glittering floors. What normal humans learned in
childhood she could not yet do, at least naturally; it
seemed she had to force her mind to fasten on each
separate thing. Every step, every breath was a conscious effort; and at the first reverse she forgot all the
rest, losing control of voice, arms, hands, innards and
all else, falling in an ungainly heap like any toddling
infant.

And at first she seemed to have no normal sense
of pain, or ability to heal. She was soon covered in
bruises and burns, and had even broken a leg, before
Savi persuaded her that pain had some value. Then
she developed it suddenly, and cried and raged like a
child; and tore off all her clothes because they hurt
her unendurably as well, and everything did. She
even broke her splints, and screamed in surprise at
the result.

And at that scream, all those who served her ran
away – not merely out of reach, but fleeing in blind
terror. Savi, though, had lingered. She remembered
her promise, and in truth she saw little immediate to
fear. She alone seemed to perceive that the nameless
girl's wrath was chiefly childish tantrum, born of
helplessness and fear and random feelings she had
not yet learned to control. So Savi treated her like a
child indeed, soothing yet firm, and brought her back
to calm, and to submit to having her leg set by a healer
once again, and being washed down and dressed. At

last she ate and slept, still like a child; and her injuries began to disappear with unusual swiftness.

It seemed to Savi as if only now the body could attend to its natural processes, without interference from the mind within. As if that strange personality was trying to control everything, instead of letting the body learn its own ways, as an infant's does. When the girl woke, Savi spoke to her of that. To her surprise the girl hung on her every word, and would not let her go away, even for a moment. From then on Savi became, in truth, her nurse.

It was no easy task, for this beautiful creature had the petulant moods of a child. She enjoyed the fear she could inspire, and unleashed it on all her servants; but Savi never found it hard to turn aside, or even chide. The girl would take reproof from her, as she would from nobody else, even the princess. And slowly she seemed to become more controlled, more restrained; and that was as well for all. The other women of the palace, from the withered chatelaine downwards, were pathetically grateful, and almost as much in awe of Savi as of their mistress. Yet even at her most infantile the girl never lost sight of her purpose, the purpose that had sent her raiders to tear Savi and the rest from their homes. She wanted their lives.

'Every moment. Every second. Not merely to know it, but to live it. I must understand what makes you what you are. How you meet every chance and change that comes, in your different ways, from palace to hovel! I must be at ease in any company, able to assume any mantle. Teach me, all of you, and you will live well, and when your use to me is done you will come to no harm. But hold nothing back!'

She had a long way to go. Even now, as they walked slowly down the long balcony that crowned the palace, she suddenly trod on the hem of her dress, leaned heavily on Savi and flushed scarlet with anger at the sound of tearing material.

'You're trying too hard!' laughed Savi. 'One foot after another, you don't have to think about it, see! Don't bother trying to look so elegant, for now. The princess is taking you too far, too fast. Learn to swing your bum naturally, like we poor peasant girls! That's what the men will notice.'

The fine-cut features twisted in disgust, and the girl made a childish vomiting noise and stuck out her tongue.

'Don't think the princess would approve of that, either!' grinned Savi.

'Men!' exclaimed the girl savagely.

'Yes, that's something we still haven't quite covered yet,' admitted Savi thoughtfully. 'Or the other way round, if you see what I mean – no, of course you don't.'

'I know all about that,' said the girl haughtily.

Savi shook her head. 'No, my lovely lass, you don't. Not by experience. And that's the only way, whatever you've stuffed your head with. Believe me!'

She had spent hours enquiring into the matter with Savi already, very strange hours. It had rapidly become clear that the girl knew practically everything about the mechanics of mating and childbearing, every working detail of a living body – everything, in fact, except what it was actually about. She had loftily told Savi all manner of fascinating things, a great deal more, in fact, than Savi had ever wanted to know. Many things she was determined to forget; and one or two, a little ashamedly, she was equally determined to remember. But the girl in turn had listened astonished and appalled to Savi expounding the human view of it, to the concepts of attraction and emotion, of pairing and companionship, of the bearing and raising of children; and where the sheer sweaty fun found its place amid all this. There had been one question, for some reason, that the girl never actually raised;

but now, after a thoughtful pause, she caught Savi by the arm.

'So you hinted. But do *you* know? By this . . . experience?'

Savi stopped in her tracks. 'Yes. Yes, I do!' Feelings and memories she had struggled to stifle came flooding back. 'What it is to be loved . . . well, not wholly. We had so little chance. There was a boy . . . he and I . . . But he's probably dead now!' she flared in sudden bitterness. 'Your butchers . . . when they took me . . . my father, and him . . .' She wrenched her arm free. 'What am I doing with you? What am I doing?'

'What I command,' said the girl quietly. 'But you have not spoken of this before. It was long ago, as you think of things, was it not? Can you not forget? People seem to forget so readily!'

'It was just a few weeks!' exploded Savi. 'I should . . . I should hurl you down that wall, not paddle along at your side like a lapdog!'

'It would avail you nothing,' said the girl calmly, leaning back against the rail. 'You cannot kill me, or hinder me. But I did not think you hated me. You stroked my hair and said kind words to me, when first you saw me.'

Savi shook her head impatiently, dashing away tears. 'I do! Or . . . Oh, I hate . . . what you really are. Or were. Whatever's behind you. It hates me, doesn't it? Along with everything else alive. But you . . . you're not it, not wholly.'

'That is true.'

'It would be like . . . hating a girl because she was kin to someone evil. Without knowing what she really was, in herself.'

'That sounds very human, to me. What I would expect. Many would hate the girl you imagine, just so. Hate, even for having a shade of skin they disliked.'

Savi whirled away, went to the wall, looked

down on the city far below, no more than a wedged mass of stinking steam and lights between the clean white walls of snow. 'Yes. Many would. But I can't.'

'So you do not think I am evil?' The girl touched her shoulder awkwardly; almost as if she was asking for something. 'I do not think so.'

Savi glared at her. 'Well, I guess those who *are* evil probably don't, not much. Most, they're just selfish. They care for their own close kin and friends well enough, but they'll shaft any other to suit themselves. But there's some . . . Some that delight in causing pain. Some that destroy for the sake of destroying. Like your raider men.'

'We did not create those desires within the *Aikiya*. We simply unleashed them. The problem has always been to hold them back, when it became necessary. Now we seldom bother. If you are to hate me for that, must you not first hate your own kind? Your men?'

It was naïvely spoken, with no apparent guile, but the shaft struck home. 'They're not all like that!' flared Savi. 'And some that are can learn better! You encourage them, instead! And there's some stranger yet, most evil of all – the black hearts, the void hearts. They'll do anything for a moment's amusement, and they think they've a right to. They've no real feelings themselves, they only learn to imitate them, and they mostly think others are only pretending, too. They can be held back, as long as there are folk around them; but in your world? They'll unleash all the evil you want, and laugh!'

'This is true,' said the girl quietly. 'We have observed it, we make use of it. But it is an arcane matter of the mind. How does a village girl like you understand so much of it? It is not from book knowledge. You speak with deep feeling. And with more hatred than when you speak of me. You have known such a man.'

Savi turned to stare at her. One minute almost
brainless, innocent. The next, a knife-sharp understanding. 'You see rightly. I did. One who thought
himself a hero. And therefore was one, to the outer
world. But who had cruel longings he could not
believe I would not satisfy. Who could not understand
why I did not leap to his call, as other girls did. And
who could not forgive me for seeing him as he was!
As no other, even his enemies, did, his heart emptier
than a black night. Vansha was his name; still is, I
doubt not. He hurt my boy, maimed him, as if
accidentally; but he did not fool me. I humoured
him, because I feared he would do worse, and I am
not proud of that. Yes, I should hate you more than
him. But at least you are something wider, greater,
however misguided you are; and you are eager to
learn. Perhaps I can make you understand us a little
better, at least. Maybe not hate us so deeply. But he is
what he is; and him I hate most of all.'

The girl gave a sudden delighted smile, and
seized her by the shoulders. 'Savi, listen! I've an idea!
If you want, I shall send the Ekwesh out for him alone,
harming no other in your village, at whatever cost to
themselves. And you shall torment him with your
own hands, for weeks if you like! Or just strike him
down.'

Savi drew breath sharply, and shook her head.
'No. No, I thank you, I'm not like him! Or you!'

'No.' The girl sighed. 'And not like most humans
I have dealt with, till now. Even our princess might
not have turned down such a chance. But since you
wish to teach me, perhaps you can also come to
understand me, a little better. Walk with me!'

The golden girl led her to the low stair at the
balcony's end. As they went down the wide stair,
the girl still a little unsteadily, fighting the long
dress the princess made her wear, she leaned on
Savi once again, and that amazing hair brushed her

shoulder. The sweet essences that dressed it sent a warm cloud of fragrance about her. Together, slowly, they made their way down through the many floors and levels of the strange building, most empty, some filled with arcane matters that were mostly kept behind doors locked, or simply melted into the wall. At last they came out into the colonnade behind the great hall, from which a few steps led down to the expanse of the floor. Heads lifted at the sight of them, servants busily scrubbing and polishing its surfaces; but the girl's slightest look and gesture was enough to clear them away. Grabbing one another by the arm, they scuttled off, glancing fearfully back.

Savi was more interested by the hall itself, though in truth she was normally afraid of it. It never seemed the same twice, its colours and patterns subtly flowing and altering. And it never seemed wholly empty, or wholly still. Savi thought it haunted by flickering, floating presences, continually at the edge of sight, gone when she turned on them, however swiftly. It was as if life dwelt within its very fabric, that was so much like marble, and yet was Ice.

Now the girl was here with her, Savi felt no fear at all, but glanced about in curiosity, seeking what she could understand. The girl watched her, and smiled faintly. She made an offhand gesture. Suddenly colours were rushing through the pillars, one to another as if they were parts of a single surface, a radiant summer blue shot with scudding wisps of white. The speckled cream pattern on the floor shivered like a wind-blown pond, and became a mighty black device with four arms quartering a circle. Then it was a flooding pool of luminous grey-blue, shot with strange black shadows that grew by the moment more solid and more intricate. Even before they took their final shape Savi understood what she was seeing in that solidifying pattern.

'The four quarters of the world!' she said. 'The

words my father always used! Only now I understand
than better! So much closer – and so great—'

She laughed with sheer delight.

'Yes, that is the world,' agreed the girl. 'Not as
it is—'

For an instant it became a globe, hanging in a
vast luminous void within the floor, glowing against
blackness; then it unravelled again, and was flat.

'But as it is convenient to overlook it, for eyes
such as I now possess. Behold!'

At either extremity of the circle a glittering point
appeared. A blinding, crystalline whiteness flowed
out from it, uneven but swift, speeding out across the
solid black shapes of the land like caressing, cleansing
hands. When the two brilliant fields had covered a
quarter of the way to the centre, they stopped,
pulsing, like eager dogs in the slips.

'Yes,' agreed Savi breathlessly. 'I understand.
The world, and your great realm within it. A wonder-
ful toy to have at your command, this.'

'It is not a toy, not a device as you would
understand it. Sooner call it a part of me, as is all
this palace. Within this nasty scrap of slime you call a
brain, no matter how I improve it, I cannot accommodate a thousandth part of my memory, let alone
my whole being. All the rest is here, at my call.'

Savi bridled. 'But you are *you*! Not mere flowing
lights in these icy walls! If you seek to live as a human,
why cling to all this?'

'Because I must.' For a moment the girl's voice
seemed to resound around the hall, vast and cold.
'Even as you see me standing before you, I am one of
the Lords of the Ice, great among the great. I must still
share in the immemorial effort of defending it.'

Savi stared at her. 'Defending? The Ice is the
attacker of all!'

The girl's hands seized her bare shoulders. 'Is
that what you believe? Poor brief vessel of filth,

oozing slime at every vent, what would you understand? Do you feel the very earth heave under the
burden of our battlements? Do you feel the Undying
Fires of Ilmarinen roil and blaze, scant leagues beneath our feet, and spurt out to confound us even
within our walls? The waves of Niarad, that smash
against our sea-cliffs? Do you feel the scouring winds
and sun-warmed breath of the Daughter of the Air?
Look there!'

The map was suddenly a mass of seething turbulence, over sea, land and Ice alike.

'Those are the circulating clouds, that can bring
snow to thrust us onwards. Those are the winds, that
can carry our chill to the world's heart, or cull its
warm airs to hold us back. Winds, that can hide the
sun's light, or release it to flay us. That is a constant
battle, in which both sides must be forever vigilant!
And it is not the only one. See there!'

The sea faded from blue to dull cream, as if the
map stood now on fine parchment. Across the great
fields of water, lines were traced about the world,
swirling lines like black veins pulsing beneath ancient
skin.

'Those are the circulations of the waters, that
men call currents. See how they play across our
boundaries and coasts, constantly striving to pull back
the water from which our battlements are built!'

The girl closed her eyes a moment, as if listening.
'Earth, winds, waters, all are set against us – and fire
most of all. You poor little creatures, the world you
believe in and know of is a petty, narrow place! The
real world is much greater, a constant warsong sung
by heroes. An undying conflict, in which no side
cares more about you than another.'

Savi made no reply, and the girl smiled sardonically. 'Oh, indeed, some of our enemies will stop at
nothing to curry aid, even from those who can least
afford it. Calling themselves Man-friends and the like.

Do not believe it! Oh, they may toy with you awhile,
not scrupling to pander to your petty hopes and fears.
They may dispense a few favours, toys and tricks. But
in the end they care only for themselves. And what
grudging help they give serves their own cause
principally. They are not mad enough to trust humans
with the least flicker of real power – any more than
we would.'

Gently, almost tentatively, she laid a hand on
Savi's shoulder. 'Whereas we do not hate individuals.
Not one or another – not you. We pity you, poor blind
helpless things with your little shreds of knowledge,
your tiny pleasures and pains, your devouring fragi-
lities and distresses. Your existence is not your fault;
you did not ask to be born, to be raised up from the
mindless beasts you were. Our quarrel is with those
who would use you to usurp our ancient dominion
and realm of purity, the austere beauty we shaped
with our deepest being. Them – oh, yes, them we
hate.'

Savi did not answer. She stared fixedly at the
swirling patterns of sky and sea, in their dance of
cohesion and conflict, held as if in deepest awe at the
scale and majesty of the world.

The girl's voice grew more insistent. 'You may
well admire it! For all this once was ours!' Her voice
was strong now, in that slender frame, almost a song
of silver, or a rushing mountain-wind, or the voice of
water splashing over sharp-edged rocks.

'*Ours!* To fashion out of the void, out of the
minutest dust, to shape, to steer, to colour, to make
fair and to direct. To love. Oh yes, child of men, we
know love! We love our long home as you love those
dens of yours, as you love the filthy things you do
inside them. Only a hundredfold more deeply!'

She leaned out over the map – like a young
willow over a pool, thought Savi. Her voice became
softer now, but darker. 'Deeply. Deep as the aeons it

cost us. And then we find our home, our gem, our
perfection becoming contaminated, infected, invaded by a spreading disease, a shapeless corrosion
called life! And that contamination we not only
cannot cleanse, but are told must inherit all we have
made! Told that we must relinquish our jewel, our
home, to the first faint stirrings of mind among the
consuming contamination. To see them ruin and
waste and despoil it! Like the wretched seed of
stinking apes that they are!'

The hand clutched Savi's shoulder convulsively,
painfully, like a sudden stab of cold. *'How much
more can the Ice lay waste, than you?'*

The voice at Savi's side was so terrible she dared
not look at the face, lest it too had undergone some
fearful transformation. She stared ever more fixedly at
those patterns, flowing so freely across the vast gulfs.
So Alya had been right, after all! There was the ocean,
upon the coasts of this very land they stood on now –
and across it there were other coasts, indeed, the
gateway to other lands.

Far off, indeed; but surely, not too far to imagine.

And between them, one to another, ran the great
veins of the ocean.

There, flowing right up along this very coast,
there was a current! A great one that went swirling off
out into the ocean, paralleling the southward face of
the Ice itself, with the winds following it as birds
follow the plough. And at the far side bending south-
wards once again, towards an island, or a group of
islands; and not far beyond those, those unknown
alluring coasts. A curving arch, a graceful shape; like
the raised neck and head of a swan. Very like, with its
last swirl for the beak; and the island for its eye.

A soft chill passed over her body, a breath out of
unknown spaces. She knew little of ships, but she
could imagine those winds driving some great craft
onward, out into emptiness that would not, in the

end, be empty. But she realised also that such a ship must have some sure way to find its direction, and keep it, once found; and that she could not imagine. Yet what the ancients surely had, the men of today could win once again.

The hand on her shoulder had relaxed. The breath by her side was calm.

'Your power is vast, lady,' Savi answered softly. 'And your burden. I see now how little I know or understand of anything. Too little, perhaps, to judge you. Perhaps I can never know. Yet I am filled with wonder, and wish to learn.'

She turned now, and met a wide-eyed smile of innocent pleasure.

'Yes! You seek knowledge, as we do! Oh, indeed, I was right to think you the best of the catch, better even than our lofty princess! You see, we are not so very far apart after all – are we?' The nameless girl giggled. 'Your mind is open, not shaken by fear. Apes I called you; yet I will allow a flash of worth among the common herd, now and again. Even of beauty.' She leaned closer, confidential. 'In fact, that's how I wish to appear among your kind. Not as just any woman, but as such an exception, wise and searching. In teaching you, I will learn . . . oh, we'll teach one another! Come!'

The girl stretched out her hand again, impulsively; then stopped. Savi winced suddenly, and cried out, only now realising that her shoulder was icy agony, that warmth was trickling down across her breast. The mark of a hand was bruised purple on to her skin, with something more than mere force. The nails had broken the skin where they touched, but it looked puckered and shrivelled. It bled only in one place; but it was bruised deep. Savi hastily pushed her fine gown down to keep the blood off it.

'Oh, I have hurt you!' breathed the girl. 'I would never have done that by design!' She touched the spot, as if wondering at the blood, let her hand rest upon it. The touch was gentle, the warmth welcome; but it seemed to start more blood. 'Come, we must have that treated. No, I shall do it myself, as a punishment, to remind me! I forget things, I forget how fragile these bodies are. I need such indignities to fix that in my mind, I must punish myself to hold them in my memory!'

The idea seemed to amuse her, as she led Savi unsteadily along the corridor to her great chambers; and again she chased all her servants out with a single imperious gesture. 'No! *I* shall salve you as if I were *your* handmaid, and you shall tell me how badly I do it! Threaten to beat me on my bare backside, for my clumsy service!'

In fact she was as fine and gentle a handmaid as Savi could wish, sitting her on the bed, washing the wound in warm water, staunching the blood, smearing on salves with tender fingers – all, Savi realised, in imitation of her, and the cares she had taken. The girl really had learned something of humanity, whether she realised it or not; and that was a great pleasure.

The warm, heady fumes of the healing stuffs, and their gentle release from pain, made Savi feel languorous and detached. She welcomed the easy kneading of the hand across her shoulder and breast. 'Does your slave-girl do well, then, my mistress?' said the voice in her ear, close enough to tickle.

Savi smiled lazily. 'It's lovely. Don't stop.'

The hand moved again, in its lazy arc, spreading the scented oils across her skin. 'I find a simple principle. I do what I would like myself, and it seems to serve. I would like you to do this to me, some time.'

Savi smiled. 'You have all those handmaids to anoint you, after those baths the princess insists you take. It's a wonder they don't rub the skin off you!'

'That's not the same!' said the voice quietly. 'I don't feel their skin as I feel yours. Shall I stop?'

Savi had moved, suddenly, shifted. 'No. Go on.'

The hand lifted, settled. 'Like this?'

The are spread gently wider, and Savi caught her breath a little.

'I know what you're doing,' she said, after a moment. 'Trying to do.'

The hand faltered, then continued, still very gently. 'Do you like it?'

'For the moment. You have a good touch. Have you been doing this to others?'

The hand stopped, this time; then started again. 'Once or twice. Some such things, not much. To the serving-girls. I was . . . curious. There were sensations I wished to explore.'

Savi nodded. 'Children do.'

'Children?'

Savi smiled. 'It is a part of growing up. You become aware of your body, in so many different ways. But other bodies are strange to you, boys' bodies.' The girl made a noise of deep disgust, and Savi chuckled. 'And they themselves are pretty strange, not easy to feel at home with. So, you turn first to what's more familiar. Did you enjoy it?'

The circling hand paused, on the slope of Savi's left breast. 'Yes. Well enough. I was not sure . . . It seemed . . . so much less than what is said of it, and written. Nor did the others respond; they seemed not to enjoy it at all. I was disappointed. It did not seem worth going on. So I did very little.'

Savi smiled. 'Because it was only exploring. And only you. The others weren't interested, perhaps. Or plain terrified of you; that wouldn't help! It's just as I told you. Feeling about's not the same as feeling. If you could only learn . . .'

The girl drew a deep breath. Her hand returned to Savi's shoulder. 'But you?' The voice was plaintive. 'You are not afraid of me? I have told you, I would never hurt you!'

'Yet you did, a little, just now. And you already have, more deeply, before you knew me. You can be really frightening.'

'I said I was sorry! I healed it. Are you not my friend, then?'

The voice sounded almost frightened. Savi sat up and looked around, and was startled to see the girl crying, inelegantly, awkwardly, tears streaming down her cheeks, nose snivelling uncontrolled over lips and chin.

'What were you saying about slime?' Savi demanded, mopping her up with a towel. 'Friends are usually more equal, don't they? Not slaves. But you don't have any equals, do you? Yes, of course I'm your friend, as far as I can be. If that matters to you! That's a feeling, you know!'

'Oh,' said the girl, and snorted loudly and liquidly – coarse as a goose, thought Savi, with that great pointy nose of hers. 'So . . . that is how you mean it? How you feel towards others? Towards your friends?'

Savi laughed a little, in exasperation. 'It's not all the same. It's always different. I loved my friends. I loved my father.' Again the chill curtain swept across her, but she drove it aside. 'Not the same way.'

'And . . . *him*? How did you . . . love him? Would you let him do . . . that?' She slid her hand back again.

'Mmmm. I did. Oh yes; and more—' She stopped, sat up in alarm. She hardly noticed the faint tremors that shook the palace, but this was worse. Icy wind whistled across the room, billowing the heavy draperies straight out, stinging her eyes and plucking at her clothes. The walls quivered, horribly, like the twitching flanks of a beast. They seemed about to come crashing inward upon her. There were cries and wails in the distance. Alarmed, she sprang up and saw the girl crouching there on the bed, intent as a great cat upon its prey.

'*You!*' exclaimed Savi furiously. 'See what I

mean? You want to be my friend, and then you
frighten the life out of me! All for a moment of petty
jealousy! D'you think I want to be *your* friend, if
you're going to act like that?'

The turbulence had already stilled. The girl's lips
were trembling. Savi sat down hard on the bed, with
her back resolutely turned. After a moment a hand
stole over her shoulder, very gently. 'I'm sorry. Is that
love, too?'

'Unfortunately.'

'So I have it. And you still have it. Enough to
make a difference? In exploring?' Soft hair enveloped
Savi's shoulder, with its scent.

Savi shook her head slightly, but only in wonder.
'I think you're learning. Definitely. Beginning to understand.'

The hand cupped Savi's bared breast, the nipple
against the palm, and moved in a slow arc. Another
hand touched her waist. Savi sighed in half-amused
indulgence, and drew it around her, feeling the long,
slender body suddenly close against her back. 'Oh,
very well then. Come here.'

Alya coughed the water out of his mouth, only for it to
flood again, with bitter-tasting grit. He spewed it out
and raised his head a little, still coughing, and
struggled to clear his sight and his mind. The black
sand beneath him brought it all back at once, and he
stared anxiously around. He saw that he had only
pulled himself up on the bar, and was lying across it
now, half in the calm pool. His sword was thrust into
the dry sand; he must have pulled himself in with it,
instinctively. Then he clapped his hand to his side. A
familiar weight was missing.

The bag. The mask.

Wrenched with panic, choking for breath, he
thrust himself up on to his knees, and cast wildly
about. The shattered timbers of boats, their enemies'

and their own, still tossed and whirled in the thrashing rapids; but of the bag, or any smaller debris, there was no sign. It might be cast up on the far side of the cavern, and beyond his reach, but most likely it had been dashed to pieces, or gone to the bottom. The loss felt sickening, diminishing, like the loss of a limb or an eye; as both it was, perhaps.

It was surely to his credit, as the tale is told, that the sight of surviving companions drove even that pain momentarily from his mind. Vansha was hauling himself up on the far side, where lay the shattered bow of the boat; he lifted a weary hand, then sagged down again, panting. Rysha was sitting further along the spit, holding her head and sniffing.

'Are you all right?'

'Just bloody brilliant. How'd you think?'

'Any sign of Asquan? Or Chiansha?'

She shrugged.

Alya looked around for Asquan, but there was no sign of either him or Chiansha. Then he saw the corpse that lay in the shallows nearby, weighted down by its mail, long hair washing in the faint current. But that was old Kalkan, surely. He was about to haul him ashore, then thought better of it, and shoved him off to where the current could get hold of him. He watched the body vanish into the thrash of the rapids. There, surely, dark forces could not touch or taint it. No quiet grave; but then the old devil might have preferred that. It was certainly honourable enough. He and his had kept their word, to the full, and to the end.

Now Alya must keep his; but the sight and presence of the Ice had daunted him, and the flurry of death and destruction about him. Now he felt the weight of the Ice above his head, the immensity of it. He had spent lives and energy reaching this place, and what was it to him? What good had he done? He had cast away his most treasured possession, and with it, perhaps, any chance of finally fulfilling the only power he felt was truly his. He might make a new mask, on the pattern of the old, engrained in his memory; but it would not have the legacy of power within it, that gave the old mask such an aura, an identity. He was surrounded by walls of white glass, impenetrable as the Wall within himself, and as impossible to surmount. Even if she was still living somewhere, how could he hope to come to her, in the midst of all that?

'*Alya!*'

It was Asquan's voice, a hoarse whisper that echoed so eerily, and had so little direction, that they all whirled around in panic, as if it spoke from a deeper shadow.

'*Over here!*'

They saw him then, an arm waving from what looked like a solid wall beyond the pool, above a heap of stones. Then, as he stepped out, the heap resolved itself into a wall, a walled platform, an obvious jetty with mooring posts and rings; its very ordinariness seemed outlandish, in this place.

'*Come on! D'you think we dare hang around here? Run, fools! Run!*'

They could hardly think straight, those left alive, but such was the urgency in that voice that they staggered to their feet as best they could, and seized their weapons. Rysha had her sword, and Vansha had lost his own; but he seized one from the shattered bow that was all that remained of their boat.

'It's Kalkan's!' he said, as Alya splashed around the pool and caught up with him. Alya thought it looked more like Darzhan's, but he said nothing. His own blade he hefted thoughtfully, as they reached the jetty. Asquan ran out to them.

'Move, fools! What's the matter with you?'

'Wait! What about Chiansha?'

'He went down among the rocks. Then I saw his

body go by. Dead, believe me! Now move! D'you think they'll leave the ways open long, when someone's got through their defences? Do you want to face more of those things?' He grabbed Rysha, thrust her staggering towards the opening – and found Alya's sword, and Vansha's, levelled straight at his breast.

'What's . . .' Asquan stared. 'Ah! You think I might be . . .'

'You might. You came out of the wreck much better than us.'

'I was ready! I leaped to those rocks there and waded – Powers, do I *look* like the dead?'

His eyes were alive enough, certainly. Alya lowered his sword. 'All right. What's this you've found?'

Asquan stamped on the stone. 'Their main landing-stage here, I think. Probably they lower the waters when they want it used, so they don't bother to guard it. But they will now! So come on! There's a stair! Unless you have any better ideas?'

Rysha was staring suspiciously up at the crevice, lined with crudely hewn stone. The steps were black rock, but the walls were concave surfaces of pure white ice, like ripples made solid, and Alya felt just as apprehensive. It was like walking into the belly of some great beast.

Rysha shuddered. 'Don't know what's up there, do we? Could be more of those . . .' She couldn't find a word.

'There might!' agreed Asquan harshly. 'But we *know* they're down here – don't we?'

Rysha plunged for the stairs. The others followed, skidding and cursing. The lower steps were slick with clear black ice from the river spray, and the walls gave no handhold – not that Alya or anyone wanted to touch them. The air was chill and heavy about them, and the pale glimmer turned them into greenish ghosts of themselves. It felt as if the vast weight above were pressing down upon them. 'This is going to be an eternal climb!' Alya shouted. 'You realise how high those cliffs were? And the stair's not that steep!'

'You can't guess how glad that makes me!' snarled Vansha, nursing a bruised shin.

'Then we'd best climb all the faster!' said Asquan. 'Unless you fancy meeting someone coming down!'

Loss, cold, fatigue, shock – Alya told himself all these were enough to explain the misery that surrounded them. They had seen so much death, and worse than death, in what he realised must have been very little time. Hours, mere minutes, had reduced them from a hardened band to a mere fragment, from possible rescuers to skulking vermin; starving vermin, soon, unless they found food somehow. Alya winced. This was his doing, the ruin of his plan.

They might as well have walked up to the cliff-foot, and knocked. They could hardly have fared much worse. Yet he was aware of more than that, tugging at his heart; more than his grief for Kalkan and the rest, more even than the loss of the mask.

He had never really been able to use the mask properly, never would, probably. It had been wasted on him. And much as they had shared, much as they owed one another, respect and much more, there had never really been any real bond between the others and himself. Never could have been.

Neither the mask nor the men – not while that fire flared within him. While it was there, he was a man apart; save perhaps from Vansha. And their bond was strangest of all. They were brothers sworn, true; but even brothers did not always stay friends . . .

Alya shook his head. His wet gauntlets had become masses of ice, and he dragged them off to massage his hands. What was putting thoughts like this into his head? The mask had worked, though in unexpected ways. He might have done more yet, much more. And Asquan, peculiar creature that he was, little though Alya liked his tastes or his nature – he'd been Alya's help and mentor from the start. He'd taught him so much, treated him like a son, little as he'd want to be any son of Asquan's! And old Kalkan – he'd liked him well enough, never mind how different they were; and the soldiers, all good enough men in their fashion. Even Rysha – she had gone the distance with him, as she pledged, even to this place that seemed to terrify her more than any of them.

So what made him think so much less of them? That tugging at his feelings again . . . .

'This *place*!' he swore.

'As you say!' panted Asquan. 'Gets a man down . . . Wearier than I should feel. Cursing you and your bloody woman for ever dragging me here . . . That's stupid!' He took his hand from his side, looked around. 'To be here – *here*, in the very Ice itself . . .' He laughed, softly. 'I'm alive, alive as I haven't felt for years! It's back there I was dead, as Volmur's deluded hatchet-man, doing his dirty work. Waiting forever for something I knew would never happen, the grace I'd never get! This has to be better! Better than dying slowly in the dark, eh, Rysha?'

'Maybe!' she wheezed. 'Maybe! I don't know . . . can't think clear . . . too afraid . . . and that's not like me! You think there's . . . something doing that to me?'

'I don't feel anything!' said Vansha sharply. 'Just the same as I've always felt. I want what I've always wanted. To find Savi, get her out of here – isn't that right, brother?'

'You sound angry,' said Rysha. 'Cold. Maybe that's what it's doing to you!'

'That's so much dung!' snapped Vansha. 'I feel as I always feel! I just don't have the spirit left for . . .' He sounded hasty, confused. 'Pretending! All this pretending. This mess! I just want . . .'

He slipped heavily, and said no more save curses.

Alya half expected the rock stairs to give way to ice; but the opposite happened. The black stone began to invade the walls, the ice to give back, until at last it was only an icicled roof to the narrow cleft along which they were slowly ascending. The steps themselves grew mostly free of black ice. 'Might even bring us right out from under, like!' exclaimed Rysha.

'It could not be too soon!' agreed Asquan, clutching his ribs; and Alya felt the same flood of relief.

'It's the Ice getting us down, right enough,' he said. 'Maybe just being shut in like that. But I don't think so . . .'

'No,' said Rysha, shuddering. 'Don't feel natural, being stuck here. It does something to you, this stuff. To your mind.' She glared at a great icicle that had come down to form a mighty column, overlain with rings of lesser ones. 'Looks slimy, almost.'

Vansha shrugged. 'It's not that bad. I liked the canes less than this.'

'They seem like a dream of peace to me now!' said Alya. 'This stuff . . .' He absent-mindedly reached up to snap an icicle with his bare left hand.

He shrank back with a cry, clutching his arm. 'What's the matter?' barked Asquan.

Alya could hardly answer. 'Painful . . . more than cold, like a shock of some sort down my arm . . . all the strength driven out of it . . .'

'This is a fine time to go losing it!' growled Vansha. 'Rub it with snow, that's the best thing for frostbite!'

'Not frostbite. As if something in me . . . recoiled . . .'

'Don't blame you!' shivered Rysha. 'I don't even like the breath of the air here.'

'Then get on!' ordered Asquan. 'It may be you sprang some alarm. Run, if you can, before they set guards here also!'

He led the way now, at a fierce trot, and the others strained to follow. The thought of being left behind down here was enough to make sure of that; and imagining some of those shadow-men tramping up from below.

But before long Asquan gestured at the ice roof, without wasting a word; and they all saw it. The glow was no longer so pallid and faint. The Ice shone now with highlights sharp and cold as diamonds, stinging their eyes with glaring rainbows. Even the black rock gleamed; and a breath of different air curled around them, heavy with strange smells, sooty and sulphurous, but in among them, the stale but welcome stinks of life.

All at once Asquan waved urgently, and flattened himself against the rock-wall, panting. For a minute they imitated him, while he watched and listened, then his hand motioned them on, urgently but silently. As they caught him up, each one of them saw it, and marvelled.

Ahead of them a green glass cavern opened up; and at its heart stood an icicle forest. Like trees upside down they hung, their broad roots in the ice-ceiling, lesser chains downturned from their fronts towards their buried crowns, like frozen foliage buried in wavy channelled patterns on the floor. It was an eerie sight, sterile yet beautiful, starkly dignified yet mocking the perishable beauty of life. From the channels Alya guessed it had been carved by some long-frozen stream-course. But they spared it little wonder; for beyond it, shading its roof and floor, streaming along a broad path cut between the columnar trees, shone the strong grey light of day.

'Now!' hissed Asquan. 'We don't run, but we move like lightning. And quietly! At the first step, the first voice – behind the nearest tree!'

He took an uneasy step on to the icy floor, and though he slithered a little, he moved as swiftly as he had ordered, in a sort of padding lope from tree to tree. The others copied it, Alya forcing his gauntlets back on; he'd no desire to touch the tree shapes. The cavern was not many strides across, and in minutes Vansha, the last of them, made it across to join the others in the shadow of the wide crevice that was the cavern mouth. They stared out, unbelieving.

'That's rock out there!' exclaimed Vansha. 'Not Ice!'

Asquan grinned. 'Rock; and fire. Earthfires mostly, I'd guess, from the sulphur stink. We've been moving along, as well as climbing. I guess that this is some kind of open vale in the Ice itself – eh, Alya?'

'Near its edge, it seemed. Between its outthrust fingers, held open by earthfires indeed. Maybe no more than five hundred strides, as the crow flies. But up and down, it would seem like a lot more.'

'Indeed. It's a good way down to the buildings there, and with little enough shelter. But all that smoke could give us cover!'

He slid forward, raising his mantle to break his outline and shadow his face, and peered cautiously out. Then he stiffened. They heard it as he did, the tramp of heavy-shod feet, the bark and yammer of fierce voices. Instinctively the others shrank back. Asquan seized Alya's arm. '*No!* Not that way! Come!'

He sprang out, hauling Alya with him, and they found themselves in a place of jagged rocks, wreathed in shadow and smoke beneath the glare and glitter of the Ice-slopes above. The only way out of it was the worn path, winding away between the rock-walls; and it was from here the voices were approaching. Asquan sprang for the shadow of the rocks, the others following.

Barely in time. Up the path, trotting, came a strong force of the painted men, their black leather armour and iron shields slashed with white characters, arrows feathered in black and white already strung to their short bows of bent horn. A tall man in an iron helmet lashed them on with a stick wrapped in hide rags. Into the cavern they trampled at his cry, their iron-shod sandals scuffing and smashing the icy floor, kicking at the icicle trunks; and in a moment only the flakes of broken ice and the waft of their stale stink, oil and hide and sweat, marked their passing.

Alya and the others needed no telling; they slipped on to the stony path and scuttled downhill as fast as they could. Only Alya paused a moment, gazing up at the cloudy sky, though he hardly knew what he hoped to read there; but a gust of yellow smoke boiled across it, and he followed the others.

The path led them down a rocky ravine as steep as the one they'd left, but it showed signs of opening out. Only some seven hundred paces down, though, the path met many others, in another stand of rocks, and they took full advantage of the brief shelter these gave them, doubled up and coughing.

'A vale, indeed!' wheezed Asquan. 'Where Ilmarinen's fires leak out under the weight of the Ice, maybe. They can't quell them, so maybe they use them. I taste other things on the air also, strange things. One thing musky, horrible; can't place it! But the rest – I'd guess there could be people here!'

'There are. We can start searching!' exclaimed Alya.

'I thought for a moment I smelt roasting meat!' said Vansha faintly.

Their chilled and empty stomachs reacted. 'We've got to find food!' said Asquan decisively. 'Fire, too, if we can!'

'I'm good for bugger-all right now!' moaned Rysha.

'Before we start any other searching!' insisted Vansha. Alya bit his lip angrily; but he too was famished. At least his strength seemed to be returning; but

that hardly seemed to depend on what he ate. With
food he would surely think more clearly.

'All right then! But watch out – the slopes, the
cliffs, the Ice! And the sky!'

So the four of them sidled warily out from among
the rocks. With the odorous breeze to guide them,
they made their way along a narrow path that wound
beneath the shadow of the Ice-cliffs, heading, as it
seemed, towards another and taller line ahead. But
when they came to a great outcrop, the path turned
under it and along, and they saw a flickering red light
on the overhang, and mirrored on the Ice itself; and
they stopped in the shadow of the rock, and, very
cautiously, peered out.

To Alya alone it was no surprise; yet to see the
vale through his own eyes was a shock, as if a dream
took sudden solidity. There below them, still in the
shadow of the Ice, though it was daylight high above,
there were all the things he had seen in his flight in
the swan-cloak – the glowing vents, the fires, the
streets shining black with perpetual meltwater and
liquid filth, and the buildings that lined them. And
searching frantically through what he remembered of
the mind of the cloak's owner, he was able to put
names and natures to many.

There towards the mouth of the vale were the
miserable slave barracks; and beyond them, hardly
less squalid, the warriors' compounds and their cone-
roofed huts. Behind them, as the valley narrowed and
sloped upwards, the quarter with the ramshackle
stone buildings, storehouses, workshops, more privi-
leged dwellings for chieftains and their kin. Beyond
those, the blank-walled, sinister towers, dwellings
turned inward as if to hide what went on there from
the outer world. It was as if the whole seething, fetid
sprawl of human habitation spilled down like an
avalanche of defeat from the wide rocky crag at
the height of the vale. That was almost level with

them, as they crouched here, riven with great cracks and crevices; yet its top had been levelled and smoothed out as if with a single sweep of a dismissive hand, to become the great open courtyard, as pale and sterile as all was smoky and dark below. Its white glazed pavement glimmered faintly with the light from the Ice-walls above; but at its heart, purer, clearer, colder, shimmering bluish even in deep shadow, gleamed the great palace of the Ice.

He had been there. He had seen her there, alive and well. So it was that she too became all the more vivid and alive to him now. It felt almost as if he could stretch his arm out across the vale and draw her to him. Or swoop down again, somehow, and bear her away like smoke on the bitter winds. Yet still he was filled with doubt, somehow; though he hated himself for it. A thought came, and he stole a glance at Vansha, leaning silent upon a rock. That handsome face was frozen into a haggard, staring mask; and he felt sure the cause was the same, the same dread. A thought he circled, unwilling to form it properly, a dark smoke-ring of half-formed horrors.

Alive, well, and here; how?

How?

How had she survived, prospered even? Had it changed her? What had been done to her? What had been made of her?

His fears were selfish, he knew that. Yet he could not suppress them. After all this time, this way, this loss, this expense of blood, could Savi still be his?

CHAPTER 10
The Masks of Ice

THE room was still now, the air warm and heavy and scented. Savi felt the sweat prickle on her skin, wonderingly idly why exactly the walls did not melt. She went on moving her hand, but slowly now, to calm rather than excite the slight shudders that still shook the body beside hers, the thigh gripped tightly between her own.

'Was all that a more successful exploration?' she asked softly, tasting the salt on her lips, the breath against her cheek. 'Did that hold understanding for you?'

A sigh answered her, and a tightening of the grip about her waist. Savi bowed her head, kissed the neck and shoulder beneath, went on moving her hand. 'And yet, since you have asked me so much – should this truly be so new to you? Did you not have another, once? Of your own kind. A – what was the Princess's word? – a consort? That is a kind of a husband, isn't—'

The body whirled out of her arms. Long hair whipped her face. The girl had turned her back on her. 'Do not name him!'

'I only . . . I did not mean to hurt you. Any more than you, me. But, like you, I wondered.' She reached out, and stroked the shaking back, very gently.

The silence stretched out. At last the muffled voice spoke again. 'You should hear, and understand. The world, nature, you would call it – that is dual. Two halves, two natures, two dimensions, two principles – the least needed to mingle their substance into a third one, new and different, and so diversify and grow. Male and female goes beyond shape, though expressed in different ways. We are paired just as you are, sometimes for better, sometimes worse. The being I was – *am!* – you would call female, paired with another. Yet in the pride of what I was and all I could do, I ceased to revere Taoune, great though he was. When he led the last assault of the Ice against men, and through his arrogance and folly this was thrown back, I would no longer bow to nor mingle natures with him. I and others went up against him, and stripped from him most of what was his, to my own great glory. And I forbade him the heights, to exist upon our margins, the Grey Lands, a lord of shadows only, eaten away by envy, shuffling his toys in darkness. A gatekeeper, no more, amid frost and snow. That is why this is so new to me; and why I give you no cause to be jealous, ever.'

Savi's stroking slowed. 'Is it so? You may tire of me, sooner. I am mortal, I will age and die. Perhaps I also am a toy in darkness.'

'You need do none of these things. You are shrouded in decay, fair as it is; but if you wish, I can take that from you, share with you some of my being. Make you a Power, though a lesser one. That is rare, but it has been done.'

Savi swallowed. 'I . . . do not know what to say! The prospect . . . it scares me.'

The body whirled towards her, once again. A hand caught in her hair, winding it in. 'You loved another, once. More than I?'

'How can I say? Perhaps. If he lived, I would love him still.'

Lips brushed hers. 'I am glad he does not. I begin to understand the sensation, as you say; though it is confusing. I pity you who must endure this turmoil, with so little mind to cope. So many feelings, bound up in one; and fear among them, fear of loss. I am not

accustomed to fear. I seek comfort.' A hand stroked
across her thigh, drawing it apart. 'Comfort, and knowledge. Savi, you have shown me love. You are love!'

'I do not know your name. You don't have one!'

'I have too many. They limit me, who would
have no limits. There is a name they called me, in a far
land; the Lady of the North. That I remain, in whatever guise. But if you insist, you may call me Louhi.'

The valley slope was treacherous. There was a broad
downward road, leading direct to the upslope end of
the town. That way the guards had come; its bed was
still scuffed with their tread. That felt too open, too
visible to anyone looking up. There was another road
further down, leading to the jumbled spill of hovels at
the town's lower end. In that warren they might have
a chance to hide. They tried less direct paths across
the slope, above the road; but the ground was
streaked with either hard-frozen snow, or a mass of
loose stones and dead soil that constantly slipped and
skipped out from underfoot in miniature avalanches,
sending them sprawling and liable to draw every eye,
or so it seemed.

'At least there're plenty of rocks to hide behind!'
panted Vansha, as they sat wheezing in the shadow of
one, shivering in their damp clothes.

'But if we go scuttling from one to another, we'll
attract attention anyhow!' hissed Asquan impatiently.
His side seemed to be paining him more, but there
was a glint in his cold eyes, as if he was enjoying
himself.

Alya scanned the skies and the ice-slopes. He
could see no sign of watchers, but that did not mean
there were none. 'You mean we should just walk
along the road? As if we're meant to be here?'

'Often the best way. From a distance, anyway.'

'It won't get us into the town. Not that place.
From what I've gleaned of it, you're either a warrior

or a thrall there, and we couldn't pass for either. The guards would spot us at once. The thralls are completely ground down, not allowed to act for themselves or raise their eyes, even. Those that aren't forever fettered.'

Asquan looked sardonic. 'Now that's the way to run a kingdom! Saw that as well, did you?'

'I *know* it. As the . . . person whose mind I touched knew it. If I could only make out all she knew!'

'Well, then.' Asquan looked at Rysha. 'Maybe we'd better wait till dark.'

They did not have to. When they first looked down into the town, it was high morning already. By the time they had worked their way downhill, less than three hours later, the sun had already crossed the cleft. The shadows of the western rim were creeping up the eastern flank, leaving the town below in twilit gloom. The days in this deep were short, and fires and lanterns were already being kindled.

Crouching among rocks above the road, the intruders watched the comings and goings, and saw what Alya had foretold. Some alert must have been given. There were patrols out on the road; and at the town end, though there were no outer walls, twenty or more black-armoured sentinels were already stationed, well able to cover the road and the land about it. All who passed had to account for themselves, hard-faced warriors and hunched, skulking slaves alike. They saw slaves too slow to answer beaten down with spearbutts; and even one warrior who angrily baulked at a body-search was speared through the kidneys, and stripped of his possessions while he still writhed. His comrades made no complaint at all.

'A hospitable folk!' smiled Asquan. 'But there lies our way, none the less. While they're busy, we can slip through in shadow – if Rysha will oblige!'

'This dunghole gives me the heaves,' she muttered. 'Like it saps me, makes everything heavier and harder . . .' She hugged herself, something like laughter in her voice. 'Thought it'd never come to this! Thought I'd be off and leg it, first time we came in sight of anywhere worth a cuss . . .'

She looked up in sudden panic. 'But there never was anywhere! Just bloody ruins, and stinking hovels, and those endless bloody canes . . . Nowhere to escape! Nowhere, anywhere, left! So now we've all come stupidly sloping up here to bloody die, 'cause there isn't anywhere else . . .'

Alya caught the edge of growing hysteria in her voice, and sympathised; his own inner fires felt strangely dim, depressed, reluctant to lend him strength. 'There may be other places! There must be! Far to the East, by the Sea – or across it! There's still hope there. And if we can only get through this, I'll take you there. As determinedly as I brought you here! I promise!'

He put an arm around her bony shoulders, but she shook it off, sniffing. 'You promise *me*? I kill men, remember. I enjoyed it! First laugh I'd had in years, watching the brat skewer his dad, then squealing when I stuck it to him. And he wasn't the first. You wouldn't like me in any of those nice hopeful places.'

'All the same,' said Alya, 'I'll take you. You've already earned that from me. Besides, it's on my way. Look, you can wait here, if you like. We'll get in some other way, and come back for you.'

'Wait? *Here?*' She gave a sudden crow of laughter, hastily stifled. 'Wanting to fill my pants every minute and nothing to do it with? Oh no, sonny boy, you don't get rid of me that easy, like. At least there's bloody food down there somewhere!'

'Ah, at last!' murmured Asquan. 'Intellect dawns!'

Rysha crooked her little finger at his groin, then

rose to her knees. Still crouching, she spread her arms wide, draping her cloak to create a pool of deeper shadow. But when she let the cloak slip back, the shadow remained like an inkstain on the ground. She muttered softly over it, and blackness flooded down from her, deepening, rolling over the stones like smoke. Alya felt something he could almost touch envelop him, like a veil or a web. He could still see Rysha, barely, her lean breast rising and falling as if with great effort, her matted hair sticking close to her cheek, her hands bunched tight between her thighs as she swayed. Slowly she rose to her feet, and the world grew dim around them. She hunched her shoulders and straightened them, and night arose from her shoulders like vast enfolding wings.

She seized Alya's hand, then Vansha's; with a toss of the head, she directed Asquan behind her. He bowed sardonically. Together they glided forward, shadows upon shadow, down towards the road.

They had to stay on the slope, to pass the brutal guards; but they did not dare stay there long. Keeping your footing was hard. The odd loose stone didn't matter, among the other sounds, the ranting and the cries. But everyone skidded, and once only Asquan's bony hand saved Alya from tumbling headlong out of the shielding shadow. Pebbles rattled down, almost in front of one of the lounging guards; but it was down the road he looked, not up the slope at all. From then on Alya trod as carefully as he could; but the slope was already getting looser and steeper, and he was a mass of sweat even in his damp clothes. Vansha was losing his footing, and signalling frantically, and Rysha was having obvious trouble. Asquan glared; they were barely twenty paces past the guards. But it had to be. They stumbled down, as carefully as they could, out on to the more solid roadbed.

None of the guards seemed to notice. They were still intent on bullying and despoiling all they could.

Rysha tossed her head again, and the little band tiptoed away along the road towards the first buildings, and the welcoming blackness of the narrow alleys between. A long low wall led to the nearest, with only a barred wicket and no windows, and they sidled along in its shadow. They could not keep from looking back, afraid the sentries would spot them any moment; and that was the root of their mistake.

Around the town, if town it could truly be called, lights began to blossom. First among them were the fires which had made it look so jewelled from above, among the snow; but from below here they turned it into a vision of torment. The rows of hut roofs stood out against the scarlet earthfires, while the blank barrack walls glimmered an evil green, as if torches burned in noxious air. Blue and green and yellow flames flared on the high stone buildings, and all the shades of light mingled and danced with grotesque shadows on the surrounding snow-walls above. Along the alleys braziers kindled, picking them out in stark light and shade. Rysha fought them all, breathing hard through her clenched teeth.

'How long can you hold out?' hissed Vansha.

'Long as need be, brat – with no more stupid questions! Long as we keep in real shadow!'

A voice interrupted them, a puzzled exclamation. A lantern gleamed not ten strides ahead. A black-clad warrior stood in the road, staring almost straight at them, rubbing his eyes.

Asquan cursed. 'Where did he spring from?'

'That gate!' snapped Alya. 'But how—' All too obvious, when he looked. Somewhere along the valley side some great vent or rift blazed open, a tongue of crimson flame. 'We're between him and the fire!'

And what was he seeing? An impossible thing, a moving blot of darkness, a shapeless cloud with perhaps a hint of more substantial shapes within.

No wonder he'd called out! Any moment now he'd shout again—

Asquan was ahead of him. He must have seemed some fell grey spirit taking shape out of the darkness, lunging with whiplash speed; and the *Aikiya'wahsa* had many ghosts to fear. The astonished warrior's hand clapped to the dagger at his belt, his eyes widened; but he wasted a moment filling his lungs to scream, and with it his life. The scream became a strangled cry as they sprawled in the dust. It was Asquan who rose, but no longer nimbly. Alya caught him as he staggered, and pulled them all hard against the shadowed wall.

Rysha was gasping now. Footsteps rang from the road behind. Two of the sentinels came running up. They stopped at the sight of the body, still feebly kicking, came no closer but levelled their spears and stared around.

Alya and the others sidled along as fast as they dared. Then one sentinel clapped a black horn to his lips, and blew a jarring alarm call.

'If I had my bow!' grated Vansha. Rysha's bony fingers clamped hard on Alya's arm. The darkness wavered about them, blacker than the night an instant, then ghostly grey, and he thought she was going to faint.

Answering horns sounded from the road, and the streets ahead, lined with low blank doorways. 'A moment longer!' he hissed, shaking her, and the blackness returned.

'*Now run!*'

Their feet scuffed on the stony road, and the sentries spun about towards them at once. But at this distance in the shadow of the wall, the intruders were still invisible; and the warriors looked dumbfounded. Then there was no more wall, and the nearest alley was still long strides away. The sentinels saw them again, the rushing blackness; and though they could

not have known what it was, they were hard men.
They shouted, and one hurled his spear. They were
stabbing weapons, not made for throwing; but it
struck sparks among the stones between them. Rysha
gasped and stumbled, and light came cascading in on
them.

The other man threw. Alya saw the heavy spear
arch down towards them, and leaping, stretched out
his open hand. The ironbound shaft slapped stinging
into his gauntlet palm. In the same flowing motion he
spun it in his fingers, poised and hurled even as his
feet hit the ground. The cast had such force that the
shaft flew almost level, and wholly true. It took the
thrower in the midriff and struck him off his feet,
dead. The other gave back, but hoarse cries were
going up on every side. Alya sprinted after the others,
catching them up as they staggered into the slime and
shadow of the little street.

Rysha was so done that she almost sank down
there and then, but running feet were close behind.
Alya and Vansha scooped her up. Asquan limped
along by himself, wheezing with pain at every step.
But suddenly they were around a corner, the fatal
firelight was hidden and shadow ruled once more.
Another knot of alleys opened up, and they plunged
down one at random. Vansha alone waited an instant
at the corner. Alya heard the feet catch up, the
sudden confusion of steel and shouting, and sprang
back to help. But Vansha came bounding up and
waved him along with his bloodied sword. 'The
closest; and the two behind unready. That'll teach
'em! What ails the old fellow?'

Alya had hardly noticed how Asquan faltered, still
clutching his side as if with a stitch; but when he tried
to help him, he saw the torn gash in the mail beside
the lower ribs, and the clotted blood like trailing silk.
'Not . . . too painful!' wheezed Asquan. 'Stimulating,
almost! And Powers, but we've a lively chase!'

They reeled and plunged down lane and street-
let, for never was there anything wider or cleaner,
rows of windowless huts whose life was all turned
inward. Filth spattered about them from undrained
ways; and the few they met in their course scattered,
appalled. At last, when they had to stop, all doubled
over and retching save for Alya, it came to him that he
could near no sound of pursuit save distant horn-calls.

'Beaten the bastards!' coughed Vansha.

'For the moment!' said Asquan, and then folded
forward over his side, wincing. His gloved hand came
away dark with new blood. 'Struck deep, for a dead
man's shadow!' he sighed, but he pushed away Alya's
hand. 'No, I shall manage.' And indeed he straightened up once again, tore off his fouled gloves,
smoothed back his soaking hair, and looked about.

'Did anyone note the lie of the town, from up
there? I did. We're well inside now; but hear those
horns! The hunt will be upon us soon enough. And
you wish to reach the palace? Perhaps if Rysha can
oblige us some more?'

'Must be bloody joking!' she muttered. 'I'm
wrung out like a tart's clout!'

'I perceive the resemblance. Well, I see my own
way clear enough. We must keep moving. Up to the
left, I think – upslope, though it's hard to tell in such
an antheap.'

'You can see the sheen of the palace,' said Alya
thinly. 'Up there, against the snow. It reflects the light
like nothing else.'

'Walk on, then. Nothing else? Have you ever seen
pearls? No? I had them once, and loved them. There
was, let me see, the clasp of a great cloak-pin, ancient
in my line. Huge ocean pearls, lustrous against silk
linings. I sold it for two horses and a good meal. I miss
the coolness of it, and the touch of the silk it fastened;
but this is better.'

Alya looked at him. 'I wouldn't have thought so. I

never had silks or jewels. Probably never will. I surely wouldn't trade them for being wounded and in danger!'

'Then you would never understand what it is to live! Comfort or danger, live either to the limit, to the surfeit. Seek the heights of pleasure, and you will find them merely another face of the peaks of pain! I have scaled both, as near the summit as now. And when you know that, nothing mortal is your master.' The old lord chuckled. 'Not all share this enlightenment, true. I have bestowed enough pain in my time to know that. You who care so much for a slip of a girl, you will never wholly understand. But it is also the way to your Wall.'

'I follow it. I find little pleasure in it.'

'And that is why you have never quite conquered it.'

'My father took no joy in pain! He took little enough in anything, I thought!'

'Nevertheless. Not everyone who delights in pain realises it. I am wiser. So are the shamans of the Ice, with their fearful rites and sacrifices. Through those they wield great powers, they do more than merely See! Their masks, their dances transfigure them, because they first endure so much. Through that, they can control forces of nature, wind, fire, storm even. The greatest of them can kindle men's hearts to some degree, it is said; or quench them. The legendary masters could travel anywhere in the space of a thought. And all that they win through pain.'

Alya sighed. 'I doubt that! They wallow in the pain. I have suffered enough to need no more! You are wise indeed, my lord, and I owe you so very much; but don't seek to shape me in your image. I will live by other means.'

'A shame!' said Asquan lightly, and yet there was sadness in his eyes. 'For I have no son I know of, and no heritage to give him, save the essence of my life, my own self. Yet I suppose it's best that you are as you are – a good man, better than I, even without the strength of the Powers within you. I would not mind such a son; but I would worry about his survival.'

Against his will, Alya was touched. 'I guess the Ice has distorted you and your life. As it has all of us, one way or another.'

Asquan laughed softly, and winced at the twinge in his side. 'That is so; and I should have expected such perception from a Seer. But you little guess how much. Did you know that there are abandoned souls who will go so far as to worship the Ice? Grovel like any Ekwesh, though they are not born to its service?'

'I'd heard something of the sort,' said Alya, slowly. 'I found it hard to imagine it was true.'

'Oh, it is, I assure you. A cult, a very ancient cult, both here and in other lands, though always secret and small. A more refined worship than the *Ai-kiya'wahsa*, of course. Involving . . . a retreat from the world, in a sense. A denial of life, and all it entails, to exalt the mind. Sounds noble enough, doesn't it? And after a fashion it is. The Powers of the Ice are pure mind, or so they imagine, greater minds than ours. Finer and higher thinkers, so they believe. So to imitate them, the flesh must be mortified, with privation, with pain, with strange experiences. Morality is a void, feeling an illusion, loyalty and honour mere self-deceptions. Things happen and must be made to happen because they *are* happening, ask not for cause or reason. All that matters is the triumph of the thought over the shell of filth that contains it. So one wallows in pain, to oneself and others, one espouses treachery in all things great and little, and above all one subjugates oneself to the higher will, believing in nothing else. Remarkable, is it not?' He looked around at Alya and smiled seraphically, as if inviting some response.

Alya, cold and damp already, felt the awful chill

of sweat along his spine, and the flickering fires did nothing to relieve it. 'My lord, that sounds very familiar, indeed . . .' He swallowed. 'My lord – why have you brought us here, then, at such cost? To what end?'

'To help you,' said Asquan mildly. 'Only that. Yes: in my rage at my loss and exile, my contempt for my fellow-men, pursuing their petty ends in the face of their peril, my fury at being so continually cheated by Volmur – in all that bitterness I bowed my head down to the Ice, once. I did its bidding, and believed in nothing, as it told me; and I did it well. The amount Volmur and his father suffered through me! The blows to their regime, their ambitions – why do you think they never felt able to move against the Forest, the Citadel, the other outlivers? And sold out, in the end, to the Ice?' Asquan chuckled. 'And I, their slighted servant, watched them sit and sweat their filthy lard away in fear! Oh yes, I served the Ice well.'

Alya shook his head, dazedly. 'But then why help us? Only that?'

'Because even those who bow their heads may sometimes raise them once again. They may, if they can but gain a shred of wisdom, see that the pursuit of pain is merely the pursuit of another kind of pleasure; that for treachery to have any meaning, so must loyalty; that one kind of tyranny is much like another; and that to believe in nothing, followed to its logical extreme, is to believe, indeed, in nothing. And so, after a time, I ceased to believe in the Ice as well. That opened my eyes to the falsity of the beliefs they imposed upon us; and to my own damnable folly!'

He sighed, and shook his head in wonder. 'They must despise us as much as their Ekwesh brutes, for all they flatter us! To sell us servitude in the guise of freedom! But at last I was free of that illusion also, free to live on without purpose, looking to little more than death. And then you appeared, a fair and foolish boy on an Ekwesh horse like a hero of old, a demon in your saddlebag, the fire of the Powers in your sinews and a desperate warmth in your heart. And it came to me that there are two ways to capture the essence of existence – to live constantly in mind of death, or in mind of life. For myself, I could manage no better than the first; but in you I saw the second, and better. And that in helping you, I could at least keep life in sight a little longer. Warm my hands at it, you might say!'

Alya, shaky with relief and confusion, smiled and shook his head. 'Perhaps I understand you, lord; or I will one day. I'm just a foolish boy, still. But I know this, that whether you believe in faith or not, you've kept it. For my part, you've given me more than many a father, already, and at great cost to yourself. You help me towards my dream, and I honour you for that. If we come through this, and I can make your name live in story, I will.'

The old lord held his head high, obviously pleased. Then, all in one onrush, he whirled on one foot and lunged into the shadows of a side-alley. There was a brief scuffling sound, a strangled gasp. Alya and the others ducked after him, not knowing what to expect – a body, most likely. But Asquan held a man pinned upright against the crumbling wall, his sword to his throat, though the newcomer was far larger than himself.

'Why were you sneaking after us? Live a little longer! Speak!'

Clearly the man understood. He flapped his brawny arms urgently, and Asquan relaxed his grip and his sword slightly.

'*Why?* Why d'you bloody think? Word's gone out, there's interlopers! Catch at all costs!'

He was a great swarthy oaf of a man, rawboned, sag-cheeked and stooped. His greasy face was slashed and scarred, eyes dull and heavy as if too little intelligence lurked there; and he stank, with the stink of the place made flesh. Yet there was steel in his voice, sharpened with terror; and something else very different.

'And you've come hotfoot to catch them?' sneered Vansha.

'To help them! I'm Chuen, me, one of the headmen here! Our own headmen, not the bastards the Ekwesh set over us! We're combing the streets, though it'll go mortal hard if the patrols catch us. We need them, those interlopers. We need 'em more than our lives!'

'You impetuous old thing, you!' sneered Asquan. 'And just what might you need *them* for, so badly?'

'Because you're here!' snapped Chuen. 'Because you found a way in! Word is, you passed the Dead and came through the Gate – that true? Anyhow, a way in. And a way in's a way out!'

Alya sighed, and abandoned all pretence. 'We lost half our number, man, and our boats in the rapid down there. What use is that to you? What use are we?'

'What *use*?' Chuen giggled. 'So it's true? Hah! Nobody, *nobody's* ever got through that before, out or in! You . . . I don't know why you're here, you're bloody mad – but what you could be to us! Hope. Life!'

To Alya's astonishment he saw that Chuen wept, great fat tears that could barely roll down his seamed cheeks. 'You're saying,' he said softly, 'that the people here want to do something? To escape?'

Chuen's teeth grated. 'The people, yes! Those as are still human. Every poor bugger who's not lost their soul to the Ice, or their wits. What'd you expect? We like it here?'

'I thought you'd be cowed. Among all . . . all this.'

Chuen nodded. 'We are. Maybe we are. Seems so fixed, so finished. There's many folk here never known aught else, save in tales. Me, I was snatched as a babe, I can hardly guess what life might be like outside. But we still tell the tales!' He looked anxiously around. 'And this is no place for 'em! Heard the horns, and came running. Others did too. Some saw you, put me on your tail. But what I know, the Ice will too, soon enough. There's a big price on your heads! More food, lighter toil. And for bringing you in, freedom, no less!'

Rysha sniggered. 'Likely they'd honour that!'

'Reckon they would,' said Chuen uncomfortably. 'What's one thrall more or less to them? A piddling matter to—' He gestured at the palace, and the cold slopes behind. '*That*. It's got bigger plans in play right now. But we'll see you safe, never fear!'

Asquan sheathed his sword. 'You've order of some sort? Even here? Where you're prisoners and thralls? I'm astonished.'

'Here, more'n anywhere! An order of our own, that all the whips and spears can't touch! What else can we have? Well, will you come, or die gabbing?'

Vansha and Rysha looked suspicious still; but Asquan nodded with grim pleasure. Alya clapped the man's arm. 'If you meant us harm, you'd have called down the patrols! Lead on!'

But from behind them came a rattle of iron-shod feet, and a challenge. The dialect was broad, but the words were all too clear.

'*You there! Stand!*'

Six lined faces, hard as treetrunks, blank eyes level and suspicious. Spears and shields at their backs, arrows nocked on their short horn bows, drawn and ready in taut arms. The leader had none, but his spear was levelled.

'Drop us, if we run!' hissed Vansha.

'Whoever would be fool enough to run?' exclaimed Asquan. 'As I said, Alya, I see my way quite clear.'

He tottered forward, cringed to the warriors, lifting his empty hands as if to seek grace. The leader grunted and struck him over the shoulders with the spear, forcing the old man to his knees. But Asquan's hands slapped tight about the shaft, behind the head, and the leader jarred as if he had struck stone. His brawny arms bulged, but Asquan's knobbed knuckles stood out stark white, and with little apparent effort he twisted the shaft suddenly upward into the leader's astonished face, hurling him back into his followers like ninepins. A bowstring twanged, the leader screamed and went rigid, and as he fell Asquan's sword swept out from beneath his cloak. Arrows tangled in the cloth, or rattled off his mail. One stuck in his shoulder, to little effect; for he slashed to left and right, cutting bow and hand apart, hurling the remaining warriors back against the wall.

So swift was all this that Alya and the rest had no chance to move; but as Asquan struck again, and two more warriors slid down the wall in bloody smears, he turned to laugh. 'Go, fools! Don't spoil my story!'

The wounded leader had spear in hand, stabbing up at him from the earth. Alya and Vansha sprang forward, but Asquan was faster still. His sweeping blow cut the man almost in two. But as his head bowed with the force of it, a spear came crashing down like an axe upon his crown. He jerked upright, blood spurting from a trenched gash among his grey hairs; but he leaned forward, almost casually, and smiled a terrible smile in the face of the man who had struck him. The warrior turned to run; but stopped dead, staring in horror at the blade that pinned him to the wall, and sagged. Cornered by the corpse, the last man cowered in dread, as well he might. Asquan, drenched in blood, slid the body contemptuously off the blade, and brought it up under his chin, so that he must rise on tiptoe or be impaled.

Asquan chuckled. 'Go, cur, tell your masters the

Inheritance of Teoquhan is avenged!' He made as if to thrust, coughed, staggered and sank down to his knees.

Alya seized the sword as it dropped, and struck. 'A dog at your feet, my lord!' he said, as the Ekwesh fell.

Asquan smiled ecstatically, throwing his arms wide as if in greeting. '*Life*—' he cried.

And slumped sideways. Alya, stooping over him, saw the eyes wide and fixed. The wound in his side gaped a handspan deep, already clotted and congealed, the last pulse of blood fading as he watched.

'He was dying all this time!' whispered Alya.

'Since the boat-fight? Think he knew?'

'Lesser men would have dropped dead on the spot! He said his way was clear!'

'Come, fools!' rasped Chuen. 'Or I wash my hands of you!'

'Washing anything's an improvement!' snapped Vansha; but he tugged at Alya's arm, and they ran.

'Brave man!' wheezed Chuen, herding them around corner after corner. 'But they'll rip the town apart to find you now!'

'Then you needn't shelter us!'

Chuen flapped his hands. 'No. We keep you, long enough. Turn here, left! Up here, now! Worth any cost. We light the fire faster, that's all!'

'What?'

'Heard what I said? The spark! Down this way, mind the footing! Kindling's all stacked. Been ready a long time.'

'What fire?'

Chuen's laugh was brutal. 'Fire that melts the Ice! That's what bloody fire! Just wants a touch of the tinderbox. That's you!'

He seized a heavy door and hurled it back. 'In here! And down to the cellar, there! Fast!'

An imperturbable pair of shovellers, man and

woman, scuffed away their tracks on the earth floor
even as they passed. Down in the cellar Chuen
tumbled old barrels aside to reveal a patch of mud
brickwork. He tore at its heart, until a brick toppled
outwards, and others beneath it. He bundled Rysha
through the gap, then Vansha and Alya, who feared
Chuen himself would stick in the gap. But the burly
headman simply carried more bricks away, and as he
tumbled through they were already being stacked up
again. It seemed to take no more than a moment
before they were shut in the dark, and could hear
mud plastered on the patch, and the barrels rumble
back into place. The loudest sound was suddenly
Rysha's agonised breathing.

'All this way!' she wheezed sourly. 'And back in
the dungeon again!'

'Like my stinking little hut,' agreed Alya, feeling
the fires in his heart burn down to mere embers. 'It
closes in about me. Chuen, is there no light?'

'It comes.' There was a crackle in the dark. A
small tongue of blue flame grew, and turned a glaring
yellow, making a horrible vision of Chuen's heavy
features. He raised the rough torch high. 'You tall sirs
will need to stoop. The way is roundabout, for we had
to dig as soil and stone allowed, and the trembling
earth. It has not been easy.'

The torch showed them an uneven roof, some of
it planks and beams like the underside of a floor, some
a rough jumble of props and timbers, all stained with
soot and grease. Chuen beckoned them on, and
indeed they had to duck, for the height changed
suddenly. Vansha almost stunned himself on a timber,
with an impact that showered moist earth around
him. 'Have a bloody care!' hissed Chuen. 'We are well
into the town now. They'll be more alert than ever!'

Vansha stifled his curses. Alya looked at the
beam where his head had hit. 'So much soot . . .
Chuen, these workings are old!'

The big man grinned, exposing worn teeth. 'Older than they seem, even. For we scrape off the lampblack for the grease, now and then. Older than I, they are; and I am an elder, having reached my forty springs, or near, as not so many survive to. Tales do not tell when they began; but they speak of a small folk, an elder race enslaved here, who began them. Our miners extend them yet, when they've a little strength to spare.'

'Duergar!' exclaimed Alya, so surprised he almost struck himself on the next beam. 'But they have not lived in ten centuries, that anyone knows of!'

'If ever!' grinned Vansha. 'What a louse-ridden warren!'

'What a feat!' snapped Alya. 'All this time! Among so much suffering, so little hope, they've been scratching and scraping away . . . Just to have somewhere, some way to get about that the Ice cannot control.' He slowly shook his head. 'The spirit of men . . .'

'Of woman, most like!' said Rysha scornfully. 'You can be sure there's a woman's hand behind this somewhere!'

'Truth,' said Chuen sardonically. 'There is. Behind the Ice itself – Cold-Hag, Frost-Witch, Iceheart and Winter's Bitch! There're others, but she's the head of all, since she threw down her lord Taoune a long age past, he who rules naught now but the Dead. And this here, this den, this sink of human refuse, this is her domain! Taounehtar Death's-Daughter, Lady of the Northlights, Queen of the Ice-Walls, Mistress of the Northwind. And the crow that pecks the eyes out of cold corpses!' He snarled, so fiercely the torch guttered. 'So bright, so fair! The snow on her breath, the ice in her breast, between her thighs the blackness eternal and the cold of the stars themselves, a chasm even Taoune her consort couldn't fill. She'd wrap the whole world in there, and she could!' He sniggered. 'Or a girl, they say now. With an icicle for a prick, I doubt not!'

Alya shook his head. 'A girl? What girl?'

Chuen's face was a glistening leer in the guttering light. 'A whole pack of 'em! Up at the palace there; we get word, one way an' another. Seems the Witch hankers after new fun these days. She'd take human form now and again – of a sort. But now she really works at it. Something to do with the new campaigns, they say – but I reckon it's just . . .' He gestured with a finger. 'Filthy whiteskin bitch! Only not your natural way, trust Her. Collecting pretty girls, she is. Up to all kinds of high jinks. Sweet stuff – high-borns and princesses, even, they say. Wouldn't mind a sniff or two at that, eh?' He nudged Alya's ribs and chuckled. 'Who knows? We may get a chance!' His face hardened. ''Cause if she's in the body, she's vulnerable!'

Alya looked at the others, but Vansha would not meet his eyes. Rysha's eyes gleamed with malicious amusement. 'Are you so sure of . . . all that?' he demanded.

'What? If she can shaft, she can bleed. Stands to reason!' Chuen licked his lips. 'Anyhow, it's a better chance at her than we've had in all the years I've been alive. Better than slaving and starving till you drop.'

Rysha sneered at him. 'Starving? You're in little danger!'

Chuen returned the glare. ''Cause I'm at the top of the heap, see? That's a sign, round here. See a man with meat on him, he's boss. But I swinked and strove for that, when other men just lay down and croaked! Done things I'm not proud of, things I don't even like t'think about. But then, so's every man an' woman you'll ever see here. Just to survive. Stolen, killed, betrayed. Sold our bodies and our souls for the next scrap of food, to last that little day, just that bloody hour longer!' He nodded, grimly. 'And when it's my turn comes, I get boiled down for me grease, same as any other! This belly o' mine, it's just held in trust, like. See, bitch?'

Alya raised a hand. 'She didn't mean to offend, Chuen. We're worried, that's all. We seek to rescue someone. A girl. From the palace.'

Chuen stared. 'From . . . ? I *see*. Well, there's plenty there that . . . that just labour and serve. But you came all this way, bursting in here, just for one girl?' He shot a glance at them, as if weighing up their sanity. '*Here?* Just for one . . .'

'Because she's ours,' said Vansha.

'Think of it in your own way,' Alya suggested. 'Because we had nothing to lose. Because nothing else seemed worthwhile, without her.'

Chuen cocked his head. 'Guess I do see. Thought it might be vengeance, with what the old-ster said. Worth tossing your lives out for that, maybe. But us, we just want to stir up a little slice o' storm here, and do a bolt for it under the smoke. And if that don't come off, why then we can make 'em smart, and be little worse off, alive or dead. We're just desperate, that's all. Yet all the same it's been hard to whip folk to the striking point. 'Cause they're so flaming feared!'

'Of this Ice-woman? Or of her warriors?'

'Both. And with good cause.' Chuen steadied himself against a rough pillar as a faint thrill seemed to course through their feet, a vibration which shivered all the way up to their groins and guts, as if fear was sent to them from outside. 'Feel that? There'll be more in a moment, harder.'

Vansha blinked. 'What is it? Earthfires?'

'Sure. Seen 'em? Whole reason this place's here. Too hot for the Ice, even; so what it can't put out, it puts to work. But there's many among the commons scared silly 'cause they still think it's some old-time dragon. Might as well be, mind you, if the Ice has the knack of whipping up the earthfires. Maybe they could send the whole place up in smoke. But there's enough ready to risk that, now.'

Chuen stopped, before a heavy blank door that blocked the way completely. 'And now that you're here, there'll be more! A sign, a gleam of hope – that's what you are to us!' He squinted at them, in the dimness, and the brutality of long despair was etched into his voice. 'So that's what you'll keep right on being, if you've any wits. Be that hope, and we'll aid you. Fail us – and, well, you'll find you've come a long long way for bugger all, right? *Right!*'

He turned and thumped on the door, a swift pattering rhythm. It was hauled back on to blackness. Pale hands reached out and hauled them inside.

Alya caught Vansha's shoulder as he bridled. 'Easy, brother! He's not used to mincing his words, that's all! Nothing he ask's beyond reason, amongst so many perils.'

The earth shuddered like something live beneath their feet. Stones and soil pattered and slithered down between the timbers. 'All right!' said Vansha. 'I'll do all you want, so long as it doesn't take me from my search.'

'Wisely spoke, young sir,' said Chuen, without turning. 'It won't. Just let 'em see the men that got in here by the Dead Stair, that's all.' Rysha snorted, and Chuen looked puzzled. The dim shapes around them hurried them on.

Alya noticed that the air was growing colder, with a heavy tinge of damp, and the earthen smell changing to one less clean.

'Nitre and human stench,' hissed Rysha. 'Back in the dungeons, like I said.'

'And sulphur,' said Alya thoughtfully. 'The earthfires, no doubt.'

'Breath of Hella!' exclaimed Vansha, and spat. 'It stinks like a whole army, down here!'

Chuen's outthrust arm stopped him. 'Well it may, young sir. Well it may!'

He held up his torch, and touched another, angled on the wall, so it billowed into flame. Another awoke, and another, dazzling lights in the dark; and with them, out of utter silence, a tense rumbling roar. The torches flared back into the distance, one by one. They were still in a tunnel, but it was a wider one and straighter, and some of it sheathed and floored with stone, though in many places repaired or supported with props and timbers. It stretched out straight before them, lined with hundreds of the torches; and every one glinted on intent eyes.

Chuen stood behind them, among six or seven other men of his stamp, burly and well-fed. But along the passageway crowded figures of another kind. They looked up from under bent brows, as if looking up was their natural way. Alya could see little else of them save outlines – hunched shoulders, ragged garments, makeshift hoods or hats, or simply spiky hair bound in rags. Here and there the torchlight showed something more, leathery faces expressionless, unreadable; and they were silent, always silent. Loose sandal soles flopped and slapped on the stone, but no word was spoken. There must be several hundred of them, squashed in shoulder to shoulder along the walls; but they did not look like an army, though here and there light gleamed on a chipped obsidian dagger or caught the curve of a stone-headed axe. They did not look like anything.

'So these are your sizzling firebrands!' said Vansha drily.

'No,' Chuen answered, no less calmly. 'Just their captains. Don't mistake their look; you learn that early here, or never, and only headmen lose it. They're eager to hear you, believe me! Just go among them, follow the passage, answer what they ask; most will understand. Then we've food and rest for you!'

'At the far end, naturally!' said Vansha.

'There,' agreed Chuen stolidly, without argument or aggression. 'Well, sirs?'

Alya hesitated, desperately weary, unable to think what to say to these featureless faces. It had seemed so easy, dragging people off on a hopeless quest, from dungeons no less hopeless, or from the subtler prison of an empty existence. But he had seen too many of them die, too recently. Their deaths had hardly sunk in yet, Asquan's especially. Was he to send all these folk to their deaths as well? He knew how little hope he could truly give them.

Vansha suddenly pushed past him. 'Allow me, brother!' he whispered, and stood tall in the torchlight, throwing his arms wide, so that his stained cloak fell away from his dully gleaming mail. There was a collective whispering rumble in the passage. And indeed he looked every bit the hero, thought Alya; every bit the man to follow. Vansha bowed deep to the assembly of eyes, and then, glancing back at the others, he led the way into the crowd.

They clustered in around the three, as they pushed through. Hands seized theirs, plucked at their cloaks and mail and swordhilts, or simply touched them as if to be sure they were not some kind of vision. And the voices around them asked the same questions over and over again, and they gave the same answers.

'From outside, for truth? From where?'

'From the south. Volmur's realm. Many weeks' journey.'

'Why'd you come?'

Vansha's constant answer echoed Chuen. 'For rescue. And revenge!'

'You really came in through the River Gate? For truth?'

'Up the Dead Stair?'

Alya nodded soberly. 'Yes! Wet, dangerous; some were killed. But, as you see, we're here!'

'You're warriors, heroes! Could we do it?' demanded others, and again they echoed him, crowding around in the corridor till it filled with smoke and the stink of filthy humanity. 'Could we? Just us? For truth?'

For truth, for truth; always for truth.

'Enough of you could!' barked Vansha, with clenched fist. 'Enough determined folk could force a way!'

'And then you'd have the current on your side, if you could find boats!' added Alya. 'Or take them! The guard was strong enough for us, but there's many more of you!'

'But wouldn't it be quicker just climbing up the far side of the vale, where it's lower?' objected Rysha. 'Make a break across the Ice, like! It's not that far!'

'Wouldn't be, but for the Ice!' snorted Chuen.

'Aye,' growled other voices. 'Wards this place like a whole pack o' hounds!'

'It's been tried!' said others. 'They didn't make it. Saw some heads. Can't be done. The cold, by night; and the watchers.'

'Can do your actual climb, easy!' added one younger man in the crowd. 'But can't walk on the friggin' Ice, once you're there! Dead smooth, that bit, save where the road goes – and they watch it! You fall, you go slow, and every breath you're breathing ice crystals, every step sucks the heat from your marrow. Got to go around, further back, maybe!'

'Fat chance!' sneered another, hard-faced and harsh-voiced. 'There's fuckin' ribs 'n' cracks 'n' crevasses, might hide you awhile sure, but that'd take you a week or more to get by! You wouldn't live so long up there. Not even if you took a cow with you!' A certain amount of harsh laughter broke out among the crowd.

'A cow?' asked Alya, puzzled. 'I'd have thought that'd be a bit of a handicap, wouldn't it?'

More laughter. Behind him Chuen coughed. 'That's a kind of a way of speaking some folks have around here.'

'Yeah,' sneered someone else in the crowd. 'Way of speakin'. Want t'know what it means? It's when a couple of big strong lads want t'get out, across the Ice. And they take another with 'em. Not so strong, somebody who's glad to get the chance o' taggin' along – lad or a girl, like. Maybe one they're lookin' after already, if you take my meanin'. Only there's no food out on the Ice; and you can't hardly carry enough. An' food's all that keeps your blood flowing. So . . .'

Alya swallowed. 'You mean—'

'Aye. They're the cow, see? Rations, like. On the hoof!' More harsh laughter.

'The human spirit!' said Rysha mockingly.

'No!' said Alya fiercely. 'The spirit of the Ice!'

'That's right!' barked Chuen, unexpectedly, radiating fierce anger. 'Looks down on all humans, because it can make some sink down t'that. And worse! And that's why it don't do t'be making a mock of it, man! Else what's the point of escape?'

The laughter faded under the heat of his anger. 'That's right,' Chuen nodded. 'You just stand back an' let these lords through. They're an example t'us all!'

'Some died!' said other voices. 'They said it!'

Vansha nodded. 'There was a price to pay. Folk died. But lives are cheap coin, when they're hostage to the Ice. And at least they died free.'

Did they? whispered Alya's doubts. *Or were they held in thrall by the power I was given – as I may be?*

But that was enough to silence the doubters, it seemed. From then on the questions were more hopeful, the touching almost reverent; and when they reached the end of that long corridor Chuen let out a long hissing sigh, and rubbed his hands. So did the other headmen, grimly cheerful. 'That's what was wanted, young sir! Oh, don't take the ill things said amiss. Hope don't leap in the spirit, not any more. There's been too much done! But they heard you, they did.'

'That is so!' put in one of the others, with a fierce flash of teeth. 'Many years, many times, we have stood on the brink, only to slink back. Too much fear, too little hope.' He whipped out his black dagger and cut at the air. 'Now we may spring! Tonight, even! While they busy themselves with their arming!'

A lean old man nodded sombrely, tugging his straggly white whiskers. 'Enough of lingering! Enough of hanging back like whipped curs! No better time! No hotter blood! Hungry to be spilt! *Now!*'

Chuen and the rest growled, but not in agreement. 'Spilt, maybe, but not wasted!' snapped one.

'Aye. We're ready, but we still must pick the moment! A day, at the least, maybe two.'

Chuen nodded. 'Won't hurt us to hold hard.'

'Nor us to rest!' grinned Vansha, and winked at Alya. 'Now, we wouldn't mind that food; and we have our own ends to consider. We need to track down this girl we seek.'

The older headman leered. 'She young, she fair? Most like she's at the palace, then, if she yet lives. Hundreds o' young things go there. Just as *She* likes 'em!' He cackled nastily. 'Best get yours away fast, right enough, little lad!'

'I've cause to believe she's there, indeed,' put in Alya.

They looked at him. 'Cause?'

'I have . . . I had ways. I . . . saw her.'

'You're a Farseer?' demanded Chuen. The old man drew breath suddenly.

'I am a Seer, as we call it. Though my training was not brought to the full.'

'What's amiss with that?' demanded Vansha. The others were looking doubtfully at one another, and here and there a hand even strayed to dagger or axe.

Chuen bit his lip. 'Here only the Ekwesh have Farseers! It's not a good name to us. Though I'll allow that legend tells of some among the thralls, once.'

'That is so!' rumbled a fat headman, his bald head dented by an appalling scar. 'Farseers and shamans could see things uncanny, it's said. But even they ended up here, for all that. And even those as weren't picked out and slain, the stories say their Sight grew dim and failed 'em, so hard the Ice oppressed their spirits!'

'I could believe that!' said Alya feelingly, seeing the doubters relax. 'In any event, I can do little now. The . . . means of my Seeing were lost in the river.'

'But *he* can still fight!' exclaimed Vansha, glaring around as if trying to fascinate them all. 'He has strength beyond human! Enough to pull down this roof around us all, if he chose! The Powers bestowed it on him, those who love life and hate the Ice! The Powers, in person!'

The chieftains stepped back a pace, in awe. It was Vansha they seemed to respond to, much as Kalkan had; and Alya could see him playing on that. Had he been leading Kalkan thus, too? An interesting question, maybe, if Alya hadn't been so weary. There were other answers he wanted, too, gnawing at him despite his exhaustion. Maybe that was souring his view. He would be wiser to wait, maybe, and be more persuasive to their new friends.

He clapped hand to sword, and his mailshirt rippled and rang. Rysha jerked awake; she had been asleep on her feet, literally. 'I have that strength!' he said, and let pride tinge his voice. That they would understand. 'But I still need rest and food, if it can be found. So does this woman; for she also has arts that have served us well.'

Chuen visibly came to a decision, and clapped his hands. 'Well, you've served *us* well. You shall have 'em. And . . .' He smacked his lips thoughtfully. 'Come the morrow, we'll bring you in sight of the palace, if no closer. You can watch the comings and goings, see if your girl's among them. More of our folk are being sent to labour there, what with these new campaigns. I've occasion to pass word to our eyes and ears there. I'll also ask them of her – and about *Her*.'

There was no mistaking the emphasis. Alya caught his arm, and Chuen looked startled at the force of it. 'You've heard something, haven't you? Already.'

'Nothing I'm sure enough of,' he grunted. 'There is this great lady or princess from far to the East . . . and others, maybe another . . .'

'She is no princess,' said Alya keenly, 'though she should have been. Just a . . . a headman's daughter.'

Chuen looked away a moment, then nodded. 'I'll put word out, 's best I can. But so many clouds gather! The Ice busies itself, even as we do. That may affect our plan. Come eat!'

The food was bad beyond belief, a thick coarse paste of boiled grains too long in store and half fermented, leavened with scraps of leathery smoked fish and rancid fat, and cold meltwater to drink. Yet it was obviously the very best these poor folk had put aside, and the newcomers ate with what grace they could. Rysha bore it best, and had scarcely wiped out her bowl and licked her bony fingers than she collapsed on the heap of rags and skins set out for them, in the little side-chamber. Vansha carefully made no complaint, not the slightest, yet somehow Alya was left in no doubt what he thought.

He himself envied Rysha, fearing what sleep would summon from memory. Yet when he also sank down among the rags, what filled his mind was the falling of vast towers of stone, taller and fairer far than the grey bastions here, and voices rising in a wave to greet a roaring wash of flame. He woke in a sweat, to feel the world shivering beneath him.

'The earth again!' said Vansha softly, invisible in the blackness. 'What a place!'

'How long have we slept?' demanded Alya, through gummy lips.

'How should I know? I'm hardly awake myself. Long, I think. Almost long enough, even. Powers, I was ready to drop!'

'I too.' Alya groped around for the jar of melt-water, rinsed his mouth and his face. 'And sick at heart. I could hardly string one word on another. You did better.'

'Is that the water there? Oh, I remembered Savi's father speechifying, that's all. And mine, spinning a few words to console folk for a bad harvest or a family quarrel. Send them off happy, that's the knack. Doesn't have to mean anything much. But there was something I kept wanting to ask about—'

'Me too. Many things, but one most of all. Apart from Savi.'

Vansha, sloshing water in the darkness, sounded surprised. 'What about her?'

Alya was startled. 'Well . . .'

'What difference would any of it make?'

Alya felt suddenly violently ashamed of himself, of his doubts, in the face of Vansha's assurance. But he could not help remembering that glimpse, how strange she had looked in that rich-hued gown. 'If she still . . . would want to be rescued?'

Vansha's tone was puzzled. 'Why should that worry you? They stole her, we've come for her, we'll take her. Or die trying. Either way, there the tale ends.'

Alya sat back in the darkness. 'Does it?'

There was a dull creak, and light flooded across them. Blinding it seemed, though it was only a tiny grease-lamp guttering in the hand of a headman. 'Heard your voices. Slept your fill? Good. Come eat again, then, and we will take you on your path. Dark approaches.'

'Dark?' demanded Rysha, sitting up, hawking and spitting. 'How long've we slept?'

'A night and most of the day following. And much has been in train, the while.'

'I'll say!' She thrust a hand down her breeches and scratched vigorously. 'We didn't sleep alone, either. Well, I need food. And before that—'

The headman shrugged at her question. 'In the corner. Where else?'

'Where else?' grunted Vansha under his breath, as they went out. He too was scratching. 'What's one more stink among so many? The place is a wallowing sty!'

'Is it their fault? At least they're trying to climb out!' Alya caught up with the headman. 'You said much was happening. Among us, or the Ice?'

'Both!' grunted the headman. 'Last night's words blow across the town like sparks from a lee fire! Where they alight, they kindle, and men strain at their chains – aye, women and children too! The mood's ugly. And all the more so, 'cause now they're being hounded more fiercely than usual. Seems the Ice believes you came to spy upon this new assault they're preparing, so they're pushing ahead—'

Alya caught his arm. 'I meant to ask! You keep talking of new campaigns, assaults – against what?'

'Against men!' said Chuen, rolling out of a side-passage. 'As ever. You'd know better than we what kingdoms there are out there. But it's one o' them the Ice means to drive against once more, and in force. They don't say where, o' course, save to their chiefs. But it's no mere raid. They've been marshalling their forces from all over the Ice, for months past now, laying in great stores, arming, drilling. Even recruiting any thralls they think worthy – you can guess what that means!' He spat contempt.

Alya felt a terrible cold urgency. 'Against the realms in the east, by the Sea? Or to the south and west? Or against others we don't know of, further westward maybe?'

Chuen rasped his bristly chin. 'Oh, to the suth'ard, I'd guess; but that's all I know. You heard any more, Tjan?'

The other man shrugged. 'Not much. A city with walls, I guess. A strong one, with those siege machines they've been building, special ones as come to bits again. So they can be floated downriver in barges, they say, an' built again nearer the spot.'

'Downriver!' exclaimed Alya.

Vansha nodded. 'Wager you a grain to a loaf it's Volmur!'

'Couldn't happen to a nicer fat bastard!' grunted Rysha. 'We should worry or something? Let's eat.'

It was only plain boiled meal, with a little salted fat, but that actually tasted better than before; and there was even a draught of wine, thin and sour, but heartening. Alya found himself thinking more clearly. 'Against Volmur first. But I guess that's because they wish to strike further afield, the realms of the coast perhaps. His kingdom sits on their main path south. He could harry them sorely if he chose.'

'If!' said Rysha contemptuously. 'If he grew his balls back, like!'

'He might, if he saw them out in force. He'd know it would be him next, or his sons.'

Vansha nodded. 'He's not a fool, whatever else. You see clearly, as usual, brother. But what difference does it make to us?'

'I don't know. If we could use it, somehow . . .

Chuen, you say the revolt's spreading. When will it strike?'

Chuen looked stolid. 'Soon. Very soon. No insult, young lords, but I will not say when. Few know, few tell. Especially if taken!'

'But we must have our chance!'

'Without us, how much of a chance, my lords? Even you! Oh aye, you might ha' gotten into that fell place, maybe – but out? And then away, with the eyes of the Ice upon you? But if those eyes are good and blackened, why, you've more of a chance, don't you?'

It was too sensible to contest. 'So what have you in mind?' demanded Vansha.

Chuen grinned. 'There's supply caravans coming in all the time now, headin' up to the great storehouses near the palace. We can borrow a cart here and there, make up one of our own. You go with it, break away, climb the hillside, get a good view over the palace. Watch the comings and goings, seek a way in.'

'But won't we be obvious outsiders?'

'Had a mind to help you with that . . .' grinned Chuen widely.

The cause of the grin soon became apparent. Alya rubbed another layer of filthy grease on to his features, and submitted patiently while an old woman streaked him with heavy white face-paint. 'What clan you want?' she demanded. 'Bear? Otter? Elk? Raven?'

'Raven . . .' echoed Alya softly, amazed there was such a thing; and she took it as an answer, seaming his cheeks with long white feather shapes. She held up a scrap of polished bronze, and he was startled at the lowering image that stared back at him, as blank and drained of humanity as any Ekwesh. He had feared his face would be too young, not hard enough; but what he saw there was gaunt and flinty. Less scarred than most, but Chuen thought that normal enough for a young man. Vansha looked worse, his handsome features dimmed and his scowl more obvious. Alya shook his head. 'So little, to make us what we most hate! Remember what Oshur said? Any of us might be *Aikiya'wahsa*, indeed!'

Rysha took to it better than either. Women were chattels to the Ekwesh, little better than domestic animals and seldom free to go about; but her lined bony face and raw-boned body looked mannish enough beneath the black leather armour. She seemed almost to relish wearing it. But though Chuen objected, she refastened a soiled scrap of black silk about her throat. 'They'll not see it, under the cloak; and it's too bloody cold up here, earthfires or no!'

Alya wondered, for he did not find it so, despite the occasional chill gusts. They soon ceased to care, though, as they sweated and toiled their way up from the lower slopes of the town. The carts Chuen had found for them were ancient, ramshackle contraptions, impossibly unwieldy. Alya had feared they would be conspicuous, till he saw others as bad or worse rattling and skidding across the uneven dirt roads. Only the caravans from outside looked at all well made, and the huge war engines that seemed to rear up like monsters behind walls. One, a great bow set upon a sloping bed and a heavy wagon, came rumbling out of a side-street, hauled by long ropes of straining thralls, with another flat cart behind to carry bolts twice the length of a man. Its huge wheels rode over the ruts and pits, but theirs could not. At every dip or rise they all had to put their shoulders to the sides and spokes, and it was no effort at all to do as the other caravan leaders did, and curse and flail at the sullen oxen that hauled them, and the ragged drivers who never raised their eyes or spoke. Nonetheless Alya let his lash fall on the cart timbers, when he could.

Other warriors paid them little heed. At first Alya kept his hand on his sword, hidden below the cover of a cart. He had had practice enough in understanding their dialect, but doubted he could speak it himself. He soon found, though, that a wordless bellow or grunt was enough to clear folk out of the way – in case, he suspected, they were roped in to help. The Ekwesh stabbing spear Vansha twirled irritably in his hands may also have helped. Only when a band of horsemen came cantering down the open way, spraying filthy mud from their hooves, did they have to check; and even then an abusive-sounding shout turned them aside.

'Well, you know what you're about, Chuen!' whispered Alya, as the wagons splashed and skidded on their way. 'Nobody so much as looked twice.'

'There's too many such caravans!' said the headman, pretending to be examining a rusty wheel boss. 'But leave its shelter, and the tale will change! And in the upper reaches, here, we must be more careful than before. Here's the homes of the chieftains, before whom common warriors are little better than slaves. And where strange things are done! Strange rites worked in the shadow of—' He cocked his head at the slopes above. 'See there!'

The light was long and low now, the sun already stabbing down between the Ice-cliffs, the shadows deepening. Fires were being lit, and among the higher buildings here they sprang up around an open space of trodden soil, ringed not by a wall, but tall jagged standing stones, like teeth. At the back of it, low and sinister, was a squat building, little more than a long hut made of slabs of unhewn stone, with crude wooden doors stopping its single opening, smoky and rotten-looking. Even for this place it seemed impossibly primitive, surrounded by the harsh stone towers; and it looked old. The earth was bare, but moss and green lichen clouded the stones. Slime gleamed on its roof.

'What's that?'

'Don't stand and stare, man!' hissed the headman. 'Sidelong! Look sidelong! Even warriors'd hardly
stare at the Mouth!'

'Mouth?' whispered Rysha. 'Some mouth! What
of? If that's a mouth, where's the throat, then?'

Chuen shivered. 'Not that kind of mouth. Like – a
crevice, an opening. That speaks.'

'An oracle, you mean?' Alya was puzzled. 'What
would they want that for, with the voice of the Ice
among them?'

Chuen shivered angrily. 'Don't use that name! I
told you, they do things there, the chieftains, the
shamans. Rites, dancing, other things! Out in the
circle, and in the House behind. And folks say that
– something speaks to them. Some . . . things, don't
know what. Like through a crack in a wall, or something.'

Alya felt a sudden shiver of recognition. '*In a
Wall?*'

'Yeah! That's what I said, wasn't it?'

'I was being slow. And these rites, these dances –
they dance in masks, don't they?'

'See for your bloody self!' hissed Chuen. 'But
don't be caught looking!'

There were men gathering, men mostly taller
than the warriors who bore spears and torches before
them. And they were clad, not in thralls' rags or black-
and-white armour, but long, heavy-looking gowns of
black or dull yellow, painted or broidered with designs in many glaring colours. Beast-heads, man-
heads, white and red on black, black and red on
yellow; but always faces, staring, leering as it seemed.
They moved with deliberate and arrogant dignity,
those men, as chiefs to solemn council; but when
they met at the gate of the Mouth, pushing past their
followers, they plunged into furious talk. A fierce low
hubbub arose around the stones, enough to attract
attention. But it was as Chuen had said; it attracted

the opposite. For those who passed by averted their eyes, and even the followers moved hastily away and squatted in the shadow of the stones, as men who seek shelter from nearing thunder.

It was a relief to get by at last, toiling all too slowly up the hill; and yet that vicious-looking circle, and the milling chieftains around it, seemed to draw Alya's eyes back. Then, as they hauled and heaved, the hubbub faded quite suddenly, and he saw men staring up the hill, and pointing. For a moment Alya feared they had been discovered, until he looked ahead. A double line of torches was advancing down the slope, striding warriors flanking a single cloaked figure tall and burly even for a well-fed chieftain. He walked stooping, as with age, under his broad-brimmed hat. But Alya, pretending to be engrossed in heaving a wheel out of a rut, caught sight of a heavy, seamed cheek, streaked with white claw shapes, and above a blade of a nose, a flash of black eyes intent, preoccupied, that marked, surveyed and dismissed him, along with all else in the scene, in remote contempt.

It was a frightening face; yet it alone did not cause the fear that washed through Alya then, but another, that bobbed at its belt like the severed head of an enemy. It was a little battered, no more; hardly disfigured, so there was no mistaking it, the intent, red-rimmed eyes, the crooked sky-beak. It was the mask of Raven. Not another like it, for Alya knew every line and mark upon it. It was his own mask, that he had deemed lost in the turmoil of the rapids far below.

Chuen's massive hand fixed on his arm; but it took Vansha's also to drag him down behind the cart again. 'I told you, don't stare!' hissed the frantic headman. 'You could ha' doomed us all!'

'That mask! Maybe I already have.'

'*What?*'

'Vansha, that's mine! My father's! They must have found it, somehow! I must get it back!'

Vansha snorted. 'Brother, sorry, I know how much it means to you – but surely—'

Alya's hand clamped on his arm. 'Don't you understand? That's *my* mask! That's *me*, almost! As good as! If their shamans try to find out about it, wear it, seek with it – and I guess they mean to! – then they'll have me, all of me!'

'What're you babblin' about?' demanded Chuen, horrified.

'I mean that the first thing they'll come to's the mind of its owner! And when they find it, they'll be able to read my every thought, if nothing worse! See everything I see, hear every word, feel what I feel – all! And everything I have seen, ever. Every memory I have!'

'Wait a bloody moment!' breathed Chuen. 'You've seen – you know—'

'The plot! Every word! Every face! Everything, even in the last couple of days!' Alya stared down at his shaking hands. 'They might even be able to control me, to turn me against you . . .'

Rysha stifled a cry. Vansha went white under the layer of grease. Concern, or fear? Alya felt almost wryly flattered.

But Chuen slapped at his forehead in anguish. 'I *knew* I should have friggin' blindfolded you, all of you! But I guessed you'd stand around arguing like the fool outsiders you are – and there wasn't time! Figured if you were no good to us, you wouldn't be coming out again! And bloody sight better you never had!' His hand clutched the hilt of a dagger beneath his rags. Rysha half rose, hesitated, hand to mouth; Vansha crouched motionless, as if in horror.

'Can't you at least change the plans?' demanded Alya, chill and bloodless.

'*No!* It's too late!' snarled Chuen. 'It's all going –

all moving. Something'd come unstuck! Thousands of us, whole lifetimes lost that somebody could try this one day, try to live free! And you go and—'

Alya felt a strange stillness descend. 'Maybe. Not yet. I'm going to get it back.'

Vansha choked. 'From there? Man, don't be mad! Strength or no strength, they'll slaughter you like a steer!'

Alya wondered if his grin looked as painful as it felt. 'Then they'll learn nothing from me, will they? Succeed or fail! They'll have to slay me to stop me, I'll make sure of that!'

Rysha was gnawing her knuckles, but she sounded earnest enough. 'If I can help – get you anywhere unseen, like—'

'No. Thanks, Rysha, but one's enough; they might get their claws on you too. Stay and help Vansha and Chuen! And you, Vansha, brother – if you see me no more, go on and rescue Savi!'

'I will! As I always meant to – brother.'

Alya drew his sword from the cart, strapped it on beneath his cloak. 'Where can I find you all? In an hour? Two, maybe?'

Chuen was trying to take all this in. 'Find you? Hah! In Hella's hands, most like! But . . . well, where I meant to take you, I guess. On the steep rock slope above the citadel. There's caves and crevices enough there that my kind use. You won't see us, but we'll see—' He stopped, glaring up and down the caravan as if to seek the support of his men. 'And they'll bloody well find that out too, won't they?'

Vansha caught his dagger hand. 'D'you want to risk an affray here, like this? Get us all caught? They'll know then, all right!'

The big man looked sick. 'Would to the skies I'd let 'em murder the bastard pack o' you! That I'd turned you in, and gone free of this whole bloody foolery!'

Alya shook his head. 'It'll go ahead, your plan.
Don't tell me when, but it will! And well! Look after
my friends! Vansha – greet her for me!'

Swiftly, even as he spoke, he ducked out from
behind the carts, and drawing his tattered cloak about
him, he set off after the torches, back down the slope.
He did not look back, something an Ekwesh warrior
would hardly do; but his heart was cold and sick
within him. It was all too easy to keep his head bowed
in the right manner. He was alone, now, dreadfully so;
and he had no plan at all, no idea of what he might do
– only what he must.

In some old ballad he might have killed a torchbearer quietly, taken his place, felled the big chieftain, snatched the mask, run . . .

With every man jack there baying for his blood.
Assuming, that is, they somehow didn't notice him
killing the torchbearer. They were almost at the
corner, anyhow, so there was no time for that. He
must look enough like any other common warrior in
his armour, though taller and slimmer than most, and
that was all he could rely on.

The procession had arrived at the gate of the
Mouth. The followers had sprung up and moved well
back, while their chieftains were gathering around
and bowing obsequiously. It was no effort at all, none,
to blend with the milling, nervous warriors; their eyes
fixed on the chieftains, they barged and elbowed him
like one of their own. Greatly emboldened, he let the
jostling slide him easily towards the shadow at one
side of the gate.

Men were bustling in and out, treading the earth
solid, fetching firewood, setting up tall wide-necked
drums of taut hide, hauling open the ancient doors of
the hut. These were evidently heavy and stiff, and
when he strode over to help, his strength was acknowledged with a harsh chuckle and a word of
thanks he understood quite well. He grunted as

intimidatingly as possible, and stood imposingly by the doors as if that was his post; and the others, daunted by his strength and size, stood back.

Barely in time, for all eyes turned to the big chieftain, sweeping free of the lesser men, striding towards the hut, carrying his own torch, and into the shadow of the doors. He snarled an order, snapped his fingers, and men leaped to close them; but Alya was already behind one, half drawing it in, and they did not see him as it ground slowly shut.

He stood there in the sudden darkness, shaking violently; but even as he did so, the fire in his limbs, so long dimmed in this place, seemed to awaken for a moment. It was a cold fire now, a frightening tingle. As if some icy breeze fanned it, he thought; as if it came close, here, to some other and chillier power.

The sudden flicker of light at the far end of the chamber seemed almost to answer his thought, and he pressed himself flat against the wall, deep into the shadows as he dared. Lamps had been lit, on some long low stone platform, crude things of some fat or oil, sickly and stinking. By their light he saw a rough pattern painted on the end wall above, glistening with sooty grease. It made little sense to him, but the tall chieftain fell to his knees and grovelled. Then from within his robe he fetched a bundle of cloth, and humming and muttering to himself, he placed it reverently on the platform and poured oil over it. His torch waved in the air, while he sang and swayed on his knees; then he touched the flame to what was there. Fire flared, lurid and smoky, with an awful sizzle. The tall chieftain stood, bowed over it a moment, still singing and humming in the one voice, like some sleepy hive of bees. Then he shrugged off his heavy robe and tossed it carelessly aside. Beneath it he wore a well-worked mailshirt over loose black shirt and breeches and heavy boots, and those also he removed, laying them to one side, with his heavy sword on top. Wearing only a breechclout, he stooped to take the mask in his hands.

He held it high, as if showing it to the fire; and his voice rose for a moment to a chanting scream. Then it cut off; and in the sudden silence he must have heard or felt Alya's swift step on the soft floor. He whirled, and dropped the mask as he reached for his sword, opening his mouth to shout; but Alya's hands were already about his throat. The chieftain was massively built, his scarred hands as solid as Alya's; and their knobbed knuckles stood out white as he tore at the grip that choked him. The fires in Alya's blood burned lower still, and for a long moment they swayed together. But he forced the grizzled giant slowly back over the low altar, and as he did so, saw the offering that burned there.

His gorge rose, at the sight and stink of the smoke. Shock and revulsion clamped his grip still tighter, and anger flared across the embers of his unnatural strength. All in an instant he felt like a roaring blaze, as if he himself were some flaming sacrifice to uncaring forces. Searing pain flamed in his wounded back, and with barely an effort he heaved the other man bodily off the ground and shook him furiously as a wolf might worry a rat. He felt the bones snap under his fingers, and snarled with malign satisfaction. He opened his grip, and the body fell in a heap at his feet, like old rags.

Alya hardly noticed it. He was scooping up the mask in caressing hands, feeling the familiar weight, the texture of the scarred wood. It was little harmed, indeed. Here and there the bright paint had chipped away, but only to reveal older paint beneath, more than one layer of it, ingrained into the very wood. His father had called it old; but this spoke of greater spans than one lifetime, or even two. Here and there it looked blackened, almost burned, as if the mask had survived some ancient holocaust. But could it survive this one?

It would make sense to burn it at once, here. Help reduce those hapless little limbs on the altar to undefiled ash, if nothing more. But that would still be defeat; and now, with the fire still thrilling along every vein, he did not feel like accepting that just yet. He looked around frantically for some other way out of the stone hut, but there was none. Cold air breathed through many gaps under the roof, but none remotely large enough. And it would not be so easy to slip out as a sentry, not now they were expecting . . .

He chuckled to himself suddenly. They were expecting a mask.

The doors ground back, and he stepped into what was now a circle of light. The sky was dark, and the torches sent shadows dancing across the ring, and the circle of faces that awaited him – a nightmarish circle, for none of them were even remotely human. A ring of men stood there, the tall chieftains, some stripped to their shirts, others naked save for stained breechclouts, but all of them masked, in a style too like his own for comfort. Lowering, stylised shapes of beasts and beings less recognisable surrounded him, wide-eyed carvings heavily lined in black and red, embodying a central clan totem or other votive spirit they hoped to call on.

For the first time ever he entered a gathering of his own kind, of Seers. And every one of them was his deadly foe.

The chieftain's clothes and mail fitted him well enough, and were better and cleaner than his warrior's guise, even if, as he found reason to suspect, their former wearer had not bathed in recent memory. It was easy enough to assume the man's round-shouldered stance, hands on hips, and glare intimidatingly around the circle. He waved a contemptuous hand at the hangers-on now clustered around the

entrance, and with the mask to muffle his voice to
imitate the chieftain's bark in a curt word or two –
'*Out! Away!*' The warriors scattered into the darkness, and many of the masks nodded in evident
approval.

For all that, the shirt already stuck to his back
with sweat. There was little enough chance he could
escape, but he had to make sure they could not
overwhelm him with numbers. He had to make sure
they killed him.

But Alya's spirit of defiance was still strong, and
seeing the men at the drums sneaking out after the
rest, he snarled alarmingly. They shrank back, and
when he snapped his fingers, they seized great sticks
of bone and struck a rolling note on the hides. The
masks half looked at one another, but he strode into
the midst of them, and clapped his hands angrily, and
the chieftains hastily leaped back into their ring. And,
wonder of wonders, they began to tread around, to
circle to the drums' dull beat, lifting their feet higher
and higher, the jaws of their masks flapping and
clapping with musical notes. They began to dance.
And, after a moment, so did he.

The drummers had clearly done this often enough. They started with a dull, thudding rhythm, so
slow that each foot had to hang hesitant in the air
before it fell, a jolting, syncopated rhythm that was
already entrancing. Their sandals scuffed and
stamped the earth with leaden deliberation, and he
felt each vibration in the mask's leather cheekpads.
The others grunted fiercely at each footfall, and so did
he, joining himself to them in the stamping rhythm.
The wind shifted, and the fires and the torches blew
little ghosts of acrid smoke about them. The drums
were thumping faster now, and he felt his body catch
them up, his heart hasten. Sweat stung his eyes and
he closed them, breathing harder; around him the
grunts were becoming soft gasps of effort. Was it the

ground shivering beneath him again? He seemed to lose all sense of his limbs, save the punishing thumping of his feet. It was as if he floated in the blackness, borne up by a great soundless updraught, propelled by his feet against an unseen ground that grew harder and hotter every instant. Then there was a glimmer in the twilight, and another, like a dark lake over which the moon was slowly coming out.

It felt now as if he had no boots on, that he danced barefoot on the blackness; and it was smooth and hard, its glassy edges stinging even his hardened soles. In the darkness around him, rising and falling, faint gleams circled; and the black mirror underfoot reflected them redly, like rising fires. They moved slower than he, more clumsily, as if still held down by weight. Thin streaks of phosphorescence, tracing patterns he knew well, images of the Trail; some strong and swift, others slow and wavering, yet none as clear or as direct as the shape that whirled into his mind like a spitting track of molten metal.

He laughed harshly and stamped harder yet to the thundering in his ears, drowning out all other rhythms, until those weaker lights were shaking and quivering to its pulse alone, reflecting it back at him. He knew what he was doing now, what he was hoping to do. Minds that encircled his like worlds floating in the void; minds that sought to join with his, to lend him their power.

And let them!

He laughed again and drew upon their strength, let the sound of drum and chant bear him up and lift him higher, so high the lights struggled and faltered to keep up. Small wonder; they were the stair upon which he climbed, leaping now from step to step with effortless floating energy. This was the way his father had told him of. This was the other way he might ascend! This was the other path to power!

And suddenly it was as if he threw back his head

and saw white clouds above the blackness, and an airy blue sky. And, rising above its dark glassy horizon, the first red disc of the sun. He reached out to it, and felt the fire in his mind blossom to its warmth, his pulse quicken and with it all the others that laboured to its tune, and whose increasingly frantic efforts only served to raise him higher. He was borne upwards, soaring, leaving the wavering ring of lights struggling below; and it was no surprise to him when the rising rays struck scarlet flame, as fresh as new blood, from the summit of the Wall. Over its margin he soared, on borrowed wings no longer, and stared into the full majesty of the sun.

In that moment he saw too much for any human eyes, too many things laid out beneath him for any human mind to take in, whole. He said, in later time, only that it was as if he did indeed look down from some immense summit, as a predator bird might, striving among a fantastically patterned landscape for the slight stirrings of its prey. Through the raven eyes of the mask, he saw minds open before him, minds known and unknown, familiar and strange; and he launched himself and swooped down upon them – upon every mind in which he saw a strange wild figure, leaping, howling, to the frenetic pace of drums, and around him, jerking like puppets, a ring of others, their gestures increasingly desperate.

Two lay sprawled and silent already. Another, on his knees, vomited helplessly. The rest snatched and tore at their masks, yet still they stamped and capered. One of the drummers lay sprawled and gaping at the sky, with blood trickling from his ears and nostrils; but the others still bent over the yammering hides, helpless prisoners of their own pulse, imprisoning the masked men in their turn.

The masks fought him. Their animal features grinned and snarled, heavy jaws twisting and snapping at the threads of pulsing fire that bound them to

one another, and to him. Their own animal fear
resisted him, a shapeless, savage, clawing mass that
lashed out at his thoughts, seeking to slash them
asunder and tear out their substance. But all that
hissed away from him without contact, like spit from
hot metal, and screamed into nothingness. And Alya
rode down its path like a sudden blinding sunshaft
with thoughts of his own, of the battle in the mists
and the grim faces of the living dead. Out of his own
fears they sprang, turned back by him now against
their source; and terror boiled up around them, far
greater than he had expected.

More than anyone else the Ekwesh feared the
Dead, he saw; those they had slain, those slain beside
them, as much as any who would slay them. For all
their fearful savagery, for all their rapacity and relentless bravery, this warrior race was a seething mass of
terrors, instilled since childhood by atrocious means,
that they might be ruled only by the greater terror of
their inhuman lords. Memories caught fire in their
own minds, memories of fearful cruelties inflicted, of
dreadful pitiless killings in the name of their masters;
and all those mangled dead awakening even in the
instant of their death, and reaching furiously out with
limbs still mangled and spurting to embrace their
slayers.

The maimed child-corpse on the altar sprang up
in the oil-flame and screamed in their ears.

The skeletons in the woods raked their withered
fingerbones across their eyes.

The slain of the Citadel came swarming up the
slopes to drag them down with bleeding fingers.

And the shadowy boats of the Dead bore down
on them, as they struggled and screamed in the river's
numbing embrace.

In that moment, as their terror-driven wills beat
against his and fell helplessly back as waves from a
towering cliff, he reached up. But before he even

touched it, the mask of the Raven dropped open, to reveal the human face of shining metal within; and in the light of that unearthly sun it blazed untarnished, with the blinding fire that Raven had stolen, for the succour of humanity.

For that instant that mask was all masks, all wills, and he that wore it commanded their minds and hearts as his own. He turned his thoughts away; and theirs turned with him, like so many sunflowers, to the face that took shape in the radiance.

They lay open before him, and he reached out a godlike hand to seize what he willed. In many the image awoke nothing save faint traces of lust and cruelty, or contempt; but in one, two, it found a mirror image, faint and distant, but clearly there. He bore down on those images, sent them seeking through others to the place where they had been seen, and with the flame within him, fed by the radiance above, he sent a thought questing ahead of him, a call, a name—

Savi!

An answer.

Eyes opened, a voice gasped. A confusion, then a realisation of place, a racing rush of images, corridors, rooms, galleries, stairs, columns of swirling ice-blue. A silhouette sat up, slender in the half-light. The glint of glossy black hair falling across a bare brown shoulder and breast, the shining of wide eyes, astonished, full of sudden feeling that flared in his vision like a corona, yet would own no name – pain or hope, fear or expectation, perhaps because it did not own itself wholly one thing or another.

A thought came to him then, a memory awoken by the awareness of the power on which he balanced, the mingled force of wills in thrall. He yearned to be there with her. He could be, now. Closer than even wings could bear him. It had been done, and therefore he could do it. He had only to reach out, but with his whole being, into the presence of the vision before him, fixing two realities in his mind, two ends of a journey in one—

He stumbled. In its outreach his mind touched, not Savi, but some other unexpected shape. Like tripping over a savage dog in the dark, perhaps. Awareness awoke and stirred, as immediate and as menacing as a low growl.

But the shape that stirred and sat up could not have been more different. Shining covers slid away from a shoulder of ivory, swept about with gold, fine features slack and half awakened, large blue eyes sleep-misted, anxious, uncertain – and as they lit upon him, abruptly flaring with fearful alarm.

Back from their gaze he cast himself, barely in time. They swept the darkness, icily intent, stabbing like steel spears even into the sunglare, reflecting the fire at its fiercest, untouched. He fell back, outwards, away—

And as he did so, he felt another thought stir in answer to that vicious will, linked to it somehow. It was no clear thought; it was more a response, that came welling up like a sudden wave upon an ocean of oily darkness, an uncoiling shadow, massive, all-embracing, monstrously malign. He called out once more, as he fell.

Savi!

A-Alya?

It was the faintest of answers, the least believing; but it was an answer unmistakable. He sought to reach out, even in his peril; but he could not. The pivot turned. The balance shifted. The dark energies that bore him into the light bucked like a frantic horse beneath him. He was plunging down out of the sun, to the Wall beneath. Plummeting down among the lights that spun and pulsed there, shattering their instant of unison, losing hold of the rhythm. The drums beat frantically and shattered, and the leash of fear snapped, and recoiled upon them all.

Their encircling minds fell howling into the void beneath him, and through them, through their masks of power, he felt the darkness leap out to envelop other glimmers there – the waiting warriors, huddled outside the Mouth, who had come running to see what was happening. Within them also the ground opened, and the bodies of the dead they had buried for so long, far beneath the reach of guilt and compassion, came snaking up like obscene plants to tear at their slayers. He saw them, through the eyes of others, scream and strike out at any other within their reach, seeing only fearful phantoms of their own cruelty; and be themselves struck down in turn, or strike at last at themselves, clawing out their own eyes to banish intolerable sight.

Then he was seeing it through his own eyes and the mask's, the screaming carnage around him. He snatched out his sword, barely in time. The bleeding maniac that rushed at him he cut down, and the snarling bear mask went bouncing away under the stamping feet and was smashed to flinders. They danced no longer at the Mouth, or it was a dance of death. The shamans clawed at one another's naked flesh, kicked and trampled those who were down even as they died. The madness had been sent out, and would not die; for its roots were in them all. Even in the street beyond the gate men fought one another still, scrabbling in the slime.

And Alya had to wrestle against the revulsion in his own mind for having occasioned this, well deserved as it was. He hauled the mask from his head, and fell back in horror. But all compunction was blown away by the stink of burned flesh from the longhouse. He would not go back in there, not even to retrieve his original disguise. He feared to bear a chieftain's robe; it would be too visible, carry too many burdens. He snatched up one of the many cast-off black cloaks all around, and a helm that had rolled away unheeded. Backing anxiously around the jagged stones of the Mouth, striking down or throwing back the men who lunged at him, he reeled out into the street and away, before the voices and the torches that were approaching, barely in time.

He staggered off through the shadows, deeply shaken. He had crested the Wall at last, if not wholly on his own, and found there a terrifying power. Had there been more minds within reach, he might have spread madness over this whole miserable township, engulfing victim and oppressor, friend and foe alike. He himself was marked by it. Yet that power had also almost delivered him into the hands of an enemy, and left him jarred to the depths of his soul.

At least he knew now where Savi was, how he might come to her, all and everything. It was what he no longer knew that shook him most: what she was to him. That other form he had seen, that mind he had touched, that had stabbed at him with a power that might shatter the Wall itself – that he could guess, and the guess itself was agony. Yet he had heard a voice speak his name; and that was to him as her cool touch had become in his fever and despair, the only fixed point in a world of infinite dark.

He clung to it, and questioned no longer, only ran.

CHAPTER 11

Winged Fire

IT took Alya a long time to reach the slopes above the palace, or so it felt. He had been right not to take the outer robe. He might have walked more freely as a chieftain, but also been too noticeable, a man of consequence going about unescorted. So when he heard the clatter of armed men running, it seemed safer to slip into whatever murky doorway or side-street offered itself, though they were often awash with muck he was glad he could not see. At least the chieftain's boots were sounder than those he had worn, and a better fit. But the way was not easy. He had to lurk for whole long hours behind a ruined wall in one foul warren, while two bands of warriors lounged and quarrelled in the street outside, and evil stenches caught at his throat. The thoughts in his mind were almost as choking.

Yet it gave him time to settle them, to come to terms with what he had done and seen. When at last the warriors shambled sullenly off, he emerged much calmer. Nonetheless he promptly lost his way, and wandered almost up to the palace square before he found the direction again. He stared hungrily at those glittering walls; but there were guards on the alert, and few others visible. He turned away towards the dark slopes of the valley wall.

There were no guards there, at least; for they led nowhere except to the Ice, that was its own sleepless sentinel. Its steep slopes seemed to dream under the moon, their dusting of powder snow glinting like pure jewels over the darker glint of the riven glacier. But he remembered that great grim awareness he had touched, and shuddered. If something so monstrous lurked out there, its dream was very far from pure. He was not going to risk awakening it.

Even down here it was much colder, well above the warm, fetid air of the vale, and he had been sweating heavily through all his clothes. The blackened steel helm was making him colder, if anything, but when he hauled it off the wind chilled his clammy hair and stung his face with it. He had to find shelter and his friends, urgently.

Chuen had spoken of rock formations, but they were all over the slopes as far as he could see. He went slipping and stumbling across the hill for some thousand paces, trying to find one that overlooked the palace. The low chittering cry of an owl made him jump, and he stared about suspiciously; there were huge white owls that dwelt among snow, he knew, but this place seemed devoid of life, even in the crevices of the stones. The cry came again, low and soft, and ducking down, he made his way awkwardly along the stony slope towards the rocks where he had heard it. But these were too low, he found; they had no view of the palace at all, and he was about to leave them and look upslope when an arm swung sharply around his neck.

His hands clamped on the coarse cloth, and there was a gasp as he pulled free. 'It's me, bugger it!' hissed Chuen, doubled over in pain. 'Sod, you nearly tore out the muscle!'

'You startled me. I didn't think you'd be down here!'

'Don't think I'd lead someone straight to our vantage, do you?' Chuen looked at him suspiciously. 'Specially someone I wasn't sure I'd see again. As it is, you're watched already. Step out without me and you wouldn't get ten strides.' Another owl cry, repeated, sounded across the slope, and he nodded. 'Well, they say you weren't followed. Might as well come up. But let me go first, if you're in no haste to stop an arrow!'

The headman led him on a winding climb among the outcrops, over slopes so steep that they were reduced almost to crawling, and up behind what looked like a solid rock ledge, but which had a deep gully within, probably cut by meltwater from above. Shadowy figures scrambled around as they appeared; and then there was a soft harsh laugh in the darkness.

'What'd I tell you, boy? Your dearest brother – he's back, right enough!'

A silhouette turned sharply. Vansha's whisper was almost appalled. '*Alya?* Powers . . . did you . . .'

Alya held up the mask, so it could be seen against the whiteness above.

'*What?*' Chuen caught his shoulder. 'I thought you'd just given up! *How? How*, in all Hella's realm?' His voice was heavy with distrust and amazement.

Alya slumped down, his back to the rock. 'I'll tell you. When I've had a rest. Has anyone got anything to drink?' He gulped down the chill meltwater gratefully. It had a strange taste, a tang of metal on the tongue, but wholesome enough. 'How have you fared?'

Rysha snorted impatiently, but it was Vansha who answered. 'Poorly enough. We've scanned the palace for hours, till the light went, but even I saw hardly a damn thing. Save a fracas a while back. All manner of folk scuttling about like an ants' nest, as if a thief'd got in. But Chuen said that was more likely over something happening down in the town. No sign of anyone who could remotely be Savi, of course, still less any sight of an easy way in . . . Wait, now. Down in the town – that was *you*?'

'I think . . . they both were. The row in the palace, over what happened in town. And we have no need to watch now.' Alya slumped down on a stone, with his back against the cold smooth gully side, and cradled the mask on his lap. 'I've seen Savi. And I know how to reach her. Every finger's breadth of the way!'

Someone among the dimness began to laugh, softly; but the laughter faltered. 'How, brother?' demanded Vansha softly. 'How?'

But Alya felt as if he inhaled the darkness. The fire in him sank to embers, and his head fell forward on his chest. He slept.

Only as he awoke was he aware of his dreams, a confused tangle of voices, of half-remembered visions, of the bulk of the Wall and the glorious sun that burgeoned atop it. But when he opened his eyes the sky was no more than a dark cloudy grey, unleashing a fine rain of wet snowflakes. They would melt when they reached the valley floor, but here settled annoyingly on hair and eyebrows, like lightly stinging reminders of the awesome wastes above. It would be hours yet before light touched the vale.

Rysha lay, mouth open and snoring thinly, on a shelf not far off, and Vansha was a hunched silhouette, unmoving. Alya yawned and stretched his cold limbs, and Chuen, standing talking to what were evidently his guards, turned his way rapidly. There was no sign the bulky headman had slept, and he looked ragged and nervous. 'You awake? There's food, but no fire. And listen, I've let you sleep, 'cause your friends insisted; but what goes on down there's my concern, all of it. I want to hear, right now!'

There was a rustle of clothes, and Vansha slid down the sheer rockface to land on his feet. 'I want to hear, too. Especially about Savi!'

Alya told them as he ate, choking down disgustingly oily meal cakes with draughts of the metallic water. He told it as best he could, putting the Wall and all about it into terms he thought they might comprehend; for it was vital that they trust him now,

Vansha and Rysha especially. They looked almost as dazed as the rest.

'Lemme get this straight!' muttered Chuen. 'This . . . power you say you've been give – an' I'm not denying that, no, not I, I've felt it! You say that's helped you over this Wall?'

Alya tossed his head, choked down some more cake. 'No. I was able to draw upon it, briefly, by holding others in thrall; but all this time . . . I think it's been preventing me crossing the Wall on my own.'

'You said something of that,' agreed Vansha. 'One power for another! Well, it makes sense. The Powers rarely give without some fair exchange, they say. Something in what those old men said, too. But you've used it now, all right!'

'Through others! And that . . . it was terrible. On my own I might have spoken to Savi. Vansha, think! I might even have flown to her, then and there! You remember, we talked of shamans who have managed that feat, though it taxes their power sorely; but then, just then I had power enough! I *had* it, for that one moment only; but I had it, I almost managed to use it . . .' His clenched fists quivered, and he laughed a little at himself. 'But as it was, I should be happy enough I escaped the other mind. That woman's. And lucky there was no other will at the Mouth to equal mine. Either might have destroyed me!'

'And all of them there you slew?' demanded Chuen. 'Every last one?' While Alya talked he had been nervously strolling up and down the gully floor, watching the lightening sky with edgy impatience; but as the tale was told, he and the others had come to sit and listen with growing amazement. Now he eyed the mask with something between horror and hunger.

'They slew one another, in their fear and guilt,' repeated Alya wearily. 'Which I only made them face.

No, headman, before you ask. It is not a thing I would care to try again. Another time it might envelop us all. We all have our darker depths. I might encounter my own ghosts. Or you, any who haunt your memories!'

Chuen backed off hastily. His men seemed to regard Alya with mingled awe and terror, as if he were something far more than human; and in Chuen he seemed to inspire feelings even more mixed. 'Well, maybe, maybe!' the headman muttered. 'Best not meddle in such matters, maybe. I'll allow it gave me a bad turn when we heard all the hubbub raised. I feared our plan was breaking too early!'

Alya sighed. 'I'm sorry. I hope it won't put the town too much on the alert.'

Chuen shrugged. 'Wouldn't make much odds. But I guess it won't. Not if it looks like a brawl, as you say. Such things do happen now and again, y'know. Clans are always touchy, ready to do each other down at the least excuse, and the chieftains most of all. One takes offence at another, and—' He clicked his tongue with relish. 'Stiffs everywhere! Running battles in the street, betimes.'

'And the Ice permits that?'

'Don't know. Seems to.'

'Likes it!' put in one of his men, and spat. 'Thinks it makes 'em fiercer!'

'Or maybe it just assumes that's the way all men behave,' said Alya softly.

'Maybe,' said Chuen, with grim relish. 'Well, I don't mind either! Maybe when our plan does break, it'll give 'em a bloody sight more to think about!'

'No doubt!' drawled Vansha sarcastically, his voice edged by impatience. 'But dare one ask just when it *is* going to break?'

Chuen surveyed him coldly. 'Aye, as it so happens, ask you may!' He jerked his head up at the sky, now bearing a trace of blue. Even as he did so, the first long beam of the hidden sun stretched out across

the snows above, and tinged the very tip of the valley
with the flame of dawn. 'Listen!'

Rysha looked around. 'Listen? I can't hear a
bloody thing!'

Chuen's piggy eyes glittered. 'Nor will you. First
light's touched the valley wall. Should be the first
stirrings in the streets already – thralls spillin' out of
the barracks, defaulters beaten, beasts bleatin' and
fartin', children cryin', cookfires lighting. Same row
I've heard each morn of my life, long as I can
remember. An' I don't hear a trace of it now. Not
a bloody trace. Not now.'

'As if the town holds its breath!' whispered Alya.

'It'll let it out soon enough!' said one of the
guards grimly. 'When the Ekwesh see—'

'Aye. A few heads'll fall, somewhere. But folk're
ready. The first heads down won't be theirs; and
better that, than live on in this stinking hole. Still want
to know when it'll begin, lad? It began a long time
back. Now's only when it reaches the light.'

Vansha said nothing. Chuen fastened his eyes on
the town with a look of real hunger. His tongue licked
his fat lips, and despite the biting wind a single sweat-
drop slithered down over his unsteady jowl. The
other men were with him, leaning eagerly out over
the sharp rocks, staring like starving wolves at a fat
quarry. Suddenly one hissed, and pointed. To the
south of the town, by the great barracks, a thread
of smoke was winding skyward. 'Not a cookin' fire!'
snapped Chuen. 'It's black. Wait now!'

'I've had enough of your waiting!' growled Vansha. 'Come on, brother; and you, Rysha—'

'No! We've got to let the uprising take hold, so
we won't be noticed! Rysha can't help us much till
we're inside!'

'Inside . . .' echoed Rysha hollowly, and hugged
herself against the gusting dawn breeze, staring at the
coldly glittering walls. But Alya paid her little heed,

for the breeze was carrying things to him. A clamour,
as of many voices; a low rumble as of feet that ran and
trampled; a faint sharp tinge of smoke less sulphurous
than earthfires, more acrid than cooking.

Chuen's fingers were clawing softly at the black
stone, until at last he hauled himself up bodily on the
gully wall, impatient of concealment. He cried out
then, and pointed; and they all saw it, down among
the still deeply shadowed streets: a thread of fire that
ran and spread, that split at a barracks wall, vanished
an instant and reappeared, stronger than before.
From further down the town a red flame blossomed,
and a moment later a rending crash came echoing
crazily out to them, off the cold walls of the vale. 'A
roof gone!' crowed Chuen. 'Burning, and nobody to
put it out!'

'There goes another!' shouted Vansha. A billow
of greasy black smoke sprang up, too heavy for the
breeze to disperse, high enough now so it caught
the sun; and beneath it, like an undercurrent, came the
murmur of many voices, rising like a spring torrent
under melting snow, the release of a force too long
held back. Screams rose, the screams of men and
women, of agony and of madness. Now they could
see the Ekwesh troops racing through streets nearer
them, like thin black threads; and when two threads
met in the same street there arose an angrier roar, and
a clash of weapons.

'They're fighting each other!' crowed Vansha in
astonishment.

'Aren't they bloody just!' Chuen's face was trans-
figured. 'That'll be your friend here! And a sleepless
night of rumours about clan clashes and massacres,
patrols charging everywhere – there'll be clans hot
for each other's blood, now! And all the better for us!
See there!'

Browner threads were filling streets higher up
the town now, brown shot with little points of flame;

and where they passed, fires sprang up, and manic howls. Alya looked up to the palace. The unrest was still half the town away, but the rumour of it was rising, and the guards there were evidently peering around anxiously.

'Shouldn't we go now?' demanded Vansha. 'Enough'll be happening by the time we get near! We don't want to find the streets blocked.'

'We'd go by the rooftops,' grinned Alya. But he too was growing impatient. 'You're right, though. No fighting unless we have to. Reach the palace and slip inside. Chuen, we must thank you and leave you!'

'Thank me?' Chuen grinned. 'Maybe you guess how much we owe to you, young sirs, and you, lady. I'm loath to let you go. But we must move soon ourselves! Our task's to clear the roads out of the town, when the Ekwesh start to barricade them, and you can wager that'll be happening soon! If you came with us—' He chuckled, the kindliest sound Alya had heard from him. 'But you won't, of course. That's not what heroes do. Still, if you find yourselves among us as we escape . . . well, feel free to come along!'

'As you escape . . .' grinned Alya. 'May you do so, headman, and find a better life indeed. Rysha, are you ready? I can get us to the palace, but we're going to need you once we're in.'

'You won't,' said Rysha stolidly. 'I'm not coming.'

Vansha gaped. '*What?* Why, you flyblown bitch, you'll come or—'

Alya silenced him with a lifted hand. 'Why not, Rysha? Are you scared?'

'I bloody well am,' she said; but evenly. 'Aren't you? But it's not that. I'm not going. I stay here, with the others. Fight or die, this is where I belong.'

Even Chuen looked startled. She laughed, harshly enough; and yet it sounded different from before. 'You ought to understand, boy. Remember? When I said I'd have broken my oath lightly enough –

if there'd ever been anywhere to go to. I didn't understand then, either. I thought I was looking for good places. I wasn't.'

She waved a hand out towards the town. '*This* is what I sought. Nobody can look down on me here. Nobody can crap all over me for what I've done or how I look, or who I choose to rub myself up against. You heard Chuen. Everyone here's done things as bad, like, or worse. I'm nothing special. I don't stink any worse. I'm not wearing fetters among you, any more. This is my level, this.'

'The gutter!' sneered Vansha.

'Lower,' she said, still evenly. 'To become a gutter, a sink for others' filth. And yet look at them! So low, yet they're still defiant, still hungering to rise. Well, that's the folk I belong with. If they can rise, then maybe so can I. Funny, isn't it? Asquan, he found what he needed here; and so have I.'

'But we seek what we need, Rysha!' protested Alya. 'And you did swear to help us to the end, didn't you?'

Rysha's lined face twisted. 'Some might say I have, already. You've seen your ladylove, and one way or another, the end is here. Yet I do mean to help.'

'How? We need your craft!'

'I don't *have* any craft, boy. Not as you have, anyhow. Not within. See this!' And she unknotted the dark rag from her neck, loosing a stray curl of her matted hair. 'Look close – aye, closer, I won't bite!' She rolled something in her fingers, freeing it gradually.

'A bit of twig?' exclaimed Alya, puzzled. It looked old and dry and half decayed, though it gleamed with grease from her hair.

She smirked. 'Even a twig may stem from a great forest! The one that once carpeted the land before the Ice came, they say. Tall trees, that cast long shadows, maybe far beneath where we stand now; and within them dwelt the Lord of the Forest, that men once called Inch'an, or Ljyest in your tongue, or Tapiau. Quite a scholard, aren't I? But those names, they were handed down in my family. Some ancestor of mine once served that Lord a good turn, somehow. I don't know how; all the stories sounded made up, to me. But he got given a gift that the Forest's said to give, in tales; a talisman. No more than a branch, but within it . . . shadow. The deepest night in the darkest dell, that never sun could pierce; and bearing it he could pass unseen, and shape sights within it to his will. My line kept that branch, though it was broken, divided, lessened in power; and though fate and the Ice ground us down, yet always we survived, because of the darkness in our hand.'

She shrugged. 'Much good it did us, at the end! There might be other fragments; but I've no living kin I know of, or care to. My father was the last, who whored me out each night to feed his drinking. I took this from him, and he died. Nobody ever took it from me, not though they stripped and raped me. They thought it just one more scrap of dirt. And so it was, and it crumbles fast. It deserves a better fortune at the last; and for that I give it you! I guess you'd suit the Giver well enough. Bind it in your hair as I did, and where there's shadow to build on it'll follow your will. Shapes – they're harder, need time. Best left.'

Alya rolled the little fragment in his fingers. It smelt of her stale hair. 'A great gift, Rysha, and I thank you. But it could save your life in all this! I cannot take it.'

'It's given,' said the woman curtly. 'Me, now, I'll skulk in shadow no more. Neither another's shadow nor another's light. What I have, I'll make for myself.'

Vansha shook his head, uncomprehending. Alya saw what he had always seen, the bleak lined face, the hard hands that had stolen sleeping lives – more, he guessed, than any would ever know. But he caught those hands in his own, nonetheless. 'Rysha, I hope you do! As much as anything I hope for myself.'

'Then you're a fool; but I knew that. A shame I'll not set eyes on this poppet of yours, to see if she were worth the trouble; but then I might've got jealous. Now get off with you. And give her a good one for me!'

Vansha looked at her sourly, but Alya chuckled with the rest. Chuen boosted him out over the rim of the gully on to the stony slope, and as he pulled Vansha after him, he saw them wave briefly, before ducking down once again. And that was the last he ever saw of Rysha the murderess, and of Chuen the headman; and whether they perished like so many amid the tumult of that day, or escaped at last into whatever semblance of freedom and a new life the outer lands could offer, no Chronicles or legends record.

Vansha did not look back. 'Give her one . . . The dirty bitch! How you could laugh, I don't know. Glad to be shot of her fell company, at long last!'

Alya was fastening the twig among his hair. 'She's an odd creature. But if half she says of her past is true, that's no surprise. Or she may simply have made it up to explain the kind of creature she is.'

Vansha looked askance at him. 'What's this? The wise Seer knows all?'

'Tries to, maybe; since I've begun to look into other minds. It needn't excuse anything. Those Ekwesh last night – pure evil, whatever one could understand. Whatever was decent there once, it's withered or been leached away. You can do that with folk, I guess. But not with her. At least, not now.'

Vansha was silent awhile, as they slipped and slithered from boulder to boulder, keeping an eye on the town and the growing uproar. 'And Savi? What do you understand about her?'

'I haven't seen her for more than an instant! And that in visions. We couldn't speak, not in words.'

'You know what I mean!' exclaimed Vansha

fiercely. 'She and this weird Ice-witch . . . Would Savi, of all people . . .'

Alya fought down his ill-formed concern. 'How would I know? But I know her, and you do too. I trust her heart!'

'She has a good heart,' said Vansha; and then, moodily, 'Too good. She's just a child. She doesn't know what she's doing, yet.'

'If that was ever true—' Alya skidded on the stones, and had to fight for balance. 'Do you think it will be now? After what she's been through?'

Vansha's voice tautened with anger. 'Yes! I keep on thinking about that. What she must have seen and felt . . . And we couldn't do a thing to shield her! Not one louse-ridden thing!'

'Unless we'd somehow rescued her right at the start. Just the two of us.'

Vansha sighed. 'If I'd known then what I know about us now, you and I, I might just have ventured it. No; I suppose we'd all have died, nonetheless. But Savi! If they've hurt her, changed her . . .' His hand went to his sword.

'We'll find out. Maybe she can be healed, if hurt. Changed back.'

Vansha nodded. 'Maybe, yes. That's true. With time. The sooner we start, the better. Look there!'

They were down at rooftop level by now, with tall outcrops to shelter them, and they could look into the streets of the lower town. 'Like a river in spate!' exclaimed Vansha, awed.

'Or the salmon spawning!' breathed Alya.

And indeed it was like both, a rolling press of bodies that surged this way and that, and here and there exploded into frenzied fighting and death. There was no solid line of battle, only scattered groups striking against one another amid the throng. While the bands of Ekwesh held their disciplined shieldwall, the thralls piled up and died against it;

but they were hurled forward by weight of numbers, unable even to fall, crushed back against their slayers. Then sooner or later the shield wall would break, and the howling mob roll over them. Alya saw men torn apart by clusters of bare hands, and their ragged limbs hurled in the air and scattered every way, like chaff.

'If *that* spreads to the upper town—'

Vansha was up and running, drawing his sword, and Alya at his heels. Then, they would never get through. Safe or not, their one chance was now.

As they clattered down into the first small side-streets of the upper town, they found them almost empty, save for drifting clouds of smoke. Guards had left their posts, called or fled, and only a few thralls were wandering about uncertainly. At the sight of two apparent Ekwesh running with drawn swords, they wisely fled. Alya slowed a little, and Vansha nodded. There might be more running, soon; and it was as well not to rush too sharply around corners.

They confirmed that almost at once. There were Ekwesh there, a dozen or so of them with draught-oxen hauling one of the great war-machines into position, to fire down the straight slope of the street into the town. They rounded on the newcomers, then relaxed as they saw armour of their own kind. Alya pushed past them with a growl, and they made way for what looked like a chieftain; but one of them shouted something at Vansha as he passed, and when he made no answer, seized his arm. Vansha was about to cut him down. But Alya, with a roar of anger, smacked the warrior across the face so hard he spun around and fell in the mire, then grabbed Vansha, kicked him and hurried him on as if on some urgent errand, ignoring the others.

'That's how they run things here!' he whispered to Vansha, who did not seem too grateful.

'Really had to boot me in the arse, did you?'

'Sorry. In character. But that's how we'll play it next time. No fighting unless we have to.'

'Something tells me that won't be long!'

Vansha was right, for as they crossed the slimy stones around the base of one of the stark towers, they ran straight into a running fight, a press of warriors driving back a much larger mass of thralls, who had no weapons but the stones they tore from the ground. The fight swirled around them before they could react, and there was no way past either side; so they turned and struck at the startled Ekwesh. They were not warriors for nothing; they rounded on the newcomers almost as quickly, but Alya felled two of them with great slashing blows, Vansha cut the arm from another, and then the thralls were at the gap and swarming over them. In minutes some twenty warriors lay dead on the street, and the slaves were snatching up their arms.

'We're with Chuen!' panted Vansha, as they showed signs of turning on him in the frenzy of revolt. He brandished his bloody sword. 'Are you with us? *To the palace!*'

The cheer was more like a maniac's howl, but they followed. The next band of Ekwesh, a patrol of six, took one look at the mob and ran. Some thralls streamed after them, beyond recall, but enough remained to clear their way, and others, seeing a force with some purpose, fell in with them, in swiftly growing numbers.

'This is a howling mob!' gasped Alya as they ran. 'Not an army!'

'They'll serve!' panted Vansha.

'But I wanted to slip into the palace!'

'There'll still be guards! See!'

There were guards, indeed, though no more than usual; at their stations, or pacing with an anxious air about the almost deserted square. There was no holding back the mob, though. At the mere sight of their armour, the maddened thralls streamed across the cobbles of the square and up the stairs, and poured out on to the white marble court with appalling speed. The guards were taken by surprise. One, at the far station, ran to wind his horn, but fell under a pelting rain of stones. A pitched battle broke out, and Alya slapped Vansha's shoulder and pointed. A group of women who had been standing on the steps were trying to reach the palace, and in danger of being cut off. Brandishing his sword, he began working around to them, with Vansha following. Out of the mêlée a thrall ran at them with a captured spear, but Vansha seized the shaft and knocked the wielder spinning, while Alya ushered the frightened women towards the huge palace doors. They were closing swiftly, but Alya hurled himself into the gap and forced them back, while Vansha chivvied the shrieking women inside. Then they ducked after them, and slammed the doors back against their own crazed allies.

The great valves closed with a dull boom that echoed massively in the building; so did the rattle and clank of the huge bars that frightened servants thrust home. Alya and Vansha fell back against the doors, panting, hardly feeling the blows that rained against the metal outside. They were inside. It was as simple as that; and as daunting. For never in their lives had either young man been inside such a place as this; and cunning and subtle minds had shaped it to impress even the strongest of mere men.

Tall antechamber; outreaching hall; walls painted and hung; column after column blazing with shifting light, filling the air with jewelled flashes; vast arching roof and soaring dome with patterns of mighty stars, Alya and Vansha saw it all as Savi had done, but with different eyes. Alya had looked not only upon the majestic mountain-walls of the Ice, but into the minds of its brutal followers; and both had

fought the guardian dead that stood fearful sentinel at
its gates.

They knew how little use the Ice had for such
display as this, for the sweet scents of the air and the
faint song of music, save to show how fully it understood the aspirations of men, and how bitterly it
scorned them. Any man, any woman might long to
dwell in such a vision of grace and majesty, to have
such servants scurrying to serve them, to command
the forces that governed the shifting hues of the
columns and the powers unguessed-at that Alya
sensed lurking here. It had been created for that
purpose; to house regal humanity, or something in
its guise, in the greatest height of luxury and dignity –
but also to mock it.

Awesome as this was, against the infinitely wider
dome of the wintry sky, jewelled with the stars, hung
with the rippling curtains of the Northlights and the
fierce strong music of the winds; against the glaciers
it covered, with their draperies of crystalline snow
and their luminescent caverns; against an immortal
beauty, this whole vast place seemed cheap and
foolish, hardly distinguishable from the meanest
hut or barrack vomited out by the town below.
And they themselves, their purpose and all they cared
about, seemed for that moment as mean.

But Alya became aware that the servants and the
few other warriors within the antechamber were
beginning to look at them curiously. He drew himself
upright, slapped his sword back and launched a glare
of such searing contempt that they turned hastily
away. He snapped his fingers, as he had seen the
chieftains do to their escort, and Vansha caught his
meaning glance, and came to his side. Together they
strode off, as men who have immediate purpose, and
no man sought to stop them.

'I hope you know where you're going!' mouthed
Vansha.

'I do,' said Alya grimly. 'And I know it won't all be that easy. There are sentinels, there will be more. And there's worse, a lot worse! And too much light. If we don't move swiftly, they'll be after us.'

Whether from Savi's mind or another, he had a clear picture of this place, and the ways he might take. Rooms surrounded it, corridors and tunnels pervaded it like great bloodless veins, quarters for servants, reserves of armouries and stores, cellars of food and fine wines, all that the denizen of this place might live as human lords did. To understand them, and in doing so to overcome them. To overawe any that came here, as some traitors must do, with the ultimate majesty and power of the Ice. To make its victory seem so certain that becoming its vassal or spy would seem the only sensible course.

It probably was, Alya thought; but sense alone had its limitations. Better to blaze like a torch, sometimes, than waste whatever was left, trying to endure the unendurable.

Along the halls they strode, and Alya ducked behind one of the great hangings, showing a city with towers crumbling before the pure white wall of an advancing glacier. There was a door hidden there, a plain servants' door that led to a stair, rough and unadorned, and at its foot, another, heavier door. They paused a moment, listening; and then Alya pulled it open. The dimly lit passage was open; but from a small room to one side a sentinel sprang to his feet with levelled spear, and challenged. Vansha was prepared; he lunged through and parried the spearblow. In the open, with surprise on his side, he would have struck the man down at once; but in the passage his blow scarred the wall, the spear lunged again, and they collided, swaying, and sprang apart, hacking at one another with short blows. This was no time for fair fight; Alya, cursing the noise and the delay, would have joined in, but he could not get through the door as the two swayed back and forth.

Then suddenly Vansha was hurled back, pinned against the wall by the spearblade stabbing between left breast and swordarm, and the guard grabbed quickly for the dagger at his belt. But Vansha threw his sword from left hand to right, and thrust. The guard choked horribly on a cry, and fell on the flagstones.

'If he'd only thought to shout, we'd have been in real trouble!' said Vansha bitterly, detaching the spearblade from his shirt.

'You're not hurt?' demanded Alya, heaving the body back into the guardroom, leaving a bloody smear on the flagstones.

'Just a scrape. My breastplate took most of the blow – see, it's nicked. Stronger than it looks, this stiff leather. But we can't keep on doing this! A mercy nobody's heard!'

Footsteps sounded along the passage that crossed this one, some distance away. 'Maybe they did!' Alya hesitated, looking along the shadowy ceiling. 'Would this have been dark enough for Rysha?'

Vansha shrugged. 'Try it!'

Alya creased up his face with the effort to think of darkness. 'Nothing's happening!'

'Maybe if you spread your arms as she did – imagine yourself like a tree, casting a vast . . .'

Blackness flooded the corridor with shocking suddenness.

'Like that!' agreed Vansha drily. 'Only maybe so we can see just . . . ah. Better. But tread carefully!'

The footsteps were drawing nearer, and they pressed back against the wall. Two men who looked like servants came by, talking animatedly about something, the riots probably; they spared the merest glance down the shadowed turning, and did not stop. Their footsteps disappeared down the other arm of the passage, and Vansha grinned with relief.

'Better than leaving a trail of bodies!' Alya whispered back, equally relieved.

'Right. Stir up the whole place! Shall we go now?'

Alya nodded, and they padded swiftly down the passage and along it, the way the servants had come. They moved swiftly now, for the way was clear in his mind, and so was the urgency. Small slotted windows gave the passages a meagre light, but they were never short of deep shadows for concealment when others came by. These were mostly servants, lowly ones by their aspect, wretches Alya was glad he need not harm. Now and again there were tense moments, as when Ekwesh warriors came striding through; and he wondered how long it would be before someone found the guard's body. He seemed to remember that they kept long watches; but he could not entirely trust the memories he had acquired. The longer he kept them, the more they blended with his own fancy, and became indistinct. Certainly it was taking too long to reach their goal.

'It's got to be a roundabout route, to stay in shadow!' he hissed to Vansha.

'Has it? It's still taking too long! The riots'll be all around here soon, as it is! And you can wager the Ice will let loose some nasty backlash!'

Alya bit his lip. 'You're right. We'll have to come up, try a run for it. If there's some shadowy corridor . . .'

'Even if there isn't! What good'll it do, if the place is roused against us? We've been twenty minutes where we should have been ten!'

'Along here, then!' said Alya. 'That door there, and up – right up, to the uppermost storey. And be ready for trouble!'

But to their wonder, though the gallery they emerged into had great windows in its walls, they were hung about with heavy draperies, and though they sent bright shafts across the floor, they left all the rest in deeper gloom. When they tiptoed over to one, they found themselves looking out over the square. The assault had been beaten back, evidently, and the square was empty of all save guards once more; but in the town the smoke and affray were drawing nearer. 'Now we've a chance!' grated Vansha. 'Along there, right to the end, through the smaller corridor and around – that right?'

'Yes. A side door, to a side chamber of some kind. Then through the door opposite. If . . . she's still there . . . and likely she will be . . . The room has windows.'

Vansha nodded, and visibly swallowed. Alya felt the same, no fire in him ready to cope with this. But there was nobody around, no sound at all, and no better time he could imagine. He touched Vansha's arm, and deepened the shadow a little; and with no word they stepped forward, for their mouths were growing too dry.

Stride upon stride, the gallery seemed endless, the sound of distant footsteps crossing and recrossing a nightmare. She . . . the other . . . she would know of the riots, of course; they would have woken her, told her. She would order them suppressed by the warriors, of course; and what then? Go back to sleep? Surely not. She would be out, up somewhere, giving angry orders . . . It was hard to imagine that in the face he had seen, so young, so strange and fair; as if she were born of living gold, not Ice. But she would surely be distracted; and that was their best chance to find Savi. She might well be still abed, here; and if not, some servant would know where she was.

Round into the corridor, and still nobody passing. No stream of orders, no messengers . . . it looked better and better. Until they were at the door, at last; with no reason even to hesitate. Vansha shot Alya one glittering glance, and he drew the darkness close about them both; then Vansha seized the strange latch, and flung the door wide.

What lay within was startling, a mass of racks and stuffs, a riot of confusing colours that swung and clung about them like a jungle of cool tendrils as they plunged through, unleashing fair but heavy scents. An opulent dressing room, and in it, dozing on a settle, a tall woman who sprang up at the sudden inrush of darkness, and opened her mouth to scream. But Vansha cuffed her flat on her back and hurled a heap of rich stuffs down on top of her, while Alya reached the inner door, strangely curved, listened one instant and kicked it open.

It opened in the base of a great pillar, on to a shining marble floor that reflected the dome above, clear as the sky. His onrush carried him half skidding across it even as he saw the dais, amid its swathes of spilled drapery. Sitting up suddenly from amongst it, black hair tangled about cream-golden breast and shoulders, her eyes wide in fear and wonder, was Savi herself.

But beside her, even as in his vision, another shape arose, taller than he had imagined and far, far more fair. Something too beautiful to be alive, surely a cunning carving of ivory and gold. Her skin was paler than Savi's, paler even than the swan-maiden's, like ice indeed, tinged only with the hint of blood beneath. And her eyes were of that piercing, eerie blue that he had seen in his vision, only still more luminous, jewels cut from the brightest winter sky. They glittered with life, and fierce awareness; and the shadow about him withered like a wintered plant. They fastened on him; first in contemptuous wrath and then in flaring astonishment, taking in his stance, his drawn sword, his evident purpose. And they widened with what, in some other, he might have taken for fear.

Wholly inhuman was the speed with which she

rose, graceless, feral, hungry as some predatory cat. In a flail of long limbs she bounded out of the great bed, spinning Savi aside, and landed on her feet before him, still as the statue she once more seemed. She was naked, she was fair beyond his dreams, yet in Alya as he looked on her there was nothing of desire.

He could not move. Terror grasped him, at a level his mind could not touch, profounder and more primal even than the ancestral chill at the predator's gaze. This was the fear that had filled the shadows beyond the caves, stalking the night beyond the failing fire, rising from the raging ocean depths. That fair face was the merest mask over that terror's deepest sources. It was every hostile purpose with which men filled cruel nature, every devouring spirit lurking in the shadow of every rock or drowning pool that faced him now, that mocked him in those chilly eyes, that worked bubbling slaver from those delicate lips. That extended a long arm to him, the skin shivering faintly, like a beast's, the index finger with its tapered claw of a nail stretched out as if to touch him lightly, delicately, the playful scratch of a pet. And though the fires seemed ready to burst out through his skin, they were of no use to him. He could not move.

'*No!*' cried Savi, from the bed's end where she had fallen. The same horror dwelt in her voice, and yet differently. '*No! You must not! This is he, Louhi! You must not! For my sake!*'

The head jerked back, tossing the ash-gold hair wildly. The face contorted as if in pain, the gasping breath rolled over him like the foretaste of evening snow. The hand wavered, came no further, quivering, as if gripped by conflicting fetters.

'You said you'd learned!' said Savi quickly, stumbling over her words; and Alya thought dazedly how sweet her voice sounded. 'You begged me to show you love. You said I had. Will you repay me so?'

The glittering gaze left him an instant, and his body shook with sudden release. Then it swung back.

'If you really did learn,' insisted Savi, 'if you really do know – then you know what I feel, also. For him; and for you. Both real; both you will destroy. Can you hurt me so, Louhi? Knowing that? Can you do that to feelings like your own? And only to hurt yourself, worse than you are hurt now?'

There was a flicker in those blue eyes, like spring waters churning beneath a frozen river.

'Need love be so selfish? Is mine?'

The arm did not move. And in that instant Vansha pushed past Alya and ran his sword straight through the woman's panting body.

She did not scream; she convulsed in breathless agony. He jerked the blade free and struck again, with ferocious strength, hurling her back against the bed; and it was Savi who screamed, once more.

'*No! Not that! You don't understand! No!*'

Vansha, snarling like a wolf, snatched free the blade once again. Alya grabbed his arm, but not in time to stop him ramming it down once more through Louhi's body. Alya hurled him back then, flat on the floor, and the sword pulled free in a fountain of bright blood. In her agony the golden woman rolled on the bed, as Savi staggered to her feet, crying out wordlessly. As if in answer the woman raised her head, though blood spilled through the three great wounds across her body, and screamed. But though there was rage in that cry, and scarifying agony, they only edged its meaning.

Vansha, scrambling up, snatched up his sword and aimed a hacking blow at her neck; but it clanged hard against Alya's sword, with a spray of sparks, and struck away harmlessly into the bed.

'*Why not?*' yelled Vansha, spraying spittle. '*Why not?*'

'Because Savi says not to. Get your clothes, Savi!'

She was already half into them, weeping, grabbing her boots, seizing Alya by the arm. 'Come on! *Come on!* We've got to go!'

'We're going!' snapped Alya, turning towards the great doors at the end, the fastest way now.

'*No!* Bar them, quickly! You heard her! She's summoned them!'

'Summoned who?' demanded Vansha, tugging at her other arm.

'The *Morghannen*! The Choosers of the Slain!'

'Hella!' breathed Alya. 'Lock them, Vansha! Then back the way we came!'

Vansha spun the wheel that barred the doors, then ran back to them as Savi, hopping on one foot, crammed on her second boot. Alya led her to the door; but she lingered an instant, staring in horror at the form on the blood-drenched bed, only twitching feebly now. Vansha, catching them up, more or less tore her away and hurled her through the door, slamming it behind him. In the chamber beyond she snatched a hooded coat of furs from a rack, then let herself be bundled out into the corridor. Behind them, suddenly, the great doors resounded like huge gongs, as some great weight smashed against them. They slammed the smaller door and ran.

Savi tore her arm free and flailed at Vansha. 'Why did you do it? *Why?*'

'Do you know what she was?' he snarled back, half choking. 'Do you know what we've *been* through, you stupid – ungrateful little—'

'What she *is*! You don't understand! You didn't wait to! That wasn't all of her! She's still here! She's all around us!'

Behind them the doors rang once more. Then there came a fearful rending crash, a sound of stone splintering, and the floor seemed to leap beneath them under the impact of the falling doors.

'Stop!' wheezed Alya, as they reached the corner;

and drawing breath, he stretched out his arms and concentrated. Shadow, deep shadow, swirled about them like a cloak, so dense they could hardly see out. Barely in time; for from somewhere within there came a high shrilling cry, full of wrath and hatred. The sound shivered through the palace as if it were thin glass, setting their teeth on edge, seething in their very bones, a summons to slaying and to war.

Ironshod feet came booming down the gallery as Alya and the others shrank, dazed and half deafened, into the shadows of the draperies. The sentinels streamed unseeing past that deeper darkness, intent only on obeying the fearful call. Others came running as the escapers sidled through the gallery, but though it took them long, agonised minutes, struggling to stifle their anguished breathing, the three of them reached the door and the stair at last.

Down it they clattered, at a speed that made shadow too dangerous, Savi weeping still and cursing, and out into the passages they had come by. But too fast; for even as they stopped to let Alya fling the shadow-mantle across them once again, there came harsh shouts, and the clatter of ironshod sandals on the flagstones. Alya swore. 'Back to the stair! We'll have to find a way out through the cellars!'

'They'll be on us before then!' snapped Vansha, hefting his fouled sword.

'Not if we meet them!'

The door slammed shut behind them. But the warriors bayed like packhounds sighting their quarry, flung it back and dashed heedlessly out on to the stair.

Darkness seemed to boil around them, blackness impenetrable, laden with the sighing weight of infinite trees. Within it swords flashed, and the first two guards died on the stairhead; those behind stumbled over them, and were cut down in their turn, blocking the stairwell with bodies. The others saw the dark-

ness seethe up at them, like an eager quicksand, and
stumbled back, but not all fast enough. The survivors
reached the door and slammed it; and the fugitives
went cantering away down into the depths. Savi held
a short sword now.

At the foot Alya had to stop, clutching his head.
He had held this whole place in his mind, but it was
growing fainter and more confused now. 'There's
only one way out I can think of,' he said slowly. 'One
that wouldn't be heavily guarded . . .'

And then it all came home to him, and he forgot
all else. Turning, he seized her in his arms. '*Savi!*'

But she was stiff, unresponsive. 'I don't understand . . .' she breathed. 'Alya – is it truly . . . How
could you . . .'

'Move, girl!' exploded Vansha. 'Or shall we die of
explanations?'

Alya stumbled heavily in the shadows. The place
was almost lightless, a mass of dark low vaulting and
uneven earth floors beneath, with doors and windows filled by strange long-corroded bars that were
not needed to keep anything from anything, and were
as often as not open from some other way. Alya
realised some older building had stood here, evidently serving as the palace's foundation; but why
would the Ice have built such a place?

It was only when Vansha tripped over a piece of
fallen masonry with graven markings that they understood. Beautifully graven, in a flowing, cursive style;
yet still unmistakably akin to the markings on his
sword, far closer even than Oshur's inscription. 'The
elder days,' breathed Alya. 'The cities of old! There
must have been one here, before the Ice and its
minions rolled over it; and for all their pride and
hatred, they've still built on its foundations! It's endured, to greet free men once again!'

'Very poetic!' said Vansha, his fine features twisting as he rubbed his agonised shin. 'It'll do well in the

ballads. But if the place would kindly show us the way out again, I'd be deeply obliged!'

'Savi?' enquired Alya. 'Do you know anything . . .'

'I've never been down here!' she said, still sharply.

'Then this is our only way! Ahead here, and down, into some kind of tunnel – if the door will open, after all this time.'

But though rusty, the door was solid iron still, much newer than the walls; and though the hinges creaked and complained, they could still force it open without too much effort. The stench that billowed up the cramped little stair made them wish they had not.

'The cesspools!' groaned Vansha, through his bunched-up cloak. 'Or drains, those sewer things Asquan talked about! No wonder they don't guard it!'

'No wonder!' agreed Alya. 'Can we even breathe the air down there?'

'We'd better try!' said Savi, in cold contempt. 'After what you've done—'

'What I did!' answered Vansha, dangerously calm. 'What had to be done!'

'I didn't much like it either, Savi,' said Alya, pulling the door to behind them. 'But she had to be stopped, or—'

'She could have destroyed you, yes! But she held her hand! She listened to me!'

'Because she loved you, I guess?' sneered Vansha.

'*Yes!*'

He shoved her ahead of him, stumbling down the stairs. 'Well, thank you for that, I suppose! But I wouldn't have trusted her another second. Chuen was right!' He laughed, with deliberate malice. 'How was it he put it? If she can shaft, she can bleed?'

Savi tried to turn and hit out at him, but the stair was too narrow. Alya hissed at the pair of them to be silent; there might be guards below. Certainly things were still afoot above, for noises filtered down to

them – distant but clear, the wash and roar of an
angry mob, breaking like a high sea against the object
of its hatred.

'We must be out from underneath the palace
now!' he exclaimed. 'That's the thralls going strong,
by the sound of it!'

Vansha laughed. 'Give 'em the fist, Chuen!'

Alya could not help chuckling. 'And Rysha! And
Asquan, and Kalkan, and – all of you . . .' He felt
suddenly, horribly weary, as if his flesh hung from his
bones, and his mind and spirit sank; as if all he had
longed for had turned to ashes, a triumph that was no
triumph.

A hand touched his arm. 'Those names? Are they
friends, who helped you?'

'Who died to help me, some of them. Maybe all!
To help you.'

She caught her breath, and let her hand fall. 'I'm
sorry. So sorry! I should have . . . I shouldn't – But if
you can only understand . . .'

The sound stopped her short, far closer than the
sounds of riot, echoing down the corridors behind
them. Another cry, so like the one that had heralded
the fall of the doors that they instinctively shrank
back, limbs taut, hair bristling, afraid something else
would come crashing down about them.

'*Down!*' cried Alya, and they spilled down the
stair and out, guards or no guards. But there were
none; nor was there the stream of sewage Alya half
expected, but instead a wide, echoing emptiness
with just a glimmer of light. It showed them, as their
eyes grew accustomed, a wide dry cavern in the living
rock, natural or very roughhewn. Its ceiling arched
high over their heads, as high as the palace, it seemed;
and its flat dry floor was a steep slope. Away to their
right hand it curved down into depths and blackness;
but to the left it rose. The air was warm, surprisingly
so. It seemed to throb with a great soundless pulse, as

if huge forces were stirring down there in the dark. He thought of the earthfires, of a rising fountain of molten rock, and shuddered.

Vansha gagged. 'What's this? They say the earth-fires give off foul gases – deadly, often enough!'

Alya wanted to spit the foulness from his mouth. 'Maybe. I'd say they're worse to the downward side, as you'd expect. But we can still breathe, more or less. And uphill the light seems stronger, don't you think?'

'Then what's holding us here?' stormed Vansha impatiently.

The cry seemed to answer him, longer and louder than before. At that shrieking, furious summons Savi clenched her hands in her hair and screamed aloud as if in answer, though over that reverberating yell she could scarcely have been heard. And it was not that far off.

'Come, girl!' snapped Vansha; and seizing her arms, though she did not resist, they bore her up the slope of the tunnel, gasping and choking as they went. But the sounds from below overtook them – a slow, grinding groan of tormented metal, loud enough to set the teeth on edge, punctuated with clanks and scraping rattles.

'Like some kind of huge device . . .' began Alya. Then they all stumbled and choked as a great hot waft of sulphurous stench and stink rolled over them, and the earth shook again, more violently than before.

'She's unleashing the earthfires!' wheezed Vansha.

'No!' exclaimed Savi. 'They're Ilmarinen's do-main, her foe! She only controls them here at the surface! I don't know—'

A second, stronger blast rolled over them, still more mephitic, and a vast moaning rumble shivered through the enclosed air. That was warning enough for Alya; but they were already too far from the stair. 'Back against the wall!' he cried, and, covering

their noses and mouths, they stumbled into the
grudging shelter of a tall splintered buttress of raw
rock, barely in time.

The vast billow of smoke and dust came rolling
up from the depths, filling the tunnel from wall to
wall, and to the height of its arching roof. Small stones
were whipped up in it, fragments fell from above, and
across its turbulent heart ran flickers of lancing blue
light, like threaded lightning. Little banners of flame
flared up and vanished ahead of its rumbling majesty,
as pockets of cave-gas ignited. It was as if they stood
in the vent of a fire-mountain.

Vansha cried out, and flung his cloak across his
face. Savi yelled, and hid her face in Alya's arm; but he
stood amazed and appalled as the waft of heat and
stench came rolling and rattling over them in a great
slow pulse. It was no volcano. The cloud reeked like
the tunnel, beneath the suffocating sulphur a sickly,
musky stench pervaded with the rotting of flesh and
greasy burning, with ammonia, dung and decay. And
within its billows, beneath the roof, massive shadows
churned, dark and inchoate, rolling with the slow
pulse of the air.

Within the smoke, fire spurted suddenly, and
above it a pair of giant glittering rubies awoke, and
another; and all along the walls the gases flamed out
in a crackling torrent. By that light they saw, and
doubted their sight. For the cloud appeared alive with
serpents, vast black worm-like forms that rolled and
writhed and churned amid the dust and smoke,
surfacing and submerging as if it were a pool they
swam in.

That in itself was terror enough, as the smoke
surged about them like a subterranean storm. But the
sight at its heart filled them with still greater horror
and awe. For within the cloud, spanning the massive
tunnel from wall to wall, there beat a single colossal
pair of wings.

They were not serpents that filled the cloud, they were not beasts at all. They were one single, massively serpentine body and tail, borne up by vast tattered wings. And set upon that body three long and snaking necks, all collared with sombre iron; three huge reptilian heads that darted this way and that, the red gems their eyes, set glittering by the brief gouts of flame they spewed from their long jaws, as lesser beasts slaver in eagerness.

Vast and incredible beyond all they had seen on their wanderings save the Ice itself, the monstrous creature bore down upon them. They might have been spied as they cowered there, for Alya was too stunned to bring the shadow about them. And all three cried out in terror as a gout of oily fire spattered the wall above and a whiplash tail's arrowed tip smashed splinters from the arch. But the monster was too intent upon its summons to bother with small specks of shivering life down here in the dark. It swept by them, heedless, on an ear-splitting crack of its vast tattered wings as they met at the bottom of their stroke, a bellowing, blasting vision of limbs and claws and scales, all scored and ragged, age-dulled, filth-choked, scarred and ulcerated; and yet horribly, brutally powerful. It had been summoned from its fitful sleep for the first time in a long age; and eager for the long-remembered taste of terror and destruction, it sped to answer the call.

In the face of fear Vansha cried out the name they all knew from childhood tales. '*Tugarin! Tugarin son of Zamai! The dragon of old is loosed!*'

How long that vast beast had lain there cannot be said, laired beneath the Ice, the roots of the palace and the mighty buildings that had stood in its place long before, which he, or his hardly less terrible sire, may well have helped to level. Their kind was bred by the Ice for its service, in an age when its ruling minds sought to torment and contort the stuff of the life itself they despised, to shape it to their own destructive ends, and many tales tell of beasts of terrible form and aspect; but none half so great, or so grotesque, as this greatest relic. None so ghastly; none so misused.

To the noise and disorder above, to the memories perhaps of ancient battles and savageries renewed that were its only joy, flew that distorted creature, and was gone. The blast of its passing tore them from their feet and bowled them about the tunnel. An earth-shaking, rumbling bellow shivered the echoes around them.

'So, it was no legend!' panted Vansha, raising himself on skinned elbows. His voice was thick with the anger that follows deep terror.

As one they looked upwards, towards the light. 'That thing . . .' Alya shook his head in horror. 'They'll be wiped out! They can't stand against it, they're not expecting it!'

'And I wouldn't give much for our chance of escape!' agreed Vansha sombrely. 'How can such a thing *be*?'

'As well ask how it can fly!' grunted Alya, helping Savi to her feet. 'I . . . have learned something of flight. With that weight . . . No. Not possible, even with such vast strength. There are other powers at work in that thing.'

'As there are in you,' said Vansha softly, and Savi looked at him, startled.

'What does he mean?'

Alya threw up his hands in defeat. 'No time to tell you now. We've got to get out while we may!'

There was no disputing that. They stumbled on, towards the light. Pale day glinted on the tunnel wall now, and the air was suddenly stronger and fresher and colder against the sullen stenches from below. In minutes they rounded the last bend, and found the tunnel mouth a wide band of hard blue sky before them. But it was tainted by many plumes and billows of smoke, and the air was heavy with burning, and alive with screams and shouting; and above it all, shaking the air, the growling, gloating bellow of the beast.

The tunnel had brought them out on the higher slopes above the middle of the town, concealed from it by a crevice half covered by the Ice. Under its jagged roof they scrambled hastily down, but despite their unease, when they came to the crevice's end they stopped stock-still, rooted in horror.

The dragon Tugarin stood high in the sky, wings beating with leisurely strength, fanning the smokes, watching the town below as a kestrel hovers over its prey. Thus far removed, it seemed almost a beautiful thing in its sinuous strength and fluidity, its black scales iridescent in the young day. But even as they saw, it stooped upon the lower end of the town, and the road they'd entered by, where many were trying to escape. Across it the creature swept, trailing blasts of flame from its jaws, that filled the narrow streets; and the shrieks that arose were ghastly.

There was no need to see what was happening. Its tail smashed rooftops down into the inferno, and its call rumbled like malevolent laughter as it beat slowly back up into the sky, to seek another gathering worth its attention.

Alya looked about him in desperation. 'We've no way out! We can't get up this wall, it's too steep! And there's no way out by the roads, with that thing watching. And the Stair . . . no. Savi, how did they bring you here?'

'Across the Ice, I think!' She pointed to the paths on the far slope. 'By there. That looks high, but it's just an outcrop of the Ice; it slopes down to another vale on the far side, more open, with a road of sorts. That was the way!'

Vansha nodded. 'That's one of the roads Chuen's men were supposed to keep open! But against *that* . . .'

'Yes. If anyone does get out on to the Ice, with no cover, it'll be like minnows to a fish-eagle! Look at it, frying thralls and Ekwesh alike! The headmen made no plans against that!'

Vansha snorted. 'What d'you think they could have done?'

And that set a thought in Alya, cold and thrilling, like a trickle from the sunwarmed fringe of the Ice. 'Maybe there is something . . . Savi, this could be dangerous, best you wait here!'

'To do what? Wait until you don't come back? Do you think I want to stay here one minute longer than must be?'

'I thought . . .' Alya shook his head. 'I don't know what I thought! Come on, then!'

Together they ran and slid down the slope towards the town, crossing great fields of scree and loose boulders like the stripped bones of a predator's prey – half riding the rubble, half falling with it as it rattled away into the vale.

'Don't suppose you'd mind sharing this latest flash of insight?' Vansha flung back at him as they staggered free, dizzy and covered in dust, and made for the opening of a mean and miserable street just beyond.

'We need . . .' Alya stopped, and pointed. Down one of the side-streets men were running, men and women, evidently thralls, and hale enough for all their terror. But behind them came others with clothing scorched and blackened, hair singed, some terribly burned; and among them were one or two of the warriors, disarmed and bewildered, shrinking back as the vast shadow passed overhead once more.

Alya seized one man as he ran past them, short and burly. 'You! You're a headman, aren't you? Chuen said they were always the best fed!'

'Chuen?' panted the terrified man. 'I know you! You're the incomers!'

'That's right!' said Alya calmly. 'And maybe we can help you now, as you helped us. But we need strong men!'

The burly man knew how to take orders, and to give them. He grabbed folk as they passed, men and women, and Alya felt few qualms at the way he hauled them aside with fist and boot to quell their panic. They were evidently used to that, and there was no time to be gentle. 'Now!' said Alya. 'Back, fast as we can, before that thing strikes again!'

He looked to Savi as they ran, taking her arm, but she shook him free. 'I'm well! Better fed than you, by the look of you! It's as if you're burning yourself up!'

He could say nothing to that, but ran with the rest until they came to the main streets leading from the palace down into the town. Here they had seen the great war-machines set up; but the riots had rolled over them, and they stood smashed or smoking. At the cobbled opening of the palace square they found some that had been bodily tipped aside against one of the blank tower walls. Vansha snapped his fingers and cursed. 'Too late!'

'Maybe we can right them!' shouted Alya. 'And the others! Lower them if you can! Drag them around – and aim them at the palace! That's the way Tugarin's been coming down!'

Many cowered at the mere mention of the name; but they ran to the machines nonetheless, and began righting them. Three were whole enough; one had not even been loosed. Its great arms were still pulled back, its cord still held in the trigger mechanism, for the warrior who should have loosed it lay crushed beneath. The huge bolt, longer than a man, had been snapped, but others were strewn about. Carefully, fearing to jerk the trigger, they lowered the machine, and it sat drunkenly on three of its crude wheels; they were shoring the fourth with rubble when more thralls came running up shouting, hustling some battered and bewildered warriors before them. 'Men who can fire 'em!' laughed one grey-haired harridan. 'Just pissin' 'emselves eager to help – eh, lads?'

One of the Ekwesh had half his face scorched raw, and painful-looking burns on breast and arms. He had evidently torn off his armour to escape the flame; and he at least went to work with a will, showing them how to wind the windlasses back.

'Hurry!' yelled Vansha. 'I can see it up there! And they're watching us from the palace!'

Alya and Savi were the only ones who looked; the others cast their eyes down, and many wailed in fear. There were figures high on the balcony indeed, though he could not make them out; and above . . .

He almost choked on the words. 'Faster! Fast! Tugarin's coming!'

And indeed they all saw it, the long snaking line against the sky, stooping, shining black a moment against the clouds and then falling, wings flung back, coming around in a great sweep that would bring him out across the town in another fearful wash of flame and death. Perhaps he had marked their preparations; for the Chronicles record that dragons had minds and spirits far above the mere beast, though very little like those of men. But they were proud and malign, and he most of all, one mind in three. Legends spoke of Tugarin's pride and battle-lust of old, and now, in his colossal age, no doubt they drove him still. Most likely he thought little of the ragged band readying their weapons beneath, save as the next sacrifice of fire he could once again make to his icy masters.

Down he dropped, and at the last, passing the top of the little valley, he spread his wings with a boom like a great ship's sail filling; and the gale that streamed from their ragged edges blasted the snow on the glacier skywards, and triggered small crashing avalanches and chiming falls of ice. Up and over the palace he rushed, trailing the snow in a glittering cloud as he had trailed the ancient dust, and the clap of his wings was shattering. Compared to it the snap of two great arbalests was nothing; yet their long bolts sang skyward in his path.

With time and fortune they might have met their mark. The great beast took little heed of them, so greatly he despised those he fought. But poorly readied and roughly timed, it was small surprise they loosed too soon. One contemptuous twitch of that snaking flank, and the bolts sang away past into the void. The third device, though, did not fire. Its release cord snagged in the damaged trigger; but Alya threw aside the Ekwesh who battered at it, and severed cord and trigger and all beneath with one great blow of his sword.

The lever fell, the cord sang free. The bow loosed, with a kick that shook its base, and the bolt rose, far more steeply than it should have. The other shots were too early, this one too late. Into Tugarin's awesome shadow it flew; but no longer into the line of the body. It pierced only the leading edge of his vast wing. In open flight he would hardly have noticed the momentary sting, would have shaken it off and flown on. But he was diving low, over a town, at great speed. There was a tower in his path, and the wing, with the great bolt stuck like a pin deep into the muscle, drooped down against it.

The towertop shattered, the rough masonry exploded outwards and those below ran out screaming from the rain of stones. But Tugarin, Zamai's dread son, tumbled in the air, and with a sickening crack the vast wing broke. The great heads jerked back as one, the fire they had been about to unleash coughed out in spraying fireballs, and with a whistling, anguished cry the ancient beast whirled sidelong across the burning town, his tail futilely lashing the air, and thundered smoking down upon the far wall of the vale.

Right on to its rim he crashed, on to the overhanging curtain of the Ice; and its snowy mantle
billowed up and flashed into steam. From all the
town a great shout went up, a wordless cry that
came from thrall and warrior alike, and it found an
echo.

Under the impact of the massive body the thick
white rim along the cliff was flung apart and shattered. Black cracks went racing away all along the
glacier's margin, the length of the vale. Great shelves
and walls of ice sagged, shivered; and then with
weighty, menacing slowness, amid spurting plumes
of snow, they broke away and slid in tumbling,
rumbling ruin, cascading and crashing down into
the upper town.

On the slopes above, the living rock, weighed
down and worn away for glacial grinding centuries,
gleamed suddenly bare and blackly fresh in the morning sun. The earthfires, so long contained, seemed to
sense the change; for the earth shook its back like a
beast newly shed of its burden, and still more ice
went crashing away.

Vansha stared. 'That . . . that's our way out! As
you said, Savi, only a short way across the Ice – but
who needs a road now?'

'I don't think you're the first to see that!' she said
drily. '*Come on!*'

They had done little else but run, it seemed, and
even Alya's legs were leaden; but she was right.

Even as the echoes of that mighty fall faded, and
the crumbling ice still rattled down among the mean
buildings below, another very different roar went up.
Of exultation; of hope, the animal that sees the trap
open, the prisoner who sees sudden rays of light
where once were only bars. It was as if the whole
town stirred itself and ran, like a welling wave,
towards that miraculously open way.

But for all her urgings Savi suddenly stopped

amidst that gathering throng, and looked back to the palace, stealing one last glance as Alya thought. He seized her by the shoulders. 'No time for doubt! You come, or stay now, forever!'

She shook him free, while others streamed around them, buffeting them. 'Not doubt! I thought I saw—' There was a cluster of watchers on the palace roof.

Vansha shook his head. 'Sorry to disappoint you!' he said caustically. 'This one's tall, yes; but her hair's as black as yours or mine. Blue-robed, pale-skinned, proud in bearing – the one in the dressing room?'

'That's the princess! Happy enough where she is, poor goose, and good luck to her. But I thought – no, you're right, Alya! I'm coming. With you!'

'With—' he began, uncertain; but she pulled him into the streaming crowd, and Vansha with him.

Even those few seconds had all but choked the streets, and they found themselves jostled, pushed and finally borne almost unstoppably along by the milling, half-hysterical crowd. Bodies ragged and filthy collided with them, work-worn faces whirled about them like visions in a nightmare, and they clamped hand in hand painfully, in constant fear of being torn apart and lost. Many in the throng, though, recognised Alya and Vansha, by face or repute, and fought through to wring their hands and slap their backs till their shoulders ached. Like leaves in a torrent they were swept along the dismal lanes towards the town's far side, and the open slopes beyond.

Yet even as it loomed above them at last, they felt the crowd change around them, like a flood abruptly baulked. The flow halted suddenly, and though frantic shouts went up, the press still swelled and deepened under the impact of those behind. The flood became a milling crush, and Alya, alarmed, began forcing a way to one side. Even as he did so, the shouts became screams, gibbering cries of panic, and a thunderous, heart-shaking growl devoured all lesser sounds. The pressure released very suddenly, as the crowd swayed back; but in the same moment the black hillside blossomed suddenly into searing yellow light.

The screams were cut off sharply. Streaks of flame laced across the bare dark slope, and the soil hissed great clouds of steam. Another growl, and spurting fire lanced high overhead and rained down among the crowd in searing droplets that slew with the agonised shock of their touch.

The monster Tugarin still lived, despite his fall; and he was blocking their best line of escape.

CHAPTER 12
The End of Strength

BARELY in time, with ruthless shoving and kicking, dragging the others after him, Alya forced his way over to the edge of the street, and through a shutterless window. They found themselves in some kind of guard-post, half wrecked by an ice-slide.

'They'll never get past that monster!' panted Vansha. 'Look at them! Like squalling sheep for the slaughter!'

The crowd was a churning well of panic. People were still running up at the rear, unaware of what was happening, blocking any retreat; and even in the thick of the mass some were fighting others who sought to turn them back. Many of the buildings around them were catching fire, panicking them further, and sending clouds of greasy black smoke rolling overhead to blot out the sun.

'The *Morghannen* must still be guarding the palace!' gasped Savi. 'But when they realise what's happening—'

'The what?' demanded Vansha. 'Those screaming things?'

'The Choosers!' Savi told him coldly. 'Louhi's bodyguard – warriors of the Ice. They spur the Ekwesh to frenzy and worse, and they are slayers in themselves. You heard their cries.'

'She's right,' said Alya tersely. 'I know their minds. We can't face them.'

Vansha threw up his hands. 'So we've got to get out, somehow! Which we already know!'

Alya cast desperately about. 'The south road is blocked by fire now, even if we could reach it. And the Dead Stair – even if we could risk the rapids, we would not face what would await us there, not again. The palace guards any northward way. And the far slope's too steep.'

'Then this is our one road!' said Vansha grimly. A rumbling roar shook down stones from the walls, and they all flinched instinctively. 'This smoke pall – could you not make that bitch's talisman work beneath it? Would the shadows be strong enough to sneak past that thing?'

Alya stared. 'I don't know! The flames give so much light . . . but we won't know till we try.'

He led them through the shattered hovel, clambering over scattered weapons and other debris, across rough stone and half-rotten timbers, and the masses of shattered ice. Flame had passed over it, so that the face of the fall was molten and slick, but already freezing again as the beast turned its fires elsewhere. The door was under the rubble, but they could just reach the remains of a narrow window on what had been the second storey. They scrambled up to it; but as Alya looked through, he ducked back in sheer fright.

'*Powers!* We're right on top of it!'

They peered tentatively out.

The old road had wound beneath this window; and whatever had stood on its far side was obliterated now by the icefalls. And by the dragon.

In the open space before them it lay, sprawled half on its side among the ruins of the hillside it had brought down, blocking all the wide ground between hill and town. Even in the tunnel they had not truly realised its vastness, there and gone in that rushing moment.

'Remember that dragon in Volmur's procession?' whispered Vansha; and Alya chuckled mirthlessly.

That toy of cloth and paint had twisted the length of a street, borne by twenty or thirty men; but a hundred could not have lifted this vast black-scaled serpent-shape. With its broken wing stuck up like a distorted sail, it looked much as he had imagined the wrecks of great ships, in the old tales. 'Imagine the real thing unleashed against him! It could have smashed his stockade to flinders and curled up in the remains!'

'Three heads!' shivered Savi. 'How can such a thing be?'

'There are monsters born,' muttered Vansha. 'Creatures with extra limbs, eyes, heads. There was a child born in the Citadel, years past, that was two children; my father would not suffer it to live, lest it be a curse. Maybe the Ice made this thing, somehow. But how could it live thus, fly even? With three minds? Fell and horrible!'

'I remember my visions!' whispered Alya in awe. 'Those cities of old must have been stronger than I dreamed. Look at it! Even that fall didn't kill it!'

Black blood seeped from the wing, and its back was twisted; and its hind limbs were broken perhaps, for though the ancient beast strove to raise itself and crawl, it could not. The other wing and the long spear-tipped tail thrashed uselessly in its fury, sending more ice and rocks cascading from the slope. But Tugarin lived still, and was strong. At each surge of the frantic crowd the three heads reared up, and sent jets of flame lancing along the ruined side-streets, and upon any who dared to show themselves.

One bold knot of men sought to run out beneath, ducking between the fires; and though most vanished in spurts of flame, yet one or two came below the great body and stabbed at it with spears. But the heads darted back and plucked them away, like lice, and they vanished, screaming, between the jaws.

'Maybe it doesn't like to use fire so close,'

muttered Vansha. 'Doesn't need it, though. Can the strongest shadow shield us from *that*?'

'I don't understand about this shadow!' complained Savi. 'But I saw things that might help!'

She scrambled down the rubble, and back into the guard-house ruin. The others, following, saw her haul a long metal plate from the rubble, an Ekwesh battle-shield, scarred and dented by the fall, but whole enough; and there were others beneath, with swords and spears and other weaponry.

'Indeed, till it turns red-hot!' grinned Alya. 'But it's a lot better than nothing!'

'Well, I've found something too!' grinned Vansha, and held up a coarse loaf and a joint of mutton. 'I don't think the guards will be needing their day-rations, do you?'

They tore hungrily at a few stringy mouthfuls. 'Take the rest with us!' said Alya. 'We can't delay any longer! Savi, stay close to us. If the thing sees us, then maybe the two of us can keep it busy enough—'

'The three of us,' she said, softly, and hefted a shield. Ignoring Vansha's explosive gasp, she threw down her short sword, and swung a broad Ekwesh spear. 'I think I can wield this well enough.'

'But if you—'

'I fought the raiders, did I not? When you lay helpless, Alya; and you were beaten back, Vansha. This is my battle, also.'

'Is it?' Vansha demanded, wide-eyed with anger. 'When we found you in *her* bed? Does the wind swing about again so readily?'

'I could explain it to you,' she said wearily. 'I will, yet, if we're spared. And if you could ever understand. Or will you tarry till the Choosers come?'

Wordless, they scrambled up the rubble once again. The shields were a burden, but Savi steadied herself with the spear, and leaned on neither of them.

'Stop at the window!' hissed Alya; and there, as

smoke rolled across the sun, he sought the answering shadow in his mind. It faltered and guttered, for forests are afraid of fire; but the shade wrapped around them nonetheless, providing what shelter it could. Alya saw little more than the glint of Savi's eyes, as she exclaimed in soft amazement; but as Tugarin spat another streak of yellow flame, he saw that only too clearly.

Silently then, they scrambled through the narrow gap, out on to the mingled mass of rock and ice that had smashed the building, and climbed slowly, painfully down, helping one another with hardly a word.

Savi was watching Tugarin – too closely, for as one great head swung their way an instant, she almost slipped, and dislodged a rock. Alya caught her arm, and the giant eyes, yellow now with the flames they had started, swept across them unseeing. To his horror, still holding his arm, she stooped, snatched up another stone, and flung it hard at the middle head. The nearer one snapped around with a thunderous bellow, and fire splayed over the walls behind them.

'Madwoman!' hissed Vansha in wrath, but she tossed her head impatiently.

'Can't you see?' she whispered. 'You wondered how it lives! I was watching it, and now I'm sure. One will guides that thing, one spirit. A thing of malice and power.'

'Aye, marvellously,' protested Alya, 'but I'm more concerned about the getting past it!'

'But that's why!' she insisted. 'It's the middle head we've got to watch! The others only serve it, like slaves!'

'What good's that supposed to do us?' sneered Vansha, but Alya broke in.

'Don't you see? When it's looking the other way—' He gazed at the girl in renewed wonder.

'Maybe you've won us our chance!' And for all the place and time, for all the doubts he also struggled to repress, Alya drew her to him as of old.

She pushed him away, but gently. 'Maybe I have. And I will tell you all – all. I promise! But now . . .'

He nodded, steadying the shield. Together, creeping as slowly as noon shadows, keeping beneath the shifting pall of the smoke, the three scrambled over the last rocks of the fall and out into the open ground, watching the necks lash this way and that, hemming in the fear-maddened crowd. There was something in the touch of free earth beneath their feet, softening now out of its frosty grip; but Alya had no chance to dwell on that. On its far side, yet another bunch of bold or panicking souls broke away, and Tugarin's heads turned sharply to follow.

'*Now!*'

Together, raising their shields, they broke into a run. Not fast, because the ground was still rough, and because they had to keep together. Fire erupted on the far flank, and terrible screams, and Savi would have stumbled if Alya had not caught her up. The bulk of the dragon seemed to fill their sight, and the stench of it made them choke, the sickly odour of the tunnel redoubled.

This close, less than a hundred paces, its flank was a horrible sight both in its ridged and hideous scales, chipped and cracked and filth-encrusted, and still more so in the corruption that ran among them, riddled with oozing sores and old wounds half healed and discoloured, running dribbles of pale humours. Dark blood leaked around its broken hindlimbs, a spreading pool that smoked upon the barren earth; and its tail lashed fitfully as it still struggled to raise itself and fall upon the crush of terrified humanity that confronted it, neither standing nor fleeing, but tormenting it, perhaps, as a wounded man is plagued by a cloud of flies.

One of the doomed men broke and ran screaming, trailing a comet's tail of liquid flame, not away
from the beast but towards it, still brandishing a spear
that was itself a living flame. In malice and contempt
Tugarin's many eyes watched him an instant, then
with one great effort the brute heaved itself up on its
massive forelegs, higher than the rooftops it had
shattered. Down the heads darted, serpentlike, ter-
rifyingly fast, and struck. The scream ended; the flame
was quenched; the man vanished. And Tugarin,
though growling horribly with pain, strove once
more to rise in its wrath. Directly before the three
escapers the huge surviving wing flailed an instant,
then beat down.

The air boomed. Dust swirled and eddied against
the foot of the vale wall. The flames bowed before the
blast, and the many smokes billowed, danced and
boiled upward and away, drawing the shadows with
them. There, very suddenly, the forest dimness became dappled and bright as a lime-glade at noon; and
the three of them stood exposed and unguarded,
close beneath the flank of the wounded dragon.

The three heads flicked towards them as one;
and as swiftly, vindictively, the main head struck.

No time for words, no time for anything save to
fling up the shield against the onrushing jaws, against
the flame that would outrun them. Alya, in horror and
defiance, felt it billow around him and melt his flesh;
for so it seemed.

But the flame was not yellow, but red as blood,
red as iron, red as the rusted earth below which the
forge of Ilmarinen blazed; and the force of it greater
and more frightening since that first searing touch,
consuming, healing. And so was the sense of strength.
Like a living flame of his own he felt, his arm as one
with the hero's sword it bore, the fire welding them
to a greater whole. As one he raised them, faster than
actual thought, and as one they struck.

Not even that, perhaps, would have been enough to turn that onrush. For the serpentine heads were all but fleshless, bone and scales large and small, even bordering the lipless arrays of fangs. But the beast's own malicious speed was added to his, and the blow caught the side of its greatest jaws.

Alya was flung on his back. The head whipped skyward, away from the agony that had cut deep into those scales. The lesser heads swung in response, as Savi had guessed, momentarily aimless, unwary.

'Strike! Strike, brother!' yelled Alya, though it pained his breast; and Vansha, as if jolted from a dream, lashed out in his turn at the lesser neck that swept above him. It was as thick as a man's armspan; but Vansha struck from below, among the smaller scales of the throat, and goaded by vengeful fury. There was a flash, a spurt of stinking blackness mingled with the dragon's dark blood. His sword passed through the scales, and cracked in two. The lesser head fell. Its jaws sagging open, its eyes dim and empty, it dangled from a single strand of sinew upon the convulsing neck.

Now Tugarin bucked like a maddened horse, and its remaining jaws howled in agony. So fell was the sound that the crowd was stunned, and cowered down in animal terror. Vansha staggered, dazed, half blinded by the foulness spraying from the severed neck. Again the surviving heads swung back, straight at him this time; but Alya sprang up, and swinging his body with the weight of his shield, he struck at the other neck.

He struck against the massive side scales, but he had aimed his blow well. Through their trailing edges it smashed, with a dull clangour, and into the quick, and across. The neck whipped up, and he fell sprawling, the sword out of his hand. Again the rush of filth and blood, and the head crashed severed to the black earth.

The agony was a goad. Tugarin, still screaming, suddenly twisted upright once more in pain and fury, rising on its forelimbs. Vansha still faltered; Alya had fallen to his knees. Their blades were heavy with smoking filth, and of Vansha's only half remained. Neither could resist. But Savi flung herself before them; and the movement caught the monster's maddened eye. It snapped at them, but head-on, no longer exposing its wounded throat; and a shade more slowly, as if to unleash the fire it had hitherto held back. But Savi, less strong than the men, was swifter, and her weapon well suited. She stabbed out her spear, not at the throat, but straight into the jaw that gaped above her.

Straight between its terrible teeth she struck, shattering them; and though the mouth was little softer than the body, her spear bit deep into its roof. The great head threshed back, blinded with pain, knocking her down; and the fire it had readied erupted in an uncontrolled vomit of flame.

A yellow fire-cloud erupted about Tugarin's head. Droplets rained about the black ichor that still dripped from the wounded necks, in great pools on the ground beneath; and they also caught and billowed like hideous blossoms. Flame raced upward, and suddenly the wounds themselves burst out in fire, a ghastly sight, as if the great beast burned from within with the stuff it secreted.

It rolled back, thrashing horribly. But then, as if conquering agony with the sheer force of its malign will, it reared high over its tiny adversaries and half fell towards them. It could utter flame no longer. Dark blood spewed from its wounded jaws and kindled in a hissing, fiery spray. But it needed none, with such a bulk. Vansha and Savi raised their weapons in desperate defiance.

Alya sprang up. He flung aside his shield and caught the hilt of his great sword in both hands; and, though his limbs were leaden and weary, it seemed to him that the fierce heat flowed up from the thawing earth beneath, and poured its renewed force into his hollow limbs, lent lightness to his legs and to his arms massive, unstoppable force. He sprang, and his leap carried him straight into Tugarin's path.

Upon scale and hide, behind that hideous head, he drove the ancient blade, and through the flesh and bone beyond. And as if it was no longer a sword alone that struck, the force that was lent the dragon for its unnatural existence, as his had been to him, crumbled before it.

Through vent and channel, through cavern and chasm, the earthfires leaped up roaring, rebellious, rejoicing at their liberation from the long containment of the Ice. Through the overwhelming, overbearing walls they blasted, striking the cold glaciers to shattered shards for long leagues about; and Alya's sword struck right through Tugarin's neck.

The severed head flew out with the force of that blow, turning in the air, and crashed down against the ruined walls. The body, already rearing, spouted flame from all its wounds now, and sank down, almost slowly as it seemed, in a growing mass of fire. It struck the ground with a massive, reverberating crash that must have travelled through that mean place like the herald of doom; and the ground shook in answer. The great wings folded, and with a rush like collapsing sails they fell limp.

Ice came cascading from the high walls of the vale, splintered, impotent, shapeless, down into the sheltered valley. The shoddy walls and crude towers tottered on their foundations, and one by one they sank down and collapsed. A great shuddering wave seemed to course down the vale, and a cloud of destruction and collapse arose in its eddy. Only the palace was left standing, fair, untouched; but the crude town over which it had stood overlord was laid waste. It reigned in emptiness now, lord and master of nothing but ruin, assailed by the very ground it stood upon. The air grew hot with spreading fire, and the fallen Ice hissed and steamed, while high above it the rippling currents blasted what remained upon the slopes, and the long stalactites began to glisten, trickle and melt.

All around that place, and the others like it that the Ice had turned to their advantage, the fires from below struck upward in a blow of massive, mocking power, a sharp reminder of what the living cold had not yet touched, and might never, in that ancient age of the world.

But the folk caught up in these events saw in them only the fall of Tugarin, son of Zamai, and its echo. Ruin encompassed the writhing, monstrous shape, consumed and shrivelling in its own yellow flame, its own funeral pyre; and Alya felt a fierce satisfaction for the fallen cities he had never known, for the images of devastation that haunted his visions. Indeed, those images never came into his dreams again; but something different took their place.

He held his sword high, and its blade dripped dying flames; and he shouted aloud: 'Tugarin is fallen! *The way is open!*'

And after one amazed breath a great shout went up from the crowd, a wordless cry of acclamation, of liberation, of unbelievable release. Thrall and warrior alike, they surged forward across the shuddering ground, out of the crumbling streets, and on to the clean black hillside that led up and out of the vale, out towards freedom.

Across the town that shout was heard, and so potent was it, so directly it spoke to the deepest feelings of men, that all fighting, all enmity was forgotten, and the cold dominion of the Ice was for that time broken. The town emptied of its last people. The lame, the sick, the wounded, the dying, all who were conscious strove to rise, to run, even if their last breath failed them in the attempt. Streaming like a river too long pent up, the human servants of the Ice fled its bitter dominion, free of orders, free of fear.

And with them, half unbelieving, ran Savi, and behind her Vansha, and Alya at her side, swept along all three by the outrush that was as much in the hearts of men as their bodies. Out they ran on to the free hillside, crying like the rest without words, for no words could match what the moment meant, for them above all. Behind them, in the ruined town, with a crash like thunder the earthfires fountained high from every seam, and blazing rock came raining down upon the palace.

And though, as the exultant hordes of men came clambering out above the valley wall at last, they saw the enormous expanse of the Ice stretched out before them, yet they saw also the cracks that crazed its surface, the steams that arose from beneath. And out on to its glittering whiteness they all of them streamed without fear or hesitation, an irresistible dark tide trampling its sterile perfection into earthy slush.

From these heights they could look out beyond it. They could see that it ended, they could see the path stretching out before them, down its narrow outthrust arm. And they could gaze out, in blue and misty distance, upon where it led, upon what to many was only the dimmest memory or the least credible legend, the infinite breadth of the still greater and more marvellous living world.

Out they poured, out without let or resistance, mocking the Ice that crunched and cracked beneath their feet, out, and down, and away. What became of them all thereafter is not told by any Chronicle, in any detail. Perhaps some perished there, in the barren lands with little food or shelter; but by their own choice they died free. But that some escaped – that much is known, some seeking their lost homes, others simply a place to live in quiet; and it is certain that many succeeded, for their tale and their descendants' reached many lands, and their kin preserved the story in all honour.

As well they might. It was no lasting victory; for it was the last rebellion against the power of the Ice in those lands, and its cold rule was scarcely affected. The palace still stood, though sadly marred; and the town, in time, was renewed. For many a century its tyranny endured, in these lands and others, its bitter walls towering unchallenged; and its servants the Ekwesh, forever renewed and bred afresh in their many other settlements, tightened their grip upon the lands that Alya and his friends had known. No realms revived there, no great campaigns were waged. Free men were few, and lived in hiding and constant fear.

Yet that day was a bitter check for the elder Powers, none the less. And it must have been felt as such, for the Ice itself never advanced its walls far beyond the limits of that day, fearing perhaps to force any further confrontation with the forge beneath the earth, and its ultimate Master. And in that, perhaps, lay the foretaste of their defeat that was to come, more than a thousand years hence – to the Ice, a time much sooner than to men.

But in these fortunes the three young folk who had most largely brought them about were not to share; for their fate was different, and set apart.

They ran with the rest, exulted with them, straggled out over the Ice in the direction of the downward road. And Alya, forgetful of all else, reached out and caught Savi's hand as they ran, and they looked in one another's faces and laughed in gladness.

Then it was as if the world exploded into darkness and agony. Alya dimly felt his legs crumple

beneath him, and fell helpless, as if he were falling
once more into the dark valley of the Citadel, a
lifetime as it seemed ago. But he landed in snow,
heard Savi scream, and struggled to move his legs.
Gasping, he rolled over into her arms, and felt the
scalding well of blood beneath his mailshirt, soaking
his back. He stared up at her anguished face, and saw
the blue sky behind her blotted out by boiling clouds
of black smoke, seamed with red and yellow light,
and the white steams of melting ice. Against them
towered Vansha in his ragged cloak, his broken sword
in his hand; and his handsome face, seamed and
scarred by the flamelight, was a mask of stone.

'What—' began Alya; but it hurt too much to get
the words out. 'Brother . . .' he croaked.

'I am not your brother,' said Vansha, calmly. 'Not
any more. I swore my oath till Savi was freed. And
now she is.'

'I feared this!' breathed Savi. 'I feared it! When I
saw you together, I wondered, when you called him
brother—'

Alya threshed his limbs. A voice rang in his ears:
he fears you, and what he fears, he strikes out at . . .

The fires had too little left to work with. 'By
both . . .'

'Freed by both of us?' Vansha shook his head
slowly. 'Did *I* have a gift of power given me, so
unfairly, so stupidly? I've been faithful to my oath,
I've swallowed your slights and endured your follies,
let you play at leading. Oh, you were good enough
company on such a quest, I'll allow! Always nice to
have a friendly face. But by the Powers, if they'd given
me such a fire as burns in you, I'd have known how to
use it! I'd have raised such a storm as they'd have
been proud of! Yet I played my part with my own
strength, I won through just as you did. And so I – *I* –
am the better man. I did the most! I kept my oath
without help.'

'You stabbed him in the back!' raged Savi.

Vansha smiled tautly. 'But only because I needed to,' he said, shrugging, as if that explained all. 'Believe me, if the Powers had only been fair, I'd have happily settled you face to face, boy, as I failed to on the cliff that day. Don't think I haven't been tempted to, since, a hundred times, when you slighted me, and went against my will! But you were too useful, and too dangerous, with that gift; and I keep my word, after all, as a chieftain must. If I'd had a whole sword and remembered that mailshirt, I'd have made a cleaner job of you now.' He reached out, and hauled Savi to her feet. 'Still, it lets me show you what must happen. She's mine now, as she always was before you came along and sneaked her away!'

'It's *my* choice!' snarled Savi, flailing and tearing at him, striving to break free or to claw at his eyes. But he only stood there, still calm, clutching her wrist with increasing strength until she cried out and slipped to her knees.

'Go ahead,' he said, relishing the words. 'You'll learn better soon enough. When I show you what a real man is. And not another woman, or this weakling puppet, propped up by borrowed strength, not even able to stand up in the snow. I didn't hurt him, I just revealed what he really is. You'll forget him, just as I will, and you'll surely forget *her*! And you'll learn to look up to me as you were supposed to.'

'*Never!*' she spat, and struck at him again, clawing at his groin. He dropped his broken sword and snatched her other hand.

'Now, now,' he chided, with the airy satisfaction of a man living out a cherished dream, and struck her so hard across the face that she sprawled back in the snow. 'Must I tame you now? Right here in front of him?'

Alya fought to move, and the fires blazed; but it taxed him even to breathe, and he was sick and dizzy.

Vansha had his own strength, all right. Even that blunted blade would have run him through, if not for the mail; and the difference might be little enough, now. Had he gone mad, his late brother? No. Vansha had always been mad, mad enough to pretend not to be, mad enough to play roles to perfection even though he did not really understand them. To play the lover, the hero, the brother in arms . . .

No wonder Kalkan had fascinated him so. Vansha had been studying another role, striving to understand the kind of person he wanted to be, perhaps; and never seeing how different he himself was, not realising that all men's feelings were not as false. And all women's. No wonder he was furious with Savi! He would never really understand why she could not ever love him, she who had seen through him from the first; and he would take it out on her, forever, with none left in this darkening world to protect her.

The fires roared. Perhaps they were helping to heal him, or perhaps the chill snow had staunched the blood, but suddenly Alya had a flicker of strength. His own sword, the hero's sword, lay beyond his reach, stuck in the snow, and he threshed frantically to reach it; but still he could move no swifter than a crawling infant, and in great pain. And Vansha planted his boot on the blade.

The icy wind plucked at Vansha's straggling hair; his face was unmoved, expressionless. 'You've seen enough, boy. I'd have left you to die, but with a rat like you it's best to make a clean end.' He seized the sword, staggering a little at the weight of it; but he could manage it. 'This should have been mine, too. With the chieftaincy! It'll be happier in a hand that's worthy of it!' Casually, brutally, he swung it high, one-handed; and Savi screamed. But she was not looking at him.

As far as sight stretched beneath that lurid sky, a tide of fleeing figures still covered the Ice, pouring out of the vale, ignoring this little drama in their desperate flight. But suddenly they were scattering to either side, shouting, as something swept among them, some thing unseen, as if a brief cold breath played across the shattered glacier. In its path, swift as a heartbeat, the snow flew up in flurries, the dark deep cracks in the Ice glazed and grew white again; and an icy blast whipped suddenly around them. Between Alya and Vansha the snow exploded and flew up in a cloud, and up through the Ice, in a hail of stinging splinters, like a white marble spear thrust up from below, arose a strange stiff shape. A statue, in the form of a woman, naked, stiff, unliving, in pure translucent ice.

Yet even as it stood, colour raced through it, an infinitely fine tracery of scarlet hues that branched and grew with blinding speed, seaming its surface like marble indeed, suffusing it with the flush of life. Around it the falling snow whirled and settled into the folds of a robe. The pale eyelids snapped open.

Vansha's cry mingled fury and fear. 'You! Witch! I settled you! I tell you, she's *mine*—' And he struck, the blow that he meant for Alya, hewed hard with the ancient sword at Louhi's slender throat.

The blade that had cloven a dragon's bones sang a high note and flew up out of his hand, notched. Vansha staggered, as if jarred, took a half-step back, his handsome face ashen and gaping. He stiffened, and the breath erupted out of him as if he were being squeezed, in a high, thin scream. And then, all over him from head to foot, the crystals of ice burst outward from his skin, through his clothes, like a thousand spears, impaling him on the very waters within his body. The blood on them froze instantly white; and without another sound he toppled face down in the snow.

Louhi ignored him. She looked much as she had in that first moment Alya saw her, a woman young and fair; yet she stood taller now, taller than human height, and of her wounds there was no trace. Her face was a mask of cold wrath, but fixed wholly upon Savi.

The fires raged within him, but he felt hollow now, as if there was nothing else within him but them; and his wound hurt terribly. Gritting his teeth, drawing what he could from the flame, he seized the fallen sword and levered himself shakily to his feet. Savi, startled, clutched him as he swayed. 'No, Alya! You mustn't—'

'You won't hurt her . . .' he grated, struggling to heft the sword. 'I have a gift of strength . . .'

She seemed to notice him at last. 'Indeed you have,' she said, with little trace of feeling. 'Ilmarinen was generous in his folly. You have used his generosity foolhardily enough. But you are in my realm now, boy, and you can neither hide from me nor fight me. I sensed you, most easily of all, the moment you set foot upon the Ice. And what a Power has given, a greater Power may take away.'

She did nothing, that he saw, not so much as blink her wide eyes. But in that moment the fires within him, like the merest candle-flame, blew out. They vanished, extinguished, as if doused in dark cold waters; and with them vanished both the feeling and the strength in his legs. They gave beneath him, and he crumpled down into the snow, striking fearful agony in his wounded back.

His sight reddened, he could not speak; but through dim eyes he saw Savi spring across him, lithe as a hunting animal, and stand defiantly.

'*You*,' said Louhi; and her voice was no longer calm. 'You promised to show it me, this human love, to show me what it felt like. Why it was important. What it was worth. Well, you have taught me its worth, indeed! Lies, wounds and betrayal!'

Alya, helpless, could see Savi's legs shaking; but

she stood firm, and her voice was low and quiet. 'The wounding was none of my doing, and you have more than repaid it. And I did not betray you.'

'I felt the pain!' raged Louhi, though her face held little expression. 'And you fled with these vermin! How could you do it? You dealt me the worst wound of all! Why? *Why?* Did I not love you, in return?'

'Alya I dreamed of, but I thought him dead. The other—' Savi shook her head. 'Him I never expected. I would have stopped him, if I could. He never learned to love, only to possess. When he hurt you in his jealousy, I feared your wrath would overtake us all, that you would not stop to listen, to understand. There was nothing then but to flee. You are who you are, after all. Say, lady, was I so wrong?'

Louhi said nothing, at first. 'You loved them. You lied to me.'

'I did not lie,' said Savi, still quietly. 'You were so lost as a human, so bewildered, so helpless, so much in need. I was sorry for you, moved by you, intrigued by you. You wanted something from me, yet it was something you could not understand. A thing that you with all your power and wealth and wisdom could never for one moment command, yet something I already had. I gave it you because you needed it, and because I hoped that you might come to understand its power – the power that brought this boy so far and so perilously to my side! And that in loving, you might come to hate and despise us the less. But what I gave to you, I could not take from him; or all my love would be false, indeed. I chose him long ago, and he has kept faith with me – how he has kept it! I must keep faith with him.'

Louhi's eyes blazed. 'And not with me?'

'As I would have with you,' said Savi, undaunted. 'I loved you sincerely. But I was still your prisoner. You have not learned the whole meaning of love. You have learned to take, but not yet to give, as I gave, despite all that you and your kind had done to me.'

'Give, girl? I would have given you life, as I promised! Life, without limit! Immortality! As a Power! Who could give more than that?' She looked at Alya, and laughed. 'Can he? Could the other?'

Savi glanced down a moment at Vansha's remains, then away. 'He could give nothing. He knew less of love than you. Yet even he would have understood that there is more to life than just existing. As you would, if you truly loved – if you were not so fettered by your own hatred for the living. My lady, you also have taught me many things: to think, to ponder, to understand. I do indeed want life – but not in any fetters, however dear. I want life as I understand it, not you. I want my own life, and I want it to the full. Life I can embrace, from the heights to the depths!'

Louhi snorted. 'Life! All its age, and pain, and sickness, and foul decay? You are fair, yet your body feeds on filth, will turn one day to carrion, unless entombed within the immortal Ice! Do you wish *that*?' She shook her head, as if to shake off the vision. 'How can you even contemplate it? I can give you more. But if that is what you truly want . . . then you shall have it. I will learn to give – to forgive – if only you will go on loving me!'

Savi said nothing, did not look down at Alya. 'Do you truly mean that, lady? Do you promise?'

'I do!' There were tears in her voice, thought Alya, astonished. Perhaps she had learned something from Savi, after all. 'I swear it!' Her voice hardened. 'But nothing more! Ask nothing for *him* – for that boy! His doom is fixed. He dies here, among our snows, for the ruin he has wrought; and will serve Taoune, who was my consort of old.'

'Do you swear?' insisted Savi; and her voice also had changed. Alya struggled to speak, but could not.

'Will you keep your oath? If then you grow weary of
me, and seek some new love, what force could bind
you then?'

Louhi stammered a protest, but Savi's voice was
firm. 'I know you, as none does, my lady! You must
swear by yourself, by all that you are, and imprint
your oath within the fabric of the Ice itself. So that
though you may still break it, you will never again be
sure of yourself! Never trust the strength of your own
will, in human form or any other. Never trust the Ice
itself to fulfil your purpose.'

'*He* cannot have his life back,' muttered Louhi
insistently, 'his strength, anything . . . You care so
little for him?'

Savi's voice was bitter. 'I know you will not spare
him, whatever I ask. When Vansha struck you down,
then their cause was lost; and I will not go down into
ruin with him, not so young, when there is life to be
lived, good I may yet do. So I ask only for my life,'
repeated Savi. 'Only for me. And I swear I love you as
I say I do, and will forever.'

Louhi gave a sudden wild laugh, and a furious
wind came whistling in off the Ice. The smokes
dispersed, to show the chill sky darkening as the
short day neared its end.

'So be it,' she whispered. 'I humble myself for
you, child of men. I swear by the Ice, by myself, by all
else that you wish. I will give you your life, in its
fullness. Teach me love, teach me all of it. Forever.'

'I will,' whispered Savi. 'I also swear.' Her words
were soft, still; but behind them was the urgency of
one who hastens along a cliff-edge, crumbling at
every step. 'I do love you. I never lied. I shall never
forget you. That love for you is part of my life, and
only one thing can ever drive it out.'

Louhi, puzzled, reached out her arms; but Savi
took only her hand, and held it to her cheek. 'Hate. If
you break your oath, you will break my love. It will

turn to hate, if you fail to give me life in its fullness.
But what that is!' She laughed a little, breathlessly.
'That you could not understand. That you could not
have foreseen!'

Numbly Alya watched Savi reach out to touch
the pale face, and heard the change that came over
her voice. 'So now, my lady – listen, and learn once
more! To live is to grow, to flourish, to change. And
for me, as for many women, it is one thing more. You
offered me immortality, Louhi, and it was a great
prize. But I will seek it my own way. I will have
children!'

Louhi's arms dropped to her sides, but she said
nothing. Savi's voice was gentle now, though she
trembled like a leaf in the wind. 'And love you as I do,
those you cannot give me! Children; and where I may
raise them free from fear and tyranny. The Ice is no
such place. And, my lady, I will have them by the man
I choose; and that can be one only. That alone is the
life I will embrace! That, and no other. If he is dead, or
crippled, or harmed in any way – as he was, first, by
your hand – it can never be. And your oath can never
be fulfilled.'

Louhi stood rigid, as if returned to ice. Her eyes
closed a moment, the lids fluttering. When she
opened them again, her very look seemed to suck
the last shred of warmth from sky and ground together. She threw back her head and laughed again,
loudly; and the stragglers who heard it ring across the
Ice clapped hands to ears and redoubled their speed.
'*I could break it more easily than breathe!*'

Savi stumbled back as if struck, and with a
supreme effort Alya reached up his hand to hers.
Instinctively their fingers entwined, chill and bloodless; and between them a scrap of warmth sprang up,
as their fate wavered on the balance, and they waited
for an end. Louhi stood frozen, staring at the sky,
ignoring them.

At last she lowered her gaze, and sighed, a very human sound. 'Stop trembling, girl. My wrath is against myself, for the most part. The fault is mine, that I sought such understanding in the first place. That I let my guard fall so, and let it draw me in. And that I let you teach me. Indeed you did so, only too well. I am become all too human, for now; and being human, I could break my word without a qualm.'

She snorted with disgust. 'Yet having already caught one of your weaknesses, I dare not catch another! Human doubt, human hesitation, human compassion, I'd have them forever hovering at the edges of every thought. And surely they would drag me down.'

She shuddered violently. 'You have learned to think, indeed, girl. An elegant paradox you have trapped me in! I must save myself, I must cut away this infection of humanity. And I will, I must do it memorably, so that the sting returns to remind me how dangerous this taste of human love has been! And how costly! As before, I must punish myself, to make the lesson stick. For that reason, more than any other, I will keep my oath.'

Her voice choked, and she whirled abruptly about, as if to look back at the smoking ruin of the vale, now glaring red in the dusk with the slow seething of the earthfires. After a moment she stamped her foot lightly, like a furious child.

'Go, idiot! Take your life, as you conceive it. Short and rotten, at the mercy of time and chance. Take your growth, that only speeds decay! And take *him*, since you lust for that, though he lives only to spoil your body with his seed! Since you must, take him whole. But nothing more!'

The light that flashed in his mind was intolerable, blinding. The shaft of pain was like white-hot impalement, and for an instant, in the agony of it, he saw Vansha stiffen and die again. Then it passed, and he felt an onrush of more normal pain, that throbbed and faded slowly. For a moment he missed the familiar tingle of the fires, winced in numb discomfort, feared he had been cheated somehow. Then he understood what he was feeling. The cold snow was stinging his feet, and its leaden bite felt sharp and delicious as a kiss. He waggled his toes, and began to laugh idiotically and cry, all at once. Slowly, awkwardly, he clambered to his feet, realising how momentous such a simple act could be, and how unnatural his former healing had been compared to this.

'Nothing more!' said Louhi, still turned away. 'He has only his own miserable strength now. I will not let such a warrior loose in the world, to challenge me ever again.'

Alya reached up, stripped off his torn mailshirt, and threw it down on his ripped and blood-soaked cloak. 'Lady, for that I thank you. Whatever your reason. Well as it served me, the gift of the Powers was a burden past mortal bearing.'

'Then you also have learned something,' the woman said, and bowed her golden hair.

She turned abruptly to stare at Savi, and her face was streaked and ugly. She had indeed learned to weep, but not to control it. 'You are a flower among filth, and you fade fast. Take your beauty to where the Ice cannot preserve it. Take it far from here! *Go!*'

Savi was draping her coat around Alya's shivering shoulders. 'But if you leave us here in the night, on the barren Ice – no clothes, no food, no way to escape – you only give us death by another way!'

'I need give you no escape!' said Louhi grimly. 'The means exist. If you are too foolish to seize them, that need no longer be any concern of mine. That is life.'

And the Lady of the Ice turned her face away, and spread her arms to the darkness.

Back to my kingdom I go now,
Bested by what I may never subdue,
Never by the strong but by the weak,
By the unshielded heart, the open mind,
By what in this illusion of a world
Reflects the faintest trace of what is true,
That even from the Powers lies hidden.

She had no music in her voice, though it was clear and strong. Darkness fell about her, enveloping her like a tide, leaving only her golden hair gleaming in the last faint light. And then even that was gone. The bitter air crackled; and the sky above them lit suddenly, from far horizon to horizon, with the great rippling curtain of the Northlights, a cascade of green and gold, so vast and fair the mere humans sank down on their knees beneath its majesty. But it shook once, and was gone, leaving only darkness and the whining wind.

'Savi . . .' managed Alya; but his teeth were chattering too much to say more, and his heart was too full.

She pulled his ragged and filthy shirt close about him. 'Ssh! Come! We've got to get you away from here, somehow, fast as we can. Can you walk now?'

'Barely!' he managed. He reached down for the sword, where it had fallen, and tried to lean on it, like a stick; but as it felt his weight, the ancient blade bent and snapped, where it had touched Louhi's neck, and dropped useless in the snow. He stood swaying and staring at it, while Savi tugged at his arm.

'It's done its work! Come! Lean on me! I won't break!'

Alya managed a smile. 'You never did. You never would have! I could have saved myself the trouble of rescuing you!'

'No,' she said softly. 'I knew you'd try, somehow, against all sense. It was knowing that that let me

endure. That let me turn to her, even; though I told
her no lies. You even warned me, I know. That
strange bird – *what is it?*'

Alya had stopped dead, gasping, reaching for his
belt. Then, pulling free of her, he staggered back
through the snow to where his cloak lay, searching,
scrabbling with frantic energy. He gave a great cry,
suddenly. '*There!* I feared I'd lost it sooner. But I must
have fallen on it when I was stabbed!'

Savi stared aghast at the ancient mask. 'It's
covered in your blood!'

'So much the better, maybe!' He held it high,
stained and cracked, and laughed quietly, and drew
the Raven image down upon his head, like a crown.
'Father, your gift comes home at last! And I have no
fires to keep me from it now!'

Savi stared. 'What good can that do?'

'Every good, girl!' He felt strong suddenly, young
and strong as a prince of men in the first bright dawn
of the world. 'Take my hands, Saviyal, chieftain's
daughter! Dance with me!'

She stared around at the howling waste, at the
bitter black sky in which the first stars were shining,
merciless and hard as gems. Even the earthfires in the
vale were fading and subsiding to a sullen glow, and
the bared black rock was turning slowly white again,
cracking in the grip of frost. Over the distant horizon
of the glaciers, the first faint gleam of moonlight
shone, mirrored from far below the edge of the
world; and by its light it seemed that distant shapes
were stirring against the dark, inchoate, huge and
menacing. Shadows flickered and swept across the
slopes above them, and the wind seemed alive with
half-heard voices, chiming like icicles.

'*Dance?*'

He seized her hands and swung her around,
singing wildly, singing anything he could think of
that had a beat, nonsense, scraps of old songs that set

his feet stamping on the stiffening snow. Wild-eyed, astonished, she shook her head and sang with him, stamped her feet, whirled about him.

'At least it keeps us warm!'

Warmth! He thought of warmer lands, of his dreams, of fertile meadows, green-clad hills, the verdant woodlands whence Rysha's talisman had come, the mighty forests by the Sea . . .

'The Sea!'

All at once the strength boiled up and burst out of him, through his very bones, more swiftly and sharply than the ice that had destroyed Vansha.

Hunger and cold . . .

They were indeed his friends. To his legacy, that the inner fires, well given as they were, had so long denied him, hunger and cold were his mark of birthright, his stamp of achievement, his endurance and his reward in one. They created the emptiness within him that the shaman's strength must fill.

His eyes were open beneath the mask, his mind clear; but it was as if he saw the Ice surge up before him, smoothly, a distortion in the world, and merge with the descending dark. And behind them, as they blended, the sudden glow burst into flame. The Trail, vaster and brighter than ever before, burned an incandescent path in the darkness, faster than sight, and exploded into glittering night.

He was face to face with the Wall, and at last he understood it – the Wall, that as his father had told him, every Seer must build within themselves, and somehow overcome. His Wall was built out of visions of his past and his destiny, of glassy Ice and overwhelming darkness, and boiling fire. He had learned to rise above it, to look beyond it, with the minds of others. Now, though, his strength was his own, and that strength was what raised the Wall in the first place. A fearsome force, that now he must confront. Go up against it, yet not over it. He must go through.

He stilled the dance suddenly, and clutched Savi tightly to him, close as the single flesh they must be. The height of black glass seemed to rush up at him, the flames burst high about him; and Savi screamed, for in that moment she also saw it. But he held his head high, and struck the release of the mask. The Raven's beak gaped wide, and revealed the human face within. The Wall reflected it back to him, but plain and featureless no longer. Within the mask shone the face of the grizzled minstrel, eyes glittering, laughing wildly; and the fires danced about and above it, like a vast crown.

And then Alya struck the Wall, and the obsidian mirror shattered. The Wall exploded about him, and was gone.

Light rushed in on him, light and confusion. He saw, as he had seen from above the Wall; but not now from a distance. Sights and sounds, visions and images whirled past him so fast they merged into a whirling grayness, and only Savi in his arms seemed real and solid. To her, and to his single thought, he clung.

The roaring in his ears seemed slowly to subside and still; and yet, as he heard his own trembling breath, it did not fade away completely. He heard another breath then, felt warm skin in his arms, and strove to haul himself up, as his vision cleared.

Savi lay beside him, looking as dazed as he felt, stretching out a hand to touch something that lay on the ground before them. It was the mask, no longer bright, no longer coloured at all, but scorched and smoking. There was a smell of singeing in his hair, and he reached up and plucked out a scrap of twig, that stung his fingers, and crumbled, smoking. He stared at it a moment, raised himself on one arm, and saw his soiled sleeve drop and fall away, as if charred.

'My hair stinks!' protested Savi. 'As if – it's burned! The ends are scorched! Yours, too!'

Alya's ears were still rushing. 'But not my skin! Are you—'

'I'm all right.' She sat up, and laughed as her thin garments dropped away, streaking her skin with char.

'More than all right!' he told her. 'You're so beautiful . . .'

She still stared at the mask, reached out, touched the ground beside it. 'What are these? Like dead leaves, but thin.'

Alya blinked at the carpet of brown stuff. 'I don't know . . . Where are we?'

'I thought you must know!' she said, alarmed again, and rolled over, ready to spring up and run. But wonder far greater than any fear held them.

'These *trees*!'

They were gigantic, far above anything that grew in any land he knew, noble columns vaster and more numerous than all Louhi's colonnades, rich brown and soft grey, with a fresh wind rushing through their strange branches. Part of the sound in his ears, he realised; yet not all. Fresh, and yet soft, scented with a strange tang he could not name, and a mildness that felt good on his newly naked skin.

'I thought of forests,' he said softly, lifting the mask. 'Warmer forests. And the mask carried us to them.'

'Carried?' Savi stared. 'But only the greatest of shamans . . .' Her eyes gleamed suddenly. 'The greatest. Of course.'

'The most foolish, more like. Look at this poor wood, it's burnt to charcoal almost. Beyond wearing. I feel the same. I doubt I'd ever have the nerve to try that again, or the strength. The mask did most of the work!'

He burst out laughing suddenly. 'As it carried me once before! Only I never knew, I never dreamed, then! But it felt the same, I recognise it now. When I wandered at the very edge of death, it took me up and

carried me southward to the kin I sought. To the
Citadel – and to you!'

Savi clung to him, wordless. But suddenly she
broke away, pointing. 'Through the trees there!
There's light – look at it! So great, glittering . . . Is
it the Ice?'

'I don't think so!' said Alya excitedly; and seizing
her hand, he led her through the sighing trees. The
remnants of their clothes dropped away from them as
they walked, and their boots with them; but the
strange carpet of needle-like dry leaves was kind to
their bare feet, and the air seemed like a caress. And
as they reached the margins of the trees, and looked
out into the open, they understood at last.

A land fell away before the forest, a downslope
of lush green grass far richer than the richest of their
plains, marshy or arid, but much narrower; for within
their sight it was bordered by a golden strip of sand.
What lay beyond that glittered as bright as the Ice, but
infinitely more mobile and alive. Its surface coursed
with enormous rhythmic ripples, like desert dunes
restored to life. To Alya it seemed that they raced to
shore with sheer elephantine joy, spilling high upon
the sand in glorious excitement, racing away again as
if to lure him down to that radiant expanse, down and
far away.

'They were what I thought of last,' he said. 'The
forests, and the Sea. Thanks to one I'll tell you of – if
only as a caution! But I never dreamed they could be
so fair.'

'Fair and terrible,' said Savi. 'As terrible as the
Ice, in their power! And the Powers that rule them,
also. But so such things are bound to be. And they
draw us to them, none the less.'

'I would have loved her, too,' he said. 'In your
place.'

Savi sighed. 'Who would not? For good or ill, she
is higher and greater than we, and that shines through

her. I will never forget her, as I promised – and yet I am so glad to be free!'

He nodded. 'As I of the fires within me. We have strayed too close to the ancient Powers, you and I; and all the ancients told that they were no safe company for mere men, even the kindly ones. We are better as we are. And together, best of all!'

He drew her close, and they clung, while the waves and the wind played about them.

'Yet are we?' she asked at last. 'Alone, without home or friends or food, or any purpose? How shall we make our lives, and where?'

Alya smiled, and pointed. Down the beach, a long way off, smoke was rising. They could make out shapes there, long straight shapes with a made look about them.

'Some kind of huge huts?' said Savi doubtfully. 'But who would build them on the sand, so near the sea?'

'Not huts,' said Alya. 'Ships. The ships that Tuma the Rider spoke of – that he besought us to join! Ships, to seek the lands across the Sea! If they can only find a way!'

She looked up at him, excitement in her eyes. 'And I know one! She showed me pictures of the world, of the seas, of great streams and currents and winds that run from shore to shore. There was one such stream – it ran almost from this shore to the other, in a great graceful curve north and east and south again, like the neck of a bird . . .'

Alya stiffened. 'A swan? With head – head and eye?'

She stared. 'Why, yes! An island in its path, that had the place of an eye! Only a short way from the other coast! I could draw it on a map—'

Alya felt a great calm steal over him. 'Then we know what to seek! What will bear us there swiftly enough to live!'

'Are you sure?' She stared doubtfully out over the rolling infinity, more like the Ice than anything else she had ever seen. 'But it's so great, with no marks or measures! The ships would need some way of keeping their direction . . .'

'*But there is!*' He clutched her hand. 'We find our way by the stars on land, don't we? And I've seen them afar, farther than any man, I guess. They move, but they don't change, not halfway across the world! There must be men who can steer boats by them, lead us along these currents of yours.' He shook his head in wonder. 'Tuma said they'd welcome us. More than that, now, I think, with the gift you bring them. A true path to the other shore!'

She smiled. 'It's your gift also. What do you think we'll find there?'

'New lands. Kind lands like these, lands where the hand of the Ice still doesn't ruin all, and root up every shoot before it can flower. Lands where we can live and love and grow freely. Isn't that the life you asked for?'

'In all its fullness!' she said fiercely, and flung her arms around him. 'You risked all to love me and to free me. Now all I have is yours. All that she gave me, all that I am I give to you! To build our life together!'

'That's all that I want, now and forever,' he said softly; and though neither of them realised it then, the ruined mask fell forgotten from his hand. 'The gifts we give one another remain our own. For our sons and our daughters to share.'

Hand in hand, naked, they ran down to the ships.

There legend leaves them, save to tell that they were indeed among those who eventually crossed the dividing sea, to a new life. For it was the great current, a secret hidden and forgotten since the days of the first voyagers, that made the crossing practicable. It was through the eye of the swan, in many senses, that it was spied out anew; and for that, and their courage and wisdom, Alya and Saviyal won great honour in their time, and remembrance thereafter.

No greater heroism is recorded of them, if any were possible; but their line flourished and grew strong in its eastern home. The Chronicles record that it gave rise, as well it might, to many great and brave folk, men and women alike; and so their story was preserved, beyond the passing of the Ice itself, and the dark days of the Winter of the World.

Appendix

OF THE ORIGINS, AND TRUTH, OF THE TALE

The story of Alya and Savi, who for a brief moment melted even the heart of the Ice, is the only major account of life in the lands west of the ocean at this time, under that bleak dominion. And yet, to judge by the way it is recorded, it would appear almost purely legendary – if it did not bear the stamp of the Winter Chronicles.

For one thing, there have been innumerable versions, surviving mostly in fragments elsewhere, which gave the tale some very different slants. The later ones especially are written more like epic romances, spruced up for courtly audiences. Alya's father is made an exiled king or duke, surviving by his sorcerous powers, Savi a princess in disguise – even, in one version, Volmur's long-lost daughter brought up in secret. In several versions they become rulers of the seaward lands. In almost all of them, other famous heroes are roped in to accompany Alya, even those from impossibly remote lands and times; they supplant or replace his original followers, and the narrative is padded out with their own often completely irrelevant tales.

One version introduces the great Zvyataquar himself, an anachronism of several centuries at least, who is made to hand over his sword in person, and with it his strength, before turning to stone, somewhat inconveniently, at the gate of the Citadel. There is even a wildly erotic version, more remarkable for ingenuity than credibility. Possibly more outrageous, though, is a separate epic of King Volmur, which all but usurps the story. He is portrayed as a wise and noble figure who leads Alya at the head of his army and does much of the hard work, inspiring the slaves' rebellion, downing the dragon and even slaying Vansha, depicted as a melodramatic, cringing traitor throughout. Savi becomes a helpless, hand-wringing cipher. However, as this account is full of sickeningly sycophantic and historically impossible references to one of Volmur's very minor successors, and appears to have been commissioned by him, it can safely be discounted.

Chronology

The extent to which all these versions obviously draw upon the Chronicle account, however, suggests that this is almost certainly the original, or as close as one can expect to get. It is told very much like a pure folktale, with little reference to contemporary events or places to give it a firm foothold in history. This, though, is common enough with records from the bleak lands, where the Ice forever strove to stamp out not only cultures but any records they might leave. It seems to have been afraid, above all, of enduring knowledge; and it acted on that fear. No complete or consistent chronicles survive; even the most authentic histories endured only as oral tales. Care was taken to preserve them, but inevitably in generations of retelling they were altered.

However, the tale of Alya and Savi passed across the ocean with them, and must have been first written down very soon afterwards – perhaps even during their lifetime. From that standpoint, it can be seen as better authenticated than most; for it was also the best known and remembered, far more so than any others. The very Chronicle book that contains it, although it treats of many matters in the lands beyond the Sea, is itself named the Book of the Mask, showing in what regard the tale was held. And in other narratives the tale is frequently referred to, even sworn by, with the evident assumption that everyone would know it and accept it as true. Alya and Savi themselves are always treated as real people, ancestors of great repute, and bloodlines traced back to them in detail.

Unfortunately the detail does not always agree; but then not every bloodline is complete, or every claim genuine. The best-authenticated ones concur sufficiently to place the lifetimes of Alya and Savi between a thousand and thirteen hundred years before the coming of Elof Valantor, and the turning of the Ice. That would be consistent with the Chronicle's own records, which set the great migrations into Nordeney at just this period. They had evidently been happening already for a very long time, beginning with a continual trickle of individual refugees and small groups, most following the ocean route whose secret was continually lost and rediscovered throughout the centuries.

Some references even suggest that the voyage Alya and Savi joined was the last great escape from the Westlands, and that they were among the refugees rescued by the mastersmiths Gille and Olvar. If one accepts the most recent date, that would just be possible; but they are not specifically mentioned in that account, as one would expect. And the refugees of that day seem to have been even more desperate and harried, and culturally primitive, suggesting that the forces of the Ice were overwhelming even the coastlands at last.

OF THE LANDS IN WHICH THE TALE IS SET

Unfortunately far less is said about these than is usual in the Chronicles. That, again, is common in stories from across the seas. The chroniclers of Brasayhal were determined to record as much as possible of the land they must lose, as the Ice melted; but not so the emigrants. To them Nordeney's craggy landscape seemed so much better and sweeter than their homeland that they hardly cared to remember it; such is the quality of freedom, perhaps. Most that can be said or deduced has been included in the tale; but all too often times and distances have had to be guessed at, or left deliberately vague.

What little information there is makes sense, however, and corresponds with what we can deduce about the land. The continent on which these events took place lay over the oceans to the west of the lands of Nordeney and Brasayhal where the Chronicles were begun, themselves forming the western shore of the continent of Brasayhal. This western continent had no single name that anyone remembered. It was then as now enormous, extending a great part of the way around the world to the subcontinental lands of Kerys, and made vaster by the fall in sea levels. Much of this expanse, though, lay under the Ice; and it was the Ice that defined the climates and conditions of the remainder.

Of the Ice in these lands

As in the lands of Kerys and Brasayhal, the Ice flowed slowly but inexorably down from the north, driving as far as it could into the warmer latitudes. As Alya saw them, the glaciers formed a wide northern icesheet from east to west, absorbing or grinding down the older mountain-barriers in their path. But while in other lands one found smaller, separate glaciers and even small ice-sheets detached from the rest, here another complete sheet almost as vast had taken shape among the mountains to the extreme west. This effectively split the whole enormous continent in half, a vast ice-curtain that had swept down to bar all of the east, where this tale is set, from the west.

There at this time the great realm of Kerys still held sway under the kings of the formidable Ysmerien line, and did much to keep the Ice at bay. But Kerys, if it considered any outside lands at all, looked across its westward oceans to Brasayhal's east coast, whence their kin fled. For what lay east they cared little, assuming it was a barrier of solid ice. Had they known otherwise, it would have made little difference. Even Kerys in its might could have done little to pass the great ice-sheet. And supposing they had, it is most likely that the later Ysmeriens, imperious and arrogant, would have only brought the suffering easterners another kind of conquest and domination. That the Ice might even have encouraged, although its roots were and are in human nature.

Of the nature of the western lands

The east, therefore, was cut off, and no true maps remain. But it is certain that this whole tale, save for its end, took place well inland, in the centre of the western continent, where the glaciers reached furthest to the south; and, as we can tell, not far from that southernmost tip.

The lands bordering the Ice

As has been noted in previous books, the effect of the ice-sheets closing about the world was to compress its climatic zones into a smaller space. This increased their extremes, so that, surprising as it might seem, the equator became distinctly hotter, and the regions in between varied more sharply over shorter distances. That, for example, is how the Ice was able to create a fertile and (relatively) temperate zone of grassland within only a month or so's journey of its southern rim, separated from it by a fairly narrow strip of tundra. This is well enough described in the tale. However, it is also obvious that at the point Alya and his followers approached, both the grassland belt and the ice-barrens were especially narrow; this strongly suggests it was the southerly glacial extreme. To east and west, tundra and temperate zone were wider, especially where mountains held back the glaciers.

It was to just such a region of the grassland belt, and a happily sheltered enclave within it, that Alya's father had fled with family and followers in the hope of founding a new community, flourishing within the Ice's own preserve, yet in a spot it could not see. It was a bold and clever action, to take refuge beneath the very claw of the beast; but in the end it did not hide him from its eye. It may be that in practising his art Alya's father even gave himself away, perhaps touched one mind or memory too many and drew the doom down upon himself. His words in the tale suggest some presentiment of his own end; but he cannot have realised it would include everyone.

The southerly lands

What lay south of that temperate zone, and the border of the canes, was not so different in clime, but much less well watered. The great rivers that flowed from the Ice were largely split here, growing wider and slower. Many streams were diverted through hillier and less habitable lands; and the others seemed to promote less fertility than they normally would. It has even been suggested that these latter rivers in their slowing deposited the silt they carried down, and that this was somehow a subtle poison for the soil, an inhibitor of growth rather than a fertiliser, containing hostile minerals or metals, perhaps; hence the faint bitter taste Alya and others remarked. That would certainly be worthy of the Ice.

Whatever the truth of it, the result was arid steppe country at best, punctuated with infertile bogs and unhealthy marshes, the kind through which Alya and his followers passed in the early days of their pursuit, and among which the tree-towns had struggled to live. At worst, in lower-lying land, it became a band of stony near-desert which increasingly desperate human farmers had only served to intensify and spread, into a barren dust-bowl; hence the deserted buildings that Alya came across. And hence the Citadel, once in relatively fertile ground, but now scraping a grudging living from subsistence agriculture at the desert's margin, its irrigation precariously dependent on seasonal flooding from the north. Its fields had moved further south since its founding, not only to help hide the place, but because the immediate soil was exhausted.

To the south there were other sources of water, not least seasonal run-offs from southerly mountain ranges not yet overwhelmed by their ice-caps. There may even have been some melt-streams from the lesser western ice-sheet, their malign effects diluted by distance, as in Brasayhal. In the south there could be greenery and even forest of a kind. And beyond that, it was still possible to create enough agricultural surpluses to build and maintain a series of kingdoms, the latest of which, absorbing the rest, was Volmur's Volaghkhan. This was still a wide country, and he or another might have founded a great realm here; but the Ice, with treachery and force, forever conspired to thwart that.

To the distant south, all ambitions were curtailed by massively mountainous country, where the earth's rocky plates ground against one another, forcing up immense ranges young, steep and sharp, their peaks the tallest in the world then as now, an easy spawning-ground for glaciers. The climate was too warm for them to flourish or spread lower down, at least for this time; but they made an effective barrier in all directions.

Beyond those peaks would have been tropical and equatorial lowlands, in that climatic compression almost certainly the same blasted, impassable deserts as the Daveth Loscaouen wastes south of Kerbryhaine, or the Seghen barrens below Kerys – ironic mirrors to the wastes of Ice that had brought them about.

The lands by the ocean

There remain the realms to the extreme west, the sea-kingdoms from which Tuma the Lynx came bearing his summons and to which the lovers at last escaped. More is said of Tuma later, but his own tale, to which we owe the only extended account of the coastal lands, records that he found no greener or fairer country in all his long journey. Sheltered by mountains and distance from the reach of the Ice, warmed by sun and Sea, it had both wide, low-lying grassy prairie inland, and fertile river floodplains and deltas free of any contamination the Ice could unleash.

At the same time, the tale describes wide reaches of swamp and saltmarsh, often spreading, and immense sandy-floored pine forests along the Sea margins that supported relatively little other life. Evidently even these lands were no paradise, by Brasayhal's standards. Nonetheless, they supported ample agriculture to keep a civilisation alive, and in those forests the means for escape to freedom.

Of the peoples of the western lands

There were evidently several races of men in the Eastlands, all of whom seem to have appeared quite distinct – to one another. It is harder to distinguish between them, at this remove, for several reasons.

They almost all seem to have shared strong

physical characteristics, chiefly jet-black hair, often though not always straight and thick. Other colours were thought to belong only to ghosts or demons, and heavy beards and moustaches were considered somewhat coarse and bestial.

Almost all races had the distinctive epicanthic fold about the eye which marks people from the same region today, and almost all had skin of the hues associated with it. However, within these common factors there seem to have been several definite physical types; but in every account they mostly lived in close company, sometimes dominating or being identified with a particular area, but never exclusive to it.

Alya and Savi were both of the commonest strain, the northern. In illustrated versions – which seem, like the tale, to follow some older original – they are always represented as handsome examples, moderately tall and well-formed, with smooth, shapely faces – Alya's with no beard or moustache – and neat, fairly narrow noses, a distinctly northern characteristic. They are often referred to as pale-skinned, despite their open-air upbringing. This probably meant a lighter, more golden shade of the slightly coppery colouring usual in the north. Most people both of the Citadel, the northern part of Volmur's realm, and of the short-lived westward realms were of this same type, such as the old man at the ruined farm.

Many among them were noticeably paler, however, such as Asquan and the princess, whose skin colour was compared to fine parchment. Both appear to have had unusually lean, tall frames, with high cheekbones and relatively long noses. Asquan, surprisingly, is shown with curling hair; this was often aristocratic foppery, but it might have had another explanation, of which more below. Certainly their light skin seems to have been considered a mark of aristocracy, and perhaps also the inbreeding that goes with it. But it also seems to have belonged to a particular physical type, perhaps one that once lorded it over the rest, and spread its genes widely. Rysha, though from much humbler origins, was of similar appearance.

Vansha, interestingly, is always depicted as a mixture of these types, clean-cut like Alya, with darker copper skin and a much heavier build, but strikingly aristocratic height and features.

Further to the south of Volmur's realm another strain became common, heavier of frame and with blunt, square features and much darker skin, from coppery red to very dark brown. They also often grew quite heavy beards, especially in middle age, and were considered to look particularly rustic. They were commonest in the extreme south; but like all the other strains they were to be found everywhere, and with them many minglings. Lord Kalkan's domain (his original title signified a feudal landowner of standing) was originally in the south-west, and most of his men, such as Darzhan, were of this type. He himself, though, seems to have been largely of the aristocratic type, though his hefty build and beard pointed to at least some local blood.

There was, however, another and more singular race, once found all over the country, but by this era much rarer. They were sturdy but usually short, their skin was also pale and their hair black; but it curled thickly, and they had heavier beards. Stranger still, though, they lacked the eyefold altogether, and their eyes are always depicted as unusually wide. Almost certainly it was from them that the aristocratic class inherited its tendency to curling hair, yet they had no special status, and their origins were obscure. It may well be that they represented an ancient northern people, perhaps kin to the largely dark-haired Svarhath who inhabited northern Kerys, who had lived in the lands now crushed beneath the advancing Ice. But they themselves also claimed descent from the

ancient and honourable race of Duergar, long vanished from the westlands. Their sometimes gnarled
and heavy features would support this, as would their
taciturn cast of mind; but both could easily be true.
Something of them may survive in the peoples of the
north in more recent times, with whom they had
things in common.

Inevitably their odd cast of face gave rise to some
racial jibes – that they had bulging animal eyes and
hair because their fathers had mated with buffalos, or
their mothers with wild horses, or both with demons.
They themselves turned this on its head by claiming
descent from primal bears, which were their clan
insignia and totem; and so it is still with the Ainu of
recent times, whose ancestors stemmed from the
same area, and who much resemble them.

Racial feeling rarely went beyond insults, however; for relatively primitive cultures the peoples of
those lands had surprisingly little tradition of actual
distrust. On the contrary, racial divergence was considered fairly normal, and they had little trouble accepting completely alien physical types. Louhi, for whatever
reason, evidently modelled herself on the exceptionally
pale-skinned Penruthya folk of Kerys and Kerbryhaine,
and on the ash-blond colouring that was rare even
among them. Perhaps she had some use for that appearance, or perhaps white simply came more naturally
to her. Yet it is notable that she struck almost all those
who saw her not as something pallid one might find
under a stone, but as extraordinarily beautiful.

There may have been underlying reasons, of
course, not least their own aristocracy's characteristically pale skin. This has been common in many
cultures, associated, understandably enough, with
leisure, youth and cleanliness – historic China, for
example, or Polynesia, where royal virgins were often
kept out of the sun or otherwise bleached. European
'blue blood' ran in veins more clearly visible through

the whitest skin. Louhi, therefore, may simply have looked supremely patrician.

Nonetheless, this readiness to accept the unusual indicated a strikingly mature culture among the people of the western lands. Unfortunately, especially in Kerbryhaine, they themselves did not always find such ready acceptance.

The peoples of the coastlands

Tuma the Lynx, also called Tuma the Rider, is another hero who is often included in Alya's band, although his own tale does not support this. It does, however, tell us a little of the coastal peoples from which he came. The most reliable version of the tale records the enormous length of his journey, and that he never once deviated from it. It is said to have taken him nine years, and that may be no epic exaggeration. He began it as one of fifty such envoys, travelled furthest and ended his journey last and alone, in great honour; and Alya and Savi, already in the east, are specifically mentioned as among those who welcomed him, and named a child for him, later to become a great chieftain himself. Tuma and his fellow messengers were sent out not by a single lord or country, but by a loosely federated state like Nordeney. The realms of the coast appear to have been small kingdoms, dispersed along the coastal lands, and their people, again, very much the same racial mix as in the heartlands – linked, despite the usual rivalries, by their common origins in some larger state, from which survived an unusual level of civilisation and culture, reflected in the courtly manners of the Princess Ulie.

Perhaps this gave them the vision to see what was happening throughout the land and that it would ultimately menace them; and that the time to act was while they still had prosperity and freedom. It may also have helped that the lands had established a joint

council of chieftains, into which, in a time of frequent
famine, were invited the merchants whose com-
merce linked the lands like veins, and later the Seers
who could help guide their destiny, although there
were always few of these. This council became increasingly powerful, till the rulers had perforce to rely
on it and rule with its consent. As the threat of the Ice
intensified, it coordinated resistance; and it was un-
doubtedly their support that made possible the great
drive to build ships and escape.

The servants of the Ice

Only one people in all these lands could have been
called a race apart, or at all exclusive; and that was by
the will of their masters. These were the human
warriors who served the Ice, the *Aikiya'wahsa*. That
is the name they took to themselves, both in Brasayhal and the western lands, or as close as we can come
to it. On both continents that name was contracted
into various common forms, in everyday speech; for
consistency's sake the Brasayhal form *Ekwesh* has
usually been used in these pages.

The tale tells us little new about them. They were
of much the common kind, although often shorter
and burlier of stature, save for their chieftains, and
darker of skin; the commonest epithet given them
means something close to 'swarthy', but with con-
notations of dirt and bestiality. Their nature is very
much as described elsewhere: ruthless, vicious, dedicated by a savage discipline and a cult of atrocity to
the service of their inhuman lords, despising all other
races as subhuman, mere fodder for rapine, enslave-
ment and ritual sacrifice.

What the tale does provide is a rare glimpse into
their own communities, if that word can be used of
the antheap settlements in the Ice. No doubt the
squalor and savagery that ruled there was partly

incidental, reflecting the Ice's low expectations of humanity and living things in general. However, it may also have served as a recruiting test, from which thralls could escape by being sufficiently strong and ruthless. The town here closely resembles a more permanent and even less pleasant version of the Ekwesh shanty town Elof encountered at the Gate of Kerys some thirteen centuries later. It is remarkable how little appears to have changed, even to the dancing-ground for the shamans; but this Mouth, with its surrounding stones, was evidently some ancient shrine, perhaps even pre-dating the town or the glaciers themselves, some early and potent site of the distorted worship the Ice imposed on its thralls.

There is one major divergence with later accounts, however, and that is in the Ekwesh themselves. Those of later years, Elof's day, or even of the Mastersmiths Gille and Olvar, are almost always described as tall and lean. Something appears to have changed them in the intervening years. The most likely explanation is a chilling one. We know that by Gille's time, probably only a couple of centuries after these events, they had overrun almost all of the land. In doing so, they must have assimilated so many of its free – and taller – peoples, including no doubt those of Volaghkhan and the Citadel, that they drastically altered their own gene pool. It conjures up a grim picture; and it also provides another reason to set Alya and Savi at a considerably earlier date.

This tale also tells us something of the arcane arts they employed as readily as their enemies; but this is important enough to be dealt with of itself, below.

Of their language

This is given in the singular, for a very good reason. Even the curly-haired easterners had one remarkable thing in common with all the rest – an error. They believed they spoke separate languages; but outsiders would have thought differently. Literally everyone across this vast continent could make shift to understand one another.

On the other hand, accents and pronunciations might differ greatly, to the point of appearing nearly incomprehensible. Many kinds of localised vocabulary were springing up, especially in towns. Isolated areas, like Alya's father's farm, or the Citadel, tended to preserve the older, higher style of speech; so that Alya and Vansha sounded not like the bumpkins they feared before Volmur, but surprisingly old-fashioned and lordly. Yet for every distinction or difference, it is clear that all these peoples were essentially speaking dialects of one great language.

This had not always been the case. It is still obvious that each racial group had many names closely associated with it, and that these originated in radically different languages and locations – those with the terminator transliterated here as -shan, for example, were largely southern, and those with -mur terminators northern. But by now, while a name or type of name might still be common in a particular locality, it would be found quite freely used in distant regions and wholly unrelated peoples. It might even lose its gender identity; as with Vansha and Rysha, the -sha terminator being originally male.

Nonetheless, however much its externals had altered, the heart of the language remained the same. Even the Ekwesh spoke a blunt and bastardised descendant of it, thickly accented and poorly pronounced, with a minimal vocabulary and limited capacity for complex expression, giving them a tendency to grunt and gesture that made them seem more barbaric and stupid than they actually were. This appeared to change little over a millennium and more, which demonstrates very clearly that it was imposed from above. When the Ekwesh, and their chieftains in particular, learned other languages they often spoke them perfectly well, though they despised any form of literature more complex than war-chants.

The forgotten legacy

Across such wide and fragmented lands, the combination of racial blending; a relatively high culture and moral sense, even in decayed circumstances; and a tenacious single language, can only point to one thing – the ancestral civilisation whose ruins and relics, neglected and incomprehensible, are strewn everywhere in the tale. Once it must have ruled all those lands, a realm at least as strong as Kerys or Morvan at their greatest; but long before their rise and fall, the glaciers ground over it also, and with even greater effect. Having crushed its physical presence into the face of the earth, the Ice now set out to destroy even its memory. As Oshur rightly says, the Ice even usurped its ancient name, and bestowed it contemptuously on the humans it enslaved and distorted into its own wolf-pack; so that when men came across it, in some old text or inscription, it awoke not nostalgia but curses, and led them to spurn their own inheritance. By the time of Alya and Savi, its characters could no longer be read, preserved, if at all, for the power still hidden in its inscriptions; and few if any remembered whence had come the strange stones in the wild, or the very words they spoke. That was the triumph of the Ice.

Of the races other than human

There were far fewer of these abroad than in the lands of Brasayhal across the ocean. The Duergar, as has been said, were long gone, and with them their craft and wisdom from civilisations more ancient still. It is suggested that some lurked still among the peaks of the eastern ice-sheet; but if so, as in northern Nordeney, they kept to themselves in the hollow hills, built strong defences and sought no allies.

And in a land that no longer had anything much in the way of forests, the lord Tapiau had little foothold, and with him his Children. Only in the coastal realms did he find any reverence; and even that was fading, as the great pines and redwoods were hewn down and sawn into ship's planking. It is possible that some of the other creatures in the Nightingale's wood were of his dominion; but of them only uncanny rumours are recorded.

What stranger creatures could still be met with were either the dark things spilled from the Ice, of which there were many; or others almost as alarming who found they could live well among the ambience of this embattled land. One such, evidently, was Nightingale; but there seem to have been many others, some far less human and aware.

He was an extraordinary creature, and there is no record in all the Chronicles of another remotely like him. His account of his origins is unusual in what it says about the attitude of the Powers to their bodies, reflected in Louhi's problems with hers. It is more likely than otherwise that a lesser Power, shaping a casual semblance of a form he could not be bothered to understand, would create himself the ability to father a child without even realising it, or caring if he did. It is also not unlikely that that child would reflect more of his mightier parent's nature, absorb some of his power, or develop abilities of his own. If Tapiau did have some presence in the wood, he either felt unwilling to challenge Nightingale, or tolerated him as a barrier against encroaching mankind.

The servants of Taoune, who brought such terror upon the travellers, might well be counted as a race apart, for they were certainly not the individuals they appeared to represent. Yet they were not always the silent phantoms of the river, either. There are many accounts which suggest that they could talk and act like their dead models, well enough to deceive even close kin – at first. Yet after even a short while unease would grow, and finally distrust and loathing awaken in all around them, so inhuman their behaviour became in a thousand small ways, so alien the thoughts they gradually revealed.

How Taoune gave his creatures their physical form is not known. He could sometimes reanimate a dead body almost at once, as with Fazdshan, but it seems he did not need to, as long as it was dark or misty. Certainly he was in scope and power the mightiest of the Ice-lords, and remained inconceivably strong even after Louhi cast him down, though his will was broken. Under certain conditions he might easily have shaped something out of nothing, as humans would see it – as the Powers shaped their own solid forms. It has even been suggested he used his own substance to embody his creatures; that the phalanx of river guards, the newcomers included, were actually some part of Taoune himself. It would explain the uniformity with which they acted, and the silence.

From later accounts, Elof's included, it appears that Taoune genuinely believed, or had persuaded himself, that he was preserving human lives in this fashion, conferring immortality – to the part that he had most use and respect for, at any rate, the pure mind. He could evidently read that at the merest contact. Some suggest that he began the practice in order to persuade the Ekwesh to risk their lives freely in the Ice's service; but even they do not appear to have been fooled.

Even so, he persisted in his attempts to make his creatures independent, perhaps the introverted obsession of a once mighty mind. One ballad suggests that he sought once to breed his creatures, to improve upon humanity, as he saw it; but the children never grew or developed in body or mind, and he could not understand why. He had them exchanged for human children; but when they fled daylight, or otherwise revealed themselves, they were found to be changelings, and destroyed.

Of the Powers

Much is said of these extraordinary beings in other books of the Chronicles, and yet the greater part must remain unknown and perhaps unknowable. It is clear, though, that they were of great mind and strength to alter the world, and of daunting antiquity. To the eldest among them had been given, once, the charge of steering this world, and bringing it to some early stage of readiness which they themselves considered to be perfection.

What this may have been is suggested by the growth of controversial modern theories. With increasing authority they claim that the world was at least at one stage in its early development under the domination of ice – not merely gripped by the extended glaciation of so-called 'Ice Ages', which covered surprisingly little of the world, but completely encased, from poles to equator, land and water alike beneath a terrible shell many kilometres thick. Once this was thought impossible; but glacial rock deposits have been found in regions which even continental drift has maintained constantly within the tropics. It has lately become clear how this could be brought about. Any event which clouded the atmosphere with dust, be it unusual vulcanism or a substantial meteor or comet strike such as is thought to have caused the famous Cretaceous extermination, would cool the world sufficiently to extend the range of the glaciers. As this ice-sheet expanded, so its white surface would increase the reflective surface of the world, its 'albedo', bouncing back increasing amounts of solar heat unabsorbed. When conditions were right this process could easily become self-reinforcing. The weight of glaciers upon the earth might increase vulcanism sufficiently to spread dust; and there are occasional but alarming references to a greater body of ice somehow beyond the world, which could well refer to the cometary belt.

However this may be, it could happen; and it resembles all too closely the plan which Louhi is known to have set in motion in heavily volcanic Kerys, a thousand years after these events. That was a last desperate thrust intended to sterilise the world not just of mankind, but of all life, from the highest to the lowest, that the Ice powers considered a corruption and an invasion of the perfect world they had shaped and loved. So, perhaps, was the earlier glaciation, when life was at its primitive stage; yet a few single cells of it lingered, clinging desperately on in shallow residual lakes beneath the Ice.

Louhi and her kind could exploit vulcanism, but she could never wholly control it; for it was the domain of her contemporary, Ilmarinen the Smith. He alone of the most ancient Powers gave any heed to living things, and eventually, feeling the need to grow and change, he allied himself with the younger Powers that arose, led by Raven, and became their friend. He was never as strong as Louhi, it appeared; or, equally likely, he feared to challenge her openly, for their strife would destroy the world as thoroughly as any scheme of hers. Perhaps also he was unwilling to strike too directly against those he had once counted as friends and more than friends. Nonetheless, by the same techniques as she had employed, unleashing vast amounts of carbon dioxide from the volcanoes to warm the world again, he forced back the Ice from its total dominion. In what must have been decades or centuries of turmoil the Ice drew back before biting acid rains and pelting hurricanes of unimaginable force, when the liberated seas themselves sprang up to aid him. And when this turmoil died down at last, in a suddenly empty world life was set free to blossom as never before. For that the Ice never forgave him; and he continued to harry and assault it at every turn.

With life came other, younger Powers, whence is not said; and they defended it against the onslaughts of the Elders with less force, perhaps, but greater wit and flexibility. A few of the Elders, such as Niarad of the Oceans, grew reconciled to life; and many among the younger ones in turn grew more like them, more entrenched and less adaptable. When humanity took shape in the world, with a mind that in some measure resembled their own, they feared it almost as much as their Elders had feared all life. Again Ilmarinen took its part, and aided those younger Powers that sought to help the struggling infant race.

Among these was the being known to almost every race, though by a variety of names, among them Raven. His greatest achievement in legend, however, was to steal the sun to warm suffering men; and there is some clue as to what he actually did. He was, it seems, a great master of weather, and it is possible that when another such wintry cloud was unleashed to send forth the Ice again, he found some way to disperse it, and clear the skies to let the sun shine once more.

Whatever the truth of this, he was seen as an archetypal trickster, strange and capricious, often apparently brutal or callous when some greater end was in view; yet often intervening with extraordinary and unexpected kindness in matters that would seem altogether small. He might not help a famine-hit city, yet restore a child's lost toy. On the rare occasions he is recorded as speaking to men, his words are often on the same theme: that the ways of destiny are devious and strange, and that not even to him were all ends clear. He evidently saw himself as a stimulant or goad. Only towards the Ice and Louhi was his enmity apparent; and unlike Ilmarinen he is known to have struck where he could, even for small ways and petty victories. In all of these, though, he preferred to make men his agents, or rather to assist their purposes – often under the guise of a bargain or exchange, however petty – and let them help themselves, where their own concerns would most interfere with the innumerable evils of the Ice.

Yet it must be said that neither Louhi nor the other Ice Powers saw themselves as evil. In fact, they cast themselves as the victims of injustice, driven out from their dearest creation by rapacious invaders who desecrated their great achievement. They strove to keep their dignity, even in actions that seemed cruel to others, and their standing in their own and each other's eyes. Nevertheless, like all who cannot adapt to new life, but remain eaten up by envy and hatred, they degenerated, and fell to fighting amongst themselves at every reverse. Three above all became great among them.

At the heart of the Ice lay a great Power, Surdar, the Frost-Lord, and many other titles; his dark will, and the myriad others he dominated, flooded it and gave it being and volition. But he was hardly conscious as humans would see it; his mind moved over centuries, and responded as much to swifter events by reflex as conscious thought. His will in turn was guided by many lesser Powers, among whom Taoune and his consort Taounehtar became dominant, by virtue of their many-faceted minds and explorative characters, more akin than most to the humanity they hated. And in the end, though she was surrounded by multitudes of others, among them the *Morghannen* and the so-called Ice-witches of evil repute, there was only Louhi herself.

Of the flora and fauna of the western lands

Relatively little is said throughout the tale of the animal and bird life in the Westlands, except as it affected the humans involved. Both the Chronicles' characteristically detailed accounts of the natural world, and the interest and pleasure that lay behind them, are lacking. To most westerners nature and all its complexity appeared as an enemy, at best a passive opponent to be conquered and exploited, at worst a continual threat. It was an attitude understandable enough in such a hard land – harder, perhaps, to us than it seemed to its inhabitants, who knew nothing better. Many Bedouin once assumed Europeans wanted to steal their deserts because they were so much more fertile than their own lands. Nonetheless, now and again a casual reference or even a flash of interest appears in the tale, and it is often possible to expand this with information from elsewhere. Many life forms were similar to those in the same regions today, and so it is possible to guess what they might have been.

Plant life

Among plant and tree types, for example, the coastal forests seem to have been a mixture of evergreens, but the tallest varieties would very probably have been larches. And the forest of canes, from the description, are almost certainly related to the modern bamboos – actually a loose term covering several genera of similar-looking grasses, living in very different environments. The overwhelming effect of this place, with its densely overhanging roof stifling the growth of lesser plants, may be read as no exaggeration; even modern varieties may grow as tall as thirty-six metres high, though they droop lower and interweave.

The brown tundra plant life, too, seems to correspond well enough to modern species, in wetter areas consisting of various species of grass including *Festuca vivipara*, with sedge species (*Carex*), cotton grass (*Eriophorum*), mosses such as the *Sphagnums*, and specialised plants such as the bush-like bog-myrtle (*Myrica gale*); and in drier ones coarse grass, reindeer mosses (*Cladonia*), Iceland moss (*Cetraria islandica*) and here and there scrubby trees such as dwarf and ground willow (*Salix herbacea* and *arctica*) and birch (*Betula nana*). What seems notably missing from so many of the descriptions, although they are mostly seen in late spring, are the flourishing flower and berry species of the modern tundras, the arctic bilberry and cranberry for example (*Vaccinium myrtillus* and *oxycoccus*) or the dwarf fireweed and Arctic poppy (*papaver radicatum*).

These and their kinds not only contribute a great deal of colour and variety to a bleak and monotonous view, but the berries in particular provide much-needed food supplements, supplying essential sugar, vitamins and so on for native diets, as for example in meat-based trail-foods such as pemmican. It may be that the malign proximity of the glaciers helped to keep them down, perhaps because the Ice valued the gloominess of its approaches, or because they encouraged other living things the Ice disliked.

Some secondary references are hard to place, notably Alya's father's reference to the mysterious 'leaves' shamans might chew. His comment was rather harsher than it appears in translation, because it seems that most shamans regarded the use of these 'herbs' with severe suspicion. They appeared to yield a short cut to the ecstatic deep trance state, but an unreliable one, avoiding austerities but also the resulting spiritual development; the heightened awareness thus achieved often proved illusory, the visions it produced blurred or worthless. They must, therefore, have contained fairly potent drugs, not unlike South America coca. This is not known to have flourished anywhere in these lands, however; so some other plant, perhaps cannabis or some other form of hemp, may have been used. In Scotland and Ireland in much more recent times hemp was grown by pipers to bind their reeds, and they were much mocked for also chewing or smoking it – and, coincidentally, famous for their visions of faerie. However, coca-like products have been tentatively identified in Egyptian mummies; so it is not impossible that some related plant still grew in the Eastlands as the Ice retreated, and lingered on at this time.

Animal life

Again, the attitude to animals is severely practical. Wild animals are prey or problems, otherwise ignored, and little more is said even of domesticated species. Horses are mentioned but hardly ever described by breed or even appearance, let alone featuring as individual animals. We do not even know the colour of Alya's Ekwesh mount, though apparently these were usually dark, or whether he rode that same horse till the end. We hear that domestic cattle existed, but no more is said; the same word is used elsewhere for what were evidently wild musk-oxen, quite different. The domesticated beasts may have been some kind of buffalo, but one reference supports the possibility that they were much the same gigantic subspecies of aurochs (*Bos primigenius nordeneiae*) as was kept in Brasayhal. Goats were more common, and perhaps also sheep. There seem to have been few animals at the Citadel, reflecting the poverty of its produce. There is some mention of domestic dogs, hounds of some kind, but very little; it is possible that they were as much food animals as hunting aids or sentinels.

Occasionally, though, the outlook of a hunter widens this view, or particular animals are mentioned to evoke a landscape – as hippopotami or lions would suggest African rivers or savannahs today. Chiefest of these are the giant herds seen first by Savi, and which the original audience would have recognised immediately, both in themselves and as a transition to rich but cooler, well-watered lands. Contrary to what is often assumed today, the various species of mammoth, even the archetypal *Mammuthus primigenius*, did not live among the snow and ice. Considering how much food any elephant needs will demonstrate why. Instead they lived in the south of the wide steppes and the margins of the forests, where their hairy coats could get them through severe winters. The sheer size of these beasts suggests the earlier forest and steppes species *M. trogontherii*, largely equivalent to the *M. columbii* that flourished across the ocean. The twisted tusks rule out any *Elephas* variety, and it was not unknown for the Ice to perpetuate older forms. There are also possible references to what must have been the immense 'woolly rhinoceros', *Elasmotherium*, living in the same terrain.

The predators mentioned as chasing them would have been equally familiar, but are not so identifiable today. As in earlier books, their name is translated 'daggertooth'; but they would almost certainly have been something different from the Brasayhal creature, *Smilodon fatalis*. There have been several 'sabre-tooth' and 'scimitar-tooth' species of big cat, with increased bulk and strength to meet often gigantic prey, and long stabbing fangs adapted to cope with unusually thick hides. The most likely candidate here is the older giant species *Machairo-*

dus, which flourished across both the Eastlands and Brasayhal; its fangs fitted into long 'sleeves' in the lower jaw, protecting them from being broken. The other common feline predator at this time, the large cave lion, lived in warmer southern areas and had formidable but conventional dentition.

It is worth noting that for the references to work, the audience would have to be familiar with these beasts, or their local equivalents – more evidence that this is a near-contemporary account.

Bird life

Where other animals hardly feature, the tale abounds in bird imagery. This is no accident. Even apart from their role in events, birds aroused a quasi-religious awareness, among the Seers especially. They were a metaphor for the shaman's soaring spirit, and to him metaphors were more than mere words. They could provide both amazing visions from the heights, and a possible means of surmounting the Wall; and they were often the dominant guide symbols, also associated with clan totems, of which more below. 'Raven', of course, also represented that Power most friendly to men, who was often accompanied by these birds, and was said to resemble them in his mocking, disruptive nature.

The bird varieties mentioned are mostly modern, found in similar regions today. This is entirely in keeping even with the earliest date. Larks, swifts, swallows, crows and ravens, all are much as they would be now. A passing reference to jays suggests much the same brilliant blue-feathered variety. Nightingale's sarcastic nickname suggests that the original was well known, and probably very like today's liquid treetop singer.

Some species are harder to place. The hawks or buzzards, herons or pheasants referred to cannot be reliably identified; although the latter might well have been one of the two ancestral strains of today's common ring-necked species, which derived from opposite ends of these lands. The great sea-eagles mentioned are also impossible to identify, but the one living closest to these lands today is also the largest, Steller's sea-eagle (*Haliaeetus pelagicus*), with a wingspan which can sometimes approach eight feet, and might once have been greater. The commonest kind of small bird seems to have been a brightly coloured seed-eater much like today's titmice, with a more 'chipping' call; for them the term 'chickadees' has been borrowed.

One or two birds, however, definitely represent vanished species. Alya refers to huge vultures of the mountains and high steppes; this would be consistent with the vast condor-like *Teratornis*, which flourished at this time, with a wingspan of some fourteen feet or greater. Less specific, but equally interesting, is the gigantic footprint seen in the Forest of Birds. If bird this was, it was surely flightless and beyond the size of all birds living, except perhaps ratite species such as the ostrich, not a forest creature and wholly unknown in these lands; or the moas (*Dinornithiformes*), then flourishing, but on the far side of the globe. More likely it was one of the many malevolent survivals or sports nurtured by the Ice from past ages. As such it need not even have been avian; fossil reptilian tracks have been mistaken for giant birds in many places, even becoming a Hopi Indian design motif. But any such monster would have been ill confined within a forest; some substantial predatory bird, perhaps a phororhacid, long extinct elsewhere, is more likely, and perhaps more dangerous.

Species of giant swan have been found from this era. However, the varieties known to the Chronicles were evidently all white, and the *Morghannen*'s black feathers must have seemed far more outlandish than today. How those fell creatures came to choose that shape is a matter of vague legend, rooted in the far side of the world. Certainly it was not their only guise; they assumed many shapes of power and terror. But it was the one they themselves seemed to favour; and interestingly, it is the most elegant and the least apt to war.

Of dragons

Exactly where the creatures known as dragons fitted into the world is hard to say. Alya's father called them 'buryakud', meaning something monstrous and utterly unnatural. They were beasts in shape and aspect, scaled and reptilian; yet their powers were wholly beyond those of any other thing living, and their minds seem to have been greater than any beast's, yet wholly predatory in cast. For the origin of all these anomalies we must look back to the Ice.

It is well established in the Chronicles that the Ice at one time bred monstrosities to lead its assault upon mankind, before it discovered that men themselves would do the job far more efficiently. Ironically, poorly as the Ice usually understood living beings, its greatest Powers showed great craft in the actual mechanics of breeding and heredity. From what the Chronicles half comprehendingly recorded, they could twist and distort the very stuff of life within the seeds and eggs of living things, changing its coils to bring forth monsters. Among many miserable sports and distortions the odd viable mutation would emerge and be refined by further breeding, natural and unnatural, over long centuries.

It seems they ultimately aimed for intelligence to rival humans; yet they came little nearer than the appalling snow-trolls, which many believe were bred from relatives or even ancestors of men. And the worst monsters they produced, terrible as they were, turned out to be less devastating than might have been expected, against human courage and determination. The Ekwesh proved far more dangerous and apt to their hand. Callous as always, they cast out their creatures to lair in the dark corners of the world, whence few survived its fall; but not so the dragons.

Their origins remain unknown; perhaps among the great reptiles who ruled the earth before earlier incursions of the Ice. These had the potential to develop minds, yet there is no record they ever did; it may be that the Ice usurped the process. Other theories suggest they were minor Powers, like the *Morghannen*, who despised the human form, and took other models to give themselves shape and potential. They do not ever appear to have had speech, in any human sense; but they had a blazing will and a vicious, constant cunning that was little less than human. Their more arcane powers, of flame and flight, may have been inherent within them, as arcane crafts were in men; or may have been lent them by the Powers that made them.

The many-headed dragons seem to have been a race apart, formed again by manipulating the germ within the egg, as many-headed beasts may be today. No doubt some were useless and helpless, pathetic wastes of life; but in Zamai of the Two Heads and his still more monstrous offspring Tugarin they created bodies ruled by a single will, weapons of appalling accomplishment. But the manipulation may have been too great; Tugarin's line failed, he had no direct offspring, and as he was needed less to subdue great cities, he was left to grow old and vast for many hundreds of years in his noisome den beneath the stone, till even the Ice's servants hardly believed in him. In youth, though smaller, he would surely have been harder to bring down and slay. In later years Louhi was to breed other great firedrakes, but Tugarin's monstrosity and majesty none approached.

OF THE CRAFT OF THE SEER, AND THE LORE OF MASKS

Throughout this book Seers are often called 'shamans', because that is roughly the meaning of the term the Chronicle most commonly applies, often with patronising undertones or even open contempt. Yet only of the Ekwesh is it really true. Elsewhere, among free people, the craft of the Seer reflected something much more complex, some survival of ancient arts half forgotten. Even though the methods used were now chiefly those of the traditional shaman, the aims and goals of the Seers appear to have been somewhat different – and even more so, the power they tapped.

Like traditional shamans in almost all cultures, they sought inner visions through a state of heightened mental awareness, by ritual and ordeal; in these visions was mingled an element of divination with one of personal development, the conquest of self that was necessary to overcome the Wall. With this went a strong tradition of healing, although this art was by no means confined to Seers, a largely (though not exclusively) male discipline.

The Chroniclers, many of whom are known to have been Mastersmiths of Nordeney, were inclined to scorn the idea that any of this had any worth. And indeed it must have seemed painfully crude, compared to their own intricate and demanding art and craft. After all, didn't the Seer rely not on ordered skill, scholarship and discipline, but on ecstatic dancing and extreme self-deprivation, almost masochistic, to induce a state of near hysteria?

These were available to anyone, requiring none of the formal study and long apprenticeship, the development of great lore and skill both mental and manual, that smithcraft demanded. Anyone could

call themselves a Seer; and it is certain that many did
who were mere charlatans, self-aggrandisers and self-
deluders, hysterical visionaries, or simply insane.
What was supposed to be trance, or at least heightened awareness, could equally be deception, its
visions delusions or lies.

And how could one compare the end result? The
mastersmiths imbued the metal they shaped and sang
over with subtle virtues to affect the world, sometimes in extraordinarily powerful ways. The shamans
sought only subjective visions, often hard to tell from
the phantoms of dreams or madness, let alone to
interpret with any authority.

Put like that, the Seer's art does seem primitive
and shapeless by comparison. Yet there is no doubt
that in the right hands it could work great wonders –
and sometimes, unfortunately, in the wrong ones; but
the same could be said of smithcraft. And when the
evidence is examined more closely, the contrast no
longer seems as strong, and the Mastersmiths' contempt no longer justified.

Beliefs and concepts

The resemblance of the Seer's art to shamanism was,
for the most part, skin deep. There was, for example,
no tradition whatsoever of cursing or blessing, as
there is in almost all shamanistic cults from the old
Norse to the Navaho; nor was there any element of
witch-finding, that embodiment of individual and
mass paranoia, which has been so bloody and destructive in cults, and won shamans in West Africa
and the Congo especially the popular name of 'witch-
doctor'. And the visions Seers sought seem to have
been clear and unambiguous, limited only by the
scope and comprehension of their vision, and not
wrapped in oracular mystery. Furthermore, there is
strong evidence of something present in no other

shamanistic belief, namely a common and systematic body of belief, knowledge and techniques.

Every shaman, even, in their limited way, the Ekwesh, seems to have shared this, although the depth of understanding varied widely. Common to them all, though, was a belief in the use of symbols to direct an ability or resource which sprang from within the shaman himself, but was ultimately the gift of others – usually understood to be those Powers who favoured mankind, and almost always clan totems. The most powerful symbols were those that emphasised one's identity with one of those Powers, major or minor, in a kind of communion that both honoured the Power and sought its attention, and even aid. Of these, the greatest were masks, considered to hide the wearer's identity in that of the image or totemic power; the Raven was one of the most popular, though best approached with caution and by Seers of some strength. The Hawk, whose mask seemed to reject Alya, appears to have been a minor Power largely associated with hunting and the open air, a favourite of independent outlivers such as Alya's father, and also of adolescents. Some, such as the feathered serpent mask the women wore, were only used by the Ekwesh, and even half-forgotten by them. As the tale shows, these masks were often of ancient lineage and extraordinary craft, carefully preserved when all other treasures were cast away, and able to acquire a *mana* of their own from the forces unleashed with their aid; of which more later.

But they were not the only form of symbol. Shapes and forms, abstract or geometrical, were often used to direct the shaman's mind in his attempt to awaken that inner force; the Trail was one of the commonest, learned until it almost became an instinctive reflex. It was compared to an incense-burner, a maze of lines along which a trail of slow fire burned; and indeed there is evidence that it may originally have been such a thing, a ritual element in some forgotten temple or place of art. When they could no longer make the actual burner, the Seers re-created it in their minds, in shamanic fashion, and found it worked as well.

It was well known that even written characters could act as powerful symbols; the effect of the inscription above Oshur's door was not uncommon, and Alya's use of it on bodies to pass unseen, though ingenious, was not without heroic precedent. It has been suggested that this was a survival of the smithcraft's practice of inscribing or incising characters on metal, or more rarely stone, to enhance or define virtues already imbued within them; and this would be in keeping with the concept of the craft's origins, described below.

It seems the concept survived down into relatively recent times in this general region, as witness the Japanese tale of Hoichi, a minstrel ensnared to play for ghosts of long-dead nobles, to the detriment of his health and sanity. A well-meaning priest covered his whole body in just such an inscription of characters, to hide him from their sight; but forgot his ears. When the ghostly messengers came again, they saw nothing but the ears. Hoichi survived the encounter, and became a famous court musician and intriguer – under the name of Hoichi the Earless.

Of the origins and destiny of sight

Altogether, the Seer's art appeared as if sophisticated thought lurked behind primitive methodology, as if civilised ends had been reduced to uncivilised means; and that may well be its origin. Indeed, however primitive the means and the ends, it is even possible that the inner forces the Seers and the Smiths tapped were essentially one and the same.

The main authority for this is Alya's tale, in which he is depicted as having been able to see fluxes of light within the metal parts of the ancient Raven mask, exactly as any smith of Nordeney could see the flow of the virtues within such craftwork. This suggests two things: that the mask had been shaped, some time in the remote past, by a smith of comparable craft; and that Alya himself, a powerful Seer, had the same talent as such a man. It would be a remarkable coincidence if the two facts were not connected. True, Alya's father saw no such traces; but his power was probably less great, as he himself suspected. Or, being a man of somewhat closed and obstinate mind, he may have dismissed any such glimpse as an illusion.

There is another strong authority, however, to be found in the Chronicles' most famous book, the Book of the Sword, and its account of the Mastersmith Elof's early years and apprenticeship. His first and evil master and mentor, the Mastersmith Mylio, lived for many years among the Ekwesh. Through them, and no doubt also their cold masters, he unquestionably gained much ancient and half-forgotten lore. The account specifically states that some of this, at least, treated of masks and symbols, in a manner that sounds very familiar; and Mylio is known, himself, to have danced as an Ekwesh shaman on more than one occasion, in the mask of the Thunderbird, with devastating results. Yet, equally certainly, he was able to blend this arcane and primitive learning with pure smithcraft of a high order, and so envisage, if not actually create for himself, those works of frightening power the Tarn-helm, and above all the Mindsword. If smithcraft could absorb Seer's lore so readily, and be so intensified by it, there is little doubt that they must once have been part of some greater wisdom, some more powerful lever by which mankind could affect the world.

In Kerys and its offshoots this remained a practical science and a craft, albeit one a large part of the people did not take seriously. But in the fragmented East it seems to have weakened and declined, perhaps because it was turned inward rather than outward, degenerating into a half-superstitious quest for personal enlightenment, without any means of applying it to the outside world. Only through ancient and half-understood symbols such as the masks could that power be directed at all. No doubt this tendency, too, had been encouraged by the Ice and its agents, turning the minds of free men away from the practical and towards the introverted, egocentric and passive, a mock-primitive belief which, as it lured folk to despise true craft and wisdom, all too soon became the genuinely primitive.

It has been suggested, in fact, that all the shaman-istic cults, of Europe and Asia, or indeed worldwide, were inspired by the memory of the true Seer's art – that they grew up in the dark millennia following the fall of the Ice, pretending to deliver what the older wisdom had delivered, by using what seemed like similar means. In just such a way the cargo cults of recent years imitate the trappings of civilisation without understanding them, as if they were magical rituals. If so, this was in keeping with the general decline, that the Ice forever sponsored, and heightened even with its fall.

From shaping metal, men fell to whittling wood; from hewing stone, men were left stacking mud-brick and wattle; and from striving to better the world they degenerated into its hunted victims. In that lay the victory of all that hated humanity, and wished its end, summed up by the Ice and its masters; but they could not have wrought it without humanity's own active aid. And the Ice, it is said, has not gone, but merely withdrawn to raise new lords, wiser and subtler than the old, with the wit to find newer and more beguiling masks of their own to hide behind, as they assist humanity in encompassing its own destruction, once again.